DISSONANCE

Unbound Book One

NICOLI GONNELLA

To my wife, Allyson.
Always and forever.

ACKNOWLEDGMENTS

More than anything I wish to thank my wife for being so incredibly supportive during the writing of this book. Whether it was hyping me up or running interference with our wonderful kids on long school breaks so I could write, without her this book would have taken far longer and been way worse.

A special shoutout goes to my best friends and TTRPG group, the Papermates: Miek Martin, Brent Kelley, Rob Hance, and Greg Painter. You dudes rule, and your enthusiasm for me chasing this thing has been a seriously bright spot in an otherwise cloudy world.

Other acknowledgments go to my friends that have helped me out in many different ways. My mom, for igniting a love of fiction at an early age. Artem Sivak, for being the eternal hype man and always being willing to bounce around some ideas. And to the Discord community The Silver Pen, whose members helped me immeasurably, of which this is a small sample: MelasD, CoCo_P, Traitorman, Nulls, and Draith.

I also need to thank the people over at Mountaindale Press, who have put in the work helping me prepare this book through editing and guidance. They're amazing people that I'm more than happy to work with now and in the future.

Finally, I need to thank you. Yes you. For picking up this book and giving it a shot. Thanks.

Now let's get that story started.

-Nicoli Gonnella, May 2022

PROLOGUE

In Ages Lost, we summoned demons to serve us. Yet their might came at a terrible cost, and their ambitions unleashed nearly brought Ruin to us all. Why then would we still seek their aid? What fool would court the Unbound?

-Sanjat Lar, Hierei of the Conclave of Amaranth

At the dawn of the third day of the fourth month in the Fifth Age, the Shining City of Amaranth, Capital of the Heirocracy, bustled with all the activity of a beehive. Chaos masqueraded as orderly progression in the wild dance of civilization and mortal enterprise. The mechanisms of the city moved as they always did.

A woman, garbed in soot-smeared robes of an indeterminate color, stood regarding the sky. In her hand was a long rod of iron, the end of which was pinched into an odd, narrow shape. Her pale hair was tied back, exposing skin too smooth for an Untempered. Her bright orange eyes regarded the eggshell blue of the sky with a curious tilt.

Clouds, white and thick, crowded above the alabaster expanse of the Shining Palace, barely visible through the press of buildings. A tower in its center stretched high into the sky, taller than all other structures in the city by divine decree. The Pathless was a jealous god, after all.

The woman tapped her rod with a manicured finger and hummed aloud.

"Ana?" said a voice, sharp and high. A Human woman, similarly garbed and holding an identical rod, stepped out of a side street toward the first. "Twin's teeth, Ana. What're ya doin' here? Yer streets're two blocks west!"

Ana did not answer, merely tilted her head in the opposite direction, eyes still fixated on the sky. A frown played at the edges of her mouth as the other woman kept on talking.

"Pathless above, you frustrate me, Ana! It's like you've got no sense! An' after I went out on a limb for ya, gettin' ya this job. Lamplightin's a quality gig; ain't nothing quite as easy for the pay. And you're like to ruin it. Quit this dawdlin' and get movin'! If the lampmaster learns of this, she'll have both our heads!"

"Shh," Ana whispered, tense. "Something is happening. Something important."

The other woman paused, outraged. "Yer shushin' me? Me? How dare ya, ya overgrown—"

An awful, terrible pressure spiked all around them. The air screamed, as if keening, and far down the street, windows shattered. The shattering spread, quick as lightning, until it rocked past Ana into the distance. Ana leaned upon her iron rod, tilted into the shockwave, and barely kept her feet. She stared up as blood trailed from her nose and ears. The sky had been riven, the clouds banished in a perfect pattern above the alabaster tower. To her eyes, the remnants of an unimaginable sending trailed upward, outward.

+1 AFI
+1 PER
Eyes of Silver Sight is level 98!

"He did it. He altered the ritual," Ana whispered. Sorrow hung from her lips before her tone sank into breathy relief. "They'll come. Thank the gods."

Ana dropped her iron rod and turned away from the tower. She stepped carefully over the prone lamplighter. The other woman moaned on the ground while her ears and nose bled profusely, but Ana paid her little mind. She had a long way to go before lying down could even be considered. Against all odds, a summons had been performed.

She prayed it would be enough.

Power lanced through the clouds, implacable, arcing along a path known only to itself. Colorless and invisible, the only evidence of its passing was a sense of concordant melody that lingered in the air long after it departed. It crossed the Continent like a tiny, contained hurricane, kindling storms along the Oscallan Plains before kissing the craggy peaks of the West.

It followed a path set into its ritual, a course unused in Ages.

The power descended from on high, blowing into a dank, fog-strewn valley filled with the stench of burnt flesh and rotting vegetation. It twisted through a row of rusted blades, each larger than any Human, sending rainbow-hued sparks cascading from their faded edges. Mana gathered along them, boosting the power as it passed.

Eyes, ancient and deep, watched from within that fog. Hungry things that lived in the dark of that place gazed, unable to venture out. One in particular woke from an atavistic slumber, yellowed bones creaking as the clutch of potent Mana flitted through its grasp. It cried out, a breathy scream that shook the earth, a moaning of hunger.

Miiine.

A thread of its crimson Intent wove among the corroded blades, tangling with the power as it wove among the odd artifacts; remnants of an ancient civilization fallen to Ruin. The flush of bloody red stained the power, but gave it the juice it needed to escape the tangle of rusted blades. It arced upward, toward the sky.

The power shifted, altered its course, and punched a hole through the icy mist and then hollowed out the clouds above. It leaped beyond the thin coating of tepid gasses far above the Continent's surface. It speared toward the moons, those eternal, celestial bodies that ruled the heavens and the net of nigh invisible power that criss-crossed the sky. Flashes of bronze, gold, silver, orange, purple, and blue-white sparked around the sending, an aurora that streamed about its crown and slowed its push for freedom.

The sanguine Intent surged, hurtling the summons beyond the ephemeral net that held it back. Free, it shot off into the Void beyond the stars, where the darkness pressed close and the songs of creation dimmed to almost nothing.

Among that darkness, the power thinned, losing pieces of itself as it passed unnaturally bright holes in the inky black. The nine strands of the summon's woven Mana were stripped raw, peeled away, and cast into the Void until only a portion remained. This one, lonely piece of the summons shot unerringly forth, touched still by a carmine glow. It continued beyond the lingering symphony of existence and into the bare echoes of its dwindling refrain.

To a blue-green marble set beyond the Void, where even echoes came to die.

To Earth.

CHAPTER ONE

He had been sitting in his car for fifteen minutes.

The radio had been on when he'd arrived, blaring some indefinable alternative rock between mattress commercials, but he'd switched it off. The silence was better. Suited him more, he found. In the confines of his small, decade-old sedan, he had a few minutes of peace.

Then, his phone started ringing.

Casting about, he pushed through fast food wrappers and empty plastic bottles on his passenger seat until he'd found it. The screen was cracked in three places, but it still worked, mostly. On the screen was the face of his sister, Gabrielle, with a big, goofy smile on her face. He tapped the button on the side, ignoring it.

He was parked outside the large gate of a private marina. The gate had a guard, but a number of folks streamed through it without worry. The area was considerably more upscale than he was used to, and he'd dressed up in his nicest button down and jeans that evening. He'd run into some old friends at a bar two nights prior, friends who had moved from college onto bigger and better jobs than he had ever managed. It had helped, of course, that they had come from money in the first place. The right word from a friend of the family had opened doors for them that people like him never got beyond.

Yet, they had all talked easily enough. The four of them were all in town for some conference and were having a party on a luxury yacht one of their pals owned. The plan was to party a bit, then set sail for international waters. He was invited along. Casually, almost offhandedly, in the same breath that they asked a waiter for more wine.

A party. On a yacht.

What am I doing here?

This wasn't his scene. There was a reason he'd dropped contact with these people; they had more money than he was comfortable with, and going out was...not his style. He was more of a stay inside and read a book or browse the internet kinda person. Except his apartment still reminded him of her, and of better times. He didn't want to be there, not if he didn't have to be.

But did he want to be *here*?

Part of him did, he knew. The part that was sick of the same dull drudgery of his nine to five gig, that groaned every morning when it was time to ditch the oblivion of sleep and commute for an hour. A party was something different. A yacht? A new experience. Why not embrace it?

For all that he was comfortable alone, he craved company. After...after, when his apartment became far more empty than before, the worst of it was the lack of connection. Sitting on the couch together, watching bad police procedurals and eating junk food had been his happy place. His gut was proof enough of that.

Then get up. Open the car door. Go to the party.

Still he sat, staring in silence at the light pollution that ruined the night sky around Fort Lauderdale. The night was mild, a brisk sixty-five degrees, and more than a little windy. A good night, all things considered, for getting shit-faced on a boat.

A sharp pinging noise alerted him to another voicemail. That made four in the past ten minutes. He didn't listen to them. That would just make him feel guilty for not picking up in the first place. Gabby knew that.

He knew what she would be saying, anyway.

"You gotta get out more! Can't move on if you're not movin'!"

Of course, she was as energetic as she was wrong. Sure, he could move on. He had been moving on for three months now. Making big changes in his life now that he didn't have...Big changes. He hadn't changed his job or apartment or his car, but he'd started going to a different coffee shop in the morning. That was something, right?

Right?

His sister was nineteen and filled with more joy for life than he had ever personally experienced. It was like every day was a new adventure to her, and with a few years left of college before the real world smacked her in the face, he could see why she thought that. He, on the other hand, was closer to thirty than twenty and found her *joie de vivre* to be exhausting.

Everything had become exhausting recently.

His phone rang again.

Might as well get it over with.

It was easy enough to get in. The guard barely looked at him as he passed the gate, and it was as simple as following the crowd onto the massive two hundred foot long boat. Lights pulsed atop the main deck, and a crush of bodies filled with the insistent bump of EDM. Men and women, mostly young, mostly clad in bikinis and board shorts, drank free drinks and danced to the frenetic music.

It was awful, so he got a drink. The liquor was doled out into a red plastic cup by a half-naked man out of a plastic bin. He recognized it from his college days as a drink made of whatever the hell you had to hand. It was red, fruity, and packed a serious punch. Pretty much exactly what he needed to take the edge off. Sipping at it with a grimace, he wound his way around the deck, feeling distinctly out of place.

Help me...

Blinking in confusion, he looked around. Had he just heard someone? It was impossible to tell; the deck swirled with dancers, all of them moving and gyrating against one another in a way that cut all his lines of sight. Someone could have been talking right next to him and he'd never have noticed.

He turned, and nearly tripped over a young woman.

"Oh my god, are you okay?" He half stumbled over her splayed legs, and it took him a moment to reorient himself on the slightly rocking boat. "Hello? Are you—?"

The girl was sitting against the bulkhead, legs out and bent, and her head was resting oddly against her chest. Worried, he knelt down, checking her neck for a pulse. Her skin felt clammy but warm, and her breath was labored. Everything he knew about medicine came from TV so when he felt at her neck, he could only guess that it was maybe weaker than normal. It wasn't racing, at least.

Did she take something? He couldn't tell and, looking around, he didn't see anyone he could actually call over to help. *Do I induce vomiting? That's a thing, right?*

Thunder crackled in the distance; an early summer storm, a dark purple against the nearly black night. This was stupid. Rain was coming, and the last place he wanted to be was on an exposed deck when a storm hit. So, hoisting the girl's limp form over his shoulder, he managed to get to his feet. Barely. She weighed perhaps 110 pounds, but he wasn't winning weight lifting competitions anytime soon. So it was a pained groan that escaped his lips as he moved toward the glass covered cabin nearby.

Somehow managing to open the sliding glass door, he staggered into the cabin and set the girl on a nearby couch. White-jacketed servers with trays full of appetizers were walking to and fro in there, and he grabbed the sleeve of the nearest one.

"Hey, uh, she needs help," he gestured to the unconscious girl. "I think she might've been drugged? Or maybe just too much booze?"

"Oh my," the server gasped, and immediately knelt beside the poor girl. Deftly, the man checked her pulse and lifted each of her eyelids as he checked for...something. "Where was she?"

"Just outside on the deck. She'd knocked out against the outer wall. Is...is she gonna be okay?"

The server's face, handsome as he was in a generic sorta way, looked grim. "I don't know. I better call 911."

Two other servers came from nowhere, checking on the girl as the original server took out a cellphone. Almost immediately, he felt superfluous. Still, he lingered a few moments longer, either worried he'd need to help or...or hoping.

For a short few minutes, he had felt important. Helpful. Now he was a bystander again as more servers bustled over to assist.

He left them to it and wandered deeper into the cabins.

The interior of the luxury yacht was, apart from the gentle roll of the water, exactly like an upscale hotel. Gatherings of people were in here, talking animatedly to one another and drinking things that clearly weren't fermented in a Rubbermaid bin. Grimacing, he set his plastic cup on a nearby table and put some distance between them.

"You're here!"

He turned sharply, surprised to find his friend Samantha nearby. Her arms were spread wide as if she was going for a hug, and, hesitantly, he stepped into it. "You invited me, right?"

"Of course, of course! I'm just glad you came," Samantha patted his back and led them toward a group of familiar faces. Brad and David, both tall and skinny, each dressed casually in a button down and khakis met his eyes and smiled. "Everyone! Our old roommate from college arrived! The one I was talking about!"

A round of 'hello's' and 'how are ya's' went off, but Samantha kept talking. "You know my husband Brad, and David of course, but this is David's boyfriend Reese," she gestured to a slightly shorter man with a well-trimmed beard. He nodded, his smile small and tight. "And beside him are my friends Kelly and Patricia."

Two women looked at him, one blonde and perhaps five feet tall and the other a brunette that matched his own five foot ten inches. The brunette did a sort of half wave, while the short blonde merely blinked at him before turning back to her friend.

"So uh, David, how've things been?" He asked, attempting to break the ice he already felt forming. "I haven't seen you in, what, seven years?"

"Something like that," David replied, his mouth smiling in a way that never touched his eyes. "Things have been good. I was just telling Brad here that I had just invested in a new gastro pub downtown. It's an excellent venue and has a six month waiting list."

"Oh, that's—" He groped for the right words. "That's neat."

Brad snorted into his drink. "Neat. Yeah, Dave here is making bank off that investment, and here I missed the boat! Wish I could be involved in something so neat."

"Hey, I told you what I was doing. You're the one who decided to fly to Italy for that job of yours," Dave said.

"A job that pays well enough, thank you," Samantha added, draping her arms around her husband. "Though an investment stateside would mean we could return here more often, right?"

"Right right," Brad rolled his eyes in mock-suffering. "My

beautiful wife, tired of the jet-setting lifestyle. Begging me to settle down and pop out a dozen kids."

"Whoa, whoa, whoa. Let's not get ahead of ourselves!" Samantha laughed, and the others laughed with her.

His phone buzzed in his pocket, and he fished it out quickly. It was Gabby again. Thumbing the silence button, he tried not to roll his eyes. *I'm here, aren't I? Stop bugging me, Gabs.*

"What about you?" Samantha turned to him, hand on her hip. "What've you been up to the past...six years since we saw you? At our wedding, right?"

He nodded. "Yeah, the one on the beach. I uh, you know, I've been working jobs here and there. Getting by."

"Getting by?" Reese said, eyebrow raised. "What's that mean?"

"Making do? Living paycheck to paycheck?" A spark of annoyance kindled in his chest, one that became a flame when the bearded Reese laughed. "You have a problem with that?"

"No no, of course not." Reese smiled consolingly at him, but condescension was written plain across the man's face.

His phone rang again. Grunting, he pulled it out and held it up. "I've gotta take this."

"Oh of course," Samantha said, her eyes flicking between Reese and his own.

He walked away, trying to quash the mixture of shame and rage he felt burning through him. With an irritated groan, he swiped his phone and put it to his ear. "*What*?"

"Bumble?"

"Mom? What's going on?" He stopped walking in surprise. "You don't usually call me this late."

"Do you know where your sister is?" His mother's voice shook, as if she was barely holding in a sob.

"Gabby? She's ahh, she isn't at home?" He sucked at lying, especially to his mom. "What's this about?"

"She's not here. She said she was going to a party and said you'd be there. Are you?"

"Yeah, mom. She badgered me into it. But I haven't seen her since I got here."

She sighed in relief, though the latent terror in her voice didn't abate. "She called and left me a terrible voice mail. Something about her and a friend being stuck on a boat? Bumble, she sounded terrified."

He thought suddenly of the phone calls he'd ignored, the volume of them suddenly taking on a different, entirely horrifying light.

"Bumble? Are you there?" The connection started to fuzz into static, and he checked his bars. He was at full.

"Sorry Mom, I'm here. Yeah, I think I know where she is. I'm gonna go check. I'll call you and let you know, okay?"

"Please, just—-keep her—afe," his mom asked, tears in her voice despite the bad connection. He replied, unsure if she'd hear him or not.

"Of course I will. You know me."

Quickly, he opened up his voice messages. Gabby had left one nearly every time, so he started with the first.

"Hey dork, hope you're on your way or else I'm gonna be mad. Call me back."

The next one had a lot of ambient background noise, music and joyful shouting. Gabby was equally loud. "Hey! Pick up! You better show up! You promised!"

The next was the same, and the next. Gabby's voice seemed more and more annoyed, and he heard another girl's voice let out several loud 'woos' before she got shushed. But the fifth call was far quieter. The ambient noise had gone, and Gabby's voice was an almost-whisper. "Ohmigod, ohmigod, someone drugged April. She's out of it! Please call me back, I need help! I can't call 911, or they'll put us in jail! Call me back!"

He swallowed, the congenial air of the space shifting toward menacing in an instant. The party still thumped outside the glass doors, a strange counterpoint to the quieter conversations in here. There was only one more voice mail.

He selected it.

"They took her! I left her by the railing for a second to get help, and they took her! Probably back into the cabin! We just got outta there! I—"

The call cut off abruptly, and a yawning pit opened up in his gut.

Oh no.

What had he done?

With a rising urgency, he pushed back through the small crowd and looked toward the couch he'd left the girl on. *April, her name is April.* But April wasn't there.

Yet he could see a few white-jacketed servers nearby, moving into an adjoining cabin. He thought he saw the girl's foot, then...yes, her shoe. A high heel had fallen on the carpet near the door.

He walked over to them, his fear singing in his veins. The door was open a crack, but before he could reach it, three tall men in polos and khakis stepped out, effectively blocking the way.

"Hey, you're the guy!" One of them said, one that he mentally labeled Chad. "You found our friend!"

"We were super worried about her, man," said another one that looked like a Derrick. "She just up and ran off."

"That girl was unconscious. She needs a doctor," he started, trying to walk around them. Chad stepped in the way. Derrick pulled the door almost closed behind them.

"Private rooms, bro. We're having her brought down to the paramedics right now, though, so don't worry." Chad shook his head in a vague approximation of sympathy. "She must've drank too much."

"Some people don't know their limits," Derrick added. The third one just scowled continuously.

If she's their friend, I'll eat that shoe, he grimaced. They didn't feel like caring friends, or even compassionate bystanders.

They felt like predators.

Yet they had him at an impasse. He couldn't push passed them as they were taller than him, in better shape, and seemed like they either owned the boat or knew who did.

"So just walk away, *friend*," Chad said, stepping into his personal space. "This doesn't concern you."

Thunder rumbled in the distance.

He was so tempted to do just that. Getting involved, that had been his choice. If he chose to believe these three Abercrombie rejects, he could step away and rinse his hands of the whole ordeal. His car was less than a quarter mile away, he'd be gone in minutes. But Gabby was involved, and that voicemail meant she was probably still on the boat. She wouldn't have abandoned her friend.

That's no choice at all.

"Can't do that, dude," he said with a nervous swallow. "Let me through. I don't trust you guys."

"Wrong move, bro." Chad's stiff arm hit him in the chest, pushing him back. It hurt, but it was only meant to ward him off.

The right hook that hit him in the jaw was meant to hurt.

He stumbled back, tripping over a leather armchair that was bolted to the deck. Chad and Derrick crowed with laughter. Spots swam in his eyes from the hit, and his jaw felt swollen and blazed with pain. He lurched to his feet, his doughy midsection all kinds of wrong for this sort of thing.

"Hey man, back off!" Chad yelled, loud enough to get even more attention in the cabin. Eyes swivelled toward them all and conversation cut off. "You can't go around pushing yourself on girls, man!"

"What?"

Thunder rolled above them, far closer than before. Chad and Derrick both moved toward him, maneuvering around the furniture. Scowls stepped forward, but still stood in front of the adjoining door.

"I said, you can't push yourself on girls, dude. That's not right," Chad repeated, louder than before.

"Sick," Derrick said with a disgusted grimace. "You better leave."

He looked around himself, not quite believing what he was hearing. People were watching them, whispering, but he could hear snippets of outrage and disgust. More than a few had their phones out, some taking a video and others trying to make calls. "What? No I didn't. I found her out..."

Somehow, a teen girl had slipped behind Scowls. Her face was serious and her makeup was streaked by dried tears. Slowly, she was leveraging the door open further.

Gabby. His eyes widened, and Chad frowned at him and followed his gaze. Panicking, he did the only thing he could think of: he made a distraction.

"Unf!" Chad fell backward into an armchair. He held his hand to his nose, which had started streaming blood. "You hit me! You hit me!"

Cradling his hand and out of breath, he backed away. It felt like his knuckle had split, hitting the man's face. He looked frantically between Chad and the spectators' faces. "I-I-"

His only warning was a blur in his peripherals, then it felt like he got hit by a truck. Derrick, the muscle-bound jagoff, tackled him away from Chad. His breath was stolen, and he literally flew through the air. As if in slow motion, he could see everyone in the room start shouting, Chad pushing to his feet, and, behind the wide-eyed stare of Scowls, he saw his sister slip into the adjoining room. Unnoticed.

They hit the glass door, and the whole thing shattered.

Thunder shook the world.

He gasped awake.

Rain poured down on him. He was...in the crowd? The strung up lights flickered and strobed in the darkness of the storm that had finally found them. He could see a number of men and women nearby, hands over their mouths. Why were they so...oh.

Oh.

Shards of glass were sticking out of his arms and legs. Dimly, he could feel his blood pouring out onto the deck. The rain was washing it away.

"What the fuck? You...dude, you okay?" Someone leaned over him, reaching out. They hesitated, clearly unsure what to do about all the glass.

He tried to push to his feet, but his limbs wouldn't work at first. Shaky seconds passed, and he managed to drag himself to the outer railing. The unknown man reached down and helped him climb the bulwark.

"Someone call 911! This guy's bleeding bad!"

"This guy too!" Someone else said, and he found himself staring at Derrick, the douchebag that had tackled him out of a goddamn sliding door. He was covered in cuts from the glass, and a particularly long one was embedded right where his neck met his shoulders. He wasn't moving. "Oh god, I think he's dying!"

There was a lot of blood.

Chad stumbled out into the rain, fingers still pinching his nose. He ran his eyes over the crowd and saw Derrick. Lightning split the sky, far above. The thunder was only seconds away.

"YOU!" Chad rushed through the rain and blood, his chest leading the charge as he screamed. He slid to a stop above Derrick, who still wasn't moving. "What'd you do!?"

Behind Chad, he could see Gabby carrying April, one arm over her shoulder. Briefly, she met his eye and she paled. She stopped.

"Go," he whispered. "Keep going."

As if she heard him, Gabby swallowed and started moving again. Thunder hit again, and the string lights wobbled with the sound.

"HEY! I'm talking to you!" Chad screamed. "You piece of shit!"

He looked again, but Gabby had disappeared into the crowd. He thought he saw her head down the gangplank.

Good. Now I just gotta follow—

He didn't see the kick that hit his gut, or even register the overhand punch that hit the back of his head. All he could sense was confusion as the world around him was tipped over and spun, until he was staring face-first into the rain.

"Hope you can swim, asswad!"

"Whoa, don't—!"

Then he was falling. Or maybe flying. It was all the same to his addled head as lightning lit up the rain all around him, reflecting off a million tiny specks. Then the ocean rose up to meet him, and a rushing wet darkness enveloped him.

Thunder, loud enough that the water roiled, slammed into the world.

The entire sky flared bright. The water filled with a crimson glow, as if he'd been dunked in blood, and the lightning somehow arced through the sea. It spread like a slow-motion video, branching and stretching in all directions as the natural world vented untold pressures.

The lightning touched him, but instead of pain he felt it only grab at him, like a thousand fingers on a hand the size of a whale. More and more of it latched onto him, the branches twisting unnaturally to head toward his floating form. He barely had the time to panic, because in the next instant the lightning's path, impossibly, *reversed.*

He was yanked up and into the howling storm. Into the light.

And then darkness.

CHAPTER TWO

He woke up on the beach.

He didn't even have to open his eyes; the loud surf and soft crunch of the sand beneath his head was enough. He groaned as he brought his hands to his face, the all too familiar surge of pressure igniting behind his eyes, the dry swelling in his mouth and throat, and the barest hints of heaving nausea.

He must have had a good time last night. He didn't even remember making it to the beach. Just the yacht, and the...his thoughts flinched away from that, his brain still too tender.

A small peek of his eyelids, and he decided blindness was preferable to the unbearable light. He reached out his hands, slowly and with excruciating effort flipping himself onto his belly. Sand mushed into his face, and he smelled something weird.

French fries?

Whatever it was, it made that pool of nausea turn into a tidal wave. He poured out all his bad decisions in two or three heaves, then curled up into a ball and laid there.

Let the beach patrol find me, he pleaded. *Let me be their problem.*

But no one came to escort him off the beach. No outraged mother shrieked about degenerates in broad daylight. He wasn't even bothered by any vagrants, looking to bum a smoke.

Despite his pain, he was curious. He slowly opened his eyes, ready to endure the blinding sun in order to get his bearings.

This isn't Fort Lauderdale.

The sky was pale, a hazy white that seemed to curve all around him. Small waves of dark green water lapped near his feet, crests murmuring incessantly. He stood on a small spit of gray sand, barely more than three feet wide, that extended into the horizon. The sky was lighter there, as if something was leaching the color out of everything. It was early morning, the sun barely above the horizon, and the moons hadn't set.

Wait.

Shit.

He rubbed his palms against his eyes and peered again at the sky. His eyes told him the same thing again. There were four...no, five moons in the sky.

"What the fuck?" He half-laughed, looking around himself for someone to explain the joke. There was no one.

Then it hit him.

The yacht. The fight. His sister.

The storm.

He took a shaky breath. "Ok so there are five moons. Ok. I'm on a sandbar in a weird ocean and the sky has five moons. I'm probably not dead. That lightning bolt didn't fry my brain, because I can see and hear and feel and—I can deal with this. I got this." Six measured breaths later, he was feeling better. Not great, but better. He suspected he still had some alcohol in his system, though he didn't remember drinking much of his cup. He stood up and looked around again, hoping he'd missed something.

The sand spit was a perfectly straight line that disappeared into the hazy horizon, a roiling fog hiding it from further sight. Behind him, the stretch of sand connected to a much larger body of land an uncertain distance away. It loomed large in the dawn semi-dark, and he couldn't make out many details, but it was way more inviting than the vanishing horizon.

Step one, he thought. *Get away from the creepy green ocean.*

He'd always feared the open sea, the idea of dark cloudy waters hiding sharks made his back itch and palms sweat. He hustled down the sandbar, moving as fast as his achy body allowed. He'd only made it twenty yards when the sand shifted beneath him. "Whoa, that's dangerous," he muttered as he adjusted his footing. Then a portion of the sandbar gave way, and his leg buckled.

He plunged into the dark water.

The water burned like fire sizzling along his flesh. He thrashed in pain, blindly grabbing for the sandy shore he knew was nearby. His hand sank into gritty sand for a moment before something suddenly tugged on his leg.

His eyes snapped open in surprise, and the caustic waters bit at his eyes as he was spun toward something in the deeper water. A giant orange eye the size of a basketball blazed in the murky depths, and a tentacle attached to it tightened on his leg painfully. He screamed, bubbles flooding his face as he tried to pull back on the sandbar, trying to escape. The shape in the dark depths was hard to make out, but it had too many writhing limbs to be anything except a monster.

A second tentacle whipped out of the darkness and latched onto his left wrist, constricting painfully and yanking his arm backward. Casually, almost contemptuously.

System Initial—
ERROR

He was barely hanging on, the tips of his fingers losing ground in the slippery sand. He spared a second glance backward and immediately regretted it. A dozen more eyes had appeared, and all were oriented on him. The dark silhouettes of dozens of more tentacles writhed in the water, hungrily reaching out for him. His left arm was pulled again, inch by inch tearing him away from his perch in the rocky sand. Desperate, weaponless, out of breath; he did the only thing he could think of...

He bit it.

A spark of bright light flashed in his eyes, gold and blue, and the creature's flesh just broke apart. Acrid blood flooded his mouth, tasting like rotting seaweed and brine, just as the acidic water ate away at his tongue and gums. More blue and gold flashes assaulted his vision, flares like fireworks exploded in his mind. Before he could focus on them, the creature's tentacles pulled back in pain, loosening their grip in the process. Frantically, he scrambled up the slope, kicking his legs in a spastic doggy paddle. His head broke the surface, and he gulped the air greedily even as he pulled himself onto the thin spit of land.

His heart hammered in his ears and fear raced in his blood. He stumbled to his feet, even as a shapeless mass broke the still waters with whipping tentacles.

Outlier Detected...
ERROR

"Holy shit!" He stuttered into a run, heading toward the dark landmass as the tentacles lashed at the spot he was standing in just moments ago. His clothes were waterlogged and burning, the awful acidic water raising welts on his skin even as he dried rapidly in the warm air. "WHAT THE FUCKING FUCK!"

**THOOM!*

An explosion behind him threw coarse grey sand over his back and pelted his exposed calf, but he didn't turn around. He wasn't sure he'd be able to handle seeing what was behind him. He just kept running, helplessly counting the seconds until he was eaten.

Ten seconds.

Thirty seconds.

Sixty seconds, and suddenly the sounds ceased. It was another half minute before he collapsed on the pale sand of a much larger beach, the treeline dark and green ahead of him. He was exhausted, mentally and physically. He finally managed to turn his head, and saw that the sandy spit was torn to shreds. Whatever had chased him had ripped it apart as it thrashed toward him. Dull horror twinged in his chest, barely registering in his exhaustion. If that thing had caught him...

Something glimmered in the dark green waters, a few hundred feet out. A thick, lashing tentacle swept into the air before diving deep into the now-still waters. A sharp trilling noise sounded in his ears, and he twitched in shock. Then, a series of bright blue boxes appeared before him.

System Initializing...
Stand By...

Target Analyzed.

Name: The Dread
Type: Blood Beast
Level: ???

HP: ???
MP: ???
Lore: The Dread is all-consuming, all-powerful, and unstoppable.

"Huh," he breathed.
He passed out.

CHAPTER THREE

For the second time in a day, he woke on a beach.

A firetruck blared into his ears, a cacophony of bells that rattled his sore head. He groaned and tried to roll over, covering his head with his arms. The tangy scent of his waterlogged clothes hit him hard, and he retched.

Smells almost as bad as that squid, he thought.

He lurched upright, suddenly remembering the sea monster. He looked around frantically, heart pounding with adrenaline. It was early morning, the sun just beginning to shine on the gray sands and dull green sea. There was a heavy mist in the air, as if the sun hadn't had a chance to burn it away yet, and it clung to the low places around him. On his left leg, where the creature had grabbed him, the skin was blistered and torn. The same was true of his left forearm, and *my god, they hurt so bad!*

He held himself still, riding out the pain until he could get a handle on it. He focused on details to cope, running his hands through the coarse gray sand (*why is it gray?*) and noticed that both of his wounds had small, circular ridges where the flesh was torn.

Suction cups. He shuddered.

A bell rang brightly in his ear three more times, spiking the pain in his head but distracting him from his arm and leg. Then he saw it: a small icon shaped like an exclamation point was flashing in the corner of his vision.

"What is this?" He thought it looked like...*No, that wouldn't make sense.*

Looking directly at it was impossible, it kept moving to the side. He stood up, his legs protesting as the blistered skin stretched tight. He tried spinning toward the blinking object, but it'd dance away immediately. After five minutes, he had had enough. "AGH! What the hell! Open!"

And it did.

His vision was suddenly inundated with small blue boxes, semi-transparent and filled with large off-white script. He couldn't place why they seemed so familiar until he read one.

"No way."

The Continent Welcomes You, Unbound!

Choose Your Race!

This is insane, he managed, his mind reeling. *It's like a game. What's an Unbound?*

Dozens of names began to populate beneath the Race header, and he caught a few. Human, Elf, Dwarf, something called a Traxik. But then there was a stuttering glitch with the screen and sparks of crimson light bled onto the blue. Three notifications appeared in rapid succession, all save the last tinged by that crimson hue and accompanied by a droning tone.

ERR0R((#)! Extra Options Granted!
ERROR#12! Race Already Selected!
You Have Chosen: Nym

Nym: Will Unyielding, Soul of Fire. A Lost Race.
+1 to WIL, INT, DEX And END Per Level, +5 Bonus Stats Per Level. -5% XP Gain.
All Choices Have Consequences.

"What? I didn't choose anythi—"

Before he could finish the sentence, his jaw snapped shut as his body was wracked with Pain. Capital 'P' pain that hurt so bad it felt like his blood was on fire. Screams tried to worm their way out of him, but his throat had swollen and his lungs felt like they'd burst. That droning tone grew louder, more insistent, more textured; it rattled through him like a subwoofer had been installed beneath his skin, shaking his bones until everything just came loose. He thrashed in the sand, in silent agony.

Then, in an instant, it stopped.

The pain disappeared, as if it had never been, and his notifications cleared and repopulated.

Race Successfully Changed.
Prepare For Your Reveal!

My what? What the hell is going on?

Congratulations! You Have Revealed Your Omen!
ERROR! Omens—ERR-0R!
Omens Are—#F(=)
Y*% H*@V3 ReVal#: (#$ F00—ERROR

More red light, more noise, though each subsequent notification was met with more and more blue and gold. A pain slowly gathered behind his eyes, intense and only getting worse at each flashing box.

A burst of blue and gold sparks inundated his vision, completely obscuring everything else and drowning out that irregular static with the sound of a ringing bell. A single stout-bordered blue box appeared. There was not a hint of red to it.

You Have Revealed: The Magician
+2 to WIL, +1 to INT, And PER Per Level.

A wave of rainbow light exploded outward from him, like an expanding orb. It happened so suddenly, he could only watch as it whisked into the distance, a receding line that didn't touch the loose sand at his feet.

What? He looked down at himself, confused and slightly terrified. *Omens? Magician?* He didn't even know what that meant!

And then he did, as if the knowledge was shoved into his brain:

The Magician: The Will To Know.

That's...less than useful. He ran a shaking hand through his dark hair, slicking it back with an increasing amount of sweat. All of this had him covered in a flop sweat, not to mention the building heat in the air. He was overwhelmed. Whatever was going on had more rules to it than he could grasp. And that light show was...concerning, to say the least.

And the pain...it still tingled his fingertips, an echo of torment he couldn't shake. The pain more than anything had him sure that this, whatever it was, was all real.

But it couldn't be...could it?

As stupid as it sounded, even in the privacy of his own head, it felt like he was in an RPG or MMO game. Fantasy races, blue menu screens, magic and monsters...it all felt terribly familiar. Save that he wasn't familiar with the Nym race in any fiction, and the term "Omen" was also unfamiliar, though he guessed it was something like a class. If this was all a delusion, his imagination was smarter than he had ever thought.

In less than a breath, another notification popped up.

Choose Your Born Trait!

This time the window was populated by dozens, hundreds, then thousands of options. A scroll bar on the side of the notification window slowly grew smaller and smaller, until he could barely see it. The error messages didn't reappear, thankfully, and he found himself staring at more options than he knew what to do with. The growing list of options ranged from useful to downright bizarre.

Mighty Thews: +2 to STR and +2 bonus to any Feats of Strength performed.
Talented Voice: +2 to VIT and +2 bonus to all Negotiations with sentient creatures that share your language.
Fish Breath: Breathe underwater, able to eat an entire fish in a single swallow.
...

"So many...."

Suddenly, he was almost glad his Race and Omen were chosen for him; if there were this many options for everything, then he'd be hip deep in these notifications for hours. He tried to close the window, hoping that he could put this off longer, but the notification just shook before returning to its original position. Looked like he had to make his choice now.

He put his hands to his temples, feeling the remnants of his hangover resurfacing. The world felt like it was spinning just slightly too fast, and he had to crouch and sink a hand into the warm sand beneath him. This was too much. First the yacht, Chad, and Gabby...*Dear god, Gabby.*

What happened to her and her friend? Had they made it off the boat? It was storming too, so—

The storm.

Again the memory of the storm and the lightning strike rose up inside him. He flinched from it, like touching a hot stovetop, but he couldn't deny what he recalled. He'd been pulled from the sea, yanked into the storm and...and left here. Beside a terrifying ocean and killer monsters. What next? He wasn't even human anymore, apparently.

"Where the hell am I?!" he half-shouted and fell to his butt in the sand. He was so tired. He tried to close his eyes, but the pop-up notification was still there. He thrashed his arms and legs in the sand and yelled. "AAARRRAAAHHHH!"

Thirty seconds later, he panted in the grey sands, physically and emotionally exhausted. His limbs were heavy from his little fit, and his left arm and leg throbbing from where he had torn open parts of his blisters. He was all alone in a strange land, with deadly monsters everywhere, and opaque RPG-style game rules.

Why? Why am I here?

He scrunched his eyes closed and tried to envision himself laying on his futon in his tiny studio apartment. He tried to remember the feel of his down comforter, and the uncomfortable slats beneath the thin mattress. But the notification taunted him, glaring bright and blue and unavoidable. He opened his eyes with a sigh.

I don't know why I'm here, or how I can get home, but if I'm going to survive this insane place, then I need some serious advantages. He set his jaw and sat up, confronting the notification.

His Omen was called **The Magician**. It had something to do with will or willpower, according to the vague description. His Race was **Nym**, and he gained bonuses to some sort of stats. He couldn't remember, exactly. He started fumbling around his display, hoping for some reminder of what those bonuses were and received a single line of text in reply.

Cannot Open Status Page At This Time

"Huh. So that means there is one."

Despite himself, he was intrigued. His fears and frustrations began to fall behind curiosity. He was blind to whatever stats he had, but he thought that his Race and Omen gained bonuses to WIL, INT, DEX, END, and PER. If this was anything like the tabletop RPGs he'd played, then those hopefully stood for Willpower, Intelligence, Dexterity, Endurance, and Perception. He had double bonuses to WIL and INT, which fed into the idea that his class had access to magic or something. His breath caught for a moment. Was magic real here?

"Don't get distracted. Maybe it is, maybe it isn't. The Trait options might clue me in. What sort of Traits do I have available?" He refocused on the Born Trait selection window, slowly making his way down.

There were thousands of options, and he quickly got lost in reading them. They covered all sorts of options and character builds, but he had no clue what to expect in this strange place. Would the ability to cleanse his blood of impurities once daily be useful? Sure, especially if there was poison or something close by. Would it be better than the other options? He had no idea.

He read through twenty or so options before he realized how stupid he was being. He had just survived a wild animal attack, and now he was sitting out in the open? He was surprised at how easily he lost himself, a powerful thrill of fear seizing him at the thought of being caught unaware by some beast. The area, aside from that terrifying squid, seemed to be devoid of any animal life at all.

But he'd never been an outdoorsy guy. Who knew what lurked out there?

He stood and stepped closer to the tree line. There was a collection of large boulders to his right, a number of which were close enough together that he had to squeeze between them. Nestled within the boulders, each taller than himself, he felt a sudden sense of relief. Perhaps it wasn't perfect safety, but he wasn't so exposed any longer.

Back to the Traits, I guess.

Three hours. He spent three hours sitting on the beach and reading the various Traits. He ended up filing them into three categories: Utility, Neat But Useless, and Overpowered. Neat But Useless was easily the largest category, filled with thousands of Traits that seemed less than optimal. He was blind to the rules of this place and his own stats, but even he could tell that being able to "eat a coconut whole and spit out the rind at high speed" was dumb.

Utility had some interesting options, including a way to jump up to three times his height at will. *That would be cool as hell,* he thought. There was even a Trait called Mageborn, which granted him a larger than normal Mana pool. It also confirmed the idea that magic existed on the Continent, wherever that might be. The knowledge thrilled him, and he couldn't help feeling excited at the thought of hurling fireballs and other wizard stuff. But the last category contained the only Trait that seemed entirely perfect.

Keen Mind - +2 INT. You have perfect recall of all events within the past 30 days, and have a 20% chance of perfect recall beyond 30 days.

The nature of knowledge meant that memory was critical, and if his Omen description was any indication, knowledge was core to his class. While being stronger or faster might help him survive, Keen Mind would let him thrive. It was just a gamble on whether he could live long enough to make it useful.

He hesitated before selecting it. He spent long minutes going over the other options, but nothing caught his eye except for Mageborn which only gave him a small bump to his Mana pool in the beginning. He didn't know how much Mana he'd be using later, but he didn't even know any spells right now. He shook his head. Screwing up his courage, he selected Keen Mind.

Are You Sure?
All Choices Have Consequences.
Y/N

That phrase again. He frowned and mentally selected "yes."

You Have Selected Keen Mind As Your Born Trait!
CONGRATULATIONS!

What Is Your Name, Unbound?

He paused. Should he use his real name? He had never really liked his name, and who knew what things he'd encounter here. Maybe it was smart to hide his real name? So, feeling a little foolish, he decided to input a name he had used in several games:

Felix Nevarre

Thank You, Felix!
Welcome Again To The Continent!
We Hope You Survive.

Then the blue window disappeared.

I'm sorry, what? He—no, Felix was worried. That last line was not encouraging.

Then his train of thought was interrupted by a metric fuck ton of PINGs and blue box notifications.

Combat Engaged Before Initialization!
ERROR! Logs Imperfect!
You Have Been Injured!
You Have Sustained Acid Damage!

Due to Attack Before Initialization, Deadly Damage Has Been Negated!
You Have Survived The Dread!

Due To Eating The Dread and Surviving, You Have Gained a Title!
Gourmand (Rare)!
Eat Your Foes! Learn Their Strength! Knowledge Fuels You!
+1 to INT and VIT!

"What?" Felix was dumbfounded. "A title? Just from biting the squid? That's...yeah, that's weird."

The notifications continued. Every time he closed one, another was ready to take its place. Most of them said he "sustained acid damage," probably from that nasty green ocean which Felix now assumed was a low-grade acid.

That's what I'm smelling! Vinegar!

That had been bugging him for a while.

You Have Learned a Skill!
Acid Resistance (Common), Level 1
Decrease damage from acid by a small amount. Amount increases slightly with Skill Level.

Felix grimaced, the taste of the Dread's ichor still faint in his mouth. At least it was good for something. The moment he closed the notification, another three appeared in quick succession:

Acid Resistance is now Level 2!
Acid Resistance is now Level 3!
Acid Resistance is now Level 4!

Huh. Felix's eyes widened as his injuries began to burn less. Now, instead of a faint burning, they just felt like a standard open wound, wet and stinging in the air. Did this mean he could train Acid Resistance by jumping in the brackish water? He glanced at the waveless sea before him, imagining the creatures squirming beneath.

He shuddered. *Hard pass.*

You have Gained a Title!
Survivor I (Uncommon)!
Your Health has dropped below 5%, but you lived to tell the tale! +1 END, +1 VIT!

You Have Learned A Skill!
Analyze (Common), Level 1
Intuit knowledge of people, places, and things! Will garner more information with further use!

You Have Analyzed Your Enemy!

Name: The Dread
Type: Blood Beast
Level: ???
HP: ???
MP: ???
Lore: The Dread is all consuming, all powerful, and unstoppable.

Analyze, huh? Felix was inordinately pleased. If he was going the route of knowledge gatherer, this would be a core skill.

That monster name and lore though...*Yikes*.

You Have Escaped The Dread! You Fled Rather Than Die A Painful Death! Wise Move!
XP Earned!

Felix let out a shrill yawp as suddenly light enveloped his body. He scrambled to his feet as a nearly inaudible yet haunting melody crashed against his ears, and the light faded just as quickly as it appeared. A new notification appeared before him, and this time the box was gilded and surrounded by a stylized border.

Level up!
You Are Now Level 2!
+3 to WIL! +2 to INT! +1 to DEX! +1 to END! +1 to PER!
You Have 5 Unused Stat Points!

"Holy shit," he said, his eyes wide. "It IS like a video game."

This only affirmed his increasingly paranoid suspicion that he had died and gone to a particularly strange afterlife. He had stats. And levels! What even was this?

The notifications continued, unabated.

Your Title Gourmand Has Garnered You Insight!
You Have Learned A Skill!

Memories of the Past (Uncommon), Level 1
Capture Memories from the Mana of your foes! Relive collected Memories to gain insight and learn from your

enemies! Memories last until relived, then fade. Percentage retained determined by Skill Level.

SYNERGY DETECTED!
Keen Mind Has Synergy With Memories of the Past (U)!
Do You Wish To Evolve Your Skill?
Y/N

"Uh, yes. Why wouldn't I?"

Evolution In Process...

Felix suddenly felt light-headed and sweaty, as if he hadn't eaten in days and tried to run a marathon. His hands shook as he held them up to his head. More flashes of blue and gold streaked across the corners of his vision, like fireworks just out of sight. That pain reawakened, flaring along his skin and burrowing up his spine.

A bell chimed, barely audible, and the pain rapidly spiked. Felix's breath was sucked from his chest, like he'd been punched in the solar plexus. His body felt like a deflating balloon, and all of his air was rushing out of him, gathering at the edges of his vision.

You Have Discovered A Skill!
Lessons of the Past (Rare), Level 1
Capture Memories from the Mana of your foes! All Memories are retained perfectly for 30 days, after which retention is increased by Skill level. Chance of capturing a Memory increases with Skill level. Chance of learning Skills from retained Memories increases with Skill level.

"Huuah!" Felix sucked in a sudden lungful of air, finally able to breathe, and he fell to his knees. His head felt stuffed with cotton and also vaguely on fire. The pain of the evolving Skill was vivid but brief, a dull burn that even now faded away. The notification hovered before him as he coughed into the sandy loam, blinking insistently until he acknowledged it. He looked up.

Ho-holy cow.

If he was reading this correctly, he could learn Skills from the memories of enemies he'd, what? Defeated? Encountered? That was wildly overpowered. His choice of Born Trait was already bearing fruit.

Memory Gained From The Dread! Would You Like To Review It Now?
Yes/Yes

CHAPTER FOUR

Felix's head rocked back, his smile faltering. A Memory from that tentacle horror? He shuddered. And he didn't have a choice? Taking a deep breath, he looked around the beach and didn't see anything nearby for at least a mile on the open sands. Before he could think too much about it, he mentally selected "Yes."

Everything went dark.

Slowly, the world lightened until Felix was surrounded by a green murkiness that reminded him uncomfortably of the Bitter Sea. Nearby, a dim light played across the waters, shining from between blocky shadows. His body spun closer, moving in a way that Felix only offhandedly thought as strange. The rest of his attention was on the strange crimson light emanating from between several columns of hexagonal basalt. They rose up from the murky sea floor, rising up and around the bloody light like a cupped hand or a copse of creepy trees. Or a cage.

Felix tried to move closer, but quickly realized he wasn't in control of his body. It felt bloated and ungainly, too big and too...squishy, somehow. He blinked. And blinked. And kept on blinking, set after set of eyes that seemed to warp around his massive skull, eyes that were just now taking in the mottled color of fleshy tentacles coiling in the acidic water. A dark presence swam in the currents beneath him, just out of sight. Then, with a sickening lurch, the presence oriented on him. Tentacles coiled and the eyes of the creature focused inward as pressure gathered on his mind. With mounting horror, Felix realized he was embodied within the Dread itself.

And somehow, it had noticed him.

"GAH!"

Soaked with sweat and face-first on the grey sand, Felix's heart thrummed in his chest. His adrenaline was racing in his veins even as he leaped to his feet and took quick glances in all directions. He was still alone, the expanse of grey beach and dull green water quiet and still. Soft lapping of the foaming edge of the Bitter Sea washed a dozen feet away, and Felix shuddered.

He climbed back into his cocoon of rocks.

That was awful. Felix shook his head as he sat down heavily. His adrenaline rush was wearing off, leaving him shaky, his limbs all elbows and knees. If that was what happened every time he reviewed a Memory, then he'd take a hard pass in the future.

As long as I can, he amended.

Lessons of the Past is level 2!

With a final steadying breath, Felix braced for more notifications, but no more appeared.

"Took long enough," he muttered. "Now what?"

The beach was silent, the soft whoosh of water and bitter tang of vinegar permeating the air. He had been thrust into this strange place, dropped into deathly danger, and accosted with changes to everything about himself. Felix shook his head, trying to get a grip. The world was like a game, so did that mean he was a player? Were there others?

"First things first," he muttered. He needed more information.

"Menu," he tried. Nothing. "Status."

Nothing. Just a grey beach and green water.

Undeterred, Felix tried to visualize what he wanted. Quickly, a blue screen appeared before his eyes.

Name: Felix Nevarre
Level: 2
Race: Nym
Omen: The Magician
Born Trait: Keen Mind

Health: 28/35
Stamina: 36/36
Mana: 51/51

STR: 2 PER: 5
VIT: 7 END: 7
INT: 13 WIL: 9
AGL: 3 DEX: 5

Skills:
Acid Resistance (C), Level 4
Analyze (C), Level 1
Lessons of the Past (R), Level 2

Title(s):
Gourmand (+1 INT, WIL)
Survivor I (+1 END, VIT)

Unused Stat Points: 5

"Whoa, cool." Excitement stirred in his chest again. He had stats, skills, and Mana. This was wild beyond belief.

Now if it weren't for all the life threatening danger. His leg and arm still twinged painfully in reminder, and Felix noticed that his Health was sitting at 28/35. It didn't seem to be getting worse, which was good, but he needed to find a way to heal up.

One thing at a time.

His stats appeared to govern his physical and mental abilities, and looked to have started...kinda low. Were these low? He had no idea what the average was.

His highest stat by far was Intelligence at 13, thanks to his Race, Omen, Born Trait, and Gourmand Title. He wasn't sure what Intelligence affected, but it was a safe bet that it had to do with magic. Did it also make him smarter? Felix couldn't tell.

Next up was Willpower, another mental stat that might have something to do with magic. The rest, aside from his Strength and Agility which were abysmal, were all middling.

He eyeballed his Unused Stat Points. His Race garnered him a huge amount of these, enough to up all of his stats by one per level if he wished (if he included the other stat bumps he also gained from leveling up). Felix had no idea if the Nym race was amazing or if this was a normal amount of bonus stats per level, but he was feeling that it was on the large side. In fact, the whole deal of his Race and Omen being pre-chosen seemed suspect and raised more questions than ever.

Felix frowned and perused his memories of the last half hour. His perfect recall showed its power here, bringing forth a seemingly flawless recreation of events. He had to put a great deal of focus on it, and his head felt like it was simultaneously splitting and overheating if he concentrated for too long, but it truly seemed perfect. At least, up until the point where he selected Keen Mind as his Born Trait. Before that moment, Felix could only rely on his natural memory. Was his normal memory improved, as well? Was that an effect of a higher Intelligence?

He flinched as his improved memory touched the edges of the Dread's Memory again. The headache flared into full force, and Felix shut it down in a hurry. He shuddered and reoriented.

"Inventory. Map," he tried to visualize them coming up. "Settings." Nothing worked. He had a Status page and that was it.

Felix grumbled in frustration. The sun, now risen above the horizon, was beating down on him with increasing intensity. He stood from his tiny fortress and walked toward the shade of the treeline, carefully eyeing the shadows for anything that might try to kill him. The Dread taught him an important lesson, at least.

The vegetation was temperate, reminding him of the northeast coastline of America. The air had a mild heat to it, reminding Felix of early spring, or maybe early summer if this was further from the equator than Florida. *Its own equator, of course.* Felix shook his head. *Another freaking world.*

Scrub and thin trees dotted the sandy soil as it built toward heavier growth farther up a small incline. As he walked, his eyes were gradually drawn to a small flowering plant near the trunk of a hearty-looking shrub. It had pale blue flowers and bright red stamen. Without conscious thought, he felt his Analyze Skill activate.

Name: Blue Heribore
Lore: Praised for its beauty, the blossom of the Blue Heribore is a well known soporific.

Felix smiled, surprised.
"Cool."

The next hour found Felix trudging deeper into the woods, Analyzing everything he could see. More than anything, he needed information. Where was he? How did he get here? Was there anything close to civilization nearby?

After what had to be four miles of arduous forest walking, Felix didn't feel he was closer to any answers. His feet and calves were sore, his leg and arm still aching from The Dread, and his mouth dry. His Analyze Skill, however, was doing fine.

Name: Velbore Tree
Lore: A silver barked tree in the Hessidae Family, known to flower only when it rains.
Properties: Unknown
Alchemical Properties: Unknown

Analyze is level 7!

Felix rubbed his eyes, a slight headache simmering behind them. He had been Analyzing everything he could, and the information displayed was getting more detailed. The Lore entry in particular had begun to drop large words in an unknown language, like this world's version of Latin. Hopefully by Level 10 he would start to see some of the Properties that were unknown, but that was just a guess. Anything beyond a dozen feet couldn't be targeted by the Skill, so Felix ended up meandering as he found various plants that seemed interesting. He had cataloged twenty-two different flowers, four types of moss, nine trees, and one slow-moving slug the size of his forearm.

Name: Rock Slug (Common)
Type: Invertebrate
Level: 20
HP: ???/???
MP: ???/???
Lore: A slug known for its highly potent acid, used primarily to digest calcium deposits.

It was busy slowly eating through a rock. He made a wide berth around that one, just to be safe.

The wildest part? If he chose to, he could remember everything that had happened today as if he were reliving it. All of those flowers, mosses, and trees were as crystal clear in his mind as the dull green undergrowth beneath his feet.

For instance, during the second hour he had found a broken branch of a Lecuna tree, its wrist-thick wood a pale brown swirled with deeper emerald tones. He knocked the small branches off as best he could and had made a passable walking stick. He had even earned a new skill for that one.

You Have Learned A Skill!
Improvisation (Common), Level 1
The ability to make what is available useful! Great for a poor crafter or a homeless vagrant.

Felix's eyebrow twitched at the memory. There was a certain level of snark in that skill description. It made him question whether this "system" was being controlled, or if it was just omniscient with sass. He wasn't sure which unnerved him more.

He'd also found a very useful herb. Small and white, they grew in bundles in shadier nooks of the forest floor. They kinda reminded Felix of Queen Anne's Lace, but with bigger petals.

Name: Yarrow
Lore: Commonly used in poultices to engage healing and stop bleeding. Can be eaten raw for lesser effects.
Properties: +1 Health per second for 5 seconds, end Bleeding Status.
Alchemical Properties: Unknown

There were seven flowers in total, and he tried one of them.

You've ingested Yarrow!
+1 Health per second for 5 seconds!

In the next five seconds, Felix's leg and arm finally felt like new. He looked down at them in amazement.

Whoa.

He wasted no time in taking the rest. Without another option, he put them in his jeans pockets and hoped they wouldn't be ruined if it turned out he needed them again.

Despite all that, he was still wandering around the woods with zero direction. He had been orienting himself by the rising sun, but the canopy had quickly grown too dense to see it much of the time. All he could manage was to head in the opposite direction of the weird Bitter Sea.

Then Felix began to hear something new. Birdsong. Chorusing insects. Even the small patter of tiny lizard feet on a branch above him. Now the sounds of life returned all around him, each step bringing more to his eyes and ears. Even the greenery was more vibrant, with deeper greens and more robust flowers.

The closer I am to the Bitter Sea, the less signs of life there are. Is that because of the Dread? That made sense. Maybe it was an apex predator or something and scared everything away.

The sway of a small branch nearby made him swivel toward a new arrival, a rodent the size of a house cat that fixed him with small beady eyes. It rotated a leafy root vegetable quickly in its paws, gnawing it with startling speed.

Analyze...

Name: Tree Vole
Type: Beast
Level: 23
HP: ???/???
MP: ???/???
Lore: Small mammal of the Phelandessiae family, noted for its sharp claws which channel Mana to pierce even the strongest bark.

Damn, he paused, pursing his lips. *Even the rodents are higher level than I am.* Despite its size Felix assumed those Mana claws would do a number on his weak frame. He wasn't even wearing armor, just his increasingly uncomfortable dress shirt and jeans. The squid had ripped up one of the legs, and the acidic seawater ate away at the rest of it. Now it was drying, and Felix was positive it was going to crust away into pieces at any moment. As he stepped back, the vole scurried away, quick as a flash.

Holy dang, that thing was fast.

Felix kept going, at first attempting to skirt around any decently-sized creatures in fear that he would be attacked. Everything looked so different than he was used to; the animals were larger and had intimidating claws or teeth or scales. But after twenty minutes of zero attacks and even witnessing several smaller creatures fleeing at his approach, Felix started to feel a little comfortable.

Maybe this place isn't too bad. I mean, they can't ALL be like the Dread, right?

As he walked, he kept Analyzing anything new in sight, trying to raise the level of the only actionable Skill he had. He was pretty sure he learned Analyze by attempting to figure out The Dread, but no matter how many times he awkwardly attempted a high kick he never saw any notifications. No Super Kick Skill for him.

Was there a set Skill list? Did he just so happen to make the right eye movement to unlock Analyze? What about his Acid Resistance and Lessons of the Past? Both of those were definitively the result of his actions, idiotic as they were. He still couldn't believe he *bit* a giant squid monster.

Felix was chuckling to himself when a sudden humming approached him. Looking up, he saw the strangest thing yet: a teal and yellow lizard hovered ten feet away from him, the blur of four dragonfly-like wings holding it aloft and producing the oddly-pitched humming noise. Almost without thinking, Felix activated Analyze.

Name: Sharpwing Skink
Type: Reptile
Level: 23
HP: ???/???
MP: ???/???

Lore: Highly territorial reptiles with four razor-sharp wings.

A grotesque gurgle snapped his attention away from the notification window, just as a wad of greenish goo splattered against his chest and knocked Felix on his ass. The goo immediately began to sizzle, eating through his tattered shirt and straight into his skin.

Acid Resistance is Level 5!
Acid Resistance is Level 6!

Ow ow ow shit ow! Felix immediately made to roll into the loamy soil, hoping to scrape the acid from his chest. Doing so, he just barely managed to dodge the Sharpwing Skink as it quite literally buzzed him. The burn of the acid fell away once he'd scraped off enough of it, and Felix got to his feet in a crouch. He readied his walking stick like a baseball bat, not really sure what he could do to a monster that was over twenty levels higher than him. But he had nowhere to run, not really, and he was sick and tired of things attacking him and getting away with it.

The Skink buzzed at him again, its mouth wide open and filled with dozens of tiny triangular teeth. It was so fast that Felix only had a bare instant to line up his shot, and he swung as hard as he could. The overgrown lizard bobbed nimbly out of the path of his clumsy stick, zipping up and around a nearby velbore tree. Before Felix could even register that he'd missed, the Skink slammed into his back and put him back onto the ground.

You've taken a Critical Hit!
Your Health has dropped below 10%!

Back and shirt shredded, Felix shook his head, dismissing more blinking notifications. The pain was overwhelming him, first his chest and now his back was a sea of fire, scorching every nerve ending and fogging his mind. Barely able to think, he quickly dumped all five Bonus Stat Points into WIL, doing nothing for the pain but immediately clearing his head. He pushed down the agony and got shakily to his feet.

Breathing carefully, Felix tried to listen for the dumb lizard. A distant humming emanated from the trees to the northeast, and without wasting time on thinking, he dove forward in a roll. A sharp rising buzz zipped passed him, just barely missing his head.

Cursing, Felix did something he should have done in the first place.

He ran.

He scrambled behind a nearby tree just in time to hear the *gurgle-hiss-splorch* of another Acid Spit landing. Felix smelled acrid smoke but didn't look back. The humming grew in pitch and volume, and he put everything he had into running as fast as he could, zig-zagging through the trees to hopefully avoid any more acid.

He wasn't sure how long he ran. All he knew was that his lungs burned with each breath, and his legs shrieked in pain as he pushed himself through the forest. By the end, his vision dimmed and black around the edges, he simply collapsed into a patch of weeds and wildflowers, folding his arms feebly over his head. After a few minutes of just breathing and no attack, he strained his senses. It was quiet. He let out a shaky breath. He'd lost it.

A small yellow icon flashed in his vision, and Felix remembered all the notifications he had ignored during his fight. He toggled them on.

WARNING! Your Stamina Has Been Depleted!
Current Stamina: 2/36

Wow. No wonder he had collapsed. It must have hit zero during his escape. He was lucky the Sharpwing Skink had given up, or else he'd be a bloody smear against some tree. *What did the Lore say again?* They were highly territorial, so once he had left its claimed area, it dropped the chase. Felix sat up, propping himself against a nearby stump, careful of his wounded back. He watched his Stamina tick down to 1/36 at this simple action, and a wave of weakness passed through his arms and legs.

He had to fix that. Somehow.

You Have Gained A Title!
Survivor II (Uncommon)!
Drop to less than 5% Health twice within 24 hours. +1 END, +2 VIT

Felix's eyes went wide, and he quickly accessed his Health.

Warning! Your Health is Below 10%!
You Are Bleeding!
Health: 2/45

Felix could feel the blood pooling behind him, oozing out of his torn-up back. That lizard had diced him up. He was amazed he hadn't fainted from the pain, and equally amazed that his desperate decision to dump all his free points into Willpower had paid off. He could feel the pain, but it seemed more distant now.

Straining his remaining Stamina, Felix fumbled into his pockets and grabbed the Yarrow flowers he'd stored there. They were crumpled and torn, but hopefully still good. He shoved flower after flower into his mouth. They tasted bitter, sharp, and almost hot on his tongue. He chewed mechanically and swallowed, moving as fast as his 1 Stamina allowed. Then, he got the blessed notification:

Bleeding Has Stopped!
You've ingested Yarrow (x6)!
+6 Health per second for 5 seconds!

You Have Learned a New Skill!
Herbalism (Common), Level 1
Increases knowledge accumulation and retention regarding roots, herbs, and natural remedies. Efficacy of gathered herbs, roots, and other natural growths increases with Skill Level.

A strange squirming sensation crawled along Felix's back, as if his skin was...rippling. It itched like hell, too. Felix toggled his Health to see the result.

Health: 31/45

Felix let his head drop into the dirt and took several big shuddering breaths.

He had almost died. Again.

He had more notifications, and wasn't doing anything except slowly recovering. He toggled them back on.

You have Learned New Skills!

Staff Mastery (Common), Level 1!
You've begun your path toward mastery of the staff! Proficiency increases with Skill level.

Dodge (Common), Level 1!
The best way to not get hurt is to not get hit. Efficacy from Agility increased slightly per Skill level.

Acrobatics (Uncommon), Level 1!
You've proven yourself capable of tumbling into and out of danger. Sense of balance increases slightly with Skill Level, flexibility increases moderately with Skill level.

Analyze is Level 10!

You Have Gained A Title!
Natural Scholar I (Uncommon)!
You have Analyzed over 500 different species! Move ever onward, scholar! +1 INT, +1 PER

Due to your efforts you have gained:
+1 STR
+1 AGL
+2 END
+1 PER

Felix blinked, surprised at the flood of screens. All this from a thirty second fight? That he lost?

What would have happened if he had won?

CHAPTER FIVE

Felix spent the next thirty minutes hiding in the weeds, mostly recovering but also frankly too worried to stand up and expose himself to other monsters that may or may not be waiting. He searched what he could of the small clearing he'd found himself in, but found no evidence of other creatures. He did, however, find a small patch of red grass called flitweed.

Name: Flitweed
Lore: A small leafy weed grown from the blood of slain beasts.
Properties: Consume to regain 1 Stamina per second for 10 seconds. Other effects unknown.
Alchemical Properties: Unknown

Despite its gruesome lore, flitweed tasted a bit like coriander and reminded him of his mother's cooking. More importantly, it was necessary.

The Stamina regeneration it offered allowed Felix to get up and take stock of his situation.

Name: Felix Nevarre
Level: 2
Race: Nym

Omen: The Magician
Born Trait: Keen Mind

Health: 31/45
Stamina: 10/51
Mana: 77/77

STR: 3 PER: 7
VIT: 9 END: 10
INT: 14 WIL: 14
AGL: 4 DEX: 5

Skills:
Acid Resistance (C), Level 6
Lessons of the Past (R), Level 2
Analyze (C), Level 10
Running (C), Level 1
Staff Mastery (C), Level 1
Dodge (C), Level 1
Acrobatics (U), Level 1

Title(s):
Gourmand (+1 INT, VIT)
Survivor I (+1 END, VIT)
Survivor II (+1 END, +2 VIT)
Natural Scholar I (+1 INT, +1 PER)

Unused Stat Points: 0

Ok, so Step One: Don't Die.

Step Two: Find Help (might assist with Step One)

Step Three: Figure Out What The Hell Is Going On.

Felix nodded to himself. Step one was difficult, but he'd managed so far. Barely. The fact that he had *two* Survivor Titles meant he was entirely too weak for the creatures around here. It was like he was dropped into a high level zone at the start of a game.

He frowned, frustrated. He had to stop doing that. This place was clearly NOT a game, no matter what the Skills and Status screens might suggest. He had to consider this place real, because anything else would kill him.

First stage of Step One is to assess what I can do. Felix looked over his Status screen and considered his assets.

His stats were growing due to leveling up, Titles, and whatever happened during that battle. So that meant, what? He could train his stats? But why didn't his stats increase during his tiring hike through the woods earlier in the day? Felix frowned, thinking.

Stats aside, he had a growing number of Skills, though most were only Level 1. He only had one offensive Skill, but all the rest were amounting to an impressive array of avoidance. If he were to train them up and increase his stats through more strenuous exercise, could he survive?

The better question was, did he have a choice? How long could he eat flowers before something ate *him*?

What I need is to learn some magic. I've got Mana for god's sake!

Though he didn't know much about this place, it was doubtful he'd find any spellbooks lying around the forest. Did they use spellbooks? Scrolls? He was basically guessing at this point.

"Alright," Felix got to his feet and took a deep breath. "Stop stalling and get to work."

Felix took off running.

Not far. He was all too aware that a level 20 creature could lie in wait anywhere. So he did laps in the forested glen where he'd found himself, approximately a quarter mile loop. It was rocky and provided uneven footing, and Felix struggled to keep up a steady pace at all, but after twenty minutes of struggling and nearly breaking his ankle he felt a burning sensation in his chest, followed by a notification.

+1 AGL

"Awesome."

It was proof of what he was trying. Bolstered by the success, he kept running.

The rocks in the ground were such a hassle that he ended up hopping between them, leaping from step to step as he kept running around the glen. After another ten minutes, he had to rest and eat some flitweed to recover his Stamina, but was back at it less than a minute later.

Running is Level 2!

+1 END

After two more rotations of this, Felix was starting to get bored. So he kept using Analyze as he ran, trying to retrieve and read the information as quickly as possible as he ran by various weeds, rocks, and trees. Ever since Analyze had hit Level 10, he found the Skill was easier to use. Smoother, somehow. He barely had to think about it before it activated. His Born Trait also helped, allowing him to memorize the info at a glance. Running as fast as he could, he jumped from rock to rock and kept up a steady stream of Analyze windows of anything he could see.

There were a few close calls, moments where nearby roars and shrill cries made him freeze up between rocks. Nothing ventured into the meadow though, thankfully. Each time, he hesitantly resumed his run, eyes wide open and attempting to watch every direction.

He took a break after forty minutes of this, ignored his notifications blinking at him, and started resistance training.

Felix had attempted to lose weight and build muscle off and on for years, but had never been as engaged as he felt now. The stat increases and Skill Levels felt euphoric, a jolt of positive reinforcement that kept him pushing that much harder. He dropped to the ground and did as many push-ups as he could. But his 3 in Strength showed itself, as he was barely able to get through five, and even that burned through nearly all of his remaining Stamina. Not even running for ten minutes used this much. Was that because he had a Skill for running? Or was the majority of his strength located in his legs, as opposed to his arms?

Questions, questions, questions.

No one to answer them. Might as well get back to work.

So it went. Felix took rests when his Stamina dropped below 5 and took breaks when he scraped his knee on a rock or bashed his arm against a tree. He'd run out of yarrow, so he'd have to find some more soon. Luckily the injuries weren't too bad. He ran as fast as he could for as long as he could, hopping from rock to rock, moving across the uneven ground with his increasingly-tattered sneakers. Sometimes, he held his walking stick as he ran, out in front of him or above his head, quickly tiring out his arms and Stamina. He did push-ups until he collapsed, recovered his Stamina, then went again. On and on and on for hours.

Before he knew it, the area had grown too dark to see well enough. It was too dangerous to run on this rocky ground, though even still Felix was tempted. Not for the first time, in the distance he heard the cry of something that sounded like a big cat. Fear shivered down his spine, like cold water on his heady enthusiasm.

He felt terribly exhausted.

Felix toggled his notifications as he trudged back toward the last of the flitweed, beginning to munch on it mindlessly.

+1 STR
+1 END
+1 PER

Running is Level 3!
Running is Level 4!
Acrobatics is Level 2!
Herbalism is Level 2!
Herbalism is Level 3!

You've Learned a New Skill!
Physical Conditioning (Rare), Level 1! Through application and hard work, you have begun a regimen to improve your health and physical fitness. Increases the rate at which your Physical Skills grow, based on Skill Level.

The burning sensation he'd felt on and off intensified, like bad heartburn or when you swallowed something way too hot. It was painful, but didn't drop his Health, and when it was over, he felt changed. Stronger.

"Hell yes," Felix whispered to himself. He'd also gained a second rare Skill.

His eyes strayed back toward his rocky obstacle course, but another cry of that cat creature and the steadily failing light was enough to nip that thought in the bud. He would have to find shelter for his first night.

"Jesus Christ, what a day."

———

Felix found the tree some distance away from his rocky glen.

It was sturdy, thick enough that three of him couldn't encompass it's trunk with their arms outstretched. It was also tall, maybe one hundred feet to the crown and filled with dark purple leaves. The bark was white with horizontal striations in pale ochre. Analyze called it a Kingsap Tree.

Name: Kingsap Tree
Lore: Ancient trees, there are only a few dozen groves left in the lands of men. To find one in the wild is a true treasure.
Properties: Wood of the Kingsap highly magical, the sap itself dense with Mana.
Alchemical Properties: Unknown.

"Ok, magic tree," Felix put his arms on his hips, considering the smooth bark and approximately twenty foot span before branches began to appear. "How do I climb you?"

It was the clear winner for safest perch in this forest. The runner up was a low dirt dugout, and that had the dual problems of being easily accessible to predators and the overpowering smell of piss. Something definitely lived in that den, and he didn't want to be there when they returned.

Felix set down his walking stick and wrapped his arms around the smooth bark of the Kingsap in an attempt to shimmy up the giant tree. His first few tries were, well...he hadn't climbed a tree in a decade. He ended up on his ass no less than five times, finally landing on a particularly knobby rock. Cursing and breathing through the pain, he turned away from the Kingsap. His eyes landed on a much smaller tree about a dozen feet away. It had low branches but was about fifty feet tall.

Struck by an idea, Felix quickly clambered up onto the branches, shimmying his weight up further and further on the tree.

When he had gotten about twenty feet off the ground, he got the notification that he was hoping for:

You Have Learned A New Skill!
Free Climbing (Uncommon), Level 1! Climb surfaces without aid of elaborate equipment. Climbing speed increases with Skill Level.

Felix grinned.

Now he just had to get down.

Felix stopped grinning.

You Have Learned A New Skill!
Pain Resistance (Uncommon), Level 1! You have learned to manage pain, pushing through it to achieve your goals.

Felix limped carefully back over to the Kingsap tree, wishing he had more yarrow. He'd come to appreciate the herb despite its bitter flavor, and it had saved his life already. This time, it wouldn't even salvage his pride.

Can't believe I fell out of a tree. All these creatures out to get me and I nearly kill myself.

Whatever. At least he learned a new Skill.

It was getting closer to full dark now, and Felix was starting to feel an edge of danger in the air. While he'd yet to feel fully comfortable in this world, he was certain that when night fell it would bring with it a whole bucket of bad. Several yowls and cries in the distance affirmed his thoughts, and he gulped audibly.

Time to climb.

It took three tries before Felix's Free Climb Skill activated, allowing him to catch onto a ridge of bark he couldn't see in the failing light. He strained upward and reached again, sliding his free hand across the face of the Kingsap. Another handhold, just barely enough to keep going. He wrapped his legs around the trunk, giving himself that extra friction needed not to fall on his ass. *Again.*

Five grueling minutes later, Felix flopped heavily onto the wide expanse of the first split in the trunk. Wheezing, the edges of his vision dark and flashing, he just laid there for a solid twenty minutes. Stamina somewhat recovered, Felix sat up and took stock.

The Kingsap was big, seeming even bigger from his perch, and the area was approximately nine feet in diameter. Easily large enough for him to stretch out and sleep. It was also oddly smooth, the bark feeling almost polished and waxed. His vantage from this height was also substantial; while he couldn't see very far due to the heavy foliage and growing dark, he could see the entire glen and his rocky obstacle course.

DEX +1
STR +1

Free Climb is Level 2!

Felix leaned back against one of the large boughs and took a deep, steady breath. This was a good place, and it seemed safe. He'd be fine as long as he kept his ears open and his stick....

"Shit."

He climbed down the tree.

CHAPTER SIX

Turns out, a night spent in a pitch black forest full of hostile creatures was not relaxing.

Felix managed to fall asleep early on, as the day had exhausted him. But something that sounded like a mix between a hacking cough and a basso roar sent him stumbling to his feet. Adrenaline racing, he stood stock still, holding his walking stick and staring into the darkness.

It was almost completely dark. Where were those five moons he saw yesterday? It was almost like he was in a cave, the sky a dark plane above him. Then he noticed the tree beneath him.

The Kingsap was glowing. Softly, too softly to notice even on a moonlit night, but more than enough to stand out like a beacon in this dark. He studied the slashing patterns of the smooth bark beneath him, dragging his fingers across its sloping surface and up one of the branches that was as thick as his waist. Halfway up, he found a gash in the branch, a small jagged hole where a bird or something must have gone looking for bugs. The glow was brighter here, radiating off a drop of pale purple sap.

Felix pulled his hand back, fingers sticky and glowing as well now. It was oddly calming, this sap. It felt like a soft breeze, and smelled like fresh cut grass on a warm morning. Without thinking, he raised his fingers up to his tongue and tasted it.

Colors burst in his vision, like a kaleidoscopic rainbow, and he tasted sunshine and morning dew and the deep, dark loam of fertile earth. It was thick, like a dense honey. It reminded him of summer days, somehow. Felix sat down and settled against a thick branch.

This place was strange and wild and weird all rolled up with RPG game mechanics. He didn't know where to go, or what to do, and yet in this moment, he felt calm. Relaxed. Above him, the clouds thinned and small silver sparks twinkled in the black.

He fell asleep.

Blink.

Blink.

Felix woke the next morning bleary-eyed and stiff from his position against the Kingsap branch. He rolled his neck, pressing down on his shoulder with his left hand, stretching out various kinks.

"Ooofa." He was tremendously sore. He hadn't worked out like that in...well, ever.

Then he noticed the "!" icon in the corner of his vision. It had been blinking at him all this time, and Felix toggled it as he sat with a muffled groan.

Congratulations!
Your Title Gourmand Has Garnered You Insight!
You Have Learned A Skill From The Sap Of The Kingsap!
Meditation (Uncommon), Level 1!
You seek the center, to become One with All. Increases Regen rates by flat percentage.

"Whoa." That burning sensation returned, in far greater force, as if something was worming its way into him. His breath caught beneath that pain, but it faded in seconds. Felix fell backward with a groan, panting.

He had completely forgotten about his Gourmand Title. It had netted him his first Rare skill from the Dread, and now an Uncommon skill from a magic tree. What did that Title say? He brought it up.

Title: Gourmand (Rare)
Eat Your Foes! Learn Their Strength! Knowledge Fuels You!
+1 to INT and WIL!

Learn their strength? So did that mean the Kingsap was particularly good at meditating? How does a tree meditate? He leaned back on his elbows, looking up at the swooping branches and fluttering purple leaves. It swayed slightly in the morning breeze, almost hypnotically. It made sense, at least as much sense as anything else in this world.

He blinked.

World. He had been avoiding that particular thought for the past day. He was very clearly in another world. Planet. Solar system? Probably. He was very, very far away from home. And for the first time, the weight of it settled on Felix like a suffocating shroud. His heart raced, he broke out in a flop sweat, and he was halfway to his feet before recognizing that he had nowhere to run.

He was stuck here.

No friends. No family. No *people* at all, at least none so far. Just angry beasts looking to eat him. He couldn't...

Breathe.

Felix closed his eyes and took a deep breath.

Just breathe.

He felt the tree beneath him, smooth to the touch and oddly warm. He took a breath. The wind rustled across his face, pleasant and cool. He released a breath. The tree creaked as it swayed, moving ever so slightly to the rhythm of the breeze.

He opened his eyes.

Meditation is Level 2!

Felix huffed a surprised breath, half laughing. Shaking his head, he stood up.

"Day two."

His second day in the Continent was similar to the latter half of the first. After some quick, painful stretches that further confirmed how out of shape he was, Felix took off running. He made irregular laps around his small glen, leaping from rock to rock, holding his heavy walking stick.

He encountered only a few creatures, mostly more Tree Voles. The cat-sized rodents watched him from the nearby branches, steadily munching their way through the canopy. Whatever lived in the smelly dugout nearby wasn't there come sunrise, though the smell of musk and urine was even stronger. He figured it must range far afield during the day, hunting maybe. If he were lucky, it wouldn't come back until he was back in the Kingsap.

Throughout the morning, he used Analyze. After Level 10, it activated smoother and quicker, small blue boxes of Name and Lore and Properties appearing and disappearing all around him. He barely thought about it; it was like breathing.

At first, Felix held his stick close to his chest, throwing it out wide when his balance failed him. After a while he tried to hold it out in front of his chest the entire time. As the day before, his Stamina quickly bottomed out. Twenty minutes of resting and meditating and he was back at it. Rinse and repeat.

How much Strength is represented by 1 point in the Strength Stat? Is that an extra 5lbs of lifting weight? Felix considered the facts as he lifted several large stones, repeatedly. Now that he had a whopping Strength of 5, he was more than double his starting Strength, if that's how it worked. He wasn't sure, but he felt stronger than before.

As the day before, he scavenged what remained of the flitweed for Stamina regeneration, and ate a plant called dewcatcher he had spotted during his runs.

Name: Dewcatcher
Lore: Collecting water from the air and made of sturdy stock, it is a filling and nutritious plant eaten by local prey animals.
Properties: Contains enough water, fiber, and basic nutrients to sustain a small animal.
Alchemical Properties: Unknown

Without fruit or meat, the dewcatchers were all he had to live on. The problem was, he was running out.

His glen was only so large, and his activities the day prior had stripped a good portion of herbs from it. His flitweed was basically gone, only a few scattered shoots here and there. With Meditation, that was less of a concern, but even still, his regeneration was not fast at all.

Felix would have to leave, soon. He had a day, maybe two left before everything useful here was gone.

Sweating and panting, he felt loose and limber. His muscles were filled with a tingly warmth. He had spent three hours on his exercises this morning, and he felt remarkably good. He shook his head. Felix would never have thought that back home.

He toggled his notifications.

+2 STR
+1 VIT
+1 END
+1 AGL
+1 INT

Running is level 5!
Running is level 6!

Meditation is level 3!
Meditation is level 4!

Herbalism is level 4!

Physical Conditioning is level 2!

The burning kept up again, but by this point Felix was associating it with growth. It wasn't great, but he kept getting better, so he couldn't fault the sensation. He opened his eyes and reviewed the notifications again.

Dang. Nice. He was making considerable gains, he felt. Again he had no baseline for comparison, and maybe natives gained twenty skill levels in an hour normally, but it felt good regardless. He felt in control.

But now I have to find food and water. And to do that...

Felix glanced back toward the northwest, back the way he had fled from the Sharpwing Skink. He frowned. That lizard had almost killed him, and it hadn't broken a sweat. Felix didn't hold any illusions; he couldn't fight back against a level 20+ monster at

Level 2. He didn't even have any fighting Skills, aside from Staff Mastery and that was...well it wasn't nothing, but he had a long way to go before he could fight anything.

There was another copse of trees to the north, however, and he stood up and headed in that direction. He'd come to notice a series of scratches in the barks of trees a few dozen feet from his glen, scratches that looked to be made by very sharp, very thin blades. Territory markings, if he had to guess. Maybe he could circle around the Skink's territory and avoid it altogether.

He still had the plan of finding civilization and getting help, though that became shakier by the hour. This place was truly wild, and Felix wouldn't be surprised to find he was thousands of miles from anyone.

That's a fun thought. Thanks, brain.

Felix walked for twenty minutes, moving as carefully and quietly as he could. His heart was pounding in his chest at every rustle of leaves, every snapped twig, or shifting branch. Then he heard it.

Buzzzzzzzzz.

He dropped low, taking cover in a patch of huge fern leaves as one, two, *three* Sharpwing Skinks flew by. Each one was a different color, but all variations on blue, green, and yellow. They had almost flown past when the trailing Skink, a yellow-spotted green one, slowed down and turned in Felix's direction as it snuffled the air. Felix's breath caught, then he forced it out as slowly and quietly as he could. He gripped his walking stick in one hand, sweat pooling in his palms.

Slowly, so slowly, the Skink hovered toward his hiding place, snorting lightly. It got so close, Felix could hear the sizzle of its acidic spit and watched as a considerable, thick glob dripped onto the ground.

Grahh!

Without warning, the Skink whipped forward, its body blurring almost as much as its wings, and Felix clenched his eyes as he heard a loud *crunch.*

But no pain.

Felix carefully opened one eye and looked up. Through the ferns, he could see the Skink flying away, happily munching on the biggest and nastiest insect he had ever seen. It was the size of his head, had wings and a hairy carapace, and far too many legs. In moments, the Skinks were gone.

Felix let out a breath that was half shudder, half relief. He carefully stood into a crouch and moved back toward his glen.

A half hour later he was back in his relatively-safe glen. He took longer coming back due to stopping and hiding every dozen feet or so. The Skinks had him jittery and nervous beyond belief. Felix hadn't ever experienced as much pain as he had with the flying lizards, and avoiding a repeat performance was a top priority.

On the other hand, scouting out the area had provided some gains.

You Have Learned New Skills!

Stealth (Common), Level 1!
Move quietly, stay hidden, remain unnoticed. The key to a long life is not being found by ravenous beasts.

Breath Control (Uncommon), Level 1!
Control your breathing, mind over matter! A step toward better bodily control.

Stealth is Level 2!
Stealth is Level 3!

Felix was inordinately pleased. The Stealth Skill would be extremely useful in scouting more areas, and the Breath Control Skill seemed tailor-made to accompany it. It made him wonder once again whether he was making these Skills himself, or being granted Skills that already existed.

Regardless, his situation was much the same as before. He had to get out of this glen to survive, but couldn't survive long against the various monsters. They were too high level.

And the Skinks are too territorial to let me through. He sighed and leaned against the wide trunk of the Kingsap. *If only I could find weaker beasts, then I could...*

Felix sat up, a revelation like a jolt of electricity across his spine.

The bug! What level was it! He searched his uncanny memory,

hoping he had...yes! Felix had been using Analyze so much recently that he was almost subconsciously activating it all of the time. Most of what he got back was the same, as he'd tagged most of the surrounding flora; it was like white noise. But for the price of a sharp headache, his Keen Mind let him pull up each and every one, including the bug.

Name: Emberfly
Type: Insect
Level: 18
HP: ???/???
MP: ???/???
Lore: Born grubs in various local trees, they transform into emberflies after twenty days and have a poisonous sting.

"Yes!" Felix punched the air before wincing and holding his temple. Level 18 wasn't much better than Level 23, but he'd take it!

Wait! The Lore mentions grubs transforming into the Emberflies. That means—

That meant he might have something his own size to pick on.

Hunting for grubs was harder than Felix expected.

To transform into an Emberfly, which was the size of his head, the grub was likely half that size. That was still huge, so he'd started off confident in finding a big nasty bug in short order. Three hours later and over two hundred trees inspected, he had still come up empty.

The search hadn't been entirely wasted though. Felix had kept an eye out for useful herbs and plants, grinding his Herbalism Skill and stuffing his strained pockets with what he could. Yarrow was the best find, though he also found a small clutch of mushrooms called Witchcaps. The little things purified blood (whatever that meant) and provided a tiny health boost.

By pure luck, near the end of his search, Felix spotted a strange pale grub undulating over a rotting log in a dry, shallow gully. The thing was roughly two feet long, mottled burnt umber and fleshy white. Eyes like jelly-filled sacs of blood sat on its face as it munched on the log beneath it. It had to weigh thirty pounds, at least.

Name: Copse Grub
Type: Insect
Level: 13
HP: ???/???
MP: ???/???
Lore: Born of eggs placed in trees, copse grubs spend their lives devouring the tree from the inside out. Once done, they transform into Emberflies.

The grub looked full and fat, having nearly devoured its entire tree at this point. The log was eaten through in several places, bored out and covered in gnaw marks. It's body was also coated in a liquid that (even at a distance of twenty yards) Felix could guess was unpleasantly goopy. It was, in a word, gross.

Gross or not, this is the lowest level creature I've seen yet. He hefted a sharp rock from the ground. They were littered all around the area, making stealth extremely difficult. *Time to squash a bug.*

Moving closer carefully, Felix ended up only two dozen feet away behind a rocky outcropping and a few clustered saplings. Breathing quietly and steadily, he hefted his rock and took aim.

Here goes nothing.

He threw.

And the rock landed with a dull thud in the dirt, easily ten feet shy of the grub.

Jesus, that's embarrassing. He wiped his hand across his face, glad no one saw that pathetic throw. Luckily, the grub didn't appear to have great senses; it didn't even react to the impact. Felix quickly gathered up a few more rocks and tried again.

This time, the rock hit the log, but still missed the grub. The weird bug twitched toward the noise, but didn't make any other movements.

With a resigned sigh, Felix moved closer. Only ten feet away now, and separated by a stand of thick trees (Beranthia Conifers, he idly Analyzed), he readied another throw.

He had made a point of gathering up maybe thirty rocks, all around the size of a baseball. They were hard and had a few jagged edges, hopefully enough to penetrate the slick flesh of this bug.

C'mon. C'mon.

Breathe in. Breathe out.

Felix spun out of cover and whipped the stone as hard and as fast as he could.

SQUELCH.

You Have Learned A New Skill!
Thrown Weapons Mastery (Common), Level 1.
Don't just stand there, throw something! Skill level slightly increases accuracy and power.

Yes! I did it!

Victory never tasted so sweet. A strike and a Skill! Now he just had to pummel the thing until it ran out of Health and kicked it. Felix grabbed two more rocks and turned around to throw them.

That's when the grub exploded.

CHAPTER SEVEN

Flesh still sizzling uncomfortably and clothing finally ruined, Felix sat behind some trees and chewed yarrow while attempting to meditate. He was too distracted, though. He was furious with himself.

The copse grub had used an area of effect skill to launch acid in a burst all around itself. Felix got a full dose, all over his chest and face. He barely survived, and his shirt didn't. It finally had given up the ghost and dissolved off of him. Only a few scraps of once-white cloth remained. He had shoved those in his pocket.

So now he had an acid-burned chest, tattered pants, and—

A Copse Grub's Acid Explosion Has Entered Your Bloodstream.
Status Condition: Poisoned
You Have Learned A New Skill!
Poison Resistance (Common) Level 1!
By poisoning your blood, you have learned to resist the harmful effects of poisons. Efficacy increases slightly with skill level, damage taken from poison decreases slightly with skill level.

Ah yes. Blood poisoning. Felix grumbled as he ate another mushroom. A debuff icon blinked in the corner of his vision, a drop of blood half colored black. As he finished the Witchcap, Felix watched the icon flicker and disappear.

Finally. He sighed in relief. He only had three Witchcaps left.

Metaphorically out of the woods, yet still unable to meditate, he focused on his notifications, which had piled up in the past two hours.

A Copse Grub's Acid Explosion Puts You In Critical Condition!

Felix waved away the battle notifications and status conditions. He already knew he took a crazy amount of acid to the chest and face. His nearly-depleted stash of yarrow could attest to that.

Acid Resistance is level 7!
Poison Resistance is level 2!
Acid Resistance is level 8!
Poison Resistance is level 3!
Acid Resistance is level 9!

Pain Resistance is level 2!
...
Pain Resistance is level 5!
Herbalism is level 5!

+2 END
Congratulations! You have earned a new Title!
Survivor III (Rare)!
Drop to less than 10% Health 3 Times In A Week. You should really take care of yourself! +2 END, +3 VIT

Breathe. Just breathe.

Felix pushed past the pain and focused on breathing and chewing more of his yarrow stash. He was lucky these magic herbs regenerated skin and blood and muscle so quickly, or else he'd be disfigured beyond recognition. The amount of acid that grub ejected was astounding. At first, Felix figured it had killed itself and tried to take him with it, but then he saw the damn slimy bastard slip down into the log. It had burrowed away!

Breathe. He reminded himself. *Breathe in, and out. I can't do anything about it until I'm back at full here. Hell, I can barely do anything at my best.*

Even a giant gummy worm kicked his ass.

On the bright side, he had gained another Survivor Title and his resistances were leveling very quickly. Probably had something to do with stress, but his Skills and stats all improved better while in combat. When his life was on the line.

What did that say about this world?

Felix let that thought go as he meditated; the past was unchangeable. There was just now, this moment, where he could recover and try again. And again. As many times as it took.

Some time later, Felix blinked open his eyes.

Meditation is Level 5!

With a smile, he stood up. The smile quickly faded as he observed his naked, pudgy torso and his beat-up jeans.

"I've gotta get more clothes." Felix turned and hunted around the trunk of a conifer, seeing a familiar grub sitting back atop its log. "But first I have to do this smarter."

———

An hour later, Felix was back in the gully, and the grub was still there, munching away. The log was almost half gone, and a quick Analyze told him its level had increased to 14.

It gains levels by eating trees? So weird. Felix stepped forward, out of the trees and toward the gully, a collection of rocks in his arms.

Felix had realized something while he was meditating. This dangerous, deadly world was misleading. He could die from the smallest misstep from even the weakest of enemies here, and his first instinct was to turtle up and hide. But without risk, there was no reward. If he didn't push himself to the edge of his capabilities, over and over, he would never escape this forest. He would never get home.

Felix climbed down the shallow walls of packed earth, sliding slightly.

No. He was done hiding in a tree while monsters prowled the woods.

He dumped the rocks out on the ground around him, hefting

two out of the pile. They were softball sized and colored a faint shimmering gray where the sunlight hit them.

Let's do this.

The first two stones flew true, hitting the grub square in its back.

Thrown Weapons Mastery is Level 2!

Felix dodged to the side, just barely in time to miss a stream of acid. The grub lifted onto its hind portions, wiggling its stubby limbs at him as a glowing green sac began to grow beneath its clacking mandibles.

Felix snatched another rock and hurled it as fast as he could.

Please please...yes!

Critical Hit!

The rock struck the grub right in the sac, and acid squelched out and upward from its mouth. Felix pumped his fist and reached for another rock. Movement in his peripherals made him turn the reach into a tumble, but his leg became engulfed in a wet heat that bloomed into agony.

A Copse Grub's Acid Stream Has Entered Your Bloodstream.
Status Condition: Poisoned

Poison Resistance is level 4!

Pushing away the pain, Felix took a quick aim and threw. The rock flew wide, hitting the log to its right, causing the grub to twitch toward the sound. Felix took a chance, limping forward as fast as he could.

Toward the grub.

He was tired. Tired of being burned and bitten and sliced. Tired of hiding and waiting and running. He wouldn't be a victim anymore. Now he was the monster.

And monsters had teeth.

Felix pulled two pieces of stone out of his pockets, lifting them up as he hop-limped toward the grub. He got within arms reach of it before it twitched back to him, mandibles spread wide and a harsh hissing noise coming from its throat.

Felix thrust downward with both stones, inexpertly sharpened. Both improvised blades struck true, sinking into the resisting, gooey flesh of the grub and causing it to release a hissing screech that hurt Felix's ears.

You Have Learned A New Skill!
Small Blade Mastery (C) Level 1!
Why throw rocks when you can stab with rocks! Proficiency increases with skill level.

Felix didn't stop. He pulled the crude stone daggers out of the grub and started stabbing again, and again. The brittle blades broke quickly, but then he was just hitting it with his fists. The grub screeched over and over, but it had fallen over in Felix's flurry of attacks, and it couldn't maneuver its stubby limbs to move.

Acid and thick blue ichor splattered with every strike, raining down on the both of them.

Then it was over.

Falling limp to the ground, Felix fumbled a handful of yarrow out of his pockets. He shoved it into his mouth, past caring that a large dose of blue blood and green acid went in too. For the next few minutes, he ate yarrow and witchcaps and the last bit of flitweed to replenish his flagging Stamina.

I did it.

The thought was dull and heavy, like the rocks all around him. As the herbs did their thing, he turned inward, meditating to stay afloat of the damage that the poison and acid was still doing to his body. Slowly, so slowly, his thoughts sharpened. Meditation began to gain ground, and Felix felt like had escaped from a dark hole.

He opened his eyes.

Sunlight, bright and golden, shone down through a break in the clouds and illuminated the gully. All around him the wood and rocks were sizzling and pitted by acid, and the savaged remains of the copse grub oozed slowly down the side of the log. Felix took a deep, exhausted breath...and doubled over coughing. The air was filled with the acrid tang of acid and boiling blue ichor. He stood up and stumbled a few steps away from the corpse.

Heh. More like Corpse Grub.

He shook his head. He was starting to get a little loopy. Focus. He toggled his notifications.

You Have Learned A New Skill!
Unarmed Mastery (Common) Level 1!
Lost your weapons? Don't stop, just punch them!

His Small Blade Mastery leveled to 2, Unarmed Mastery leveled to 3, Acid Resistance leveled to 10, Pain Resistance leveled to 8, Poison Resistance leveled to 6, Dodge leveled to 2, Acrobatics leveled to 3, and he earned a level in Improvisation back when he made his sharpened stone "daggers." His Endurance, Agility, Strength, and Vitality all went up by 1, while his Willpower increased by 2.

Overall, an impressive amount of stats and skill levels in a ten minute span. Felix supposed his theory about stress and skill levels was correct; the greater the difficulty and need, the greater the growth.

Now, if only it didn't hurt so much. He groaned as he rubbed his tender chest, still red and raw from acid burns.

You have defeated a Copse Grub!
You have gained a Level!
You have gained a Level!

You are now Level 4!
+6 to WIL! +4 to INT! +2 to DEX! +2 to END! +2 to PER!
You Have 10 Unused Stat Points!

Congratulations! You have earned a new Title!
Giantslayer I (Uncommon)! Defeat an enemy at least 10 levels higher than yourself! +1 STR +1 AGL

The pain dimmed as Felix felt a rush of power flood his body. His blood buzzed in his veins, his muscles squirming as his skin tightened and shifted. It was painful in a different way, like he was being stretched beyond limits he didn't know he had. After a few moments, the feeling faded, leaving him shaking on the ground.

"God damn," he managed, his breath puffing dust from the dry gully. "Leveling didn't feel like that last time."

Was it because he leveled up twice? If so, he didn't plan on doing that again. Felix could just imagine how that would work mid-battle. He'd get killed in seconds while he writhed on the ground.

But still, I feel stronger now. He pulled up his Status screen.

Name: Felix Nevarre
Level: 4
Race: Nym
Omen: The Magician
Born Trait: Keen Mind

Health: 70/70
Stamina: 82/104
Mana: 119/119

STR: 9 PER: 10
VIT: 14 END: 20
INT: 19 WIL: 22
AGL: 8 DEX: 8

Skills:
Acid Resistance (C), Level 10
Lessons of the Past (R), Level 2
Analyze (C), Level 10
Running (C), Level 6
Improvisation (C), Level 2
Staff Mastery (C), Level 1
Dodge (C), Level 2
Acrobatics (U), Level 3
Herbalism (U), Level 5
Physical Conditioning (R), Level 2
Free Climbing (U), Level 2
Pain Resistance (U), Level 8
Meditation (U), Level 5
Stealth (C), Level 3
Breath Control (U), Level 1
Thrown Weapons Mastery (C), Level 2
Poison Resistance (U), Level 6
Small Blade Mastery (C), Level 2

Unarmed Mastery (C), Level 3

Title(s):
Gourmand (+1 INT, VIT)
Survivor I (+1 END, VIT)
Survivor II (+1 END, +2 VIT)
Survivor III (+2 END, +3 VIT)
Natural Scholar I (+1 INT, PER)
Giant Slayer I (+1 STR, AGL)

Unused Stat Points: 10

"Dang." No wonder his body ached from his level up. Combined with his stat gains and Title bonuses, his stats were getting up there. Well, everything except his Strength, Agility, Dexterity, and Perception. They were still his lowest, most not even above ten.

Felix still had no clue on the average baseline for stats, especially for natives of this place. Assuming ten was average, he definitely didn't want anything below that. He had 10 stat points to allocate now, and he mentally set aside half of them to get all his lagging stats up to ten.

Where should the rest go?

Vitality was linked to his Health, obviously. Each point in that seemed to add five points to his maximum Health score. Endurance was definitely linked to Stamina, but something else was mixing in there too...perhaps Strength? Same with Mana, with Willpower being the driving force, with maybe Intelligence adding some extra?

So increasing those would increase his three main attributes. His Mana was largely useless, and his Race and Omen bonuses took care of both Willpower and Intelligence, so increasing it was pointless at this time. Health and Stamina were always good to have, especially since he kept nearly dying. But both Vitality and Endurance were pretty high already, and he was still getting the shit kicked out of him.

His natural instinct was to avoid damage altogether, and that would mean increasing his Agility, which seemed to affect speed and flexibility. Maybe upping Agility and increasing his Dodge Skill? Maybe. He had theory-crafted for many different games in his day, but making decisions like this when his actual life was on the line was hard.

Felix took a breath and allocated his points.

A rush of energy filled his body, the stat points altering his muscles and nerves and who knew what else. It wasn't painful this time, just weird, and immediately after his entire body felt oddly tingly.

He called up his stats.

Health: 75/75
Stamina: 105/105
Mana: 119/119

STR: 10 PER: 10
VIT: 15 END: 20
INT: 19 WIL: 22
AGL: 14 DEX: 10

So Strength definitely affects the Stamina total. It adds, what, one point of Stamina per two points of Strength? He nodded to himself, happy to have solved that small mystery.

Felix stood up and stretched. His joints popped and he could have sworn his muscles creaked. He flexed his hands and looked down at his fleshy torso and tattered jeans. Was he getting more defined? It was really hard to tell without a mirror. He felt stronger, he thought, and his movements felt smoother, maybe?

Shaking his head, Felix looked at the grub. Its body was battered and mashed to bloody pulp on the log it was born in, though its face was mostly intact. This was due to the strange hard pieces all around its face and jelly-like eyes. Having left his walking stick back at the treeline, he found a thin, discarded branch to poke at the corpse, pushing its face...until two jagged pincers latched onto it.

"Ahh!" He stumbled backward, letting go of the stick as he groped for another stone.

But the grub didn't move.

He drew closer, and the grub was just as lifeless as before. Its pincers were fixed firmly around the stick, holding the piece of wood nearly vertical. He must have hit some muscle or something, making it latch on. Felix grabbed the stick firmly and tried to yank it away, but the pincers were lodged nearly halfway through it, about a quarter of an inch. A few sharp tugs and the stick broke.

Huh.

Felix looked at the broken branch in his hand and back at the pincers. He had a weird idea. He didn't know if it would work, if it was even possible, but he did know one thing:

"This is gonna be gross."

CHAPTER EIGHT

After bashing the grub's face with a rock over a dozen times, the pincers finally came loose. At first, Felix was worried they'd be damaged by such harsh treatment, but after being delicate did nothing except slice his fingers, he resorted to blunt force trauma.

He held up the pincers and examined them in the bright sunlight. They were approximately six inches long, way longer than he'd have expected on a grub that was only two feet long itself. They had a gristly bit at the ends, but were otherwise made of a thick bone-like material. Chitin, he assumed. He wasn't really a bug guy.

"Hope this works," he muttered. He pulled out the scraps of his tshirt and wrapped them around the bases of the pincers. He had enough torn pieces that he was able to wrap both pincers halfway up their lengths. An icon blinked in the corner of his vision, and he quickly toggled it.

Improvisation is Level 3!

"Haha!" Felix held his two new knives up in the air. "I shall call you Grubstickers!"

Felix turned, triumphant, and met the eyes of a Tree Vole sitting on the log. It blinked its large orange eyes at him, slowly chewing a large leaf. Suddenly embarrassed and on edge, Felix put his arms down and shifted his feet. In a flash, the tree vole scurried away.

"Phew," he breathed. That vole was level 22, and he was still hurting from the grub fight. He wasn't ready to take on that challenge.

Cautiously, Felix packed away his new knives and climbed out of the gully. He retrieved his walking stick from a copse of conifers, and headed back toward the Kingsap.

———

Back at the Kingsap, Felix prepped for his journey.

He collected all of the remaining yarrow, witchcap, and dewcatcher that was in the nearby area. There wasn't much. It took some doing, but he fashioned a sort of sack out of the wide purple leaves of the Kingsap, binding them all together with some crawling vines called Agatha's Curse.

Name: Agatha's Curse
Lore: Strong and invasive, named for a famed Alfein naturalist whose garden was befouled by this creeping vine.
Properties: Strong and fibrous, cannot be digested.
Alchemical Properties: Unknown.

What's an Alfein? He supposed they were some of the other people here in the Continent. Something that kept a garden, at least. Maybe that meant they were close by? Or no, invasive species were usually ones that spread far and wide, right? He couldn't remember.

Maybe I'll find out once I'm out of this forest. He considered the vast and towering trees before him, too tall to even see beyond. If there *was* a beyond.

Felix had a plan. He was going to find some more Copse Grubs and grind them until he was as high level as possible. The closer to level 20 the better. If need be, he would seek out Ember-flies after that. He gathered up a leaf's worth of sap (maybe a couple ounces, max) from his magic tree and headed out.

Felix sought out several of the trees he had checked previously. Before, he hadn't found a Copse Grub in any of them, but realized he was looking in the wrong places. He needed to check where the grub got its food. Since he couldn't look inside the trees, he figured he'd put some food on the outside.

Using a stick, he spread a small amount of magic tree sap onto the lower trunk of the white *arrol* tree before him. Then he waited.

It didn't take long. Within minutes, the trunk was torn up from the inside as a two-foot-long gummy worm burrowed its way out. He didn't know how they sensed the sap, but during his fight, Felix had noticed that the grubs were exceptionally sensitive to anything impacting their tree. He had guessed that it would sense food, especially something as interesting as Kingsap. In moments, the grub had scurried down the tree and started gnawing at the sap-coated bark.

Taking careful aim, he hurled his walking stick straight at the bug's head. Except it wasn't a walking stick any longer; he had used his Grubstickers to whittle down the point until it resembled the crudest of spears. With a wet *sklorch*, the spear sunk into the back of the Copse Grub.

Thrown Weapon Mastery is level 3!

Immediately, it began to writhe in a panic. Acid jetted out in several arcs, burning sizzling tracks through the underbrush but easily avoidable. Felix picked up the first of a dozen rocks and hurled them as quickly and as accurately as he could manage. Within minutes, the grub was down to dregs of its Health, but his crude spear kept it from burrowing away. He had meant to pin the thing to the ground, but flubbed the shot. Regardless, the ungainly length of wood stuck firmly into the grub's back, keeping it from fitting into any burrowed tunnels.

Suddenly, he was out of stones. Quick as he could, Felix ran forward, knives out. He reached out to stab into the grub, and that's when it happened.

He had forgotten about the AOE.

"AHH FUCK!" Acid exploded all around the Copse Grub, inundating Felix in what felt like gallons of green, putrid muck. His skin sizzled even as his Acid Resistance fought back.

Acid Resistance is level 11!
Pain Resistance is level 9!

But that was it for the grub. Obviously spent, it fell limply onto the ground. Fighting against the agony of his skin on fire, Felix gripped his knives and dropped to his knees. It was all he could do to not fall on the creature, but he forced his right hand up. His breathing was labored, tight in his chest as the acid peeled back his skin in layers. He shook, but kept his fist up.

Pain Resistance is level 10!

"*Fuck you*!" Felix screamed as he forced his arms down with all the strength he could muster. Over and over again, until his Stamina bottomed out and Felix fell gasping to the earth. But it was enough.

The Copse Grub was no more.

Felix wiped blue ichor from his face as he shakily took his feet a few minutes later. Red blood dripped from his hands where he gripped the knives too hard.

"Who's next?"

He didn't realize that he was smiling.

For the next nine hours, Felix began a strange routine. He would find dying trees and spread some Kingsap sap on its trunk. The Copse Grubs, as he suspected, found the magical sap to be irresistible. Once they burrowed out of their trees, Felix would hit them with his spear and rocks from a distance until they discharged their AOE Acid Explosion, then moved in close to take it down with his Grubstickers.

After his first battle with the Copse Grubs, his Acid Resistance had hit level 10, and much like Analyze, it changed in a way he couldn't quite quantify. The damage reduction seemed stronger, but more than that, it felt like his skin replenished faster or corroded slower now. He couldn't quite tell, but it was welcome all the same.

Now his Pain Resistance had hit level 10 as well. While he hadn't noticed less pain than before (being burned still hurt just as much), it was easier to push past it. Coupled with his high Willpower, and he felt he could handle a lot more punishment than ever before.

If this was the effect of a level 10 Skill, then he planned to get all of his Skills up that high as soon as possible.

By the end of the day, Felix's abilities had reached a new peak. He had killed fourteen Copse Grubs in the area, each time sustaining less and less damage due to dodging, increased proficiency with his knives, and acid resistance. That was fortunate, since his stock of Yarrow had run out by late afternoon. He was healing exclusively with Meditation and his own innate regeneration.

What made it all easier was that, after the fifth grub, his Analyze seemed to unlock more information on them.

Name: Copse Grub
Type: Insect
Level: 13
HP: 51/51
MP: 34/34
Lore: Born of eggs placed in trees, copse grubs spend their lives devouring the tree from the inside out. Once done, they transform into Emberflies.
Strength: Acidic ranged attacks and a defensive acid based area of effect skill.
Weakness: Piercing damage and removing them from contact with their birth tree.

All of this seemed based on his own experiences with the grub, but seeing it quantified was something else. Now he could see how much Health they had and made sure to dislodge them from their tree as quickly as possible. The remaining grubs fell much quicker.

He managed to salvage another three pincers, wrapping their hilts with Agatha's Curse as he'd run out of tshirt material. He had lost a few using them as ranged weapons at first, but his Throwing Weapons Mastery had gained quite a few levels in the process, so it wasn't a total failure.

Sitting back in the Kingsap, Felix toggled open his Status screen, pleased with his growth.

Name: Felix Nevarre
Level: 7
Race: Nym

Omen: The Magician
Born Trait: Keen Mind

Health: 100/100
Stamina: 126/126
Mana: 167/167

STR: 12 PER: 14
VIT: 20 END: 24
INT: 25 WIL: 31
AGL: 18 DEX: 16

Skills:
Acid Resistance (C), Level 12
Lessons of the Past (R), Level 2
Analyze (C), Level 11
Running (C), Level 6
Improvisation (C), Level 4
Staff Mastery (C), Level 1
Dodge (C), Level 6
Acrobatics (U), Level 8
Herbalism (U), Level 5
Physical Conditioning (R), Level 5
Free Climbing (U), Level 2
Pain Resistance (U), Level 12
Meditation (U), Level 9
Stealth (C), Level 3
Breath Control (U), Level 1
Thrown Weapons Mastery (C), Level 8
Poison Resistance (U), Level 6
Small Blade Mastery (C), Level 7
Unarmed Mastery (C), Level 3

Title(s):
Gourmand (+1 INT, VIT)
Survivor I (+1 END, VIT)
Survivor II (+1 END, +2 VIT)
Survivor III (+2 END, +3 VIT)
Natural Scholar I (+1 INT, PER)
Giant Slayer I (+1 STR, AGL)

Unused Stat Points: 15

Felix had gained three levels from the fourteen grubs, which was nice but not nearly as much as he wanted. His usual level up bonuses applied, and also netted him another 15 (!) free stat points to use how he wished.

He toggled his notifications:

+2 STR
+3 END
+5 VIT
+3 DEX
+4 AGL
+1 PER

His base stats seemed to be getting harder to raise through exertion alone. It took combat and near death to really pump them up, though he found plenty of that in the forest. His greatest gains were in Vitality and Agility, and he assumed that both increased due to dodging streams of acid, and ironically, not dodging streams of acid.

Luckily Felix's pants were still whole, more or less. He didn't think he could handle being loose and free in these woods.

His Skills had grown as well, proving that doing was the best way to learn. Dodge hit level 6, Acrobatics leveled to 8, Pain Resistance leveled to 12, Thrown Weapon Mastery leveled to 8, Small Blade Mastery leveled to 7, Analyze leveled to 11, Acid Resistance leveled to 12, Physical Conditioning leveled to 5, Improvisation leveled to 4, and Meditation leveled to 9.

So close. Felix's eyes widened as he thought about his Meditation Skill hitting level 10. It seemed that the first five levels of Skills usually progressed quickly, slowing down slightly as it hit 5-9, and then again 9-10. After 10, it was difficult to level them at all, at least with his current usage. Analyze had only just hit level 11, and it had been at 10 for more than 24 hours of constant usage. Yet Pain Resistance had hit 12 just as fast as Acid Resistance. It was likely that he was missing something.

Questions upon questions. Felix rubbed his eyes, suddenly tired. *Nothing is easy.*

Felix could feel the results of his stat gains, but did not feel the same pain as before when he leveled up. Admittedly, he was only increasing one level at a time now, with the occasional stat bump. Much more gradual, but obviously effective. His Strength, while still low compared to his other stats, was enough that his knives easily punched through the grubs' tough flesh.

He wasn't sure how his mental stats were affecting things, but he found it easier to keep going, to push past his pain and fear and worry to ensure he survived. Maybe that was his Willpower in action, or maybe his Skills were working on him, but by the end of that day, Felix felt he could do this. He could survive.

Now, sitting in the Kingsap and letting the evening winds rock him gently to sleep, Felix was feeling good. It was a dramatic shift from just that morning, but it was amazing what hope could do. Hope and a clear goal.

He would be the strongest thing in these woods. He would become a monster, if only to keep the rest at bay.

This goal had him contemplating his knife as the light finally faded from the sky. Stars sparkled briefly in the distance, but clouds kept them veiled. The Kingsap beneath him glowed gently, turning the blue blood on his knife black. It was the blood of a Copse Grub, a remnant he hadn't wiped clean.

What if I...?

It was disgusting. Stomach-turning, really. This thick liquid had come from one of the grossest creatures he had ever seen, one of a species that had burned him with acid so many times he had lost count. But still, the thought persisted.

The grubs have Mana. Which means they cast spells, or at least spell-like Skills.

The logic was sound, but his tongue twisted at the thought of it. He wasn't even sure if it would work. After all, he had gotten plenty of grub blood in his mouth over the course of the day, and nothing to show for it.

Even still. If it worked on a tree, then....

Without wasting further thought, Felix licked the blue blood off his knife.

CHAPTER NINE

The night air stilled as everything dimmed, just slightly. Then the world...flexed, somehow.

Everything went dark.

You have gained a Memory from a Copse Grub! Would you like to review it now?

Yes/Yes

Everything was still dark. Dark, comforting, damp, and safe. Life. Food.

Flexing and pulling...crawling, inching through dissolving food. Delicious.

Light. Sudden. Dangerous.

Pain. Food torn away.

A face. Wrong. Broken. Metal. Unmade.

Lost.

They're all Lost.

A claw, sharp. Stabbing pain flooding body. Hurt.

Hurt.

Release the Burning, the Foodmaker. Over and over, until empty. Flee. Burrow down, down, deep as possible.

Into the dark.

Where it's safe.

"Urghlgh."

The sound of his own retching hit him before anything else. Felix groaned and rolled over, his body limp as a dead fish and somehow sore all over.

These Memories hit like a truck. Felix groaned, cradling his head. *Feels like my brain is trying to escape with an ice pick.*

Some time later, he managed to roll to his knees without vomiting again. The tree stopped spinning long enough to show him morning was well underway. He'd managed to lose the entire night.

Blacking out this much can't be healthy. He steadied his head, feeling like his eyeballs were pushing in the wrong directions. *Yeah, no. Definitely not healthy.*

He settled back against his branch and considered his hands. A short while ago, they were just nubby feet meant to push him through the delicious white wood of his mother tree. The *grub's* mother tree, he corrected. It was hard to keep the grub-Felix and himself separate. The Memory was so seamless that it felt baked into his mind.

After a moment longer, he accessed his notifications.

Pain Resistance is level 13!
Lessons of the Past is level 3!
Lessons of the Past is level 4!
Congratulations! Lessons of the Past Has Garnered You Insight!
You Have Learned A New Skill!
Acid Stream (Rare), Level 1!
Manifest a stream of acid to launch at foes!

"Holy shit, it worked." Eyes wide, Felix considered the implications as he fought down the burning in his chest. His Gourmand title gave him some sort of percentage to learn his opponents' strengths by eating them. Apparently he didn't have to eat them whole, as proven by the Kingsap and now the Copse Grub's blood. The percentage was also very low, maybe less than 1% based on how often he had gotten grub blood in his mouth during the previous day.

Not only that, the first skill the title had acquired for him was Lessons of the Past, which also created some sort of chance to gain skills from experiencing the Memories contained in his foes' Mana. Metaphysical implications of memories stored in blood aside, the skill and title combination was amazing. While he obviously didn't gain a Memory from the Kingsap, he had still had a chance to learn Meditation due to the Mana that flowed through the magic tree. And, though his Gourmand title didn't activate on the Copse Grub, he still was able to grab a Memory and learn from that.

"This is amazing," Felix laughed and was about to stand up when a blue box appeared in front of him.

Congratulations!
You Have Received Your First Spell!
You Have Received A Quest!
Advance Three Spells To Apprentice Level!
Reward: Title

"Oh man," he began. "Quests too? Fixed rewards? This is—"

ERROR...
Lost Race Detected...
Adjusting Quest...

Quest Received!
Advance Five Spells To Apprentice Level!
Reward: Variable, Title

"What."

The bottom dropped out of Felix's stomach. He had gotten a quest, but his race—his stupid, XP-penalty-having, not-his-choice race—altered it? Not only altered it, but made it harder, apparently!

He rubbed his temples. At least the rewards appeared to increase, though "variable" could mean almost anything.

And what did Apprentice level mean? It was higher than level 13, the level of his highest Skill. Pain Resistance didn't mention a word about Apprentice anything. Frowning, he pulled up his Status screen and consulted his Skills.

"Oh man, these are a mess." He'd been gaining Skills rapidly the past few days, and the result was a Skill column that was a mish-mash of types, rarities, and levels.

"Could I get these reorganized or—" Before he finished the thought, another blue box appeared.

Do You Wish To Reconfigure The Skills Section?
Yes/No

"Creepy," Felix grimaced. "But yes."

The reorganization was simple enough, basically drag and drop. But it took him close to an hour before he was satisfied with the layout.

"Ok. Accept."

Skills:
Resistances: Acid Resistance (C), Level 12; Pain Resistance (U), Level 12; Poison Resistance (U), Level 6

Utility: Analyze (C), Level 11; Improvisation (C), Level 4; Running (C), Level 6; Stealth (C), Level 3; Breath Control (U), Level 1; Free Climbing (U), Level 2; Herbalism (U), Level 5; Meditation (U), Level 9; Physical Conditioning (R), Level 5; Lessons of the Past (R), Level 4

Combat: Dodge (C), Level 6; Small Blade Mastery (C), Level 7; Staff Mastery (C), Level 1; Thrown Weapons Mastery (C), Level 8; Unarmed Mastery (C), Level 3; Acrobatics (U), Level 8;

Spells: Acid Stream (R), Level 1

Broad categories but effective. More importantly, it wouldn't make his eyes bleed every time he accessed his Status. That done with, Felix clapped his hands and quickly climbed down the Kingsap.

Free Climbing is level 3!

"Time to practice some magic!"

Felix was beyond excited. While he had many Skills at this point, this was his first truly magical Skill. Fixing his eyes on a rock about ten feet away, Felix activated Acid Stream. Quickly, maybe half a second or so later, a bubble of acid manifested a half inch from his palm. The bubble grew until it was about the size of a grapefruit, then suddenly burst outward in the direction his palm was facing. Bright green acid, looking very similar to the Copse Grub's attack, arced gracefully out toward his target. It missed by several feet, hitting around seven feet away and splashing into a small puddle.

Felix kept the stream up for a few seconds, watching his Mana tick downward steadily. Acid Stream took 5 Mana per second and was a continual cast, lasting apparently as long as he had Mana to fuel it. With his current stats, he could keep it up for 33 seconds.

"This is so cool," Felix grinned. He walked to the small green puddle and inspected it. The small grasses and thin weeds were sizzling away, burning down to nothing in the acid. However, the larger weeds and plants with thicker stalks and tougher flowers were just trampled down, like a garden hose being sprayed into a flower bed. He channeled a quick stream against a nearby rock, letting it splash against it for a few seconds. The acid sizzled and bubbled, but the rock was unaffected.

"Dang. The grub definitely had more power than this," Felix bit his lip, thinking. "I wonder at what level the spell can melt rock?" And would leveling it improve the cost, speed of casting, or anything else? He hoped so.

Oh, how does Intelligence affect this? In many RPGs, Intelligence dictated the power of spells, while wisdom (or Willpower in this case) affected the amount of Mana and regeneration. *Does it work the same? My intelligence is pretty high.*

"Welp, one way to find out."

An hour later, Felix realized he had hunted all of the local grubs. If he wanted to experiment, he'd have to attack the level 18 Emberflies...but he wasn't ready for that kind of heat, not yet.

It seemed it was about time to leave his little glen and his magic tree. Despite the danger, Felix found he was a little excited at the thought of exploring beyond the Skink's territory.

But, before anything else, he focused on his free stat points. He had fifteen of them to use, and had to consider this carefully. All of his stats were getting fairly high, with the exception of Strength at 12. While it was tempting to increase his Willpower and Intelligence and thus his Mana score, his race and Omen did a good job at keeping those high.

No, he had decided to follow his instincts and up his physical stats. This would keep his stats in balance, and while he might regret it later down the road, he didn't know all of the rules in this place and would rather play it safe. After all, in a world where his Strength and Vitality scores were actual representations of how likely he was to die? Yeah. He was fine with balance.

He dumped 2 into AGL, 4 into PER, 1 into DEX, and a whopping 8 into STR.

Health: 100/100
Stamina: 126/130
Mana: 167/167

STR: 20 PER: 18
VIT: 20 END: 24
INT: 25 WIL: 31
AGL: 20 DEX: 17

Once he hit accept, Felix's body flooded with energy, causing his flesh to almost vibrate. Related to the burning in his chest, a weird, tingly sensation made his bones ache and his muscles squirm. It faded quickly, much more quickly than before. Maybe he was getting used to it?

As the sensation faded, Felix regarded his bare chest and stomach. An amount of pudge still existed, but a good chunk of it had disappeared, replaced by barely-visible muscle. He felt...strong. A lot stronger, if he was being honest, with more energy than he knew what to do with, like he could run forever.

"Now, this I could get used to," Felix grinned as he flexed his hands and stretched his legs. Previously, his 12 in Strength just barely allowed him to pierce the toughened flesh of the Copse Grubs, even with his makeshift knives. With a 20 in Strength, he was nearly twice as strong, and should be able to deal with them much more easily.

Searching around his glen and surrounding areas, Felix was able to find another cache of dewcatchers and a small grouping of yarrow. They had been hidden by hanging moss, right along the pathway he had been using for days now, and his eyes had been almost magnetically drawn to them as he passed. Increasing his Perception had definitely been worth it. If he hadn't caught a slight glance of them out of the corner of his eye, he would have missed them. And that would have been bad, since he was totally out of healing herbs and nearly out of his water supply.

It wasn't a lot, but it would have to be enough. With his supplies nearly gone, his food supply nonexistent, and his chances of survival nearing zero, Felix had little choice but to attempt to escape the Sharpwing Skinks' territory.

Taking a steadying breath, Felix hefted his wooden spear and headed due east. Into the woods.

It was easy going at first.

The difficult, forested terrain he had struggled through two days ago felt much less arduous. His Stamina was keeping pace with him, despite having to duck and hide at every loud noise. He evaded three different Skinks by hiding in the underbrush or under massive logs. While it was stressful and dangerous, it did wonders for his Stealth Skill.

Stealth is level 4!
Stealth is level 5!

Each level increase made him feel more at ease with hiding and moving quietly. He still forced himself to move as slowly as possible, or not at all during these moments, not trusting his low-level Skill to make up for a lifetime of inexperience.

After two nerve-wracking hours, Felix began to hear a weird sound. He had traversed deeper into the forest than ever before, and the ground had been sloping upward for quite some time. With the huge trees and heavy foliage he couldn't be sure, but it felt like he was climbing a small mountain...or at least a big hill.

Turning a corner along an exposed rocky wall, the sound suddenly became twice as loud and Felix knew exactly what it was.

"Running water!" He whispered, excited. There must be a river nearby and, judging by the sound, it was quite big. This was perfect; he only had a few more dewcatchers left in his makeshift leaf-bag. He quickly ate an oblong fruit he had picked up a short while ago. It had pale lavender skin and tasted like a cross between a pear and an apple. It was good, soothing the ache that had been building in his stomach for the past few hours.

Just a little farther to go. Hopefully, the river means an end to the lizards' territory. He had noticed the Skinks sliced up various trees with their wings throughout the forest and assumed it was their way of marking. Like a dog pissing on a fire hydrant. He just had to find an area without the markings, and he was golden.

Felix took a few steps down a rocky incline, being careful of the loose rock all around. He was excited to get to the river, mostly to bathe. After several days in the forest, he was getting awfully rank. And judging by the sound, it had to be only a short distance away. He could probably make it without—

Bzzzzzzzzzzzzzzz.

Shit, no, not now. Felix had come to dread that sound. Especially now, with the river so close. There was little underbrush along the incline, and the treeline was about twelve feet away. He couldn't make it without causing a *lot* of noise. And he couldn't hide in plain sight, either.

Fuck. God damn it!

He started running.

Shale-like rock fell and clattered around his feet as he careened down the remaining twelve feet and stumbled into the treeline. As he hit the trees, a teal Sharpwing Skink wheeled into view and let out a warbling *yarp!*

Let's race, lizard. Felix took off, pushing himself as fast and as hard as he could. The Skink's wings buzzed as it chased him, but it didn't close in. He was doing it! He was gonna win!

Then a second Skink zipped across his path, nearly cutting his head off. A quick duck and tumble saved his life, even as he hopped back onto his feet and kept running. Now the buzzing increased, rattling his teeth unpleasantly as the two Skinks amped up their pursuit.

Notifications started popping into his vision, but Felix waved his arms. "Not now! Minimize!" The blue boxes closed, just in time for the ground to drop out from beneath him.

CHAPTER TEN

Felix plummeted into a raging river.

He tumbled, head over heels, the water surging around him violently. He briefly saw the surface, but was so disoriented that he couldn't tell which way he had to swim. The water around him was murky, churned into a swirling froth of bubbles. It was absolutely frigid, and his skin quickly turned numb. Felix kicked, straining against the current to orient himself, pushing toward the bright light that flashed across his eyes. Bursting back to the surface, Felix reoriented himself just as the Skinks zipped to the edge of the embankment.

Then they buzzed toward him.

"Oh, what the hell," Felix gasped. He had no choice. Unfortunately, his guess had been correct: the river was wide, too wide to swim across before the lizards took him out. He took several quick breaths before inhaling as large a lungful as he could. He dove beneath the surface just as the first Skink slashed its razor sharp wings at him.

Below the water, the world was suddenly quiet. A faint rumble in his chest was all that remained of the surface noise. Felix pushed down toward the bottom of the river, a good six or seven feet below. Straining, even as the current pulled him along, he was able to grab onto the edge of a mossy rock. Clinging with all his strength, Felix pulled himself down toward the bottom of the river and he waited.

And waited.

From this vantage, he could see everything. The water wasn't murky here so much as roiling; once he was deep enough, it was like a strange other world. Weeds and moss grew all around him, filling in the spaces between large, river-round boulders. From his angle, he could just barely look up and behind himself, where the blurry shapes of the lizards zipped to and fro above the surface, like obese dragonflies.

C'mon. Leave already.

His lungs were starting to burn. He wasn't entirely sure how long he had been down here, but it was definitely a couple minutes. His enhanced body was apparently better at holding its breath than Felix had ever been, but even so, he was pushing the limits of his Endurance. He tried to close his eyes, focusing only on controlling the burning ache in his chest.

Of course, that's when he slipped.

Felix's hands, one then the other, slipped away from the rock beneath him. He flailed, trying to latch onto another, even as the strong current ripped him off and away. His lungs screamed, his urge to inhale almost impossible to resist. Felix was spun about, arms spread as he careened off of one boulder after another. He smashed his elbow into one, then his ribs bashed against several upright rocks. The pain was like hot lava in his bones, burning him from the inside out.

Then, for one beautiful moment, all of the rocks around him disappeared. He floated, free, unimpeded. Consciousness dimming, his vision dark except for occasional flares of bright yellow and blue at the edges, Felix barely had time to register the sudden shape of the rushing water. He zoomed along, pulled at breakneck speed toward an edge where all the foaming water rocketed away.

Oh, he thought, *a waterfall.*

Felix started awake, slamming into something.

Laughter, muffled by cubicle walls. Bright fluorescent lighting smeared his eyesight, and he rubbed the heel of his hand against them, attempting to clear it.

He was at his desk at work, standing on a rubber mat in front of a chest-high desk. This standing desk is what he had slammed into. His keyboard was askew, and the mouse was dangling by its cord off the edge of the sliding tray. He righted them both and took a step back.

Why was he...?

"Felix!"

A voice slithered across the cubicles, and the clip-clop of heels sounded on the hard linoleum flooring. Felix turned, just in time to see a woman with sandy brown hair step into his space, arms akimbo.

"Felix, what are you doing? The big meeting is starting in five minutes!"

Felix blinked several times, his vision still oddly blurry. "Uh, meeting?"

The woman rolled her eyes at him, a beautiful pair of blue-green eyes framed by thick lashes. "Yes, a meeting. This is your big chance! Designing the main attraction! You can't tell me you're getting cold feet?" She arched a perfect eyebrow at him.

"My—" This wasn't making sense. He was—he had been—

Then he remembered. A water park. Yes, of course.

At some point, the woman had guided him out of his cubicle and into the aisle. They were halfway to a large picture window looking out over the city skyline. Bright, beautiful sun filled the office. Felix found it blinding.

The water park. He was working on it. Right? The main attraction, called—

"Roaring Waterfall, right?" The woman prompted, nudging his ribs. Felix flinched, his chest aching for some reason.

Must have hit it on the desk...

"Crazy what you engineers come up with," she continued, her hands never stopping moving. She mimed someone going down a slide, then off a sharp edge. "I mean, sending a man off a waterfall would be death in your world. Good thing this isn't, yeah?"

"Hm? Yeah. Ah—" Felix's head felt like it was stuffed with cotton. He was fuzzy, and the light from the window was so bright. What was she saying?

Hands grabbed his shoulders and soft blue-green eyes stared

into his dull brown ones. Felix couldn't quite make out her face, but she was...she was...words were spoken. He couldn't make them out.

"What?"

"You've got a long way to go, Felix. I can't have you giving up yet."

"What? What do you mean?" Felix's head spun, but her words were like fire. He felt like he was burning up. "Why are you calling me—?"

Then, in an instant, the fog burned away. His eyes cleared, his mind sharpened. They stood at the end of the aisle, the view of the city spread out beneath them.

“Where am I? I’m not an engineer...” He looked at the woman, but could only make out her vivid blue-green eyes. The rest of her was blurry, occluded by a floater in his vision. She smiled and her teeth..."Who are you?"

"Felix, Felix, Felix," the stranger sighed. "If I told you that, this wouldn't be any fun."

Then she pushed him out of the window.

"WAKE UP."

"*Ghaaaaaah*!"

Gasping like a fish, Felix emerged from the calm blue waters like a breaching whale. Splashing frantically, he flailed until soft, yielding ground emerged beneath his feet, half walking through the water until he fell, exhausted on the shore.

"Still...alive," he breathed.

Felix's pants were waterlogged, and his acid-raw chest was turning blue. The water was damn cold, far colder than the summer-like weather would suggest. He shook, muscles contracting rapidly against his will. Two icons flashed in his vision, a blue snowflake and a head silhouette with a jagged line through it. Teeth beginning to chatter, he toggled them.

Status Condition: Exposure (Mild)

Status Condition: Concussion (Mild)

"O-oh, c-cool," he managed. "N-n-new ways t-to die." The warm air against his freezing skin chafed like a steel wool pad, scraping him raw. Everything was too bright, and the ground wouldn't stay in place. It kept squirming around. Forcing himself to breathe deeply, Felix clawed his way up the shore, pulling himself onto a large flat rock after a few minutes.

He must have passed out again. When he opened his eyes, the shadows all looked different, and it wasn't as bright. More worryingly, the blue snowflake icon had turned red and was pulsing. And he was *freezing.*

Status Condition: Exposure (Severe)

Don't panic.

Warmth seeped into him from the rock he laid on, but it wasn't enough. His guts felt like ice, and his arms and legs were numb clubs. His breath hitched in his chest, coming out in stuttering gasps. This was it. After everything, he was gonna die. Not because he was sliced apart by a lizard or melted by acid or even because he fell down a huge waterfall.

But because he got too chilly.

"No," he growled, or tried to. It came out as a shaky whisper, but his eyes narrowed in anger. He refused to give up.

Pulling his arms and legs into the fetal position, he tried to marshal what remaining heat he had left. The sun-warmed rock helped, but a light breeze started up and chilled his skin even more. Felix grunted and tried to focus. How could he get out of this? He didn't know how to start a fire, and none of his Skills would be of any help. He only had his tattered jeans and sneakers, and they were still damp and bitingly cold. He huddled there, fighting just to breathe without gasping.

Inhale.

Exhale.

Wait.

Something. Something was...there! He felt it. A flash of heat, dim and buried in a mountain of cold. The burning in his chest! He focused, trying to find it, visualizing a flickering flame right above his navel. Lower than he anticipated, but it was there. A candle flame he could cup with his hand, protecting it from the frigid wind. Yet, Felix realized it was slowly dwindling, even as he felt his limbs shake harder. He doubled down, thinking warm thoughts; bonfires and sunlight and standing before a heater after walking a mile in the cold.

Did the flame grow? He wasn't sure, but he kept on feeding it.

Red electric stove-tops, pizza pockets that were molten hot inside, hot soup that burned your throat as you swallowed it. The flickering fire grew this time, he was sure of it. His core felt warm, nearly hot, burning with a brightening fire that Felix could almost *see*. It made no sense, but he persisted.

Limbs shivering, Felix pushed that heat from his core, moving it outward in big loops into his arms and legs, desperately trying to warm himself up.

You Have Learned A New Skill!
Fire Within (Rare), Level 1!
You have discovered the fire that burns within, animating the cold clay of your body and filling it with strength.

Warmth surged into his limbs, suddenly moving much more freely as the Skill activated. In twenty seconds, his limbs were awash in pins and needles as feeling and mobility returned.

"Ow ow ow ow." Felix gritted his teeth against the discomfort, but it was a small price to pay to see the blue snowflake disappear from his vision. He kept circulating the heat inside of him another thirty seconds before his Mana guttered out. A faint headache pounded at his temples, and the light was still a little too bright. Probably from the concussion.

Felix struggled to his feet, muscles tight and sore from the swim, the cold, and all the rest. Slowly stretching and practicing measured breathing, he had time to check his stored notifications.

You Have Learned A New Skill!
Swimming (Common), Level 1!
Swim like a fish, or sink like a stone. Wise choice.

Swimming is level 2!
Swimming is level 3!

Breath Control is level 2!

Breath Control is level 3!
...
Breath Control is level 8!

+1 STR
+1 END
+4 INT
+6 WIL

This time, the burning sensation didn't return, but that internal fire grew just a bit brighter. Strengthening.

"Intelligence? Willpower?" Felix was surprised at the sudden stat bump. Whatever the reason, he was grateful for anything that increased his chances at surviving this place.

You Have Earned A New Title!
Daredevil I (Uncommon)!
You've proven your bravery! Or was it stupidity?
Survived a fall of 50 feet. +1 STR +1 VIT +1 AGL

You Have Earned A New Title!
Daredevil II (Uncommon)!
You're a madman! Survived a fall of at least 200 feet. +1 STR +2 VIT +1 AGL

He shook his head in disbelief, mouth flattening in a grim line. He kept earning Titles for not dying.

He felt dizzy for a moment, but it passed quickly.

Notifications through, Felix looked around at where he found himself. The lake before him was huge, easily miles across at the far end, and blue as the sky above. The forest surrounded it all, the same type of trees as the other parts he'd navigated. The shore was wide and empty of trees or even much undergrowth. He stood on a series of large rocks, but much of the shore was bare, sandy earth. Three hundred feet to his left, the waterfall pounded away at the lake, pouring its frigid waters from far above him.

I fell down THAT? Felix couldn't believe it. How was he not a bloody smear in the water? Did his enhanced Endurance and Strength allow him to survive? He glanced at his Health.

Health: 23/115
Stamina: 10/136
Mana: 3/199

Health almost gone, Mana nearly gone, Stamina bottoming out. It was a miracle he could even stand. His head pounded, temples throbbing, Felix leaned his arms against his knees and tried not to throw up. This was no good. He immediately began Analyzing the surrounding flora.

After a few minutes, he found a decent collection of yarrow, flitweed, two new herbs, and a dozen strange fruit trees. The herbs were called bellock and aram leaf, and neither had straightforward lore entries.

Name: Bellock
Lore: Highly toxic, believed to disrupt Dark Murmurs.
Properties: Unknown.
Alchemical Properties: Unknown.

Name: Aram Leaf
Lore: A flower with sharp, angular leaves; powerfully affected by the Blood Moon.
Properties: Unknown.
Alchemical Properties: Unknown.

Luckily the yarrow and flitweed was what he needed at this point, and he was fortunate that it was common as weeds in this death forest. As he ate a handful of both, he investigated the nearest fruit tree.

Name: Kelaar Tree
Lore: Indigenous to the Foglands, the tree produces a fruit that was once a staple of the region.
Properties: Very nutritious.
Alchemical Properties: Unknown.

Analyze is level 12!

Foglands, eh? Is that where I am? Weird name for a place without a stitch of fog.

Feeling better as his Health and Stamina regenerated at a visible clip, Felix picked a low-hanging Kelaar fruit and inspected it. It was red with white splotches radiating from the stem. He took a tentative bite, and a soft, savory flavor filled his mouth. It wasn't bad, just odd; he was expecting sweet. He ate the whole thing. At the center were a bunch of seeds that tasted sort of like peanuts. He grabbed another and sat down.

The sun was getting low by this point, and Felix eyed the shadowed forest with increasing unease. He had maybe three hours before full dark. He quickly ate the second Kelaar fruit and walked down the shore, back toward the cliff.

He Analyzed everything he could, the grass, ground, trees, water, everything. He made it nearly to the waterfall and cliff face before he felt his eyes being pulled toward a wild patch of shrubbery. Cautiously, Felix stepped forward, moving as quietly as he could. He had lost his spear and leaf sacks in the river, so he only had a single grubsticker in hand as he carefully prodded at the undergrowth. His Perception had pegged something. But all he could find were vines and weeds, despite—

"*Ah*!"

Felix recoiled, falling back onto his butt, nearly stabbing himself with his grubsticker. Buried in the weeds were the pale white bones of a skeleton.

"Fuck, I hope this skeleton isn't alive," Felix swallowed nervously, the plot of too many games and movies running through his head. But the pile of bones didn't move. Slowly, he approached the corpse. It was human-ish, he decided. Two arms, two legs, same general shape and position. Its skull looked odd. Long, with sharper cheekbones and a wide jaw. Probably not human. He tried to Analyze it.

Name: ???
Race: Henaari
Level: N/A
HP: N/A
MP: N/A
Lore: The Henaari are a matriarchy that reveres the Endless Raven. As such, they long to explore the unexplored and find the unfound.

Endless Raven, dark murmurs, blood moons. Analyze's lore entry is getting more specific. Felix sighed. *And I have no idea what it all means.*

Using his makeshift knife, Felix carefully cut away the weeds that grew up and through the bones of this Henaari corpse. Quickly, it became clear that his Perception hadn't guided him wrong; lying beneath the skeleton was an intact leather satchel. Eyes wide, he pulled it free.

The satchel was made of a dark leather, still supple despite how long it must have laid out here in the elements. Despite the dried mud crusting the side, the satchel was in perfect condition. A simple bronze clasp secured the top, but before he could open it, Felix's eye caught on a metallic sheen from beneath the Henaari's pelvis. Tearing away a few more weeds and dirt, his hand closed on a simple wire-wrapped hilt that he slowly pulled from the earth.

"Whoa," Felix's eyes were wide and his heart raced.

He had found a sword.

CHAPTER ELEVEN

The sword looked like it was made of bronze, and had a weird curved shape. It was straight near the hilt, then it bowed outward in a distinct curve. Like an axe or something. The hilt was a simple cross guard, and the handle wrapped in dark wire and capped with an oblong pommel. The whole thing was in surprisingly good condition.

Name: Unknown Sword
Type: Slashing
Lore: Unknown

Interesting. No damage range or anything. This was the first time Felix had Analyzed a proper item. All of the improvised weapons and tools he had made offered nothing to the Skill. The details were both more than he expected and less than he wanted. Noticing there was no sheath or belt to put this sword in, he set it down at his feet and moved on.

The corpse was wearing the tattered and rusted remains of clothing and armor, but unlike the satchel, they were utterly ruined. Time and weather had rotted away the organics, and rust had done in the rest. This person had to have been lying here for months or years. Honestly, Felix had no idea how fast metal armor rusted away like that.

Turning back to the satchel, Felix found several interesting items within it. A small, thin rope called a brightweave coil, made of a slick, silky material was of particular note.

Name: Brightweave Coil (50ft)
Type: Tool (Enchanted)
Lore: Brightweave is the process of weaving Mana into a material, typically silk or something of similar quality. This rope was woven with an enchantment for durability, and with a limited ability to obey commands. It can tie itself into a knot upon command and release said knot as well.

"Wow," Felix was stunned. "A magic item." It was an extremely useful item, though he shook his head. Was it strange that his first thought was that his Free Climbing Skill wouldn't level if he used the rope?

Additionally, there was a hard leather case in the satchel. It had a simple catch, and was made of boiled leather plates. When he opened it, he found ten small loops filled with glass. Six of the ten loops held only shattered remnants, but four had intact vials capped with a blackened cork of some sort. Two vials were red, one was blue, and the last was a strange silver. He Analyzed them, and they were Health potions, a Mana potion, and the silver concoction came back with nothing.

Name: Unknown Potion
Type: Consumable
Lore: Unknown

The Health and Mana potions each cured 50 points per dose. A huge amount, especially in the middle of battle. Felix grinned and hugged the hard leather case to his chest, gently, careful not to smash the fragile vials. Excited, he reached back into the satchel and rooted around, looking for anything else.

His hand hit a hard, heavy object. Felix pulled it out and inspected it. It was a slightly blunt and very heavy iron spike. One end was a blunted tip and the other was flattened out, like a tent spike or something. A hole was formed into the flat end, as if it were meant to be threaded in some way. Felix looked around, expecting to see the rotted remains of a tent or something, when his eye snagged on a dark shape up on the cliff face. He stepped closer, walking to the base of the cliff and looking up. There, nearly ten feet up, a black iron spike had been hammered into the cliff face. Felix looked back at the corpse and the pile of rope at its feet.

"Why were you climbing this cliff?" Felix scratched his chin, his stubble irritating his usually clean-shaven skin. His eyes roamed over the cliff face, trying to pick out any more black spikes in the harsh late afternoon light. One, two, three more pitons could be seen, all together making a meandering path toward the waterfall itself. Stepping closer to the waterfall and rocky bank, Felix peered upward through the haze of chill mist. After nearly a minute, he caught a glimpse of the darkness behind the waterfall.

"A cave!" He gasped, excitement and relief flooding him. A cave meant shelter, and the out-of-the-way location meant he didn't have to worry about any beasts in the area attacking him. He grinned.

"Time to level up Free Climbing."

It took him a few minutes to gather up everything he would need. The satchel was a decent size and could hold plenty of herbs, roots, and Kelaar fruit. He packed it to the brim, just barely securing the clasp on the front. A few leather straps on the top of the satchel were convenient to tie down the strange hooked sword. Slipping the rope around his shoulder and the satchel around his chest, he began to climb.

His Stamina bottomed out shortly after he made it past the first iron piton. Dropping back down, Felix fell into a seated position and Meditated. As his Stamina ticked back up to full, Felix considered his options. His Free Climbing Skill was only level 3, and this cliff was obviously much more of a challenge than the Kingsap tree. But it stood to reason that if he just kept trying, his Skill level would increase and his Stamina consumption would drop accordingly. Nodding to himself, he got back up.

After an hour, he had fallen six times, but Free Climbing had risen to level 6. He could now make it past the second piton, and the fall was beginning to pose a significant danger. The sandy embankment helped cushion his falls, but he was pushing past forty feet and it was extremely easy to break a bone if he landed wrong. Luckily, his Acrobatics Skill took this time to shine, and a lucky tumble allowed him to reduce the damage a little. Acrobatics had risen from level 8 to level 10 quickly, and as before, Felix felt a portion of the Skill's power flow into him. He felt more graceful and flexible than ever before in his life.

After two hours, he made it up to the third piton. At this point, he was being showered in a constant icy mist. Still, without protective garments or even a shirt, Felix had to keep activating Fire Within to force away the cold. The main problem was that he couldn't really move while he used the Skill; he had to hunker down and hold tight for several minutes each time. Luckily, the cliff was craggy and had plenty of handholds that he could rest at. Not quite as luckily, the mist began to thicken into watery spray as he neared the final piton. He was forced to keep Fire Within activated constantly, pushing himself to keep climbing as he did so. His Mana continually dropped, the Skill taking approximately 3 Mana/second and reducing him to zero in a little over a minute, which meant a spiking headache that made him pause his climb.

Three hours later, the sun had almost completely set over the treetops, and Felix pulled himself up onto the final ledge. He lay there, panting and heaving and letting the icy spray settle over him. He was so tired, so drained of Mana and Stamina that he didn't even activate any Skills. He just laid there, seeing the sunset through a curtain of water. He toggled his notifications.

Free Climbing is level 9!
Acrobatics is level 10!
Physical Conditioning is level 6!
Physical Conditioning is level 7!

Meditation is level 9!
Meditation is level 10!
Meditation is level 11!

Fire Within is level 2!
Fire Within is level 3!
...
Fire Within is level 9!

+4 STR
+1 END
+1 WIL

What a workout. With a groan, Felix rolled over and up onto his feet. He was exhausted from the river, the hypothermia, and the climb. If nothing else, he was excited to have a safe place to sleep again. As he stumbled forward, the extent of the waterfall cave stretched out before him. It was perhaps fifteen feet deep by thirty feet wide, but that was it. Much of the area was wet and slick, but a sizable portion near the rear was quite dry.

"It'll do," he huffed.

You Have Learned A New Skill!
Exploration (Uncommon), Level 1!
Only by traveling into the unknown can your horizons expand. Skill gains related to exploration and information gathering are increased a small amount by Skill Level.

"That's...yeah, that's the weirdest one yet," Felix grunted as he sat in the back of the cave. The rock wasn't smooth, but it wasn't uncomfortable either, not with him as tired as he was. He briefly considered Meditating before his eyes drooped closed and he fell asleep.

It was full dark when Felix woke back up. He knew that because he could see the stars.

Wait. He blinked and squinted. Were the stars *moving*?

With a grunt of effort, Felix stood up from his seated position against the cave wall. A number of blue-white specks loomed beyond the waterfall, even out of the opening to the side of the cave, where the water didn't distort everything. His sore body protesting with every step, he hobbled closer to the edge. Had this been daytime, he would have been able to see all of the surrounding area, but it was night, and as it had been the past few days, night meant utter darkness.

Except for the glowing specks of blue-white light.

They fluttered and flowed around the area, not so much illuminating as radiating. They moved like birds, flowing in and out of liquid seeming flocks of light. They were...beautiful.

Something inside Felix loosened as he watched them. A knot in his chest he hadn't noticed, something that had been growing tighter with every passing hour in this strange and deadly land.

"Mom would have loved this," he sighed. His mother had loved fireflies, back when she had dragged him and his siblings out camping each summer. She would spend hours on the KOA picnic benches, watching the light fail as lightning bugs floated between the wildflowers. He closed his eyes. He could almost hear the clicking of the cicadas as he breathed in the warm night air.

When Felix opened his eyes, a couple of the glowing creatures had floated closer to him. Now in range, he tossed out a quick Analyze.

Name: Wisp
Type: Elemental
Level: 9
HP: 10/10
MP: 345/345
Lore: Bewitching travelers with their alluring light, wisps are commonly mistaken for light elementals. They are in fact bundles of raw kinetic energy.
Strength: Unknown
Weakness: Unknown

"Huh, weak."

It was the lowest level creature he had seen so far. Its HP was extremely low, too. If he tried, he could really mop these things up and probably get a decent amount of experience—

Felix shook his head. Easy experience? That was a fucked up way to look at a world, no matter how tempting. What would that turn him into down the road? Felix preferred not to find out.

He held out his arm as one of the Wisps drifted closer, appearing curious. The light they emitted was almost too bright to look at directly, but it was gorgeous. Felix watched, enthralled as another and another Wisp alighted on his arm.

Ha, alighted. Felix smiled, happier than he had felt in a long while. In fact, it reminded him of something—

Another three Wisps landed on his shoulders, their small bodies giving off a faint pressure. He could almost see something in the light, something twisting and twirling, casting a shadow within its bright center.

"Ow!" Felix recoiled, a sting radiating across his forearm. Quickly, a half dozen more sharp pains struck his arms and shoulders.

Frantic, he brushed off his arms and shoulders, spinning away and across the small cave. The Wisps drifted after him, their blue-white light pulsing slightly as they drew close. An invisible wave of force suddenly swept him off his feet, tossing him easily to his right, directly into the rough cavern wall.

"UFF!" Felix slid to the ground, winded. The Wisps pulsed and flowed toward him, and he counted seven in total. Bracing himself against the wall, he got to his feet and awkwardly drew the hooked sword from his pack.

"Why couldn't you just be pretty lights?" Then he stepped forward and swung. Again and again; but the Wisps floated away from the blade with preternatural ease. It was like trying to catch a dandelion puff in your hand. A Wisp darted forward and bit at his shoulder before flitting out of reach. "Ah!"

Frustrated, Felix swung wide then brought his empty left hand up to point his palm at the nearest Wisp. Quickly, a ball of acid formed and launched itself in a steady stream at the creature.

Acid Stream is level 2!

The glowing bug now disoriented, Felix followed up with a quick slash of his hook sword.

You Have Killed A Wisp!
Experience Gained!

You Have Learned A New Skill!
Long Blade Mastery (Common), level 1!
Wield the blade to defeat your enemies and protect what is yours!

"Now, that's more like it." Felix smiled as he turned toward the other Wisps. "Who wants some?"

The Wisps were floating in place now, obviously hesitant to face him. Or...Felix's eyes widened as a river of lights flowed toward his cave.

"Oh no," Felix raised his left hand and let loose a gout of acid, spraying it in an arc over the cavern. The Wisps wilted and flickered, some dying, but the rest dodging the unfocused stream. But then it was too late. A torrent of blue-white lights flooded the cavern, and a vast force ripped him from his feet and threw him toward the back of the cave.

CHAPTER TWELVE

Felix hit the ground and tumbled backwards onto the hard stone floor. Head swimming and aching from that full-body push, he stumbled to his feet with his new sword in an awkward grip.

"Bring it—" His half-snarl caught in his throat. A wall of blue-white light stretched before him, completely filling the small cavern with near-blinding radiance. Felix's heart hammered and sweat swiftly beaded on his forehead and back as he regarded his certain doom.

But nothing happened.

The Wisps milled about, swirling and eddying like currents of phosphorous waves, but didn't advance on him. Nor did they use their strange magic either. They just...floated aimlessly.

"'What's going on?' he asks himself for the thousandth time today," Felix grumbled aloud. Then his eyes snagged on a piece of dimly-glowing script, nearly impossible to see in the flood of blue-white light. A series of symbols was carved into the floor just inches in front of him. In fact, the carving extended in a line separating him from the mass of Wisps. Felix's eyes tracked the impossibly-straight row of symbols across the room, up the walls, and even across the ceiling. They framed an opening the size and shape of a set of large double doors. Each of the symbols shimmered with a faint yellow light, like a weak light bulb.

"Is this protecting me?" As he muttered, the script lit up. "Why

—" The symbols directly in front of him lit up again, flaring as he spoke.

It's preventing sound from escaping the area. Probably light too, since the Wisps obviously can't see me. He smiled wide, genuine joy flaring in his chest. *This is amazing!*

Felix's heartbeat quickened, excited at the idea of real magic. This was the kind of stuff he had been expecting when he found himself in a magical fantasy world. Then his smile froze. If there was a magic seal here, how did he get through? And what was it protecting? Slowly, Felix turned around.

Behind him was a massive room carved into the rock. It was a cave, certainly, but Felix couldn't make himself call it that; the floor was covered in hexagonal tiles, and the walls and ceiling were at near perfect angles. The room was around forty feet wide and maybe twice that in length. Most of the space was open, filled with those hexagonal tiles and nothing else. Toward the far end there was a raised platform, probably a foot tall and quite large. It was hard to tell from his vantage. More importantly, there were five doors: two on the left, two on the right, and a large set of double doors on the far wall.

Exploration is level 2!

It's like a dwarven temple or something. Or wait, is that racist? There's probably loads of underground builders in a place like this.

The room was empty, though no dust covered the ground near his feet and everything looked to be in good shape. Carved pillars lined the walls, creating shallow alcoves between them that held what looked like mosaics. Strangely, there were no shadows, and ambient light proliferated, though Felix couldn't tell its source. It was a warm, buttery light, unlike the beautiful if harsh wisplight.

Reminded of their presence, Felix turned back toward the swarm. If the magic rune seal kept him hidden and safe, then he had a huge advantage he felt he had to exploit. Not to mention, he had a decidedly different view toward the little creeps than he did just a few minutes ago. He quickly sheathed his sword in the backpack and raised both of his hands, summoning twin orbs of green liquid into his palms with a small burst of effort.

"Bite me, jerks."

Then he unleashed his acid streams.

The magic poured out of him, across the barrier and directly into the milling horde. Handfuls of Wisps died every few seconds, even as they panicked and began to pull up and away from the acid. Packed as they were, it was nearly impossible for Felix to miss. He focused on shaping the stream, trying to flatten it out to cover more area. With a brief burst of his Willpower and a flare of pain, the spell changed. The streams fanned outward, spreading horizontally until they covered nearly ten feet altogether. That's when the Wisps began to fall en masse.

Acid Stream is level 3!
Acid Stream is level 4!
...
Acid Stream is level 10!

You Have Learned A New Skill!
Dual Casting (Uncommon), Level 1!
Deal more damage for a higher Mana cost! Damage increases greatly with Skill Level, Mana cost decreases slightly with Skill Level, speed increases moderately with Skill Level.

Meditation is level 12!
Meditation is level 13!

Congratulations! You Have Earned New Titles!
Butcher I (Uncommon)! Kill 100 creatures in a single battle! +1 STR, +1 WIL, +1 DEX

Butcher II (Uncommon)! Kill 500 creatures in a single battle! +3 STR, +2 WIL, +2 DEX

Butcher III (Rare)! Kill 1000 creatures in a single battle! +4 STR, +3 WIL, +3 DEX

You Have Gained A Level!
You Have Gained A Level!
You are now Level 9!
+6 to WIL! +4 to INT! +2 to DEX! +2 to END! +2 to PER!
You Have 10 Unused Stat Points!

By the time the last Wisp was gone, Felix was panting and had a splitting headache. He had meditated the entire time he had attacked, attempting to shore up his regeneration and keep pace with his spell. It had worked, more or less, though he had to pause a couple times to avoid bottoming out. He leaned heavily against the wall, careful not to touch the still-glowing inscriptions.

"Holy hell, that took a lot out of me," Felix tried to swallow but coughed instead. His throat was dry and dusty. A symptom of too much Mana use? Or just thirst?

He glanced at his notifications and his jaw dropped. 9 Skill levels, three Titles, a new Skill, and two level ups? And to think, he wasn't going to kill the little bastards at first. Shaking his head, he carefully crept back into the waterfall cavern. The humidity hit him like a slap in the face; he hadn't realized how dry it was in the hidden room. The Wisps were gone. Even their corpses had faded away, somehow. Perhaps an aspect of being an elemental? Either way, the path forward was clear.

Creeping forward, Felix reached out and tried to scoop a handful of water from the thundering waterfall...and almost got thrown off the cliff for his efforts. Windmilling his arms, Felix just barely kept his footing. He felt like an idiot. Of course he couldn't just reach out into a huge waterfall.

Spotting a pool of water on the cave floor, he pushed aside his pride and laid down next to it, drinking from the pool with big slurping gulps. Instantly he felt better, the headache retreating somewhat and his throat clearing up. With a sigh, Felix pushed back up to a sitting position. Then he saw something.

Perception keeps paying dividends, I have to remember that. Felix spotted a single Wisp fluttering nearby. It moved haphazardly, obviously injured. The light it cast was fitful and weak. Felix raised his hand up, ready to use the small bit of Mana he had regenerated to melt the magic mosquito, but paused. His memory, ever active as it was, pinged on a dumb idea. Dumb that is, if it hadn't worked already.

"I'll probably regret this," Felix grimaced as he reached out and snatched the weakened Wisp, cupping it in his palms. Then, before he could think about it anymore, he tossed it into his mouth and bit down.

Light exploded from his mouth, crackling along his teeth and gums with a jolt of incandescent pain.

Pain Resistance is level 13!

Felix felt a sharp crackling sensation soak into his tongue and throat, like he had swallowed a battery made of pins. His head snapped to the side as the muscles in his neck spasmed. His chest felt tight and empty, and he couldn't draw a breath at all, as if a wall blocked all air from entering his lungs. Damage notifications sparked across his vision, and Felix's Health bar dropped visibly. Attempting to Meditate, he tried to focus his thoughts on absorbing the Wisp's riotous power. He mentally pulled it toward his center, where he thought his Fire resided, nestled just below his ribcage. It fought, pushing back against his efforts even as his high Willpower nudged it ever closer.

Sweat beaded on Felix's forehead and a vein pulsed at his temple. He brought everything he could to bear on the Wisp's Mana, pushing it the final distance into his core. Suddenly, Felix's inner fire began eating up the Mana, burning it for fuel. In moments, it was gone.

"Huh," he breathed, slightly disappointed. "I guess that didn't—"

A pulse of energy thrummed through his veins, and a flare of blue-white light discharged around him, scattering a number of tiny pebbles.

Congratulations!
Your Title Gourmand Has Garnered You Insight!
You Have Fully Digested Your Opponent's Mana!

You Have Learned A New Skill From A Wisp!
Tides of Vellus (R), Level 1!
Born of the Moon of Eternal Storms, the Wisps have a sliver of its power, and now so do you! Strength increases greatly with Skill Level, accuracy increases moderately with Skill Level, distance increases slightly with Skill Level.

You Have Learned A New Skill From A Wisp!
Influence of the Wisp (R), Level 1!
Just as Vellus once enthralled with its majestic light, so

now do you. Duration increases slightly with Skill Level, Strength increases moderately with Skill Level.

"*Two* Skills?" Felix was shocked and delighted. And what Skills they were! Rare, both of them. Both obviously magical in nature, though they had less-than-useful descriptions. Whatever. He'd figure them out.

Standing with a groan and stretch, Felix happily walked back to the false wall at the back of the cavern. Despite his headache and how this night started, he was in a remarkably better mood.

He couldn't tell where the opening was by sight, partly due to whatever illusion was going on, and partly because, without the Wisps this cave was *extremely* dark. Pulling out his hooked sword, he poked around until he saw a flash of golden light, nearly blinding him as it came from...the sword itself.

"Huh." He held it up before him, watching a line of symbols appear along the entire length of the blade. As he moved it closer to the wall, an opening he hadn't noticed was suddenly there. The strange temple was beyond the open archway. Felix stepped through with a shiver, the humidity vanishing to be replaced by a steady, drier warmth. The moment he was through the archway, his sword stopped glowing.

"It's a key. *That's* why I could get through," Felix grinned. "This is so cool."

Felix walked across the room. This was the first evidence of civilization he had found since arriving here, a genuine alien species. Why had they built this place? The room was an absolutely massive space that someone (or something) had built for unknown reasons.

No chance this is just someone's house. Seems like a lot of effort for something so simple, Felix thought.

The floor wasn't tiled so much as carved segments in the rock floor, but they appeared to be perfectly-made and polished. The buttery yellow light that came from nowhere painted almost everything in that color, but the floor was a darker stone than the walls. He glanced up, noting that the ceiling was probably four or five of him high, making it around thirty feet tall. The effort in excavating this on Earth with medieval technology would have taken years, decades maybe. But, Felix reminded himself, he didn't know if this world had a medieval technology equivalent, and more importantly, that didn't take magic into consideration. Who knew what was possible with magic?

Pillars, hexagonal like the tiles beneath his feet and made of the same darker stone, extended from the ground all the way to the thirty-foot ceiling. They were unadorned except for vertical fluting, much like Greek and Roman columns back home. He stepped toward a space between two columns (there were six on either end of the room), one of the small alcoves he had noticed before. In the alcoves, large, five-foot tall murals stretched, made from different bits of colorful stone. The mosaics depicted a figure in elaborate robes and armor, holding a three-pointed star made of a brightly-colored stone. Disappointingly, the figure looked like a normal human with dark skin and dark curly hair, with two arms, two legs, and all the normal features.

"Man, I was hoping for some weird magic race or something," Felix sighed.

The mosaic depicted the human figure surrounded by nature: trees, mountains, various creatures that he assumed were analogous to squirrels, rabbits, and deer. He even saw a small depiction of a turquoise lizard with four wings. As he moved to the next mosaic, he saw much of the same. Another human figure in robes and armor, holding a bright star and surrounded by scenes of nature. He made his way toward the other end of the room, glancing at these alcoves and holding his sword in a tight grip. Felix had been through too much to expect this all to go smoothly.

He approached the central platform, a dais raised up about a foot from the tiled floor. It was made of a lighter stone than the floor and pillars, and shaped like a star. Well, a nine-pointed star anyway. It was maybe twenty feet across, tip to tip, and absolutely filled with carved lines that criss-crossed the entire surface. They appeared to be random to Felix, making straight lines and curved ones that had none of the glow the script near the entrance did. Felix assumed they were decorative.

Felix reached down and ran his hand across one of the arcing lines, tracing it with his fingers. It was a flawless cut, something a machine would have had to do on Earth. Following the line, his eyes landed on the huge double doors at the far end of the chamber. Stepping around the platform, he slowly approached the massive portal. It was made of some sort of green metal with a dull finish, and even from a distance, he could tell it was absolutely covered in carvings. Etchings? Or were they cast into the metal? He stepped closer.

On each door, facing the center, was a figure. The figure was the same humanoid being as he'd seen in the various mosaics, wearing elaborate robes and holding stars in their hands. These stars had nine points, however, much like the raised platform. How many points did the mosaic stars have? Thinking for a moment, Felix pulled the memory of the few he'd inspected. The stars varied, starting with a three-pointed star and moving up to a six-pointed star. A quick glance to the side confirmed it; the nearest mosaics had eight pointed stars. The points increased as they approached the door. Why? Did that mean anything?

Shaking his head, Felix kept inspecting the doors. At the center where they would open up, there was a raised relief of jagged tree-like objects. Lightning, maybe. But there were many, all bursting from one point and surrounded by a much more elaborate eighteen-point star. Script surrounded these figures, covering every available space on the metal doors. Finally, rounding the platform, Felix stepped closer to the doors, but stopped when the inscriptions suddenly flared with a powerful green light. Shielding his eyes and stumbling back, he tried to blink the afterimages that burned into his eyes.

"What the hell was that for?" He growled, rubbing at his eyes. When he could see again, the script was still lightly glowing, brightening every time he tried to move closer. Now that they were glowing, a secondary set of symbols lined the floor in front of the doors, inscribed in an arc and leading up the walls and around the frame. At the very top was a single character that looked like a precise 'V' cut with flowing lines and hash-marks.

Felix stepped away and the light disappeared.

"Ok. Do not touch the creepy metal door. Got it."

Felix turned instead toward one of the side rooms. These doors were made with thick wooden planks bound in what he assumed was bronze; the latch was made of the same metal. The door was also in a strange shape, formed like a regular door except the top which had three points like a star. "They really ran with the theme, huh?" He depressed the latch, and the door opened without a creak.

CHAPTER THIRTEEN

The first room was filled with empty stone shelves. It was narrow, probably ten feet wide between the heavy shelves on either side. It seemed like a pantry or larder, storage in any case. However, the shelves were empty of anything, even dust. Felix backed out of the room and moved to the next.

The second room was almost completely empty as well. The tiled floor extended uninterrupted throughout, spanning approximately thirty feet square. Felix almost turned and left but noticed that there were over a dozen hexagonal pillars hanging from the ceiling. They only extended ten feet before all of them terminated at a 45-degree angle. A large gash in the ceiling hinted at some sort of violence occurring here. But what could cut through solid stone like this? With a worried frown, Felix started to back out of the damaged room, but paused.

What?

Along the back of the room, obscured by the hanging pillars, Felix made out some sort of mural. Taking a few tentative steps around the center, he saw the image of a humanoid etched into the wall. Neither male nor female, they were spread-eagle, arms and legs out like in a medical diagram. And just like a medical diagram, there were a number of details picked out on the person's form. Swirling, looping lines trailed through the figure's arms and legs, each of them coming back toward a circular shape nestled just above their navel.

Felix blinked in recognition. *That's what my Fire Within feels like...*He let his eyes roam the diagram again. *Is this...are these veins? For the fire?*

What purpose did *that* serve?

There was little else in the room of any note, but Felix couldn't quite tear his eyes off the diagram. It had the feel of an educational tool. He just wished he knew what he was supposed to be learning from it.

Felix had to cross the hall to get to the third room, this time giving the green metal door a wide berth. This door looked more damaged than the rest, with deep gouges all across its front. They looked like claw marks. Sword held to the side, Felix pushed open the third door.

Inside was around the same size as the damaged second room, but it was filled with shelves similar to the storage area. Except, the majority of these shelves were built into the walls, and small bits of script decorated their edges. They were inert as he approached, dull and lifeless to his touch. The wall opposite of the door was dominated by a heavy stone desk, along with shelving and drawers built into it. The drawers were impossible to open, appearing to be either carved faux drawers or requiring someone with MUCH greater strength. No chair sat behind the desk, just a low stone ledge against the wall where perhaps someone once set knick-knacks.

There was one more room left. Said room was smaller than the study and diagram rooms, but bigger than the storage area. And what's more, it was filled with things: A tent, blankets, a bedroll, even a larger, more complicated-looking backpack sat against the side wall. Whatever this room was used for in the past, it had been turned into a temporary camp by someone. And if Felix had to guess, it was done by the Henaari currently decomposing down on the shore.

A quick peek into the backpack nearly caused him to cheer. Rolled up and stored among a variety of food, a waterskin, and sundry other small items there were several sets of *clothing*.

"Oh, hell yes!" Felix closed his eyes and hugged an armful of clothes to his chest. "Finally."

For the first time in what felt like weeks, Felix had a restful night's sleep.

Partly because he felt safe; the hidden chamber was secured by those magic inscriptions, and the door to his room had a thick wooden beam he could drop to lock it. It was luxurious, this safety. For once, he didn't feel like a monster was going to rise up and eat him in his sleep.

The other part definitely had to do with the bedroll. The thin padding was sumptuous after sleeping on tree branches and cave floors. Felix woke the next morning feeling more refreshed than ever. For a few moments, he reveled in the fact that he was warm, comfortable, and fully dressed. Before he had drifted off, Felix had put on a short, beige woolen tunic, a pair of dark leather pants, and even a set of thin woolen socks. Socks!

Sitting up, Felix rubbed the sleep out of his eyes and assessed the room. Before, he had been tired and excited about the clothes and had only given the Henaari's camp the most cursory of investigations. In the light of morning (not that any natural light could be seen), Felix found himself questioning just why someone was up here in the first place. Did it belong to the Henaari? No, that didn't track. Why would he be camping out if he owned the place? Despite the suspicious lack of dust and rust, the structure had clearly been abandoned for years. Decades, even.

Felix scratched his chin. Centuries? Who knew with magic in the mix.

He idly checked his notifications from the night before.

Explorer is level 3!
Explorer is level 4!
Explorer is level 5!

*Huh, makes sense. This place is an amazing find for me. For anyone, even....*Felix's mind clicked.

So, the Henaari was just exploring. Like a fantasy archaeologist. Which made sense considering the Henaari Lore he had pulled:

Lore: The Henaari are a matriarchy that reveres the

Endless Raven, as such they long to explore the unexplored and find the unfound.

Whatever the Endless Raven was, it encouraged exploration. And the Henaari was extremely prepared. The backpack was similar in structure to a hiking pack back home, and contained numerous pockets, pouches, and compartments all filled with various oddities. Most of it was obvious; dried rations, a waterskin, a flint and steel, even a hammer and a few more black iron pitons. There was also a handbound journal filled with little drawings and cramped handwritten passages. The language wasn't one Felix had ever seen before, more a gathering of pictograms than letters. He set that aside for later.

Two items in the pack made his heart race. A dull blue rock on a leather strap, and an unadorned ring made of the same bronze material as his sword.

Name: Farwalker's Finder
Type: Necklace (Enchanted)
Lore: Made from the first stone found by a Henaari Farwalker on their first excursion, it has been enchanted to lead them to interesting places.

Name: Gathered Light
Type: Ring (Enchanted)
Lore: Enchanted by the Dawnspeakers of the Henaari, these rings are meant to collect and disperse light as a means of uncovering the dark places in the realms.

He wasn't about to argue against two more magic items. As far as Felix was concerned, the more magic tools he had, the better. The ring even seemed pretty useful as a means of lighting his way, if he could figure out how it worked. The necklace was another matter; the Lore entry was vague on the effects of the enchanted necklace, other than specifying "interesting places." That could be a whole host of things. Felix decided to keep the necklace in the pack, for now.

Items cataloged and sorted, Felix turned toward his notifications. Specifically, his unused stat points from his most recent levels. He took a bite of a kelaar fruit as he pondered his Status screen.

Health: 115/115
Stamina: 157/157
Mana: 266/266

STR: 35 PER: 20
VIT: 23 END: 28
INT: 33 WIL: 50
AGL: 22 DEX: 25

Felix's Willpower and Mana was off the charts compared to the rest of his stats, but most everything else was in a decent balance. His Intelligence was keeping up, but surprisingly his Strength had outpaced it due to his recent Butcher Titles.

Honestly, I'm not sure how I feel about those Titles. I mean, I can't argue with them. I did slaughter all of those Wisps. But being called a Butcher feels...not great. But his Titles were powerful, especially the rare variety. The bonuses increased as the rarity and the series increased, rank III giving much more than rank II. Which made sense, considering the prerequisites for his Butcher Title; gaining rank IV would mean he'd have to kill many more enemies in a single battle, probably several thousand. Could he even do that?

Idly, Felix wondered how his Strength compared to other creatures at this point. How much lifting power did 35 Strength represent? Would a sword strike from him overpower the average person? Or was he still weak? After all, he was only level 9. His lack of information and comparison frustrated him. With a breath, he tried to let it go.

Considering a balance between his stats, he decided to place +2 in Vitality, +3 in Agility, and the remaining +5 in Perception. More Health is always good, better reflexes and speed would compliment his increasing Strength, and his Perception had been clutch in multiple situations at this point. As far as he was concerned, he'd never go wrong with more Perception.

Health: 115/125
Stamina: 157/157
Mana: 266/266

STR: 35 PER: 25
VIT: 25 END: 28

INT: 33 WIL: 50
AGL: 25 DEX: 25

That done, Felix decided to do a little more exploration of his new home. Maybe he'd climb down the cliff and inspect the nearby forest, too. He felt good, like he finally had a handle on things. Smiling, he reached out to unbar the door when another notification appeared with a trilling sound.

You Have Received A Quest!
Home Sweet Home!
You have found a safe place in the wild Foglands, an ancient Temple long thought lost. You are charged with securing your ancestors' Temple from all threats. Be wary, young Nym, for your trials have just begun.
0 of 5 Threats Eliminated
Reward: Title, Home, Variable

"What?"

Felix's mind stuttered to a stop before whirling wildly. It was his Race again. The mosaics! They weren't humans, they were *Nym*! The same as him, apparently. What were the odds of that? And this place was a Temple of some sort, which meant religion probably. Felix scrunched his nose in distaste. Religion wasn't a favorite subject.

He didn't like that last sentence, either. What trials did he have to look forward to? And what were these "threats" he had to eliminate? Wait, no, they were probably monsters. Big nasty, level 35 monsters. He was sure of it.

Felix squeezed the bridge of his nose. He was feeling a headache coming on. However, at least there were rewards. A new Title (which could be a big boon), a "Home" (whatever that meant), and some more stuff depending on how he did. What did the Home reward mean? What if he didn't plan to stay here? He was still interested in finding civilization, after all.

He shook himself. He was spiraling again. Felix sat down, closed his eyes, and *breathed*.

Ten minutes later, feeling much calmer, he exited his Meditation.

Meditation is level 14!

"Huah, ok." Felix stood up and stretched.

During his Meditation, Felix had whittled down his situation until he was presented with two options. One, he could flee this Temple and the safety it offered, taking his chances with the forest and monsters and hoping he'd find a town somewhere. Two, he could secure his position here, establish a foundation where he could get stronger. Then, when he was ready, he could travel beyond the forests and find civilization again.

Amazing how much easier thinking is when I Meditate. This Skill really helps. I need to learn to keep it on at all times. Felix resolved to practice ongoing Meditation as much as possible in the future. For now, he had to get geared up, because his choice was simple. He would seek the strength to survive, and staying here was the best route to that. For now.

The weather was too warm for the padded leather jacket he found in the pack, so he kept his woolen tunic and leather pants he had put on the night before. He belted on the spare scabbard and bronze blade, checking to make sure it was free in its sheath like he had seen in a movie once. It unsheathed with a soft, metallic sound, moving easily despite the sword's strange shape.

Felix actually found a short knife in the pack as well, the blade about the length of his palm and very sharp. Its blade was made of steel, or at least something that looked like it. It came with a small sheath that he fixed to the opposite side of his belt. His last Grub-sticker got tucked into the satchel, along with his potion case, the magic rope, finder necklace, the hammer, and a single piton.

Finally, he considered his beat up and torn sneakers. They had served him well the past few days, and they weren't brand new when he arrived here either. After a brief hesitation, Felix kicked them off and put on the tall leather boots he found. They were a medium brown color and came to the middle of his calves. At first, he was worried they wouldn't fit, but a couple of ingenious brass buttons on the outside of the boot adjusted them to fit his legs.

"Huh, not bad," Felix said after a few testing steps. He flexed his hands and took a deep breath. Time to go.

Climbing down the cliff face was both easier and harder than he had anticipated. Felix had to hammer a new piton into the floor of the waterfall cave, but it only took a few swings of the hammer to drive it into the stone. Felix was concerned at first, worried the ground was soft or weak, but it seemed like normal rock and a quick tug proved it wasn't going anywhere. Quickly he put the brightweave coil into the piton's loop and considered how to make it tie itself into a knot.

"Tie," he commanded.

The thin rope just laid there.

"Knot," he tried.

Nothing.

Felix scratched his head and thought about it. He could always tie it himself, but...why? The Lore entry said the magic rope would tie and untie at command, but there had to be more to it than that. What else did it say?

Lore: Brightweave is the process of weaving Mana into a material, typically silk or something of similar quality. This rope was woven with an enchantment for durability, and with a limited ability to obey commands. It can tie itself into a knot upon command, and release said knot as well.

"Hm, if the rope is woven with Mana, then is more Mana needed to make it work?" It was worth a shot. But how to get his Mana into the object?

Felix held onto a part of the rope and tried *willing* his Mana into the Brightweave Coil, as if casting Acid Stream. Briefly, he felt a stirring in that core above his navel, where his Fire Within resided and where he had devoured the Mana of the Wisp.

Felix focused on his core as he once again tried to *will* his Mana into the rope. He felt a lurching sensation again, but this time tried to guide the power up and across his chest, over his shoulder, and down his arm into the hand holding the rope. The power felt hot, like standing too close to a bonfire but *inside his veins*. It hurt, but not as much as the Wisp's Mana. When the power burned into his fingers, it hit a barrier. The Mana wouldn't bridge the gap between his fingers and the rope.

Felix grunted and doubled down, applying his considerable

Willpower toward the effort. Pressure mounted in his fingers, and he had a brief thought that maybe this wasn't a good idea, when something *burst.* A shimmer of white light dazzled in his grasp before sinking into the Brightweave Coil, which immediately lightened in color and moved in his hand like it was alive.

Panting and covered in sweat, Felix held the rope with a shaky grip, sending it a single mental command. *Knot.*

And it did.

Fire Within is level 10!

Congratulations!
You Have Learned A New Skill!
Manasight (Uncommon), Level 1!
Your eyes can perceive the spectrum of magical forces that inhabits the world. Increases detail, strength, and distance moderately with Skill Level.

You Have Learned A New—
ERROR!
#(##$*

That burning pain hit him again, harder than ever before. It clawed at him like he'd swallowed knives, and it didn't stop until he dismissed the latest notification. Once he did, the pain receded, and Felix hit the ground.

Hodang, what was that? He had started to feel the rush of another Skill hitting level 10, even as he had clearly spent too much Mana on that rope. And then errors. Again. *What Skill did I learn?*

He checked his Status, but could only see the addition of Manasight. Nothing else. His head spun as he sat there, worrying at his lip. With some effort, he cleared his mind and tried to Meditate. A few minutes of that set him right and he put the strange experience behind him. Felix was getting good at that.

He climbed down the cliff a short time later.

Climbing the enchanted rope was remarkably easy compared to his ascent the previous day. Sure, gravity was in his favor, but he had expected it to be a little challenging. His Strength let him hang on easily though as he just hand-over-hand let himself down.

Hitting the ground below, he scanned the area for any obvious threats. He saw nothing but early morning light and a forest that swayed in a warm breeze that promised a scorcher of a day. *I'm gonna regret this wool shirt, I think....Nah, way better than being half naked all the time.*

With a quick glance at the Henaari's hidden corpse, he crept toward the treeline, trying to look in all directions at once.

CHAPTER FOURTEEN

He felt bad as he walked away from the Henaari explorer. After all the help they had inadvertently given him, Felix felt they deserved a proper burial, not to be just left in the woods.

When I come back, he promised himself. *For now, let's see what my new spells do and get some experience.*

Watching the ground avidly, Felix searched through the multitude of tracks in the soft earth of the embankment. As what was probably the main source of freshwater in the area, he assumed there were tons of beasts close by, which made him both nervous and excited. Felix followed a set of paw prints that were small, maybe the size of a big bunny. He might be eager to try out his power, but he wasn't insane.

Felix tried to move as stealthily as he could, but his sword sheath kept tangling in his legs. He had to keep a hand on the pommel at all times in order to walk normally. It was very frustrating. However, due to his focus and effort, he was able to raise Stealth by two levels.

The small tracks quickly led off into the brush, and they were singular, without any other small tracks around it. Hopefully that meant it was a small lone beast that wasn't too terribly high level. There were even a few places where he could tell the creature had run, probably from the other things in the forest.

You Have Learned A New Skill!
Tracking (Common), Level 1!
You have taught yourself to read the world around you for signs of life. Increased utilization of Perception per Skill Level.

Felix pumped a fist. Another Skill always seemed to help. In fact, as he looked down at the tracks again they appeared to light up, as if the prints were glowing. He could see the glowing tracks for about five feet before it cut off.

"Ooh, yeah. Very useful," Felix grinned and crept forward.

The landscape around the lake was the same as nearer the coastline where he arrived, temperate forests in the height of summer. The air was hot with a slight humidity that made his woolen shirt stick uncomfortably to his back. The plants all around him were green and vibrant, filled with colorful flowers and fronds. Distantly, insects and small beasts flitted through the air and branches, but they were entirely too fast for him to Analyze. He wondered how high their Agility was to be so speedy. Likely, more than twice his own.

A half hour later, Felix found himself in a grove of Caplan Sprouts, massive twenty-to-thirty-foot plants that had a proliferation of leafy fronds at their tops and thick, banded trunks with mazes of heavy roots that piled around their bases. But the most interesting thing about the grove wasn't the immense vegetation or even the spicy, yet appetizing scent they wafted on the breeze, but of a large creature covered in a heavy brown pelt. It was shaped like a weasel in that it was long and sinuous, but it was the size of a sedan. As Felix watched from behind a rocky outcropping, he could see the fluid grace in its movements. The monster had six, no, seven legs, each tipped with black claws that looked razor sharp. A short, bushy tail stuck up in the back, whipping about as it attempted to burrow under one of the Sprouts.

Felix threw a quick Analyze at the thing.

Name: Seven-Legged Orit
Type: Blood Beast
Level: 20
HP: ???/???
MP: ???/???

Lore: Strengthened by dire rituals, the Seven Legged Orit has altered itself beyond its limits. Be wary.
Strength: Agility
Weakness: Unknown

This thing is way bigger than what I was tracking. And what's up with that Lore entry? Felix watched it carefully, barely tilting his head beyond the wide wall of the Sprout he hid behind. *Does this count as a threat?*

He toggled his Quest list.

Quests
Advance Spells!0 of 5 Apprentice Spells
Home Sweet Home! 0 of 5 Threats Eliminated

Home Sweet Home! 0 of 5 Threats Eliminated
Threats:
Seven-Legged Orit
Unknown
Unknown
Unknown
Unknown

That answers that. No way am I 'eliminating' that thing any time soon, though. Felix started to back away, trying to make as little noise as possible. The rustle of digging continued, followed by a large nose snuffling in the dirt. It was distracted, so he figured he wouldn't have any problem getting away. Next time, he'd—

Something cried out.

A high pitched wailing cry came from the roots that the Orit was digging into. It sounded frightened, and it tore at Felix's heart. Cursing silently, Felix crept back toward the edge of his Sprout and looked again. The giant weasel had moved, digging at a different angle, and a small creature huddled in the shadows beneath the heavy roots. He only got an impression of fur and feathers and large, limpid golden eyes. This is what he'd been tracking.

Tracking is level 2!

Am I really doing this? But he was already casting a spell, an orb of green acid generating in the palm of his left hand. A pitiful yowl came from the roots as the monster crushed them against the ground, pulling and tearing at the thick wood. As the Orit pounced at the roots, slashing into them with its long black claws, Felix stepped out of his cover and let loose an Acid Stream. The concentrated acid jetted from Felix's hand, tearing across the distance and against the Orit's back.

SCREEEEEE!

The Orit stumbled to the side, all seven of its legs undulating its body as it tried to avoid the corrosive liquid. Felix was on it though, pushing his hand forward as he pumped more Mana into the spell to try and increase the flow. He stepped further out from the outcropping as the spell widened and pushed what felt like slightly more acid out, dropping his Mana at an even greater rate than before. The Orit screeched and ducked behind a Sprout. Felix cut off the spell and dropped into a defensive crouch, watching the vegetation for movement.

For a moment, all he could hear was the pathetic mewling of the small golden-eyed beast. Slowly, he drew his sword, the soft scrape of metal on leather loud in the sudden silence. The wind rustled the fronds above them, gently tickling against the back of Felix's neck. His leather boots creaked as he shifted in place, and his tunic felt heavy with sweat around the collar.

Where—?

A sudden feeling of terror made Felix tumble forward, pulling himself into an awkward half roll. He came up in time to see the Orit drop from above, claws and fangs slashing at where he just stood. Just barely climbing to his feet, the beast was already on him, slamming his body backward and sending him flying twenty feet. Felix landed in a heap, cracking his head against the trunk of a Sprout and losing his grip on his sword. He dimly saw it wedge pommel-first between a tangle of roots, just out of reach. His Health dropped over two dozen points and a familiar blinking icon of a skull with a jagged line through it appeared in his vision.

Status Condition: Concussion (Minor)

Head trauma, we meet again.

Felix grunted and attempted to stand up, but fell down in a bout of dizziness. Which saved his life, as the Orit slashed at where his head once was. The follow-up strike with the monster's fourth leg, however, connected.

"AGH!" Felix's right arm and chest burned where the Orit's black claws ripped through him. Skin and muscle shredded, his tunic torn and covered in blood, he bit back his pain and forced himself to roll away from the giant weasel. Felix stumbled to his feet, leaning heavily on his left arm. He was done. Absolutely done. Of all things, this?

"I JUST GOT THIS SHIRT!"

Felix used Tides of Vellus.

Everything within a five foot radius of him was launched violently backward. Weeds, rocks, even a small sproutling, all blasted back like an invisible explosion went off. A faint haze of blue Mana rode the air, slowly dissipating as he watched the Orit rear backward, its forelegs pushed into the air by the Skill. The giant beast fell back to all paws with little actual damage done, but it eyed Felix warily and dropped low, snarling at him.

"Fuck off," Felix threw his Grubsticker at the beast's face, striking it directly in its sensitive nose. The Orit squealed in pain and pulled its face down as it tried to claw out the makeshift knife.

Glancing at the rock shelf behind him, he swallowed and raised his left hand. Then he began to pour acid onto the loamy ground between the Orit and himself. He needed time to think, and if he could ensure the Orit could only attack him from the front....

Felix increased the amount of Mana to the spell, causing a strange haze of green mist to gather around his left hand as acid continually spat out. Meditating and channeling Acid Stream, Felix's focus barely registered that the giant weasel had pulled the dagger from its snout. Suddenly, his Mana bottomed out, and a whale of a headache pounded across his eyes.

An eight-foot expanse of acidic mud separated Felix and the Orit in a semi circle, with the rock shelf guarding his back. The Orit kept well away from the acid, which was great because Felix's vision was blurring intermittently and his legs felt weak from blood loss. Still, he was able to finally get a good view of the creature, and it was terrifying. It was all of the worst qualities of a snake and a rat somehow combined and magnified. It's neck was serpentine in its movements as it inspected the mucky earth before it. Watching the monster snort at the still bubbling terrain, Felix carefully reached into his satchel and pulled out the hard leather potion case. Just as he was easing a red potion from the case, he heard something he hadn't expected.

"Why...do you...fight?" The Orit growled at him, it's voice a basso rumble.

Felix blinked, so surprised he stopped fiddling with the wax seal on his health potion. "Uh, what? Why? Why am I fighting you?"

The Orit nodded, its black eyes never leaving Felix's face, and its knife-sized teeth showing as it panted.

Felix stood there, unsure how to respond. The Orit could speak! It was sentient! Felix had a sudden spasm of conscience. Had it just been hunting, like himself?

"Why are you attacking the, uh, that beast?" he waved in the direction of the small creature. The Orit made a horrible grinding noise in its throat, and it took Felix a moment to understand that it was laughing.

"Fun."

Felix grimaced. "Fun? How is that fun?"

"Screams...Pain....Fear...it all tastes so sweet, mmm." A tongue the length of Felix's forearm slurped out and licked its snout, tasting its own blood. "A scent I cannot resist. Hunger...gnaws at me."

Felix's skin crawled at the naked lust in the Orit's face, a disturbing mixture of appetite and libido that he had no desire to decode. Then it snarled, hackles rising as it prowled the other side of the muddy pool. The Orit shook its head and sneered, something Felix didn't know animals could do, and looked Felix up and down. He felt a thrill of fear, cold lightning that crawled up his spine.

"You, too smell...gooood." The Orit's black eyes bored into him, and its wounded nose twitched. "Too good for this blasted waste."

Felix frowned, confused. *Waste? What does that mean?*

Another grinding noise in its throat, and it shook. "You will stay, I think." Then the giant weasel began to bark in sharp, high pitched whines, raising its head up toward the sky.

That's ominous.

Felix immediately broke the seal and quaffed his health potion. He could feel it immediately begin to work on him, flesh reknitting and pulling taut. It was both intensely uncomfortable and a significant relief. Carefully, he stored the glass bottle back in his satchel as a sickly red glow surrounded the Orit, gathering a mist-like ambient light around itself like a shroud. It felt violent and spoiled, like a river of coagulated blood, and Felix barely stopped himself from retching.

Is this Manasight? He chewed back bile. *It's godawful.* But thanks to his Skill, he could see the bloody Mana gathering around the Orit as it continued to bark rhythmically. As it collected, it formed a funnel above its body, like a small tornado of bloody energy. Whatever it was doing, it was very, very bad.

Manasight is level 2!
Manasight is level 3!

Felix pulled out his only blue potion, broke the seal and chugged it. It felt like electric fire as it raced down his throat, scouring his veins as it went. A sudden weighty sensation appeared in his core, and his Mana bar rocketed up. Felix considered his options; he had trapped himself on a small island, his sword was wedged in some roots about thirty feet away, and he had barely 100 Mana left. The Orit's strength was its Agility stat, and it was definitely faster than him. If he was going to have any sort of chance, then he needed to slow it down or....

He had an idea.

It was a terrible idea.

The Orit's strange ritual was reaching a crescendo, and some instinct told Felix that he didn't want to be here when it finished. He took a single, steadying breath. Pouring everything he had into his last spell, Felix channeled his Mana up from his core and into his arms and legs. He cast Tides of Vellus, except this time, he focused on putting all of the force down and behind him.

That's when the beast's ritual ended. "Mine!" It roared, and a torrent of blood-red energy blasted toward him.

Pressure built in his head and chest, but Felix willed his power to obey, threw his arms back, and *released.*

Felix *exploded* from the ground, thrown ten feet into the air at an angle. The focused force of his spell launched him well over the shocked face of his enemy. He landed in a roll, coming awkwardly to his feet at speed as he raced toward his fallen sword. Behind him, the bloody power smashed into the rock face, scorching it black as the Mana transformed visibly into crimson fire.

"NO!" The Orit roared again, spinning around and running toward Felix. "Mine!"

Felix had angled toward the hiding place of the small beast, the creature that had started this. He pushed himself, trying to use all of his Strength and Agility to get just a few fractions of a second ahead, but the monster gained on him. The terrible sensation of a bloody quagmire suddenly surged behind him, and Felix made a final desperate leap over a section of roots. Even as he fell, he activated his last spell, one he hoped he understood.

The world lit up in surges of blue white and bloody crimson before it all went dark.

CHAPTER FIFTEEN

After the lights faded, the grove seemed pitch black in comparison.

Felix blinked afterimages out of his eyes, only to see the Orit's toothy maw inches from his own. He fell backward with an undignified yawp. Blood and mud splashed up his arms and soaked into his pants. The giant beast huffed and panted at him but wasn't moving. Craning his neck, Felix could see a nasty wound on the Orit's underbelly, dark blood and ropes of wet, grey intestines spilling out and pooling around a blade lodged firmly in the Sprout's roots.

HIS blade.

The Orit rolled a black eye at him, breath coming in pained gasps. "You...saved prey?" Its chest heaved as it thrashed weakly, blood oozing faster from its wounds. "They are...meant to be...ours. Weak...worthless...they only exist...to be devoured. Why?"

Felix leaned against the Sprout trunk, sucking in heavy gasps as well. His Health and Stamina were less than 10% again, and his Mana no more than a sliver of blue in his vision. He didn't know what to say to the beast. Felix had no clue why he'd risked himself to save a creature that, even if they both survived, was probably going to be eaten by another predator in a matter of hours. But words came to his mouth anyway.

"Because....someone has to," Felix said, flushing in embarrassment.

The Orit, however, had a different reaction. It became still, and it's black eye burned with a dangerous, bloody light. Teeth bared and streaked with its own dark fluids, it snarled at him.

"What...are you?" It strained forward, unable to push closer, and snorted, a gnarly suction of blood and air. It's eyes widened as it whispered something.

"What?" Felix couldn't hear it, so soft were the giant beast's words. He leaned forward, caution warring with an uncomfortable sort of pity for the Orit. It was a messed-up thing, but nothing deserved this. Its words were still almost too quiet to hear.

"You...should not be!"

Felix heard a terrible ripping sound as the monster lunged, and his weak attempt at dodging failed when his left leg buckled under him, too drained to move. The Orit's jaws crashed shut just inches in front of him, the force expelled enough to push Felix down into the bloody mud.

"Lost...one...!"

A last, guttural sigh and the bloody light went out from the beast's eyes. The Orit was dead. Finally.

The plan had worked.

Huh, he thought, lying in the mud. *This is usually where I pass ou—*

A strange yipping cry woke him.

He was covered in mud, blood, and other things that were thick, grey, and...and chunky. *Eugh.* Carefully, eyeing his nearly depleted Stamina, he rolled onto his belly and squirmed toward his satchel. It had somehow gotten free and sat a few feet away from him. Falteringly, Felix pulled out some yarrow and flitweed, devouring them in a few quick bites.

Moments turned to minutes as he attempted to Meditate and put the herbs' regenerative properties to best use. Try as he might, though, he couldn't maintain the necessary mindset for the Skill. But with enough herbs (all his stock), he was on the mend, at least.

Though Health and Stamina were nearing 50%, his Mana was still in the low teens when he heard that strange cry again. Felix glanced toward it, surprised to see the small creature that started all this hadn't yet run away.

Ah, of course. The Orit had crushed the cage of roots it had been hiding in, effectively trapping its meal.

With painstaking slowness, Felix got to his feet and made his way over to the roots. Each step was an effort, his sore muscles starting to cramp from the cold mud, but he pushed through it. *Pain Resistance is probably part of that equation,* he thought. *Good thing I fell from that tree.* A grim smile flitted across his face, but melted away just as quickly; for as he neared the trapped creature, he saw something else just beyond the Sprouts. It was a corpse, ravaged by teeth and claws, but pieces of it showed that it once had black and russet fur mingled with dark feathers. And it was approximately the size of a horse.

That could have been me, Felix thought with a lurch.

Golden eyes flashed in the shadows of the crushed roots before him, and he could barely make out a tiny form pulling back into deeper darkness.

"Hey, little guy, er, girl?" Felix cooed as comfortingly as he could. His shoulder was still in pain, despite the fresh healing, and the rest of him was damn sore. But he knelt down in front of the roots and waited.

Minutes passed, but the creature did not emerge. Felix fished out a kelaar fruit and bit a piece off. He put it down into the roots, fitting it between the lattice work so it plopped into the dirt near the dark thing. "Here you go, I'm sure you're hungry."

The food sat there, untouched.

Felix sighed. He hadn't expected it to rush over and thank him, but...oh hell, he wasn't sure what he wanted. To comfort it? Felix shook his head. This place was as savage as anything he'd seen in nature documentaries, and it was probably used to this.

What am I doing? He wiped his face with a groan and stood up. Reaching into his satchel, he pulled out the rest of the kelaar fruit and set them down at the edge of the root cage. Using his hands, he gripped a few of the roots positioned as far away from the little creature as possible. With a grunt, he pulled them apart, ripping a wide opening in the roots. It was surprisingly easy, despite how tired he was.

With one last glance at the dark nest of roots, he hobbled away.

Shaking his head, he checked his notifications as he started back toward the Orit's corpse. He had a slew of skill ups, a remarkable amount really. Thrown Weapons Mastery and Acid Stream gained one level, while Stealth and Influence of the Wisp gained two. Running and Fire Within jumped up three levels, Acrobatics gained four levels, Dual Casting and Dodge gained five whole levels, and Tides of Vellus gained a whopping seven levels.

Felix felt his mind thrum with a barely discernible music, a faint humming almost, as two more Skills crossed the unnamed level 10 threshold. Dodge and Acrobatics instantly felt more natural and easier to perform. If he wasn't so sore, he'd try a backflip. He'd always wanted to do a backflip.

+3 INT
+3 END
+2 DEX
+1 PER
+2 AGL
+1 VIT
+1 WIL

You have leveled up!
You have leveled up!
You have leveled up!
You are now Level 12!
+9 to WIL! +6 to INT! +3 to DEX! +3 to END! +3 to PER!
You Have 15 Unused Stat Points!

Felix shuddered as a powerful heat coursed through his veins, entirely different than his Fire Within, flooding him with energy that screamed to be spent. He went from exhausted to wired in the span of four seconds, and it was a serious whiplash on his mood. He could practically feel endorphins pumping out, soothing his aches and worries.

"Whoa," Felix's eyes were wide. "That's a lot."

It almost made him feel better about ruining his new shirt. Almost.

Felix was glad Influence of the Wisp worked like he figured it would. Digging through the battle notifications, he found where the spell activated and smiled.

Target is Enthralled for 2 seconds.

Just as the Wisps had lured Felix into allowing them to land all over him, the Skill allowed him to influence the target's mind. Two seconds wasn't very long, but it was just enough to convince the Orit to keep running even as his lodged sword pierced its belly.

Felix shuddered as he limped up closer to the beast. Even though it had saved his life, he found Influence of the Wisp to be a frightening Skill. If he gained a Skill like that, then there were others out there who could, too, and he would do well to remember that. Was there such a thing as a mental defense Skill?

Moreover, Felix was surprised that Tides of Vellus had increased so much. He guessed it was an effect of his manipulation of the spell and his own Mana that had given the level boost. Forcing his Mana around his body like that hurt like hell. Even now, the channels he felt his magic run through felt sore and strained. Even the thought of another casting made him wince.

Eugh, I'm not getting over this way. The ground before him was soupy with fluids from the car-sized weasel. He limped around the Sprout trunk, taking the long way around. Ducking beneath several low-hanging branches, Felix glanced at his next notification and smiled wide. He had been hoping for something like this. He had gained a few new Titles, five in fact.

You Have Gained New Titles!

Unconquered (Rare), +4 END, +6 VIT, +4 WIL - You are the line in the sand. You have survived against all odds again and again.

Giantslayer II (Uncommon) +2 STR, +2 AGL - Defeat an enemy at least 10 levels higher and one-half stage higher than you.

Spellslinger (Common) +2 INT +2 WIL - Fight a battle of Mana and come out the victor.

Racial Adjustment: Gains doubled.
+4 INT, +4 WIL

Face the Charge (Rare) +4 WIL +1 VIT +2 STR - You have faced down the charge of an enemy much stronger than you and lived to tell the tale!

Bulwark of the Innocent (Epic) +10% to STR and VIT - Not all strength is plundered, and some lines must never be crossed. You are the shield against predation, a champion of all.

"Holyyy shit," Felix gasped. He forgot his attempts at stealth and stood straight up, bumping his head against a branch. He barely noticed. "This...there are so many things to unpack here."

Unconquered seemed like a progression of his Survival series, and what a doozy it was. His highest stat bump yet, and proof yet again of how he couldn't go more than a day without a near-death experience. Felix shook his head. He'd be delighted to see the end of these Titles, great as they were.

Another Giantslayer Title, which was gratifying. Nice to see the system acknowledging how hard it was to fight the Orit, though the stats weren't anything to write home about. And what was a half stage? More questions, as always.

Speaking of the Orit, the Spellslinger Title indicated it was a magic user and that their fight was technically a "battle of Mana." Which was a roundabout way of saying "wizard fight," as far as Felix was concerned, and that tracked. What else would he call something that could wield all that bloody Mana? His weird Race even earned him double rewards on that one, and for once he wasn't mad about it. About time it started paying dividends.

Face the Charge was a rare Title and quite good, though it wasn't like he needed the boost to Willpower. He'd take what he could get; Felix just wouldn't recommend the experience. Being charged by a monster the size of a car wasn't something anyone should have to go through. He shook himself and moved on. *Don't think about it, just...just keep going.*

His last Title was, well it was a game-changer. Bulwark of the Innocent gave him a percentage boost to his Strength and Vitality. Ten percent wasn't huge, but it would only increase in significance as his stats grew. Felix noted the rarity of the Title. "Epic, huh? Are all Epic Titles percentage awards?" If so, he needed to get as many as he could.

He laughed. *Yeah, I'll charge right out there and get some more.*

Quest Updated!
The Seven-Legged Orit has been destroyed!
1 of 5 Threats Eliminated!

Felix frowned. It was no question that the Orit posed a threat to him, but did it have to die? Did everything have to be tooth and claw here? Why was it like this?

He paused that thought as he came around the Sprout's trunk and saw again the massive corpse of the Orit. In the short time since it died, rot and decay had set in to an alarming extent. Even as he watched, the corpse was almost...sublimating into the air, a faint greasy smoke all that was left of it. Thankfully, that meant retrieving his sword was surprisingly easy. Covering his mouth with his left hand, he reached down into the bowels of the beast and grabbed the crossguard. Wiggling it back and forth, Felix was able to pull it from the tangle of roots after only a few moments. He pulled it out and held it at arm's length.

"Ugh, that's nasty," Felix fought back his gorge as he inspected the blade. It was foul, plain and simple, and Felix immediately rejected the burgeoning idea of learning a Skill from the Orit. The bloody corruption of its Mana permeated its body, and his stomach turned even considering putting that blood in his mouth.

It was a Blood Beast, according to Analyze. Felix muscled down his urge to vomit as his thoughts started to churn. His memories, perfect as they supposedly had become, felt gelatinous. Bogged down almost. Then it snapped into place. *The Dread was a Blood Beast. Are they...related? Like a dog and a wolf? Or a cat and a...catfish, maybe.*

After taking a long drink of his waterskin, he used the rest of it to rinse off the filthy sword. That done, he sheathed the blade and turned to leave. But something caught his eye.

A flash of red glimmered in the Orit's chest cavity. The light...pulsed, like a heartbeat. Unsheathing his sword again, he used it to cut back the beast's chest, sawing away at gristle and tendons even as more of the monster's remains floated away as smoke. After a minute of effort, an irregularly shaped stone the size of a large marble fell onto the ground with a THUMP. The red light contained within the marble intensified for a moment, before dimming back to a pulsing glow.

Name: Blood Remnant
Type: Consumable
Lore: Remnants form under unique circumstances and are useful to a variety of professions.

Felix reached down and plucked the blood remnant up, feeling a considerable heft to the small stone. The Remnant had hints of that bloody Mana he sensed before, but it didn't have nearly as much of a...stench was the only way to describe it. This felt like warmth and a coppery aftertaste in the air; not pleasant, but not agonizing either. Felix secured it in one of the satchel's inner pockets. *Maybe it'd be useful later*, he rationalized. But really, he found the Remnant extremely...enticing, for reasons he couldn't figure out.

The moment he pocketed the Blood Remnant, a notification appeared.

You Have Received A Quest!

A Light In The Dark
You have found the Remnant of a blood ritual attuned to Hunger. Shed light upon this dark ritual and seek out the remaining Remnants.
Blood Remnant 1/4
Reward: Unknown

Accept?
Yes/No

Felix blinked. "Seriously?" He rubbed the bridge of his nose. He was too tired for this. He mentally accepted the quest, and it joined his queue. He could worry about this later.

With a final look at the still-untouched pile of kelaar fruit, Felix started the long trek back home. He focused on Stealth, attempting to remain as invisible as possible during his journey. He was a ways from the waterfall, and he couldn't risk getting caught up in another fight. The fight with the Orit and aftermath had taken up most of the daylight hours, and the sun was dropping low in the west, almost obscured by a line of mountains he could see in the hazy distance. He must have been out longer than he figured; hours, even. It was a miracle he wasn't killed while unconscious, though Felix admitted the giant monster corpse nearby likely dissuaded others.

Against his expectations, he didn't encounter a single creature on his way back to his camp. He heard plenty of scurrying in the forest, but it sounded small and was gone before he could see anything. Within a short period of time, Felix was back at the waterfall, idly picking a few more kelaar fruit and herbs to replace his diminished stock. He bid a silent hello to the Henaari explorer, reminding himself to properly bury them in the morning.

"Ah damn, I left this up all day," Felix groaned. He had left the brightweave coil tied to the cliff, dangling for anyone to see. What if someone had climbed up? What if...what if they were waiting for him?

Gritting his teeth in frustration, Felix checked his sword in its scabbard, making sure it was clear and no longer sticky with monster blood. He had to be ready for anything.

He climbed up.

CHAPTER SIXTEEN

Halfway up the cliff, Felix nearly smacked himself in frustration.

He had fifteen free stat points to spend. If there ever was a time to stay ahead of the curve, it was when he was expecting an ambush. Wedging himself against the rock face, he quickly allocated points to Perception, Agility, and Vitality. Felix clutched at the cliff face, feeling his heart race and his limbs burn with energy as his physical body changed rapidly. He didn't realize quite how hard he was gripping.

Crack!

Felix pulled his hand back, watching in shock as his handhold broke away. Apparently, he didn't know his own strength anymore. He laughed, the sound drowned out by the roar of the waterfall, and started climbing again, this time without the magic rope. In less than a minute, he was near the top, barely panting, and listening to that near audible music as his Free Climb Skill shot up past the level 10 threshold.

Just below the cave, he checked his health and stats one last time.

Health: 201/238
Stamina: 174/211
Mana: 150/383

STR: 43 PER: 31
VIT: 47 END: 38
INT: 46 WIL: 72
AGL: 32 DEX: 30

Good enough.

With a sharp pull, Felix was up and over the edge, rolling quickly to his feet. His levels in Acrobatics showed their worth as he did so, the movement feeling effortless. He scanned the dim interior of the cavern, but saw nothing. Quickly, Felix grabbed the rope and commanded it to untie. A pulse of his Mana and it did so, even going so far as to coil up into his hand. Forcing himself to stop gawking at it, he stowed it and warily walked to his hidden Temple.

It wasn't until he was several steps into the ambient light of the Temple that a soft clicking sounded from behind him. Felix spun, holding his hooked sword out and gathering a liquid ball of virulent green in his left hand. Sitting on the hexagonal tiles in front of him was a puppy. Sort of.

"Wha-?"

It was small, likely a foot tall while sitting, covered in russet fur, with dark black coloring its four paws and neck. Its head, shaped like an odd bird of prey, tilted inquisitively, huge golden eyes bright in its dark face. *Those eyes...*

The pup barked, a high-pitched yipping sound. *Of course! The little animal. But...it followed me all the way here, without me noticing? How'd it even get in?*

Felix wasn't skilled at listening for pursuit, but he figured his Perception of 31 would have at least caught something. He looked over the pup, and it definitely was a dog of some sort, despite the fact it had a bird head and two small grey-fuzz covered appendages on its back that twitched. *A dog-bird?* He focused on the creature.

Analyze is now level 13!

Name: Tenku
Type: Chimera
Level: 1
HP: 40/40

SP: 35/35
MP: 35/35
Lore: A chimeric beast, tenku are pack hunters and are equally at home in the sky and the land.
Strength: High Perception and Agility, they are speedy strikers.
Weakness: Low Strength and Endurance, a drawn-out battle is the worst case scenario for them.

"Chimera? Aren't those bigger, usually?" He muttered to himself, but soon remembered the savaged horse-sized corpse he found near the Orit. *Right. That was probably its mom or something...Poor little guy.*

The tenku regarded him with a second head tilt, sniffing in his direction as it yipped again. Felix followed its gaze to the satchel at his hip, and when he looked back he saw it lick its dark beak. Felix laughed. "Oh, I see. You're hungry." He looked off to his room, only a dozen feet away. "Wait here, little dude."

Moving slowly at first and without turning around, Felix navigated to his room and grabbed the last few fruits he had stashed there earlier. When he turned around to leave the room, he found the tenku sitting in the doorway, mouth open and tongue lolling.

"Uh, hey buddy. You like these, right?" Felix tossed one of the fruits to the chimera, the red and white food bouncing once before fetching against the doorjamb. "Eat up."

Felix looked down to grab another fruit, and when he looked back, the tenku had already eaten half of its own. It was impressive, really. A few more bites, and that fruit was gone. Felix stepped a bit closer and rolled another at the pup. The tenku pounced and devoured it in seconds. Felix went through his entire stash in the next few minutes, but thankfully the last one seemed to satisfy the ravenous beast.

"Holy hell, dude. You can really pack it away, huh?" Felix scratched his head as he regarded the tenku, who proceeded to walk into his room, growl once or twice, and plop down right onto his bedroll. It was asleep in seconds.

Felix smiled, and despite his dire straits and constant battle to survive, despite everything, he felt pretty good. Maybe he shouldn't be trusting this strange little creature, but he found it hard to be worried about a puppy.

Laying down a few feet away, Felix eventually let himself drift off to sleep. It had been a long day, and tomorrow would be longer still.

Laughter, edged with something darker, danced through the room. But Felix was already fast asleep.

Two hours after dawn found Felix stripped to the waist and covered in sweat-soaked mud. A hole approximately six feet long and six feet deep lay in front of him as he panted in the early morning sunlight. His Strength made it a far easier task than it should have been, even though all he had to use was his hands. Were he normal, human Felix would have been at this for most of the day. Reaching over, he gently picked up the Henaari explorer's skull and hopped into the grave. With as much reverence as he could manage, he placed the skull down with the collection of its other bones. He had found all of them, he thought, and had arranged them in a general humanoid shape in the dark dirt. Standing over the body, he paused. He wasn't sure what to say.

"Thank you, stranger. You've helped me a whole lot. I'm not a religious guy, and I wouldn't know the first thing about yours, but I hope you've gone to the best afterlife out there. Whoever the Eternal Raven is, I'm sure they're happy that you found the Temple."

Nothing left to say, Felix hopped out of the grave and began to fill it back in.

Another ten minutes, and Felix was tamping down the disturbed earth with his feet. He had moved a sizable rock to the head of the grave, to serve as a marker, though he had no way to carve the thing, let alone knowledge of what he would carve it into. The tenku watched him the whole time, his eyes bright as he constantly moved around Felix in a wide circle.

Felix had been surprised to find the tenku still there that morning, though not so surprised to find it rooting through his satchel, hoping for more food. They had quickly come down to the forest to find more food and take care of his Henaari benefactor, as promised. He had harvested nearly fifteen kelaar fruits and five bekl berries, each the size of his fist. By the time he was halfway through digging the grave, the hungry chimera had devoured all of them.

Wiping sweat and dirt from his face, Felix laughed as the tenku ran up to him and sat up on his hind legs, mouth open expectantly. Reaching up, he grabbed another kelaar fruit and tossed it over. *That'll keep it busy for a minute or so.*

...Or less.

The pup ate the fruit in twenty seconds. With the rate at which this beast was eating, he doubted he could sustain it on fruits and nuts alone. Not if Felix planned to eat anything himself, that is.

"And my mom called *me* a bottomless pit," Felix chuckled, watching the tenku scratch itself. After a moment, he growled and bit his foot, gnawing on it before falling into a fuzzy lump on the forest floor. "Huh. That's not bad. Pit. What do you think? Are you a Pit?"

The chimera rolled over, exposing his belly, offering a happy yip as he smooshed his back into the kelaar rinds.

"Ok," Felix laughed. "Pit it is."

That was most of his day. Foraging for food and avoiding some of the gnarlier higher-leveled beasts that stalked the edges of the lake. Felix made it a point to sneak everywhere, hoping to grind out the Skill while getting what they needed. Pit was a constant joy, either skulking around in imitation of Felix or pouncing on every flower he saw. Felix just shook his head, urging the little beast from making too much noise. To his credit, Pit seemed ready and able to listen.

Except when they encountered a trio of rabbit-like creatures. The tenku barely hesitated before it darted after them. Two dashed away, faster than Felix could even track, while the third spun in a circle as Pit charged. The little chimera was freaking fast, but when it reached the rabbit, he was sent sprawling.

"CHIRRUP!" Pit quailed as he fell over.

Acid Stream!

A sharp jet of green acid darted from Felix's hand, striking the rabbit directly in the face. It had been too preoccupied with Pit. Its smooth, brown fur withered and its skin bubbled under the assault. Felix was surprised when Analyze told him they were only level 9.

It died soon after. Pit got up as if he'd been fine all along, walked happily over to the half-burnt rabbit-thing, and took two quick bites from its chest. Felix winced and looked away. Fruit was one thing, but this...*Eugh.*

Things continued on that way for a while. Two hours later, Felix and Pit had traveled further down the lake shore than he had been before. Felix kept Analyzing everything he saw, and continued to interact with new and interesting plants, many of which proved to be edible. This was occasionally foiled by Pit as he stomped on various flowers, but the amusement was worth the twinge of annoyance. Another worry was preoccupying Felix, however. Despite filling up his satchel, he guessed it would barely get Pit through two meals. They hadn't seen another of those rabbit creatures again.

I'm foraging for two, now, he thought with a smile. It was amazing how much better of a mood he was in now that he had Pit to keep him company. The strange tenku was cute and clumsy, but also remarkably quiet, often sneaking up on him even when he was fully aware the pup was nearby. *If only I could see his stats. I'd like to know how high his Agility must be to get past my Perception.*

A sharp bark sounded from the brush, different from the happy yips to which he'd grown accustomed. Pit suddenly jumped forward, beak open in a strange snarl, as a large beetle nearly the same size crawled onto a nearby log. Pit sailed through the air, an impressive jump, but was met by a flare of light as the beetle bucked its large horn at the tenku. The horn caught him in the chest and sent Pit flying nearly six feet straight up.

Felix watched all of this at once, his Perception and Intelligence working overtime to give him all the disparate details. That's when he noticed the tenku was set to fall back onto the beetle's jagged horn. Instantly, Felix's body was covered in a bright blue fire as he used Influence of the Wisp. The same fire encased the beetle.

Javlik Beetle is Enthralled for 2 Seconds.

Influence of the Wisp is level 4!

Felix drew his sword and struck down at the bug, knocking it aside even as Pit fell onto all fours nearby.

The chimera didn't get up.

"No," he gasped. Felix focused all of his Strength into his sword blows, striking as hard and as fast as he could, cracking the

Javlik's tough exoskeleton until it smashed into gooey pieces just as the blue fire around it disappeared.

Long Blade Mastery is level 2!

Huffing a few breaths, Felix immediately ran over to where Pit lay unmoving on the mossy ground. He took hold of the tenku for the first time, feeling his soft baby fur and small limbs. But he was too quiet, too limp. Felix carefully flipped him over, and seeing a bleeding wound in his chest, quickly Analyzed him.

Name: Tenku
Type: Chimera
Level: 1
HP: 0/40
SP: 2/35
MP: 0/35

"No..." Felix whispered, suddenly crushed.

He was an idiot. *Of course* there would be real monsters nearby, *of course* they would be too much for a level one baby. Had he really let a single rabbit throw away his caution? What was he thinking? Warm, fat tears rolled down his cheeks. For all that, he had known the tenku less than a day, he had rapidly grown on Felix.

He'd always wanted a dog, and—how had he let this happen?

His tears were interrupted by the rude appearance of a notification.

Do You Choose To Save Him, Lost One?
Yes/No

What? Really? Of course! Yes!

A Choice Is Made.
All Choices Have Consequences.
Bear Your Burdens Well, Lost One.

The ominous words disappeared, and Felix was suddenly inundated with a shimmering blue and golden aura. He glanced down at his hands, still holding the small pup, and saw that Pit was covered in the light as well. The aura intensified, climbing to blinding brilliance that filled the forest with golden-azure radiance. Felix felt pain, like something was dragging a sharp blade on his insides, tearing something precious away from him. With a sudden lurch, Felix saw a flash of black and red, small and fragile, pour into that same tear inside himself. More pain, unlike anything he had felt so far, like someone was burning his soul.

Then all at once, the light was gone.

Suddenly exhausted, he stumbled forward, legs weak and knees like jelly. The lack of pain was better than a drug, and his equilibrium was briefly shattered as the forest tilted all around him. A slew of blue boxes filled his vision.

You Have Gained A Companion!
Pit the Tenku, level 1.

Congratulations! You Have Earned A New Title!
Pactmaker (Rare)!
You have formed a pact with a denizen of the Wilds, gaining benefits even while binding your life to theirs. +4 AGL, +3 DEX, +4 PER

You Have Learned A New Skill!
Companion Pact (Uncommon) Level 1!
You have formed a pact with a denizen of the Foglands. Increasing Skill Level and Affinity will net larger gains from the pact, for both you and your Companion.

Congratulations! As A Pactmaker, You And Your Companion Share Level Benefits!
Overlapping bonuses do not stack.
You Gain: +1 PER, +2 VIT, +4 AGL, +3 DEX Per Level!
Companion Gains: +3 WIL, +1 END, +2 INT Per Level!

"Wait, what? How?" Felix quickly looked down at his hands, but the tenku was gone. Frantic, Felix spun in a circle, thinking he had unconsciously dropped the little guy.

A sharp bark shattered the silence, deeper than before. Felix looked up. Pit was standing five feet away, tongue lolling happily and eyes wide and bright and clear.

"You're ok! And you...you're bigger." The tenku in front of him was a few inches taller than before, and his wings looked fuller, with the start of real feathers on them. "We're...Companions now?" Felix looked over the notifications in front of him, reading and closing them rapidly. "You can do that?"

Pit barked, excited suddenly, and ran headlong into Felix's legs, nearly bowling him over. Almost idly, Felix bent down and scratched the chimera's birdlike head, noticing for the first time the feathers that started to grow in among the fine fur. Pit panted and leaned into the scratches.

A small blip in his vision alerted Felix to a new icon in the shape of a small feather. He toggled it.

Name: Pit (Companion)
Level: 1
Race: Chimera - Tenku

Health: 40/40
Stamina: 35/35
Mana: 35/35

STR: 1 PER: 15
VIT: 8 END: 7
INT: 10 WIL: 6
AGL: 32 DEX: 14

Skills:
Bite (C), Level 1
Rake (C), Level 1
Cry (R), Level 3
Skulk (C), Level 15
Companion Pact (U), Level 1

"You can gain levels?" Felix breathed. "And Skills too?"

Felix laughed.

CHAPTER SEVENTEEN

In the grey light of dawn, on the sixteenth day of summer, Magda Aren found herself on the Haarwatch wall overlooking the approach to the Foglands. Here it was summer only in name. Thick, land-bound clouds drifted and swirled amidst the shadows of winter-bare trees, ominous in what they hid. She leaned against the crenelations, feeling somewhat naked without her shields. But being armed and armored for war at all times wasn't something she could afford, not anymore. She fingered the silver medallion hanging around her neck, symbol of her prestige and authority. Chains, as far as she was concerned, as good as any manacles.

It was saying something to her state of mind that she didn't notice the man until he was nearly on top of her.

"Ye can't go, Maggie. It be too dangerous out there, now. The fog blinds us, and the beasts be gettin' worse." A heavyset dwarf with a short, bristly beard growled nearly in her ear, while his two bright blue eyes creased in concern. He was dressed in a combination of leathers and mail, effective armor for defending the wall of Haarwatch or wading into an army of monsters. Magda stood up, towering over him by over a foot as she crossed her arms in front of her fine silk tunic and embroidered tabard.

"The Culling be only six months past, but we've yet to see a drop in the chimeric hordes. They've retreated, aye, but our scouts say the wilds are full to bursting. Ye enter there, ye ain't coming out," the dwarf said, brows turned down.

Magda smirked at the dwarf, her hand on her belt. "That sounds like a challenge, Rory."

Rory groaned. "It ain't, ya loon. It's a warning, and a fair one too." Rory turned toward the heavy mist that rolled across the wilds, the area of the Continent folks called the Foglands. "I've been up here for close to twenty years now, and I know how these things go, Maggie. The Culling shoulda cut back the mists and chimeras both, as it always does. But they only went quiet, leavin' us alone in our turtle town. I know they're out there, getting stronger while we wait."

"Then why wait? Take the fight to them, beat them back like you have before." Magda's eyes twinkled; her mouth curved upward in a slow grin. "Don't tell me Raging Rory is afraid of a little fog."

Rory grunted, frown deepening. "It be more than that, and ye know it. Politics, fah." He spat off the side of the wall, and they both watched it disappear into the roiling mists. "The new Governor in Setoria wants a show of force at his festival, a display o' Haarwatch's best. So I'm left with the dregs to man this fog-cursed wall." Rory sighed, a deep, bellows gust of air expelling from his sturdy lungs. "Truth be told, I'd rather wade into it with you than watch over a bunch o greenhorns who know the hoe better than their pikes."

"We can't all go walking into the lion's den; someone's got to keep them safe," Magda replied with a smile and a jerk of her thumb backward, toward town. "And besides, I've got greenhorns of my own to shepherd."

Rory grunted, this time smiling. "Oh, aye, I heard you've been lugging some dead weight. Who hired the Guild to powerlevel their brats this time? Who had money enough to earn the services of the Shieldwitch herself?"

"My sister, for one."

"Little Evie's old enough to face the wilds? I must be losing track o' time; last I knew, she weren't any taller than me."

Magda snorted. "Everyone's taller than you."

"Aye aye, laugh it up, human," Rory grumbled, grin still not gone. "So Evie is going out, I assume to earn her Omen? Who're the others?"

"Atar V'as, some prodigy from Te'thys," Magda's expression soured. "And Vessilia Dayne."

Rory's eyes widened. "Yer shittin me."

"No shit involved, dwarf. Not unless I fail to bring her back in one piece," Magda laughed, but the humor was gone.

Rory leaned against the crenelated wall, armored gauntlets scraping against stone. "Twins' teeth, woman. Here I am, complain' about monsters at the gates, and you've got em in your lap." He slapped his thigh and let out a sharp bark of a laugh. "That's some damn luck, Maggie."

Magda's eyes hardened, her mouth a grim line. "Don't I know it."

A dozen blocks east of the wall, a grizzled and scarred man sat in a well appointed office, lounging in an expensively-crafted chair in a row of near-identical copies. He wasn't much to look at, wearing rumpled woolens and a sweat-stained jerkin. But at his waist were two exquisitely-crafted hand axes, and around his neck hung a silver medallion. Two heavily-armored guards at either end of the room kept eyeing him as if he were a dangerous animal, both of their hands hovering near their weapons.

A desk carved to look like gryphons held it up on two corners sat across the room, and a woman in a pale green dress worked silently on various piles of paperwork. Suddenly, she raised her head, curled hair bobbing in place. "Sir? The Lady is ready for you now."

Slowly, the man stretched his long limbs and stood up. With a rolling gait, he strolled up to the heavy oak door nearby. On its surface was a fine carving of a shield crossed by a sword and spear. To either side of it, a gryphon and a creature that was a mixture of a cat and snake. Snorting at it, the man pushed the twelve-foot door open and entered.

Within was another very well-made office, heavy with wood, rare out here at the edge of the Foglands where harvesting trees could not be done without bloodshed. Dark stain and expensive waxes shined in the light of a series of wrought iron everlamps, and delicately embroidered tapestries filled a couple dedicated alcoves. The faint scratching of quill on paper caught Harn's ears as another woman took notes and watched him, twin to the receptionist outside save for her faded blue dress. To her right, on the other side of a massive wooden desk, a stately woman in a complicated outfit of silks and armored gauntlets stood, staring idly out of the large picture window behind her. It was only early afternoon, but the sky still looked dark, despite the season.

"What a strange town, Haarwatch. I see people everyday, laboring, trading, training, working their hands to the bone to eke out a living in this fog-touched outpost. They could live out different, more comfortable lives elsewhere. Setoria is not far and is a safe enough journey with a minimal escort. But they stay, and because they stay, so must we.

"The Guild is the wall on which the frenzied hordes break. We are the first defense of the Heirocracy. But we live in rural squalor compared to Setoria, bloated city that it is. Underfunded, understaffed, and expected to save the empire from the chimeric hordes." The woman, Lady Eliza DuFont, sighed dramatically and turned to look at her guest.

"You're quiet today, Harn. Not happy to be back?"

"Hm," he grunted. A man of few words, today he did not feel inclined to indulge. The woman laughed like a bell, and waved at him. Her assistant scritch-scratched another note on her parchment.

"Sit, sit."

He remained standing, but she paid him no mind, adjusting her dress and sitting in a plush chair behind the massive desk. She poured two cups of wine and offered one to the silent man. He begrudgingly took it, holding it but not drinking.

"I imagine you're wondering why I've asked you here—"

"I have an inkling," Harn said, eyes surveying the ceiling and walls.

"Hm, yes. I suppose you would," she said, regarding him. "I need to ensure that your operation goes off without a hitch. You understand if something...untoward happened to Lady Dayne, it would reflect disastrously upon the Guild."

"In the form of cutbacks, you mean," Harn lazily suggested, sucking at his teeth unpleasantly. Lady DuFont frowned.

"Indeed. I don't have to tell you that the funds given to us by the Hierocracy are subpar. Even in the best of years, we barely have enough well-trained Guilders to man this wall. And this has not been the best year." The woman shuffled a number of papers around, clearly searching, before plucking one sheet from the pile and holding it triumphantly. "Here we are! Scouts are reporting an increase in chimeric activity beyond the third front." She glanced up from the paper, meeting Harn's gaze. "That is as far as they could penetrate, the hordes too numerous to risk any further."

"Sounds like fun," Harn tried to smile, but it always came out as a smirk. He wasn't sure why, but it irritated people, especially Lady DuFont. He couldn't bring himself to care.

"Fun? We have—"

"Listen, Lady, Maggie and I know our business," Harn growled. "We've been hired to do a job, and we never go back on a contract."

"Which I applaud, Master Kastos. You and your teammate are valued assets of the Guild, worth more than a dozen lesser teams. Which is why I am having this conversation with you. Even your team cannot withstand a swarm of ten thousand beasts. No matter how strong Onslaught and the Shieldwitch become, you can never best the entirety of the Foglands alone." Lady DuFont leaned forward, eyebrows tilted up and blue eyes worried. "I beg of you, reconsider your contract. The Lady Dayne can attain her Omen in a much safer way. I even have a Priest of the Pathless here in Haarwatch that could—"

"Priests! And what did they pay you to recommend that, *my lady*," Harn snarled, wine spilling from his chalice. "The Pathless aren't worth the hot air they pump out. Revealing an Omen takes challenge and danger, not gibberish before an altar. Those three kids are strong, and revealing their Omens in battle will make them stronger still." Harn dropped his chalice, thoroughly crushed in his bare grip. "You would have us betray our client's trust and smear the name of the Guild, over *politics*? You go too far, Eliza."

Lady DuFont had steepled her hands during his tirade, and regarded him with a cool gaze. "Very well. You have heard my objections, as has the record." She glanced at her secretary, who was writing furiously with her quill, then glared at Harn with steel in her eyes. "However, Silver Rank or not, you speak to me like that again, and I'll end you, Harn Kastos."

A sudden flare of power and her armored limbs were limned with a yellow light as her aura smothered the room. Harn stumbled, knees bending briefly before Lady DuFont retracted her aura. He straightened slowly, meeting her eyes as he nodded.

"Very well, Elder," Harn growled. "You've been heard."

He marched out of the room.

———

The oak door, larger than two men put together and weighing nearly five hundred pounds, slammed shut as Harn stormed out.

"That went well," Lady Eliza DuFont observed. Her secretary (either Vera or Tera, she was never sure) stood up from her desk and sprinkled sand over her parchment.

"The meeting is fully recorded in the Guild Logs, as you requested, my Lady."

"Good," Eliza stretched her arms, feeling her shoulders cramp from exerting her aura. It was not a tool used often in polite society, but it had its uses, shutting down belligerent fools being one of them. "Have the Logs taken to the record-keepers and notarized."

"As you wish, my Lady."

Tera (or Vera) left the room, a bundle of parchment in her hands. The moment she exited, Eliza let loose a sigh that had been building for the past twenty minutes. She was just about to sit back down in her chair when a soft scraping noise grabbed her attention. Immediately, Eliza had her arms up, yellow light flowing around her limbs as she activated a Skill. "Who dares?"

A shadow detached from the edge of her office, neatly forming from cast-off scraps of light until a figure about five and a half feet tall materialized on her expensive Denarian rug. Wearing flat plates of boiled leather dyed variations of grey and black, a half mask of featureless, matte-black porcelain covered their upper face, leaving plump lips stretched over a generous smile. The figure took an elegant bow, white eyes never leaving Eliza's own.

"I bid you a good morning, Elder DuFont."

"Illia, you fog-touched wretch," Eliza breathed, her Skill fading as she lowered her arms. "You are as unnerving as ever."

The pale woman smiled even wider, if that were possible. "The Lady is too kind."

Eliza composed herself, straightening her silk brocade and tugging on the edges of her custom gauntlets. Their presence always helped ease her mind, a weapon constantly to hand. "You saw the whole thing, I presume?"

"It was quite the show," Illia said. "I could have sold tickets."

"A necessary fiction, if our plan is to work. I can't be seen supporting a decision to take the Duke's only daughter into the Foglands." Eliza shook her head, still marveling at the audacity of the adventurer team's plan. "That the Duke and the Guild green-lit this contract is pure madness. I aim to be on the correct side of history."

"With some help, of course," suggested Illia.

Eliza smiled. "Of course. And you are prepared for your part in our arrangement?"

The woman in black flexed her shoulders, an impressive array of blades secured across her torso. "Always. I'll shadow the team the entire way, keep the Duke's brat safe, and extract her once the team falls."

"Good."

"What if they don't?" Illia asked.

Eliza raised an eyebrow. "What if they don't what?"

"Fall."

"They will," Eliza promised, sipping her wine and turning toward the picture window behind her. The Guild Hall was the largest building in Haarwatch, and she could see clear to the walls. Men and women patrolled them, clear as day to her enhanced Perception.

"One way or another."

CHAPTER EIGHTEEN

Felix rolled to his feet, small cuts all over his arms and face from another exploding stone pillar.

"GWAAAARRH!"

What could only be described as a gorilla mixed with a rhinoceros charged at him as it screamed. Dusty brown Mana surged around the ape's arms and legs as the ground rumbled. Felix threw himself to the side as a blocky pillar of stone speared out of the forest floor.

"Would you *quit it*?" Felix spat, picking himself off the ground. Again.

Felix was exhausted; this battle had gone on too long. He was covered in wounds and his Stamina was dangerously low. Thankfully, the Irontooth Ape was also on the ropes.

Name: Irontooth Ape
Type: Chimera
Level: 20
HP: 120/545
SP: 151/324
MP: 5/21
Lore: A wildly aggressive chimera born of the earth. Do not taunt.
Strength: Strength and Endurance

Weakness: Agility

Well. On the ropes was subjective. It still had plenty of juice left to clobber Felix.

If it weren't for Pit's preemptive attack against the wounded Ape, it would have passed them by. But the little Tenku got aggressive. They had been fighting out in the forest for the past three days, testing their mettle against a variety of small game. They had learned how to fight well together, but not, apparently, how to cool off. Even now, Pit was snarling and hissing, flaring his small wings wider in an effort to appear menacing. The Ape turned toward Pit, clawing at the ground with a heavy paw.

"C'mon, Magilla!" Felix suddenly cried. He stood his ground and held his arms out wide. "Come and get me, you big, stupid monkey!"

The Ape turned and screamed at him, blood pouring down its shoulders from several deep cuts Felix hadn't made. Something clearly had attacked this creature previously. It slammed the ground several times, making nearby trees shake. Then it charged.

The ground exploded into plumes of dark dirt and small stones, and the Ape rushed at Felix like a train. Its weakness might have been Agility, but it had serious power. It was all he could do to brace and hold up his hands, turning his thoughts toward his Mana as he activated Tides of Vellus.

Felix had spent a lot of time working on this spell, casting it with varying levels of Mana to replicate his trick against the Orit. It was tough. Moving that much Mana and changing the flow of the Skill itself was a challenge, one that bucked against him. He had spammed it countless times against the lower level beasts that Pit would hunt down, slowly but surely raising its level. All for this.

Crackling blue light blasted outward, focused in a cone to his left, tearing up earth and roots before catching on the heavy rocks and trees around him. Felix was thrown bodily to the right, the force picking him up into the air. The Ape kept charging, its momentum too great to stop even as its prey zipped out of reach. The Ape hit the massive rock where Felix once stood, smashing into it with the roar of an avalanche.

Smaller boulders the size of Felix's head sheared and shattered onto the ground, thoroughly entombing the raging rhino-ape. Felix stood up, brushing himself off gently. The beast seemed quiet, perhaps dead. Focusing, Felix used his Manasight on the creature. Through the swirl of green and brown Mana that flowed over nearly everything in this forest, he couldn't make out the Ape's signature earth magic.

"Huh," he breathed, still out of breath. "Wasn't expecting that. Good." At best, Felix had figured the Irontooth Ape would gravely injure itself against the rock, or at worst, smash right through it. He looked at Pit. "I barely had anything left—"

A surge of dusty brown Mana assaulted his senses, and Felix jumped backwards, just in time to avoid another earthspike as the Irontooth Ape exploded up out of the earth itself. It snarled and thrust a hand forward at him.

"*Ah*!" Felix screamed, forced to jump repeatedly as the earth-spikes erupted wherever he landed. "Bad monkey!"

Felix held out a hand and pumped a full blast Acid Stream into the Ape. Sizzling flesh splatted as the viscous green liquid sprayed onto it, and the Ape cried out in pain. Felix poured everything he had left into the blow, the stream a torrent as it pummeled the beleaguered beast, pushing it back onto all fours.

With a final grunt, the Irontooth Ape fell to the ground. Dead, at last.

Dodge is level 15!
Pain Resistance is level 15!
Meditation is level 19!
Running is level 14!
Long Blade Mastery is level 6!
Acid Stream is level 15!
Tides of Vellus is level 11!
Manasight is level 10!

+2 STR
+2 INT
+1 VIT
+5 END
+1 AGL

You Have Gained A Level!
You are now Level 13!

+3 to WIL! +2 to INT! +4 to DEX! +1 to END! +2 to PER! +2 to VIT! +4 to AGL!
You Have 5 Unused Stat Points!

Your Companion, Pit Has Gained A Level!
+2 VIT! +2 PER! +4 AGL! +4 DEX! +3 WIL! +1 END! +2 INT!

You Have Earned A Title!
Workhorse (Rare)!
You have pushed your body to the limit, drawing every measure of Stamina until you collapsed. Then you did it again. +4 END, STR, +3 VIT

Felix collapsed onto the ground, drained. Pit flopped down next to him, blood coating his normally lustrous fur. Felix stretched out a hand and scratched him under the chin, too tired to move more than that.

"You see," he panted. "You see what...you got...us into?"

Pit yipped at him, excited. Then he started to lick the blood off his feathers. Felix rolled his eyes.

He had gotten the hang of Meditating and fighting, but it still wasn't as effective as when he was at rest, so long drawn out battles like this were not in his favor. He was beat, bleeding, and sore all over.

But, he had to admit, his Skills were getting serious workouts.

Skills:
Resistances: Acid Resistance (C), Level 13; Pain Resistance (U), Level 15; Poison Resistance (U), Level 17

Utility: Analyze (C), Level 17; Improvisation (C), Level 4; Running (C), Level 14; Stealth (C), Level 11; Swimming (C), Level 3; Tracking (C), Level 11; Breath Control (U), Level 8; Companion Pact (U), Level 5; Dual Casting (U), Level 9; Free Climbing (U), Level 12; Exploration (U), Level 9; Herbalism (U), Level 14; Meditation (U), Level 19; Manasight (U), Level 10; Lessons of the Past (R), Level 6; Physical Conditioning (R), Level 14

Combat: Dodge (C), Level 15; Long Blade Mastery (C), Level 6; Small Blade Mastery (C), Level 7; Staff Mastery (C), Level 1; Thrown Weapons Mastery (C), Level 9; Unarmed Mastery (C), Level 3; Acrobatics (U), Level 14

Spells: Acid Stream (R), Level 15; Fire Within (R), Level 14; Influence of the Wisp (R), Level 9; Tides of Vellus (R), Level 11

In just three days he had upped many of his Skills, some nearly into the 20s. This battle alone pushed up so many Skills and provided some much-needed stat bumps. It was a fine line to walk, fighting harder and harder battles to push himself without going so far that he died. It was effective—on that he couldn't argue—and not only for him.

Felix brought up Pit's status screen.

Name: Pit (Companion)
Level: 4
Race: Chimera - Tenku

Health: 43/70
Stamina: 10/50
Mana: 28/83

STR: 4 PER: 21
VIT: 14 END: 10
INT: 16 WIL: 15
AGL: 44 DEX: 26

Skills:
Bite (C), Level 8
Rake (C), Level 7
Cry (R), Level 9
Skulk (C), Level 18
Companion Pact (U), Level 5

There has to be a way to increase Pit's base stats. His Agility is extremely high, but his Strength is abysmal. Companions don't seem able to gain Titles. Maybe if Companion Pact gained more levels, it'd provide something?

He had already leveled Companion Pact to 5, and aside from a sense of accomplishment, he hadn't noticed any differences in the Skill. Honestly, he wasn't entirely sure what it did. He brought up the Skill description.

Companion Pact (Uncommon) Level 5
You have formed a pact with a denizen of the Foglands. Increasing Skill Level and Affinity will net larger gains from the pact, for both you and your Companion.

What's Affinity? He checked his status again, but there was no entry for Affinity. Based on the wording, it would indicate some sort of compatibility between him and his Tenku friend. How it measured that was anyone's guess.

"Another question for the list," Felix sighed, pulling out the Henaari's old journal. While filled with various notes and observations from the explorer's journeys, it was written in a language Felix couldn't decipher. It was also little more than a quarter full. Plenty of space for Felix's own notes. Using a thick grease pencil from the Henaari's pack, he had filled up several pages with all of the questions he planned to ask someone once he got out of this dang forest. He jotted down "Affinity - What is it?" onto the page.

Felix looked down at the notebook, the breadth of his ignorance eliciting a tightness in his chest. This place was trying to kill him. Every day he fought against creatures that wanted to eat him, and every day he made it out alive, but it was so hard. He never knew where he was going, only that he couldn't stop. If he stopped, he would die.

Breathe.

Pit nudged his hand, raven-like head pushing into his palm. Felix smiled and started scratching at the side of his neck. It didn't matter. He'd get through it. He had to.

He still hadn't made any further progress on his three quests. Felix's newest quest was a big question mark; he had no idea where to find more Blood Remnants. His Apprentice quest was...well he hadn't hit Apprentice in any of his spells, though he didn't really know what that meant. He assumed it was a certain level threshold, but what if it meant he had to apprentice himself to a wizard or something?

Meanwhile, the Home Sweet Home quest had 1 of 5 eliminated, but he had yet to run into anything else the quest considered to be a "threat," though Felix disagreed. The Irontooth Ape was a gnarly opponent, and clearly a threat to Felix's well-being, if nothing else.

Felix sniffed. A scent like burning offal and hair had begun to fill the air. "Dang, I'm taking too long."

Groaning with exhaustion, Felix stumbled to his feet. His Health and Stamina were barely at 25%, but he had to move before the Ape's corpse disappeared. Already, parts of it were turning to a greasy sort of smoke, the flesh rapidly disappearing. Felix walked over to the corpse and put his finger in the creature's blood, pulling back a red soaked hand.

He had attempted to activate Lessons of the Past and his Gourmand Title multiple times the past three days, trying it with various bugs and small animals that they had hunted down for meat and experience. It hadn't worked at all, though he'd gained levels in Lessons of the Past despite the failures. And while the meat part was questionable, the experience certainly racked up.

Regardless, he had to try again. His gains from Lessons of the Past and Gourmand were too great to not attempt this whenever he could, though he stood by his decision to not eat the Orit's blood. That thing had been nasty.

Aware he was just stalling, Felix shoved his finger into his mouth.

And nothing happened.

"Dang," he looked down at Pit, who was eyeing the Ape corpse hungrily. "I guess you can—"

The world turned grey.

It was like a wave rolled out through the ground, the trees and leaves, even the air. Then a pulse of sickening vertigo upended his vision like a glass of marbles, his senses bouncing and scattering in all directions.

Even still, Felix *burned.*

You Have Gained A Memory From An Irontooth Ape!
Would You Like To Review It Now?
Yes/Yes

Felix could see the notification even though he couldn't even feel his legs. Couldn't see his legs either, or any of his body. Quickly, he selected the only option he had.

Reality swirled, like a waterfall spinning into a black hole. Like a tornado inside a teacup. Like nothing and everything he had ever seen.

Then he was somewhere else. Some*one* else.

Balfur was running, slamming his heavy fists and stout legs into the earth as he barreled through rugged terrain. Large monolithic stones rose up all around, surrounded by a pervasive fog, thick as soup. A scream sounded from his right, then cut off. Another one was taken. Balfur sped up, heart thudding in his chest, breath pumping like a bellows as he fled.

"Aktu et rakna!"

Voices from the fog, deep, powerful, cruel voices. Fear ran through him, fear like he had never felt. All his life, none were strong enough to challenge him. Now, he ran, bloody and broken.

Another few screams of his brothers and sisters, all cut pitifully short. They were coming. The blue-skinned hunters. The giants had returned.

Minutes passed, but nothing had caught him yet. As he reached a rise, he risked a look back, toward home. Stone spires rose up out of the fog like small mountains, piercing the sky with their impossible, dangerous heights. His family had only kept to the bottom of those hollow mountains, preferring to keep steady earth beneath their feet. Now, he feared he'd never see them again: his home, or his family.

A guttural cry sounded, not far off. They were closing in.

Balfur turned, eyeing the dark cavern before him. He had no choice. If he were to survive this day, he must enter the Other's den. Snorting, he stepped within the cavern and turned around. He faced the fog-drenched valley that had been his home all his life. Then, with a grunt of effort, called upon the Mother's Gift. She answered, and a dozen stone columns rose up and sealed off the cavern opening.

Only one way out, now.

Balfur trudged into the cave, taking dangerous paths long forbidden by his people. For hours he walked, smashing any blind creature that groped for him, and ultimately avoided the Other. How, he did not know, only that the Mother had given him her blessing. For eventually, he saw the light of day shining upon another forest, thick fog swirling just like home. Balfur trudged through the wood, seeking a new home, somewhere it could recover from its many wounds.

A yipping growl caught his attention, and then a small winged shadow attacked Balfur, raking at him with tiny claws. The thing's attack caught the edges of a wound, tearing it further.

Balfur roared in anger and pain. Rage boiled in his blood, and the Mother's Gift answered.

This time, he would fight!

The darkness lifted suddenly, and Felix gasped a desperate breath. He tripped and fell backwards, sitting down hard on the packed earth.

That was intense. Felix looked down at his hands, marveling at his human skin and clothing. *Just like the grub. I felt like I* was *the ape. But this one was...*Felix looked up at the Irontooth Ape's corpse, which had almost completely dissolved. It had been intelligent, sapient even. He had killed it in self-defense, but still...

Felix stood up and approached the remains. He knelt down by its head, its expression gone soft in death. "I am sorry, Balfur. I wish..." Felix looked up, sniffing and seeing the trees dance in the afternoon wind. "I wish it could have been different."

He sat there a long time while the remains of Balfur dissolved into nothing.

Ultimately, Felix felt hypocritical.

He had been seeking these challenges and monsters, using them to level up and improve his Skills so he could survive. It hadn't bothered him too much, the killing. But then, he had never *become* someone he had just killed. It threw him, and Felix wasn't beyond admitting that he felt less after killing it.

He had sat in that clearing for an hour, digesting everything. By the end, he didn't have an easy answer to his dilemma, only more questions and moral ambiguity. But he had a plan. He had to reach people to answer his questions, and while the Ape didn't recognize them, Felix certainly did. Those hollow mountains were stone towers.

There *had* to be people there, right?

The Iront—Balfur was chased from its home, a valley covered

in heavy fog and accessed by a cavern. The Memory contained Balfur's journey through the cavern, and his Keen Mind Trait held a perfect snapshot of it. The only confusing part was where he entered Felix's neck of the woods. He had a general idea of a mountainside with a deep crevasse, but thick fog encompassed the area, much like his home valley.

Felix hadn't seen a single speck of fog since he'd been here. For all that this was the Foglands, it'd been mostly clear and sunny. It hadn't even rained in the past week.

Not really important, I guess. Felix checked his satchel and made sure he had enough food packed away. He didn't know how long he'd be underground, though it had only seemed like a couple hours in the Memory. *What* is *important is that I find civilization and get out of this death trap.*

With a sharp whistle, Felix started off. Pit trotted behind, his tail swishing happily.

CHAPTER NINETEEN

Late afternoon in the Foglands was no better than full dark. The soupy murk of mist occluded everything around them. Even their torches, burning bright, were barely enough to penetrate the dense covering. Sounds echoed and stretched strangely in the fog, distances hard to guess, and the smell of winter pervaded all: cold, blank, dead.

Ice on the wind.

Magda held up her torch, casting light upon several twisted trees that bore blackened fruit. They looked like they were once red and white, but now looked more like blood on pale flesh, eaten away by whatever sickness corrupted this stretch of the Continent. Beyond the trees was the start of a stone wall, ten paces thick and half shattered by some enormous force.

Suddenly there was a yowl from the left, and the screech of metal on metal. The yowl cut off abruptly with a steely squelch. A tall man appeared out of the fog, wearing a suit of plate marred with countless scratches and now covered in gore. A frog-mouth helmet encased his head and face, like a menacing juggernaut of steel. He flicked his axe, tossing blood off of it, and grunted with a slightly echoing voice. "More harnoq. This place is crawling with chimeras. Rory wasn't lying."

"He never does," Magda replied. She was wearing a steel half helm and a combination of mail and leather, much as the dwarf in

Haarwatch. She hefted twin kite shields on either arm and nodded her head at a few figures behind her. A fair skinned woman with raven black hair stepped forward lightly, almost as if she were dancing. Tight-fitting leather armor encased her, leaving her legs and arms less defended in exchange for mobility. A spiked chain was wrapped around her left arm as she surveyed the area.

"Not a great view, is it?"

Magda rolled her eyes. "Next time I bring you out for your Reveal, I'll make sure it's more scenic, Evie."

Evie flushed and gave her sister a smile. "You know what I meant. Visibility is terrible, even with my Perception. How do you Guilders enact a Culling in this murk?"

They had stepped out onto a cliff top ruin, and the remnants of battlements rose above the fog. Beyond that, there was the faint horizon and the skeletal shadows of bent trees. The armored man tilted his strangely-shaped helmet as he regarded the ruins.

"They don't usually travel this deep, kid," the man said with an echoing sigh. "No reason to, when the beasts come to them. Stand on top of a wall, throw spears and arrows, and just rake in the experience. A cushy job if there ever was one."

"Are not the Guilders on the Wall rotated? You could spend some time up there, too, if you so desired, yes?" Emerging from behind Evie, a tall woman with dark hair and darker skin smiled shyly in the light of their torches. She wore off-white enameled armor made of thin metal plates etched with flowing designs, an elegant hybrid between leather and platemail, and in her hands was a towering spear at least eight feet in length.

A young man with olive skin and light blond locks laughed from the side, resting against a thin staff of metal. "Sure he could, if he wanted to get laughed out of the Guild."

"Atar, don't be a pain," Magda said offhandedly, causing the olive-skinned youth to flush in embarrassment. "Wall duty is for Tin boys and girls, and is punishment more often than not." Magda peered into the fog ahead, eyeing the ruins. She straightened abruptly.

"Eyes up, enemy incoming." The woman started forward, shields up and ready, Harn following close behind.

"Don't worry about him," Evie said in a stage whisper to the dark woman, arm draping around her shoulders. "He's a dick."

"Hey!" Atar, only ten feet away, was outraged.

"Quiet, Sparky!" Harn's barked order straightened all of their spines reflexively. Four days in the Foglands with the indomitable Onslaught had taught them to listen first, talk back never.

"Yikes, Sparky," muttered Evie, grinning. "Gotta be careful out here. Fire can't solve all your problems."

"And, what? Flipping and giving lip does?" Atar tossed his expertly-tousled hair back and followed after their team leaders.

Evie stuck her tongue out at his retreating shadow."C'mon, Vess. Before we lose the light." Her green eyes flashed in excitement. "Time to kill some monsters."

"Yes, of course," came the reply as Vess fiddled with the haft of her spear. "Right behind you."

"From above!"

The cry was urgent, if not particularly loud, and Atar fell to the ground in an ungainly heap. Just in time to avoid the buzzing swipe of a gnarly chimeric beast with two heads, glowing eyes, and four razor-sharp wings. A grunt from nearby and the scrape of metal on metal, then the buzzing stopped. For now.

"What are they?" asked Vess, her hair in disarray and spear leveled. She watched the swirling fog for any sign of movement. "My Analyze is not working properly. It is only giving me question marks!"

"Chimeras, what else?" Atar snapped, pushing himself up to his knees. His robes were ruined, Magda noticed. He'd be even more annoying to deal with now. "AH! There's mud all over my Parnen battle robes! Do you know how much these cost?"

"Quiet, Sparky," came the reply, followed by a bop on the head. Magda winced inwardly. Harn was a good friend and even a passable teacher, but he didn't pull his punches. Even when he should. Atar sucked in a breath and held his head with both trembling hands.

Twin's teeth, he's terrified. Magda felt pity once again for the greenhorns who had followed them into the Foglands. They had signed up for a journey into danger in exchange for their Reveal and some levels. None of them knew they were headed into this nest of vipers.

"Analyze doesn't work right in the Foglands," Magda supplied, looking around. She pointed to a darker shadow in the night. "There, we'll make camp near the bluffs."

"Why?" Vess asked. She was a curious one. Brave, too. Magda hadn't missed how the noble held herself during that chimera attack. She was ready to spear the thing, and would have if they weren't so Twins-cursed fast.

"Magic, mostly. Too much ambient power here to fully rely on information-gathering Skills. This fog fools the eyes and dulls the senses, and it does no less to our Skills." Magda sped up. "Now, c'mon. Everyone, with me."

They marched in near silence toward the dark shadow, which revealed itself to be a tower, ruined by time and whatever war ravaged this land in the past. The others trudged past her, Harn right behind them. He gave her a quick finger sign. *All clear.* She nodded and pulled off her pack.

"We'll rest here tonight," Harn growled.

Whispered conversation sounded behind Magda as she rooted around in her large rucksack. She only half-paid attention as the girls set up their bedrolls and discussed the monsters.

"Did anyone else notice something off about that flying chimera?" Vess asked.

"Sure," said Evie. "Lots was off. The chimeras are pretty freaky."

"I will give you that. But why does every monster look...I'm not sure. Fuzzy, I suppose. Like they're more fog than beast."

"My master says that the Foglands are invasive. Any beast that stays here long enough is corrupted by it, turned toward a...darker nature," Atar said, his voice dripping with an attempt at mystery. Magda heard a very Harn-like snort, and Atar quickly added, "But no one truly knows. It's one of the more mysterious places on the Continent."

"Ya know, you could'a just said 'I don't know' like a normal person," Evie teased.

Magda could practically hear the boy's ramping outrage, like a teakettle about to boil over. Then it subsided. *Huh,* she thought. *I guess the kid can learn.*

"If I wanted advice from—"

"Enough. Take these and place them evenly around the inner walls." Magda had stood up and held out a handful of perfectly-spherical blue orbs. They were palm-sized, dark, seemingly made of glass, and had fine scratches all around them. The three Tin apprentices took them and placed them quickly. Once done, Magda nodded and held her left hand out.

"That which binds, hold together within, to shelter from without," Magda chanted, and the orbs all began to glow a brilliant sky blue, the scratches on them lighting up and casting designs of light upon the walls. The designs, dense scriptwork, shifted and flowed until they were all connected, and with a sudden shimmer of light, they sank into the stone itself.

Vess reached out and touched the wall, her hand pushing against something just before the stone itself. Magda smiled, remembering her first time with wardstones. It felt like thick air, or jelly, pushing back on her hand. To enemies, it would hide them, dulling their scent, camouflaging their appearances, and muffling their sounds. But only so much.

"No fire, no loud noises," Magda ordered.

"No fire?" asked Atar, hands already shimmering with heat over a pile of wet twigs. A sharp look from Harn made him pull back his hands and pout. "Been cold for days," he muttered.

"Quiet and cold is something you'll have to get used to in the wilds, kid," Harn offered, settling his pack down between Atar and the young women.

"Is everything you do about shields?" Evie asked, nodding at the wardstones. "Ever try a sword? Or a chain?"

"She is the Shieldwitch, no?" Vess asked, slightly confused. "Shields are what she does, as I understand it. And I am grateful. I doubt I would feel half so comfortable without your support, Lady Aren."

Magda frowned and waved her hand. "Just Magda, please. I'm no noble."

"Eh, you're as good as one, though," Evie said between bites of dried meat. "Silver Guilder and all. You shouldn't downplay that."

"And you shouldn't speak while chewing, kid," Harn said as he took off his tall helm. Underneath his face was blocky and grizzled, a visual representation of his voice, complete with at least four scars across his chin and nose. He scrunched his nose in disgust. "You're spitting all over my bedroll."

Evie tossed a rock at him, pinging it off his pauldron. "Hush, you. I'm a decorious young woman, with worldly airs and whatnot."

Vess struggled to keep a straight face. Magda ignored it, since it was a valiant effort. Last thing she wanted was an embarrassed noble on her hands. She cleared her throat.

"Get some food and some sleep. Tomorrow is a big day, and we still have a ways to go—"

"Where *are* we going?" whined Atar, hands busy rubbing his arms and legs. "You haven't let us kill anything for days, just defend ourselves. I thought we were out here to Reveal our Omens and gain levels?"

"Yeah, you never said," Evie asked, finishing off a bread roll. She lazed backwards, leaning on her elbows. "And that's weird even for you, Maggie."

"*You* may call me Lady Aren." Magda smirked as Evie pouted. *Ah, might as well tell them something.*

"We're headed into the interior, where we'll find true danger. This, out here? This is nothing. Just a bunch of predators with too little prey. I keep you from attacking so that you don't gain any levels before your Reveal, help maximize your gains for later." Magda pointed to the west, where their destination lay. "We're headed due west from here, over country few have traveled."

"True danger?" Atar looked pale, though it was hard to tell in the low light. He swallowed, his boyish features never so apparent as now. *Blind gods, they're so damn young.*

"Oh yes, kid. True danger lurks in the Foglands. Things even I can't kill," Harn added with an evil grin. "They say there's even a cabal of Lost sorcerers here, hidden from the world. Practicing magic so dark, it'd burn your soul clean out!" Harn's voice rose to a dramatic whisper as he leaned toward Atar. "Boo!"

Atar jumped, nearly landing on his feet if not for his robes, and instead face-planted in the dirt. Harn laughed, a quick and loud chuckle that became a wheezy guffaw.

"Enough, enough," chided Magda. She glanced up at the moon, hazy and indistinct in the fog. When she looked back, Atar was giving Harn a venomous look before he rolled over, blanket pulled on to ward off the chill of the foggy night. Evie was giggling quietly, and Vess looked clearly uncomfortable.

Magda sighed and walked away. "We move in five hours." She stalked to the edge of the ward, script light illuminating her face. "I'll take first watch."

Wasn't much to say to that, it seemed. They all turned in

within a few minutes, leaving Magda alone with the blissful silence. She settled down by the edge of the ward, watching the cloudy darkness beyond the ruined tower.

We're close, Callie, she thought, eyes searching the dark for some clue.

Just hold on.

CHAPTER TWENTY

It took five hours to find the cave.

Felix's uncanny memory led him true, but the strange fog that pervaded Balfur's recollection confused him. There was no sign of it. The forest was the same as always, full of a variety of trees, dangerous beasts, and a plethora of interesting herbs.

Congratulations!
You Have Gained A Title!
Natural Scholar II (Uncommon)!
You have Analyzed over 1000 different species of flora and fauna! +3 INT, +2 DEX, +2 PER!

Felix had gathered dozens of different plants, all with an increasing variety of uses, and his Herbalism Skill jumped up by 3 whole levels. Some were regenerative for Health, Stamina, or even Mana, but most were focused on curing status ailments like Bleeding, Dazed, even one that supposedly cured Petrification. The implications of that one worried him.

The journey was further complicated by no less than fourteen monstrous beasts, ranging from a level 20 snake creature to a level 24 moth bigger than him. The levels seemed to increase as he moved further, closing in on this cave. Felix crept around most of these enemies, content to observe rather than spend hours fighting them off. His Stealth Skill even raised by 4 levels, along with Breath Control.

There were a few, however, that were too Perceptive for him to avoid. Felix and Pit dealt with them, but it drained them. More time was spent recovering back to peak before moving on. All in all, his Dodge gained 4 levels, Acrobatics increased by 3, Dual Casting by 3, Physical Conditioning by 3, Long Blade Mastery had jumped up 2 levels, Running gained 1, Manasight by 1, Meditation by 1. Even Unarmed Mastery gained a single level when a serpentine cat had knocked his sword from his hand. It was exhausting, the constant fighting, but Felix couldn't deny he felt a primal sort of glee every time he survived a fight.

His magical Skills progressed as well, each of them gaining a few levels due to heavy use. Mana was his highest attribute, and it recovered faster than Health or Stamina. He still wasn't sure what determined regeneration, though Felix was convinced it was a hidden stat of some sort. *Something* was affecting it.

It was as he struck down a yellow-furred squirrel the size of a dog that he finally saw the cave. It was heavily obscured by several large fern-like plants all around it, neatly blending into the rocky terrain.

Your Companion, Pit, Has Gained A Level!
+2 VIT! +2 PER! +4 AGL! +4 DEX! +3 WIL! +1 END!
+2 INT!

You Have Gained A Level!
You are now Level 14!
+3 to WIL! +2 to INT! +4 to DEX! +1 to END! +2 to PER!
+2 to VIT! +4 to AGL!
You Have 5 Unused Stat Points!

"Huh. Nice." Felix smiled and wiped his bloody sword on the matted fur of the big tree rat. He looked over at Pit, who had already started eating another one of the giant squirrels. "C'mon, Pit. We'll take a break in the cave."

Pit yipped and grabbed one of the corpses, dragging it in for a meal. The Tenku had grown again, and was now nearly two feet at the shoulder. He was easily able to carry the dog-sized squirrel in his beak, though most of it dragged on the ground.

Exploration is level 10!

Just inside the cave was fairly dark, the late afternoon ambient sunlight illuminating only a short distance within. Felix strained his Perception, looking for any sort of threats in the cavern. His Memory detailed this as quite the labyrinth, filled with numerous beasts that hopefully would stay within, for now. Sensing nothing, Felix sat down on a rock and assigned his bonus stats.

He quickly allocated 1 point to Endurance and the remaining 4 to Perception. He had noticed a significant improvement since hitting 50 with his other stats and wanted to bring the important ones up to snuff. Felix shook his head. As much as he used his magic, he couldn't get away from the urge to balance out all of his stats. Maybe he'd be more powerful if he'd focused on Strength and Vitality over spreading himself out like this. Maybe. And maybe he'd end up too unbalanced and would die because he was strong but not fast enough. Balance, as far as he was concerned, was life or death.

Name: Felix Nevarre
Level: 14
Race: Nym
Omen: The Magician
Born Trait: Keen Mind

Health: 242/283
Stamina: 210/276
Mana: 238/417

STR: 53 PER: 47
VIT: 56 END: 50
INT: 55 WIL: 78
AGL: 45 DEX: 43

Skills:
Resistances: Acid Resistance (C), Level 13; Pain Resistance (U), Level 15; Poison Resistance (U), Level 17

Utility: Analyze (C), Level 17; Improvisation (C), Level 4; Running (C), Level 15; Stealth (C), Level 15; Swimming

(C), Level 3; Tracking (C), Level 11; Breath Control (U), Level 12; Companion Pact (U), Level 6; Dual Casting (U), Level 12; Free Climbing (U), Level 12; Exploration (U), Level 10; Herbalism (U), Level 17; Meditation (U), Level 20; Manasight (U), Level 11; Lessons of the Past (R), Level 6; Physical Conditioning (R), Level 11

Combat: Dodge (C), Level 19; Long Blade Mastery (C), Level 8; Small Blade Mastery (C), Level 7; Staff Mastery (C), Level 1; Thrown Weapons Mastery (C), Level 9; Unarmed Mastery (C), Level 4; Acrobatics (U), Level 17

Spells: Acid Stream (R), Level 17; Fire Within (R), Level 16; Influence of the Wisp (R), Level 11; Tides of Vellus (R), Level 15

Title(s):
Gourmand (+1 INT, VIT)
Survivor III (+4 END, +6 VIT)
Natural Scholar II (+4 INT, +2 DEX,+3 PER)
Giantslayer II (+3 STR, AGL)
Daredevil II (+2 STR, AGL, +3 VIT)
Butcher III (+8 STR, +6 WIL, +6 DEX)
Unconquered (+4 END, +6 VIT, +4 WIL)
Spellslinger (+4 INT, WIL)
Face the Charge (+4 WIL, +1 VIT, +2 STR)
Bulwark of the Innocent (+10% STR, VIT)
Pactmaker +4 AGL, PER, +3 DEX
Workhorse +4 END, STR, +3 VIT

Unused Stat Points: 0

Felix laughed at himself. Focusing on his stats and Skills kept his mind off the dangers he was about to face. He was a long way from the man he was on the beach, but he still wasn't enough to survive all the dangers here. There was always something worse out there. Chances were, that something was inside this cavern. Even if it weren't, *something* had chased Balfur out of that stone city, something that made even a level 20 Irontooth Ape mortally afraid.

Shaking himself and slapping his knees, Felix redirected his attention. It was much easier to focus himself recently, likely due to his huge Willpower and rising Intelligence. Thinking felt a lot faster, like the gears were all lubricated and juiced up, and he was having ideas he wasn't sure he'd have thought of a few weeks ago.

Pit lounged nearby, picking clean the bones of that giant squirrel. He was still eating a ton everyday, but it was much less of a problem now that he could hunt for himself. Felix watched him, smiling slightly. The little guy had been an invaluable companion to Felix, lightening his mood considerably just by existing. Suddenly, Pit's head perked up and oriented into the darkness.

"What is it, bud?" Felix slowly stood, unsheathing his sword. He focused on the darkness, trying to leverage his Perception to glimpse whatever it was his Companion sensed. There was nothing.

Then nothing attacked.

Shadows whipped from the edges of the cavern, tendrils of darkness that tangled around Felix's legs and yanked. He fell with an "Oof!" and the tendrils pulled him toward the cavern.

Grunting with exertion, Felix sat up and hacked down at the shadowy tendrils, bronze sword striking true. As he did, the runes on the blade flashed a bright gold, and the shadow screamed as it partially dissolved. Felix scrambled to his feet, holding the still-glowing sword in front of him like a torch. Something moved in the darkness, silent save for the slight hissing from its wounds.

An idea struck, and Felix held up his left hand, the one wearing a simple bronze ring. A flood of light bloomed from the ring as Felix activated its enchantment; it had been passively gathering light for the past few days, and should have plenty to light his way. The shadow creature squealed in alarm and perhaps pain, and Felix could finally see its full form.

It was made of rock, or looked like it; it was shaped like a pill-bug, covered in plates of rocky material, with six heavily-jointed legs spread out for balance. It sat low to the ground, and it had four tendrils made of darkness whipping wildly in the air.

Name: Rockstrike
Type: Elemental
Level: 23
HP: 289/342

SP: 260/252
MP: 72/72
Lore: An elemental born of a confluence of Earth and Shadow. It is eternally hungry.
Strength: Strength and Agility
Weakness: Light

It did not like the light, hissing from beneath its armor, and the tendrils struck back out against him. They struck Felix across the chest, wrapping around his right arm as it attempted to disarm him. Felix cried out, the shadow-stuff burning against his unprotected skin. He wrenched his arm away, but an angry red welt was left on him. The tendrils coiled back, then launched once more at his face. Too fast to dodge, Felix tried to tuck and roll away.

He knew he'd be too late.

A sharp cry tore through the cavern, and Pit was momentarily surrounded by a haze of red.

Pit used Cry!
Rockstrike is Stunned for 1 second!
Cry is level 10!

Felix glanced up, seeing the Rockstrike's tendrils drop limply to the ground. He burned Mana, forcing power through the looping channels in his arms as he cast a focused Tides of Vellus. A cone of blue light blasted forth, throwing the Rockstrike back and into the cavern wall. It smashed into the jagged surface and fell onto its back. Before it could recover, Felix jumped toward it, his 53 points of Strength propelling him fifteen feet toward the elemental, and struck downward with his hooked sword. The glowing blade cut into the elemental's body like it was paper, sizzling and spitting as the wound released gouts of shadowy miasma. Felix had to stumble back to evade the noxious cloud.

Doing so saved his neck, as the Rockstrike went berserk, whipping its shadowy tendrils in all directions. One smashed against Felix's chest, throwing him back ten feet, directly into a stalagmite. The breath exploded out of his lungs, and Felix felt like a vice gripped his chest. He was still stumbling to his feet when his friend leaped onto the flailing elemental.

He tried to cry out, to tell Pit to stop, but he couldn't get a breath. He could only watch helplessly as the Tenku ducked the powerful tendrils and began to savage the Rockstrike's wounded underbelly. The elemental tried to attack, but Pit was too close, the tendrils not quite flexible enough to hit his small form. Despite his condition, Felix could almost sense Pit's fury, his fox-like tail bushy and stiff, wings tucked close to his body.

Bite is level 9!
Bite is level 10!

Rake is level 8!
Rake is level 9!

Pit was a flurry of primal fury, his claws and beak tearing into the Rockstrike with abandon. Before Felix even got to his feet, it was done. The Rockstrike's tendrils fell limp to the ground, its legs slowly curling and stiffening up. Pit pulled back, holding a strange chunk of black rock in his beak as he trotted happily back toward Felix.

"What have you got there?" Felix wheezed, his breath coming back to him. Pit came up to him and dropped the rock into his palm before settling back with a smug look on his face. "Good job, buddy. Didn't know you had it in you."

The rock was odd. It was definitely stone, but it felt slick like oil and radiated a strange sense of...he wasn't sure. Hunger? To his Manasight, the stone leaked a cloud of brown and black, swirling together in a way that tasted like deep dark earth. He Analyzed it.

Analyze is level 18!

Name: Rockstrike Core
Type: Elemental Core
Lore: An elemental core is the central node of any elemental. While not always solid, it provides the majority of their power as they live and evolve. Can be used for many purposes, from smithing to enchanting.
Rarity: Common

"Oh, it's like the Blood Remnant, I think," Felix offered,

holding the core up to his face. "It was really smart to take this ou—"

Pit snapped the core from his hands, and gulped it down.

"Dude!" Felix lunged forward to stop him, but Pit scurried backward, pleased as punch. Then he started to glow. With a yipping cry, Pit suddenly shimmered a brilliant black and red, and his wings snapped out to full. Dark red feathers filled out along his wings, primaries and secondaries bursting forth like crimson spears, while the inner coverts filled with lustrous black. As the light faded, Pit was no bigger than before but seemed...

Felix toggled Pit's status.

Name: Pit (Companion)
Level: 6
Race: Chimera - Tenku

Health: 75/75
Stamina: 64/64
Mana: 83/83

STR: 6 PER: 21
VIT: 15 END: 12
INT: 16 WIL: 15
AGL: 45 DEX: 26

Skills:
Bite (C), Level 10
Rake (C), Level 9
Cry (R), Level 9
Skulk (C), Level 18
Companion Pact (U), Level 5

"Holy hell, how'd that happen?" Felix was flabbergasted. Pit had...absorbed the core? And it gave him a stat bump? How? Wait, no, that didn't matter. What DID matter was if it was repeatable.

"Pit, little bud. Wanna eat some more elementals?"

Pit barked and flapped his wings, clearly ecstatic.

They traversed the cavern, pushing deeper and deeper as they sought out more elementals like the Rockstrike. Felix was following the Memory map from Balfur, but wasn't above taking a detour. His Keen Mind kept him from getting lost, so the two of them moved carefully and inspected as much as they could.

Barely fifteen minutes into their trek, however, Felix's Tracking Skill noted odd marks along the floor and walls. Sharp divots, less like footprints and more like depressions left by iron spears, they nevertheless faintly glowed in his vision. His Skill pegged them as tracks, but they were easily a dozen feet apart, much wider than the Rockstrike's. A huge creature had come through here, then disappeared. The tracks vanished before he made it to the next intersection. Felix shivered, memory of Balfur's fear of the "Other" rising to mind.

Tracking is level 12!

Felix changed his mind. Delving deeper into these caverns was a mistake. The risk of encountering a foe they couldn't handle was too high. Level 20 might be doable for them at this point, but Felix doubted that was the limit of the monsters here. After that, they kept to the Memory path.

In the interest of training as well as survival, Felix exercised his Stealth while Pit used Skulk, which operated in much the same way. Felix kept his ring to a low burn, casting only a dim light around them, enough to see without completely giving away their position.

The caverns were beautiful, in their own way. Bioluminescent fungi lined the walls in the deepest places, and the constant *drip drip drip* of water echoed through many of the passages. The cavern walls were smooth and worn, likely thousands of years old, and in the light of his enchanted ring, he could make out the striations of layered sediment. These were the bones of the world, and like much of the Continent, it seemed very similar to Earth.

If it weren't for all the monsters and moons, this would be like some wilderness back home.

They encountered a number of Rockstrikes along the way, each one fast and dangerous. Felix and Pit developed an effective strategy against them: they would stun them with Cry or Influence of the Wisp, flip them, then hack at their unprotected underbellies.

Due to their strong armor and hides, this would take a few minutes unless they got lucky, and that was provided they didn't get lashed with those shadowy tendrils. There was more than one close call.

Felix still tried to better his use of Tides of Vellus. It was his most versatile spell, as well as his personal favorite. The problem was the conical burst, which in the tight confines of the cavern was too much. Most of the force was lost as it rebounded wildly off of the rock around them, often pushing Felix around more than the enemy. He focused on trying to reduce Tides to a sharper, more precise angle. It was hard work, costing him more Mana and concentration, but Felix hoped it would pay dividends eventually.

After four hours traversing the deep dark caves, they had delved into most of the tunnels and were on track to reach the end of the cavern system within thirty minutes, if Balfur's Memory was to be trusted. They had gathered a total of twelve cores out of fourteen Rockstrikes, and he fed all of them to Pit. Each core was like a mini level up, granting a smattering of stat points in Strength, Agility, and Endurance. The points were often only 1 or 2 per stat, and it was a crap shoot on whether all stats would bump up or just some of them.

Felix wasn't sure how it all worked, but he was glad it did. He was finally able to increase Pit's Strength by a significant margin, and now his Rake and Bite attacks actually had some oomph behind them.

Health: 135/135
Stamina: 195/195
Mana: 115/115

STR: 30 PER: 25
VIT: 27 END: 36
INT: 20 WIL: 21
AGL: 57 DEX: 34

Pit also leveled up three times, which not only boosted his stats, but also netted him a new Skill.

Your Companion, Pit Has Learned A Skill!
Wingblade, Level 1!
You have learned to shape the ambient Air Mana into

weapons. Increases range and accuracy moderately with Skill Level, damage increases slightly with Skill Level.

Beasts, it seemed, gained preset Skills as they grew. It was a welcome addition to their growing arsenal. Pit was becoming a formidable creature, though he hadn't grown any larger, being a little smaller than a medium-sized dog.

The hunting was good for Felix, too: he had gained another two levels. He also put his Gourmand Title to the test and tried Rockstrike blood six times. It was gross. Their blood was a rotten orange color, like something had gone wrong with it, and it made him gag every time. It wasn't until Felix had a moment of inspiration and bit directly into a fading shadow tendril that he had results. The shadowy flesh burned on the way down, but Felix immediately felt his Fire Within begin to grab and digest the power. The pain was excruciating, radiating from his throat and belly and into his limbs, as if acid was being pushed through his channels.

Pain Resistance is level 16!

Felix watched his Health begin to drop as he circulated the caustic Mana, but he restrained his panic. *It hurt when I ate the Wisp, too,* he reminded himself. *Just circulate it. Push. Through. It.*

A few more excruciating minutes and the burning stopped.

Congratulations!
Your Title Gourmand Has Garnered You Insight!
You Have Fully Digested Your Opponent's Mana!

You Have Learned A New Skill From A Rockstrike!
Shadow Whip (Rare), Level 1!
Manifest a tendril of pure elemental shadow. Range, accuracy, and damage increases with Skill Level.

Felix grinned. With this spell, he now had another offensive skill, *and* he finally had five spells for his quest.

He was still celebrating inwardly when he turned a corner and found the end of the caverns. His grin faltered, and Felix took a quick glance behind him, making sure he hadn't gotten lost.

Balfur's Memory was particularly clear here, and there weren't any branching tunnels for a mile. Then it came to him. Balfur had used his earth magic to seal the cavern.

Just as Felix realized this, his enchanted ring guttered and cut out, plunging them into darkness.

"Shit."

CHAPTER TWENTY-ONE

Felix stood in the darkness, chewing his lip.

He'd encountered this flaw with his Keen Mind Trait before. His head was like a computer with a huge amount of memory, but his RAM was limited. Keeping track of all those memories had started to feel exhausting, and this was the result. He had "forgotten" that the cavern was sealed behind Balfur.

"Okay," Felix reasoned. "Not the worst outcome. I just have to figure out how to drill through solid stone." He reached out and touched the rough surface of the cave wall. He could find no opening or flaw in the rock. "Right. Easy."

Then he heard it.

Skittering.

The sound of small stones clattering against bigger ones, but softer, as if a rock slide was attempting to be stealthy. It was all around him now, moving quickly in the darkness. Felix put his back to the wall, Pit sidling up to his right. It was pitch black, and the movement echoed in the cavern. Felix's pulse jumped, adrenaline pumping into his limbs as he readied to run or fight.

Wafts of brownish-black smoke drifted all around, and it took Felix a moment to realize what he was seeing. There was no light, so it wasn't smoke. It was Mana. Flexing his Manasight, Felix suddenly saw a dense cloud of Mana all around him. Deep shades of brown covered it all, but grey-black smog choked the brown tones of earthen Mana, something he could only recognize as shadow.

But within the clouds, he could just barely discern shifting movement. Bundles of black and brown twitched and flowed from one spot to another, the clack of their limbs following them.

Manasight is level 12!
Manasight is level 13!

Rockstrikes. They surrounded him. Their shadowy tendrils lashed angrily in the air, even as they focused on him with their beady eyes. They were here for vengeance; he could hear it in their seething silence. It was so strong, it felt like the earth itself was shaking.

Wait. Oh, that sucks so much.

The earth *was* shaking. The ambient Mana began to swirl, like a breeze in heavy smoke, churning it wildly. The Rockstrikes shifted and several began to run away, their panic as palpable as their rage.

Then the ground split open, and the earth itself engulfed them all.

Felix tumbled down, falling without sight,surrounded by the cacophony of an entire mountain crashing down. Thunder and darkness, his fear was electricity in his veins, even as his stomach lifted into his chest and his unseeing eyes burned with the rush of air. When he impacted the ground, it was almost a relief.

Almost.

Hitting the ground felt like a jolt of lightning, a shearing pain that splintered across his nerves. Agony was a red fire across his shoulder and chest, his vision black except for a few glowing status icons.

Status Condition: Broken Ribs (Major)
Status Condition: Dislocated Shoulder (Minor)
Status Condition: Shock (Severe)

"F-fuck," he groaned. It hurt to breathe, and his vision was hazy with brown and grey smudges atop the inky void of his surroundings. Thinking was hard, his mind stuttering under the pain. He forced through a single thought, however, and activated Meditation.

You Have Entered Into The Domain Of Another.
Beware!
It Approaches!

The darkness deepened as Felix felt his mind recede, reflexively pulling away from the ruin of his body. Everything faded.

Time lost meaning. Minutes, hours, days? Felix had no idea. A sense of red hot ruin coursed through him, pulsing like a second heartbeat. A slithering giant passed him, arcs of jagged light piercing the darkness, dancing across his wounds like knives of fire.

Suddenly, thunder crashed, carmine light galvanizing the sky as the nothingness all around him swelled into a roaring sea. His mind was abruptly afloat on a raft of blue light, tossed in a turbulent sea that threatened to engulf him at any moment. Beasts roamed these waters, twisting shapes beneath the acidic water, limbs thrashing and coiling. Serpentine bodies rolled beneath him, their dorsal fins raking against his raft, tearing holes and flooding his feet with dark water that burned his flesh. Terror gripped him harder than his pain, his mind filled with the image of vast jaws and innumerable teeth.

Somehow, Felix understood that if he didn't repair his mind, he would fall, never to rise.

Felix stiffened his Will, forcing the raft to repair itself. Gouges from innumerable claws filled in with a shimmering blue light, the gouges shining brighter than the rest of the raft. He wasn't sure how he knew to do that; it was like flexing a muscle he hadn't known he possessed.

That's not enough. Felix looked up at the oncoming waves, each reaching higher than a two-story house. He focused, shaping his Will in a way that felt both alien and utterly familiar. Blue light crackled as a hull rose up around him, a shape only vaguely boat-like, angled to cut through the dark waters all around him. Waves crashed over him, a deluge of fire and acidic lightning that made his nerves scream in agony. Trembling, Felix raised his arm, pushing his Will up and over him in a rough wedge.

The waters crashed all around him, and he was tossed into the air only to be slammed immediately back onto the deck. Felix gritted his teeth and held on.

Felix knew he wasn't here on this deadly ocean. Somehow, he was also underground, pinned beneath tons of rock and choking on darkness. He knew. Yet it did not matter. The world raged all around him, his Will a thin shell against the red lightning and corrosive waves. He tried to focus, to snap himself awake or something. But his mind ran in circles, thoughts chasing each other as all of his agonies this past week filtered through him, carried on the acrid gales.

Acid burns, slashed flesh, bludgeoning, sharp teeth on weak skin. Memories of pain, of torment, they piled against him and threatened to capsize his vessel. He fell to his knees, then onto all fours. Felix was tossed by the unending strength of the sea, and the crimson thunder shook his azure sanctuary. Whispers rose from the water all around, their voices soft and sweet as they offered surcease to his torment.

Just let go, they sang, their voices as smooth as silk and cold. *You have done enough. It is over.*

Felix's Will felt strained and brittle, little more than a wisp of fog against a hurricane. He ached, his body broken and his mind starved for familiar voices, familiar places. Their voices were a song he had never heard, but yearned for just the same. *Your home is waiting, wanderer. We will take you there. You need only let go and let us in.* Their voices twanged with a note of needful, hungry ruin.

"..don't give up yet..."

This voice was different. It was harsh, but warm. A face surfaced in his eyes, a smirking mouth and nondescript face from a dream, one that he couldn't quite remember. Except the eyes. Blue-green eyes like leaves against a summer sky.

"You have so much more to do, Felix...

"...others are counting on you..."

There was an ache in his chest, one quite separate from the ocean of pain that surrounded him. This was already there, something he'd been nursing ever since he had saved Pit. It hurt, throbbing like the memory of a sunburn, but inside his chest. Inside his soul, maybe.

Deep in that hurt, Felix could feel a thread of emotion; one that he identified as not his own. He could feel a stubborn, foolish anger. Anger that burned bright enough to risk attacking an Irontooth Ape, anger that would attack anything and everything that threatened him.

Because he knew his Companion would be there for him.

Companion Pact is level 8!

Let us in, wanderer!

Felix's eyes snapped open. "No," he stood up, shaky as a newborn colt. "Never." Their voices felt like teeth on his neck, like a discordant note in an orchestra. He knew, deep in his bones, that to let go would be to fall forever. Felix had made a promise to himself. He would survive. He would persevere, despite all the odds against him.

The voices howled, enraged at him. Memories of pain, escalating and unending, cascaded through his mind. Felix braced himself, drawing on his Willpower as never before. He might not be strong enough, or vital enough, or fast enough, but he was a tower of will. He reforged the ship around him, draining the water that had begun to accumulate, making the hull thicker and stronger. Azure light gleamed in the dark sea, and the creatures below retreated.

He was iron, his body unfeeling and cold. Unbreakable. He would survive this.

The water dropped all around him, bottoming out as a wave approached. Felix braced himself, his Will wrapping tight around himself. The wave was a tsunami, a mountain of dark water that crackled with red lightning. Twisted shapes coiled within it, each the size of jetliners.

Felix punched forward, his small ship suddenly accelerating across the water. If all this was a function of his mind, then he would make it his own. He forged the ship into a battering ram, slick and aerodynamic. He rocketed toward the wave, hull barely touching the sea even as it climbed up the face of it.

As he neared the crest, Felix grinned.

He would prevail.

The mountain dropped. And everything went dark.

You Have Survived.
The Challenge Is Incomplete.
Be Wary, Young Nym.

When he woke, it was to utter darkness.

A brief moment of panic set in as Felix scrambled up to his feet. He smashed his head against a rock as he stood up, and bright colors flashed before his eyes.

"*Fuck*!"

His voice was deadened, as if the darkness around him absorbed it.

Blindly, Felix cautiously stepped forward. He traced his hand along the wall behind him, his left arm out and swinging from side to side. Eventually, he hit another wall. And another, and another. The cave was maybe 10 feet square and was completely sealed. And he was alone.

Where is Pit? His mind conjured images of him being crushed and swallowed by the hungry earth. Of him being trapped somewhere like Felix, but hurt.

No no no no. A voice inside Felix started wailing, only moments from taking him over entirely. Felix slapped himself across the jaw, focusing on the pain. *No. I can do this. I just...let's take it one step at a time.*

He inspected his body, checking his Health and Stamina. Everything was full, and the dangerous status conditions had healed while he'd been unconscious. What was his regeneration at, now? How long did it all take?

A blinking icon distracted him, flashing in the corner of his vision. With a breath of relief, he toggled it.

Pain Resistance is level 17!
...
Pain Resistance is level 23!
Meditation is level 21!
...
Meditation is level 26!

Congratulations! You Have Reached Apprentice Tier in Meditation!
You Gain The Following:

+10 to all Mental Stats (INT, WIL, PER)
+10% to all Regeneration

You Have Unlocked A Harmonic Stat!
Resonance - Affects mental recovery. Confluence of Intelligence and Willpower.
Current Value: RES - 12

You Have Unlocked A Harmonic Stat!
Resilience - Affects physical recovery. Confluence of Endurance and Vitality.
Current Value: REI - 8

You Have Learned A New Skill!
Deep Mind (Epic), Level 1!
You have delved deeper into the mind than most, traveling upon a dark confluence of truth and perception. Increases Resonance per Skill Level, increases potency of mental Skills by a moderate amount per Skill Level.

Deep Mind is level 2!
...
Deep Mind is level 23!

You Have Learned A New Skill!
Mental Resistance (Rare), Level 1!
Gain resistance to mental assault, control, and other attacks of the mind. Increases mental defense significantly per Skill Level, increases mental flexibility moderately per Skill Level.

Mental Resistance is level 2!
...
Mental Resistance is level 21!

"Holy hell," he whispered, memories of his journey on the dark sea rushing back to him. "It was all real." Or real enough to affect the physical world, at least.

Apprentice Tier, huh? Felix smiled, finally able to cross that question off his list. Apprentice Tier happened at a certain level; he assumed level 25 based on his notifications. It could be 26, but that felt...wrong, somehow. Now, he just had to get his spells up to level 25 to complete one of his quests.

If I can even get out of here.

He slapped his cheeks again, focusing. That wouldn't help him.

What else did he learn? Felix went over the notifications again. He attained Apprentice Tier in Meditation, and that netted him some benefits, for some reason. Did this happen with all Skills when they hit level 25? That would be both amazing and insane. He had just gained 30 stat points in an instant. He had also gained a flat 10% bonus to his regeneration, which was huge.

Speaking of regeneration, he had also unlocked something called Harmonic Stats. Reading the prompt over again, Felix clenched his fists in excitement. He had been right! There *was* a hidden stat for regeneration, two of them in fact. Resonance and Resilience, for mental and physical recovery. The notification said they were a confluence of two of his main stats, but how did that affect anything? Felix's hands reached for his journal, even in the dark, but a thrill of terror ran through him as he patted his empty waist.

His satchel and sword were gone.

"God damn it," he swore softly. All his food and water was in that bag, not to mention his various herbs and last health potion. Everything he owned in this world was in there, and now it was probably crushed under a bunch of rock. Felix felt himself spiraling again, and wrenched himself back on task.

This high Willpower thing was paying dividends. He could practically feel the iron control he had over his mind and actions, his thoughts clear and firm simply because he wished them to be. *Would I have survived that dark ocean without my bonuses to Willpower? Or would I have fallen into the depths?*

Felix shuddered, unable to stop himself from recalling the serpentine shapes that flooded that violent sea. He still didn't understand why he had appeared there, or what it all meant, but he had survived. That was all that mattered.

Well, that and his new skills.

He had gained more Pain Resistance, which explained why his head didn't even twinge anymore, but more importantly, he gained Mental Resistance, too. It was a resistance Skill that he had been wanting, seeing how good his own Influence of the Wisp was at enthralling monsters. Remembering the deadly song of those creatures beneath that dark sea, Felix felt he had truly earned that one.

The biggest get was Deep Mind, his first Epic-rarity Skill. Likely a result of his struggles against mental assault, it increased the potency of mental Skills and, much more powerfully, it increased his Resonance with each level. And he was now at level 23. Felix sat back against the wall, doing some mental calculations. He brought up his new stats.

Harmonic Stats
RES: 38
REI: 8

Resonance is 38 and Resilience is 8. So assuming each level of Deep Mind increased Resonance by 1, that means I started with a 15 in Resonance? That seems high, based on my other stats. Felix's eyes widened. *Wait, I got a 10% boost to all regeneration, which means base values were 12 and 8, respectively. So then...*

Felix's body was suddenly limned in blue fire, lighting up his tiny cavern. Influence of the Wisp quickly wore off, the Skill more designed for bursts than continued use. Felix checked his Mana, which had dropped 10 points. Counting out the seconds, he watched as it refilled. It took slightly less than ten seconds to return to full. It appeared that Felix's Mana regeneration was somewhere around 1 Mana per second.

Oh wait, I'm still Meditating, aren't I? He barely noticed anymore. After hitting Apprentice Tier, it was like the level 10 bump he felt before, but exponentially greater. Meditating was like breathing, even as he stood up and moved around. He cast another Influence and watched his regeneration without Meditation. This time it was more like 0.5 Mana per second. *So that means the Harmonic Stats are multiplicative with my base stats. In this case, that's Willpower and half my Intelligence. And then the whole thing is, what? Divided in half? Yeah that makes sense.*

Huh, that's more mental math than I've done in a decade. It was so...easy.

Felix's Mana regeneration was formidable now. He didn't want to test his Health regen at this point, but it was likely good enough to restore him if given an hour or two. That would mean he'd been down here at least that long. He wasn't hungry or thirsty just yet, but he had to imagine that would be coming soon. Panic gripped him again, and he forced it down.

He felt more centered after going over his notifications. The primal excitement over raised levels and new Skills helped him forget, for a moment, where he was. But it came back, unavoidable and inevitable. He was trapped.

He was trapped, and Pit was gone.

Then, the ground trembled. For a moment, dark anxiety gripped his heart, but he quickly recognized that it was nowhere near the same intensity as before. That was an earthquake; this was a tremor at best. But the tremors grew until he could feel vibrations through his feet and heard the sudden, unmistakable sound of stone grinding upon stone.

Rushing to his feet, Felix activated Influence of the Wisp. As his body burned, he could see three yard-long worm-like creatures pouring out of the solid stone ahead of him. They were as thick as a two-liter and covered in an intimidating rocky carapace.

Name: Wurmling
Level: 14
Type: Wurm
HP: ???/???
SP: ???/???
MP: ???/???
Lore: Able to swim through stone like water, they sense their prey through vibrations. They prefer to attack in groups.
Strength: Agility and Endurance
Weakness: Unknown

Influence wore off in moments and the chamber was plunged into shadow.

Then they attacked.

Pain tore into his legs and arms as the Wurmlings snapped at him. An awful, sickly heat flooded his wounds, and Felix could see a brief reddish glow as they grabbed onto his limbs. He screamed.

You Have Learned A New Skill!
Fire Resistance, Level 1!

Through the fire and the flames, you come out stronger. Increases resistance to fire damage per Skill Level.

Felix whipped his arms up and out, attempting to launch the Wurmlings off him. They held on tenaciously, and wriggled their bodies to tear into him further.

"Fuck!" Felix ran directly at a wall, holding up his arms. With the Wurmlings still attached, they had nowhere to run, and he smashed them hard into the stone wall. They let out an nearly inaudible *squark* and dropped off of him. Felix stomped down hard on the last one at his ankle, and something inside it gave way. A kill notification populated his vision.

He was stronger than them.

Felix made sure Meditation was still running and slowly circled the room. He still couldn't see in this lightless cavern, but he had other talents. He activated Manasight, and his vision was inundated with clouds of dusty brown light and swirls of grey darkness. Earth and shadow Mana dominated the space, understandably, but within that fog were motes of orange. The motes blurred, each one whipping at him from a different angle. Felix ducked and dove forward, attempting to evade their attacks. Instead, he smashed head-first into a cavern wall.

"*Ahh*!" Felix gripped his skull, blood pouring out. Dizzy and disoriented, he gasped as another set of jaws latched onto his thigh. With a muffled scream, Felix rolled over and grabbed the coarse armor of the Wurmling. His hands struggled to grip it, the monster's body undulating wildly. It suddenly flared orange in his Manasight as its entire body became red hot, and Felix dropped it and fell backwards, bumping the cavern wall again as he fell to the ground.

Pain wracked him, but it was nothing. Compared to his fall and that ocean of monsters, these were mosquito bites. With a roar, Felix spun to his feet and tackled the still-glowing Wurmling. With his Manasight flaring, he smashed his hands repeatedly into the body of the Wurmling, knuckles bleeding as he cracked the rocky carapace. He grabbed its body and whipped it up into the air, feeling it crunch against the low ceiling before he brought it crashing to the ground. The Wurmling splattered into viscous goo, its orange glow snapping off in an instant.

Breathing heavy, Felix's Manasight pegged the other Wurmling off to his right, a faint orange glow in the brown-grey Mana-murk. Its glow was also dimming, becoming more diluted by the earth Mana all around. It was trying to run away, he realized. Screaming, he turned and lunged for its tail. His fingers gripped the last few inches of the Wurmling, and he pulled.

The Wurmling fought, its strange stone tunneling Skill attempting to pull it into the rock wall, but Felix overpowered it. Inch-by-inch, he pulled it out of its tunnel, the stone carapace buckling and popping in his hands. Burning hot liquid coursed over his fists, scalding his skin; but he never let go. With a final grunt of effort, the Wurmling ripped free of the wall, and Felix slapped it down onto the ground like a dirty rug. A final pop and *splortch,* and he received the final kill notification.

Felix sagged against a wall, almost too tired to stand. Numerous wounds littered his skin, and he couldn't tell what blood was his and what was the monsters'. He licked his dry lips, tasting blood as they cracked.

Blinking notifications flashed in the corner of his vision, but for once Felix swiped them away. He just...he was tired.

Then the ground rumbled again. Felix grunted as he stood up, just in time to sense four more Wurmlings arriving.

"C'mon then," Felix rolled his shoulders and put up his fists. "Round two."

CHAPTER TWENTY-TWO

"Haah, haah."

His heavy breathing filled the small cave. Felix collapsed on his knees in the center of the chamber, as far from any wall as he could manage. The Wurmlings liked to tunnel out of whatever wall he leaned against, so restricting them to the floor beneath him was the best he could do.

He was exhausted. He'd been fighting the Wurmlings for what felt like hours. They had gotten stronger, too. They started at level 14, but the last batch he had killed were level 19. Felix considered his torn knuckles, his Manasight showing him a rich gold aura shot through with flows of blue-white lightning. His aura, apparently? Manasight had grown by leaps and bounds during the past few hours, as Felix had to rely on it almost exclusively to fight. Now he could make out the space around him, and even something of the textures on the stone.

Well, not the stone itself. What he figured he was seeing was brown earth Mana formed into regulated bits of matter. He was seeing the aura of everything around him, echoed into the physical world. It was a far cry from the cloudy smoke he perceived only that morning.

Yesterday morning? Felix couldn't be sure how long he'd been trapped here. He was getting thirsty, though. All the heat put off by the Wurmling's bite attack had made the small cavern into a sauna. Felix wiped sweat from his face, his arms burning and heavy. He scanned the area around him for enemies, but the slight orange specks of the Wurmlings' fire Mana were nowhere to be found. Maybe he'd earned a break.

He laughed. It hurt.

Felix watched his Health, Stamina, and Mana all tick up steadily, healing his wounds and burning the fatigue from his body. It was amazing, frankly. The closer to full he was, the steadier his mind and body became, which almost went without saying. But, in practice, it was a miracle.

He shook his head. His mind was still muddled after using too much Mana. He had a brief respite, and he had to make use of it.

He checked his notifications.

God damn, there are a lot of these.

Normally, growth like this would have had him agog, but he was entirely too tired for all this bullshit. A few experiments later, and he condensed all of it.

New Title Gained!
Blind Pugilist (Rare)!
Even without your sight, you fight 'til the end. +4 PER, +3 DEX, +3 AGL

New Skill Learned!
Blind Fighting (Rare), level 1!
You've learned to hone your senses and battle without sight. Chances to hit while impaired increases moderately with Skill Level, chances of critical hits increases moderately with Skill Level.

Fire Resistance is level 11!
Influence of the Wisp is level 18!
Blind Fighting is level 17!
Unarmed Mastery is level 22!
Dodge is level 24!
Acrobatics is level 21!
Manasight is level 25!

Congratulations! You Have Reached Apprentice Tier in Manasight!

You Gain The Following:
+10% Perception
+25% Toward Identifying Mana

+5 REI
+1 RES
+2 STR
+1 AGL
+2 DEX
+4 PER

You Have Gained A Level!
You are now Level 17!
+3 to WIL! +2 to INT! +4 to DEX! +1 to END! +2 to PER!
+2 to VIT! +4 to AGL!
You Have 5 Unused Stat Points!

Felix grunted in surprise as he heard the almost-there crescendo of music. The rush of stats burned through him, cutting through most of his exhaustion in moments. His bones shifted, creaking as his muscles grew denser and heavier, even as his aching joints suddenly loosened and strengthened. His Manasight clarified immensely, the world becoming a clearer patchwork of ambient Mana, something he could even vaguely feel on his skin. Earth Mana felt like soft, ghostly sand, and shadow Mana felt like the cool, damp shade beneath a stone.

Taking a deep breath, Felix exhaled sharply. His mind was clear and his body whole. He clenched his fists and stood back up. The Wurmling has been coming at regular intervals, but the last few had been much more spread out. Felix figured they were running out of monsters.

Or maybe they were afraid of him now.

He tipped his head back and closed his eyes, the action all but meaningless in the dark. It helped center him, though. Thankfully, he was running out of distractions. While fighting the Wurmlings had netted him some excellent advantages, he was still trapped in a hole in the ground. He had to get out, and soon. He settled in to focus on his Meditation again.

After fighting the Wurmlings for so long, Felix had watched them burrow into and out of the stone like water. His Manasight had been too simple to determine how they did it, though it was surely a Skill of some kind. He had even tried to eat their blood and learn the Skill, but that had been a bust. Their blood was corrosive and burned a hole right through his tongue.

Acid Resistance is level 14!

That would have been horrifying if not for his regeneration.

He stood there, letting the cool sensations of earth and shadow Mana wash over him, mitigating some of the rising heat. Felix breathed, steady and slow, letting his mind fall into that strange sense of calm he found deep in the Meditation Skill. He drifted and let his mind flow. Tunneling through stone. The idea floated along his thoughts, aimless. It felt so familiar, though.

That's it!

He had seen a Skill like it before: the Irontooth Ape had done it. He revisited Balfur's Memory, examining it from every angle he could. His sense of his tiny cavern disappeared as he focused entirely on the Memory. He watched the Ape run from the monsters in the fog, then escape into the tunnels above. It sealed the exit and...

Yes. The Mother's Gift, he called it. That's what I need.

Felix honed in on that moment, no more than a second, where Balfur thought and the stone acted. Was there a twinge? A flow of power? He couldn't tell. It felt like...like breathing to Balfur, an extension of himself.

Breathing..just like...

Felix pulled from the Memory, focusing his mind on the flow of Mana through his body. His Fire Within flared, coursing in loops and whorls up and down his torso and limbs, blue lightning in his veins. Felix breathed, twisting his Mana flow, feeling as Fire Within shaped his Mana into strange new forms, altering the density and composition of the Mana itself. It felt like...a spectrum that fanned out into infinity. He wobbled, his concentration drifting as he perceived that expanse, but steadied himself with an effort.

Fire Within is level 20!
Fire Within is level 21!

His channels hummed with power, his Mana flowing like a

rushing river through these new, complicated forms. Felix grunted distantly, physical sensations lost amid the powerful torrent of fire across his belly and down his legs. He flexed his pathways, mimicking the casual grace of the Irontooth Ape, letting it all flow from the soles of his feet and into the earth itself.

He released it!

Felix stumbled. Knocked from his concentration, he took two tripping steps to his left, his Mana snapping like a rubber band stretched too far. Pain like sharp, targeted explosions went off behind his eyes and sinuses, shivering echoes rattling his teeth and ricocheting down his spine. Felix muffled a scream, biting it back as he wrestled with his Mana. The power within him wobbled, a gyroscope out of balance and threatening to rip him apart from the inside. He knew it, deep in his bones. So he fought back, pushing and shaping the Mana until it was contained completely within his core.

Fire Within is level 22!
...
Fire Within is level 24!

"Haah, haah, oh d...dang," Felix panted, squatting down and resting his head in his hands. "That was the hardest....that...I don't know *what* that was."

Felix felt like he'd run a marathon while doing calculus and balancing a bowling pin on his head; his mind and body were both sore in ways he never knew he could be sore. His hippocampus hurt, and he was reasonably sure his brain didn't have nerve endings. His Manasight was acting up, like he had stared into the sun for too long, so he shut it off. He crouched there awhile, just breathing really, because that was all he could do.

After a few minutes Felix leaned forward and put his hands to the ground, shaking off a sudden dizzy spell. Messing with Mana like that was no joke, he...

What?

The stone floor before him had a dip in it. Felix blindly traced his fingers around the area, measuring out a near perfect circle of stone that was just a fraction of an inch lower than the rest of the ground. The ground was uneven, he knew that, and that could be it...except for the two perfect shoe prints in the center of the depression.

Felix's jaw dropped. He had done it.

Now do it again, better.

Felix focused, tracing back the way he had shaped his Mana just minutes ago. His memory was crystal clear, though the effort still sent a spike of pain across his mind, but he managed to hold it in place for a few seconds. He felt the rock beneath his hand...peel away, gathering at the edges of an inch deep hole.

New Skill Learned!
Stone Shaping (Rare), level 1!
Through blood, sweat, and tears, you have wrested control of the earth itself! Increases control and speed with Skill Level.

+1 RES
+5 WIL
+2 INT

New Title Gained!
Exemplary Student (Uncommon)!
Learn Skills from the examples of others! +2 PER, +2 INT, +1 DEX

Due To Rarity Of The Skill Learned, Reward Increased! +5 PER, +5 INT, +3 DEX!

"Hell yeah!" Felix punched the air, his body flooding with energy as the system pumped him full of stats.

"I'm coming, little buddy."

It took longer than he had hoped, tunneling through the walls.

Felix tracked the next batch of Wurmlings that headed his way, using his tentatively-recovered Manasight to peer through the earth around them and watch their orange sparks slither in his direction. He dispatched them quickly, bringing his Unarmed Mastery to 23 and his Blind Fighting to 18. After the Wurmlings were gone, Felix oriented on their origin and started Stone Shaping.

While using the Skill seemed to automate much of the process, it was still a strange sort of magic to perform. Unlike Acid Stream or Influence of the Wisp, this wasn't just a spell he could pour Mana into and have it do what he wanted, at least not at low levels. He had to focus, keeping his thoughts toward the stone in front of him, and utilize the rhythmic Mana-shaping he had experienced in Balfur's Memory and his own recent attempts. It was slow going, but within a half hour, he had created a tunnel nearly six feet deep.

Stone Shaping is level 2!

...

Stone Shaping is level 8!

He had also used up all of his Mana twice by that point. He had to take breaks, often.

As he used the Skill, the stone he targeted pulled up and around, flowing like water until it settled behind him. The stone accumulated there, filling the tunnel as quickly as he made it, eventually encapsulating him into a bubble of emptiness between the stone. It was unnerving, but as long as Felix didn't dwell on it, he could shrug it off, his Willpower no doubt helping him. It grew easier eventually, the effort and concentration required becoming less and less as he leveled the Skill, even though his finesse was sorely lacking. After nearly two hours and many rests between, he broke through a section of stone and ruddy light streamed into the tunnel.

Felix flinched back from the light, overwhelmed. But he felt a giddiness in his chest as he pushed once more with Stone Shaping, creating an uneven hole big enough for his body to squeeze through. Without waiting, he pulled himself out of the tunnel and into the light. He sucked in lungfuls of fresh air, his grip on his anxieties finally relaxing now that he was out of the tunnel.

Stone Shaping is level 13!

He landed on tiled flooring, and was so disoriented from the journey and just attempting to breathe that it took him several seconds to recognize something was wrong. He was in a hallway, one carved entirely from the stone around him, but it was sideways.

Exploration is level 12!

Mostly sideways, at least. Felix had tunneled up at the back of the long hallway, and as it moved away from him, it buckled and twisted, as if the earth had turned liquid at some point in the past. Also, the air felt hot. Far hotter than his small cavern had been, though obviously larger. Hot and...eggy?

No, sulfur. It smells like brimstone.

The red-orange light seeped from the chamber ahead, illuminating far more than Felix was used to. He even let his Manasight dim back to a low burn. Even now, orange clouds of energy floated through the air, buffeting him like waves on a beach. Heat followed those waves, rapidly rising now that he was out of the earth, and a sweat quickly gathered on him. Felix stood with a light grunt, and started walking down the hallway, peering into the shadowy recesses all around him.

The walls were carved into columns and alcoves that might have once held fine sculpture or tapestries, but now held nothing more than tinted shadows. Dust and stone powder lined everything, the heat sucking all the moisture out of the air like an oven. It only grew worse as he approached the end of the hallway, the light itself growing brighter and brighter. Felix paused at the edge of the hall, peering cautiously out onto a wide balcony that ran for dozens of yards to the left and right and whose edge was protected by a sturdy stone railing. Everything seemed carved of a single stone, as if someone had used Stone Shaping to sculpt it all into existence. As his eyes grew used to the light, Felix looked up, breath catching as he noticed the ceilings nearly two hundred feet above him. The walls were carved with vaulting buttresses, massive stone archways that supported the distant roof. The walls farther up were lined with even more balconies and railing-lined pathways, going up at least two dozen levels.

New Skill Learned!
Heat Resistance (Uncommon), level 1!
Not everything hot burns, but it can still kill you.

The heat ratcheted up another level as he walked out onto the balcony, hot winds blowing up from below him. Squinting against the intense heat, Felix peered downward, noticing at least another level below him before a large courtyard could be seen at the ground floor. Part of the room was lit up with orange and yellow light, shifting slowly across the lower walls. The light came from a small river of lava—actual, honest-to-goodness lava—that coursed along the side of two walls and disappeared into tunnels built into the ground floor. The rest of the floor was filled with black, hanging chains which were affixed somehow in midair and ended in either cruel-looking hooks or rough cages.

Exploration is level 13!
Heat Resistance is level 2!

Felix blinked the sweat from his eyes and looked closer. The heat was making everything distorted and wavy, and his eyes were both swimming in sweat and drying from the hot breeze. His throat ached, burning with thirst that he hadn't quenched in at least half a day now. He shook his head, and *looked*. Below him were dozens of Wurmlings and four huge wurms that were twice the size of their smaller brethren. He quickly Analyzed them as level 20 Yungling Wurms.

"Fuck," he croaked softly. The wurms were smacking a few iron cages around with their tails, a few of them containing the distinct shapes of Rockstrikes that struggled against the metal bars. There were too many to take on, so he'd have to move much more quietly. But just as he was about to pull away from the edge, a sudden ache in his chest drew his eyes down and to the left, to a single iron cage that was being knocked about by one of the Yungling Wurms.

Companion Pact is level 9!

In that cage was Pit.

"No..." Felix's eyes widened despite the drying wind, and his fist clenched so hard his bones and tendons creaked. Pit had been put in a cage much too small for him, and his wings were awkwardly jammed into the bars. Each time the wurm hit the cage, he'd let out a pitiful whine and cower away from the beast. The ache in his chest magnified ten times, becoming a burning pain that drenched his insides with hot acid and demanded he take *action*.

"Hey! Let him go!"

And Felix jumped off the balcony.

As he fell two stories, he had only two brief thoughts. The first was something along the lines of, *what the fucking fuck aaahhhhhhhh!*

The second was to activate Tides of Vellus and to pour nearly a third of his Mana into it.

A brief, powerful blast of blue light and projected force rocketed out below Felix's body, countering his momentum and slowing him down just enough that he landed on the ground hard instead of deadly hard. Small debris, black iron chains, and a few of the smaller Wurmlings were knocked aside and crushed. Several kill notifications spammed across his vision as he stood up from a slight crouch. Felix fixed the Yungling Wurm with a glare and cracked his knuckles.

New Skill Learned!
Make An Entrance (Uncommon), level 1!
All of life is a stage, and you have an uncanny knack for timing.

"Pick on someone your own size."

CHAPTER TWENTY-THREE

While the wurms seemed taken aback for a moment, Felix checked his Health. He had lost nearly 10% from his landing and his left ankle twinged painfully, even through his resistance. Still, he smirked at the wurms as if he was fine and raised his fists up in what TV told him was a boxing stance.

New Skill Learned!
Acting (Common), Level 1!
You stand upon the stage, now make it yours. Convey emotions and intent with greater fidelity per Skill Level.

Then as if a switch flipped, all of them surged forward, their mouths open and glowing with an orange flare of light.

He went to work.

Fighting the Wurmlings was routine at this point, and maybe it was the higher levels in Unarmed Mastery and Dodge, but their attacks were predictable. Felix ducked serpentine strikes and wove between their armored bodies even as he laid about him with heavy slams and punches. In moments the skin on his knuckles burst open again, each stroke hitting heavy, rock-like plating, but he didn't stop. He crushed the Wurmlings one after the other, even as his Stamina depleted faster and faster.

Heat Resistance is level 3!
Physical Conditioning is level 14!

The heat was excruciating down here. Those movies where the heroes fought above a pit of lava had it all wrong; they should have been cooked alive. The dry air pulled moisture from his body like a sponge, his sweat evaporating as fast as he produced it and his skin cracking as it dried, creating fissures up his fists that expanded slightly with every swing. More agony that he firmly pushed to the back of his mind. Now wasn't the time to be weak. These monsters wanted to fight?

Felix would show them his claws.

Six Wurmlings fell to his strikes, crumpled beneath his superior Strength, but then one of their older brothers joined the fight. A Yungling Wurm surfaced from beneath Felix, taking him by surprise and tossing him into the air. He landed nearly thirty feet away, only a stone's throw from the open channel of lava at the end of the room. Felix stood quickly, unsure where the wurm was going to emerge. The large group of them still milled over toward Pit's cage, but the Yungling that hit him was nowhere to be seen. Then he felt it...rumbling beneath his feet.

Flexing his Manasight, he could see a torch-sized flare of orange Mana zip upwards through the dark earth. Felix rolled out of the way just as the Yungling Wurm breached the surface, its large, three-foot diameter body crashing onto the ground like a hydraulic press. It left behind shattered stones wherever it traversed.

This is taking too long, Felix thought. He glanced back toward Pit, who was watching him with fierce eyes. *I've gotta end this now.*

As the Yungling barreled toward him along the surface, Felix summoned an Acid Stream, hoping to pour it down the wurm's throat. But a sudden burst of speed put the wurm too close too soon, and Felix had to abort the casting. But that didn't mean it wouldn't get hit. Grimacing against the pain, Felix gripped the half-finished orb, splashing green acid all over his palm and fingers, and delivered a sharp right cross.

The wurm's skin crumpled like paper, its head ricocheting off the ground like a ball.

New Skill Learned!

Corrosive Strike (Rare), Level 1!
Imbue your strikes with the power of acid, destroying their defenses even as you pummel them into submission.

Felix stared wide eyed at the notification.

You can do that?

Ideas flooded his head, and his fingers itched to find his journal so he could write them down.

The Yungling Wurm rolled woozily to its belly, slithering toward Felix. He dismissed the Skill notification and regarded the wurm. With an effort of Willpower, Felix released a concentrated blast of Tides of Vellus, knocking the ten-foot-long wurm to the side again. The monster was hurt, but it wasn't down for the count, not by a long shot. He quickly Analyzed it, checking it's Health.

Health: 344/899

Felix frowned. Then he did the only thing he could think of: he cast everything he had. Influence of the Wisp paused the wurm for a few seconds, giving him a chance to tie it up with Shadow Whip. A single thick tendril of darkness shot forth, wrapping itself tightly around the wurm. Holding it in place, Felix cast Tides of Vellus as fast as he could. Shock after shock after shock, the Yungling Wurm was rocked back by the kinetic force of the spell, and each time its movement was arrested by the Shadow Whip. Felix strained, his Mana draining rapidly even as his muscles screamed in protest. His strength was high, but this was dancing at the limit of his ability. After the tenth time casting Tides, he saw a kill notification come across his vision.

Shadow Whip is level 2!
...
Shadow Whip is level 6!

It was dead. Finally. But he had no time. In his struggle, he hadn't realized that the other Wurmlings had surrounded him.

Pausing for a few breaths, Felix checked his peripherals, his enhanced Perception giving him a clearer view than if he had eyes in the back of his head. There were at least two dozen Wurmlings still left, and three more Yungling Wurms. And they were all surging toward him.

Shit.

Felix let out a pulse of Tides of Vellus, using the original pattern to launch a pulse in 360 degrees. It was enough to push back the smallest of the Wurmlings, and Felix rushed to his right, using Corrosive Strike to make a hole. His strike devastated two Wurmlings, his acid-enhanced fists tearing through them like tissue paper. Felix stumbled forward, not expecting the lack of resistance, turned it into a forward roll and came up just in time to get his core tackled by one of the Yunglings.

"Ooof!" Breath wooshed out of him as he was lifted up into the air. The snout of the Yungling tipped, flicking Felix behind it, before it dove into the stone floor. The bigger wurms were much more graceful at tunneling, and the ground barely moved as it swam through it like water. Felix had landed hard on his back and saw his Health dip 40 points; he was pretty sure he was bleeding somewhere, too.

Regardless, he forced himself to his feet, even as he scanned the area around and below him with Manasight. As he guessed, the Yungling came up from beneath again.

"One trick pony, huh?" Felix gasped, still holding his sore gut. He straightened and gathered earthen Mana to his hands, reaching and grasping the ground beneath him. "Check this out, then!"

Stone Shaping!

Felix wrenched his arms apart, the stone beneath him parting and revealing the ugly mug of a surprised Yungling. Swinging his left hand down awkwardly, Felix bashed a Corrosive Strike directly into the wurm's face. Between the strike and the wurm's own momentum, its skull shattered into shards of carapace and gallons of purple goo. The ichor fountained up all around Felix, drenching him and everything around him for feet. Coughing, he stumbled back from the hole and now completely dead wurm.

Corrosive Strike is level 2!

...

Corrosive Strike is level 8!

Whoa. That had been much more effective than he had thought. How fast was that thing going?

Felix glanced at his Health and Mana; he was at a little under 50% of both, but they were regenerating steadily. He glanced up at the rest of the wurms, which were converging on him again.

It would be enough.

He charged out toward the oncoming horde, releasing pulse after unfocused pulse of Tides of Vellus to move and disorient his foes. Then, utilizing his Acrobatics and Dodge Skills, bobbed and weaved between their horrifying maws and craggy carapaces as he moved toward Pit's cage. The dog-sized tenku was whining in pain, his cage still swinging from a previous wurm strike. He was only a few yards away, but the third Yungling Wurm crossed his path. The wurm split the four sides of its mouth open, revealing a tunnel of razor sharp teeth soaked in bright orange illumination. Moments later, a torrent of fire streamed forth, dousing everything for forty feet.

Felix threw up his arms and rolled away, but not fast enough. Fire engulfed his right arm, shoulder, and back. It ate into him like a living thing, the flames hotter than anything he'd ever felt before. Felix screamed in pain, but his resistances let him keep his head. He immediately rolled himself on the ground over and over until the fire went out.

Pain Resistance is level 24!

Fire Resistance is level 12!
Fire Resistance is level 13!

Heat Resistance is level 4!
...
Heat Resistance is level 7!

Before he could stand, a burst of fiery Mana surged beneath the earth, directly below him. Felix pushed off the ground, attempting to dodge the incoming wurm, but he misjudged his own strength; Felix launched himself up and to the side, his body spinning rapidly in the air until he smashed painfully against one of the rocky walls. A resounding crack echoed through the chamber, even as Felix stood up and inspected himself. Not only was he burnt and sore all along his right side, and his clothes would have to be replaced (*again, god damn it*) but his Health was also down another 20%.

Another couple hits like that....

Felix let the thought go. He was doing this too inefficiently, and his Stamina was taking a serious hit from all this heat. It had to be depleting at twice the normal rate. If this went on, it wouldn't matter how much Mana and Health he had left, he'd pass out and these wurms would eat him. They'd eat Pit, too.

No, not gonna happen. Felix mentally shook himself, reorienting. He was facing...fourteen Wurmlings and two Yungling Wurms, each with basically full Health and Stamina. The Wurmlings had that heated bite attack, but he could work around that easily by this point. The real problem was the last two Yunglings, which in addition to their greater speed, strength, and size also had fucking fire breath. One of them was uncoiling from the tunnel it had just made, and the other was swiftly advancing on Felix from his left. He had to kill them before anything else.

Only one Skill would give him the chance he needed.

Felix stood tall and held his hands out, palms outward.

Influence of the Wisp.

Felix's entire body blazed with a blue-white fire, his illumination casting the magma orange air into stark contrast. He tried to duplicate a feat he'd once done with Acid Stream, increasing the amount of Mana into the spell to sort of supercharge it. He felt a tugging in his mind, but it was like a hand getting caught in a spiderweb. He pushed through it, and Mana thundered out of his channels and into the spell. He blazed brighter than ever before, and then so did everyone else within fifty feet. Blue-white fire limned them all, and variations on the same message popped up in Felix's vision ten times.

A Wurmling Has Been Enthralled for 2 Seconds.
A Yungling Wurm Has Been Enthralled for 1 Second.

Influence of the Wisp is level 19!
Influence of the Wisp is level 20!

Most of the wurms stopped dead, and the few outside his range collided violently with their brethren, knocking both to the ground. But Felix was already running toward the nearest Yungling, pushing himself as fast as he could go. Just as the Wisp-light began to fade from the first Yungling, Felix swung down with a Corrosive Strike, putting his entire body behind the blow.

The ground beneath them caved in, cracks racing outward and splitting the uneven stone. Unwilling to rely on chance, Felix swung three more blows, each as powerful as the last, until he noticed his hands were simply splashing in a gelatinous puddle of purple muck. Disgusted, he leaped from the depression he had made and turned to the rest of the wurms. He was covered in gore, and bubbling green acid dripped from his fists.

Corrosive Strike is level 9!

"C'mon!" he roared, all of his anger and frustration and fear pouring out of his lungs. "We're not done yet!"

New Skill Learned!
Intimidation (Common), level 1!
They say honey catches more flies than vinegar, but you've found blood works just as well.

Felix blasted out Tides of Vellus, throwing the smaller Wurmlings back and killing a few of the nearer ones. He rushed forward, stomping on any wurms that got too close and striking out at the rest. Corrosive Strike tore through their bodies like tissue paper, and even Acid Stream simply dissolved jagged holes into their carapaces. The last Yungling Wurm had retreated to the row of hanging cages, obviously smarter than the rest of its kin. As Felix dispatched the last Wurmling, the Yungling held up its whip-like tail, covered in bony protrusions and rock-hard armor, and poised it over the cages. Its meaning was immediately clear.

"Fuck you," Felix spat, holding up his left hand as shadows gathered in his palm. "I've got a whip too."

Felix snapped out his Shadow Whip just as the Yungling hissed and swung at the cages. Thankfully, his high Dexterity and Perception made the shot easier, and the Shadow Whip latched onto the wurm's tail. Felix pulled, his strength just enough to redirect the force of the swing, causing it to slam powerfully in the stone just ahead of the cages. Quickly re-gripping the strange shadow substance, Felix pulled hard and jumped forward at the same time.

Shadow Whip is level 7!

Rock dust billowed, driven on by the hot volcanic winds, but Felix didn't need eyes to see his enemy. Manasight made the wurm's position clear, and as he rocketed through the dust cloud, he already had a fist prepped for the opening maw of the beast. He swung, and the blow knocked the Yungling Wurm back a step, its serpentine body thrashing to keep upright even as Felix was knocked backward by the force of the collision.

He landed gracelessly on the rocky ground, tumbling a few times before he could get his feet under him. When he did, he glanced up to see the Yungling Wurm only feet away from him, four-part maw opened and poised to swallow him whole. Felix threw up his arms, catching the top two jaw segments even as the bottom two sunk deep into his thigh and calf. Screaming in pain and terror, Felix pushed with every ounce of Strength he possessed, even as his blood poured down his legs and his head grew light. An orange light bloomed deep in the nightmare creature's tooth-lined throat, flickering with a growing strength and heat.

"Not," he grunted, still pushing against the wurm's massive jaws. "Today," he shifted his legs, bracing himself against the ground below. "You...piece...of..shit!"

Tides of Vellus.

Tides of Vellus.

Tides of Vellus.

Felix spammed the spell three times, sending waves of concussive blasts directly down the wurm's throat. Teeth snapped and membranes ruptured, flooding the creature with putrescent purple blood. His Mana plummeted, the shaped and boosted spell costing far more than the vanilla version, and Felix's already light head began swimming. Despite that, he held his trembling arms up and pushed his feet down into the shattered stone beneath him, and he whispered.

"T-tides of Vellus..!"

The interior of the wurm swelled for a brief instant before it exploded in all directions, its insides becoming very purple, very messy outsides.

Blue lightning crackled around the impact site, the rest all darkened stone and sundered meat. Felix stood up on shaking legs, throwing a fist into the air even as purple offal and pulped flesh sloughed off his shoulders and chest. He oriented on the last remaining Yungling, positioned farther down the chamber, and pointed a suddenly steady finger at it.

"You're next."

The wurm went extremely still, then turned and dove into the stone wall.

It ran.

Intimidation is level 2!

Felix watched with his Manasight until it fled out of range, and only then did he collapse bonelessly onto the ground.

"This world sucks."

CHAPTER TWENTY-FOUR

For a minute, Felix just laid on the ground.

He was so damn tired. And thirsty.

Waaghk. So so thirsty.

Status: Dehydrated (Major)

Yeah, that makes sense.

In the corner of his vision, a tiny exclamation point icon blinked furiously at him.

Acid Resistance is level 15!
...
Acid Resistance is level 20!

Heat Resistance is level 8!
...
Heat Resistance is level 11!

Tides of Vellus is level 19!
...
Tides of Vellus is level 25!
Congratulations! You Have Reached Apprentice Tier in Tides of Vellus!

You Gain The Following:
+10 WIL, INT
Rarity of the Skill has upgraded!

Tides of Vellus (Rare) has become Reign of Vellus (Epic)!
Reign of Vellus (Epic), level 25!
As if descended from Vellus itself, you command a greater portion of its true power. Greatly-increased power, control, and precision with Skill Level, moderately increased distance with Skill Level.
Skill Level is retained.

Felix's eyes widened, though he still laid uncomfortably against the ground. A crescendo of nearly-there music swelled in the distance, like a phantom orchestra a dozen rooms away. A flood of joy rushed through his veins, the mental stats spiking a sense of delight in his brain.

That made him pause.

Are these stats changing my brain? I do—

You Have Gained A Level!
You are now Level 18!
+3 to WIL! +2 to INT! +4 to DEX! +1 to END! +2 to PER! +2 to VIT! +4 to AGL!
You Have 10 Unused Stat Points!

+13 STR
+10 END
+4 VIT
+1 PER
+5 INT
+13 WIL
+6 REI

New Title Gained!
Hero (Epic)!
Face adversity again and again, fighting against impossible odds! Must have Unconquered and Bulwark of the Innocent Titles and have raised all stats at 70 before level 25. +5% All Stats

Felix's body spasmed as he was flooded with power again, the music rising; a stereo blaring in the dark. His limbs felt like vibrating strings and his head like a gong, ringing and clashing and never quite stopping. Thoughts burned through his mind, ideas too fast to recognize or hold onto, even as he felt a sudden increasing mastery over them.

"Oh, whoa." Felix viewed his new Title with wide eyes. "Hero?" He groaned as he sat up, looking around him again. The wurms' remains were everywhere. Purple blood and off-white offal covered most of the uneven stone ground, and it sizzled where it had begun to eat into the rock.

"Huh, didn't even notice it burning. Acid Resistance is getting up there."

Purple blood coated his arms, chest, and legs. It had eaten through much of his clothing, leaving him once again nearly naked, but it barely harmed his skin.

Is that because of resistance, or because of my increased stats? His Vitality and Endurance were...wait a sec. He pulled up his stats.

Health: 122/370
Stamina: 102/405
Mana: 318/723

STR: 74 PER: 97
VIT: 74 END: 76
INT: 100 WIL: 134
AGL: 74 DEX: 74

Felix blinked.

This...this is incredible. My stats are skyrocketing past my expectations. He regarded his bare fists, which were already healed from his bare-knuckle fist fight. *It's like I'm not even human anymore.*

Felix grimaced. *Right. I'm not. I'm...Nym...an. Nymian? Nymean? Whatever. I seem human, and as far as I can tell, the Nym weren't too different physically. Human-ish.*

Felix stood up carefully, expecting further soreness from his fight. But the sudden stat gain had scoured his body, and he felt remarkably good, if uncomfortably sticky. The purple gore was everywhere, and it was all he could do not to get it in his mouth. When he tried before, it burned right through him...but with his higher resistance maybe....*No.* Even if it worked, the last thing Felix wanted to do was pass out in a monster lair, even if he might gain a cool new Skill.

Felix hesitated again, but shook his head.

Too risky. Don't be dumb.

He stepped carefully over to the row of cages, some still swinging from the aftermath of the battle. Only a half dozen of them were filled, most Rockstrikes within burned to a crisp by an errant fire breath, while the rest rustled weakly. Thankfully, Pit's cage was uncharred, though the little tenku looked awful. His wings were bent at painful angles, and his forelimb was covered in blood. A hot wave of rage flowed over Felix, then a sudden creaking tear and a hot flash of pain flared in his hands. Alarmed, Felix looked down: his grip had split the skin on his knuckles again. Grimacing at the pain, he looked back at his Companion.

"Pit! You ok, buddy?" The cage was at about eye level, so Felix reached his less-injured hand through the bars, skritching his friend's neck. Pit cooed in relief, his eyes closing for a moment. "Don't worry, I'll get you out."

Felix cast around for some way to lower the cages, but soon realized that nothing was holding these cages up. The thick black iron chains at their tops were suspended nearly twenty feet up by...nothing. He had thought it a trick of the light, or the heat haze, but this was clearly magic.

Felix looked at his hands, slender but growing tougher with calluses on his palms, still bloody but healing as he watched. He could use a Corrosive Strike on the cage, but while it might break the bars, he had no way to prevent it from hitting Pit. That was a nonstarter.

I could just...try to bend the bars.

Heat Resistance is level 12!

Am I strong enough to bend iron bars? Felix felt his heartbeat speed up, and a giddy sense of anticipation built in his gut. He shook his hands to loosen them up but hesitated before putting his hands on the cage. Felix pulled up his stats and invested his 10 free points. Five into STR, five into VIT.

Sudden strength and vibrant energy rushing through him, he gripped the bars of the black iron cage and pulled. His skin, dry and already wounded, split open further and dribbled blood down his arms. But slowly, and with a loud screech, the bars bent until they broke open in his hands. He kept bending them until he had an opening big enough to let Pit escape.

Releasing the bars, Felix reached carefully through the opening and helped Pit pull his wings out of the too-small cage. Pit trilled weakly, his wings twitching and his paw held close to his body as he clung to Felix's shoulder. The tenku's heart rapidly beat against his arm, and a faint trembling wracked his haunches. Felix frowned even as he softly stroked Pit's back.

"It's ok, little man. It's ok."

Felix looked around the area, for the first time noticing that there were a number of empty archways lining this level. Then, he spotted a single door in the nearest archway and headed toward it. The door was made of the same black iron as the chains and cages, and as he approached, Felix noticed that no other archway even had a door. It shook something loose in his brain that had been preoccupied with surviving up until now.

"How'd a bunch of wurms get you into a cage, Pit?" Wurms didn't have hands. Why'd they even *have* cages?

Pit trilled again, softly but insistently. A damaged wing shuddered and pointed toward the iron door they were approaching, almost as if to say, "let's find out in there."

Companion Pact is level 10!

The door had a simple latch, just a single lever that released a bar, but even that much invention made Felix worried. The wurms weren't the original inhabitants of this place, that was certain. No matter how faded, the artistry of the walls and flooring were amazing, nearly equal to the Waterfall Temple. The place was ancient, its creators probably long dead. But the wurms couldn't use floating chains and cages, and with that tunneling Skill, the wurms definitely didn't need doors.

The question was: who did?

Felix crouched low as he tested the door. It was metal and this place was crazy hot, but the black iron was cool to the touch. So was the cage, now that he thought about it. *What did* that *mean?* He shook off the stray thought and concentrated on easing open the latch as quietly as possible.

The latch groaned slightly, but pivoted on mostly-greased pieces. With seemingly infinite slowness, Felix pushed the door inward and peered through the small opening. He could see no movement inside, and his Manasight only noted flows of earth, shadow, and...blood? Felix opened the door the rest of the way.

Exploration is level 13!

The room beyond looked like a small antechamber to somewhere more important, maybe twenty by thirty feet in size, windowless but with two large doors on the right and far walls. Felix stepped through the door, watching his step as he took in the details of the chamber, simultaneously noting that it was considerably cooler in there. The walls were less warped than elsewhere, too, and the splendor of the original carvings was better preserved. Geometric lines and blocky design was belied by delicate fluting on faux columns and small figures etched into nearly all surfaces. The floor was a series of five-sided tiles, only slightly disrupted and cracked along the edges. It was amazingly-designed, and put him in mind of the Nym Temple again. It wasn't exactly the same, but similarities were definitely there.

By contrast, two oversized tables were set up in the center of the room, each made of rough-cut wooden boards. They were crude and stuck out against the nicer surroundings, ruined though they were. The tables were tall, nearly five feet high, and were covered in misshapen plates of iron, while bits of bars and half-assembled iron cages were stacked to one side. Odd, jagged metal tools sat next to them, a set on either table. They looked like blunt scalpels, a cylinder of silver metal with a tapered tip. An equally rough pair of stools were next to the tables, one tipped over onto the ground.

Someone had been here, someone humanoid enough to use a stool, and they had left in a hurry.

Did they hear me fighting? He frowned. *Of course they did. That was loud as hell.*

"Is this where you were taken, before?" Pit bobbed his head in confirmation.

So someone captured us, put me in a stone hole and Pit in a cage. Why?

Felix scrutinized the tables and floor, noticing heavy scratches all over the soft wood and lightly covering the harder stone tiles.

Suddenly, faint-glowing boot prints appeared, one set large, the other significantly smaller. The tracks moved all over the room, appearing to pace in some instances, before they both disappeared through the door in the back. Despite the proliferation of the tracks, Felix could tell that only two figures had been in here.

Tracking is level 13!

Pit sniffed delicately at the air before huffing out a sneeze.

"I agree with you there," Felix said, his own nose wrinkling in disgust. "Something smells spoiled in here."

Felix padded over to the table despite the persistent stink, and studied the scraps of iron. Crude shapes were scratched into the metal, the steel styluses nearby likely used to mark the hard surface. Felix spun a piece around. There was something familiar about the shapes. Then it clicked: these were the same as the script in the Temple. Just...far cruder. He set Pit down on top of the table as he looked closer.

He ran his fingers over a symbol that had been repeated at least a dozen times. It was shaped in arcing loops around a central boxy formation; like a cube on fire. Felix recalled this same symbol along the walls of the Temple, situated fairly evenly. But it wasn't fire. Something about it was off, like the maker didn't know quite how to draw it. Felix picked up a stylus and scratched the design from memory, adding a small swooping slash across the top. It was crude and rough, only barely scratched into the metal plate.

Yes, that's it. He picked up the metallic strip. *It wasn't fire.*

It was *light*.

Abruptly he felt a tug on his Mana, as if something was pulling it rapidly out of his core and into the scrap metal. The shape before him began to glow with a golden radiance, like a piece of the summer sun.

Felix jolted in surprise, dropping the metal with a loud *clang*. The light cut off.

New Skill Learned!
Sigils of the Primordial Dawn (Epic), level 1!
You've learned to read the language of the ancients, a sorcerous script made of magic. Proficiency increases with Skill Level.

New Skill Learned!
Invocation (Rare), Level 1!
You can invoke the power of sigils, pulling Mana through them to activate their power. Efficiency and channeling capacity increases with Skill Level.

Pit crooned in interest, dipping his beak toward the inert piece of metal. Felix pushed him gently away.

What in the world? Felix picked up the iron scrap again, half expecting it to light up once more. It didn't, the carving unlit and slightly charred around the edges. *What caused this charring? The magic?*

Sigils of the Primordial Dawn is level 2!

Felix shook his head, bemused. This felt...terribly familiar, though the only time he'd seen script like this was in the Temple. Moreover, what exactly were these people trying to do? He looked around. What was this place for?

His gaze landed on the two doors. One was made of that same black metal and led off to the right, and the other was made of a pale wood. That was where the footsteps led.

As Felix strode closer to the metal door, he noticed a row of cubbies in the wall. Tall closets without doors were built into the stone walls, five on either side of the room. In the closest one sat a pile of black iron pieces, obviously more material for whatever practice was going on here. The next few were the same, but the last one was great news.

"My stuff!" Felix knelt down and snatched up his leather satchel and sword. The leather was scuffed in places but remarkably fine, and the bronze blade was similarly unscathed. More importantly, Felix flipped open the bag and rooted around until he found an oblong leather waterskin, then proceeded to chug half of it. The other half he gave to Pit, who lapped it up just as quickly. After that, the two of them tore into the remaining fruit he had stashed away, all in all reducing the weight of the satchel by a considerable amount.

As they ate and drank, Felix kept an eye on both doors, watching and listening for the approach of their jailers. He knew they weren't out, not by a long shot, but it was a much-needed respite. In fact, Pit seemed to be recovering swiftly. His wounds had healed for the most part, and he was able to move around on all his legs. Felix wasn't sure how, but it seemed Pit had benefited from the recent battle as well. He seemed taller, his legs more gangly.

Then, as he was finishing the last bekta berry, the unmistakable sound of voices came from beyond the metal door.

They both froze, and Pit's head swiveled toward the sounds. The voices grew in volume slowly, as if they were walking steadily toward the door. Felix shoved the waterskin back into his satchel and grabbed his sword. Pit skulked over to the wooden door, Felix right behind him.

The voices rose to a louder pitch, and Felix sensed a strengthened waft of the rotting stink. It was coming from beyond the metal door and moving closer. It smelled like death and blood. It smelled like the Seven-Legged Orit.

Heart pounding, Felix opened the wooden door and slipped through just as he heard the metal one unlatch.

Stealth is level 18!

They made it. With a soft breath of relief, Felix turned and saw that he was somehow, inexplicably in a wild garden.

And the rotten blood smell was even stronger here.

CHAPTER TWENTY-FIVE

Exploration is level 14!

The garden was immense.

The door behind him was built into a thick stone wall heavily carved into rigid geometric designs, but after a dozen feet in any direction, the stone was completely consumed by greenery. The uneven flagstones slowly but surely were devoured by the constant creeping of thick moss and small weeds, until it was less a walkway and more a rolling grassy path. Except less of a path and more a meandering suggestion. Plants of all sizes and colors erupted in all directions, wild and untamed. Sunlight even streamed from above, several rays shifting from moment to moment, but resolutely golden and bright.

What IS this place?

Felix couldn't tell where the cavern ended and the garden began, but judging by the height of the unseen ceiling this place was easily a mile in diameter. And every inch of it was coated in growing things. Creeping vines flowed across the walls and the odd square pillar that rose from the ground. Flowering trees were grouped together, ones with odd, tear-shaped fruit the color of rubies that glittered in the sunlight. Tall, sprouting weeds with violently purple bell-shaped flowers hung heavy, curving over the growths of small, reddish blossoms that emitted small puffs of fire.

In one section, conical gourds proliferated, supported by thick moss and sharp coils of thorns.

It was so wild, Felix briefly entertained the idea that he had escaped back outside. Had he not noticed the darkness high above and several instances where plants had been pruned back or replanted, then he might have just kept on believing that. Unfortunately, he was certain that this was a garden, one maintained by whoever or...whatever was controlling the wurms.

Moreover, that bloody stench was stronger than ever here. It drifted in the air like an invisible fog, clinging to him like the world's worst perfume.

Ugh, it's in my mouth. Felix grimaced and stayed low, as both he and Pit began sneaking through the underbrush.

I need to find stairs or an exit or something. Felix strained his senses, attempting to see farther or hear better, pushing himself and his Perception. Meanwhile, he kept Analyzing everything that came within range. By this point, it was more than reflexive, it was damn near compulsive.

Analyze is level 19!

Hundreds of previously-unknown plants, trees, fruits, even small, minor insects filled the space immediately around him. The proliferation and variety of life was remarkable, and if he weren't so keyed up, this place might be wonderfully relaxing. However, as Felix began reading the lore entries on the various plants around him, a strange disquiet crept into his heart. Of the two dozen types of plant within range, all of them contained a variation of the same two phrases.

...affected greatly by the Blood Moon...

...enhances the effects of Dark Murmurs...

Just like those two herbs near the waterfall. Aram Leaf and Bellock. He shied away from a particularly sweet-smelling blossom called an Entreating Lotus that apparently doubled the effects of Dark Murmurs. *Dark Murmurs and Blood Moon. Both sound bad. It can't be a coincidence that nearly all of the plants in here relate to those two things, right?*

Felix looked around with Manasight, watching that bloody mist curl around the garden, almost...caressing the plants.

Yeah. I gotta get outta here. The corrupted Mana was unsettling to watch, constantly moving and undulating around the vibrant green-gold shimmer of the plant's life Mana. He watched as it swirled near the base of the Entreating Lotus before being sucked quickly toward the roots.

Oh shit. It's feeding them. Felix looked all around, his eyes suddenly seeing a sinister forest of dangerous plantlife. *What is this all for?*

"We fail you, master."

Felix stopped walking, gesturing for Pit to freeze. The voice was sibilant and high pitched, loud but muffled as if to suggest it came from some distance away. He focused his ears, listening as hard as he could. Somewhere ahead, leather creaked and metal scraped.

"Sorry be we, master," another voice said, this one deeper and more rough, like two rocks rattling against each other. Again, metal and leather shifted against each other as something moved up ahead.

They're just beyond those Gigantrees, he thought, nodding at Pit to keep going. They started skirting in a wide circle around the cluster of trees, moving as slowly and quietly as they could.

"Endless sorryness—"

"Enough!"

The voice was a whip-crack, sharp and final. Felix stopped in his tracks, suddenly afraid they'd been heard. He couldn't see through the thick foliage and assumed the enemy couldn't either. He hoped he hadn't been wrong.

Stealth is level 19!

Whew. Still good.

"You are fools, but I am more the fool for spawning such wretches. Of course you cannot master the Elderscript; you've the mental capacities of an emberfly." A heavy sigh followed, breathy and dry. The voice was commanding, a deep baritone that brought to mind an older man still in his prime.

Felix flexed his Manasight, trying to pierce the greenery. Earth brown and life green Mana streamed all around him, but he focused, applying his intent to see beyond as he did in his cell. It was far easier now that he had reached Apprentice Tier, and slowly the image of three figures resolved, though they were still fuzzy around the edges. Strangely, all three of them were oddly muted, painted in grays, as if they'd been leached of something vital. While the wurms were a pale ochre touched with stripes of vibrant orange, these figures' only spot of color were the ribbons of bright crimson pulsing up and down their spines. The sight of them tasted spoiled, like meat left in the sun.

Two of them were kneeling on the ground, one big and bulky and the other slimmer and shorter. Both were draped in silver-brown slabs of Mana, and Felix somehow instinctively knew it was metal.

Armor? They're wearing armor.

Then he saw their master. It was pacing, its body flowing like liquid smoke in his Manasight, shifting and twisting without ever truly dissipating. Twisting veins of bloody Mana traced out its limbs and spine, collecting together in its chest and radiating back up its neck and face. Eyes like mini suns burned as they regarded the two kneeling figures.

Holy shit, what is THAT? Felix could sense the being's power now, a cresting wave of force that filled the garden. His Manasight had picked out pieces of it, seeing them as clouds of corrupted Mana that swirled around and fed all the plants, but it was all coming from this...*thing.* He was suddenly struck with a deep and abiding fear of this creature. It was unlike anything he had seen before.

"You are both lucky that I have more interesting toys to play with," the figure continued, an edge of terrible glee in its voice. "Ones made of *much* stronger stock."

The dread figure raised its hand and gestured vaguely upwards, its limb curling smoke veined with pulsing red.

"The Hoarfrost has gifted a bounty upon us, though they know it not," the creature sneered. It moved as if it were pacing, getting louder and softer by turns. "Settling into Shalim means the Coldwrought Children have entered my domain, an idiotic gamble had they actually believed me still living." It laughed. "I'll show them! Oh yes! I have set the bloody bait. Now I only wait for the snap of the trap!" The two kneeling followers dutifully laughed, their reaction too delayed to be genuine.

"W-we caught prey..is good, yes?" The slender one shifted its head up, looking at its master. "More of the shadow crawlies, a-and a chimera—"

"Bah! Mindless Rockstrikes! Useless to me! But...a chimera, you say?" The master thumbed what Felix supposed was its chin. "Rare creatures, despite what the *ilenii* profess. Perhaps we can make use of that one."

Felix swallowed, glancing down at Pit. The tenku's feathers and fur were ruffled up, his wings tucked close and body low to the ground. Pit could feel the awful vibes coming off this master creature, same as Felix. Electric fear snapped down his spine, tingling his back and shoulders with pinpricks of gooseflesh and hot nerves.

"Hm? Where is Helga? Where is my dearest child?" The voice pitched louder suddenly as it called out. Felix and Pit backed away, slowly, moving as carefully as they could through the thick underbrush.

Stealth is level 20!

Distracted by the swirling presence of the creature, Felix had no warning when the earth beneath him bucked and rippled, throwing him to the ground. Earthen Mana pulsed like a disturbed pond, the ground flowing so smoothly it was more liquid than solid. Within that flowing liquid, a near literal bonfire of orange fire Mana blazed, stretching across the majority of the garden before circling back toward the creepy voice. Something absolutely huge surfaced nearby, the sound of it breaking ground like an excavator biting into rocky soil.

"My sweet, you have returned to me," the voice crooned. Felix shook himself and started moving again, heading away from the voice as quietly as he could. The overgrown greenery proved to be a mixed blessing; it was perfect cover, but moving through it was challenging while remaining silent. His heart hammered and his skin was coated in a sheen of sweat despite the relatively-cooler temperature. He focused on controlling his body, creeping forward at a snail's pace. He couldn't Analyze that thing at this distance, but Felix knew it could squash him like a bug.

Breath Control is level 15!

Stealth is level 21!

Felix could barely hear the voices now, the distance stretching farther as the seconds ticked by; in fact, just as he passed another lone stone pillar crawling with ivy, he saw a rocky wall with an open passageway. Then he heard that voice, much louder than before.

"No! Here?" it asked, incredulous. "What bliss! We have a visitor!"

With a cacophony of groans and cracks, greenery all around Felix suddenly pushed away from him, bending back like opening a book. A few of the less flexible trees were snapped in half or ripped straight out of the ground. Felix froze, his shoulders tight and eyes wide. He was exposed. He slowly turned around, and could finally see the owner of the voice.

It was nearly ten feet tall and covered in plates of tarnished, golden-hued armor. Sunbeams played across it like a halo of light, and an errant breeze stirred the tattered cape at its back. The armor was layered with plates of various sizes, smaller and more intricate at the joints, and covered the entirety of its body. Felix couldn't see a single piece of exposed flesh or even hair. Twin red lights burned in its dark visor as it gestured at his side. There, the massive, car-sized head of a wurm protruded from the ground, its four-way mouth splitting open into a gruesome sort of smile.

"When my dear sweet Helga told me of your capture, I couldn't believe it!" Its shoulders creaked as they shook in a mimicry of laughter. "A Human, here! In the Foglands! How exotic." The armored giant gestured again, this time at Felix himself.

An impossible force held him in bands of invisible iron, and Felix was lifted bodily from the ground. He was pulled through the air quickly, levitated in a manner that Felix found both terrifying and strangely familiar. Jostled, he was deposited into the arms of the two armored lackeys, who gripped him in callous hands made of leather and iron. Felix grunted in pain, and saw that the two figures were similar to their master, though encased entirely in black iron armor. They only came up to the giant's chest, but were still far bigger than Felix himself.

It was all he could do not to retch. They smelled like death, blood, and curdling corruption oozing into the air around them.

The golden giant flexed his immaculately-jointed hand, releasing the Skill it had used once the lackeys were holding him. The fingers were completely encased in the tarnished armor, tiny golden plates covering every joint and seam. As the Skill deactivated, a reddish electricity sparked around the golden giant's fingers. His eyes opened wide.

It's like Tides of Vellus...but his control is insane.

"My, my, my," whispered the giant, his voice breathy from beneath his gargantuan helm. Its armor made it look like a knight had been sealed alive in their armor. "How did you get all the way out here? And into my tunnels, too? My Helga says you were slaughtering poor Rockstrikes in the upper caverns. Chasing some levels, were you?"

The armored hand never dropped from before him, but also never quite touched Felix. It flexed and twitched ever so slightly, almost as if turning the pages of a book.

"Just got lost, is all," Felix offered, watching that golden hand warily. He took the moment to Analyze the giant.

Name: ERROR
Type: Archon
Level: ???
HP: ?????/?????
SP: ?????/?????
MP: ?????/?????
Lore: Golden guardians of the Nymean people, Archons were the last defense against calamity. It was not enough.
Strength: Unknown
Weakness: Unknown

Error? Nymean? What is with *this race? And that's the first time I couldn't see someone's level. This is bad.*

"Lost? I, too, have been Lost." The archon sighed like a bellows. "It is a grave sadness in your soul, a diminishing that lingers like a riven limb." It tilted its head at Felix, curious. "You...are familiar with such exile, are you not? I sense a kinship here."

The archon loomed over him, fixing Felix with its glowing ember eyes.

"Why have you entered my Domain, *ileni*?"

Felix felt drawn to those eyes, like a moth to flame, and his thoughts stuttered and twisted dangerously. The thread of his mind felt taut, yanked and unspooling into those unending fires.

Mental Resistance is level 22!

The grip on Felix's mind slackened ever so slightly. He rasped out the first thing that came to his head.

"I'm exploring! For the Endless Raven!"

The golden archon tilted back, its fiery eyes growing incrementally wider. The mental pressure on him almost disappeared entirely. "You claim the right of Wander, *ileni*? You have not the mark nor the badge of the Seeking Eye, unless you hide them most cleverly."

"Oh uh, wait, in my bag," Felix extemporized, an idea already blooming even as the lackeys gripped him harder. "I have my necklace, ugh, in there."

After a nod from the archon, the smaller of the two lackeys started rifling through Felix's satchel. It roughly shoved aside his waterskin and threw some half eaten rinds into the bushes. Felix Analyzed him and his companion while waiting.

Name: Arcid #54768
Type: Archonic Construct
Level: 35
HP: ???/???
SP: ???/???
MP: ???/???
Lore: A bastardization of life and magic. It has no soul, yet it screams in eternal torment.
Strength: Unknown
Weakness: Unknown

Name: Arcid #54772
Type: Archonic Construct
Level: 35
HP: ???/???
SP: ???/???
MP: ???/???
Lore: A bastardization of life and magic. It has no soul, yet it screams in eternal torment.

Strength: Unknown
Weakness: Unknown

Dumb names. How about Slender and Big Boy? His thoughts were spinning madly, still reeling from whatever the Archon did to him.

The sound of something ripping marshaled Felix's thoughts, causing him to gasp. "Hey! Hey!"

Slender dropped the satchel back against Felix's thigh, and held up a small medallion. It was the Farwalker's Friend, the necklace he found with the Henaari's belongings. The Arcid handed it over to its master, who took it delicately in hand. The archon vaguely gestured for his lackeys to drop Felix, and they did so immediately.

"It has been a long time since I have beheld a Farwalker. You are...shorter than any Farwalker I've seen before. Though admittedly, it has been a few centuries. Why did you not proffer this to my guards when you arrived?"

Felix swallowed as he climbed to his feet, his throat suddenly drier than it was in the lava room. His mind flipped through everything he knew of this world, of the Henaari and—

That's it!

"I'm on a...secret...mission. I am to find a lost Temple of the Nym, said to be in this mountain range," Felix lied, as glibly as he could.

Acting is now level 2!

"Hmm, and how did you discover this so-called Temple?" The archon stroked a thumb along its golden mouth-guard...the closest it had to a chin, Felix supposed. "Farwalkers are brave and wily, but not so foolhardy as to venture into the Foglands on bare speculation, mm?"

Felix felt the mental pressure again as the archon's eyes shimmered a deeper red. He squirmed against it, unable to get free entirely, but able to slip past the worst of it.

Mental Resistance is level 23!

How is it doing this? This mental pressure was unbearable and exhausting, despite his rising resistance. Felix opened his mouth, but was overcome by a wave of ennui. He suddenly questioned why he'd ever want to waste his breath lying, not when the truth was *so* much simpler. He could just spill the beans and it'd be over. The pain would go away and he'd be free. Just let go, and sink into the abyss.

Let us in.

NO. GET OUT OF MY HEAD!

Mental Resistance is level 24!
Mental Resistance is level 25!

Congratulations! You Have Reached Apprentice Tier in Mental Resistance!
You Gain The—

Felix pushed the notification away, focusing his swimming vision on the golden giant trying to break his mind. The archon's eyes were points of vile flame, burning in the darkness of its helmet like the last guttering torch before true night fell. He licked his lips and steadied his breathing.

"The Henaari told me of it."

Breath Control is level 16!
Acting is level 3!

"Hm, intriguing." The golden giant leaned back again, Felix only then realizing how close the metal creature had loomed. "Your mind is strong, and your will is not weak either. You speak of things that you have no knowledge of, yet I find your words compelling. You are an enigma, *ileni*."

Felix gulped, his hands shaking despite the tight grip of the Arcids. The metal monstrosity idly petted the enormous wurm at its side, golden metal rasping as it slid over its rocky carapace.

"Now, I have been patient. I have listened to your fumblings and childish acts of wordplay, and it has amused me. But my humor thins by the second, and so I will ask you this once only." The archon turned fully toward Felix, its entire body a threat of imminent violence. "Answer me truthfully, and you will have a just reward. Lie to me and, well, you shall experience horrors beyond your comprehension." The massive wurm next to him snapped its four-way jaws, globby bits of drool splatting against nearby ferns.

The archon leaned forward, its torso somehow crossing the gap between them like a dark mountain.

"How do you know of the Temple?"

This time the pressure was like an avalanche, subsuming every bit of Felix that wanted to lie or obfuscate the truth. He gasped, his mind floundering in an ocean of pain and darkness, and the denizens of the deep began to erode his thoughts. A sick, cloying corruption oozed over him, a smell that tasted like violence and desperation, the color of hunger and hate. The ground dissolved beneath him, the air boiling away, and even the light deigned to shine elsewhere. He was sinking into blood and acid, hate and darkness, and there was only one way out.

"I-" he struggled to push the words through his chest. They stuck like burrs, tearing into his heart and lungs. "I've been there!"

With a sudden twist, Felix flourished the hooked bronze blade. He held it out between him and the golden giant in a way that he hoped was threatening, but suspected only appeared desperate.

"Ha! You draw your weapon on *me*?" The archon thundered, his eyes flaring into torches of flame. "I've withstood the countless blows of a cataclysm; you've no—"

The archon paused, his eye-fires fixed on the sword Felix held.

"That is a Crescian blade...and those..." The golden giant stepped backward, as if struck. "You-" it gasped.

"You are Nymean."

CHAPTER TWENTY-SIX

Reign of Vellus!

Felix exploded with azure light, the force of the upgraded Skill discharging into actual bolts of lightning as it sheared into the Arcids beside him. But they were heavy, far heavier than anything he had tried to move before, and instead of throwing them, Felix was launched backwards like a rocket. He smashed into a crumbling, ivy-covered column, gasping in pain as the resounding impact shuddered through him.

"Impossible!" The archon raged, his armor suddenly blazing with carmine light. "*Kill him! Destroy the Nym!*"

Groaning, Felix shoved away the pain and tottered to his feet. Slender and Big Boy were thundering toward him, and while he had flown nearly fifty feet and they were remarkably slow, their huge strides were eating up the gap. Felix spotted Pit cowering behind a toppled tree and jerked his head backwards.

"C'mon!"

Felix paused, looking back at the looming giant and the Finder's Necklace loosely in its grip. Shaking his head, he ran.

They raced toward the back of the chamber, Felix hoping all the while that he had been correct. When the heavy greenery eventually opened up into a dim stone corridor, he grinned wide and glanced to the side at Pit...just in time to see the massive rock that was hurtling in their direction.

"Watch out!" Felix dove forward just as the boulder would have crashed into them, grabbing Pit and tucking into a roll. He was back up on his feet, this time carrying the chimera in his arms as he ran as fast as he could. The boulder hit the ground with a huge crash, jarring Felix's bones and teeth as he ran. He didn't stop. He couldn't.

If I stop, I die.

Running is level 16!

The dim hallway tilted toward the right, meandering through the mountain around him as if a drunk burrower had made these tunnels. A sudden thunderous crashing came from behind, though Felix refused to look. The walls shook and cracked, small crevices chasing their way down the hall as the cacophony of a landslide barreled toward his unprotected back. Pit gave a challenging squawk over Felix's shoulder, his fur and feathers sticking up in a puffy display of dominance. A bright flash and Felix felt a burst of wind as Pit launched a Wingblade at the Arcids.

Kwiiiiiiaaaaaaahhhhh!

The Wingblade splashed against their pursuers with little effect. Big Boy let loose a mighty bellow, shaking the air with a voice that sounded like high speed car crashes; metal on metal, compacting and rattling at incomprehensible speed. It tore through the passageway, its larger size neither fitting nor caring as it crashed through the stone walls. The smaller Slender was moving a bit ahead, faster than its brethren.

Pit let out a pitiful *eep* before tucking his head into Felix's shoulder.

The corridor twisted worse the further they went. Floor tiles were missing in many places, tilted up on their edges or knocked entirely out of the ground and piled in the corners. It took all he had to keep up his speed with the difficult footing, pushing his Agility to the edge of his capability as the iron Arcids thundered behind him. He risked a look over his shoulder.

Slender was steadily gaining ahead of its bulkier counterpart. While the latter was shearing through the narrow hallways with the force of its charge, the former stomped ahead, only fifteen feet behind Felix. With a startled yelp, Felix put on more speed, pushing his body harder than before.

Running is level 17!

Physical Conditioning is 14!

His Stamina was depleting rapidly. The heat was mounting again, his resistance not high enough to negate the consumption penalty it inflicted. It was only his high Endurance that allowed him to press on, leaping over dislodged blocks of stone as the corridor became increasingly dilapidated. A sudden sharp turn in the hall had Felix skidding as he negotiated it, his shoulder bashing painfully into the rock even as chips of stone debris scattered from the impact. He stuttered forward again, pushing against the earth for all he was worth.

Just in time. A violent breeze blasted past his back as he jumped forward, and the wall behind him exploded.

The sound of impact was the loudest thing Felix had ever heard, and it sent him careening wildly down the passageway, falling to all fours several times in an effort to remain moving. Rocks pelted him, drawing sharp, bloody trails across Felix's back and legs.

He glanced back again and caught a glimpse of Slender woozily extricating himself from the shattered wall. Unable to make the same tight turn as Felix, the Arcid hurtled full force into the stone. It was buried nearly to its waist in rubble, but it was moving the weight quickly.

Felix slid to a stop, focusing on the smaller Arcid. He had to delay them. He couldn't run forever. And if Slender couldn't manage that turn...

Influence of the Wisp.

Felix blazed with blue-white fire, and a moment later, so did Slender. The ironbound creature looked at its limbs in evident confusion, even as Felix received a notification that it had been Enthralled for 1 second. It looked up at him, the cold fires in its helmet flaring wide in realization before turning to look back the way it came.

That was when Big Boy hit him.

Like a freight train, the bulkier iron lackey plowed into Slender and the wall beyond. Unable to move or even cry out, Slender tangled with Big Boy as the wall before them gave out. Ominous rumbles shook the corridor, and Felix quickly spotted expanding cracks tracing cross the walls and ceiling. He jumped backward as a slab of stone fell, powdering the ground as it slammed down, and more cascaded after it. In moments, the two Arcids and the hallway itself were buried under several tons of rock.

But the rumbling continued. Felix ran, eyes up for any more collapses, but the vibrations petered out after several hundred feet.

That was close. His heart was racing, and he was unable to shake the image of an entire mountain falling on top of him. *I gotta get out of here.*

Two more turns, all left, and he found himself at the base of a large set of spiral stairs. Each step was three feet tall, making it an awkward climb, and there was enough space for even the golden giant to fit through here. Cautiously, Felix climbed the stairs, keeping as quiet as possible. After three revolutions, the stairs opened up onto a large landing which contained a single wooden door.

The door was huge, easily twelve feet tall, and it had an elaborate metal lock affixed to its oversized latch. Felix considered the massive lock, nearly the size of a watermelon, and aimed a Corrosive Strike at it. The metal groaned and snapped in two hits, twisting and melting by turns. He ducked into the door and shut it behind him, panting as his Stamina ticked closer to empty.

Did I lose them? If he was lucky, the tunnel collapse had taken care of them. However, Felix hadn't gotten any kill notifications for the Arcids. *Tough bastards. Hopefully they're at least busy for a while.*

Felix gulped the warm air, tasting a sour flavor even as he reveled in being alive. It was hard to place, tasting faintly metallic. The chamber was similar to the others he'd been in: geometric engravings, squared pillars along the edges of the room, and pentagonal tiles once etched with details now lost to time. Then he noticed the giant desk, easily twice as big as a standard desk and paired with an equally large and sturdy-looking chair. An inkpot the size of a coffee mug sat on the surface, which was just barely visible from Felix's vantage, set next to several reams of thick parchment.

Felix had stumbled upon the archon's chambers.

Exploration is level 15!

He immediately crossed the room, inspecting another door

opposite the one he entered. It was heavy, metal, and silvery; a departure from the wood or black iron doors he'd seen so far. It had five different raised panels, and was molded with the image of three seven-sided stars across the central one. The stars stacked vertically, and were made with a 3D depth, like the interior of a cake mold.

Oh god, I miss cake. I haven't had cake since Gabby's birthday...

When was that? A month ago? He'd only been on the Continent for two weeks or so, but it felt like a lifetime. His life from before he woke up on that sand spit was like a continually-fading dream, and the longer he struggled here the more real this all became. Felix sighed and looked back at Pit.

"C'mon buddy. We have to keep moving," he said, but the tenku was busy attempting to climb onto the chair of the archon.

"What're you doing? Those things could be here any second!" Pit didn't listen, instead flapping his wings vigorously to pull his oddly-proportioned body up onto the chair. Once there, he trilled happily, turning toward the desk and hopping nimbly atop it. Felix pulled at his hair, exasperated. Then Pit started kicking things off the desk.

Parchment rained down on him, and Felix had to swat away a particularly large stack that slapped onto the stone floor. Glancing down, Felix saw that many of the pages were blank, but a few had a series of sigils scribbled onto them. He bent over and picked them up, leafing through the incredibly detailed designs. Each of the pages were roughly 11x17, and their entire surface was covered in densely-packed markings. He didn't understand any of these, but he recognized them as similar sigils to those in the Temple, the same ones the lackeys had been trying to reproduce onto scrap metal for some reason.

On the last page, he saw an odd illustration. Made out in the same hand as the rest, it depicted an oblong-shaped stone, faceted and hovering over an incomplete pillar or altar. There were a series of sigils listed next to this drawing, each one more convoluted than the last, and they were almost...upsetting to look at, somehow. As if they each held a terrible secret hidden in their designs, like branches obscuring the horrid flesh of a corpse.

Sigils of the Primordial Dawn is level 3!

With an effort of will, Felix tore his eyes away from the page, suddenly breathing heavily. The room seemed warmer than before, the air more cloying as if thickened, hugging close to his skin like a thin film. Felix swallowed, his saliva gone dry as helplessness and constraint assaulted his senses, pressing against him like the walls in a shrinking room. Then, something inside him pushed back, Felix's mind unable to take the vertigo-inducing sensations. The emotions intensified, as if fighting against his will, but a short moment later, they shattered into nothing.

Bastion of Will is level 26!

The effect suddenly cut off, and Felix fell on his ass. The papers landed next to him, ink staring menacingly back in his direction. Felix grabbed them and shoved them into his satchel. He'd look at them later. Or never.

Wait. He toggled back his notifications and stared. *What the hell is Bastion of Will?*

Scrolling backward, Felix saw the notifications for increases to Running and Physical Conditioning and...

Oh shit, that's right.

He had hit Apprentice Tier for Mental Resistance, thanks to the archon's repeated attempts to rip apart his memories. He pulled up the notification.

Congratulations! You Have Reached Apprentice Tier in Mental Resistance!
You Gain The Following:
+10% WIL
+5 END and VIT
Rarity of the Skill has upgraded!
Skill Level is maintained.

Mental Resistance (Rare) has become Bastion of Will (Epic)!

Bastion of Will (Epic), level 25!
Your mind is a fortress, and your Will is fierce. Let crash the might of your enemies, you shall not be moved.
Resistance greatly increases with Skill Level.

"Whoa," Felix huffed. "Hell yeah." This was his second Epic Skill in as many hours. This trip into the mountain hadn't been a total waste.

Though that'll change sharply if I don't get out soon. That Archon isn't the type to give up, and that wurm of his—

Felix's eyes widened as realization hit him.

I'm an idiot! The wurm can tunnel through solid stone!

"Pit! We have to go! Now!" That wurm wouldn't be stopped by a measly cave in, and the moment the golden giant realized his minions were stuck, he'd sic his precious Helga on him. Felix stood up and saw his tenku companion attempting to push an entire locked metal box off the edge of the desk. It was about the size of a cigar box, but seemed considerably heavier.

"Oh jeez, dude, really?" Felix reached up and grabbed it, stowing it in his satchel. The leather bag creaked ominously, but it held for now. Happy, Pit lightly hopped from the desk, using his larger wings to glide gracefully to the floor.

They rushed toward the three-star door. The latch was clear and didn't have any sort of lock, so Felix whipped it open and stepped out into a short corridor ending in two staircases. One led up, and one led down, and both were choked with debris. Growling in frustration, he reached out his right hand and cast Stone Shaping.

The flow of earth Mana was suddenly brought into stark contrast all around him, and Felix felt as if he could reach out and shape it all to his will. Focusing, he mentally commanded the stone before him to shift and open the way forward. With a scraping groan, the stone flowed like thick oil, pulling away from a central pathway no more than two feet wide and extending nearly ten feet up. With a gasp, Felix felt a large chunk of his Mana disappear immediately, eaten away by the Mana-hungry spell.

Stone Shaping is level 14!

Wiping his brow, he hustled up the stairs, squeezing himself through the narrow crevice he had created. Even if the Arcids got free, they weren't following him through that gap. The stairs were clear after that, save for the occasional rocky debris. The next level expanded into several well-preserved hallways, but he kept going up.

Gotta make the surface. Gotta go up.

Felix climbed nearly six flights before he could go no higher. The last level opened out into a wide landing containing only a set of double doors surmounted by a stylized frame covered in elaborate geometric patterns. Blocky and angular, like everything else here, the doors were fifteen feet tall and appeared to be made of stone as opposed to metal or wood. Felix approached them carefully before shoving one of the doors lightly, but nothing happened. He pushed harder, and they made a grinding noise before shifting ever so slightly. Felix's muscles protested as he dropped his arms, the release of tension almost worse than the weight itself.

Heavy. Really *heavy*.

Felix put his back into it, this time shoving on one of the doors with both hands. Slowly, the door swung open, grinding loudly into the floor as it went. It took four hard shoves to get the door opened enough for him and Pit to slip through, but even then, the gap was under two feet wide. These doors were incredibly heavy, even for his 78 points of Strength. He could imagine someone else being trapped here forever, unable to budge these behemoths.

Pondering these thoughts, Felix emerged from the double doors to find himself in a cavernous space. The walls were perhaps 300 or 400 feet away in every direction but back, and the ceiling was probably twice that. It all looked like rough stone, arcing above him and strangely devoid of anything like stalactites. The air was incredibly hot, hotter still than that courtyard where Pit had been caged, and sweat dripped from his pores almost instantly.

Exploration is level 16!

"Uff, I'm getting sick of this heat, Pit." Felix wiped his forehead with a ragged, dirty sleeve. Pit chirruped back at him, his wings drooping. Felix glanced at the ground, noticing it was flat and relatively level, despite the disturbances in the lower tunnels. Whatever seismic activity warped the structure below didn't affect this place too badly. The ground extended out a couple hundred feet, though not all the way to the edges of the chamber, he could tell. A ruddy light emanated from the edges of the cavern, and swirling gusts of sulfuric fumes filled his nose. Not quite believing what his senses were telling him, Felix walked to the edge.

A surge of hot wind buffeted him. Below him was a massive pool of lava that neatly encircled the stone platform he was on.

Heat Resistance is level 13!

"I'm in a volcano?" Felix panted through the increasing heat, his Stamina visibly ticking down. "What the hell?"

Slam!

Suddenly the doors quaked, as if something huge had smashed into them. Felix spun around, hand on his sword. Dust rained down from the carved edifice above the doors, cracked and worn but still as beautiful as anything else down those tunnels.

Slam! Slam! Slam!

The cracks spread further, splintering the stone and sloughing off entire sections. Whatever was behind those doors wasn't giving up. Felix gasped a breath, panic rising as the doors began to break down. He cast about, looking for anything, any possible escape route.

There! At the far end of the chamber, a platform extended nearly flush with the ground, making it all but invisible from straight on. It stretched outward in a sort of stone bridge toward the far wall of the cavern, which featured a shadowed archway. *A bridge! The exit!*

That's when he realized the slamming had stopped. Felix turned toward the stone doors, sensing a sudden something moving at high speed. He activated Manasight, and aside from the absolute deluge of orange fire Mana, there was an ochre blur the size and shape of a city bus barreling toward the surface.

Toward him.

"Fuck, fuck, fuck!" Felix launched into a sprint as the ground exploded into a geyser of liquefied stone. Helga, the massive wurm reared back with a screeching roar, breaching like a shark after a seal, her entire body clearing the ground for the briefest of instants. She landed with a bone-jarring quake, snaking toward Felix even as she hit the earth.

Felix ran with everything he had, but he could hear the wurm gaining on him with every step he took. He risked a glance backward, and saw a nightmare: Helga slid forward, her body twisting like an impossibly large serpent, her four-way mouth wide open and filled with drool-soaked teeth the size of swords. Fear ran like cold electricity up his back and down his limbs even as he pushed himself to run faster. Faster.

Running is level 18!

Then he was at the bridge, the stone tapering to only five feet wide as it arced over the bubbling magma below. But his relief was short-lived: only thirty feet out, the bridge ended, sheared off long ago. The far edge of the cavern was beyond a nearly fifty-foot gap, an impossible distance.

Pit was at his feet, racing alongside him. He had grown bigger, but was still faster than Felix, and his wings...

"Pit! Jump and fly! Fly to the other side!"

Without a beat, Pit chirped and raced ahead, running to the edge of the bridge and jumping as far as he could.

Reign of Vellus!

The kinetic forces of the spell were leagues easier to shape than before, and Felix's quick mind and Fire Within Skill activated in unison. Azure lightning discharged from his body, and Pit let loose a surprised *squawk* as he was pushed up and forward twenty feet. Felix had hoped the tenku's smaller mass and increased speed would allow Reign of Vellus to give him enough oomph to make the jump...and as Pit hit the zenith of his boost, his red-black wings snapped outward in a glide.

Reign of Vellus is level 26!

"Yeah!" Felix cried out, right before Helga ate him.

CHAPTER TWENTY-SEVEN

The wurm's jaws chomped down on Felix, the four-way mandibles snapping from all directions. Teeth the size of his arm rushed toward his body, but Felix was able to catch two of the jaws with his hands. The lower jaws however, pierced his thighs with impossible speed and force, exactly where the Yungling had got him before.

"GAHHHHHHH!!!" Felix screamed, veins in his neck bulging as he fought with Helga's upper jaws. His arms trembled, the power behind the giant wurm too much to withstand, the pain in his legs nearly incapacitating were it not for his resistance. Felix cracked open his eye, blurry with tears, to the rapidly-approaching end of the bridge.

She's still—!

Felix didn't think. He didn't plan.

Felix made magic.

Stone Shaping!

The sheared end of the bridge suddenly morphed, lifting up into a precarious incline that Helga barreled toward, her momentum impossible to defy. Felix staggered as his Mana drained to half, the spell cast sloppy and wasteful, and Helga's jaws suddenly slackened as his resistance disappeared. They hit the incline.

And they were airborne.

Helga screamed, a voice like a rattling timpani roaring from her throat as she found herself momentarily midair. Felix's stomach rose into his throat and his body briefly lifted weightlessly, before the wurm and Felix inside it were sent hurtling downward.

Not a chance! Reign of Vellus!

At the apex of her climb, Felix blasted forth. He clenched his body into a ball, skin and muscle ripping and tearing as he exploded out of the massive maw of the wurm. Purple blood and shattered teeth spiraled out around his body, carried on the force of his Skill, and Felix was launched toward the cavern exit.

The only problem was that he was aimed a solid fifteen feet too low.

"*Ahhh, shit! Stone Shaping! Stone Shaping!*"

Felix forced his pathways into the arcane patterns of the Skill, twisting his power until it drilled into the earthen Mana before him. His Mana guttered out, suddenly flashing red in his vision, yet the cavern wall liquefied even as Felix collided with it at forty miles an hour. A great gout of thick stone sludge jettisoned from the wall, and Felix landed shoulder-first on the small five foot by three foot indent he had created.

Crack!

"*Aghh! Mmmffff!*" Felix howled, clenching his teeth until his jaw ached and the veins in his neck stuck out like cables. Pain Resistance let him keep his wits about him, and he didn't move, agonizing as it was. He was pretty sure he had just dislocated his shoulder, too.

Stone Shaping is level 14!
Stone Shaping is level 15!

Pain Resistance is level 25!

Congratulations! You Have Reached Apprentice Tier in Pain Resistance!
You Gain The Following:
+5 VIT
+5 END
+5% END
+New Skill Learned

New Skill Learned!
Armored Skin (R), Level 1!
Requires Apprentice Tier in Pain Resistance, Unconquerable Title, Face the Charge Title, Blind Pugilist Title. You've taken abuse that would cripple most, and you keep on fighting. Gain physical damage reduction per Skill Level, reduces Stamina penalties by small amounts per Skill Level.

This place sucks so much!

His lungs struggled to fill up, and something felt like it was leaking inside of him. The heat had disappeared, and he only felt cold now. Dimly, Felix could hear the enraged roar of Helga until that disappeared, too. Worried, he saw an icon of a dazed-looking face in the corner of his vision.

Status Condition: Shock (Major)

Grunting with the effort, Felix squeezed his uninjured hand into his satchel, feeling around for his healing potion. It was agonizingly slow, and the dislocated shoulder didn't do much for mobility. With a surge of Willpower, he suppressed his pain long enough to wrench the last vial from the bag, uncapping it with his thumb and pouring its contents down his throat.

The potion started working instantly, his flesh re-knitting painfully as his Health jumped up. The flashing icon dissipated in a few seconds, and Felix's head felt suddenly clear. He tried to sit up, only to feel a jolt of pain through his shoulder and chest. His left arm was weak and nearly useless, his fingers barely responsive. The potion had not fixed everything, not by a longshot.

Banging echoed from the platform, followed by minute but definite rock grinding against rock.

The Arcids. They're at the doors. He looked down at his shoulder, already feeling it swelling, and bit his lip. *I really hope this works.*

With a breathy grunt, Felix pushed himself up on his right arm, then slammed his left shoulder directly into the ground. An explosion of pain lit his entire body on fire. Felix's vision blacked out for a few seconds, as if his nerves couldn't handle the sheer agony.

"*Motherfuuugh! How the fsghghhhh!*" Felix howled. Distantly, the slamming paused before resuming at a far more frenzied pace. *Oh god, TV has failed me!*

Then Felix got a most welcome notification.

Helga the Pendlewurm is dead!
You have gained EXP!

You Have Gained A Level!
You are now Level 19!
+3 to WIL! +2 to INT! +4 to DEX! +1 to END! +2 to PER! +2 to VIT! +4 to AGL!
You Have 5 Unused Stat Points!

Your Companion, Pit Has Gained A Level!
+2 VIT! +2 PER! +4 AGL! +4 DEX! +3 WIL! +1 END! +2 INT!

"*Ahh!*"

The swell of that near silent orchestra vibrated across Felix's senses, his mind only catching the bare hints of their vibrations as power flooded through his body. Thinking fast, Felix dumped all five of his points into Vitality, then as the stat-gain high reached its crest, he jammed his shoulder once more into the ground.

Pop!

"*Fffffffffuuuuuck!*" He screamed, half with joy, half in pain as his body still squirmed with the unspent level up energy. His body arched in agony, then dropped limply to the ground as his nerve endings seemed to stop feeling entirely.

Armored Skin is level 2!
Pain Resistance is level 26!

Felix panted, exhausted. But his Health started rising again, slowly. What's more, the slamming above continued, and it was starting to be accompanied by the crunch and crack of breaking stone. He had to go. *Now.*

Mustering his energy, Felix stood up, wobbling slightly as he nearly fell out of his shallow alcove.

"Whoa," he gulped, staring down at the bubbling magma a good hundred feet down. He glanced back at his tiny hole in the wall. "I really cut it close this time." He shuddered, briefly imagining burning to death in lava. Much the way Helga died, he figured.

Good riddance. He spit over the edge; or tried to, he was too dehydrated to actually have saliva at this point.

Heat Resistance is level 14!

Felix looked up, seeing only the knobby wall of the cavern as it stretched up and up and up. Then a small black and russet head popped out from a space within twenty feet and chirruped at him.

"Pit! You're OK!" A weight dropped off his chest, and he started climbing. The natural rock wall had tons of handholds in it, making it a short work for his Free Climbing Skill.

Free Climbing is level 13!

He made it to Pit in less than a minute, yet by the time he stood atop the exit platform, a cacophonous crash sounded from across the cavern. Felix's heart raced, and he turned toward the exit, not bothering to see what he feared would be the golden Archon. Before him was another massive set of doors, also made of stone, yet bigger by half than the previous set. Glancing at his Mana, which had barely recovered to 50%, he gulped and tried to focus. Shutting out external distractions, he homed in on the Mana pathways that traced through his body.

A sudden panicked squawk was his only warning.

Terror echoed across their bond, hitting Felix at the same time as Pit's cry. He started dropping to the ground, but was too slow. A slab of rectangular stone the size of a basketball clipped his right shoulder as he fell, spinning his body around like a top, and he hit the ground *hard.* Hot blood coursed down his arm. He twisted his head and looked back.

A half-demolished Big Boy stood there, one arm crumpled, the other still extended from its throw. There was no sign of Slender.

"Pit! Get back!" The tenku growled and retreated. Felix struggled to his feet and glanced at his Mana. He had only lost about thirty Mana from his aborted spell, but it wasn't great. His head was swimming from the backlash of built up Mana, and flashes of blue and gold sparked in the corner of his vision. So far, that had only happened when he was at his worst. But that didn't matter. Felix crooked his left hand toward the Arcid.

Reign of Vellus!

Big Boy lurched backward, the rock it held falling as it nearly lost its balance. Small blue bolts of lightning sparked from its metal appendages as it regained its footing. Something wet dripped down from Felix's nose, but he couldn't waste the momentum. He stood up, feeling the magic twist in his veins.

"C'mon Big Boy! Do your worst! You couldn't hit lava in a volcano!"

The Arcid's eyefires narrowed. It slammed its fingers through a massive piece of stone, nearly half of the broken door. It screamed as it lifted it one-handed.

"Oh," Felix gulped. "That's...yeah that's the worst."

Big Boy roared as it started spinning the massive slab, gathering enough momentum to crush Felix to paste even fifty plus feet away. It spun forward, looking to ensure it hit its annoying target.

Just a little more...c'mon...

The Arcid spun, the huge door only a grey smear in the orange light. It stepped up to the edge of the platform, Big Boy's feet thudding and digging into the rocky ground. Felix focused on the patterns in his Mana channels, the ones responsible for his Vellus Skill that he hadn't stopped circulating since his first shot.

Now!

Reign of Vellus!

The shaped spell discharged, a flood of azure light ripping toward the Arcid. Bolts the size of Felix's leg crackled and arced between Big Boy's metal body parts, but Felix didn't push.

This time, he *pulled.*

Muscles and tendons on his arms pulling taut, Felix used his body as much as his mind to shift the Arcid's weight even the slightest bit forward. He slid forward himself, only barely catching himself on the edge of an upturned paving stone. Gritting his teeth, he pulled on the already overbearing weight of the door slab, yanking it over the edge of the platform. It tried to let go, but it's arm wouldn't respond as blue electricity arced across its limb, and as the slab dropped...

...so did Big Boy.

Felix stumbled as he released the Skill, blood pouring from his nose freely. He grimaced as he straightened, bone-weary ache radiating through his shoulders and neck. A few moments later, he received a kill notification for the Arcid.

Oh god, I'm—I've gotta—

Felix spun, heading back to the massive doors he hoped were an exit from this god-awful place. His shoulder was torn, his head still swimming from Mana backlash, and as he tried to pull on the large metal rings in the doors, they refused to budge.

"Shit shit shit," Felix whispered, eyes stinging from the acrid fumes of the lava. "I'm low on Mana, low on Health, and remarkably okay on Stamina. I have to Meditate."

Felix sat down before the door, closing his eyes and getting as comfortable as he could. He had been maintaining Meditation while moving, fighting, even while casting spells all this time, yet it hadn't leveled in hours. There had to be more he could do.

His Fire Within pulsed in time with his heartbeat, fast and agitated, and Felix slowed it down. He felt the flow of his Meditation Skill as it thrummed within his core, ephemeral but strangely physical, much like Mana itself. If leveling a Skill was all about expanding capabilities and garnering a better understanding, then he had to figure out just what Meditating actually *was*.

A way to increase my regen. A search for "oneness" or whatever. Contemplation? A...a steadying of the mind and body to...improve the functions of both...by channeling the power of my mind and body....

Meditation is level 27!

What, really? Felix's brows drew down in concentration, falling deeper into his thoughts. *Then, by using Health, Stamina, and Mana, the Skill forms a sort of loop, speeding up recovery by feeding them into one another? Did stats have anything to do with it? What were those called? Harmonic Stats, Resonance and Resilience; pertaining to mental and physical recovery, respectively. Harmonic. Harmony. That's a music thing, right? What—*

Felix's eyes snapped open.

Does it have to do with the faint music I hear when I level up?

Meditation is level 28!
Meditation is level 29!
Meditation is level 30!

+5 RES
+5 REI

"Huh," Felix gasped. "Music?"

A sudden bellowing shattered his calm, the air itself shaking with the power of it. Felix scrambled to his feet to peer in the direction of the platform, but the broken doorway was still dark.

Not for long, I imagine. Felix looked at the exit. *Gotta move.*

Careful to keep Meditation active, Felix breathed and waited ten, then fifteen seconds. His Mana rocketed back up by nearly 60 points; it'd have to do. He could already hear the thunder of approaching footsteps. He didn't have much time.

Using his Fire Within Skill, he visualized his pathways, feeling the flow of his Mana through his body. He Willed his Mana through his chest, belly, arms, and legs, flowing it in progressively complex patterns that were nevertheless increasingly familiar to him. Felix only had one chance at this; if he got it wrong, he wouldn't be leaving this volcano. As the power built and twisted into the required patterns, he released it.

Stone Shaping!

A five-foot portion of the stone doors before him liquefied, flowing into an amorphous tunnel that Felix and Pit quickly stepped within. It was like stepping into pudding, except upsettingly warm. The thickened stone sludge flowed around and behind him, sealing up the pathway back even as a titanic scream shook the air.

"*Helga—!*"

The scream cut off, and Felix sealed himself in stone.

Felix took a moment to breathe.

His heart had jumped into his throat when he heard the Archon's voice. He was very angry, and Felix figured he knew the reason.

"Next time, don't sic your dog on people," Felix muttered. "Golden jerk."

Shaking himself, Felix moved forward, his thoughts only on keeping the pattern tight and controlled. Stone shifted and moved around them, leaving only a small six-foot-by-three-foot bubble within a mountain of impenetrable rock. Using the Skill carefully like this was far easier than the sudden alterations he had done before. This way, his Meditation could ensure his regen kept up with the expense, if barely.

Felix kept his head in the game and kept moving. He wasn't out of the woods yet.

The way wasn't entirely solid, almost as if most of the rock he cleared was large rubble. Or not even stone. Flickers of light flashed occasionally around him, bright in the dark. Something had collapsed, a long time ago. Every few minutes, a puff of stale air rushed into his bubble, the massive boulders around him melting and shifting. However, as an hour went by, Felix still hadn't cleared the path.

How deep beneath the earth was he? Was this not an exit? He felt as if he were wading through waist deep snow.

What if he never got out?

The spell nearly cut out as his concentration wavered. Felix caught himself, firming his mind even as he poured slightly more Mana into the spell. His regen couldn't quite keep up with the increase, though. He'd have to take a break sooner rather than later.

Two hours.

Three hours.

Four hours and twelve breaks later, the bubble around Felix burst open into a blazing, brilliant light.

For a moment, Felix was blinded, his eyes used to the darkness of the mountain. He stumbled forward, tripping slightly on scree that slid and clattered beneath him. When the world came into focus, Felix's breath caught. It was gorgeous.

Beneath bright blue, cloudless skies, Felix observed a towering mountain range that spread to his left and right, or north and south, he amended with a glance at the setting sun. The mountains overlooked a wide valley that extended well into the hazy blue distance, and was filled with a variety of pines and leafy green trees.

And there, off in the distance, stone towers rose up into the sky.

"That's so far away," he sighed, shoulders drooping for a moment before he started moving down the mountain. "C'mon, Pit! We've got a lot of ground to cover before nightfall."

Pit let out a low squawk behind him.

As they stumped down the mountainside, loose stones cascading around him, a booming voice echoed across his consciousness.

Challenge Complete!
You Have Survived!
Return To The Domain To Receive Your Reward!

"Wha?" Felix dragged his hand over his face as he minimized all the notifications trying to pop up. "Under the mountain? No fucking chance of that, mysterious system voice. You hear this, Pit?" The tenku merely chirruped tiredly and kept shuffling sideways down the mountain. Felix shook his head, his face pinched. "Unbelievable."

They trudged down the mountain in silence.

CHAPTER TWENTY-EIGHT

"Down!"

Magda dove forward, left shield extended to deflect an acidic projectile from a hissing Tree Serpent. The kite shield didn't quite reach, but the attack deflected anyway, much to the surprise of Atar cowering behind her.

"How'd—?"

"Get back behind the wall!" Magda shouted, ignoring her own advice and charging forward at the serpent. She didn't look back to see if he listened. If he didn't, he'd likely die.

Magda wasn't worried about the boy.

Evie and the Dayne girl were fighting off the Tree Serpent on their own. Harn was too busy fending off the marauding chimeras behind them. Evie swung her spiked chain around her body, expertly weaving the twenty-foot-long weapon through her arms, legs, and around her torso. Each rotation added momentum to its strikes, and in an expert's hands, it was a deadly implement.

Magda felt pride wash over her, even as she desperately charged toward the battle. Evie was good, but she was still only barely into Apprentice Tier for Chain Mastery. The thirty foot long Tree Serpent easily bobbed and weaved through her assault, wedge-shaped head and single flame-colored eye staring fixedly at the nimble fighter.

Vessilia was moving about with almost as much grace as Evie, hopping here and there, lining up strikes with her eight-foot spear. She was strong, too, as each hit did considerable damage when it connected. The Tree Serpent threw its looping coils up and away from the vicious duo, dodging Evie's latest attack while lunging to bite Vessilia.

"No, you don't! Wall of Force!"

A shimmering field of energy suddenly warped the light between Vessilia and the Tree Serpent, cutting short its lunge as it bounced off. Rearing back in anger, the serpent moved to strike again, but Magda was already on it.

"Clarion Call!" She held her twin kite shields in front of her as she emitted a high-pitched wail. The Serpent froze in its tracks, it's single eye widening as if mesmerized. Then it went wild, snapping and lunging at Magda with abandon. The Shieldwitch punched outward with her shields, each time meeting the attacks at an angle, deflecting the majority of the strikes to either side of her body. "I've got it's attention! Flank it!"

Evie and Vessilia looked at each other and took off. Evie ran along the ground, nimbly negotiating the root-filled terrain despite the pervasive fog that limited her Perception to a measly half-dozen yards. She came up beneath the serpent, near the tree where the majority of its body was tethered.

Whipping her spiked chain in a tight loop around her shoulder, she launched the weighted end of it straight up. The chain flew far faster than it should have, bridging the gap in a fraction of a second and hitting with the power of an Iron Guilder. The Tree Serpent cried out in sudden pain.

Then Vessilia came down on it.

Somehow the girl had climbed atop the nearest tree, and using it as a springboard, she jumped a full twelve yards into the sky. She landed on the serpent's head spear first, the eight-foot polearm sinking three feet deep into the serpent's glowing eye.

SCREEEEEEEEE—

Vessilia twisted her blade, and the serpent suddenly fell limp. The Duke's daughter rode the corpse to the ground, where it hit with a boom of displaced fog.

"Yeah! You kicked his ass, Vess!" Evie was ebullient, but then she always was. Magda let the Force Wall drop as Vessilia pulled her spear free of the gooey remains of the serpent.

"Well, I would say we did it together," Vessilia smiled brightly, her teeth straight and extra white against the dark orange blood that streaked her face.

"Yes, good job, now back to the group! Now!" Magda cut them off and hustled them back to the first Force Wall she had put up. Evie rolled her eyes and nodded her head at her friend. The two smiled and ran back to Atar and Harn.

Blind gods, that girl can make friends with Avet himself. Magda shook her head ruefully, thundering behind the pair as they retreated to her temporary bulwark. A hazy orb appeared out of the mists, visible mostly due to the fog that rolled up and over it. The orb became permeable as Magda approached, and all three quickly entered. "Harn! Report!"

"Chimeras have been routed, and the fliers have been scared off for now," Harn growled, still watching the darkening skies. Night was coming on them quickly. "How'd you kill the snake?"

"Didn't," came the reply. Magda jerked her thumb over her shoulder at Vessilia. "She did."

"Oh, aye?" Harn's grim face watched the Dayne girl look proud, blush, then wilt under his stony regard. Magda suppressed a smile. The man was a brute, stubborn as an ox, and as hard to impress as any Guilder trainer she'd ever met. Which made sense, considering his background.

"We must seek shelter for the night," came an insistent voice. Magda glanced over at Atar, eyeing his torn robes and mud-splattered hems. He didn't have a single wound on him, or even any monster blood. The rest of them were practically painted orange and crimson, by comparison. "It is getting too dark to keep going."

Harn looked over at Magda with a raised eyebrow. The Shield-witch glanced at Atar before turning back toward the setting sun. "We keep moving. We're close."

Muffled groans came from the Tin Guilders, but they hoisted their discarded packs and followed after. The five of them trudged along the darkening path, following game trails barely visible even to their enhanced senses.

Game trails, Magda snorted to herself. *As if we're the ones doing the hunting.* Even now, she could vaguely sense the prowling of chimera, sniffing them out.

They were deep into the interior of the Foglands, the terrain largely unmapped and unexplored. Not that the land could be trusted, for it appeared to shift and change randomly, moving a tree or a hillock from one glance to another. Whatever cataclysm created these lands, it scarred them deeply; magic oozed from everything, confusing even their Skills at times. The chimeras were out en masse as well, and the Tree Serpent was only one of five such encounters they had endured over the past seven hours. Add in the strange commotion to the west earlier that afternoon, when rage boiled up from the earth like a near physical vapor, and all of them were on edge and due a rest.

But we're too close to rest. Magda's mouth thinned as she viewed the narrow ravine before them. It extended perhaps twenty yards before opening back up, and there didn't seem to be a convenient way around it. *We have to take a chance.*

Before she could step inside, the little shit stepped in front of her.

"That's enough! We've been following you blindly for nearly a week," Atar yelled, red in the face, making his wispy blonde mustache stand out. "You've let us kill one or two beasts between the three of us, keep us moving for hours on end, and what's worse, have yet to help us Reveal our Omens!"

Atar squared his shoulders and clenched his fists at his sides. "Now you expect us to keep moving, through a twisty and obviously trapped ravine as true night begins to fall! I demand to know just what is going on here!"

Atar huffed and puffed, his skinny shoulders trembling with either rage or fear. Probably both. Magda looked back at Evie and Vessilia, the same questions echoing in their eyes. Harn simply shrugged at her, his helm covering an expression that was surely some variation of "I told you so." Magda put her hands on her hips.

"You're an arrogant pissant, and you only deserve to know what I deem appropriate," she growled, and the boy flinched as if struck, his thin arms crossing over his chest. Magda glared at all of them, her dark eyes barely visible through the slit of her half helmet. "From here on out, you are responsible for yourselves. We are encroaching upon a place that is truly dangerous. It is enough to put pressure on both Harn and myself, let alone the three of you. Follow my lead and do. Not. Stray."

She punctuated the last three words with a jab of her thick, gauntleted finger. The last was to Atar, who flinched again.

"Understand?"

Mute nods went all around, and Magda stomped past the small mage and into the ravine.

"Good."

He was back in the ocean.

Opaque green water, sizzling against his skin even as the last vestiges of his clothing dissolved away. Carmine lightning skittered across the skies, thunder following close on its heels. The storm was on top of him, and the waves swallowed him whole.

He fell, sinking faster and faster.

Into the darkness.

Slender shapes encircled him, twisted and slithering through the murk. A flash of scales, of spines, of awful claws and teeth. They spun closer and closer, appendages meant to rend and tear and eat and eat and eat and eat—

Then something brilliant shimmered beside him. The warmth of the light chased away the twisting creatures, sheltered him from the corrosive waters, and stilled the tossing seas. A hand laid on his shoulder, his muscles going soft and weak at its touch.

"You have survived...I am surprised."

Felix's body relaxed entirely, the feeling he mistook for weakness instead being a delightful relief in all of his muscles. But he couldn't quite look up into the blazing light. Who was this?

"This is good. You're strong. I'll need you to be stronger still if you are to find me."

The presence drifted closer to him, a blinding light just beyond his periphery, and he was struck by the impression of lips close to his ear as it spoke again.

"Can you do that, Felix Nevarre?"

Felix sucked in a breath, pulling in tainted water that suddenly wanted to dissolve his body from the inside. He reeled, the light fading, his body thrashing in the darkening depths.

He screamed.

Pit leaped backward with a startled squawk, fur rising and wings spreading wide.

"Pit?" Felix realized he was sitting up, braced precariously between two thick branches. His heart thudded in his chest as he belatedly noticed the danger he was in; they had climbed this tree to sleep. Though it wasn't a magic tree, it was a very tall conifer with remarkably little sap on its bark, and that meant it was the winner. Felix looked at the night darkened forest around him and regarded Pit, who was delicately poised two branches away.

"What's up? What happened?" The skies were clear and filled with dazzling starlight, the majority of the moons having set already, leaving only the smallest two hovering over the horizon. It was early morning, something like 3AM if he were to use Earth time here. As far as Felix could tell, the days and nights felt a good deal longer than back home, but he wasn't sure.

Pit rustled his feathers a few times, taking a moment to preen his wings with his eyes closed.

"Oh, c'mon," Felix pled, rubbing an eye with the back of his hand. "I was having a nightmare. It was...it was not great. I'm sorry for scaring you. What happened?"

Pit chirped happily, regarding Felix with his big golden eyes. Felix couldn't help but smile. Then the tenku turned and gestured with his black-dipped front paw, toward the east. Felix turned.

It took him a minute to see it, but between the shifting branches and thick foliage, he could see fire.

"People," Felix gasped. "Pit! We've gotta check it out." Felix shifted to climb down, but a blinking in his vision arrested his attention.

Oh right, my notifications. Guess I was too tired to go through them last night. This night? Earlier. He sighed. *I should check them. There could be something useful in there.*

Felix settled back against the tree and with a placating gesture to Pit, toggled his notifications.

Stone Shaping is level 16!
...
Stone Shaping is level 23!

Fire Within is level 25!
Fire Within is level 26!

Congratulations! You Have Reached Apprentice Tier In Fire Within!
You Have Gained:
+10 WIL
+5% Control Of Internal Mana

Deep Mind is level 24!

Felix clenched his body as a rush of information and power flooded his system. He reached a steadying hand to a nearby branch, but his sudden spastic grip snapped it in two. As the feeling faded, he regarded his hand with dull eyes.

I'll never get used to that. The burst of stats and Skill levels seemed to be hitting harder recently, and Felix wasn't sure if that was because he kept getting them in big batches or another reason. He had to get that under control. Now that his Strength was so high, he was afraid he'd hurt himself or others someday.

Shaking his head, he focused on the last few notifications. He'd reached Apprentice Tier in Fire Within, which made sense after he'd used it to escape the mountain. If its past utility was any gauge, having that Skill in Apprentice Tier would be extremely useful. As a reward, he'd gained more Willpower and greater control of internal Mana. While the Willpower was welcome, he could honestly say it was his least-needed stat. He almost wished he'd earned Strength or Vitality, but Felix wasn't one to look a gift horse in the mouth. Especially here; horses probably had razor-sharp teeth and ate people on the Continent.

However, the percentage of increased control for "internal Mana" was definitely cool. Felix figured the pathways and looping of his Mana he sensed when using Skills was all internal Mana, and that had only brought him benefits so far. Sitting up in a tree, about to climb down and investigate a mysterious fire in a dark forest, Felix honestly felt excited to find out what else he could do.

How strange life had become.

Felix carefully climbed down, fully utilizing his Born Trait to recall the exact handholds it took to climb this tree in the first place. He made it to the ground easily enough, but not faster than Pit, who glided from tree to tree, bouncing here and there until the tenku padded quietly to the earth.

"Showoff."

Pit rubbed consolingly against his legs.

Quietly, the two of them crept forward into the dark, Stealth and Skulk both activated as they maneuvered through the plentiful shadows. They separated several times due to the terrain, but Felix could always feel the general location of his friend, like an extra limb or something.

Is this because of the Companion Pact? He could sense Pit like a warm bundle of emotion in his chest, comfortable in a way he couldn't quite verbalize. Pit felt like eagerness, joy, a little aggression, and a lot of hunger. Whatever this Skill was, however it worked, Felix delighted in it. Pit was one of the few good things he'd encountered on the Continent.

Fifteen minutes of skulking through the darkness, and Felix started to notice stone structures rising from the wild overgrowth all around him. Vine-choked walls and ivy-covered archways that led into empty grottoes were the remnant marks of a place long abandoned. Trees dominated much of the spaces, greenery bursting up from stone pavers and filling the wind-worn cracks in the structures all around him. A sinking feeling assaulted Felix as he regarded the ruin of a stone causeway, pitted and overrun by tree roots as thick as his thigh.

Exploration is level 17!

This place has been abandoned for decades. How long does it take for a forest to reclaim civilization? Ten years? Twenty? Again, magic threw his guesses off, but this place had not seen much settlement in a long time.

Maybe this is just the poorly-maintained outskirts? He tried to remain hopeful as he moved closer to the fire, the light of which was starting to fill much of the causeway. Felix kept to the shadows as he crept closer, keeping his breathing even and his steps light. If he weren't moving so carefully, he was sure he would have missed it: there was a thin coating of ice on the ground.

Kneeling to inspect it, Felix was surprised to find how cold it felt. The evening was chilly for late spring, but couldn't be colder than 60 degrees. *Why isn't it melting?* Waves of cold pulsed from the small bit of ice before him, and the ice before him had coated a large portion of the road and even crept up the side of a few crumbling walls. Ahead, the road opened up into a square of some sort, though it was mostly filled with fifty foot tall trees. The ice extended for some distance into the square, though it did not approach the trees themselves.

What is this? It wasn't natural, that was certain. Felix regarded the ice with his Manasight, and he discovered a whirling pattern of pale, purple-white Mana that pulsed steadily outward. *It's growing,* he realized. *What is doing this?*

Felix padded into the remains of a building, barely more than two walls and a section of roof, and peered out of empty window casements. His breath caught, only moments from eliciting a loud gasp.

Breath Control is level 17!

Just beyond his ruined shelter, the world was absolutely coated in frost. Ice was several inches thick on the undulating pavers, exploding outward from the center of the half collapsed ruin of two large buildings. At some point, the structures had fallen into one another, and now they supported the other's weight like a precarious stone tent. Ice covered the crumbling details of these buildings, cascading across their surfaces horizontally, as if a bomb of wintry weather had detonated here. A few footlong spikes dotted the ruins and ground, all angled away from the center, where a cheery bonfire burned as bright as the sun in the dark night.

All of this would have been amazing, were it not for the two hulking figures within the ruin.

Eight feet tall with dark blue skin, they were bald save for scraggly beards of white hair. Overlarge ears stuck out from their heads, and their jaws were heavy and thick. The creatures wore dull iron armor covered in scraps of discolored fur, and Felix spotted a couple large, blunt weapons laying on the ice.

Name: Unknown Risi Warrior
Type: Giantfolk
Level: 26
HP: ???/???
SP: ????/????
MP: ??/???
Lore: Giantfolk are known for their great strength, boundless stamina, and poor intelligence. Be wary.
Strength: Strength and Endurance
Weakness: Intelligence, Dexterity

Analyze is level 20!

Felix gulped. The two came up with the same information; both of them were Level 26. One of the two stood up and paced, grabbing its metal club off the ground. Muscles the size of Felix's head flexed as it easily hefted the club onto its shoulder.

"Ak tu shum rata," the Risi said to it's companion. It seemed agitated. The other waved its hand in their direction, still reclining against an ice-covered rock.

"Eva ka ratu tel," the seated one said, it's voice languid and sleepy.

Felix eyed their armor, and Analyze didn't let him down:

Name: Crude Iron Armor
Type: Armor
Lore: Crudely made with the simplest of smithing techniques, this armor was meant to be mass-produced. It is very heavy and trimmed with Ice Fiend fur found only in the Hoarfrost.

Big, strong, armed and armored to the teeth. That's a big ol' nope.

Felix decided to creep backward and get out of there fast. These Risi were more trouble than they were worth. Felix almost made it out of the small ruined building when a bright trilling noise sounded from his system. Seeing an icon for an open book in his vision, Felix reluctantly toggled it.

Quests
Advance Spells! 2 of 5 Apprentice Spells
Home Sweet Home! 1 of 5 Threats Eliminated
A Light in the Dark! 2 of 4 Remnants Found

Wait. What? When did these update? The Apprentice quest makes sense, but the rest...

Felix opened up the quest that worried him the most: Home Sweet Home.

Home Sweet Home! 0 of 5 Threats Eliminated
Threats:
~~Seven-Legged Orit~~
The Risi
The Archon

Unknown
Unknown

Felix stared at his screen for a long moment, then closed his eyes.

"Fuck," he whispered.

CHAPTER TWENTY-NINE

Harn scowled.

Things weren't going how they were supposed to.

The fog rolled, thick as ever, but now it blanketed a treacherous ground covered in ice. Ever since they entered these city ruins, bigger and bigger chunks of the path had been coated in the stuff, as if something was walking around and freezing all it touched. To Harn's knowledge, there was no record of a creature capable of this, not in the Foglands.

Something's changed. Harn made eye contact with Magda, seeing his own uncertainty reflected there. *What's going on here?*

Magda had been increasingly reclusive during this trip, leaving most of the training to him. If he were being honest, that was how Harn preferred it anyway, since two captains could muddy orders. But Maggie and Harn had worked together for nearly five years now, and they had worked out all the kinks of their partnership. Usually, the duo would take some trainees into a dangerous area, bring them close to death to activate their Reveal before pulling them out and eliminating any threats. They'd done this close to two dozen times now, and while they had some higher-profile trainees this time, nothing should have changed.

But then Callie went missing.

Calesca Boscal was their third member in the beginning, but had left a few years back to pursue a promotion. She was Silver

Rank, just as they were, but her skills as a finder of lost things gave her an edge in the Guild's acquisitions department. She'd go to remote locations, scout them, find any treasures she could carry, and report back on the rest. The Guild would send others to get the remainder, while Callie would get shipped off on another mission. It was perfect for her, and she had seemed truly happy.

Maggie hadn't liked it.

The two of them had a complicated history, and their on-again-off-again relationship was part of the reason for Callie taking the job. At least in Harn's opinion. Never one to mix his personal life in his job, he saw the warning signs long ago and stayed far away from it. It all blew up quite spectacularly, but Maggie still carried a torch, that was clear.

Harn stepped up toward Magda, speaking in a low tone. "This is getting bad. Reminds me of Neven in all the wrong ways."

Magda nodded absently, her eyes scanning the fog. "It's too quiet."

Harn fingered the axe blade at his waist, thinking. "I know—listen, Maggie—"

"—there's nothing here!" Came the furious whisper behind them. Harn turned to see Atar leaning aggressively toward Evie and the Duke's kid, arms spread wide as if to encompass the whole area. "It's been hours! They said this was filled with monsters that would push us to our limits! HAH! We haven't seen a beast greater than a mouse since we passed that ravine!"

"Shut it, Sparky," Harn growled. The kid was getting on his nerves, even if he was making some good points. "There are—"

"No!" The kid puffed himself up, his face red from outrage and hands balled into fists at his hips. "You're not in charge anymore! You don't even know what you're—"

"I said quiet, fool!"

Harn heard something. A soft crunch not coming from their own boots.

THUD.

"What was that?" Atar asked, his voice finally softer.

THUD.

"That?" Harn asked, unsheathing his axe and rolling his shoulders to loosen them up.

THUD.

Four hulking humanoids loomed in the fog, easily twice their size, blue-skinned, and covered in crude metal armor. They hefted large metal clubs and axes, a dangerous gleam in their dark eyes.

"That's a monster, Sparky." Harn grinned under his helmet, his blood rushing through his veins as his Brawler's Physique was unleashed. "It's time to hunt."

"RAAAAHH!"

I can't believe it.

Felix had huddled in the shadow of the ruined home for almost ten minutes now. He felt paralyzed, alternately looking at his Quest update and the giantfolk that were still visible through the window. Not only did his Home Sweet Home quest list the Risi as threats to be eliminated, but also the Archon? That big golden douche with the pet sandwurm?

This quest is trying to kill me, he decided. How—what possible way did he have at his disposal to—

Felix took a breath.

It'll be...fine. I-I can figure it out.

Felix crept back toward the window, careful not to touch the sill which was slowly being covered in the encroaching frost. One of the Risi were agitated, and the other seemed like they couldn't be bothered. He could use that.

Think. Use the environment against them. Felix scowled as he inventoried his available Skills. He had built up quite the diverse range of tools, so he had options. *I just have to make the most of them. Gotta lure them away, handle them one-by-one. Those muscles suggest high Strength, and those weapons...*

He Analyzed the nearest club, a great beast of a weapon at five feet long and nearly a foot wide at the tip. Like a brutal iron spike, it tapered toward the handle, shaped into a rough pyramidal shape. His range had extended since hitting Apprentice Tier, pushing him well past twenty feet.

Name: Crude Iron Club
Type: Bludgeoning
Lore: Made of crude iron, it is a raw and rough weapon, being both extremely heavy and poorly balanced. But it is brutally effective.

Ok. I can use that—

A high-pitched scream cut off his thought. A third Risi warrior stomped into the square, carrying over his shoulder a squirming figure wrapped sloppily in a huge rope. The giant dropped its captive roughly onto the ground, where they hit the ice with a clatter of metal armor. The captive stopped moving, and Felix sucked in a breath. He ducked low as the giant turned toward his direction, and he motioned for Pit to stay back.

"Lathu. Ikta na raatu!" The newcomer roared. Felix peered up and saw the blue-skinned humanoid gesturing to several slash wounds on its arms and legs, where the armor didn't protect as well. It was gesturing back the way it came, and for the others to follow. The uneasy giant wanted to follow almost immediately, bounding over to the new arrival like an eager puppy. Felix narrowed his eyes. It was hard to tell with their craggy features and white beards, but it seemed like that one was much younger than the rest, less experienced. The younger giant turned toward the other, who was still sprawled on the ground attempting to take a nap.

"Atcha, Jurvo! Klepas ta nata!" Young urged Lazy to get up, gesturing with his hands. Lazy ignored him and rolled over, muttering something in their tongue that Felix couldn't make out. The meaning was clear, however, and the newcomer pointed at the unconscious captive and back at Lazy. They did this repeatedly, vigorously, until Lazy waved them off and nodded. The other two left, quickly jogging out into the dark.

Felix's heart was in his throat. This was perfect, but only if—

Thunderous snoring began to fill the square. Lazy had fallen asleep.

Hell yes!

Felix crept outside the fallen building, coming as close to the outer corner as he could without passing into the square. Asleep or not, he didn't want that giant to have a chance at line of sight on him. At the corner, the captive was just within range of his Analyze.

Name: Unknown Human Woman
Race: Human
Level: 19
HP: ???/???

SP: ???/???
MP: ???/???
Lore: Humans are adaptable and prolific breeders. They can be found in many corners of the Continent.
Strength: Strength, Agility
Weakness: Endurance

She's human! There are *people here!* The sudden relief he felt was palpable, so powerful it almost made him dizzy. For a period of time, Felix feared he had entered a world of monsters, that this endless terror field was all there was.

He just hoped she survived that body slam.

I have to get her out of there, before any of them come back. Eliminating the Risi is secondary compared to that.

Felix crept back into his shelter and started to plan.

He could use Stealth and sneak his way over to her, untie her and carry her away...No. Too slow, too much of a chance of waking the giant. And besides, was he strong enough to lift a full-grown woman wearing what looked like plate armor? He didn't know, and Felix sure as hell wasn't going to gamble at this point.

He could use Stone Shaping to...make a barricade? Felix shook his head again. Too loud, too Mana-intensive despite his internal Mana control.

Reign of Vellus could work, pulling her to him. Felix was still amazed at the changes in that spell. The evolution of that spell gave him some insights into how it worked, and while it could now push or pull, it still tended to discharge big gouts of electricity toward its target. There was probably a way around that using Fire Within, but not without practice and time he didn't have. The other giants could be back at any moment.

Felix had other options, but nothing was perfect. Plans and tactics rattled through his head, ideas that could work or fail depending on this or that variable. One thing remained constant, though: he would have to untie her first and go from there. The sleeping giant...well he'd have to make sure he didn't wake up. But the first priority was the captive.

I'll have to go with option one.

Felix looked over at Lazy, busily snoring away. The giant had pushed together its thick Ice Fiend ruff, forming a pillow, and had its long, blue arms in a tangle. A club similar to the others' was resting within easy reach, standing up and leaning against the ice-covered stone wall. His Perception could pick up the Risi's heavy, steady breathing and even the faint burbling sound of drool pooling in its open mouth. With a grimace, Felix refocused.

Pit was next to him, and Felix kneeled down toward his friend. He couldn't speak, worried to wake the giant, but he tried to somehow...push his thoughts toward the tenku. Companion Pact worked something like that right?

Stay back. Stay safe. Watch out for danger.

Pit...just looked at him blankly, tilting his birdlike head.

Felix sighed, silently. He could feel the warmth in his chest; the connection to Pit he'd been endowed with just a few days ago. He touched his chest and pointed toward the unconscious woman. He pointed at Pit and then at the ground. Pit looked between his hand and the ground several times before plopping himself down—rather grumpily, if he were being honest.

Sparing his friend a smile, Felix crept out of the shelter. He made sure Stealth was activated as much as possible and stepped out into the open.

Despite being as quiet as he possibly could be, Felix felt like each soft pad of his foot was agonizingly loud, his leather boots crunching against the ice. But he reached her without incident.

Stealth is level 22!

Up close, Felix could finally make out the captive's features: she was breathing, and she was a young girl, maybe twenty years old. Younger than him by a fair margin at least, with dark brown hair and slightly darker skin. She was wearing a strange collection of enameled steel plates and flexible leather pieces. It looked really expensive. She didn't have a weapon he could see, but that made sense. She was a captive after all.

Maybe she's a mage? Felix's eyes lit up at the thought. *Now that'd be something. Maybe she can tell me—*

A sudden snort sounded and Felix went absolutely still. Carefully, he turned around and was relieved to find the giant still sleeping. It had just rolled over.

Whew. Gotta hurry.

Felix tried to untie the rope. But it wasn't tied. It was just wrapped tightly around the girl, held mostly in place by her own unconscious weight on top of it.

Shit. I can't hold her and *untie her.* Felix tapped his lips before swallowing carefully. *I'll have to improvise.*

Acid Stream

Felix formed a small globe of green liquid in his hand, but did not push it in any direction. Instead, he let it pool there, spinning like a tiny planet above his palm. The spell fought against him, wanting to be released, but he flexed his Willpower, and it stopped. Then, very carefully, he dragged the orb across a thick rope section. With a hissing sizzle and three seconds time, the rope dissolved and fell apart. He did a silent victory dance in his head and kept on moving. It took nearly two minutes, but he had cut her loose without getting any of the corrosive liquid on the girl.

He had just pulled the last of the ropes off her body when he heard the faint crack of ice behind him. His Perception suddenly blaring in warning, Felix turned just in time to see a massive metal club swinging for his head.

Felix jumped back, using the same motion to kick the unconscious woman away from him and Lazy. She slid across the ice with the force of his push, fetching up against the wrecked building where Pit was hiding. That was all the attention Felix was about to afford however, because the Risi started swinging again.

The giant was strong, so strong that his swings felt like standing too close to a subway train. All wind and metal and instant death if he stepped in the wrong place. Felix backed up again and again as he dodged around the Risi Warrior's brutal attacks.

If just one of these attacks connect, it will destroy me. Felix was sweating, but the giant wasn't even breathing hard.

Then Felix saw Pit drag the poor girl into the ruined building, and a weight lifted off his chest.

Felix rolled out of the way of another strike, came to his feet, and leapt from an ice-coated boulder. He jumped back toward the giant, making it to eye level before he let loose a Corrosive Strike. Except, Felix didn't stop to realize that once you were in the air, you could no longer maneuver. The Risi knocked him from the sky with a swipe of its metal club, smashing him into the ice and stone with a cracking report.

Felix hit hard, and felt his bones creak. The ice beneath him shattered, and his Health dropped by 40%.

Fuck! He spit up blood onto the ice.

Armored Skin is level 3!
Armored Skin is level 4!

Felix felt a sudden rush of wind behind him, and he rolled to the left quickly, barely evading another strike of the club. Coming to his feet, he squared off and fired an Acid Stream at the giant. The acid hit the Risi square in the chest, sizzling and bubbling against the metal armor, but failing to eat through it.

"Tch," Felix clicked his tongue, annoyed.

Reign of Vellus!

The giant, who had taken two steps toward him and was winding up his club, was sent stumbling as Felix tugged on the Risi's unsupported left leg as it stepped forward. Felix rushed forward and swung a vicious uppercut.

Corrosive Strike!

His fists, enhanced with his acidic magic, blasted a large dent into the giant's chest plate. Lazy even popped up momentarily into the air, and Felix followed up with a jump-assisted double-fisted slam onto the giant's back.

Crash!

Lazy hit the ice hard, shattering it further as frozen chips scattered up and into the air. Felix panted with effort, his arms almost numb from the vibrations of striking the giant's hard skin.

The giant, however, simply stood back up. And grinned.

"You suck," breathed Felix. Then he charged back in.

CHAPTER THIRTY

Vessilia Dayne was not having the greatest of days.

Battered and bruised, the pain woke her more than anything else. She lacked the Pain Resistance Skill, and she regretted it dearly. Agony lanced across her limbs and lower back where the giant had smashed her against the ice. She blinked blearily at the half-fallen roof, covered in bits of ice and green vines as if winter and spring were fighting one another. Her mind felt muddled, and two blinking icons flashed in her vision:

Status Condition: Concussion (Mild)

Status Condition: Injured (Minor)

Slowly leveraging herself into a sitting position, Vess let out a hiss as her back tweaked and sent more flashes of pain out to her legs and made her fingers tingle.

That is not good, she thought. *Minor means sprain or bruising usually, so perchance not as bad as I—*

Her inner dialogue died as her eyes finally adjusted to the gloomy interior. Standing only two feet from her was a shadowy presence with two sets of eyes, each burning gold with a fiendish fury, and clawed appendages stretched out to either side, dark and fuzzy like the fog that it lived within.

"Chimera!"
Dragoon's Footwork!

Dragoon's Footwork is level 26!

Vess flowed like quicksilver, her body moving almost without conscious thought, and she was suddenly ten feet away and upon her feet. Instinctively, she reached out to grab her spear but found nothing but empty air.

Damn! The giant! That monstrous foe had disarmed her during their initial melee. She grabbed at her waist and pulled a small dagger from her belt sheath, wincing as pain shot through her back. *This will have to do.*

She advanced on the chimera, who had oriented on her remarkably quickly. *Its Perception must be sky high to notice my movements through this blasted fog.* Even now, the ever-present mist had begun rolling into the ruin's darkened interior. The fiend blinked owlishly at her, tilting its head curiously before snarling and dropping low. The two of them circled one another, giving Vess a chance to really look at this beast.

The chimera had four legs that looked like they belonged to a small wolf, a bushy tail, and two clawed appendages on its back. The claws spread out like gnarled wings, quivering with each step. It was hideous, its hide rippling and twisted like all the chimeric beasts she'd encountered, the edges of its form fuzzing off into the fog itself.

Each step was painful, a jolt of discomfort that was growing into an almighty blaze of agony in her back. Vess swallowed and eyed the collapsed wall in her peripherals. *If I can outsmart it...*

Vess activated Dragoon's Footwork again, this time in a feint toward the left before spinning to the right and diving out of the ruined building. The chimera fell for it, its remarkably fast reflexes still not enough for her advanced movement technique.

Thank you, Mother...

Vess landed on an uneven stone thoroughfare, nearly identical to the one her team had followed. Perhaps they were close. She heard the sound of fighting nearby, including the unmistakable sound of a giant's pained roar. Quick as a blink, she took off toward the sound.

Behind her she heard frantic scrabbling in the ruins as the chimera gave chase.

Night! She cursed, not wasting time looking back, just focusing on rounding the corner of the building ahead. The street was covered in ice, thickening as she went, but more disconcerting was the increasing amount of shattered walls she was seeing. Vess passed four broken walls, newly destroyed to her eye, and through the fifth she saw a massive cloud of grey blue dust.

It was distinct from the ever-present fog, instead rising up in a large plume amid a mountain of stone fragments and ice chunks. The great, terrible sound of ice shearing away from masonry filled the square, and a number of broken walls rose all around; whoever was fighting was demolishing this entire area. In her mind, only one person could have done this.

"Lady Aren!" Vess called, before trying to bite back her words. The last thing she needed was to draw the attention of whatever monster made *this* happen, nor distract her mentor during such a battle.

Then the fog shifted, and the plume of dust and ice settled to reveal a human man step out. Much to Vess' surprise, it was not Harn or even the pompous Atar. No, it was a stranger with pale skin, dark hair, and absolutely shredded clothing. His tunic had perhaps once been beige, but was now a dark grey-brown and largely useless as a covering; the sleeves were torn off and several huge rents in the fabric exposed entirely too much trim flesh.

Vess felt herself blush. His pants seemed to be leather and more or less intact, save for the bottom of the legs which had been eaten away by something and were a tattered mess. Simple boots covered his feet, wet and coated in patches of frost. Wounds covered the man's arms, and blood stained much of his torn clothing, but he did not seem to care. Instead, the man stepped forward and quickly oriented on a point in the fog to his right. Vess saw nothing at first, but then a silhouette emerged from the fog.

It was huge and heavily-built, much as the ones her team had faced, its skin blue and body covered in dark metal armor. It even had the same five-foot metal club slung behind its back. The key difference, however, was that this giant looked to be in rough shape. Its armor was dented and busted in several places, and a number of angry patches on its arms and face were bubbling and leaking a dark blue blood that plopped heavily to the ground.

"C'mon, you lazy piece of shit!" The man's face split in a wide smile despite his injuries. "Let's go!"

The giant roared, its own face lit up in a predatory grin. Then it charged, exploding across the ground so fast that Vess could not quite track its movements. Just like the bastard that had captured her, this one was unbelievably powerful, and Vess found herself wincing in anticipation. The giant was too strong, too fast, too much to overcome. A great boom sounded out, rattling loose stones at her feet and sweeping away the fog for a few instants. Vess blinked against the wind, and found herself looking at an unexpected sight.

The man was alive.

And he was...*winning?*

The dark-haired man ducked beneath the giant's heavy swings, each strong and fast enough to blow back any debris that was around them. Small pebbles and stones scattered with each haymaker, the giant's attacks growing increasingly fast and complicated as it fought. But, somehow, its opponent dodged around nearly every attack as if he were dealing with an unruly child.

How is he doing this...?

Vess was confounded. The man was faster than any Tin she knew, but he did not fight like an Iron Rank. He was too wild and uncontrolled. In fact, he moved unlike anyone she'd ever seen. Were there other Guilders out here?

"Vakta rok est!" The giant cried out in its guttural language, swinging its massive fist around in a sweeping cross-strike.

Vess watched as the giant landed the hit, flipping the man backwards in a sideways spiral. He flew backwards ten feet, twisting his own body so that he landed on his two feet even as he continued sliding for another five. Vess gasped and raised her hands to her mouth. *That would have shattered all of the bones in my shoulder, I have to—*

"Fuck, that hurt!" The man laughed, rolling his injured shoulder in its socket as if loosening it up. "Notched up my Resistance though, and a few other things!" He cracked his neck and charged back in. "You'll have to do better than that!"

He's insane, Vess decided. *Why else would he fight with his fists? He's even got a sword! Use your sword, fool!*

But the man ignored her silent advice, and the two combatants charged at one another again. In a blink, the giant was on top of the man, slamming a massive metal club onto the ground before it. It shattered the earth, digging a crater nearly ten feet wide and a foot deep into the square. But the mad warrior was no longer before it.

He had slid between the giant's legs, holding onto some strange length of stretchy black material. The material was somehow wrapped around the giant's ankles, and as the warrior finished his slide he braced and yanked backwards. The giant stumbled, just barely, causing it to rip through the strange whip with pure brute strength.

I have to get in there. I have to do something.

Yet before Vess could muster an idea for aid, the man did something else completely unexpected. He raised his right hand, palm out, and shouted.

"Reign of Vellus!"

A brilliant surge of lightning blasted up around the blue-skinned giant, arcing up from the ground itself. The monster, still unsteady on its feet, suddenly slammed backward onto the ground almost as if the lightning yanked him down. Stone and ice shattered again, the crater this creature had made now oblonged by its own fall. The giant's metal club soared into the air, propelled by the creature's flailing arm, but it stopped midflight. Vess blinked, unable to trust her eyes, because then the club reversed direction and slammed directly onto the chest and throat of its former owner.

The giant screamed, blue blood spitting from its open mouth and drenching its white beard. Yet the metal club, surrounded by small arcs of lightning, lifted up into the air again and into the waiting arms of the dark-haired man.

"You're not the monster here," Vess heard him mutter, his voice ringing as if he had shouted. With a grunt, he hefted the heavy club up onto his shoulder and gripped it with two hands. The giant below him unsuccessfully tried to suck in a breath, flailing its limbs uselessly.

"I am."

He swung the club down, directly onto the giant's unprotected head.

Once.

Twice.

Three times.

Thick blue blood splashed outward, and the giant went absolutely still.

Blind gods, Vess held her hand up to her mouth, horrified.

The man dropped the club, the heavy weapon not even bouncing as it hit the stone with an earth-shaking thud. He turned directly toward Vess, orienting on her as if he knew she had been there all along. Vess froze. This man...his eyes burned with blue light.

"Oh, huh," he said, smiling. "You're awake."

Then the chimera was on her.

They were losing.

Magda watched Evie tumble across the ice, her body sliding just enough to stay ahead of the giant's powerful blows, and opposite her, Atar flung bolts of fire repeatedly at their shared enemy. They fought valiantly and not without skill, but it wasn't working. The giant shrugged off Evie's spiked chain, even when she altered its weight; and while Atar's flames were painful for the blue-skinned behemoths, they appeared to do very little damage.

Magda growled as Harn tanked a strike from yet another giant, this one having just appeared as reinforcement only moments ago. The man's armor shimmered and appeared to thicken just moments before the hit landed, and Harn was only tossed back a few feet before he recovered. The warrior stayed true to his nickname as he raised his twin axes and charged back into the fray.

Bang!

A massive concussion rang out above, and Magda quickly took her eyes from the fights around her. Two giants assaulted her position, one larger than the other. The furthest away and larger of the two was a massive specimen wearing the same crude armor as the rest, but wielding a massive double-headed axe that appeared to be made entirely from ice. Luckily, this one seemed content to let his lesser brethren take the brunt of the assault, only occasionally taking swipes at her Force Wall. The closest was the bastard who had been heavily wounded by Vessilia, the same one who had knocked her out and ran off. Now he had returned with a second giant in tow...and the girl was nowhere to be seen.

Girl, you'd better not be dead, she threatened. The wounded giant reared back with its stolen spear, and Magda knew the shield couldn't handle much more abuse. So she did what she had been trained to do: be unexpected.

Just as the giant's spear would have connected, Magda dropped the Skill and hurled a massive boulder up at the monster. The rock, heavy as it was, flew through the air deceptively slowly, and while the giant staggered from the lack of resistance, it had no time to dodge it. The boulder hit the giant square in the chest.

Stone Break!

The boulder shimmered with an amber-colored energy and exploded. Thousands of razor-sharp pieces scattered in all directions, piercing the giant and throwing it stumbling back. Magda raised her own kite shields up, blocking the majority of the shrapnel from herself. The rest of her allies were far enough away that it wasn't a true danger. The wounded giant, the bastard who took her trainee, was bent over, unable to fully stand up as thick, blue blood poured from its chest. Its stolen spear fell to the ground with a clatter.

"Had enough?" The giant snapped its eyes up at her taunt, its wide eyes frenzied and wild. It stood up with significant effort, and Magda saw the results of her attack. Its crude iron armor breastplate had been utterly shredded, the metal pierced by innumerable shards of stone. It roared, loud enough to shake the air, and then bull-rushed the Shieldwitch.

But Magda trained every day with Harn Kastos, who was not only quite proficient in Unarmed combat, but could alter his armor's weight. With a practiced motion, she met the giant by grabbing hold of its upper arms, and with a twist of her own shoulders, she sent the blue brute into the dirt. The monster hit, sending a cascade of ice and dirt fountaining into the air, even as Magda staggered under the creature's immense weight.

Twins' teeth! That thing is heavy. Are their bones made of metal?

The giant swung an elbow backwards at her, catching her squarely in the chest. Magda was thrown several feet, and a sudden shortness of breath meant it had dented her breastplate. With a grunt of effort, she swung her arm forward, casting the leading edge of her kite shield at the creature's elbow. Even from this distance, her expanded shield hit easily, and the giant howled in pain as she penetrated nearly three inches into the joint.

The giant thrashed, its body twisting on itself as it tried to simultaneously cradle its injury and lash out. Magda blocked the haphazard strikes, even as she threw up another Force Wall around them both. Straddling their back, she crouched over the eight-foot tall giant and grabbed the stone directly next to their face. Leaning toward their ear, she whispered, "Die screaming."

Then she exploded the stone beneath it.

Stone Break!

The cowering giant suddenly hopped and stuttered, arms and legs flailing as the ground beneath it shattered into thousands of projectiles. Barely protected by the flesh of the giant, Magda rode through the explosion like a boat on a stormy sea, holding her kite shields tight beneath her. Its screams of agony were quickly swallowed by the deluge of stone, until everything went still.

You Have Defeated A Risi Warrior!
You Have Gained XP!

"No," Magda gasped. She hadn't been sure.... "Harn! They're Risi Warriors!"

"What!" Harn kicked his opponent away, buying himself a few seconds. "They're supposed to be in the Hoarfrost!"

"The Hoarfrost?" Atar's voice cracked, strain evident in his bearing as he sent bolt after bolt of fire at the giant attacking Evie. "That's weeks away! Why are they here?"

"Stop talking! Just keep casting!" Evie growled as she backflipped off the chest of her target, throwing a small dagger at its blue face. The giant snarled and knocked it away with a fist, but was too distracted to defend from the flurry of Sparkbolts that lit up its backside. It roared in pain, the off-white fur at its waist finally starting to catch fire. "It's working! Keep it up!"

Atar groaned, obviously pushing the edge of his reserves. He called up another Sparkbolt, chantlessly, as he had been doing the whole fight. Magda was impressed, to be honest. Maybe the kid *wasn't* useless.

Then she saw it. Looming out of the fog, the leader of these Risi suddenly leaped toward Atar, ice axe raised above its head. A purple-white radiance bloomed from the weapon, dropping the temperature instantly.

"Atar! Move!" Magda cried out and started running. But she was too far away.

Atar looked up, face pale and body freezing as a sudden frost crept up the boy's legs and locked him into place. The massive giant came down, its axe leading the way.

"No!" Magda couldn't accept this...she could make it!

Then, a metal club spun out of the fog-filled darkness, smashing into the ice at the boy's feet and sending him stumbling backward. The giant leader's axe smashed into the stone where he had been standing, only barely catching the young mage. Atar fell, blood trailing in his wake as he collapsed onto the ground fifteen feet away. Magda made it to him moments later, recasting Force Wall around them both as she rifled through her pack.

The giant snarled as it stood up, glancing from the metal club to the swirling fog in the near distance. The clatter of rubble falling echoed across the area, and a sudden breeze thinned the fog as a man stepped out onto the crumbling edge of a structure. His features were hard to make out at this distance, but he was bloody and torn, his clothes barely holding together, and one of his arms was extended.

Then a second figure stepped up beside him.

"Vess?" Evie joyfully cried out.

CHAPTER THIRTY-ONE

15 Minutes Ago:

"AAHH!" The young woman screamed and jumped away from Pit, who had Skulked up toward her back.

"Yeah, he's pretty sneaky," Felix chuckled to himself, before wincing at the sudden movement.

Status Condition: Strained Shoulder (Minor)
Status Condition: Bleeding (Major)

Health: 74/470

Shit.

Felix reached into his pack and pulled out a few sprigs of yarrow, chewing them down quickly. He watched as his Health jumped up, tick after tick, and reached for more. But he was out. All he had left in his bag was his side knife, his enchanted rope, a bunch of loose papers, and that bulky cigar box. He suddenly noticed a large hole in the bottom of the bag. He frowned as he remembered the Arcid's rough handling of the satchel.

Double shit. All my herbs...

His Health steadied out at around 70%.

Guess that'll have to do, for now.

With a grunt, he hopped over the giant's corpse and made his way over to the young woman. He swung his arms, trying to loosen the tightness in his shoulder. Lazy had hit him pretty hard back there, if it weren't for Armored Skin, he'd have probably lost the arm. Idly, Felix pulled up his notifications editing it mentally until it only contained the max gains.

Armored Skin is level 14!
Pain Resistance is level 27!
Corrosive Strike is level 15!
Shadow Whip is level 11!
Acid Stream is level 22!
Influence of the Wisp is level 21!
Physical Conditioning is level 18!
Unarmed Mastery is level 24!
Acting is level 5!
Make An Entrance is level 3!

+5 STR
+2 END
+10 VIT
+2 AGL

New Skill Learned!
Blunt Weapon Mastery (C), level 1!
Swords and fists are good and all, but why use those when you could be using a big fuck-off mace? Skill Level increases proficiency.

Blunt Weapon Mastery is level 3!

What a haul. Maybe clearing out all the Risi won't be such a bad—

"Step back, creature!"

Felix looked up to find the young woman and Pit circling one another, the tenku warbling confusedly while the woman held a long knife in a strange grip.

"You!" She oriented on him, suddenly including Felix in her defensive gestures. "Who are you?"

Taken aback, Felix said the wittiest thing he could manage.

"Uhh-"

"No, it matters little now," she brushed the question off. "Help dispatch this foul chimera!" She whirled back toward Pit, who had tried walking over to Felix and who now cowered under her glare, his primaries dragging on the ground.

"Hey, no don't do that," Felix raised his hands and stepped up to the lady, keen to explain. "Pit is a-"

"YAH!" With a panicked cry, she spun and planted the knife directly into his chest. Or she tried to. Felix watched her move as if underwater, his Perception catching her attack before it even started. That she was attacking him was a surprise, but honestly Felix was more preoccupied with the advent of blue and gold shimmers at the corners of his vision. His mind...*tingled*, warm like his legs after a short run, primed almost. With an almost casual motion, he lifted his bare hand and awkwardly deflected the woman's knife, dislodging it from her grip to clatter to the stones below.

New Skill Learned!
Parry (Common), level 1!
Sometimes dodging doesn't work, or is too slow, or hell, you don't want to. Now you've got options! Accuracy and speed increases with Skill Level.

The shimmers of light dissipated, like turning off a switch.

What the hell?

"Oh blind gods! I am—I did not mean—" The woman (girl, really) stammered, gripping her wrist as she stepped backward. A sudden angry screech made her jump, leaping nearly a foot off the ground somehow.

"The monster! It attacks!"

Felix looked at the young woman and frowned in annoyance; she had landed a bit away from the both of them. "What's your name?"

"Vess...Vessilia Dayne, Tin Rank Guilder." Felix chewed on the inside of his cheek in thought.

"Vessilia, my name is...Felix Nevarre, and this is my *friend*, Pit." He stressed the word, and gestured to the small tenku who took the moment to sidle up to his Companion. The young woman's face pinched in confusion even as she bent down to retrieve her blade.

"Your friend? A chimera?" She seemed baffled. Felix couldn't figure out why. Sure, Pit was a little aggressive at times, but he was basically a puppy. "*Why?* They are abominations, and highly dangerous."

Pit sat down and groomed his left wing, adjusting feathers with his beak. Vessilia flinched, her knife going up again as she eyed the tenku warily. Felix shook his head.

"I don't care. You put that knife away, or I'll do it for you."

Slowly, reluctantly, the woman sheathed her knife at her waist. Her hand, however, didn't stray far from it.

Whatever. As long as it isn't out.

Perturbed, Vessilia settled her hands on her hips. "Where are you from? Why are you in the Foglands, and how in Avet's name did you kill a frost giant with your bare fists?" Her voice rose slightly with each question, and her dark eyes were intense.

Felix scratched his left shoulder awkwardly and dodged the question. "What is a Guilder? Or a Tin Rank?"

Vessilia fixed him with a suspicious stare. "How do—? Why would you not know this?"

"Let's say I'm stupid," Felix smiled in a disarming sort of way, he hoped. He was never really good with this interpersonal stuff.

The girl gave him a weird look, like he'd just farted in public or something. "A Guilder is a member of the Protector's Guild, a coalition of adventurers that work to protect the Continent from monsters. Tin Rank is the lowest of the Guild, essentially a...trainee."

"Oh, huh," Felix huffed a breath. *Adventurers? For real?* "So where's your trainer, then? Is that Lady Aren?"

"Ah, well, she is technically my mentor but..." Vessilia appeared nervous for some reason, and Felix quirked an eyebrow.

"You don't know where she is?"

The girl huffed out an aggrieved breath. "Fine, yes, I am a bit turned about. I was carried here against my will, I will have you know."

Felix smiled. "So, you'd recognize how to get back if I can get you on the path?"

"Sure." Vessilia shrugged. "The idiot left me awake the entire trip, only knocking me out once he got here. Enormous git," she muttered under her breath. Felix clapped his hands, startling both the girl and Pit, who warbled and fell over in surprise. Laughing lightly as his Companion stood back up, he glanced at Vessilia to find her clutching the hilt of her knife and staring daggers at his friend. Gently, Felix placed a hand on hers, causing her to look up at him in surprise.

"He's a good boy, Vessilia," Felix looked her in the eyes, and tried to convey this simple fact again. "He won't hurt you."

After a moment, the girl's brows relaxed and her grip loosened. Felix grinned. For some reason he couldn't figure out, she blushed.

"Okay! Let's get going; I can see the destination from here. Sooner we find your mentor, the better!"

Hopping back toward the giant, Felix picked up the discarded Crude Metal Club and slung it over his shoulder. It was *very* heavy, even with an 84 in Strength, but it was manageable. It was a good weapon against the giants, and also added a dash of irony to each strike.

Felix walked off, leading them back to the original square with Pit hot on his heels. Vessilia followed slightly more cautiously, picking her way over the rubble and remnants of his battle against the Risi Warrior. He knew his fight had destroyed several of the more rickety walls around the area, but Felix was a little surprised that he'd gone so far off course. They walked for about 400 feet before entering back into the iced over square, which even now was starting to melt. Reaching down, Felix ran his hand through a small puddle of water.

"Why is the ice melting?" Vessilia asked from behind him, her steps loud and heavy on the thin ice.

"Not sure. Maybe the giants were maintaining it?" Felix shrugged and stood back up. He pointed across the square. "I saw the wounded giant carry you from that direction."

Vessilia stepped ahead, looking around the ice and noting the acid-scorched ropes still laid in a pile. She seemed to be searching for something, but after a few seconds, she seemed to have given up. For whatever reason, she seemed to be squinting a whole lot.

Maybe it's a sight Skill or something.

They took off shortly after that, Vessilia in the lead. It was sometimes slow going as the girl seemed to have trouble navigating some of the more treacherous rubble and ice slicks, almost as if she hadn't noticed them until she was on top of them. Did that mean her Perception was low? Her Agility didn't seem terribly high either when she attacked him, nor her Strength.

She said Tin Rank was basically a beginning adventurer, so low level. But she's level 19? That's the same level I am, but my stats are clearly higher than hers. What's the difference?

Felix pondered as the armored young woman picked across the ground, moving with less and less caution. She was in a hurry. After only ten minutes, a roar of rage preceded the telltale clashing of metal. Felix's gaze snapped up as surges of bright orange Mana burst and evaporated not too far away. They were spots of vivid color in the gray, brown, and purple white miasma that was the ruin all around them.

"Fire magic," Felix breathed, both curious and nervous. His last experience with fire magic was an awful case of bad breath, though this was likely an ally. Felix didn't imagine Frost Giants would be using fire spells. Vessilia confirmed it.

"That must be Atar." She paused, sucking in a sudden breath as she must have noticed the lights reflecting in the ruins ahead. "They're all fighting, I can hear them! Come quickly!"

Shooting her a curious look, Felix easily outpaced her, even with the giant club. Pit chirruped curiously at him.

"Don't know what we're getting into, buddy. But keep an eye out and stay to the side. Things might get weird for a while." Felix felt his chest grow warm, that bundle of emotion that he recognized as his connection to his companion swelling and shifting. He was coming to recognize that the feeling meant agreement.

Companion Pact is level 11!

Moments later, Felix crested the ruins of a two-story building that had collapsed, turning its second floor into a strange ramp. Once there, he had a clear view of a fierce battle. Nearby, a figure in full plate armor was duking it out with a blue-skinned Risi, one he almost didn't recognize due to the preponderance of bloody injuries.

It was Young, the smoother-skinned giant that left with Wounded. Speaking of Wounded, they were getting their ass handed to them by another armored warrior, this one wielding dual shields on their arms. As he watched, he saw the person pick up a boulder the size of Felix's torso and chuck it at the giant. It exploded in a brilliant shower of jagged shards.

Felix felt a chill. These people were strong. He didn't think he'd survive an explosion like that, even with his Armored Skin.

The rest of the battlefield was dominated by a much larger giant with an icy axe that didn't seem to be doing much, and a fourth Risi Warrior battling two humans. One of them was using some sort of chain to whip and bind the giant, with little success; she was also remarkably...flippy. *Acrobatic, that's the word. She's good, way better than me.*

The other fighter was a young man with curling blond locks and disheveled robes. He was busy conjuring small orbs of fire that he'd then sling at the Risi from behind. He didn't look to be in great condition, robes torn and stained by blood.

Fire mage, huh? He hadn't worked with fire yet. Maybe the kid would let him learn.

A sudden, explosive boom diverted Felix's attention back to the center of the field. The shield warrior had somehow blown up the ground itself, and had put up a...magical force field? Agog, he was so focused on the swirling shield of yellow energy that he nearly missed the movement of the big, axe-wielding giant leader. It had hefted its massive ice axe and was running toward the mage, lifting the weapon to deliver a devastating blow.

Felix panicked. He glanced around the field, noticing that nearly everyone else was preoccupied.

No way I can make it over there in time...

Ice encroached up the mage's body, and a quick glance told Felix the giant leader had cast something. Streams of purple-white Mana radiated off its hulking frame, and its ice axe started glowing as well as it stepped ever closer.

What if I...no, I could—

The giant made a final leap, pulling its axe high into the air.

"Damn it!" Felix hauled back and, like he was doing a hammer throw, spun and released the massive club he'd looted. It felt like throwing an I-beam, and Felix staggered a few steps as the club whirled off into the darkness. Thankfully his Perception, Strength, and Dexterity were good enough that the club flew true, and it smashed hard into the ice-covered ground at the mage's feet. Almost at the same time, the giant's ice axe cleaved into the ground, sending the boy flying off over a dozen feet.

Thrown Weapons Mastery is level 10!

"Holy shit," Felix gasped, wide eyed. *I almost hit that guy!*

"Avet's Eyes, how did you do that at this range?" Vessilia had come up behind him while he winced. He turned and saw her face; she looked impressed.

"Uh, practice, I guess," Felix managed.

"Vess?"

The cry came from below, specifically from the chain-wielding woman with the sky-high Acrobatics level. Vessilia's expression brightened, and she waved as the chain-wielder continued to dodge her opponents' attacks. Felix took a breath as a wounded giant lumbered closer to them, pushed back by the axe-wielding man.

"Time to help, yeah?" Vessilia nodded, and they both turned back. Once he was ten feet away or so, Felix turned and dashed back toward the edge.

"See you down there!"

"W-what? Wait!"

Felix jumped.

Reign of Vellus!

Blue light flashed as he fell, arcs of lightning rising up to meet him. He slowed, then landed with a muffled *thud*, knees bent. Felix quirked his mouth to the side. *That was easier than before.*

Then the giant was on him.

Wounded badly and wielding their metal club, the Risi Warrior roared in rage at Felix, charging him with what he was coming to understand was characteristic gusto. Felix braced, ready to dodge or strike or cast, but found it was unnecessary. An armored blur shifted before him, slashing twin blazes of silver light at the blue behemoth before resolving into a warrior with two axes. The Risi's left arm and neck were suddenly bisected.

Blue blood rained down on them both.

"Gross." Felix grimaced, then smiled at the warrior. "Hi, I'm Felix."

The warrior grunted and flicked his two axes, wicking the blood off them and onto the ground. They wore a strange frog-mouth helmet, and it made them look like a medieval murderbot a little bit. Felix's palms started to sweat as they tilted their head, looking up. Felix followed their eyes, seeing Vessilia leaning over the edge in surprise.

"He with you?" The murderbot's voice was surprisingly deep and raspy. Vessilia nodded.

"Yes! He helped me, Harn!"

The murderbot (Harn, he supposed) grunted and turned back toward the battle. "You helping us, too, little mage?"

Felix swallowed. "That's the idea." Harn nodded and started running toward the next giant.

Felix followed, excitement rising unbidden.

CHAPTER THIRTY-TWO

"Help them, mage," Harn pointed at the flippy girl and the mage, who was just getting to his feet. The shield warrior was helping to steady him, and Felix noticed an empty glass vial in her hand.

Healing potions? Maybe I can get some refills.

"What about you?"

The man cracked his neck, small overlapping plates allowing his weird helmet to flex. "I'll be keeping this one busy."

Felix nodded, checking his Mana.

He was still over 80%. More than enough, probably.

Felix started running toward the giant, moving as fast as he could. The lightly-armored young woman was fighting alone at this point, the mage still orienting himself as he passed by at speed. The shield warrior and mage gave him a strange look, but Felix didn't bother with them yet.

"Magda! Let's do this!" Harn called, apparently to the shield warrior.

The giant was fighting in a section of the ruined city that had several remnant walls and columns. The agile fighter was weaving in and out of them, trying to stay one step ahead of the powerful creature.

Analyze

Health: 344/890

Stamina: 210/488
Mana: 15/75

Felix reached out a hand and formed shadow Mana, Fire Within on blast as he shaped the Mana internally. The twists of Shadow Whip were strange to him, not as complex as Stone Shaping perhaps, but weirder somehow. The Mana pattern felt sticky and pervasive, yet tightly compacted in a way that made him briefly dizzy. Shaking his head, he dropped his attempt and kept it simple. Once he was within range, he activated the Skill as normal.

Shadow Whip!

A tendril of darkness latched outward, tangling up the giant's legs. It was like a spider web, tacky to the touch and shining dully in the moonlight.

The giant, who was running toward the young woman, stumbled and fell to its knees.

Shadow Whip is level 12!

At the same time, the young woman with black hair flung her chain around a column, tightening it and somehow slingshotting herself around it, throwing her up into the air above the giant. The chain unraveled, pulling back into her grip as she fell like a rock onto the giant's back. The chain, which he now noticed was definitely bladed, looped around their head with a quick flick of her arm, and Felix saw her grin.

It was a manic, irrepressibly gleeful sort of grin.

Then he was at the giant himself, who reared back, suddenly leashed by the small woman on his back and shoulders. Taking the opening, Felix wound up a Corrosive Strike, blasting the Risi Warrior right in the gut. The armor dented, and the giant doubled over even as the woman on its back started choking it.

The giant slammed its hands around, smashing into the ground and throwing Felix off into a wall. The wall cracked, and the ice on it sheared off in large sections.

Armored Skin is level 15!

+1 VIT

"Uugh." His Health and Stamina were both down below 60%.

Wobbling, he got back up.

The chain fighter was hanging off the giant's back, who was now on its feet and smashing blindly into ruined pillars.

Felix ran back in, this time directing dual Acid Streams at the blue skinned warrior. His acid ate into its exposed flesh, burning it with an audible sizzling.

"UGH! That smells terrible!" The warrior gagged and did a running leap over a ruined wall, yanking her chains backwards with her. Using the wall as a fulcrum, she leveraged the giant back as it flailed his arms at the chain tightening around its neck.

Felix dropped his Acid Stream and darted forward, throwing Corrosive Strikes as fast as he could into the giant's center mass. After the fifth shot, its breastplate fell apart. It swung at him, but it was simple enough to dodge back, then close again. Three more strikes, and its ribs gave way with a crack. After the twelfth shot, the giant's eyes rolled back into its head and it collapsed.

Corrosive Strike is level 16!
Corrosive Strike is level 17!
Corrosive Strike is level 18!
Physical Conditioning is level 19!

The chains suddenly tightened and cut into the Risi Warrior's neck, half decapitating the monstrous giant.

A Risi Warrior is dead!
XP Earned!

"Not a fan of that." Felix blanched as he saw clearly into the creature's ruined neck meat. A leather-clad blur flipped up and over the wall, landing in a perfect gymnastic dismount next to him. She turned to him, pulling her hair out of her face.

"Hi! I'm Evie!" She beamed, her rounded face appearing younger than he suspected. The girl flicked her forearm, and her spiked chain unraveled from the corpse. A second flick wrapped it back around her own arm. She had pale skin, green eyes, and straight black hair that hung from a convoluted braid around the crown of her head. "Who are you?"

"Evie! Your help, if you please!" Vessilia's proper voice shouted out from nearby.

Felix looked at Evie and shrugged. "Time to go, I guess." He headed toward the voice.

Evie followed after. "It's just so weird to see someone out here! How long have you been fighting these things?"

"Uh," Felix ducked under a low column. "Like a half hour?"

"Ahh!"

Vessilia landed before them, holding the mage in her arms, who was covered in a layer of frost. The slender mage pushed Vessilia away from him.

"Enough! I'm not a child!"

"You need to stay back here," Vessilia said, looking back toward the cloud of smoke and debris she had just escaped. She had found a spear somewhere, eight feet long and entirely made of metal. "That leader is extremely powerful. Not even you could take it alone, Ser Nevarre."

Felix felt their eyes orient on him, but he was too busy trying to pierce through the smoke cloud. Silvery sparks and flashes of purple-white Mana flared and faded, and the sounds echoed of at least...three people moving and grunting in combat.

"Damn this fog! I can barely see my feet, let alone the giants. How many are there?" Atar's hand lit on fire as he raised it up, as if it were a torch. "It sounds like an army!" Felix looked at him, askance.

Fog? He looked around. *What fog?*

"Put that out! You'll draw their attention!" Evie snapped.

"No need to worry about that," Felix said, refocusing on the dust cloud. It was like watching a cartoon fight; he could only occasionally catch glimpses of the white axe or metal bodies. "There's only one left." He nodded toward the cloud.

Do I just...wait here? Those two seem extremely capable. Felix mulled it over and shook his head. There was no point in risking his life here...

"How do you know there is only one left?" Evie asked him. Felix started, not realizing she had gotten so close.

"Hm? Oh, I don't see any others? Plus, there were only four on the field when we arrived. Your shield warrior killed one of them, murderb—Harn killed another, and you and I killed the last."

"Fah, you fool," scoffed the mage. "Four? There were at least a dozen attacking us! Each of my Sparkbolts found unharmed targets with every cast!"

"I'm pretty sure your *Spark*bolt wasn't doing much except annoying them, Sparky," Evie said with a smile.

The mage—*Sparky? Was that really his name?*—scowled. *Ah, probably not.*

"I am the best fire mage in all of Te'thys!" Sparky was apoplectic, a vein in his forehead pulsing against his mussed coif of blond curls.

Felix tuned them out as they continued to bicker. He flexed his Manasight, trying to watch the battle and see if he needed to run away or not. Those two seemed powerful, but if they got overwhelmed...no way was he handling an enemy like that alone.

Crescents of glowing purple-white light flashed and slashed across his senses, followed quickly by muted yellow orbs of light and silvery shimmers of metal. The attacks and defense and retaliations came thick and fast, with a Skill he likely couldn't match by a long shot.

They must be above Apprentice Tier, right? What's that called? What kind of bonuses—

There was an immense flash of purple white and the dust was blown away. Moments later, an arctic gale roared past them, frost growing in its wake. Felix crouched forward, feeling it sap his strength as he leaned into the sub zero wind, barely able to keep his feet. The others weren't so lucky.

"Waagh!" Metal clattered behind him ,and Felix turned to see Evie and Vessilia both falling back. The mage however, still coated in frost, suddenly ignited in a layer of orange flame. As if given new strength, he stood up against the gale and spread his arms wide. An aura of heat bloomed around him, nullifying the chill winds.

"You can't...defeat...Atar V'as!" The mage struggled as the winds grew briefly stronger, his flames guttering but still burning.

Then, just as suddenly as it began, it was over.

Felix looked back toward the fight, expecting to see a slain giant, but only saw a metallic shape fast approaching.

"Down!"

Felix tackled the still-burning mage and brought him down to the ground. Just in time; the massive shape of Harn rocketed past, shattering several stone walls as he blasted through. The fire covering the mage burned him mercilessly for only a moment before it extinguished.

Fire Resistance is level 14!

Felix stood up, pulling the surprisingly thin mage to his feet as well. "You okay, man?"

The fire mage seemed a little punch drunk, his burning man routine and knockdown taking a lot out of him. "I—I'm fine."

"We need to get out of here. That thing is too strong," Felix said as the two women stood up as well. Their armor was rimed with frost.

"Maggie can handle it," Evie said, her tone confident though her voice still unsteady. That frost had been nasty. Some sort of Stamina-sapping Skill?

"Is Harn alright?" Vessilia asked, steadying herself on her spear. Ice cracked and broke off her pauldrons as she moved. "I cannot see where he landed."

Felix glanced back, clearly seeing the armored warrior rising from the rubble a mere sixty feet away. Ice had accumulated on his armor too, much more than a thin layer. Felix looked at Vessilia, who was still squinting in the slightly wrong direction.

Can they not see? I thought it was some sort of sight Skill but maybe...maybe something is blocking—

Roar!

The sound was deep and sharp, as if a cave had teeth. Felix whipped back toward the fight and saw the shield warrior barely keeping the monstrous leader in check. The giant was easily twice the size of the others, with the Strength that came with it. She used her shields masterfully, somehow deflecting attacks and taking blows that would have reduced his bones to dust. She wasn't particularly fast, but damn, she was precise. And tough.

Her Endurance and Vitality must be sky high to tank that kind of assault. I want to help, but I'd get creamed if I waded in there...

"Hey, punch mage," a gruff voice came from behind. Harn had walked up, ice still falling from his strange armor. He pointed at the fight. "You comin'?"

"Punch mage?" Felix asked. *Makes me sound like a concessions magician.* "Uh, you need my help?"

The murderbot glared at him. At least, it felt like that to Felix. "C'mon. Now."

Harn walked past them, thick ice still coating much of his armor. Felix glanced at Vessilia and followed.

"Where in Siva's name did you find *him*?" Evie whispered.

Felix didn't hear the reply, not that he couldn't. His Perception was high enough that it would have been easy. But it was embarrassing, he found, hearing others talk about him. He walked swiftly away.

"How long?"

"Sorry?" Felix asked.

"How long have you been fighting out here?" Harn kept walking, not even looking at him.

"Two weeks or so," Felix estimated. He'd lost time under the mountain, he wasn't sure how much.

"Ever fight something like this?" The massive giant jumped onto the shield warrior's glowing magic shield, causing it to flare with power. The jump actually brought it into Felix's Analyze range, finally.

Name: Unknown Risi Commander
Type: Giantfolk
Level: 35
HP: ????/????
SP: ????/????
MP: ???/???
Lore: Giantfolk are known for their great strength, boundless stamina, and poor intelligence. But there are always exceptions. The Commanders are uncommonly intelligent and excellent tacticians, in addition to their physical might.
Strength: Strength, Endurance
Weakness: Unknown

"Uh," Felix gulped. "No. Sorta. Does a giant weasel count?"

Hoarse laughter echoed from Harn's frog-mouthed helmet. "You've got more ranged spells than that lightning one?"

Lightning? Oh, he means Reign of Vellus. "Yeah, a couple."

He nodded, raising his twin axes. *When had he gotten those out again?* "I'll go in there, cover my approach."

"Wait, how—"

Harn took off, kicking the ground and launching himself forward.

He's pretty fast. Was it his Strength or Agility that did that? Felix mused, but as the armored man approached, the Risi Commander spun away from his assault. They swung that massive ice axe as they did, and a sudden flurry of icicles filled the sky, launching in the path of their strike.

Reign of Vellus!

Felix had no intention of moving all of those icicles, some of which were the size of his entire body. Instead, he altered the pattern of the spell and focused on the narrow corridor containing Harn and himself. A spike of pain lanced across his head as azure lightning sparked and jumped between frosty spears and several dozen were acted on all at once. Felix strained, sweat beading on his brow, the icicles speeding toward Harn first and Felix second.

"Yrrraagh!" Felix screamed, blood pouring down his nose as his Mana drained. A storm of lightning erupted all around him, and the icicles shifted slightly to either side of both Harn and himself. Icy spears struck the ground all around him like bullets. Their impact shook the earth, splintering the stone itself and cleaving into the ruins all around him.

Fire Within is level 27!

Reign of Vellus is level 26!

"Gah!" Felix panted, gulping big breaths as a headache mounted behind his eyes. That one had drained him. His Mana was down to less than 30%, but if he used it properly, it'd be enough. He hoped.

Meanwhile, Harn kept running. The metal bastard never stopped, turned out. Whether that was because he had faith in himself or Felix was uncertain, though Felix was sure it was the former. The axe warrior kept leaping powerfully forward, the earth splintering beneath his feet, his body low and weapons extended to either side. The shield warrior, Magda, suddenly dropped the yellow-colored magic shield she had been maintaining all this time and rushed forward. Somehow, Felix couldn't tell how exactly, Magda's shield bashed the Risi Commander from a dozen feet away, throwing the massive blue bastard onto their backfoot.

Harn kept running, drawing closer and closer.

The giant wasn't a fool, though. With a roar, they slammed their immense axe down into the ground and a twenty foot wall of ice spikes erupted from the pitted causeway. It instantly cut Harn off from the battle between Magda and the Commander. Repeated impact resounded from the other side.

Shit. Can that lady survive long enough for Harn to get over this wall? The warrior had started violently attacking the wall with his axes, but aside from a slew of ice chips, the wall seemed unharmed. *Can't lift him, but maybe...*

Stone Shaping!

Altering his Mana flow in the pattern he'd previously discovered, Felix was able to keep the spell more efficient. But he needed speed too; so Felix dumped nearly 100 Mana into the spell and *pushed.*

From beneath a startled Harn, a stone ramp exploded forward at an angle, shearing through the top portion of the ice wall. Harn rode atop it, wobbling as he kept his balance, but by the time it stopped growing, he was already running up its length. At the top, he vaulted over the last ice spikes and landed somewhere beyond the wall with a deafening BOOM.

Felix ran forward, unable to see any of the action. As amazing as spellcasting was, he couldn't do anything if he couldn't see anything. He awkwardly navigated up the rough stone ramp, stopping just shy of tumbling off the edge. Beyond stood the massive giant, currently in a fierce altercation with Magda and Harn. In fact, Harn was trading serious blows with the Risi Commander, coming away from them the worse for wear.

"Step back!" Magda shouted, throwing several fist-sized stones at the giant. They each exploded on contact, sending a sharp rain of shrapnel in all directions. Harn and Magda covered their faces, and the giant commander flinched back, but then they returned to swinging their axe.

Felix had an idea. He waved frantically at the shield warrior until she looked up at him. She seemed surprised to see someone else there at all. Felix exaggeratedly pantomimed looking at the ground beneath her. She glanced down, and Felix began to cast.

All around Magda, the ground erupted into irregularly-shaped columns, each four to five feet tall and six inches in diameter at least. Shaping the stone at such a distance was painful, and it ate away at the majority of his Mana pool, leaving him with barely 5%. Felix's nose started bleeding again, the coppery taste creeping into his mouth. He gave a tired thumbs up to the shield warrior and sat down.

Stone Shaping is level 24!

Magda hesitated a moment before snapping off the nearest column and throwing it, javelin style, straight at the giant.

"Stone Break!"

The five-foot stone exploded, littering the Risi Commander's back with lacerations. They snarled in pain, half-turning from Harn, who was assaulting them from the front. That was a mistake. The heavily-armored warrior exploded with ferocity, swinging his axes like a machine of death, drawing gouts of thick blue blood with each strike.

"*Raaaargh! Akta ra foluu!*" The Risi screamed, their white beard dyed blue as they spat blood.

Harn roared back, spinning like a whirling dervish, driving the giant backwards even as two more stone spears exploded at their back. The giant threw themself into a forward roll, smashing violently against the earth and nearly pancaking Harn. They recovered, spinning on the two warriors and brandishing their weapon.

"Korta jav riktanu, tor atta!" the Risi Commander growled, their voice so deep Felix could feel it in his chest. A haze of purple white began to gather on the icy greataxe they wielded, congealing around it like stormclouds of Mana. Felix glanced at the others, but they only stared down their opponent, using the moment to rest.

"Hey, Harn," Magda spoke as she rolled her shoulders.

"Yeah, Maggie?"

"Do you speak asshole?" she asked. The Risi snarled, hands tightening on the shaft of their weapon with an audible creak.

"No, can't say that I do," Harn replied lazily.

Magda grinned, her teeth very white and perfectly straight. "Good. I'd hate for anyone to say we didn't try." The two of them advanced as one, rushing across the cracked causeway.

CHAPTER THIRTY-THREE

"Rokta fo valla, humans," the giant snarled, their voice suddenly dipping into English. *Or whatever they call English here. Wait, is it English? Or am I speaking another language?*

Magda and Harn didn't stop running, though they shared a look.

"You have come too late, prey. We are nearly finished." The giant continued, their arms never lowering that two-handed axe.

"Too late for what?" Magda laughed. "You're already dead, frostborn!"

Felix could just barely sense it, powerful swirls of purple-white Mana and a familiar crimson congealing along the edge of the Risi Commander's axe. A shimmering blade, conjured from Mana, nearly invisible.

He wasn't sure what was about to happen, but it wasn't going to be good.

Influence of the Wisp!

Blue-white fire flickered around Felix before it guttered out.

No Effect

Shit!

The giant was already swinging. Magda and Harn were within ten feet of the giant, too close to dodge, going too fast to stop.

Reign of Vellus!

Felix poured the pitiful remains of his Mana into the spell, yanking upward with all of his mental might. He twisted his body, too, muscles straining as he fought against the incredible weight and inertia of the icy weapon.

The greataxe and the Mana blade at its end tilted ever so slightly up.

With an explosion of crimson and purple light, a blade made of bloody ice screamed through the air. It tore across the thoroughfare, neither air nor stone ruin giving any impediment to its furious speed. The edge traveled for nearly 100 yards, shearing straight through several buildings before it dissipated into purple-white vapor.

Still not stopping, Magda and Harn moved through the giant's body as if he weren't there, blunt force and slashing trauma shattering limbs. The giant recoiled, losing their grip on the weapon as it pulled back. A solid, powerful kick from Harn sent them tumbling backward. Barely able to stand, the giant looked drained of something vital. Their cheeks were hollow beneath their stained beard, and their eyes were dull.

Without another word, the Commander fell to the ground, their body shattering like ice.

An Unknown Risi Commander is dead!
XP Earned!

You Have Received A Quest!

An Incursion of Risi - The giants are descending from the Hoarfrost, threatening your home. Find out their purpose and eliminate them before they achieve it.
Purpose 0/1
Risi Killed 5/500
Reward: Title, Varies

Accept?
Yes/No

Felix's eyes bulged at the sudden prompt, his eyes zeroing in on the most important number.

There are 495 more of these guys?

He fell back onto his ass, legs suddenly weak. Felix dismissed the quest notification without choosing an answer, resolving to worry about that later. Lying down and taking a good long rest was all he wanted right now.

And of course, that's when he heard the sound of approaching footsteps.

"Punch mage? You alive up there?" The voice was slightly strained, but he couldn't mistake the raspy voice.

"Yeah, still alive," Felix mumbled, rubbing his eyes.

"Good. Come down. We have questions," Harn added. Part of Felix rankled at the tone. He wasn't being asked, he was being ordered. With an effort of will, he shrugged that off and stood up. His head throbbed, but not as bad as before. After 10 seconds, his Mana was already back up to 5%.

Felix half slid, half walked down the crude stone ramp he'd made, a portion of his mind marveling at that fact. The rest of his thoughts were turned toward meeting all of these people outside of combat. What was he going to say to them?

Hello. I'm from another planet, and I have no idea what's going on. Also I'm human. Or I was. Before. On the alien world that I mentioned...?

Felix palmed his face, groaning. *This is impossible.*

By the time he came down the ramp, most of the adventurers had gathered together. Felix approached them cautiously, noticing how they all grouped themselves. Evie and Vessilia stood together, the former whispering something to the latter that Felix couldn't make out. Atar sat on an overturned column, head in his hands, but looked up as Felix stepped forward. At the fore, the large-framed Magda and heavily-armored Harn stood like powerful sentinels. Surprisingly, Harn had a giant axe made of ice hanging across his shoulders, though it seemed...reduced somehow.

"Uh, hi," Felix managed a small wave. For the first time in a while, he was acutely aware of the state of his clothing. His tunic was just a collection of rags at this point, and his pants were torn up to the knees. His hair was a shaggy mess that stuck out in all directions, and he had at least two weeks of un-groomed facial hair.

"Who are you, and why are you here?" The shield warrior stepped forward, her face only partially visible through her half-helm. She looked like a viking mixed with a brick house, physically huge and topping him easily by half a foot.

"I'm Felix and I, uh live out here." Felix decided to lie, unsure whether he'd be believed or branded as crazy for claiming to come from another world. He could always revise his story once he figured this all out.

Acting is level 6!

Magda raised her eyebrow, visible through her helm's protection. "Live? For how long?"

"How long? Well, it feels like my whole life—"

"We can chat later," Harn interrupted, looking off into the distance. "More are coming. We need shelter."

Felix swiveled in the same direction, suddenly hearing the stomp of large feet and light clatter of metal armor. When he turned back, all five of the adventurers were moving down the shattered lane. He hesitated as they walked away, unsure if he should call out or ask permission to follow them.

Then Vessilia turned and beckoned him. "Are you coming, Ser Nevarre?" Magda snorted but kept moving. Vessilia smiled at Felix's reluctance. "They are good people, I assure you. And we will all be safer together."

Felix rubbed the back of his neck and let himself be led away.

Maybe this will work out.

"I don't trust him," Magda whispered, glancing back at the strange man who followed them. His footsteps were eerily quiet as they navigated the iced over cobbles in the city ruins, and his eyes...

"Seems capable," grunted Harn, stepping over a fallen column.

"Too capable," agreed Magda. "I saw him run at that Risi Warrior faster than Evie, and she's specialized in Agility. And his *bare-fist* punches were putting dents in iron armor. He might not be as strong as you, but he's up there."

Magda squinted into the dark, thick fog weeping across their path. She knew it was around here somewhere.... "He's not even Tempered yet, and is out here alone? Why? You know how hard it is to get out here...unless he had help."

Harn shrugged, still apparently nonplussed. "C'mon, Maggie. He's probably some noble brat who lost his retinue. We've seen the type, hell, we *have* the type now." He stepped forward and placed a hand on his friend's shoulder. "You need to calm down. This Cassie situation has got you all tense. Let's make camp and plan from there."

Magda and Harn stared at each other for a few seconds, years of teamwork and communication bridging the gap between them, giving even silences a deep meaning. Old words and old thoughts wore comfortable ruts between them.

"Your helmet is stupid," she muttered, for perhaps the thousandth time.

Harn barked a laugh and walked off.

Traversing the shadowy city was a lesson in quiet terror. Felix crept beside Vessilia and the pale mage, trying to stay quiet and unseen in the looming darkness. The bones of a once prosperous city were all around, mostly toppled and cracked, with heavy evidence of nature crawling back among them. Carpets of wild grasses emerged from between sunken cobbles and flowering stalks covered in night-closed blooms spread across tumbled walls. It would have been picturesque, were it not for the occasional thump-clatter of large creatures moving in the distance.

Giants.

They weren't being followed, not really. It only appeared that way because there were 495 of them moving in clumps all around the ruins. But then...maybe they *were* gathering together? Maybe the movements were organized and these eight-foot-tall behemoths were drawing them all into a trap?

Breathe. Get a grip. Felix clenched his jaw and focused, steadying his mind. Fortress walls rose in his mind's eye, a dozen feet tall and half that thick. His fears flailed themselves against it, exhausting their power over him.

Bastion of Will is level 27!

It was easier after that.

The path they took was fairly straightforward, though their

leader Magda led them on a confusing trail. Twice they went down the same alley, and there was a particular minaret he'd seen at least four times. It was obvious she was avoiding the giants' ice, but something else seemed to bother her. Much like Vessilia, Magda would often squint into the distance. He still couldn't figure out why, and it was nagging at him. But after fifteen minutes or so, they came upon a set of stairs into the ground which led to a thick iron door. Magda opened it with a solid yank and remarkable lack of noise.

As they piled in, Felix felt a small surge of anxiety. Confused a moment, he quickly realized it didn't belong to him; *Pit* was upset. Casting his eyes about and following the warmth in his chest, Felix spotted a dark shape near the top of a nearby fallen cathedral. He wasn't sure what else all of the towers and complicated buttresses could be. Pit was nestled between the eaves of the fallen roof. Making eye contact, Felix tried to convey a sense of calm.

Just hold on, buddy. Stay safe.

He turned around and ducked into the open door. Harn gave him a strange look as he came in, looking outside behind him before securing the portal.

The building above had collapsed so long ago that several trees were growing in the remnants, and as he entered the subterranean space, several thick roots coiled across an earthen ceiling. Using his Manasight, Felix gauged the room around them. Dusty brown earth Mana predominated, along with thick wisps of smoky gray shadow. Most surprisingly, the roots above them shone with a green-gold radiance that slowly pulsed along their lengths, like a heartbeat of summer sunlight. It was honestly delightful, and Felix smiled as he enjoyed their light.

Thump!

Felix's eyes snapped open, abruptly reminded that he was among strangers. His hand was at his waist before he recognized that Magda had slammed her pack down onto the ground.

"Same as usual. No fire, no light. Never know what might leak out. I'll set up the wardstones, and we can get some rest." She fished a number of strange blue orbs from her pack and started placing them around the room. Felix was immediately curious, but with a narrow-eyed glance from Magda, he kept his distance. Once the last orb was placed, the shield warrior muttered something under her breath, something that, despite his enhanced Perception, he could not make out. It was all echoes and distortion. All at once, the orbs lit up from within, casting bright blue designs on the walls that twisted and converged, becoming a singular ring of mystical glyphs.

I know these shapes, he realized as he picked out the various sigils he had seen before. *Wardstones, she called them. That is seriously cool.*

The sigils blazed on the walls a moment longer before seemingly sinking into them and disappearing.

"Where have you been sleeping?"

"Gah," Felix replied, surprised again to find the girl Evie so close. *How does she keep doing that?* She regarded him with bright green eyes that almost glowed in the dark. *Weird.*

"Um, in trees, mostly," he said, taking a step back away from the enthusiastic girl.

"Trees?" She made a face and stepped away from him. "One of those sickly, diseased things? Eugh!"

Felix furrowed brow and squinted. "No, nothing like that...most recently, it was an evergreen tree, called a Rodan Pine. Nothing special really, just tall enough so most beasts wouldn't notice me."

"What about flying monsters? We've seen a few gnarly things, like the ones with four wings sharp as swords."

"It—" A chill raced down Felix's back, his mind casting back to the Razorwing Skinks. "They haven't—as long as you keep out of their territory, they'll leave you alone."

Jangling metal and heavy footsteps drew his attention away from Evie as both of them turned toward the approaching Magda. She had taken off her helm, revealing a dirt-stained face and sweat-mussed sandy brown hair, cut short at her ears. Her jaw worked soundlessly, clenching and unclenching as she watched the two speak. Focusing on Felix, she grunted. "You, it's time to start answering some questions."

Evie adroitly slunk back, moving out of the line of fire. Felix turned fully toward their leader and nodded, a flutter of apprehension in his guts.

"Sure. What do you want to know?" The others gathered around them, sitting or standing as they listened in. Harn stood near the door, helmet off and tucked under an arm. He had a squarish face covered in scars, and his expression was lazily disinterested. *Does he practice that look?*

Magda leaned forward with a creak, the smell of sweat and

leather and cold metal wafting toward Felix. "Where are your people?"

"Uh, I don't have people," Felix swallowed, thinking briefly about home. "I'm alone out here."

"How?"

"How, what?"

"How do you survive? You're, what? Level fifteen? You can't have more than a handful of Skill levels." Magda gave him a once-over that was surprisingly embarrassing considering the state of his clothes.

"Nineteen, actually. Just hit that yesterday."

"Us as well. Though we've been stuck at level 19 for several months..." Evie gave Magda a look that Felix couldn't entirely parse. It reminded him of the way his little sisters would needle him when they were younger. For her part, Magda ignored it.

"What have you been doing out here?" Magda asked.

"Exploring, I guess you'd say. I've even got a Skill for it." Felix was kinda proud of that one. Didn't even have to lie, not really, though his Acting Skill didn't level. A downside of being truthful, or being himself? *Wow that's a dangerous rabbit-hole to wander down.*

Magda was still talking."That *is* strange. Exploring is usually a Henaari Skill. You don't look particularly Henaar. Too short."

"So I've been told," Felix laughed. "Despite your obvious distrust of me, this is really nice. You're the first people I've spoken to since...in a long time."

"Since when?"

"Do monsters count?" That brought her up short, for some reason. Magda suddenly loomed closer.

"Explain."

The gut-flutters increased, and Felix shrugged. "There was a monster, a giant weasel thing called an Orit; he spoke. Didn't have anything nice to say, so I don't really count him."

"Interesting." Magda sat back, mouth turned up at the corners. "So, mini farwalker: have you explored this area?"

"No, I just got here. I had heard there was a city here...didn't know it was a ruin."

"Of course it's a ruin. Hasn't been anything in the Foglands since the third age," added Evie, who was across the small chamber and stuffing her face with some sort of biscuit.

"How silly of me," Felix deadpanned, then brightened. He was determined to make the best of this. "But at least I found you folks."

"So, you haven't seen any other humans?"

"No you're the first, but I just got here. Do you expect to find others in the city?"

"Not sure we could find anything with this blighted fog," muttered Atar, rubbing his arms as if cold. *Maybe he has low Vitality? Or just not enough meat on his bones. He's pretty spindly.*

Wait.

"The what-now?" Felix asked. This wasn't the first time he'd heard mention of it, and even Balfur's memories featured a heavy fog he still hadn't experienced.

Magda looked at him, eyebrow raised. "He said the fog. You should know, being out here so long. It's murder on Perception and fouls even the best tracking."

"What fog?" he asked. This time, everyone looked at him in varying degrees of confusion. "Wait, is that why you all keep squinting?"

"What do you mean, 'what fog?'" Magda asked, slowly.

"I mean, I didn't see any sort of fog. It was a clear night out tonight."

Magda rocked back on her heels, face clouded.

Should I have kept that to myself?

Abruptly, terrible howls echoed into the night. The sound pierced from outside, muffled but unmistakable.

"Those sound...big," noted Vessilia, her hand already holding her spear.

Ice crackled, and in the dim light of the wardstones, trails of frost began to form along the ceiling. They gleamed purple-white in his Manasight. Shortly thereafter, the howling faded off into the distance.

"Noctis wept," cursed Magda.

Noctis? God, I'm gonna run out of pages in my notebook for all these questions.

"Hoarhounds," rasped Harn, a grimace crawling across his face.

"Hoarhounds? Here?" Atar gasped, eyes wide in the dim blue light of the wardstones. "First giants and now hoarhounds? What is going on here? Why would they stray so far from the north?"

"Why indeed," Magda muttered, and her eyes lingered on Felix for more than a moment. Then she turned back to her bedroll, already laid out, somehow. "Get some rest. Harn'll take first watch, then me, Evie, and then Atar."

"Aw, beans," Evie muttered, already bundling herself up in her thick woolen blanket. Atar also looked peeved, but didn't say anything, only rolling over with a *humph*.

Settling back against the softest rock he could find, Felix found himself too worried to be tired. Pit was out there with what sounded like giant wolves. Wait, no, giant *ice* wolves. Felix was a worrier by nature, and this grated at his mind.

"He will be safe," said a soft voice.

Felix turned to see Vessilia half-sitting on her bedroll, watching him. She was very well lit in his Manasight, the soft blue water Mana of the wardstones underlighting her sharp features.

"Who?"

"Your...friend."

Felix smiled. "Thanks. I'm sure he will, but I can't help but worry." Vessilia laughed, a deep throaty chuckle he didn't expect. "What?"

"You remind me of someone."

"And that's funny?"

"It would be if you knew them." Then she rolled over and, apparently, went to sleep.

Felix sat up for a while longer, mind turning over, not because he had fallen in with aliens from another world or because their leader seemed to distrust him entirely.

Nope.

It was because he wasn't sure if he had just gotten dunked on or not.

CHAPTER THIRTY-FOUR

Felix woke with a start.

It was dark, cramped, and unpleasantly moist. For a few frantic moments, he couldn't remember where he was or how he'd gotten there. Visions of four-way jaws, of buzzing wings, and the far-off feel of twisting tentacles pushed at him, scraping at his sanity before suddenly disappearing. The dark walls of a powerful fortress reared for a moment in his mind, shearing the impressions off at the base. Calmer, Felix looked around.

The dim blue light of the wardstones revealed the sleeping forms of his new...associates? Certainly not friends, not yet. They didn't trust him enough. For his part, he wasn't entirely sure he trusted them. There were currents here he didn't understand, and though he was excited to finally see people, he was wary.

Wary had kept him alive so far.

Sitting up, Felix's stomach grumbled. They had passed around some basic rations before they all turned in, so at least he wasn't starving, but it was hardly filling. Salted and dried meat followed bricks of bread-like food that were harder than most rocks. Chewing it was a challenge, let alone swallowing it. Putting aside his stomach, Felix wiped off a slight sheen of sweat and fanned himself. The temperature and humidity had climbed in the room, likely due to the press of bodies. So it boggled his mind when Felix saw most of them were bundled up in blankets.

They can't ALL have low Vitality. What if—

A thought occurred to him: the fog. The others had spoken of a persistent fog in the countryside, one that befuddled the senses. Maybe it was also chilly? But why could Felix neither see nor feel it? Curious, he flexed his Manasight.

Generally speaking, his Manasight was always on in some ways. He absently noticed the flow of what he had come to call Mana Vapor in just about everything, seeing it as though out of the corner of his eye. When he activated the Skill, that's when the depth came to the fore. At its current level, the Skill no longer inundated him with smoky Mana clouds, instead showing a refined world made of pulsing power.

The room around him was awash in the deep blue shimmer of water Mana, originating from the wardstones. These soaked into the dusty brown earth of the walls, tinting the shadow Mana with faint blue tones. That same green-gold light shimmered from above, evidence (he thought) of the life growing all around him, but pieces of it had gone dark while others had a faint touch of purple-white ice Mana.

So the Hoarhounds' power killed the plant-life. Makes sense. Crops can't survive an ill-timed frost.

He saw all of this, shimmering and shining in their various hues, but he saw no fog at all. At best, there was that faint, smoky haze he always saw when he used Manasight.

Wait. As Manasight leveled, I started to see in greater detail. But the haze hasn't gone away...

Felix narrowed his eyes, trying to focus on the literally ephemeral haze in his Manasight. It was like trying to watch one of those eye squiggles that drift across your vision, nearly impossible to actually pinpoint.

Floaters, that's what they're called. And if it behaves like that...

He stopped moving his eyes, instead focusing on the middle distance in front of him and letting that Mana haze drift around him. As it passed, he used his peripherals to inspect it, flexing his Manasight as best he could. For a long few minutes, there was nothing until...

What?

A flash of thin white mist, hanging low to the ground, there then gone in an instant.

Manasight is level 26!

"Huh, it *is* there."

"Muh? What?" He wasn't sure who spoke, but Felix ducked his head back down and pretended to be asleep. After a moment, soft snoring resumed.

Quietly, Felix checked on his Quests.

Quests
Advance Spells! 2 of 5 Apprentice Spells
Home Sweet Home! 1 of 5 Threats Eliminated
A Light In The Dark! 2 of 4 Remnants Found
An Incursion of Risi! 0 of 1 Purpose; 495 of 500 Risi

His spell quest was obviously his Fire Within Skill and Reign of Vellus. He was close with Stone Shaping and Acid Stream, too. Felix idly wondered what Title and reward he'd get for completing his first quest. Hopefully something useful.

Home Sweet Home and An Incursion of Risi he passed over. One was brand new, and the other hadn't changed since he last checked it. Plus, he was still a little ticked off at the system for giving him such monumental tasks.

Not that I HAVE to finish them...I think.

A Light In The Darkness had updated...and Felix didn't know why.

A Light In The Dark! 2 of 4 Remnants Found

I found the first one on the Seven Legged Orit...but I haven't killed anything like that since.

Felix felt around in his satchel, taking quick inventory of its scant remains: a torn waterskin, an empty potion case, the bright-weave coil, his beat-up notebook and grease-pencil, and a stack of loose papers. *Wait. The box Pit found...*

Pulling the cigar-box sized chest out of his satchel, Felix carefully set it onto his lap. He moved quietly, attempting not to rustle much and awaken his new associates. Slowly, he poked and prodded the lock on it, but was unable to find a latch or release anywhere obvious. Gently, Felix shook the box, hearing the soft thump of something moving inside.

Is that the other remnant? Maybe one of these adventurers knows how to pick a lock.

Using his Manasight, Felix could make out the locked box as having an exceedingly neutral aura to it. Compared to the vibrant colors all around him, it was a muddy rock on the ground, completely boring and unremarkable.

Well that's a dead giveaway. The remnant has gotta be in here.

Setting the box back into his satchel, Felix laid back and tried to sleep.

Sleep was elusive.

It was a couple more hours before everyone else woke up. Unable to let himself be idle, Felix spent the time Meditating as deeply as he could, searching for a way to level that Skill up even more. He had figured out that it was linked to harmony or harmonics, but what that actually meant was a mystery.

He dove deeper, trying to ignore all outside distractions and contemplate only the swirl and flow of his Mana channels. His Fire Within sat in his torso, slightly higher than his navel, spinning and flaring with various colors: flashes of electric blue, emerald green, bright gold, and even hints of black and crimson buried in the roiling light. The Mana spooled around his body in complicated loops and whorls like living light or phosphorescent water that gleamed as it moved, never settling and always circling back to his core. But, after hours of watching that interplay, he was still no closer to a single level up in Meditation.

Frustrated, he resurfaced to find most of the others already up and talking softly. When they saw him sit up, they all fell silent, then Magda spoke.

"Hold to the wardstones. They will last the day, and we will be back by nightfall." She nodded at the three trainees (*apprentices?*) and turned toward the exit.

The others all stood back, watching as both Magda and Harn hefted their weapons and cautiously exited the heavy iron door. Once it closed, Evie let out a frustrated sigh.

"Wait, they're leaving?" Felix asked as he stood up, a part of him still marveling at the lack of aches and pains he'd normally associate from sleeping on hard ground.

"Yes. They wish to scout the area first before we make any movements," Vessilia offered. "They are not sure how many giants have come south, and what their disposition is within the ruined city."

"They're leaving to have fun without us," grumped Evie.

"Again," agreed Atar, his flesh-colored mustache quivering in annoyance.

"Oh," Felix felt there was more history here than he cared to parse out. Then his head rocked back in alarm. "Oh no! I forgot to tell them! I know how many giants are in the city."

"What?" Evie shot upright.

"How?" Atar asked.

"I got a quest yesterday after we finished off the Risi Commander. It asked that I eliminate the remainder of the giants and find out why they're here," Felix said.

"A quest! And how many were there?" Evie was bouncing on the balls of her feet.

"500. 495 now."

Silence reigned in the small basement as the three trainees chewed over his words. Felix felt bad he hadn't mentioned it before, but so much was going on that it slipped his mind.

"Um...I suppose Lady Aren and Ser Kastor will be able to handle themselves," Vessilia haltingly began.

"Pff, she'll eat em and spit em out. That's not the point! We were supposed to have a proper adventure! Now they get all the fun, while we twiddle our thumbs." Evie grumped even harder this time, plopping onto her bedroll.

A high-pitched laugh rang out, one Felix was surprised belonged to Atar. It was almost musical despite its sour tone. "Never trust the Shieldwitch to involve us with anything. I mean, it's not like we *paid* to be here or anything."

Silence again, this time awkward and filled with things for which Felix had no context. Blowing a deep breath out, he turned to Vessilia, who was still staring at the door.

"So, ah, where are you folks from?"

God that sounds lame. He cringed inwardly. *It sounds like you're trying to pick her up.*

"Mm? Oh, we are from all over. I am from Pax'Vrell, Atar is from Te'thys, and Evie is from...Setoria, right?" Vessilia looked at her friend, who was currently balancing a small throwing dagger on her fingers.

"Sorta! I've lived the past five years in Setoria, but before that, me and Maggie have been all over. Bel Atol, Valspire, even spent a few months in Levantier." Evie spun the dagger and caught it neatly.

"Busy life," Felix observed. "That's a lot of places for someone who's only, what, seventeen years old?"

"Twenty, thank you very much. It is what it is," she added with a shrug.

"And where, exactly, are you from, Felix Nevarre?" Atar's reedy voice asked, so at odds with his laugh. "Don't think we didn't notice you evading that answer."

Felix smiled ruefully. *Jig is up, I guess.* "I come from far away, probably nowhere you recognize. But I've been in the Foglands for two weeks or so, trying to survive."

"You've been here alone, right?" Asked Evie, her eyes glowing a brighter green. Now that he thought about it, he looked between all of them. All of their eyes were glowing green.

"Yeah, it's been pretty rough." He cleared his throat. "Why are all of your eyes glowing green?"

"Oh? Ah yes, it is because of Nighteye," said Vessilia.

"What's that?"

"You don't know Nighteye? How do you see in the dark?" Atar scoffed.

"I don't? Are you saying Nighteye is a Skill that lets you see in the dark?" Felix was immediately interested.

"Yeah, it's a spell we got drilled into us when we joined the Guild. Every Guilder has Nighteye." Evie tapped the corner of her eye, her irises flaring with neon green.

"Oh cool, can you teach me?" Felix smiled, hands itching to try out a new spell.

"I don't think we can? Skills are hard to teach and learn. Usually takes a specialist trainer to pass them on. And besides, why waste a Skill slot on it when you don't have to? You seem to be doing fine, and most only get a couple dozen Skills our entire lives, ya know?"

It felt like a trap door beneath Felix's stomach dropped out, sending his guts into freefall. Only a couple dozen Skills? But what if he wanted to do more spells, or other cool tricks? Was he stuck with the mishmash of Skills he had stumbled upon?

No, that can't be right. Two dozen. That's way too low. Quickly, Felix pulled up his Skill list.

Skills:

Resistances: Acid Resistance (C), Level 20; Fire Resistance (C) Level 14; Heat Resistance (U), Level 14; Pain Resistance (U), Level 27; Poison Resistance (U), Level 17; Armored Skin (R), Level 15; Bastion of Will (E), Level 27

Utility: Acting (C), level 6; Analyze (C), Level 20; Improvisation (C), Level 4; Intimidation (C), Level 2; Running (C), Level 18; Stealth (C), Level 22; Swimming (C), Level 3; Tracking (C), Level 13; Breath Control (U), Level 16; Companion Pact (U), Level 11; Dual Casting (U), Level 13; Free Climbing (U), Level 13; Exploration (U), Level 16; Herbalism (U), Level 17; Meditation (U), Level 30; Make An Entrance (U), Level 3; Manasight (U), Level 26; Lessons of the Past (R), Level 9; Physical Conditioning (R), Level 19; Deep Mind (E), Level 24

Combat: Blunt Weapon Mastery (C), Level 3; Dodge (C), Level 24; Long Blade Mastery (C), Level 9; Parry (C), Level 1; Small Blade Mastery (C), Level 8; Staff Mastery (C), Level 1; Thrown Weapons Mastery (C), Level 10; Unarmed Mastery (C), Level 24; Acrobatics (U), Level 21; Corrosive Strike (R), Level 18; Blind Fighting (R), Level 18

Spells: Acid Stream (R), Level 22; Fire Within (R), Level 27; Influence of the Wisp (R), Level 21; Invocation (R), Level 1; Shadow Whip (R), Level 12; Stone Shaping (R), Level 24; Reign of Vellus (E), Level 26; Sigils of the Primordial Dawn (E), Level 3

I count 46 Skills already. There's no way two dozen is the limit. Did they mean more than two? Like three or four? Felix cleared his throat.

"So what if, hypothetically, someone had fifty Skills?"

Vessilia and Atar both laughed, though their intent seemed wildly different.

"That would be...unwise. A person only has so much time in a day to cultivate their Skills. Gaining and training that many, aside from the difficulty, would be hardly efficient or necessary. Most people claim there is an upper limit and stick to a core grouping. Something to do with the Human soul, at least according to the Priests of the Pathless," Vessilia mused.

"The Pathless is a false god, and your priests are jackanapes. My Master says that your spirit can only handle so much stress, and that each Skill has a multiplicative effect on straining the spirit. Once you've hit your limit, that's it," Atar said. "I cannot believe you don't know that. Who trained you, anyway?"

Felix ignored him, mind spinning furiously. *Well, one way to find out.*

"Can you teach me anyway?"

The next hour was filled with Evie and Vessilia trying (and failing) to teach him the Nighteyes Skill. Felix mechanically ate the hard-tack and jerky offered to him as Evie finished retelling the tale of her own learning experience.

"...and then he put me in a dark room with a bunch of Ratlings," Evie finished.

"No!" Vess gasped, hand over her mouth. "How did you get out?"

"By learning to see in the dark and killing them all." Evie shrugged, clearly not phased by it. "It was the same thing with most of my Skills: get into a stressful situation, line up the right prerequisites and mindset, and bam. Skill gain."

"That's...not very helpful," Felix winced.

"Well, I'm not a trainer, so there ya go," Evie rolled her eyes.

Felix pondered. The commonality in both of their stories was stress and need. He had neither in this particular situation, but that wasn't how he always gained Skills, either. There were a few times where he simply did a thing and learned it. Easy as breathing.

Or stole it from a monster, he amended. That was a bit of a cheat.

"Can you deactivate the Skill and reactivate it again? I'd like to see if I can notice anything."

"Um, sure," Vessilia said, her eyes going dark and unfocused. Felix realized that without the Skill she was blind in here. "Ready?"

"Go for it," Felix flared his Manasight while watching her eyes closely.

Something flickered in her eyes for a moment, then they burned a bright green. Vessilia flinched back.

"Ah-I, uh did not know you were so close." She looked flushed for some reason.

"Yeah, had to see the details," Felix said offhandedly. "Can you try it again?"

Swallowing, she nodded and deactivated the Skill. With a flicker, tendrils of Mana coalesced behind her eyes, spiralling up into her irises and causing that bright neon glow. But the how was eluding him.

"Ah dang, that's not giving me anything. Maybe I'll try your way, Evie."

"Sure, let me go find some rats." Evie smirked. "If you really want to learn it that bad, just join the Guild when we get back to Haarwatch. You've got skills, more than most Tin Ranks out there."

Felix leaned back, squeezing his eyes closed and rubbing the bridge of his nose. "Vessilia mentioned that before. Tin Rank. What does that mean?"

"It's a power rating. Guilders use it to determine who can do what missions or help with certain kinds of projects. Maggie says it reflects your 'poise under pressure, strength of arm, and solidity of mind.' Or something like that. I tend to tune her out when she starts sounding like a Guilder brochure," Evie smirked.

"So, it's all about getting more powerful to do more jobs to get more powerful?" Felix asked.

Evie touched the side of her nose and pointed at him. "He gets it."

"It is also about helping the less fortunate. Sheltering those without our gifts and abilities from threats. Monsters, rampages, incidents of all stripes." Vessilia had a gleam in her eyes that Felix hadn't seen before; it was like watching someone talk about their heroes.

"Huh," Felix grunted. *That's...really nice, actually. I can't believe it actually shakes out that way, though. Not all the time. Not unless humanity here is wildly different than back home.*

"So you're all out here to get stronger then? To rise in ranks?" Felix asked.

"We're *here*," spat Atar, joining in on the conversation for the first time in an hour. "So that we can Reveal our Omens and get some practical experience. Not that it's actually happening."

"Reveal your Omens? What—?" Felix began, but Evie interrupted him.

"Yeah, we *are* kind of young to attempt it, but that's only because we're just *that* good."

"The sooner we get our Omens, the more advantages we can accrue," added Vessilia. "A handful of extra levels with an Omen can make all the difference in a battle."

Felix didn't say anything, lost once again to contemplation. *They don't have their Omens revealed yet. They only have a few Skill slots. Why is my experience so different from theirs? Why did I start at level one with my Omen already revealed?* Despite his perfect recall, Felix itched again to jot this all down in his notebook for future reference. He'd have to manage it when they weren't looking so closely.

"So, is your Omen predetermined? Or do you pick it?" Felix asked, as innocently as he could manage.

"Pick it?" Atar asked, incredulous. "You don't *choose* your destiny, you *reveal* it."

"Yeah, an Omen is something you're born with, most folks agree. It's just you need high stress and violence to unlock it, usually," Evie added.

"Usually? Not all the time? Are some people just born with it revealed?"

"Haha! You mean like an Unbound?" laughed Evie. "That'd be wild, for sure."

Felix noticed Vessilia was suddenly uncomfortable. She opened her mouth a couple times before words came out. "Ah...Ser Nevarre, I was curious. How, exactly, did you receive the giant quest?"

"Oh uh, I just got it when the Risi Commander died. Popped right up." Felix mimed a box in front of him. "Why?"

Vessilia blushed again. *She must be really shy.*

"It is nothing, just a personal curiosity. They say that quests aren't given to just anyone. They are selective, and some claim the gods are the final arbiters."

"Gods?" Felix asked, uncomfortable with the idea of actual, literal gods existing.

"Ehhh," moderated Evie, waving her hand in the universal sign for "maybe." "Most people think it's about opportunity and novelty. Be the first to do such and such, the first one to see or go somewhere, that sort of thing. It's all chance. The gods...I love you Vess, but the gods don't mix into the lives of mortals. Not like the stories say, anyway."

"Pfhah! Blind pagans. You're both wrong," Atar said, so snidely that Felix wanted to kick him. "Your gods have no say in this world. Quests are by virtue of spirit alone! I'm sorry to say that you found the quest because you were worthy of it. That's all."

"Did your master spoon-feed you that bullshit, or was it more of a do-it-yourself thing?" Evie rolled her eyes.

"How dare you!" Atar leaped to his feet, fire sparking around his body as he did so. "My master is worth twelve Shieldwitches, make no mistake!" Fire continued to build around the mage as he spoke, until he blazed just as he did during the giant battle. The other two canceled their Nighteye spells as the mage lit up the entire room.

AwoooooooO!

The sound was distant, but pierced into their hideaway just the same. Everyone froze, and even Atar let his fire cloak Skill lapse. Shortly after, a gargantuan roar sounded out. It sounded *much* closer.

Felix looked at everyone. "What was that?"

"More giants?" Vessilia guessed.

"Definitely more giants. And at least one Hoarhound." Atar's voice was small in the sudden dark. Moments passed, quickly turning into minutes that dragged slower and slower. But no further sounds rang out.

"Okay, that's about all I can stand of that," Evie said as she stood up. Quickly gathering her supplies, she wrapped her spiked chain carelessly around her neck and shoulder. "I'm going out."

"What? Why? We were told to stay put," Vessilia objected, clearly not comfortable with the idea.

"Because it's boring here. And because my sister is hiding things from us. Why are we out here?"

"I thought you were out here to Reveal your Omens?" Felix asked, not quite sure what was going on.

"We could have Revealed them days ago. Maybe even been back in Haarwatch by now." Atar added, also standing up. "I've said it since the beginning, but the Shieldwitch has an agenda. I'm going, too."

Evie gave him a sour look, but didn't protest.

Vessilia gave Felix a look before standing herself. "I guess I have to go to keep you both out of trouble." She looked back at Felix.

"Are you coming, Ser Nevarre?"

"I told you, I'm not a Sir anything," Felix protested. Then he stood up and stretched. "But yeah. Let's do it. I was getting bored in here, anyway."

CHAPTER THIRTY-FIVE

They made it out onto the street quietly enough.

Since they didn't know how to deactivate the wardstones and weren't planning on straying too far, they simply walked out. Passing through the ward was awfully similar to passing through the rock-turned-liquid of his Stone Shaping spell; the air was thick like pudding, charged with a certain warmth, though it smelled distinctly of rain.

Petrichor, that's what it's called.

Thankfully, Felix was able to shift the door despite how heavy it appeared. It was a strain but not unmanageable. They filed out, and he closed the door again, making sure to lift slightly to prevent it from squealing. Felix caught Atar staring at him, his eyes green in the deep shadows. "What?"

Atar said nothing, just frowned and turned away.

Bemused, Felix strode past the haughty mage and stepped onto the uneven cobbles above. The street was empty, and the hollowed-out buildings leaned drunkenly together in places, deepening the shadows that covered them all. However, through gaping holes in the various facades, patches of blue sky and a bright sun streamed from the east. It was beautiful, like waking up in a new city. A city ruined for centuries and filled to the brim with murderous giants.

But still, he insisted to himself. *Blue sky, sunlight. Could be worse.*

He paused a moment, the edges of his smile fading. "Do you all still see the fog?"

Vessilia looked at him over her shoulder, eyebrow raised. "Yes? Do you—oh that is right! You said you do not!"

Evie eyeballed him again and made a point of looking around. "You blind? It's everywhere."

"Not to me. All I see is clear cobbles, dark alleys, and a bright blue sky."

"No way. Blue?" Evie craned her neck, looking up. "All I see is overcast grey. That's a good hallucination you've got. I'd kill for some real sunshine."

"It's not—" Felix started, but didn't feel it was worth it to continue. Maybe he was hallucinating. *I mean, this entire journey has been one bonkers thing after another. It'd make a certain kind of sense if I was tripping balls.*

He shook himself, unwilling to follow that thought. It led nowhere productive. Instead, Felix focused his Manasight, reveling at the sudden color and crispness everything around him attained. His sense of Mana flows had increased a lot since he began, and the morning sun (even when not shining directly onto him) seemed to amplify everything. The Mana haze still drifted atop of everything, floating everywhere across his vision without moving at all somehow. As before, he focused on the haze with his peripheral vision, willing himself to see beyond the obvious.

I know you're there. Show yourself...

Felix's Mana suddenly dropped, the blue bar in his vision losing about twenty percent as a thick cloud of white fog utterly pervaded his vision. As if the world was wrapped in white cotton, distances were difficult to perceive, sounds appeared muffled, and even the patches of sky above became monotonous shades of grey.

Holy shit. This *is what they see? How do they do* anything*?*

Something whirled above him, disturbing a layer of mist atop one of the ruined buildings. Felix turned, startled, but only got the impression of a dark form slipping away.

A bird?

The vision stuttered and crackled, quickly fading away into static on an old television. In seconds, it was gone.

It's an illusion! Right? Do those exist—?

Manasight is level 27!

...
Manasight is level 31!

Felix's eyes widened. He was right.

Evie clapped her gloved hands together, the sound soft and muted. "Ok, Felix. Do you have a sneaky Skill?"

"Mm?" Felix turned back toward the group, having made his way into the middle of the alley. "I have Stealth, yeah."

"Oh good! That's two of us. We'll have to account for the stompers over here."

"I do not stomp," argued Vessilia, her voice slightly exasperated. Then she tipped her head to the side, conceding the point. "But I am wearing heavier armor than you."

Atar, surprising no one, snorted in derision. "Stealth is a tool for liars and ruffians. Doesn't surprise me that *you'd* have it, Aren!"

"Cram it up your ass, flame boy," Evie said in a sing-song voice.

"Hey!" Felix hissed, spreading his hands out toward the both of them. "Cool it! Stealth does jack all if you're shouting."

An abrupt clatter sounded further down the alley, followed by the thumps of dislodged rubble, the rustle of scattered debris. They all froze in place. Felix heard the click of claws on stone. Evie slowly reached up toward her spiked chain, carefully gripping its end as she scanned the thick morning shadows. She nearly jumped out of her skin when Felix's hand suddenly clamped onto her own, keeping her from drawing her chain. She pushed as hard as she could, but she couldn't make his arm budge an inch.

"Don't. It's a friend," he said, already stepping forward; because while the others had to contend with the cloying fog, his vision could clearly make out the winged form of his four-legged Companion.

"Heya, Pit. Who's a good boy?" Felix leaned over and patted his legs, urging the tenku to run to him. Pit let out a happy chirrup as he accepted a couple scratches on the side of his head.

"Yyero's blighted ass! That's a chimera!" Evie exclaimed, her voice less a whisper and more a high pitched cry.

"Ah, yeah," Felix scratched the back of his neck, feeling an uncomfortable flush heating his skin. "I was meaning to tell everyone, but with the way Vessilia reacted originally, I didn't think it'd go over well. I just kept putting it off." He stood to the side and gestured down at the dog-sized tenku. "Everyone, this is Pit. Pit, everyone."

Pit warbled in a friendly way, but all of them flinched. Even Vessilia, who had gotten a bit better about Pit previously.

"Oh, he uh, he won't hurt you. Unless you try to attack him, maybe. He's still a baby for the most part," Felix smiled down at his friend.

"A baby? That's a fog-touched chimera! They're feral killers!" Atar was backing up, but stopped as his shoulder blades hit a stone wall behind him. "We've had to fight them all the way here."

"Atar's right, much as I hate saying that. I don't know how you got caught up with it, but it's best to just put that thing down," Evie's hand slowly crept back up to her chain.

Felix held out his hands in a placating gesture. "Look, it's fine. He's my Companion. We made a Pact."

Silence met his words, and all three of his new acquaintances gave him confused looks. "A what?" Evie asked.

Huh, I figured they'd know what it was...Hell, I was half-convinced they'd start listing off reasons why it was a bad idea. He shook his head. "Doesn't matter, I guess. Just...stand down, folks. He's harmless."

Vessilia reached a hand out and placed it on Evie's shoulder, giving her a look. Biting her lip, Evie looked between Pit and her friend before reluctantly nodding. Vessilia smiled at Felix and nodded too. "You saved my life, Felix Nevarre. You have earned some trust here."

"Thank you," Felix said.

They all turned to Atar.

The teen mage swallowed, his Adam's apple visibly bobbing, before he straightened himself under their gaze. "O-of course. I'm not afraid of some pet."

Felix caught Vessilia's eye. She shook her head, hiding a small smile.

"Good," Evie regained her joyful tone. "Let's go find what my sister is hiding."

Exploration is level 18!

The pathways were far clearer in the daylight, though the bright sunlight provided its own issues. Unable to slink in the deep shadows, their Stealth had less useful applications.

Or so Felix thought.

When the first Risi Warrior crossed their path, they were traversing a wide thoroughfare with zero cover or shadows. The giant stepped casually out from a hidden side path, at an angle from their vantage, perfectly aligned to see their passage. The thump of its feet was unmistakable, and all of them froze on the spot.

The giant simply waltzed past them, a mere 60 feet away, trudging in another direction.

Analyze...

Name: Unknown Risi Warrior
Type: Giantfolk
Level: 28

"What? Why didn't it see us?"

"I'm not sure how close it was, exactly, but..." Evie gave him a look. "The fog can be used to hide *us*, too."

Felix's mouth made a silent 'O' as he realized what she was saying. *The fog is affecting the giants, too. So it* can't *see us clear as day, because it's...not...a clear day.*

He winced. He actually felt bad about that one. It wasn't even a good pun.

Pit slunk through the shadows with them, easily keeping pace as they moved across several city blocks. Felix was happy that the tenku was fine; he had been half-convinced Pit was going to start a fight with one of these horse-sized hoarhounds, so it was nice to be wrong in this case. Still, he kept close to the chimera, making sure he was occasionally casting a glance back at him.

Nearly twenty minutes passed as the five of them traversed the sprawling city in an ever-widening spiral. Felix was astounded at the variety of architecture; it was unlike anything he'd seen before. Large, wide windows surmounted complicated bas-relief sculptures on the face of nearly every building. The doorways and eaves were all covered in tiny depictions of odd humanoid figures. He wandered close to one such example, and while time and weather had smoothed most of the features, it appeared each of these bumps and ridges were people. A tiny people, it seemed, as they were paired next to animals of all sorts ranging from quadrupeds to birds.

Analyze...

Name: Ruined Pavilion
Type: Structure
Lore: Little is known of the Foglands, especially of the interior portions. This ruin was built by sapient beings, but who they once were is lost to time.

So my guess is as good as any? I say tiny people. Unless all *animals are giant here?* He racked his brain a moment. *There was that Tree Vole back near the shore...that wasn't too big. But was it a baby? Have I seen a normal bird since coming here?*

He didn't think so. And he'd remember, obviously.

Felix acted as scout during their search, which Evie begrudgingly allowed after he stopped her from stepping into a fairly large sinkhole. While he could tell they didn't quite believe his claims regarding the fog, they listened to his warnings. Due to that, they skirted past several Risi Warriors on patrol through the streets. However it didn't look like any sort of patrol Felix had ever seen; they were listless and unaffected by anything around them. They simply walked, club or axe in hand, eyes fixed forward as they passed by.

Now, they were either extremely bad soldiers, didn't care about their jobs, or there was something wrong with them. Felix was leaning toward the latter as they progressed further in their search. He counted fourteen different Risi Warriors, and every single one seemed...distant, as if they weren't entirely present as they moved. When Felix explained his feeling, the women shrugged, but Atar tilted his head thoughtfully. Surprisingly, he didn't spout anything awful, but kept his thoughts to himself.

Huh, guess he can't be the worst all *the time.*

That first sinkhole wasn't the last they found, as Felix noted an increasing number of buildings were half-subsumed by the earth. It reminded him of home.

Nothing like a sinkhole to make you feel nostalgic for Florida. Just need some more humidity and a shit load of mosquitoes.

Despite his snark, he felt a real pang for his home and family.

What were they doing at this point? Did they worry about him? Felix pulled back from those thoughts, like a hand from a hot stove-top. That was just pain for no reason.

Focus.

They had come to the largest sinkhole yet, and the ground fell away sharply, the street nearly whole but tilted at a wild angle down into the earth. Some buildings still stood, held somehow in place by what must have been astounding engineering.

"Blind gods, would you look at that?" Vessilia peered into the sinkhole, her eyes squinting. "Whatever structural magics were worked here must have been powerful to still hold those buildings together after all this time."

Oh, right. Magic engineering.

"Where do we go from here?" Atar asked, looking around. "I don't see an easy way around this. It has to be at least a mile wide."

"I'm not sure," Evie chewed her lip, squatting at the edge of the sinkhole and peering down. "Do you think there's anything down there?" Pit wandered to the edge as well, sniffing the air curiously.

"Not for all the gold in Vanpuur," Atar vowed, slashing his hand in the air at what she was suggesting.

"Hey," Vessilia piped up, pointing forward, across the sinkhole. "What is that?"

Felix looked up at the sunlight's gleam against a brassy-colored dome on the far side of the sinkhole. The dome was squat and wide, and even from this distance, he could see a number of blue-shaded figures moving around it. It was situated at the edge of the hole, and some sort of wooden scaffolding had been erected, leading straight down. Ice hung from all of it, and Felix found the disparity between it against the heat haze unsettling.

"I think that might be what we're looking for." Evie grinned after Felix described what he saw. "Let's go."

The walk around the sinkhole took an hour, each of them having to pick their way across oversized debris and fallen buildings that hadn't stood the test of time. As they drew closer, muffled howls grew more distinct, as did the grunts of the guttural giant language. Exchanging nervous glances, Evie and Felix took the lead, though Pit was not far behind. Leaving Vessilia and Atar some distance behind, Evie and Felix split around the tumbled ruin of what was once some sort of temple, if the fluted columns were anything to go by.

In near silence, Felix and Pit moved up along a broken rooftop nearly a block away from the bronze dome, his boot whispering against the stone. Peering over the edge, Felix had to fight back a gasp. Nearly a dozen Risi Warriors filled the open area before him, and he could see at least twenty more in the distance.

Not only that, but a handful of huge blue-white hounds prowled alongside them, their jaws open and slavering steaming drool wherever they went. The hounds were the size of horses. The area was once a large, rectangular plaza, but now was mostly dilapidated and utterly filled with ice, and drifts of snow collected in the various nooks and crannies. Only a few buildings still stood, one being the domed structure, and another was a circular construction with large fluted columns on the front that reminded him of a frost-rimed tholos. Very Hellenistic.

Exploration is level 19!

Didn't expect that knowledge to come in handy. Thanks Mrs. Thomlin.

The giants were loosely grouped together, some talking, others acting as lazy lookouts, while a few even had fallen asleep. They were distinctly different from the near-mindless giants he saw on patrol. A handful moved with purpose toward the round colonnade, disappearing quickly within.

Then he heard the horn.

Three long, measured blasts, the sound was deep and piercing, like a conch shell the size of a bus. The hoarhounds all picked up the note, howling in their terrifying voices until the horn stopped. The sound of chains replaced the horns, as two giants led a large line of prisoners out of the tholos and into the plaza. He couldn't make them out individually, but judging by their sizes and coloration, they were humans.

They ranged in age from mid twenties to sixties or seventies, if the silver hair was anything to go by. They wore ragged remnants of what might have once been armor, but would provide very little protection now. A few of the humans looked in better condition than the rest, but the majority of them looked dirty, beat up, and generally malnourished. Felix frowned as he counted, watching the procession creep toward the bronze dome.

Forty-seven. They have forty-seven captives. Why? How? I thought this place was super dangerous?

The giants stopped the prisoners directly in front of the squat building that seemed to be the center of the Risi's operation. There was some milling about for a minute or two, and Felix started to get nervous. He glanced down at Pit to confirm the tenku was still nearby, but that was when he felt a sudden wash of icy air. Quickly staring back over the edge, Felix saw that an absolutely huge creature had emerged from the bronze dome. It was close to twenty-five feet tall and was covered in giant slabs of iron armor; it had to weigh several tons. Its head was as bald as the rest, and from its jaw grew a magnificent beard of wild white hair.

As he watched, the enormous giant was circled by several large shards of ice, orbiting him like a tiny solar system. Winds kicked up around the figure, blowing icy gusts in all directions as it glowered toward the assembled prisoners.

Holy fuck. That's a big boy. Felix's eyes were wide, fixed on the creature's craggy face, which had split open into a gaping, predatory smile. Then the giant surprised him again. It spoke; what's more, Felix could understand it.

"You have survived another night," it rumbled, its smile sharpening. "Be thankful! Praise your dead gods! Consider it your great honor to be used as stepping stones on our path to victory." The Risi Warriors all cheered, their basso voices like a landslide. The leader let the cheering fade before continuing.

"We, the masters of ice and blood, predators of the eternal frost have long sought the rising note, the Song of the Deeps." The giant's voice was a baritone so low it sounded like rocks rubbing together. Felix had only ever read of voices like that. "In the Hoarfrost, the Holy Depths are frozen, locked away and taken from us. But here, you pathetic creatures bask in her Song, even as you refuse to listen. Instead you follow a million untrue paths, relics of the Lost. The strong devour the weak. It is as it always was, time before time."

More cheers, and this time Felix heard an edge to the voices, a hunger. Teeth jutting at the edges of a vast precipice, something upsettingly familiar.

"Your flesh, weak and pitiful as it is, will be our bridge; your sacrifice, unwillingly given, our path to enlightenment. Prey serve the predators. Remember that. Carve it into your short memories and burn it into your souls." The giant licked his lips and showed his teeth. "The Mother calls. Time to die."

With a roar, the giants yanked the prisoners forward, chains jangling loudly against the ice. They cried out, some in anger, most in fear. A few fell to the ground, but they were dragged forward without pause, their bodies scraped raw against the uneven ground until they found their feet. Some did not. Felix couldn't pull his eyes away, watching until the last of the prisoners were dragged into the squat, bronze-topped building and followed by the immense leader.

The doors, easily twice the giant's size, slammed shut.

CHAPTER THIRTY-SIX

Felix slid down the roof as quietly as he could, his mind whirling. Popping to his feet, he kept low and moved as fast as he could back toward the group, Pit dutifully by his side. The things that giant said...much of it lacked context, but Felix had a very bad feeling.

Hopefully Evie had gotten closer and saw more.

It was a good quarter hour back to where the others had holed up, and Felix took it slowly, exercising his Stealth as best he could. Last thing he wanted was an entire camp of frost giants coming down on them.

As he rounded the final corner, however, Felix came upon Atar, Vessilia, and a wincing Evie standing with their shoulders hunched and eyes on the ground. Spinning toward his sudden arrival, the half-helmed Magda snarled.

"You! Of course it's you," she turned in contempt, her eyes going to Evie. "Do you know what we've stumbled onto? What could have happened to you?"

Felix felt Pit about to round the corner, and put his hand out. *Wait*, he sent through their connection, hoping it would work. He could feel the chimera pause at the edge.

Companion Pact is level 12!

"We scouted," Evie said, still not meeting her sister's eyes. "We were careful."

"Careful, my ass! You could have been seen! You could have gotten the others taken as well!" Magda gestured violently at the others.

"Take—So you know about the prisoners?" Felix interrupted. He really didn't want to get in the middle of a sibling tiff, but he was getting tired of Magda's attitude. "I thought you were here to Reveal their Omens and gain some levels?"

"Prisoners? There's prisoners?" Atar's eyes went wide. "The giants have captured people?"

Felix nodded. "I counted forty-seven humans."

"Noctis wept," Vessilia swore, her hand going to her mouth.

"Why *are* we here, Magda? You dragged us out here, specifically here, to train. Why?" Evie had her hands on her hips, her bright green eyes defiantly trained on her elder sister's.

"Rescue mission," came the metallic, echoey reply. Harn walked in from the left, stepping carefully around stones and making surprisingly little sound for a big metal man. His voice reverberated slightly within his frog-mouthed helmet. "We didn't know it was this bad, though."

"Rescue—!" Atar's pale face flushed, his flesh-colored mustache popping in contrast. "That is a direct violation of the terms of our agreement!"

"I know, kid! I know!" Magda tore off her helmet, her sandy brown hair wild. "We thought we could do both. My—our friend is in there, somewhere! We came to find them and get them out."

"And you thought that bringing Tin Guilders would be a great idea?" Atar laughed, a nasty sound. "Let me guess? Intelligence is your dump stat!"

"You little—!"

Awooooooo!

Magda froze midstep, hand just about to grab Atar's collar. Everyone turned back toward the giant's camp, the fear palpable. The howl lasted several seconds before fading.

"Prisoners have escaped!" A high pitched cry sounded out from nearby. Felix whipped his head around, but he couldn't tell the source. "Over here!"

A brilliant flare of light streaked up into the air above them, burning like a mini sun as it hovered there. A sudden thunder rolled through the ruins, the ground itself rattling and snarling barks bounced back and forth.

"They're coming!" Magda pointed at Harn. "Split Circle! Rendezvous at the wardstones! Go!" Harn grabbed the mage and Evie by the arms, nearly dragging the two of them down the left hand path. Magda put her hand on Vessilia much more gently. "Come, Lady Dayne!" Without so much as a backward glance, they took off.

Felix was left standing there alone. Pit padded up to him and nudged his hand. "Why are we even with these people, Pit?"

The tenku chirped worriedly and looked toward the approaching noise.

"Yeah, yeah. They're my only lead on getting outta this hell-hole." Felix looked up.

"C'mon. I've got an idea."

Felix considered the wall before him. It belonged to a broken three-story building, and he hoped it would hold up. Pit spread his wings and dug his claws into the stone, apparently extremely good at climbing, and fairly flew up. Surprised, but without the time to show it, Felix also rushed up the ruin, grabbing ledges and propelling himself up to the next one with all the Strength and Agility he possessed. He only had to be careful not to grip too hard; he didn't want to crush the stone beneath his hands like back at the waterfall.

Free Climbing is level 14!
Free Climbing is level 15!

Felix clambered to the top floor, nearly fifty feet up, his breath a little short and his Stamina having dropped by a tenth. Pit hopped lightly over the ledge, and Felix swung his body over the top just as he heard footsteps below. Holding his breath and keeping low, Felix strained his senses, listening for the giants and hearing them mutter something deep and incomprehensible. He focused, trying to make out their actual words as he pushed his Perception. There was a rush of sound, and then...he could.

"Rok tonah! Rato lat yikana," a giant muttered, his voice sounding disappointed. Many others stepped forward, their feet heavy on the uneven street. There was a muted clang, like metal against metal but quieter; likely the giants' Ice Fiend fur muffling their armor.

"Ikki tak, vokala," groused another voice, also displeased. Felix could hear what sounded like dozens of giants, each muttering to themselves.

"Pata! Ti roka! Kieh! Kieh!" Another voice, much louder and angrier, shouted the other voices down. The sound of snarls and growls wove between the shout, making the hair on the back of Felix's neck stand up. Shortly after, the street below was filled with thunderous footsteps, all of them quickly moving away.

Stealth is level 23!

Felix waited twenty seconds before poking his head up and checking. The giants were gone. What's more, when he stood up, he could see them scattering through the ruined streets, groups of two or three spreading out along the pathways.

They're hunting us now.

Felix looked at Pit, who met his eyes stoically. "We've got to meet up with the others. If nothing else, we stand a better chance together." Pit nodded, his big, golden eyes fierce.

They leaped from building to building, sticking to the rooftops in order to keep their vantage point. Most of the Risi Warriors had dispersed by this point, and even in the clear summer sun, Felix could only see so far. There were many stone buildings that blocked his view, though he could make out some beyond them due to their lattice-like sculptural designs. Whoever built the city were master artisans, and Felix couldn't help but be impressed.

Imagine this place when it was alive, Felix mused, pausing at the top of a leaning four story structure. *It's easily as big as a mid-sized city back home. There must have been millions who lived here.*

A cool breeze rushed across the rooftops, chilling him for a moment despite the mounting mid-morning heat. He looked up at the sky, blue as a robin's egg and wisped with thin cirrus clouds at the edges. *Not the worst weather to keep ruining my shirts in.* He fingered his tattered sleeves, barely more than scraps at this point. As he did, he noticed movement out of the corner of his eye.

There was a large group of giants coming down a nearby alley, four or five of them with two giant wolves. He had been tracking them as he moved, attempting to keep ahead of them as they both moved toward the subterranean hideaway. As he trained his eyes on them, he saw that sudden movement again....it was on top of one of the walls. A black...blur.

What is that?

The blur flitted across rooftops, heading in the same direction Felix was, just on the other side of the street. Felix crouched down, hiding quickly behind a lumpy, faceless statue. The blur drew closer, and Felix saw that it was more like a moving shadow, a blot against the bright backdrop of day racing across dilapidated ledges. His Manasight flared, and it was clear he was perceiving some sort of shroud made entirely of shadow Mana. As he watched, the shadow flicked one of its strange limbs, followed quickly by the sound of cobbles breaking down below. The giants, only a few hundred feet behind, roared and raced after the sound.

Is it...leading them? Felix gazed in the direction the shadow was moving. It was as if it knew exactly where to go, exactly where the others were holed up. *If I let them go on, then...*

Felix took a couple quick breaths and eyeballed the street below.

This is very stupid.

Felix spun, setting his feet against the far ledge before pushing off. He raced across the rooftop and on the last step pushed with all of his Strength. The stone cracked beneath him, its sharp noise loud as a gunshot, and he was flung headlong into the thin air.

Fffffhhhhhhaaaaanooo!

Faster than he could anticipate, Felix zipped across the intervening distance and collided bodily with the shadow creature. For a brief, impossible second, it started to orient on him, but it was too late. He was going too fast to stop. The two of them tumbled, ass over teakettle, their bodies tangling and then disengaging as they crashed through a couple rickety chimneys before skidding to a stop along the roof.

"Uugh," Felix groaned, fresh bruises throbbing along his ribs and thighs. He stumbled to his feet just in time to see the shadow burst into a puff of smoke, resolving into a figure wearing blackened leather armor and some sort of mask. It was matte black, giving off zero reflections in the bright sunlight, and covered the top half of their face.

With a growl and a kick of her legs, the figure spun to her feet. Felix didn't even see her use her hands.

Another flippy one.

She had a bandolier of knives across her chest and a few dark handles stuck up from her hips. Whoever this was, she was loaded for bear.

"Who're you?" Felix asked, drawing his hooked sword. He might be better at unarmed combat, but a bare sword felt like the more threatening gesture.

The woman (and she clearly was a woman, judging by the molding of the dark armor) grimaced and glowered at him, her eyes an unnatural blank white beneath her mask.

That's creepy.

"Why are you baiting the Risi?"

The woman's smile stretched wider, but then suddenly faltered, her eyes growing wide.

"Behind you!"

Her voice reverberated strangely and Felix dropped to the ground, rolling forward and spinning around. He came to his feet in less than a second, sword still up, and saw...nothing. Just a dilapidated stone wall.

Oh my god, did I—"URK!"

A long stiletto had slid two inches into his side, right where his kidneys were. He looked down, disbelieving, as the masked woman's full lips stretched into a nasty grin.

"Sorry, kid. Nothing personal."

Status: Poisoned (Major)

Poison Resistance is level 18!
Poison Resistance is level 19!
Armored Skin is level 16!

With a grunt, she yanked the blade out, taking three tugs to pull it free. Felix felt a burning sensation from the wound, and suddenly his legs stopped working. He fell to the ground.

Poison Resistance is level 20!

"Noctis' tits, he nearly broke my dagger..." she muttered as sounds started to echo strangely. The weakness crawled up his spine, and his gut went cold. Everything around him started to go dark, as if the world was dimming. Or he...was...?

Poison Resistance is level 21!

Sound cut off the same time his vision did. He couldn't even feel the air on his skin anymore. He was completely numb, cut off from all sensation. Panicked, Felix turned inward, where he could still see his Fire Within surging and flowing. He grabbed at it, orienting on it, feeling it burn against his limited senses.

Poison Resistance is level 22!

Felix sank into his inner power, the magic crackling like an electric storm. It soaked into him as it raged, burning, cooling, charging him with indelible life even as the weakness in his body grew larger and larger.

He...he was....

He was dying.

Ilia inspected her dagger, noting a serious bend in the tip. She huffed a little breath.

That kid bent my favorite blade! Little shit!

Ilia looked back at the boy, who even now stared blindly into the sky as his body curled up on itself. She hadn't realized there would be any Iron Ranks on this expedition. Where had he come from?

Was he one of the prisoners?

That had surprised her, and she wasn't used to surprises anymore. No others were supposed to be in the Foglands; they were locked down for the past six months. She was certain they were all Guilders, too, and *that* was more than intriguing. Something to speak with Elder DuFont about, though it was not her main concern.

She was being paid for a very specific task. And fighting an army of frost giants wasn't in her contract.

This blasted fog is a menace. She'd gotten separated from the Shieldwitch after they had entered the ravine, the foul mists leading her astray. *No longer.* Now that she had found her quarry again, it was time to go to work.

She carefully sheathed her stiletto, mindful not to touch the blade herself. It was coated with a particularly nasty poison harvested from a monster called an Inevitable; it shut down the five senses before seizing the heart and causing it to rupture. It only needed a touch in the bloodstream to go to work, and it was fast. The final death wasn't as quick, but usually the target was out of commission long enough that she could just kill them at her leisure.

How did he even see me? That worried her, and indicated she was being too lax. Her Stealth had reached Journeyman Tier, but she hardly had to flex it here in this foggy wasteland. That was a mistake, it seemed. *I'll rectify that.*

With the big idiot out of the way, though, it was time to lead the giants toward the others. Ilia smiled, her teeth white and slightly crooked. It was the perfect opportunity, a way to frame the monsters of the Foglands as truly terrible and the Shieldwitch as incompetent. A win-win, as far as her employer was concerned.

And if I can secure a hefty blackmail from Elder DuFont along the way? Pure gravy.

She walked to the roof's edge, the thick fog swirling like she was trapped in clouds. All around her, bits of stone and masonry poked up through the mist, islands at sea. She couldn't see much farther than fifty yards, but she could feel the giants and their thunderous steps. One of the many benefits of the Brightsense Body she had acquired. Orienting on the nearest group of giants, she got moving.

She didn't notice the chimera.

Poison Resistance is level 23!

Felix couldn't feel anything anymore. His body might as well have been gone.

What was on that dagger?

Slowly, his resistance rose as his body fought off the toxin, but Felix had no idea whether it would cure him. Not to mention, he had no idea what that scary shadow lady was doing. She could be stabbing him to death right now, and he wouldn't feel a thing.

Felix's core flared with heat and light, blinding his "vision" for a moment. A burst of blue-white Mana burst outward, looping off into the dark distance like a solar prominence. This kept happening, a close up view of the Mana channels deep within Felix's body. He wasn't sure how or why he was here, but at least he could feel *something*.

Sure enough, as the Mana raced through his pathways, the distant sensation of burning assaulted Felix's mind. It was faint, like an echo of pain more than torment itself, but it was likely coming from his actual body. As he watched, the pain was carried back by the looping Mana and deposited in his core. It looked like a blackened stain, and it was slowly eaten away by his core.

It's...devouring the pain. No. The poison. The poison!

Felix pushed his Mana out and watched as the electric fire raced along his channels. The moment he felt the distant pain, he reached out and *pulled*. A sudden, terrible rush of agony flooded him, but as he drew the pain in, his surroundings lightened. The shadows were drawing back.

Again.

More loops of Mana, more speed, more pain. Even as he sent out a second and third burst, Felix pulled back on the original Mana, drawing it into his core with a deep breath. The pain was like a cloud of thick ink, and his internal fire devoured it. Purified it.

Again.

Poison Resistance is level 24!

More darkness, more pain. It felt like his world was burning, as if biting insects crawled over every inch of his body, each sting more excruciating than the last. But he pushed onward, rallying his Willpower as his mind flinched at what he was doing.

Again!

Felix's core burned like a storm on steroids. Fire and lightning crashed within the terrible maelstrom in his center, fury and power expanding out along his pathways. The inky pain dissolved faster and faster, barely reaching the core now before it was consumed. With a flash of blinding, coruscating light, the pain suddenly stopped.

Congratulations! You Have Reached Apprentice Tier in Poison Resistance!
You Gain The Following:
+5 VIT
+5 END
+...

Rare Essence Detected During Formation!

Choose A Feature:
Inevitable
Deadening
Heart-Rending

Still dizzy from the lack of pain, Felix chose the first one, barely reading it.

Congratulations!
You Have Absorbed The Essence Of Inevitability!

What does—?

Intense pain speared across his mind, agony enough to dim the effects of the poison itself. Electricity rolled across his spine and into his ribs and hips and shoulders, crackling along his bones like a toothache turned up to a thousand and buried in his deepest places. His inner world flashed with light, then went dark.

Moments or minutes; later, he could perceive again. In fact, Felix thought he could feel his limbs again, as well as a new sort of torment as blood returned to them. The dark world around him lightened until he could see a galaxy of stars all around, some fixed and some drifting like wayward fireflies.

Felix blinked.

And opened his outer eyes to the strangest sight yet.

CHAPTER THIRTY-SEVEN

Skraaaaaaaawwwww!

Sharp gusts of wind buffeted Felix as he blinked awake. Before him, the dark-armored woman was doing her best to dodge the attacks of an enraged chimera. Pit was a blur of feathers as he sped around her in circles, flapping his wings every few seconds to send a near-invisible blade of wind at his enemy. The tenku screamed out again, and Felix could feel his rage.

Briefly, the woman froze, Pit's Cry ability working its magic. Pit launched another Wingblade.

Pit! You beautiful idiot. Felix felt his heart lurch in his chest; whether that was elation or a side effect of the poison, he wasn't sure. He tossed an Analyze at her.

Name: ???
Type: ??
Level: ??
HP: ???/???
SP: ???/???
MP: ???/???
Lore: Humans are adaptable and prolific breeders. They can be found in many corners of the Continent.
Strength: Strength, Agility
Weakness: ???

That's...less than useful. Does she have some way to block Analyze?

"Damn chimera!" The dark woman rolled and tumbled away from a sharp blade of air, somehow pushing off of nothing to reverse her direction and dodge a second blade that sped past.

Pit's Wingblade is level 5!

Felix tensed his limbs, feeling excruciating pain as feeling returned to them. Wobbly, he pushed himself up into a crouch, then into a stuttering stance only a breeze away from falling. Pit let out a warbling cry of joy, and the deadly rogue fixed him with a frustrated exclamation.

"You've got Journeyman Tier Poison Resistance? How?" She half-stepped and dodged another wingblade. "You're like, twenty?"

Felix didn't answer, focused more on keeping his feet. He leveled his gaze on her, letting Meditate activate and begin to regenerate his wounds. "Why?"

"Why what?" She asked, bemused.

"Why try to kill me? Why—"

"Because I could, kid," she interrupted him and brandished the long daggers she held in a backward grip. Felix hadn't even noticed them being drawn. "Good job surviving this time. You won't again."

Shadow Mana swirled around the rogue, stretching from nearby sources to pool at her feet. Quick as a blink, the power swarmed up her body, which de-materialized right before his eyes.

Oh no, not falling for that one! Felix threw his hand forward, his eyes suddenly feeling warm.

Influence of the Wisp!

Influence of the Wisp is level 22!

Blue-white fire flickered around her form, briefly banishing the gathering shadows. The woman's eyes grew wide, before something around her neck flared and shattered. She stumbled backward, surprise still writ large across her features.

"Tricky bastard!" Her white eyes flared brightly behind her half-mask. The woman's body undulated, bending in ways Felix was positive humans were unable to, and abruptly half a dozen knives flashed forward.

Felix couldn't dodge; he was barely standing up. So instead he just relaxed, letting himself fall to the ground. Still, a sharp line of fire traced across his scalp, while another blade lodged into the meat of his left shoulder. "MHFF!"

The pain was manageable; he had felt worse. Felix pushed, forcing his still-numb palms down onto the shoddy roof, throwing his body up and into the air nearly fifteen feet. In a moment of inspiration, he whipped out a hand, conjuring his magic.

Shadow Whip!

A tether of matte black shadow Mana coalesced, snapping out at the woman's outstretched hand.

Shadow Whip is level 13!

Gotcha!

Felix hauled on the line, which did something he should have expected: While he was strong, perhaps stronger than the rogue, he was up in the air. He had zero leverage. Instead of pulling the woman to him, Felix was yanked toward *her*.

"Ah!" Felix twisted his body by tugging on the line, which only accelerated him more. He crashed into the rogue with his right foot half extended, the rest of his body awkwardly splayed. His foot missed, but his jack-knifed torso bashed directly into the woman's legs, sending them both into a tumble toward the edge.

"Blighted ass!" The rogue pushed at Felix, stronger than she looked, and started grabbing for something. Before she could knife him again, Felix struck out blindly, kicking again and this time pushing her away from him. She slid only a couple feet away, but Felix clearly heard the *tink* of steel on stone.

Marshalling his Strength and Endurance, Felix pushed up to his feet. He was recovering slower than he wanted, but he had *something* in the tank. He took several steps backward, bending down to retrieve his hooked sword with his right hand; when had he lost that?

"Who are you?" He panted, wiping away at the blood pouring down the side of his face from his scalp wound. "Why are you helping the giants?"

The woman got to her feet slowly, watching him all the while. She seemed reluctant to turn her back on him, now.

Good, maybe she'll wait before she attacks agai—

She blurred forward.

GAAH!

Felix brought his sword up in a reflexive parry, catching one of her long daggers on the axe-like bow of the blade. But that left his chest wide open for the second of her daggers, which zipped toward his heart.

Parry is level 2!

"SKRAAAW!"

A blast of wind cut between them, knocking the dagger aside as Felix spun to his right. He put some more distance between them and slashed out again, this time feeling his blade scrape along her forearm armor thing.

Bracer?

"Thanks Pit!" Felix flashed a smile, feeling the general placement of his Companion. "Stay back on this one. I've got her."

"Oh you do, do you?" The rogue arced an eyebrow at him...*I think.* "How'd someone like you get captured by the giants? Lose your bodyguards?"

"What?" Felix was annoyed and confused at her change of tack. *She thinks I was a prisoner? Why?*

"Was that it? They certainly did a number on your armor. What happened? Daddy scrimp on the quality of guards? Go for the bargain bin for his least favorite?" Her voice was thick with syrupy sarcasm and Felix felt his hackles raise. A sharp, itchy heat built up along his back and neck, his skin crawling as a rage he hadn't felt before rose up.

This asshole thinks that I was captured? That's ridiculous! It's—

Felix took a step forward, jostling the knife still stuck in his shoulder. The blaze of pain ate into his rage, and sent a chill snaking down his back as his senses tingled in warning.

Holy shit, she's using a Skill on me!

Bastion of Will is level 28!

The rogue frowned when Felix stopped moving, silently snarling when he started backing away.

"I'd appreciate it if you kept out of my head." Felix smiled, happy to see the woman angry. He also desperately wanted to pull the dagger out of his shoulder, but couldn't afford to split his attention. *This lady has a whole bag of tricks.*

"Strange noble," she scoffed. "Awful polite, even if you are a cockroach."

"And you're awfully...stabby," Felix finished lamely. "Listen, putting aside the fact that you just poisoned me, then stabbed me, then *attempted* to stab me again, I'd really rather not fight. I'd also appreciate you not luring the giants toward my uh, associates."

"So you *are* a Guilder. Interesting." The lady smirked, which annoyed Felix more than he expected. "I can let you go, sure. No can do on the second part, though. Professional pride, you see."

A lightbulb went off in Felix's head, dots connecting in a way that was painfully obvious in retrospect. "You're an assassin! Of course! Dark armor, creepy mask, poison and daggers, why didn't I see it before?"

"...Creepy mask?" Felix heard her mutter.

"If you're an assassin, were you hired to kill Magda and the others? By who?"

Instead of answering him, her hands blurred as Felix barely perceived several knives zip his way. He leaped to the right again, the roof below creaking beneath his feet in protest. The knives flew by harmlessly, and Felix felt awful smug for about a second.

Then she reappeared directly next to him, daggers held low.

Ahhh! Reign of Vellus!

A burst of blue lightning blasted forth, ripping the rogue from the roof and slamming her into the dilapidated wall. The same wall she had tricked Felix with before, he was happy to note. Without waiting for her to recover, Felix darted in, moving close with his crooked sword held to the side. He led with a slash, catching a glancing blow across her bandolier of knives, his bronze blade striking golden sparks on the steel. She recovered, though, and caught his second swing on her long dagger, quickly twisting and following up with a series of lightning quick thrusts.

He jumped back, more agonizing lines of fire ripping along his stomach. Her daggers further shredded his once-beige tunic. Felix eyeballed his Health, noting it was barely over 25% while his Stamina was hovering just above 10%. His left arm hung limply, his shoulder spasming around the knife still lodged there.

I can't keep this up. I've got maybe two more good hits left in me.

"You're looking haggard, roach. You need a nap?" The assassin taunted him, smirking despite her obvious fatigue. If Felix was exhausted, she wasn't too far behind. He supposed her Endurance wasn't too high...she seemed to be focused heavily on Strength and Agility. "Here. Let me help!" She rushed forward.

Felix stepped forward to meet her, knowing he couldn't outrun her in his state. He did the only thing he could.

The unexpected.

Pit!

He slashed low to high, trying to simultaneously shove her daggers aside and drive her back. The assassin was ready, angling her weapons and flowing around his strike like a wraith. And then, she tripped.

Which, of course she tripped. That's what happens when a terrier-sized tenku runs headlong into your legs.

"Ahk!" She cried out, Felix's sword somehow catching her across her face as she stumbled. It was only a second, but it was enough. He dropped his blade once it had connected, rearing back with his right arm and put everything he had left into a single uppercut.

Corrosive Strike!

The rogue took the blow straight to the gut, and Felix thought he felt something crack, before her entire body suddenly rocketed backwards. The force of the strike propelled her up into the air, literally launching her off the roof. For a moment, Felix only stared at the space where the assassin once was, dumbfounded. Then he rushed to the edge.

She was gone.

Pit cautiously walked up to him, peering out into the darkened alley below.

"You think she's gone?" Felix asked. His Perception and Manasight was picking up nothing. Either she had exploded into a thousand pieces, or she had used some sort of escape Skill. He was hoping for the exploded option.

"Ugh," Felix huffed. "Assassins, now?"

Pit's only reply was to chirrup twice and nuzzle his beak against Felix's leg. Felix smiled, reaching down with a groan to scratch the tenku's neck. "Thanks, Pit. You're a lifesaver."

Pit chirped brightly and walked back onto the roof as Felix followed, still keeping a watchful eye out for the assassin's reemergence. She'd caught him off guard too many times, at this point.

In a flash, it came to him.

"Vambrace! That's it!"

That would have bugged him for the whole day.

Looking down, he regarded the flat steel knife that was lodged in his deltoid. Pulling it out wouldn't be pretty, but it had to be done. Felix had been able to put the pain out of his mind during the fight, but it had severely hampered his movements. He vaguely remembered something about leaving a weapon in a wound to prevent blood loss, but that was before he could heal himself by sitting for a long time.

He grunted as he pulled it out. The blade was small, only five inches long, but it was wide. It had a weird etching on the flat of the blade, like a nautilus or curled horn or something.

Name: Steel Throwing Knife
Type: Piercing
Lore: Unknown

He pocketed the knife for later and applied pressure to the wound to prevent the Bleed status, focusing on Meditation for a few minutes. When the worst seemed past, it was time to move on.

As Felix scooped up his hooked sword, he pondered at his increasingly frequent encounters with near death. The shock value of it had decreased a lot since he started, but he still wasn't comfortable being brought low by every enemy he encountered.

Granted, they're all higher level than me, but still. I need to figure out how to do this all better.

Ultimately, he wasn't dead, so Felix counted it as a win.

Felix hefted his curved sword, looking at its bronze length. Despite heavy use, the thing was still in pristine condition, the edge unmarred by burrs or nicks.

What did the Archon call it? A Crescian blade? He held it up, examining it in the midday light. *Aside from the enchantment to bypass the Temple wards, it seems normal enough. Oh, what's this?*

The blade had a thick rivulet of blood streaked across it, bright and red. The assassin's blood. Felix bit his lip in consideration, then reached into his satchel and pulled out an empty vial from his potion case. Carefully, he scooped a dollop of blood into the vial and corked it.

Later. It should be worth it. He couldn't afford to go into a Memory trance out here, not when that woman might come back.

Again, Felix considered whether leaving the Guilders to their own devices would be the smarter play. He'd survived so far on his own, and this situation was getting complicated *fast.* Yet, Felix couldn't quite convince himself to leave. He had no clue how to get out of the Foglands, and his only guides were being hunted by giants and an assassin. It didn't leave him much choice.

"C'mon Pit. We have to catch up. The others need to know about this."

As the boy and his monster sped off, Ilia watched. She had been tempted to attack him again, but he'd thrown surprise after surprise at her, and honestly, she was worried.

Who is this kid? Wish this damn fog didn't interfere with Analyze. She considered him as he started to fade into the fog. *He's gotta be a plant. Doesn't make sense, otherwise. He couldn't have seen me luring the giants, not in this murk. No, someone told him.*

Ilia fingered the cut along her cheek, feeling the wound slowly stop bleeding. He had cut her...somehow, he either had incredible Strength, or his sword was heavily enchanted. Either way, something didn't smell right. Ilia climbed out from her perch, keeping Stealth at full burn as she started to follow. She wasn't going to make the same mistake this time.

Ten more minutes and Felix was nearing their basement camp. While before they had searched in an ever-widening spiral pattern, the way back was a straight path, one that Felix recalled perfectly well.

Perfect recall never gets old.

This meant that, despite his detour, he wasn't long behind the others. However, as he got closer, he heard the definite sound of combat. Felix rushed down the street, still on the roof level wherever he could manage it. Hopping from the third floor roof of a half-collapsed building (*a bank, maybe?*) through a gaping hole in the side of a five-story residential complex, he crossed the building to peer down below.

Three stories below him, the others were fighting against a pair of Risi Warriors and a lone Hoarhound the size of a horse. Magda was tanking their attacks while Harn brought the heat. Felix spotted Evie engaging the Hoarhound, keeping it busy and away from their back-line fighters, Vessilia and Atar. Felix hadn't really seen Vessilia in action before, but she moved fluidly and decisively, wielding her eight-foot spear with precision, supplementing Evie's attacks with her own while Atar flung orbs of fire at the beast. The mage was actually doing some significant damage, too; the Hoarhound was covered in scorch marks and looked to be on the ropes.

Wow. They're...good. Really *good.*

Seeing it from up here shed new light on this team's fighting ability. So far, he'd been very impressed (and a little terrified) of Magda and Harn's prowess, but the other three seemed lackluster by comparison. *I mean, I guess they're apprentices or trainees or whatever, so I can't expect them to be expert anything, right? But still. They know their shit more than I do. Heck, I don't even know if I should go help or not. They've got this in the bag.*

Movement out of the corner of his eye drew Felix's attention south, back the way he had come, down an angled alley behind the fight. Focusing, Felix saw blue-white fur moving toward his allies, directly toward Atar and Vessilia.

Shit. Me and my big mouth.

Felix ran across the room, hopping back onto the three-story bank's roof with as much grace and stealth as he could manage. He made it to the ledge and peered over. A blue-white furred Hoarhound stalked the alley below, its draft-horse-sized body slung low as it padded nearly silently toward Atar's back, only a couple dozen feet away. Three stories up, Felix tossed an Analyze at it.

Name: Hoarhound
Type: Elemental
Level: 27
HP: ???
SP: ???
MP: ???
Lore: Formed from the Hoarfrost itself, Hoarhounds are

the wrath of nature given breath. Strong and hardy, they are deadly foes on the frozen tundra.
Strength: Strength, Endurance
Weakness: Willpower

Analyze is level 21!

Hmm. Willpower, huh?

"Pit," Felix whispered, turning toward the tenku. Then he imagined himself jumping down and attacking the Hoarhound from the front, while Pit flew in from behind. He *pushed* that thought toward his friend. Pit jerked his head, eyes wide in surprise, but Felix felt agreement echo back through their bond.

Companion Pact is level 13!
Companion Pact is level 14!

It worked! Felix grinned. He looked down below, where the elemental beast still stalked forward and then across the street, where several pillars held up the tottering remains of the city. An exciting idea occurred to him, something he absolutely had to attempt.

Time to check off the bucket list.

Shadow Whip!

A matte black tendril shot out of his left hand, wrapping around a crumbling pillar across the alley. Felix tugged on it, took four quick breaths and did a running leap off the bank roof, slightly ahead of the Hoarhound. The wind rushed through his ears as he dropped, then as the Shadow Whip pulled taut, he swung at speed in an arc directly toward the beast. The Hoarhound's head snapped up as Felix came into view, and it's tire-sized maw opened up into a gleeful snarl.

Influence of the Wisp!

A Hoarhound is Enthralled for 1 second!

Blue fire covered both Felix and the hound, locking it in place as the Nymean crashed his booted feet directly into its snout. The huge dog's jaw snapped shut with a crash as its head whipped backwards; its body followed suit, lifting up in the shockwave of the attack. Several Windblades sliced into the Hoarhound from above, even as Felix dropped to the street before the elemental and grabbed the only foreleg that remained on the ground. With a strained groan, Felix lifted and twisted his body, dropping the Hoarhound to its side with a muffled *boom.*

"Yiiipe!"

Without letting it up, Felix started pummeling the elemental about the neck and face, dropping blow after blow of Corrosive Strike. Launching himself from another building, Pit swooped in again on his wide black and red wings, flapping them every few seconds to send out a shearing Wingblade of compressed air.

It was over in less than thirty seconds.

Felix stumbled back once he saw the kill notification, gulping air and putting some distance between him and the monster corpse. Exertion over, Felix started to sweat profusely, his body overheating as his work caught up to him. Pit landed gracelessly next to him, thumping to the ground like the weird dog-bird he was. "Didn't stand a chance once we got it on the ground, huh?"

From behind him, he could hear the muffled sounds of continued battle. Felix looked over his shoulder and saw that the others had pushed their Hoarhound further down the road, toward the giants. He was alone.

Good. Don't really want others to see me do this. Felix fetched another empty vial from his potion case and dipped it into an open wound of the Hoarhound. Dark, purple-blue blood oozed out, entirely too viscous and smelling like the inside of a freezer. The blood easily filled the vial, which started to frost over the moment he corked it.

I have to get stronger. Anyway I can.

He tucked the vial away and turned toward his new allies. Their fighting was getting louder, gaining a frenzied note. "C'mon, Pit."

Pit trilled three times, a high flute-like sound that made Felix feel like he was being poked repeatedly in the chest. He turned back to his Companion in exasperation. "Okay, what?"

In response, Pit pointed his beak toward the Hoarhound corpse, which even now had started to dissolve into greasy smoke. Felix's eyes traced the path of Pit's beak and saw a faint glimmer of purple-white light in the monster's chest. Realization dawned.

Right! It's an elemental!

Felix rushed forward and, using his enchanted hook blade,

fished the gory morsel out of the beast's innards. In seconds, a luminescent purple-white stone plopped onto the cobbles. It glimmered with radiance, muted only by the thick syrup of Hoarhound blood.

Name: Hoarhound Core
Type: Elemental Core
Lore: An elemental core is the central node of any elemental. While not always solid, it provides the majority of their power as they live and evolve. Can be used for many purposes, from smithing to enchanting.
Rarity: Uncommon

"That's, wow," Felix was impressed. "That's much prettier than the Rockstrike cores." He reached out a hand to touch it...but Pit pounced on it before he could. The greedy little bird snapped it up, tipped his head back and swallowed it in a single gulp. Felix pulled his hand back and flexed his fingers, happy he hadn't been holding the elemental core. He worried Pit might take a chunk with him next time.

Elated, Pit spread his wings and trumpeted out a strident cry, far louder than usual. The tenku, usually the size of a big terrier, suddenly expanded and grew into a Collie. The feathers along his crown and nape filled in even further, and his legs grew gangly while his wings became slightly darker and pilot feathers just a bit longer. Beak open wide and eyes glittering, Pit chirruped brightly.

"Holy shit," Felix managed. "What was *in* that?"

Then Pit growled, and his eyes flashed with purple light, before he let out a deep unmistakable *bark*...and an ice spear launched from his maw. It traveled only a short distance before smashing against a wall, but it still gouged out a divot.

Congratulations!
Your Title Gourmand Has Garnered Your Companion Insight!
They Have Fully Digested Their Opponent's Mana!

Your Companion, Pit, Has Learned A Skill From A Hoarhound!
Frost Spear (Common), Level 1!

Utilizing the stolen Mana of a Hoarhound, Pit can form and fire spears of refined ice! Increases range and accuracy moderately with Skill Level, damage increases with Skill Level.

"Wait, what?"

CHAPTER THIRTY-EIGHT

Your Companion Pit Has Gained A Level!
+2 VIT! +2 PER! +4 AGL! +4 DEX! +3 WIL! +1 END! +2 INT!

"You can—" Felix pulled up Pit's stat sheet.

Name: Pit (Companion)
Level: 8
Race: Chimera - Tenku

Health: 219/219
Stamina: 268/268
Mana: 179/179

STR: 44 PER: 33
VIT: 43 END: 49
INT: 25 WIL: 33
AGL: 70 DEX: 47

Skills:
Bite (C), Level 16
Rake (C), Level 18
Cry (R), Level 19

Skulk (C), Level 23
Companion Pact (U), Level 14
Wingblade (U), Level 5
Frost Spear (C), Level 1

Active Titles:
Gourmand
Survivor III
Butcher III
Unconquered
Face the Charge
Bulwark of the Innocent
Pactmaker
Work Horse
Blind Pugilist
Hero

"Gourmand...you have it, too. And Survivor III, Unconquered...all of the big weight Titles are here. Everything that was Rare or Epic. Holy shit!"

Felix was floored. *This...this has to be an effect of the Pact, right? I gain, he gains?* He scratched his scalp, the newly-healed laceration itching slightly. Dried blood flecked off and onto his hands, but he didn't notice. *But he didn't gain anything like this from the twelve Rockstrike cores he ate...just a few stats.*

He brought up the Skill description.

Companion Pact (Uncommon) Level 14!
You have formed a pact with a denizen of the Foglands. Increasing Skill Level and Affinity will net larger gains from the pact, for both you and your Companion.
Upon reaching level 10, all Titles ranked Rare or higher will be shared with your Companion at a 2:1 ratio.

"Ho dang," Felix muttered. That answered that. Pit ran in circles next to him, chasing his bushy red tail as he enjoyed his suddenly larger frame. His little buddy was getting bigger...and deadlier.

A sudden groaning and thud from around the corner pulled him out of his reverie. Felix hustled to the end of the alley and peered out to see another collapsed Hoarhound mere feet from him. The creature twitched weakly before expiring, and with his Manasight still going, Felix could see wisps of purple-white Mana smoke fade from its body. The sound of a meaty squelch made Felix look up, and he saw Vessilia standing atop the beast, eight-foot spear in hand and covered in purple-blue blood. She blinked when she saw him.

"Felix!" She hopped off the hound lightly, almost floating in the air before landing neatly beside him. She looked tired under all the blood. "Where have you been? We lost you."

Felix fought the urge to snap at that one. *I think that was the point.* "I got...sidetracked. I'll tell you all about it later. First," he pulled out his hooked sword, placing it against the chest of the Hoarhound. "I've gotta get something."

It was the work of seconds to cut into the beast's body and yank out the elemental core. This one was the same color, but slightly smaller. Holding it high up to avoid the snuffling of his greedy bird, Felix looked into the core depths with Manasight. Inside was a storm of energy, predominantly that purple-white hue he associated with ice Mana, but also slight streaks of other colors, too vague to be picked out. At least not by him.

"That's an elemental core! What are you..." Vessilia began as Pit started whining. Rolling his eyes, Felix tossed the core to the tenku, who snapped it up. Pit glowed with a slight shimmer before it died away. Felix checked Pit's status, noting a +3 in STR and +1 in END. *Not too bad. No other Skills, though. Shame.*

A gasp came from the spear woman, and Felix looked at her.

"Did he just eat that?" Vessilia was shocked. "Those are—"

"What is taking so long? Oh, you caught up. Wonderful." Felix didn't need to turn around to recognize that voice, snide as it was.

"Are there any enemies left?" Felix ignored the kid and addressed Vessilia again as he looked down the road. There were a couple Hoarhound corpses that hadn't been there before, and a number of toppled columns that blocked line of sight. Vessilia snapped her mouth shut and nodded.

"Harn and Magda are fighting the last two giants now. We should see if they need help." Felix nodded and they got moving, leaving Atar behind.

"Hey! Don't ignore me!"

"Oh, are we ignoring the mage again? That's always fun." Evie hopped down from a terraced building, leaning but still mostly intact, like much of this city. She looked just as tired as the rest. "Where've you been, Eyes?"

"Eyes?" Felix asked, his mouth twisting.

"Ya know, cuz of your glowy eye thing," Evie mimed her eyes popping open, wiggling her hands to the sides of her head.

"That's a terrible nickname," Felix laughed. "I don't even have Nighteye. When do my eyes glow?" Vessilia and Evie both looked at each other and then at him.

"It happens when you—"

"Look out!"

All three of them looked up to see a nine-foot Risi Warrior leap over a fallen pillar, streaming blood, but with its metal club raised high. Evie and Vessilia quickly hopped aside, but Felix, startled, did the thing he'd been practicing over nearly every encounter.

Reign of Vellus!

A surge of blue light unfolded from Felix's body, pushing back against the falling giant. Azure lightning crackled up from the ground, burning the creature's flesh even as it was spun sideways by his pulse. As it fell, Vessilia surged forward with her spear, a sudden flurry of blows happening faster than Felix could perceive.

Simultaneously, a spiked chain reached out and wound around the giant's arm and weapon, binding it tight before a shimmer of silver-brown energy made the chains fall hard to the ground, bringing its body down with a resounding crash. A single, flaring ball of fire even zipped across the street and splashed against the creature.

You Have Killed An Unknown Risi Warrior!
You Have Gained XP!

It was over in seconds.

Felix blinked at the two women, clearly impressed.

"Haah, hah, it's when you do that!" Evie panted, and Vessilia laughed, equally out of breath. Evie jerked her head toward the pillar and started walking. "C'mon, can't let my sister have all the fun."

The two young women hopped over the large column, easily six feet tall on its side. Atar walked up beside Felix, looking between him and the departing women before huffing and following after.

Felix narrowed his eyes, letting them move further ahead. Once they were all beyond the stone obstruction, Felix activated Stealth and pulled out his last empty vial. He crouched and quickly but carefully filled the vial, leaving only enough room to cork it. The blood was significantly thicker than the Hoarhound blood, and more blue in color. *Gonna need wax or something to seal these. Hope they don't spill in my bag.*

Putting the vial away in the potion case, Felix stood and dusted his hands off.

He followed the sound of continued battle.

Turned out that Magda and Harn had everything under control.

Felix arrived to find the three Tin Ranks standing in a semi-circle while Magda and Harn beat the piss out of the last giant. Felix threw a quick Analyze its way.

HP: 184/843

That'll be over soon, then. Looking to the side, Felix spied another dead giant that was slowly turning into greasy smoke. And another. There were four more giants here, all similar in size to the one being fought. *Does size determine level with Risi Warriors? That commander was almost fifteen feet tall and level 35. That must mean the leader back at the bronze dome is probably like, level 50. Shit.*

A resounding boom came from behind him, and Felix turned to see Magda standing over the last giant, her shield smoking with a purple-white Mana vapor. The giant struggled for a moment longer, choking on a crushed throat before falling limp for good. Magda walked over to their group, seemingly unfazed by her battle. Harn had disappeared.

How strong are they? Felix had no frame of reference. He figured he had high stats for his level, what with all the Titles he had accrued, but he was positive he couldn't hold up in a fight against either Harn or Magda. He once again tried to Analyze them.

Name: Magda Aren

Race: Human
Level: ???
HP: ???/???
SP: ???/???
MP: ???/???
Lore: Humans are adaptable and prolific breeders. They can be found in many corners of the Continent.
Strength: ???
Weakness: ???

Same as before. He'd Analyzed everyone the night before, but he'd hoped that increasing his Skill level would do something. Apparently not. *Maybe I have to wait until Apprentice Tier. Gotta keep grinding Analyze.*

"We're clear. No giants for at least a few blocks, and none of them are heading this way." Harn hopped down off a building, having climbed it when Felix was distracted. Harn used a hand to catch himself every story, so that when he landed, it was with only a light flexing of his legs.

That was cool.

"What is *that* doing here?"

Magda's voice startled him out of his thoughts, and Felix quickly followed the woman's pointing finger toward Pit. The tenku tilted his head to the side, releasing a curious coo.

"*He* is named Pit. He's my friend," Felix interposed himself between Magda's finger and his Companion. *Who knows what a finger point can do, here?*

"Your...*friend*?" Harn's voice sounded confused from inside his helmet. "How are ya friends with a chimera? They kill everything on sight."

"It is true, Ser Kastos," Vessilia said, stepping forward. "Pit has followed Felix around since we met. He appears to be perfectly tame."

"Why are we just hearing about this now? Where was he last night?" Magda demanded, and Vessilia flushed slightly, opening her mouth to defend Felix again.

"It's ok, Vessilia. Thanks." Felix fixed Magda with his eyes. "I sent him away, so you wouldn't be suspicious of me. I saw how Vessilia reacted to his presence, and I wasn't sure I'd be welcome with him at my side. Turns out, I shouldn't have bothered, since you've been suspicious of me since we met, anyway." Felix sighed, but didn't break eye contact. "Pit is my friend. We made a Companion Pact, and I trust him. That's it."

Harn looked to Magda, his body language weird to Felix, but he couldn't spare the attention to figure that out. Magda also refused to break eye contact with Felix. She stepped forward, coming well within his personal bubble and pushing a finger toward his chest, almost but not quite touching him.

"Let me make this clear. I do not trust you. I do not trust your chimera. You are hiding things, and I'll have my answers once we're safe again." She turned away and marched down the road.

Pot and kettle, lady.

"As of now, we move. The temporary base is likely compromised, and we have to get the wardstones back, as well as the other supplies you left behind." She didn't turn around, but Felix noticed Evie's shoulders slump slightly. He raised his voice.

"Yeah, it's definitely compromised." He tossed the steel throwing knife he had retrieved from the assassin onto the ground, letting it clang loudly. Harn walked up and picked up the blade, turning it over until he saw the spiral etched into one side. Swiftly, he looked up at Magda before turning back to Felix.

"Where did you find this?" Harn's rough voice was urgent, a stark difference from his usual lazy intonation.

"I uh, got caught up trying to follow you. Since no one waited, I took the rooftop route. Along the way, I ran into this woman luring more giants in this exact direction. We fought." Felix shrugged. "She ran off."

Magda had walked back at this point, and Harn handed the knife to her. He kept talking. "What did she look like? Was she human? Wearing dark armor with a black mask?"

Felix was taken aback. "Yeah, yes exactly. She had white eyes under the mask and it was extremely unsettling."

Harn looked to Magda. "We have to go. Now."

Magda didn't argue. They both turned and started running, calling back while they did so. "Keep up!"

The four of them all exchanged glances, then ran after.

Only a few more city blocks and they were back. Felix could see the remains of the collapsed building and the giant trees growing from them, and it was only a few hundred feet away. Several tumbledown structures stood in their way, having come along a different path than before. Harn signaled them all to stop, holding up a closed fist. He started making several hand gestures, some of which were familiar in a vague sort of way, and others which were complicated wrist and finger flexes that meant nothing to Felix. Everyone else understood, apparently, because they all got low and freed up their weapons.

Special hand signals? The only one I'm sure about was the "stop" motion.

Felix could infer, though. Something was up ahead. Or worse, something was waiting at their basement hideout. Harn crept forward, his armor not making a single sound, somehow. Felix wondered at that, but then saw a dark brown, near-black sludge-colored Mana swirling around Atar's left fist. The kid was mouthing a series of syllables, too. *That's not earth. What kind of Mana is that shade of brown?* As far as Felix could tell, every type of Mana had a corresponding color, at least in his Manasight. He'd have to ask Atar what he did later.

Now, Harn had disappeared around the corner. They sat there, crouching in the lee of a crumbling wall for a very uncomfortable set of minutes. Felix took the time to Analyze everything he could, a practice he had fallen out of during recent trials.

Much of the ruins came back the same as his previous tries. Ruined archway, ruined colonnade, ruined residence, etc. ad nauseum. But he did pick out bits here and there. The various carvings, once intricately detailed and now weathered heavily, had begun to give him snippets of something. He spotted a larger than usual sculpture across the road.

Name: Weathered Sculpture
Type: Art Piece
Lore: Once a well-crafted working of stone, the marble has long since lost its luster and definition.

The sculpture, barely two feet high, only vaguely resembled a humanoid figure. A too-large head on top of a narrow body suggested non-human proportions, though the shapeless lump of stone at its feet was mostly unidentifiable. But Felix now knew the stone was marble, at least this sculpture, and that it was once well-crafted. That meant skilled artisans. Which perhaps was obvious given the design of most of the ruins, but any tidbit felt useful to Felix, and he carefully filed it away.

Felix was able to Analyze at least four dozen objects, as well as his allies again.

Name: Evie Aren
Race: Human
Level: 19
HP: ???/???
SP: ???/???
MP: ???/???
Lore: Humans are adaptable and prolific breeders. They can be found in many corners of the Continent.
Strength: Agility, Perception
Weakness: Endurance, Strength

Name: Vessilia ???
Race: Human
Level: 20
HP: ???/???
SP: ???/???
MP: ???/???
Lore: Humans are adaptable and prolific breeders. They can be found in many corners of the Continent.
Strength: Strength, Agility
Weakness: Endurance, Vitality

Name: Atar ???
Race: Human
Level: 17
HP: ???/???
SP: ???/???
MP: ???/???
Lore: Humans are adaptable and prolific breeders. They can be found in many corners of the Continent.
Strength: Intelligence, Willpower
Weakness: Strength, Vitality

Hm, some of it's new. The night before, he could only make out their names and level. *It's interesting to see their strengths and weaknesses. I could have guessed at them based on what I've seen even in that first fight we had. Atar is no surprise. Interesting that Vessilia has higher Strength and Agility than other stats.*

A very slight scrape ahead of them made Felix whirl toward the noise, but it was only Harn returning. He gestured everyone close and made a complicated series of hand movements at the mage. Atar swallowed and frowned in concentration, both hands now moving in a circular motion while they fairly blazed with bright yellow Mana vapor. Felix watched as that vapor expanded and engulfed their entire group, though at a diameter of perhaps five feet, they all had to press fairly close together. Once inside the Mana vapor, Felix realized the outside world was extremely muffled.

A silence spell. So is the bright yellow sound Mana? Is sound a function of magic here? Why not use this on Harn before?

Harn spoke up in a quiet grumble. "We have four giants holed up outside the basement. They're poking around some of the other buildings, and don't seem to know what they're looking for, but they're way too close. Another half block down is a group of three Hoarhounds. They're likewise sniffing around, but haven't caught any scents as of yet." Harn spread his gauntleted hands wide. "Magda, you and I can handle the giants, but if the hounds join in, we'll have trouble. And that's if the Sworn isn't bringing more giants our way. Which I highly doubt."

The Sworn? The assassin?

Magda nodded, and slowly cracked each of her knuckles. Felix didn't understand the warrior, really. She had been a bundle of suspicion and nerves ever since he met her, but she was cool as a cucumber now, slowly deliberating. The spell Atar was casting died away. Apparently, he couldn't hold it very long. Finished with her knuckles, the Shieldwitch nodded at the mage who slugged back a familiar blue potion before casting again. Once the yellow Mana vapor swept out over them, Atar nodded back.

"I'll go. Harn, you hold them off long enough for me to get in and get out." Magda turned, ready to go.

"That won't work, Maggie. The hounds are too fast. You won't make it in before the battle gets too heavy."

"And won't heavy fighting alert more of the giants? How many are nearby?" Vessilia asked, looking between the two leaders. Harn only shook his weird helmet.

"Too far. The fog hampers even our senses. There could be none in earshot, or there could be twenty."

A heavy silence weighed in on them as everyone mulled it over. Atar was sweating profusely, enough that Felix was starting to get concerned for him.

"We need the stones. Too much has been...we need them," Magda said, glancing at the Tin Ranks and Felix.

"Unless you can turn invisible, we're gonna have to call this a loss. Maybe come back for them another time."

"You know we can't, Harn." Magda rubbed her temples, clearly frustrated.

"I'll do it!" Evie volunteered, but her sister simply fixed her with a withering glare, and her ebullience died. "I'm fast and stealthy. I can do it. Especially if Atar gives me a boost with this enchantment."

"It's too minor. He can barely cast it for long now. It won't last long enough to make it there and back," Harn said, gentle in his gruff way.

Felix cleared his throat. *They have to learn to trust me.*

"I can go."

Magda's expression narrowed, and Felix held his hands out, palms open.

"What have you got to lose? Worst case, the giants catch me and I die, right?"

If he were being honest, Felix definitely did not like the way Magda smiled at him.

CHAPTER THIRTY-NINE

Ok Pit, on my signal. Felix sent the image of him holding up his hand and nodding, and then of Pit running out toward the giants. He pushed it, the sensation becoming a little easier than before. Pit nodded his head three times, clearly excited.

Dumb bird. He smiled.

The tenku had been beside himself when Felix tried explaining what he was doing. It had startled him when Pit sent images back toward Felix, blurry edged impressions of a winged creature flying around giant blue collections of smells. It was both visual and olfactory, though the smells were more potent. The blue lumps smelled of cold metal and ice and a weird sort of musk. It was easy enough to figure out what Pit was suggesting, and Felix honestly had no reason to say no. He needed the help.

Just be careful, buddy, he sent worriedly as the tenku padded forward, activating Skulk and sticking to the shadows. Ahead of them, four Risi Warriors rooted around several of the ruined structures. Eight or nine feet tall, they easily filled up the first floor sections of the buildings, often having to fold double to get in and out of doorways.

They weren't gentle, nor were they quiet. They stomped about, yelling and smashing into archways, ripping up the various plant life that filled the city's skeletal remains. Small patches of ice spread out as they roamed, almost as if they passively generated it, though it was far less than in other portions of the city.

Felix held still, eyeing his target. The underground room was two hundred feet away, nearly a third of the block, and the Risi were all nearby. The basement stairs were faced away from him, luckily, so he only had to drop down into the stairwell and muscle open the door... after crossing the street, navigating several questionable ruins, and sprinting the last stretch out in the wide open. *Hoo boy. Sure, Magda. I got this.*

No problem.

Pit crept closer, now lost even to Felix's eyes. Somewhere along the way, the tenku had dipped into a building; Felix could only feel his general direction through their pact.

Pit's Skulk is level 24!

Felix shifted, pressing his feet against the ground like a runner at the starting blocks. Except the ground felt...soft. He flexed his feet and felt the cobbles loosen beneath him slightly, wobbling and making a loud *clack* sound. Felix froze, barely moving his eyes to see if the giants had heard him. Their grunts and shouts continued, unabated.

Breathing a silent sigh of relief, Felix activated Stealth and made himself ready, careful this time not to press too hard against the road. Then he saw it, Pit's bushy tail waving from a second story window three houses down from the Risi Warriors. Two golden eyes, mere specks at this distance, looked at Felix expectantly.

Ok, he held up his hand and nodded. *Now!*

Felix took off, trusting his Companion to follow their loose plan. He crossed the road at speed, the sound of his feet against the cobbles lost amidst the abrupt explosion of squawks and roars down the street. Felix made it to a small patch of shadows before leaping forward through the window of another dilapidated structure, racing within a darkened area filled with soft moss and a couple pale patches of fungus.

Pit's Rake is level 19!
Pit's Bite is level 17!

He's getting a workout. Felix came to a low window near the end of the first building, one with just enough of an angle to see his Companion jumping off of a Risi warrior's chest before darting away. *Now let them chase. Just be safe.*

Felix couldn't help but keep his mind on his friend, even as he hopped over another sill and into an adjoining alley. He was moving as fast as he could, ducking between shadows to try and stay hidden, but the last stretch was ahead. Nearly fifty feet of wide open road, bright sunshine pouring from the clear blue skies as midday moved onward.

But it's not *bright out, is it?* Felix reminded himself. Flaring his Manasight, he let his focus drift as he, paradoxically, zeroed in on the faint haze he saw. This time he felt a sharp jab of pain behind his eyes, and saw his Mana bar drop down 20% as the world was engulfed in thick, rolling fog.

It poured out of buildings and down the streets like a living thing, vapor practically on the cusp of being water again. A soupy haze occluded his vision, one that even his high Perception could not see past. Beyond fifty-sixty feet, the street appeared empty; the only indication of anyone was the continued roar and crash of the giants chasing Pit, and the tenku was a street behind him.

I got this.

Felix took a careful step forward, then another, and another. He hugged the wall, sticking close to the edges just in case. He was more than halfway to the stairwell when the building in front of him toppled to the ground.

Pit's Cry is level 20!

It was an absolute cacophony, dust and debris from shattering stone and snapping trees; all of it pouring only feet before him. But what was worse was that in the midst of all that, two giants stumbled out of the collapse, blue hands waving away thick plumes of dust and hobnailed boots crushing the remains of trees. They roared and called out, grunting something he couldn't understand back in the direction they had fallen.

Shit shit shit shit shit!

Felix dropped low, holding his breath and flaring Stealth as much as he possibly could. He kept his Manasight going, willing himself to continue to perceive the fog. He had to trust the illusion to cover him, or else this whole thing was blown.

Breath Control is level 17!

The Risi paid Felix zero attention and instead were immediately focused on finding something missing in the mess. The two eight-foot creatures rooted around in the pile of debris, grunting and pushing stone aside as they got increasingly angry with one another. A cry came from the other street, a roaring that rose in pitch, as if in question.

"Rak talla! Watta kel no!" One of the giants screamed in answer, still digging furiously.

They don't know I'm here. Felix closed his eyes briefly in relief, before padding forward as slowly and quietly as possible. In order to pass by the Risi, Felix had to make a wide curve around both them and the collapsed debris. The swirl of fog was all that was between the giants and his discovery, a barely there, *illusory* curtain of vapor. Step by step, tortuously slow, and all the while he felt a thrilled exuberance in his chest, a sentiment echoed by his Companion as he ran wild and free among the streets. Felix wasn't quite sure which was him and which was the tenku, but his heart was racing, and adrenaline made his limbs shaky with energy.

Step.

Step.

Step.

Felix was only ten feet away, a simple jump down into the stairwell and through the door. He was gonna make it. He just had to figure out how to—

"Lalla! Watta lakka!"

The Risi's jubilant cry was followed by a creaking groan. Dropping his Manasight, Felix's vision cleared in time to see a looming, two-story pillar the approximate diameter of a redwood tilt and crack as one of the giants pulled its massive metal club out from beneath it. With a single, powerful tug the club came loose, and the giant crowed in success.

"Lalla!"

Then the pillar started to tilt.

Nononono!

Felix dove forward, stone breaking under his feet as he

launched himself over and down into the stairwell. He hit the iron door hard, denting it as he rebounded. Without pausing, Felix pushed his hands forward and swept them apart, flaring the only Skill he could envision at that moment.

Stone Shaping!

Earthen Mana flexed and dissipated against the door. The metal didn't respond in the slightest.

GAH!

Rock sheared above him, the pillar crumbling under its own weight as it lost its long fight against gravity. A spray of pressurized marble geysered into the stairwell. Felix nearly slapped his head as he remembered. *It's a pull door!*

Stone Shaping!

The smallest of gaps appeared on the edge of the door. Enough for a hand. Felix grabbed it and yanked with all he had, the door groaning in protest before popping open.

The pillar broke apart above him, sections of the ancient stone tumbling down like massive millstones and burying the entrance.

Felix was alive.

He unclasped his arms from his head and risked a glance backward. It was totally dark, the collapse blocking out even the slight light from the door frame. With a minor effort, Manasight activated and the room became a series of vibrant colors.

He had rolled ten or so feet into the room, but large, chunky rubble had scattered everywhere, rolling uncomfortably close to him. Felix stood up, quickly orienting himself in the small space.

A wash of dark blue water Mana was coming from several spots along the walls, and though one of them was uncomfortably close to the blocked in door, it seemed fine.

There, the packs. He could see all five of them, left around the area. Though it looked like Magda's had been mostly crushed by debris. Felix winced. *Probably nothing* too *important.*

Felix went about gathering all of the packs, which were roughly shaped like a backpack he was familiar with, just without any cinches and made entirely out of some soft leather.

Name: Avum Skin Rucksack

Type: Container
Lore: It's a bag made out of a large avian. Holds items, usually.

Avum, huh? Like a big ostrich? His eyes lit up. *Like a chocob—*

A sound distracted him. A...crinkling. Felix looked all over, but it stopped after a moment. He shrugged and moved on.

He grabbed Harn's, which was the largest of all the packs, and started dumping the smaller ones in. No way was he carrying all five—er, four of the packs. It just wasn't physically possible.

Harn's bag was pretty dang big, but eventually it reached capacity. Felix took a bit of the overflow items and put them in his own satchel, mostly consisting of extra food, water, and even another case of empty vials. The vials would come in handy for future blood collection.

Felix paused, grimacing. *What a gross thing to have become my new normal.*

A few more items had fallen out of the larger bag when it had overflowed, but it was mostly bric a brac that seemed either useless (a hair comb) or unnecessary (a bottle of oil with a painting of a...*sensual*-looking dragon on it). Frankly, the last one worried him, more than anything.

While he was picking through the remains, he came close to where Magda's rucksack had been buried. Only a small corner of the pack protruded from the large stones, and it had split from the pressure. Dangling out from that corner was a gold-colored necklace. Felix reached down and picked it up.

Name: Twin-Touched Locket
Type: Enchanted Accessory
Lore: Used by many to keep images of their loved ones close. Always paired.

The locket itself was on a thin chain, shaped like a triangle and covered in small engravings. Felix had no clue if they meant anything, but they were probably magic of some sort. *Analyze said they were enchanted. What kind of magic is that, I wonder?*

Unable to restrain his curiosity, Felix clicked the catch, letting the locket pop open. When nothing happened, he turned it over and looked inside. Within there was a small, exquisitely detailed painting of a woman with blond hair and fierce eyes. A woman that looked extremely familiar.

For a moment Felix couldn't figure out why, his mind grasping at the vague impression like anyone would. But then, it came to him. At the giant encampment. When the leader was speaking on the ice.

The prisoners.

This is her, he realized. *This is their friend. Maybe more than friend.*

This same blond woman was among them, one of the few still in some sort of armor. One of the few who still looked defiant.

She was alive.

He quickly put the locket in his satchel and moved to the edge of the room to gather up the wardstones. There were seven of them, and he went to the nearest one. The problem, however, was that the wardstones were still active.

Do I just...turn it off?

He thought back to what Magda did with them. He had watched, but he hadn't *watched,* really. She had whispered something, likely some sort of incantation to activate them, but he hadn't heard her clearly. Reliving the memory wasn't very useful if he didn't see anything in the first place.

Felix put his hand on one of them, feeling the current of water Mana pulsing within. It swirled, currents hidden in its darkness. It was as if it contained an entire lake within it's incredibly dense depths. He felt a shiver run through him, a sense of cold washing over him.

Doubling down, Felix peered into it with his Manavision, but it was a solid ball of water Mana, indistinguishable from a giant marble. Scratching his head, he picked it up.

Immediately the orb stopped glowing and the strangest sound filled the small cellar. It was that crinkling again, as if impossibly small, atonal chimes were being tapped, over and over. But this time, it didn't stop.

Felix pivoted, staring up at where the sound was coming from...and saw frost beginning to cover the entire ceiling.

"Oh fuck."

The ice snaked across the roots of the trees above, the purple-white glow of ice Mana slowly encompassing and engulfing the life Mana. A muted scratching sound came from beyond the ice, and Felix felt his stomach drop as he realized what it meant.

They're digging.

He had to get out.

Quickly, Felix ran around the room and collected the seven wardstones, shoving all of them into his satchel. Squatting next to the overfilled rucksack, he slipped his arms into the straps and stood up. It was extremely, *annoyingly* heavy. It made him feel top heavy and pulled him backward slightly.

Regardless, he made his way over to the edge, watching the ceiling the entire time. Bits of dirt had started to rain down from the root system, sprinkling across the floor. Felix raised his hands and started channeling Stone Shaping.

C'mon, c'mon. Let's see if I can dig out before they dig in.

His Mana coiled and looped through his pathways while Felix focused on keeping the spell efficient; he couldn't risk running out of Mana in the middle of his tunnel. The stone wall melted before him, becoming that sludge-like consistency with which he was familiar, and Felix hurriedly stepped through.

The stone parted around him, shifting and flowing behind him as before to create a tunnel without digging. As the stone re-solidified behind him, Felix could no longer hear the encroaching ice and imminent arrival of his enemies, and his heart unclenched.

A minute later, panting and sweating from the effort, Felix emerged onto the street. The cobbles shifted before him, and he stumbled woozily onward. Despite utilizing his Fire Within, his Stone Shaping spell was still very Mana-intensive over extended periods.

But just as he was catching his breath, a shadow loomed over his shoulder and a chill wind huffed across his neck with a rumbling growl.

"Shit," he said, heart thundering.

Two more shadows joined the first.

Magda rubbed her temples again, though it did her no good.

She didn't really have a headache. Once you've Tempered your Body at least once, normal physical ailments dropped to pretty much zero. That didn't stop the habit though, or the certainty that her head was going to explode from the stress.

But mostly, she did it so she didn't have to look at her sister.

<Rescue mission? For who?>

Evie was needling her with questions, and especially that one, ever since that boy had left to get her wardstones. She was using handspeak, which made it easier to ignore her, but somehow her little sister made even a silent language annoying.

<Not the time> Magda signaled back, punctuating the line by putting her half helm back onto her head. Again, she avoided her sister's gaze, staring out into the swirling fog instead.

As much as Magda was disappointed that Evie didn't stay holed up and safe during their scouting, she was more disappointed in herself. Magda didn't have the mind for all of this skullduggery...it went against her nature and chafed her every sensibility. If it weren't for Callie, she....

Please trust me, she silently pled. *Just a little longer.*

Roooooaar

Awooooo!

The world was suddenly awash in screams and calls of both the giants and their Hoarhound pets. Magda spun toward Harn, who already had his axes out and was facing the way the boy had left.

Moments later, the thud of boots on stone filled their ears, quickly followed by the young man looking worried and carrying Harn's amusingly large rucksack.

"We gotta go!" Felix skidded to a stop, eagerly handing the pack to Harn, who shouldered it without an issue. The kid glanced sourly at her partner for a second before turning back to the rest of them. "I got mostly everything. Where's Pit?"

The Tin Ranks all looked at each other, shrugging. Magda also shook her head. *Maybe the thing sacrificed itself to distract the giants?* She mentally shrugged. *At least it was useful.*

But Felix didn't look worried, just confused. Then he swung around, looking up at the wall they sheltered behind.

"We need to run. We need to run *now*!" Without waiting, he took his own advice.

Magda stared after him, but soon heard a warbling cry as a dark shadow zipped above her head, passing directly through the window of the wall behind them. The creature had four glowing eyes and dark wings that looked like fanged claws, and it sailed gracelessly down onto the ground, where it landed heavily and kept running.

Harn turned, eyes wide. "You heard the kid! Run!"

The Tin Ranks took off, Magda right behind them as the stone wall simply *exploded* into ricocheting rubble.

Three Hoarhounds and a single, bleeding giant charged through the wreckage, their bodies simply bashing through it all.

Magda ran.

CHAPTER FORTY

They skidded to a stop along a paved hillock, the buildings around them a bit more worn down by the wind. All of them were breathing hard, even Felix, though Harn and Magda seemed fresh enough. After a few dicey interchanges, they hadn't heard the sound of pursuit for a few minutes now, and Felix was starting to hope they'd lost them. They took quick shelter in shadows cast by a jumble of fallen porticoes.

"We can't stop; those hounds have our scent." Harn hitched the giant rucksack further up his back and moved to get a clear view ahead.

"Wait...w-wait..." Atar huffed, olive skin slick with sweat and his normally carefully-done hair in disarray. "I can't go much longer."

"We stop at this point, and it won't be one pack that surrounds us. It'll be dozens. Hoarhounds are a menace for a reason, Sparky." Harn started walking.

"You need...to focus...on your Endurance more," gulped Evie, resting against her knees. "Or get that...Running Skill up higher."

"Shut...up...flippy...ass."

Pit pushed against Felix's legs, also eager to move onward despite his heaving sides and panting tongue. After sneaking into the cellar, tunneling out, and running away from the Hoarhounds,

Felix was feeling it too, but he had to trust Harn's judgement. The man was no-nonsense and frighteningly capable.

Harn pointed off in the distance, where a handful of stone towers loomed, some of the highest buildings he had seen so far. Apparently, they were so big the others could see them even through the haze.

"We go there. Gain the high ground and watch out for ice patches."

He started off. With a groan, everyone followed.

Going downhill was easier, but it looked like a mile at least until the towers. Harn in the front and Magda in the back kept everyone on pace, and it wasn't one meant to coddle them. To keep his mind off his body, Felix toggled his dismissed notifications.

Pit's Frost Spear is level 2!
Pit's Wingblade is level 6!

Nice to see Pit moving along. He glanced down at his friend who was keeping pace at his side. The tenku's wings were tucked tight to his body, perhaps to decrease wind resistance as they were getting quite big. He shook his head, wiping sweat that poured from his forehead. Despite Felix's high Endurance and Running Skill, this constant pace was getting to him. The Running Skill decreased the usage of his Stamina during the activity, but it didn't do anything yet for the buildup of soreness and fatigue settling in damn near everywhere. Idly, Felix wondered what Apprentice Tier would make of the Running Skill; he had 7 more Skill Levels before he found out.

Awwooo!

"Shit," Magda swore. Felix turned slightly to see her behind him; she was looking off to the right, and Felix followed her gaze. Beyond a tangle of cored-out-but-still-standing homes, he could see the flash of blue-white fur. "It sounds like there's at least five now."

Felix tried counting as he ran, not quite able to. Instead, he took a mental picture and checked it over. He counted at least ten.

"More than that," he panted. "At least double."

Magda shot him a look, but quickly glanced away. "Harn, we gotta get outta here!"

"I know!" Harn hollered back, no longer worried about silence. "Here!"

All of them took a tight turn into a fire-gutted shopfront. Felix wouldn't have guessed it was a shopfront, but his Analyze hadn't been wrong yet.

Name: Ruined Commercial Structure
Type: Structure
Lore: Anything could have been sold in such a place before whatever calamity befell this place occurred. The inside has been almost utterly destroyed by a recent fire.

Calamity? What happened to this place?

Felix wasn't allowed much time to muse. The sound of paws and claws came closer and closer, and the seven of them hustled up a set of stairs in the back of the shop. Ash and charred wood stirred and cracked beneath them, a number of small saplings having been torched to charcoal. The stairs were stone, thankfully, but they creaked ominously beneath their hurried feet.

Once up top, they heard barking that sounded much closer. The hounds were coming, fast.

"Come," whispered Harn, gesturing toward an open window much like the rest, glass and shutters all long gone. It faced onto a flat roof leading toward another building, this one with three levels above the shop's second floor. "Climb out onto the roof. Evie, you first."

The Tin Ranks and Felix did so quickly, filing out the window as quietly as they could, while Harn and Magda hung back. Soon, they were all on the flat roof, and Harn made a series of gestures at Evie who nodded then ran toward the edge. There was a small alley separating the shop from the five-story ruin next to it, but it wasn't any more than five feet; an easy jump for any of them.

Evie sailed over the gap, slipping through a gaping hole in the wall before coming neatly to her feet. Vessilia went next, followed by Felix and Pit. Atar, still visibly winded, made his best effort at the jump but fell short. Felix barely had time to react, but needn't have bothered. At the last second, the mage threw his arm forward and a small metal rod expanded and pierced the stone.

DANG!

The sound was like a gunshot in the air. Magda and Harn went stock still, and Felix reached down and yanked the mage up by the front of his robes. Just in time, as they all heard loud sniffing abruptly coming from below. Felix was locked in a crouch, his arms holding Atar so close that he could smell the floral fragrance he was wearing.

Guh, that's cloying. Probably better than I smell, though. Haven't had a bath in...four, five days? Suddenly Felix felt bad for holding Atar so close. He was probably *rank.*

Ice started creeping up the side of both of their buildings, and Harn began making wide sweeping gestures in their direction. Unable to understand, Felix looked to the ladies. Both Evie and Vessilia watched Harn a moment longer before nodding and padding quietly toward the stairs leading up. Felix helped the mage to his feet and disengaged, careful to not rustle their clothes or kick any loose stones.

Atar followed after, his face pale and bloodless, still holding the strange expanding rod in his left hand. The rod was maybe the width of Felix's thumb, but was easily six feet long and tapered to a point on one end. Had he had it this whole time?

They picked their way up the stairs. Everything was coated in a fine gritty dust, as if, in the absence of wind and rain, the stone had been reduced to powder by the weight of time itself. Felix was still amazed at how many of these places were still standing at all, considering that they were easily hundreds of years old. If not more, considering magic.

As they neared the fifth and final floor, metal crashed and sudden howling pierced the near distance. The noise was too far away to be an immediate threat, but too close to not be important. He strained his senses, but his Perception picked up nothing else. The others didn't stop, though, so Felix kept on. Shortly after that, they made it to the roof.

"What are we doing?" Felix whispered. The others turned to him, fingers on their lips. Vessilia made a couple of complicated hand signs, but when Felix's blank stare registered, she tilted her head in confusion. Instead, she silently waved him to come with her.

All of them moved to the center of the roof, as far away as possible from any edges, and she made four signs toward Atar.

With a roll of his eyes and almost pained grunt, his hands flashed with bright yellow Mana that swelled and covered the five of them. Sound ward in place, Vessilia spoke up.

"You cannot read handsign?" Vessilia asked.

"No, definitely not," Felix said, shrugging. "I've just been following you guys and working off context clues."

"Huh. Well, Harn had us head to the roof. Said he and Maggie would join us soon," Evie clenched her jaw, clearly upset. Vessilia put her hand on her friend's shoulder.

"They'll be fine." Evie nodded, jaw still tight.

Felix cleared his throat, a little uncomfortable. "So do we continue onward?" He nodded toward the towers Harn had in mind. They were a little less than a quarter mile away, if he was judging the distance right. "We should be able to do it if we stick to the roofs."

Evie grunted softly. "Yeah. That's the plan. We go ahead, get to the nearest tower and get in."

Felix made an impressed face. "That's a lot to say in a few gestures."

"Handsign is pretty compact," agreed Vessilia. "I can..uh, I can teach it to you sometime, if you would like."

"Oh sure. That'd be fantastic," Felix said, already thinking about how easy languages might prove with perfect memory. "Ok, then, let's get moving."

With a gasp, Atar released the silencing spell, and Felix watched the colorful Mana vapor dissipate into the air. He turned and saw the mage regarding him with his usual annoyed expression.

"What are you doing?" Atar's expression fairly screamed. Felix only replied by putting a finger to his lips and making a series of complicated nonsense gestures. Then he walked away.

Magda huddled close to the edge, watching the Hoarhounds prowl the streets below. There were at least fifteen of them now, all spread around the area as they hunted for their group. Harn caught her eye.

<How many?>

<Fifteen. Three packs. Any more Risi?>

Harn hesitated, his face hidden, but Magda knew he had an expression of extreme concentration.

Harn's hands flashed. <Only four. More perhaps, further out.>

Magda nodded. The fighter's Brawler's Physique Skill granted him some distinct advantages, and his Body Tempering had enhanced his senses well beyond what Magda could perceive. But even his powerful senses were defeated by the distorting veil of the Foglands' magic.

<Any sign of the Sworn?>

<None.>

They both knew that meant little. Magda was tempted to believe the boy had lied, but that knife was impossible to fake. Giving herself a little shake, she focused on the problems she could solve.

<Time's up. Distraction, now.>

The Tin Ranks would have gotten far enough by then. Time to do their part.

———

The day wore on as Felix and the others navigated across over thirteen rooftops and passed through structures barely strong enough to hold them. While it astounded Felix that much of this was still standing, it still meant that nearly everything was on the brink of collapse. Most of the time, it seemed hope and probably magic was all that kept the worst of them together.

Regardless, they had made it.

"So this is it, huh?" Felix stared upward at the tower, an impressive construction that rose at least fifteen stories and was utterly covered in complicated statuary. A number of flying buttresses supported the lower levels of the tower, adding width to the base of the building. Felix eyeballed the distance between their three story ruin and the nearest bit of the tower, estimating perhaps twenty feet or so separated them. Whoever had once inhabited these structures had obviously been important, too much of a big shot to be rubbing shoulders with common folk. "Think we can make it?" he whispered.

Atar scoffed, but Vessilia simply smiled, her teeth bright and perfectly straight. Felix's pulse picked up as his thoughts turned.

How do they have such nice teeth? Do dentists exist here?

Vessilia backed up without a word, then took a running leap off of the edge.

Whoa!

With a powerful rush of air, the spearwoman leaped nearly twenty-five feet, easily clearing the distance and landing amid the crowded statues. Felix gaped.

"Dragoons, ya know?" Evie remarked, pushing up his hanging jaw. "Me next."

"Wait," Felix said, riffling through his satchel until he pulled out his brightweave coil. He unraveled it and handed Evie an end. "Here, take this."

"Sure," Evie shrugged, smiling herself. "Always happy to help the less capable." She held onto one end of the rope with one arm as she unwound her spiked chain with the other. After taking a run up herself, Evie threw her chain out, the end of it moving faster than Felix could track. With a metallic clank, the links struck and wrapped around a weather-worn oblong statue. A simple tug, and somehow Evie sailed through the air, propelled by some force directly onto a ledge above.

"How did she...?"

"She's cheating, sort of," whispered Atar. He had long ago collapsed his metal rod and was looking after Evie with something close to envy. "Her Born Trait has to do with altering the weight of herself and her chain."

That's seriously cool.

"Do you mind if I...?" Atar gestured to the rope in Felix's hands.

"Oh! Sure, yeah, not a problem. You go first." Felix handed the brightweave coil to the mage, looking up to see that Evie had tied it off around another statue. It was elevated now, the rope reaching back at an angle to their roof. "It's an enchanted rope, so you—"

The coil suddenly knotted every five feet or so, creating an easily-climbable surface. Atar's hands flared with orange Mana as he fed power into the rope.

"Oh yeah. Of course you know how to use it."

With Felix steadying the rope from behind, Atar was able to cross the distance relatively easily. While the mage might have low values in most physical stats, he apparently had more than enough to climb the rope.

Pit glided across the distance, jumping first to gain some more height, and climbing up the outside of the tower until he reached the Tin Ranks' level. Last to go, Felix gripped the rope and sent a pulse of Mana through it. The rope began to coil up, and once the slack was gone, Felix took a breath and jumped off the side of the building.

Swinging, Felix fairly flew toward the lower tower walls, and braced himself to hit. With a *thump,* he landed feet-first against the tower wall, low enough that he was below any statuary. The magically coiling rope yanked him up the wall, like a slow-moving grappling gun. Unwilling to just hang and wait, Felix complemented the magic rope by climbing with his free hand and legs the rest of the way.

Sadly, his Free Climbing didn't bump up at all.

Felix retrieved his coil, directed it to unknot and loop around his shoulder, and climbed the last few feet up into what appeared to be the fourth floor window. It was dark in here, the afternoon sunlight fighting to penetrate much farther than a few feet, though Felix could make out a large room supported by several round columns. The others were waiting around, though Atar and Vessilia were busy inspecting the far wall, eyes bright in the darkness.

"Took ya long enough," Evie jibed, her voice still not much more than a whisper. Felix grinned and dusted his hands.

"Not all of us have magic weight powers to give us a boost," he joked. Evie grinned even wider, green eyes flashing. Then she looked down at Pit, who was on his haunches at Felix's feet.

Felix read the nervousness in her body language. He wondered what freaked them out so much about Pit. *Was it just that chimeras usually attack them, like they said?* Felix reached down and skritched the tenku's neck, causing his back leg to twitch uncontrollably.

"Don't worry. He's a good boy."

Evie's eyes flashed back up to his, then looked away. He wasn't sure if she was embarrassed or what, but she quickly diverted her attention.

"Hey you! Quit gawking at rocks, and let's get going!"

"There are murals here. They are exquisitely detailed!" Vessilia's smile was wide as she turned back to them. "They've hardly been weathered at all!"

Intrigued, Felix made his way over despite Evie's groan. Vessilia excitedly gestured at the walls where Atar was busy fixedly staring.

In keeping with the architecture of this city, the carvings were everywhere. The spots where the ceiling and floors met the walls were the most heavily detailed, repeated patterns of greenery and small four-legged forms among the friezes. The center of the walls featured a sort of scrolling scene, moving across lush natural vistas like mountains and rivers and forests. Felix stepped up to one and ran his hands across the surface, feeling the very slight bas-relief detail worked into the stone.

Wow. This is incredible.

In fact, the designs and markings reminded Felix heavily of the underground dungeon where he had been imprisoned. He glanced at the floor beneath him, scuffing dirt and dust aside to see the neatly-made edges of pentagonal tiles. He looked back up at the main sculptures, the sprawling depictions of nature and picked out a few small figures dotting the landscapes.

Just like under the mountains. Same tiles. Even similar small figures. Did the same people build both? They're pretty close to each other, so that would make sense.

Yet everything in this city and even under the mountain had been made for people much larger than the small figures depicted. *Why?*

"Ahem, I like uh, rocks as much as the next gal, but we need to get some distance from the ground," Evie said, starting to walk toward a shadowed alcove. Pit was right behind her, and she gave him a wary glance. "Harn said the Hoarhounds are powerful trackers, and I really don't want to wake up to find an ice wolf chewing on one of ya."

The three of them reluctantly followed Evie, discovering that the alcove was actually a series of winding stairs. In fact, it was two series of stairs built into one: the main set of stairs was made for a human (or human-like) stride, while a path along the center was made for much smaller legs. It was two steps for every one.

"Fascinating," Atar murmured.

It was very dark in the stairwell, and Felix had to flare his Manasight to see. The stone all pulsed with a dusty brown laced with flashes of silvery gray. *That's metal, same as the bits of armor I've seen. So iron, probably?* He wasn't a metallurgist, so it could have been titanium for all he knew. Analyze told him nothing, only that it was "quarried stone." Light carvings decorated the outer wall of the stairwell, scrolling vines and leaves twisting and knotting together in an intricate design, and his Manasight could pick out other flashes of metal and stones in the dusty brown earth Mana. He could Analyze those, though: bits of green copper, blue lapis lazuli, and even a smattering of actual silver. The colors swirled and shimmered within the earth Mana, dimming and brightening in turns like a distant night sky.

It's even more beautiful in Manasight than my normal vision. Felix looked around, enjoying the shift and flare of Mana as it flowed through literally everything in this world. *It's like I'm standing on empty air filled with colored light.*

"Oof!"

Felix ran right into Atar's back, who tilted into Vessilia. The spearwoman was braced, though, and kept everyone on their feet.

"What in Avet's name is going on?" Atar whispered, furiously.

Felix could see that Evie was holding up a closed fist. She made several quick gestures, and the other two shifted their stances. Atar looked back at him, eyes wide, and mouthed two words.

"Someone's here."

CHAPTER FORTY-ONE

The room ahead was as dark and quiet as the stairwell had been, but in Felix's Manasight it all swirled with color. Evie stalked ahead, moving low to the ground and as quietly as possible. Felix couldn't see much, being stuck in the back, and after two gut-wrenching minutes, Evie returned, her eyes brightening significantly as she stood up straight.

"I was wrong. Can't find anything," she whispered. "If someone *was* here, they left no trace. Even the dust ain't disturbed. Everyone fan out, though, see if you notice anything I missed."

The other four climbed the rest of the way into the room, inspecting it for the first time. Felix's vantage widened until he could see an oval-shaped room containing four open archways and a single odd depression in the center. He stepped closer and found that it was a pentagonal hole, with two tiers of seating in it. The very center was the lowest and contained a boundary of carved stone.

It's a fire pit with...tiered seating. Reminds me of those old conversation pits from the 70s.

Weird, but not too remarkable. Felix kept looking.

The floor was more of the same pentagonal tile, mazed with stress fractures and coated in a thick dust that, just as Evie said, was undisturbed until they trudged through it. There was no sign of anyone, either via his Tracking Skill or his Manasight, no matter how he strained the ability.

Felix turned back to the women, his Manasight still flaring from his inspection of the room. Both of them were vaguely humanoid shapes dominated by the green-gold of life Mana, a blurry line of power that branched like small saplings along their spines. But for a few flickering moments, he could spot flashes of other colors sparking within their bodies. He blinked and they were gone.

Ugh. He rubbed his eyes, feeling them strained after relying on the Skill for so long. *So no one is here. What did Evie sense, then?*

"Nothing is here," announced Atar, walking from one of the side rooms and dusting his robes. "Just dust and more impeccable sculptures. Who exactly lived in this place?"

"Not a clue. My father's library is extensive, and still I have not heard of an entire city within the Foglands." Vessilia put her hands on her hips, clearly entranced by the stonework all around her. "It is truly fascinating."

Atar smiled in her direction, a familiar light in his eyes.

Felix smiled to himself, turning toward one of the archways and noticing yet another stairwell. This led upward, much as the last, with the same smaller stairs set into the center.

"Third and final check. Nothing. Anyone else?" Evie asked from across the room.

"...No," offered Atar while fiddling with a pouch at his belt.

"Zilch over here. Just dust," Felix added.

"Vess?" Evie prompted when the young woman didn't reply. She looked up guiltily from inspecting the walls, eyes wide.

"Mhm? Oh! No. Nothing at all."

"Okaaay," Evie drawled, stretching her shoulders and arms. "Then we make camp. We can't stray too far; gotta let Maggie find us somehow."

They did just that. In a short piece of time, the five of them had settled in, not having their packs or even blankets to lay out. Instead, as the wait turned to an hour, Vessilia and Atar had drifted back to the walls, and Evie paced and fretted near the stairwell. She wasn't nearly as calm about her sister going off into danger as she projected.

Does she have the Acting Skill, too?

Unsure what to do with himself, Felix sat at the edge of the tiered depression, idly petting Pit's fur/feather combo. Somehow, the combination was smooth and soft, not nearly as coarse as he would have expected.

I need to get away. Gotta take care of these vials soon. Can't imagine they'll last much longer without refrigeration.

Unwilling to wait any longer, Felix stood and made his way to the stairs on the far side of the oval room, Pit close behind him.

"Where're you going?"

Felix looked back over his shoulder at Evie, who, despite her question, was barely paying attention to him. "Can't sit still, so I'm checking out the floor above us."

Evie nodded, then brightened. "Good! Keep an eye out for anything weird, and don't do anything I would do."

"I think you got that backwards," started Felix.

"No, I didn't." She was already back to pacing.

Felix felt a chuckle bubble up in his chest. *What a weird girl.*

He started up the stairs. *Cute though.*

The stairs spiraled upward for a few minutes, decorated much the same as the previous one. So a galaxy of magic guided him upward, his Manasight having to work double time in order to pick out what was stair and what was the flash of inlaid precious material.

Why do simple materials like these make my vision strange? It was more than colors, it was a vibrancy to these metals and gemstones that almost oscillated in his eyes, as disconcerting as it was beautiful. *Analyze doesn't ping them as anything special. Just silver and copper, lapis lazuli and serpentine. Not even really rare fantasy metals like mithril or anything.*

So caught up with these sights, Felix only barely registered that the stairs were ending. So, he was startled when he found a solid wall directly before him. Painfully so, as he thunked his forehead against the rough stone and stumbled backward two steps in surprise.

"Ow! What?" Felix rubbed his head. "Why's there a wall here?" Felix considered the mortared stone before him, eyeing the makeup of its dusty brown Mana shot through with jagged veins of silver. It was like any other wall in the tower and completely unremarkable for that fact. Annoyed, he turned around.

Then he turned around again.

W-where are the stairs?

They were gone. Felix was in a narrow room; a hallway, really, no more than five feet wide but stretching forward another fifty feet. Triangular alcoves lined the path, each heavily-shadowed but filled with sculpture of some sort. Pit whined, picking up on Felix's distress.

The stairs had vanished into thin air. Or had he been teleported? Was that a thing? Or...

Or did the walls move?

Felix wasn't sure why he found that more creepy than being translocated by magic, but it was. He tapped the walls again, pushing against the floor and baseboards in the hope that he could activate some hidden catch. But nothing was there. Analyze sent back the same information as any other wall, and his Manasight caught nothing else. So, with a rapid pulse, he took step after step down the new corridor, Pit padding behind him with his wings tight and tail low.

There was no dust, he noticed. His steps brought back the clean sound of hard leather on harder stone, with a slight scrape as he pushed off his back foot or pivoted. Every sound felt close and immediate, as if nothing else existed except him and his boot noises. As he passed the first of the alcoves, he saw white statues of animals on simple, fluted display stands. He Analyzed them as he went. There were detailed recreations of large cats called Kanwar, birds called Fellhawks, Grey Wolves, and even small, Fat-Tailed Lizards. But as Felix strode further down the hall, the statues grew...strange.

Each subsequent alcove repeated the same types of creatures as before, except each of them had been altered in some way. The Kanwar had grown scales and small horns, the Fellhawk had gained fangs, the wolves grew another set of legs, and the lizards...they gained wings.

Oh what the hell. Skinks are gonna follow me forever. What is all this?

The corridor came to an end with each of the animals having gone through a complete metamorphosis, turning into altogether different beasts than they started. Felix Analyzed them and came up with four new names: Harnoq, Tenku, Wendigo, and a Wyvern.

Not Skinks at all. Something totally different.

"Tenku, huh?" He eyed Pit, who sniffed at the sculpture. "One of your aunts or uncles, buddy?"

Pit simply snorted in disdain and walked ahead. Felix smiled and followed.

The room opened out into a larger chamber, an ovular one almost identical to the one below, only without any adjoining rooms, just a single darkened alcove on the far side. It even had the same tiered pit. The two largest differences were the total lack of dust here, as if someone had just cleaned the room, and the absolutely massive bas-relief murals dominating every single wall.

Exploration is level 20!

Much like the ones below, they were far better preserved than the countless carvings outside. They also heavily featured natural formations. One wall was entirely filled with a split-peaked mountain made of thick, dull iron, heavily forested and featuring two peaks that appeared to have been sundered in two at some point. The second wall had a sprawling forest rendered in silver and serpentine stone. And the last wall featured a waterfall above a sprawling lake, the water picked out with lapis lazuli and pieces of near-translucent alabaster.

On top of that, the walls were crawling with depictions of animals. Most were unidentifiable to Felix as they seemed to be a mish-mash of multiple species spliced together. Some, however, greatly resembled the statues in the previous hallway.

Chimeras.

Repeated over and over were small white figures, rendered as caring for or otherwise interacting with the chimeras. Unlike any other carving, they were made of a smooth white stone.

Are these the caretakers of these ruins? The original inhabitants? Felix found himself fascinated by it all, especially the similarities between this place and the Nymean Temple. *The Temple also had naturalist style art. Is it similar ideology? Or were the two connected?*

Across the far side of the room, the shadowed alcove resolved into another archway, this one with a set of stairs leading up...and back down a level.

Good. Not sure how I got turned around, but I can get back to the others easily. He ran a hand across an immaculately-rendered tree on the wall. *I'd hate to use Stone Shaping and ruin some of this.*

Mind more at ease, Felix made his way back to the tiered depression. He seated himself within it and took a breath. Then, he laid out his blood vials.

Hoarhound blood. Risi blood. Assassin blood. Felix set them all on the bench beside him, eyeballing them in turn. The first two were dark-colored and rimed with literal frost, the hound blood most of all. The power of this blood hadn't seemed to have abated, and the idea of eating them was challenging at best. The last was the simplest, but also the one he was worried about the most; the liquid had darkened considerably, and it was normal human blood. Not magical creature ichor or whatever. Just like, A positive.

Just take it slow. I'll do the Hoarhound first. Chances always seemed better for Skill gain rather than Memory gain, but it was a crap shoot as far as Felix was concerned. He hoped for a Skill, in this case.

Felix lifted the container, hands sticking slightly to the cold surface. He popped the seal and ice cracked from the vial. With a grimace, Felix tipped it back quickly, except the blood within was viscous and moved like tar. It rolled, stretching and drooping until, all at once, it plopped right into his mouth.

OUGH! It was vile, a thick, terrible paste that Felix had to actually chew to swallow. What was worse, the viscous liquid was so cold that he felt pain radiate from his tongue and throat, a sensation that burned a line of agony down his entire esophagus.

New Skill Learned!
Cold Resistance (Common), level 1!
You've felt the powerful effects of frost and have grown stronger for it. Damage reduction increases with Skill Level.

Felix pushed the blood down, actively shoving it toward his core. He cycled the thick sludge, pouring it into the furnace of his Fire Within, willing that his power devour it. After a moment, his blue-white Mana surged, and the power began to eat up the ichor, burning it for fuel.

Pain.

Frost crackled across his back and ribs, extending down his

arms and legs with a burning ferocity. Cold poured off his body like steam, and Felix could sense a purple-white Mana vapor begin to pool around him in the tiered pit he sat in, his own special fog that rolled out from his chest.

It was agony.

But he could handle this.

Cold Resistance is level 2!
Cold Resistance is level 3!
...
Cold Resistance is level 6!

Pain Resistance is level 28!

Congratulations!
Your Title Gourmand Has Garnered You Insight!
You Have Fully Digested Your Opponent's Mana!

You Have Learned A Skill From A Hoarhound!

Mantle of the Long Night (Rare), level 1!
The cold of the Long Night cannot be stopped, only delayed. Extends an aura of cold centered on yourself. Range and strength increases with Skill Level.

Yes!

The pain stopped as sudden as the notifications appeared, and it was like a drug all by itself. Then, his brain flooded with palpable relief, easing through his bones even as his appetite surged. It had worked.

Thank fuck. Felix rubbed at his chest, memory of the burning pain going nowhere soon. *I hope this Skill is worth the pain.*

His stomach growled, loudly.

How long since I last ate? He honestly wasn't sure, so he fumbled with his satchel and pulled out a few servings of jerky and hard bread. Between heavy chewing and hearty swigs of his rescued waterskin, Felix made short work of the meal. By the end of it, he felt remarkably more human.

That was...more food than I've had in a while. I feel like I could eat more, too. Is this because of my stat increase? More power, so more fuel is necessary? He'd have to test that at some point, but he shook his head and checked his Health and Stamina. Both had recovered adequately during his meal, so Felix meditated a bit longer to top himself off before uncorking the vial of giant's blood.

This vial smelled awful: distinctly gamey and extremely cold, like a distillation of a piercing winter wind pushing through a bloated carcass. Steeling himself, Felix quaffed it.

Thick, but more corn syrup to the Hoarhound's molasses, it rolled down his throat quicker than he anticipated. A slight burn emanated as it did, still obviously cold, but almost refreshing compared to the first.

What a cool life. I can now add knowledge of the palatability of different monster bloods to the ol' resume.

He laughed, touching his chest, the blood feeling like gnarly heartburn. *At this rate I—*

The world pulsed, a familiar ripple pushing out around him like a stone in a still pond.

You Have Gained A Memory From A Risi Warrior!
Would You Like To Review It Now?
Yes/Yes

Felix's eyes widened, but then he was gone.

He was somewhere else. Some*one* else.

Lork was pissed.

Pissed and uncomfortable.

Lork hawked, reaching deep before spitting a wad of phlegm the size of Felix's fist onto the ground. It landed with a great, gooey splat and made a few of the prisoners scatter. Even seeing the Humans run didn't cheer him up.

It had been a bad day.

Lork had been part of a hunting party in the city, and had gotten separated during a commotion with free Humans. The Mother-cursed fog turned him around, and by the time he found his crew, they had all been killed. Even the Commander.

Fie on that fat bastard. *Lork wouldn't lose any sleep over him.*

But that meant he *was the one who had to report their defeat to the Circle. As a result, he got stuck with guard duty and half rations.*

"Damn those Humans!" They had cost him three entire meals at this point! The moment he found them, he'd show them the meaning of fear. He'd eat their entire faces off and make 'em watch!

Still, *he mused, digging a finger through his wide nostril.* Could be worse. *Lork was doing guard duty but was in easy reach of the icefire and their frostbanks, keeping his body in better condition than it had been running patrol out in the city.*

Kept my mind, though. The Daughters ain't taking no chances with patrols. *Lork had seen a few of 'em, empty eyes and empty skulls for twelve hours, just puppets for the frost witches.* Some ain't even come back.

Lork shifted on his rock, still uncomfortable. Despite his rocky perch, this was the closest to home they had in these insufferably warm lands. It was nice to bask in the frostbanks.

Even if *he had to watch a bunch of pale children shiver in their cages.*

"Oi, Lork. Meal time." A gruff voice came from the left, closer to the icefire than Lork was allowed. The only exception was meal time. Lork traded off with a fresh warrior, this one barely bearded. Lork snorted, getting a venomous look from the kid as they passed.

Closer to the fire, Lork found a pile of charred meat, seared over the icefire and stacked on a large flat rock. Other kin were seated around the icefire, breathing in its healing smoke and basking in its radiance. His mouth watered as he considered the array of meat before him, aching to take all of it, flee to a cave, and gorge himself. Before he could act on it, a burly kin got in his way.

"Short rations for you, Lork," the kin growled, white beard fluttering. He grabbed a couple thin haunches and shoved them toward Lork, not moving until the punished guard had started walking away again.

Lork made his way to the edge of the icefire light, barely close enough to enjoy its power. Disgusted at his own weakness, Lork tore into the haunches, quickly stripping them of flesh. The others started talking once Lork moved away, some disappointed there had been no fight. Lork barely listened.

"...entered the labyrinth. Ain't none of 'em comin' out." One darker blue kin was saying, his white beard greasy with meat juice. A taller and more slender kin reclined next to him and burped loudly.

"They got that leader though, right? The angry one." The slender kin made a face, pretty comical on his larger and exaggerated features. "She been through like seven times now, I think. She ain't dead yet."

"You think they'll get it?" asked a hopeful voice, another beardless kin with wide eyes.

Mother's breath, how desperate are we? Taking in

children. *Lork snapped the bones in his hands, beginning to suck on the marrow as he lamented the state of his people. The others kept talking.*

"Grimmar will make 'em get it, even if he has to puppet them himself," vowed one scarred veteran, hands filled with a thick slab of meat that he had barely touched. "Blood will show, and we'll get ours. Make no mistake."

Grimmar. *Even the name made Lork shiver. Their leader and ruler of the Circle was kin enough to inspire his people to travel three thousand miles to this cursed land, and witch enough to put fear into the hearts of all who might oppose him. It was Grimmar's mad plan, this journey to the south, Grimmar's visions that guided the Circle, and it was Grimmar's might that would claim it all.*

He'll do it, *Lork agreed. Nothing could stop Avet's own.*

CHAPTER FORTY-TWO

Felix became aware of the sound of a single, low-pitched chord. It sounded like hunger at the end of a long night, like cold held close by the dark, of teeth not used.

With an awful clarity, he became aware of his body: the pleasant fullness of his stomach, the delicious flavor of the meat the giant had eaten, and the terrible certainty that it wasn't pork.

URGK!

All at once, Felix fell forward and vomited. His hastily-eaten meal dashed against the fire pit, easily filling up the carved ring. He hacked and coughed, his stomach and mind refusing to believe he was empty, muscles wringing him out like a dishrag. When he was able to sit straight, Felix found Pit sitting close to his back, gold eyes watching with concern.

"I'm a—*ghlk*, I'm ok," Felix insisted, wiping at his mouth. He *knew* he didn't really eat what the giant ate, but he found it impossible to convince his mind that two meals were separate. Even the thought of the greasy, charred haunches of meat made Felix's stomach turn, so he pushed down the thought. Or tried to. Having perfect recall wasn't always great.

Lessons of the Past is level 10!
Lessons of the Past is level 11!

That's something, at least. Felix leaned back carefully, resting his body against the tier seating behind him. The stone was hard and cold, but Pit nuzzled up against his shoulders like a fluffy body pillow. He smiled when he heard the distinct sound of cooing coming from the tenku.

Ok, I got a Memory that time. What did I learn?

Felix retrieved his battered notebook, fishing out an even worse grease pencil. It had snapped in half at some point. *I'll have to see if I can borrow a spare from their big bag of supplies.* He found a clear section of paper, drew a line of demarcation from the other packed notes, and started writing.

Labyrinth. Something inside it? Something about this "Mother."
Leader's name is Grimmar, who rules the Daughters of the "Circle," and controls the others.
Puppets = mind control? Explains the dead look in the patrolling giants' eyes this morning.
Prisoners being led by the "angry one."

Notes finished, Felix regarded the page. Technically speaking, the Nym didn't need to write any of this down, but it helped him organize his thoughts. Having perfect memory was well and good, but only if he knew how to think in the first place. Something his mother taught him a long time ago.

First step to doing right is thinking right. Hey, Bumble?

Felix's breath hitched suddenly, his nose burning and throat aching. *That...it was like hearing her voice.* Why hadn't he thought of this before? His memory had a chance of perfect recall beyond thirty days, but he'd rarely used it, too preoccupied with the now. He tried again, thinking back on anything, summers and vacations, long evenings near the beach, anything. But it was all just noise, vague impressions of washed out scenes. Just like any other memory.

But still. Makes me feel a little less alone.

Felix smiled to himself, lightly stroking Pit's crown. After a minute or two, he took a breath and centered himself. It was time for the last vial.

I wasn't able to learn any Skills from the giant's blood, but the Memory at least gave me more information on them. Maybe I can learn the Risi's language? He scratched out another note. *I'll try that later.*

Carefully, Felix picked up the last vial. This one, unlike the others, was simply cool to the touch. No ice or magical phenomena had formed around the glass. It was just blood, darker and thicker than it had been when he'd collected it.

It's congealed, a little. Ugh. Maybe I can pass on this one...I mean what do I need from an assassin I beat up?

Felix smiled sourly at himself, unable to even speak that lie aloud. The assassin had wiped the floor with him. If he hadn't fought off the poison she had used, he would have died there on the roof. And if he hadn't put her on the back foot somehow, Felix doubted she would have fled. She was capable and ruthless, attempting to kill him simply because she could.

Speaking of, what happened back there? What was it called? Right. "Essence of Inevitability." What the hell does that even mean? Felix tightened his grip on the vial and let his mind drift, recalling the experience within his own little world of torment.

"Rare Poison Detected During Formation!

Choose a Feature:
Inevitable
Deadening
Heart-Rending

Still dizzy from the lack of pain, Felix chose the first one, barely reading it.

Congratulations!
You have absorbed the essence of inevitability!"

He cut off the memory as pain started to mount. Felix opened his eyes, and they shone blue for a brief second before dimming to nothing.

Holy...that's a rush. Like reliving the moment. Felix could still recall the pain he had felt just hours ago. It tingled at the edges of his nerves, the memory dangerously close to rehashing the agony. Shaking his head to clear it, Felix tried to make sense of it all.

Inevitability. He looked for a blue box to appear, hopefully one with helpful information. No such luck.

Essence.

Formation?

With a nearly soundless chime, a new screen appeared before him.

<u>Formation, Apprentice Stage, Essence(s)</u>
Body, 1 of 3, Inevitability
Mind, 0 of 3, N/A
Spirit, 0 of 3, N/A

Ok! Now we're getting somewhere!

Felix poked at the words Body, Mind, and Spirit. But nothing happened. Apprentice Stage, at least, he thought he could make sense of now. He had reached Apprentice Tier in Poison Resistance while that gnarly concoction was inside his body. So he...took something from it? Absorbed it? Why?

Moreover, he had chosen "inevitability" instead of a super cool one like "heart-rending?"

But what did that mean?

Felix probed the Essence column and finally, finally, something happened.

You have absorbed the essence of inevitability!
Continue to temper yourself and reap the rewards!

Huh. Temper myself? He rubbed his eyes, feeling a headache coming on. Those guilders need to get back soon. I've got so many questions.

Tempering sounded like strengthening to Felix, and he wasn't against that idea. This has to be a common thing, right? The how was a bit of a mystery, though it clearly had something to do with reaching Apprentice Tier. He nodded to himself. He'd ask the Tin Ranks about it when he went back downstairs.

In fact, Felix was convinced he'd taken the wrong route with them. The Tin Ranks especially were very accepting of him and his particular circumstances. Despite Magda's suspicions (and Harn's to a lesser extent), Felix figured it was time to be honest.

I'll explain what I can. They don't seem to have an issue with my Race, after all, despite all my worry at having a "Lost Race." They had to have Analyzed me by now.

That decision firming up in his mind, Felix lifted the vial which had warmed slightly in his grip, though the blood was still disgustingly chunky. Taking a deep breath, Felix uncorked the vial and tipped it back.

"OUGH GAWD," he coughed. "That's ughk! That's horrendous."

He expected it to be coppery. After all, he'd bitten his own lip before. He had even expected lumpy sour curdles. But he hadn't expected it to be cloyingly sweet!

"Oh damn! Oh fuck! That's -erup- bad," Felix pushed down his gorge, forcing himself to swallow the chunky mess even as the taste of it invaded his entire mouth. Several thumps on his chest and it passed, leaving him with what felt like a slime trail of salty sweetness.

Deep breath. Any moment now, and your core will burn it all up. Deeeep breath.

But nothing happened.

"Well...shit." Felix felt at his chest and core, prodding. "Does it not work on humans? That's a waste. Pit, it's time to—"

Felix turned around, but there was no one there.

There was nothing there.

Blackness, pure and complete filled his vision. Not a speck of Mana swirled or shined, not a soul moved. Felix looked down at his hands and he could clearly see himself, fully lit by a sourceless light.

This is terrifying. His words swept around him, jangling like out of tune bells as the not-air shivered. But his chest didn't rise, his breath didn't move. Definitely not a fan of this.

What the hell is going on?

The discordant chime of his words shook the darkness, the void...thinning, somehow. Felix reached out a hand, attempted to grasp the shadows but there was nothing there. No substance at all around him. Or below him. Felix had a dizzying moment as he regarded the endless dark beneath him, a negative space so absolute it was like standing on a featureless black painting that was at turns flat and terrifyingly 3D.

AHH!

More atonal noise, more shivers in the world around him. Felix fought down his panic, applying his mind instead.

Move.

The nothing shuddered, but less. Like a taut tarp in a gentle wind.

Move!

A wobbling, as if the darkness was balanced on the edge of something else. Felix channeled all of his fear and adrenaline into a single shout, pouring all of it out of him.

Move!

With a soundless explosion, the void shattered into ten trillion pieces, each one rotating and oscillating into a cascading spray of people upon a white background. The people flickered outward, shot forward as if shot from cannons. Behind them trailed imprints of themselves, footprints that were their entire past, crawling forward at lightning speed like a billion caterpillars shuffling into infinity.

It was, in a phrase, trippy as balls.

Felix held his head, his eyes ready to explode from his skull. He looked up, and the figures extended upward, too, and down, and behind him. Felix stood in an epicenter while infinite permutations of people spread like a fractal map of armored women.

Wait. Armored...Felix scanned their faces, noting their darkened leathers and brace of blades. These are all the same woman. The assassin!

Holy shit, what was in that blood?

In some iterations the woman was wearing no armor or mask, just simple clothes or heavy jackets. Sometimes she was even dressed in elaborate finery. But mostly it was the mask and armor, over and over.

A single person in an infinite span of moments, the thought struck him over the head as he watched the assassin unfold endlessly into the white void. She reached in all directions, echoing across his mind like a ringing chime. It was a sublime chord, plucked and shuddering as she spiraled away from him in a dance that was pure chaos. All movement without meaning.

Then, without warning, a terrible discord shuddered through the music, a defect in the crystalline tones that spread like cracks across the person's spiraling self. The cracks mazed the void, spreading like broken ice, shearing with inevitable finality.

Blindly, Felix thrust his mind forward, moving somewhere, anywhere he could. Anything to escape.

He touched one of the infinite moments and flinched as time splintered like a shattering stained glass window. It enveloped him even as it fell in on itself.

And he was gone.

Ilia squatted on the ledge, wearing the shadows around her like a familiar cloak. Below her, human prisoners toiled between the frosted colonnades. Giantfolk stood watch, not closely, but certainly not far away enough for any of them to attempt escape.

The prisoners were too smart to try that again, though she could hope.

Certainly would cut into the drudgery of this assignment, she thought, rolling her shoulders and flexing her leg muscles, trying to stay limber in the cold. At first, Ilia had been intrigued by this spot of monster on human slavery, but it had grown tiresome quickly.

If I hadn't gotten separated from my quarry, I'd have better things to do. Ilia rolled her eyes. They're headed here, though. Sooner or later, they'll show up.

The prisoners were mostly human, and were largely pathetic and weepy. Broken, by all accounts. Barely a hundred of them left, too. Ilia had been listening to them whisper among themselves, everything from curses at the gods to stillborn attempts at good humor. These men and women were desperate, the bare remnants of a grand expedition into the Foglands. Something that hadn't been tried in a hundred years.

It would have been audacious if it had succeeded.

Now it was blackmail fuel, because no matter what Ilia was hired to do, she knew Elder DuFont would pay good money for this never to come to light.

To have wasted so many resources on an expedition this size...and to have not one person return with anything? An absolute scandal.

Did the Elder think I wouldn't find out? Ilia scoffed.

She jumped across the ledges, using Cloudstep to tap off a platform made of air when the footing disappeared.

Interestingly, there was a leader among the prisoners. A

woman with honey-colored hair, cropped short, and wearing light drakeskin armor. She was fresher than most, even still had some fire in her eyes. Most of the others were barely above livestock at this point.

Ilia watched as the woman ordered around the few who would listen. With many surreptitious glances back at the giantfolk, she went about teaching them how to fight, detailing how to survive in the labyrinth below.

Poor fools. You'll all be dead by dawn. Ilia had no doubts that whatever these behemoths were after was deadly; after all, if it was easy, they'd send their own folk in.

Unable to Analyze in this blasted fog, she could still feel the power contained in the giants. Especially what emanated from the bronze dome near the sink hole. Whatever dwelt in there was terrifying.

A dark crack sheared across a nearby pillar, though Illia did not look at it. She continued watching below, noting the prisoners' ragged clothing and lack of shoes. When the second crack spread across the ground below, she did not notice, either.

When the third and forth cracks branched across the sky, Felix looked up.

Pulled from the assassin's body, a powerful vertigo destroyed Felix's sense of balance. He tipped and fell from their perch, landing on the heavy snow with a muffled thud. But it didn't hurt. Felix felt nothing, even as the memory around him began to splinter into a thousand pieces.

The prisoners stared at him in fear, their faces only half finished from this angle, a hodgepodge of misaligned features that gaped in terror at him. Horror mounted in his chest, but his screams wouldn't come.

He had no voice.

And then the world was rent asunder.

Vvim was old.

Far older than they had any right to be. And they were bored.

They were old enough to remember this place as it was, before the end. They remembered when Shelim was strong and beautiful, a jewel in the crown of the greatest kingdom ever known. The valley had been lush then, filled to the brim with life and laughter, so much that the mountains rang with it.

But that was long ago.

Before the Ruin, before the great work was finished. Before the curse.

They once had family, even after the Ruin. Now, Vvim only had the shadows of the past for company, and their memory dimmed with every passing year.

Vvim let out a sigh that was as dusty as the room around them. They rarely breathed anymore, just as they rarely ate. Why bother? When it all turned to ash in their mouth, it was better just to remember food.

Then, against all odds, something happened.

A tingle of discharged Mana surged across Vvim's desk, lighting a decrepit crystalline deposit set inside the surface. With a palsied hand, they pushed the inches thick layer of dust away and peered at the deposit. It glimmered blue, gold, then surprisingly, green-gold.

"It...cannot...be," Vvim wheezed, breath again pumping their withered bellows. They had felt a few Humans enter the tower some time ago, but they had withdrawn their attention when their senses detected nothing remarkable about them. But that had changed.

They were using sorcery.

Not magic. No pitiful rote Skills and Spells. True, honest sorcery. Now that he was aware of them, Vvim could feel the harmonics subtly shift the air itself. They raised a hand and manipulated the resonance, feeling the texture of the working.

It felt...discordant. Wrong. Not like a song half sung, but like a snapped string or punctured drum. It felt like an ending.

Vvim smiled, their skin creaking as their fur stretched. Small fissures appeared on their cheeks and chin, though no blood came forth. Their teeth showed, sharp and white.

Vvim felt their heart stir in their chest, a weakened, shriveled thing that caused their ears to practically roar as fluid pumped through their veins.

They were ancient. Far older than they had a right to be. And they were happy.

After millennia, death had come.

CHAPTER FORTY-THREE

Lessons of the Past is level 12!
Lessons of the Past is level 13!

Felix woke up in the fire pit. His entire body felt like he'd been beaten with one of those giant metal clubs. He was sore and aching and it hurt to *think.*

He didn't move, kept his Manasight deactivated and eyes closed. The sound of his breathing was loud, and the smell of his sick was sour, but he laid there unmoving for a long time.

At some point, he roused himself. His brain began to work, small bursts flashing in the dark of his skull.

That Memory...what was any *of that? Are humans so different from monsters?* Why did he see that insane M.C. Escher print of a landscape? Eyes closed, he could still perceive his interface. Felix noted his Lessons of the Past Skill had risen to level 13...and that before the assassin's blood, it had risen above level 10.

Level 10 has been a milestone for Skills, I've noticed. Did...did the Skill change?

If so, Felix didn't like it. He'd have to be more cautious in the future, especially if those...fissures reappeared. The thought of them, of their deep void color, sent shivers of pain across his skull. It shrieked like nails on a chalkboard or squeaky styrofoam with existential terror thrown in. He squeezed his eyes shut and tried to forget it.

It didn't work.

Finally, Pit's confusion and concern radiated through their link, and Felix forced himself to a sitting position.

Puke had dried to him and his tattered shirt. He finally stripped it off and threw it away from himself. No shirt, just pants. Just like old times.

"I gotta get more durable outfits."

Massaging his neck, Felix stood up and activated Manasight. He found his three vials, though it took a moment to locate the last cork. Climbing out of the pit, he leaned over and washed his three vials out with his waterskin before taking a long pull himself.

He felt remarkably better after that. He had probably been slightly dehydrated.

I'm sure I gotta eat some more, but... his stomach flopped over at the idea. *Maybe later.* Though the food didn't excite him, it was filling at least. He missed stupid corner store pizza, and gas station hamburgers, two staples from his life before.

Admittedly, my diet and exercise regimen has certainly been better since I came here. Felix looked down at his bare torso, seeing muscles he had never had before. The fat on him was nearly burned away, only a little sticking to his love handles still. He ran his hand down his stomach, feeling the distinct impression of *abs*.

"Quest Received," Felix said in a serious voice. "Fight monsters, almost die, do it again. Reward: Aaabbbs." He chuckled to himself.

Yeah. He breathed in again and let his arms rise and fall with a soft slap. *Coulda been worse. Ok!* He clapped his hands together, then bent and retrieved his notebook and grease pencil.

"What have we learned, Pit?" The tenku tilted his head at Felix, letting out a half chirrup. "Well, the assassin's name is Ilia. Good to know for the future. Maybe the Silver Ranks will know who that is?" He jotted down the note. "There were a hundred prisoners when Ilia was there. Unsure how long ago the Memory was. Check with the Guilders and ask how long they've been out here. Maybe figure out a timeline?"

Felix tapped the pencil nub against his lips, considering the Memory, focusing to keep it from overwhelming his senses. Bits and flashes of it replayed, a strobe light of moments. "Ah, ok. She said they were *mostly* human prisoners, so not all of them. Maybe that means there are a lot of intermixing peoples?" Felix chewed his lip, more of the Memory playing out in his mind's eye. "Apparently, the fog inhibits her ability to Analyze people. Which means it probably stops the Guilders, too. Which means they don't know jack about me, except what I tell them," He sighed and leaned against the wall, the stone cool against his back. "So I have no idea if being a Nym is good or bad to them. Dang." He underlined that note a couple times, writing a big "Be Cautious" in the margin.

He took another breath.

"Hokay, onto the important bits," he took up his pencil again, adjusting his grip so his knuckles stopped hitting the page. "The prisoners were being led by someone. Honey-colored, short hair, leather armor. Is she the same 'angry one' the Risi mentioned?"

That part was *a bit strange. Why would both memories concern the prisoners? Is there an element to this I'm missing? Probably. I could fill books with what I don't know about this place.* He laughed, annoyed at himself. He was doing just that, wasn't he?

He made a few more marks onto the page. "Who is Elder DuFont? They hired Ilia, clearly. Mention that to the Silver Ranks. And as far as I can tell, Ilia was using two Skills in that Memory: some sort of shadow cloak and a way to walk on the air, what she called Cloudstep." Felix snapped the book closed and stowed the pencil.

"And I know which one I want to learn."

An hour later, Felix decided that learning shadow cloak was impossible.

This was for two reasons: one, Ilia's Memory had not been focused on the Skill, instead letting it run in the background. He figured it was likely some sort of passive benefit, or otherwise worked in a way that made zero sense to him. And two, the...slipperiness...of shadow Mana prevented him from properly manipulating it. Which made no freaking sense, considering his Shadow Whip spell was more tacky than slick.

So what's the difference?

Using the hints he could tease from the Memory, Felix had attempted to recreate the Mana patterns using Fire Within;

Shadow Whip was a reference point. Felix was surprised to find how dissimilar the two were. The spell had slipped from his grasp and rebounded on him four times before he gave up, and the end of the hour found him nursing a massive headache against one of the carved walls. The iron mountain loomed above him, shining with a silver-brown radiance in the corner of his vision, and Felix had to deactivate his Manasight.

At least in the dark, he didn't have to see how much he didn't know.

Frankly, I'm surprised I've managed to figure out this much. All of this magic stuff is wildly out of my league. Felix drank some more water, the liquid sloshing loudly in the total darkness. *The Skills I've been learning are changing me in ways I hadn't expected. Fire Within alone has me contemplating a weird internal world of Mana that I definitely never had before. It's amazing and thrilling and terrifying and...*

And it means I need a teacher.

That was abundantly clear. There was so much that he wanted explained, so much that he had probably fucked up already. Sure he'd amassed a lot of stats and a considerable amount of Titles, but that was luck and circumstance. How did everything work? What was after Apprentice Tier? What even *was* an Omen?

Felix sighed.

I'm in the dark unless I can get the Guilders to help me. Considering Magda's suspicious nature, that might take some doing. He leaned his head back against the wall, looking up into the black. *All of this is changing me. The stats, the Skills, even my pact with Pit. Piece by piece, I'm becoming someone other than who I was when I arrived here. It scares me just as much as it excites me. Who will I be when this is over?* What *will I be?*

Pit settled against Felix's left side, beak slightly nipping at his hand. Dutifully, Felix started scratching the little beast. The image of the assassin ran through his head, her cold condescension and dismissal of his life. Anger welled up inside him, hot and righteous and burning for an outlet.

At least Ilia taught me a truth: I either get stronger, or I die. It's my only way forward.

He leveraged himself to his feet, and Pit squawked in dismay. Felix still had another Skill he could try, and at least a little time left before anyone came looking for him. He dragged his fingers through the Memory, stopping once he found what he was looking for: Cloudstep.

He focused on the Memory, letting his mind drift back into the grip of his past, just enough to see it again. He was Ilia again, making a casual leap into thin air, only to have it solidify beneath him before pushing off again. It was a brief and well-executed move, and at first blush seemed miraculous.

Felix backed up, reliving the moment again. But this time, he felt for the rush of Ilia's senses, which were very acute, and tried to feel out the patterns of her Mana. The moment her leg left the ledge, there was a stirring in her core before surging down into her legs...but he lost it once the air solidified again.

Shaking his head, Felix started again. It was activating too fast. He couldn't keep up.

Again.

The Mana surged, the pattern formed and twisted down the pathways in her leg, expelling into the world...and—!

She was pushing Mana out into the air? Just unattributed Mana? He checked again, but the Mana he sensed was almost colorless, a translucent cloud of power that puffed from her feet and solidified. *How?*

He did it again. And again, but the how of it never revealed itself.

So Felix practiced.

He attempted to mimic the feel of the power, tracing its path down his channels and into his foot. It was easy enough to manage after a few minutes, moving the magic within him, but expelling it was another story. It seemed...stuck, for lack of a better word. Bottlenecking at his foot, the Mana simply gathered there until he stopped focusing, then would flow immediately back to his core.

Frustrated, he copied the shifts and twists of Ilia's magic, tracing out a complicated whirling pattern much as he did with his Stone Shaping Skill, yet very different. Where Stone Shaping was all curving lines and steady flow, these were twisty and loopy, prone to making abrupt changes in direction and reversals. It was extremely difficult to get the hang of, and Felix felt his headache edge back into his temples.

The twists and patterns of each spell I gain all seem unique. They're like magic words, almost. But instead of a string of vaguely-Latin word-jumble, I get the equivalent of throwing rocks in a pond to make waves hit the shore in just *the right way to set it on fire. Craziness.*

Wait. Felix opened his eyes, his Manasight showing him the sleeping form of Pit at his feet. *I'm worrying about the wrong thing here. I've done this before, with Reign of Vellus. How does that work?*

Felix reviewed his kinetic spell, watching as the blue crackling wave of force washed outward from him before dissipating. *Was the Skill automating the action? Is that why it's so easy to do this with Reign of Vellus?* He looked closer, watching as the Mana flowed from Felix's body and out of his hands, the azure light sparking with electricity as it jumped away from him.

It seems like intent and momentum. Build up enough of both and it'll just...flow. I hope.

Felix tried again, gathering up his Mana and surging it down his right leg. He focused, willing his vision of reality to occur just as he pressed down with whatever mental muscle controlled his pathways. There was a build up of resistance that felt awful, then suddenly *whoosh!* A cloud of blue and gold puffed into appearance at his feet. It disappeared in moments.

Fire Within is level 28!

New Skill Learned!
Mana Manipulation (Uncommon), Level 1!
You have learned to manipulate Mana itself! Good job! Don't kill yourself! Increase in precision and control with Skill Level.

"Holy shit, I did it!" And he got a cool new Skill from it, too. Felix wasn't sure what the difference between Fire Within and Mana Manipulation was, but he was eager to find out.

But first, he had some stepping to do!

Surging his power, Felix forced out another cloud of blue-gold Mana but this time immediately placed his foot down on it...and stumbled forward.

"Gah! Shit."

The cloud sparked into a thousand bolts of static electricity as his foot just smooshed right through it.

"Do I need more Mana?"

Felix tried again, and again. Turned out, he had to put nearly five hundred Mana into the little cloud before it would even start to hold his weight. Finally, after entirely too long, he pushed his foot down onto the Mana cloud and felt it mush beneath him...but hold. For two seconds. Then it disappeared again, evaporating into the air itself.

Fire Within is level 29!
Mana Manipulation is level 2!
...
Mana Manipulation is level 4!

New Skill Learned!
Cloudstep (Uncommon), Level 1!
Like running, but very different! Step to the skies! Durability and duration increase with Skill Level.

"Hell yeah!" Felix pumped his fist into the air, savoring the victory. But he had wasted so much of his Mana, and had nearly emptied himself out this time. Felix tottered toward the nearest wall, letting himself fall against it. His body felt overheated, as if he'd been working out, and the cool stone was a balm.

Can't believe that was so hard. Felix huffed, trying to slow his breathing. *Why is that? Sometimes I feel like I gain a Skill without trying, and this I have to fight tooth and nail for.*

Felix didn't let his mind wander down that path. It was useless to speculate without someone to teach him. *Speaking of which, they should be back by now, right? I should go find them, at least to ensure that they don't leave me behind.*

Felix stood up, pushing off the carved wall as he gained his feet. Then he heard a ringing sound; but ringing wasn't quite right. It was more felt than heard, a ringing chime that shook his bones and tingled against his skin.

What is that?

Felix turned toward the wall he was touching, feeling it strongest through the stone surface. The chime came from his left, toward the stairs, somewhere along the wall itself.

Cautiously, Felix approached, one hand on the wall while the other was clenched, ready to summon a Corrosive Strike in an instant. But when he reached the center of the mural, he found the silent chiming was coming from the depiction of a waterfall arcing into a wide lake.

Something is...it's coming from under the blue inlay. The lapis lazuli was layered thickly on the mural, carved and altered to depict a stylistic water feature, and the vibrations were coming from...the waterfall itself. Felix flexed his Manasight, and instantly he noticed that the surface Mana of the mural was rippling.

Abruptly, thc blue stone waters began to flow and shift, as if real. Drawing closer, Felix watched as the stone poured over the waterfall and splashed powerfully into the lake below. The mural was so detailed, so immaculately done, that he could even see the barest hint of a ledge beneath the waterfall, as if....

The stone parted, and revealed a small, jagged piece of bronze metal *inside* the waterfall. Like a bronze fish surrounded by jeweled waters. The vibration grew more powerful as his hand neared, practically singing as he reached out and touched the metal.

The moment he touched it, the ringing multiplied a thousand-fold. It coursed down his arm and between his ears and danced across his heart and guts. It was so strong, so omnipresent, that it took Felix several seconds to realize the sound was coming from behind him, too.

He looked down and saw his sword, strapped to his pack, was nearly chiming along with the vibrations. With his left hand, Felix grabbed it and held it aloft.

Slowly, the runes along its length ignited in a strange sequence, flashing out of order and in differing intensities. Then they quieted.

The vibrations stopped.

Felix was dumbfounded.

What is this?

He touched the waterfall again, the chime gone now. But then he stepped back and looked at the scene, hoping for more answers. There was a river coming from up on a distant mountain before dropping off the cliff, and pouring into a large lake that was surrounded by white and red trees. *Odd.* He focused on the bronze piece, shaped like a small hook almost. Kinda like...

Kinda like his sword.

Exploration is level 21!

"Holy shit!" Felix stared down at the sword in his hand. "This is the Waterfall Temple!"

He looked around at the other murals. "Then, does that mean...?"

He rushed over to the other walls, peering at the silver forest and the split-peaked mountain. But despite his search, he could find no bronze inlaid into their designs. His Manavision found no spark of gold hidden beneath their depths.

Are there Temples hidden at all of these places? Why? The one I found only had a few mostly-empty rooms and a big magic door that wanted to kill anyone who got close...Shit. Based on what he knew of this world, nothing good was behind that door. And Felix was willing to bet that each Temple had one...if there *were* other Temples.

I don't even know if these are even in the Foglands. But if his hours of watching the History channel meant anything, it was that no one carved elaborate scenes into walls without a purpose.

Questions, questions. They never end.

Another noise caught his ears, freshly acclimated to the lack of ringing or chiming. It was the sound of metal on stone, and the soft murmur of voices from below.

They're back. Good. Felix squared up his shoulders and moved toward the stairwell. It was past time they all had a chat.

Vvim gripped their cane with whitened knuckles, and though their hands were palsied with age, it was not time that shook their limbs.

The youth ran off, dashing down the stairs to seek his companions, and Vvim did not stop him. They dared not. Though others might be fooled, Vvim was untouched by the grand illusion erected Ages ago.

Little could be hidden from the Geist.

Still, they were not to be hurried. Things could be more complicated than it first seemed. Vvim's eyes shined a pale, robin's egg blue, their whites stained as if their irises had burst and overflowed. Their eyes were shrewd and powerful, but their nose...yes, their nose was much stronger.

Vvim hobbled forward, cane clacking against the stone. Their nose wrinkled and twitched, and they bared their teeth slightly at the sour scent of vomit.

Salted meat? Hardtack? No...something else.

Vvim searched until their finger found a small dab of red. They lifted it, bringing the wet to their nose and breathing deep.

Blood of a Human. Why? Their eyes fell upon the far wall, the blue water glistening in their senses, still radiating a faint heat from the boy's presence.

A sigh of wind, and Vvim held withered hands before the sculpture, feeling the texture of thc warmth that stubbornly clung to the wall. Brows furrowed, Vvim clacked their teeth and gestured at the waterfall. The blue stone parted, revealing the jagged piece of bronze embedded deep within it.

The Herald's Hook.

Quick as a blink, Vvim checked the other two murals, running their senses across them.

Still there. Still unclaimed.

Vvim looked down as if peering through the stone slab at their feet. *Who are you, child?*

CHAPTER FORTY-FOUR

Felix slowed his descent, taking each step carefully. He held his Manasight at full burn, watching the floor, ceilings, and walls for movement. Felix was determined to see if anything would happen a second time.

Pit bristled behind him, clearly displeased with the pace. Felix absently pet the tenku on his head, eyes never blinking.

Half way down, Felix heard something. A shift, like stone against stone. But when he turned, he saw nothing. The Mana was stable, the shadows thick. He kept walking, step by step, trying to watch everything all at once. After a few more turns in the spiral stairwell, he caught sight of a faint light falling onto a landing.

Felix stepped down, still unable to notice anything strange. But when he looked through the archway, the oval chamber opened up where he had left everyone, and it was...off. The room looked normal, not blurry or hazy or darker, but Felix found that even with his Manasight, he couldn't quite focus on what was in front of him. His eyes kept sliding to the side, making him focus on the walls or ceiling.

That's an odd feeling. They must have set up the wardstones. How do they do it? He knelt down by the archway and pushed his hand forward, feeling the jellylike consistency of the air. He ran his hands through it, enjoying the strange feeling even as he saw zero reason for it to exist. His Manasight picked up nothing but the soft, near-invisible flow of air Mana.

Must be too low level, or the wardstones are high quality. Without further hesitation, Felix stepped through the jellied air, and suddenly the room was full of people.

Harn stood to the side, nearly thirty feet away, staring at one of the murals. It was the one depicting a rolling meadow beside a thin stream. Strange animals cavorted across the fields, and they seemed to fascinate the strange man.

Vessilia was moving pieces of wood into a pile in the tiered pit, while Atar, surprisingly, helped her. He couldn't see Magda anywhere.

It was apparently early evening, the sun close to setting. The windows weren't visible here in the central area, but Felix could make out a sliver of light slanting in from one of the side chambers. In a moment, even that was gone, as Evie finished putting a thick blanket up and over the opening. Felix turned his head, noticing that all the archways were similarly covered, cloth secured from top to bottom.

The preparations made perfect sense when, a moment later, a bright fire sparked alive in the central depression. Atar looked exceedingly pleased with himself, and he put his hands on his hips and surveyed his work. Vessilia placed a few more pieces of wood down into it before dusting her hands and climbing out.

"Oh! How long have you been there, Felix?" She seemed surprised to see him, though her smile was warm.

"I just came down the stairs when I heard you folks making noise," Felix gestured behind him. "Glad to see everyone made it back in one piece."

Vessilia made a face, her eyes narrowing and brow furrowing just slightly. "Oh..alright. Well, come closer and join us." She waved him over, smiling brightly again. "We have much to do."

Though her expression confused him, Felix was happy to move closer to the warm fire. As he walked toward them, he cast a look back behind him and stopped dead.

The archway was missing.

Felix strode back over to the smoothly-made wall, simple stone blocks set with mortar that looked no different than all the rest. He set his hands against them, feeling the thickness of the air where the ward pressed against it. The wall held firm, even as he applied the full measure of his Strength against it.

I missed it! How is it doing that? Felix could see no seams, sense no magic. It was just...a wall. Much as before.

He turned and moved back to the fire, fully intending to ask Vessilia about the door that was no longer there. But when he drew close, one of the side chambers flapped open and Magda strode in. Everyone stopped, turning to look at the Silver Rank, and she surveyed them all in turn.

"We have....much to discuss this night. But before we do, we need our strength. First, we eat."

The fire crackled merrily, Vessilia adding a stick or two every few minutes. Above the fire, a large rack of ribs and other meaty bits were skewered with a wooden pole and turned on a crudely made spit by Harn. It was definitely monster meat, and judging by the thick purple-blue blood that dripped and sizzled from it, that monster was a Hoarhound. Felix had been hesitant to eat it, worried about upsetting his tender stomach, but honestly, it had been a long time since he'd had fresh meat, and he was craving it something awful. And it smelled extremely good.

Felix had never eaten anything quite like it. Harn had added some seasonings to it but it looked like simple salt and pepper, and it didn't explain how the meat just melted in his mouth. It smelled savory with an edge of chill, like the cooling sensation of mint without the flavor. It was delicious, and he cleaned off four ribs in just a few minutes.

After ten minutes, Felix leaned back, stuffed. He watched the others eat and enjoyed the heat of the fire. With the power of the wardstones and heavy cloth on the archways, there was no chance any light would escape their room, and he was grateful for it. The fire was warm and comforting after so long upstairs in the dark with only cool stone beneath him. Though he had often overheated during his exertions, it had only left him feeling that much colder now that he was still.

The others slowly picked at their food, and Felix could see them flick their gazes toward Magda and Harn, each of them waiting for her to speak. Tossing his bones down to Pit, Felix crossed his arms and waited as well.

The minutes dragged by, and Magda seemed to be sorting things in her own head, often fiddling with her food and pushing her sandy brown hair back behind her ears. She even had a strange tic where she'd touch her collarbone occasionally before letting her hand drift back down to her plate. Smacking his head, Felix reached into his satchel and pulled out the golden locket. He stood and walked over to Magda.

"Here. Most of your stuff got crushed by the falling building, but I grabbed this before I got out," he slipped the locket into her open hand. "Figured you'd want it back."

Magda just stared at her hand for a long moment, and when she looked up at Felix her eyes were round and wet. "Thank you," she managed, her voice catching slightly. "I thought it was lost when I didn't find it in Harn's rucksack." She slipped it carefully around her neck, securing the delicate clasp with her large hands with ease. With the triangular amulet resting against her chest, she stood up. Felix took a step back, worried for a moment as Magda loomed nearly a foot taller than him, but she simply turned to everyone and spoke. "I think it's time to talk."

There was a sound of shuffling as everyone, Harn included, repositioned themselves to face their towering leader. Felix walked back to his seat and got comfortable. He had a feeling this was gonna take a while.

Magda cleared her throat. "First I wanna apologize, to all of you. You've been caught up in something that you didn't ask for, and it's my fault." She swept her gaze across all of the Tin Ranks. "Our plan...My plan—no, let me start at the beginning."

She stepped over to Harn's rucksack, shuffling a few items around as she kept talking. "There was a Guild operation in the Foglands, put into motion over six months ago, that was bent toward uncovering a set of important ruins." She gestured around them. "This city, in fact. At first, I figured it was just an artifact dive. Get in, find some relics or treasures, and get out. They even planned around the chimeras, going into the interior when most of them would crowd the edges and attack Haarwatch. In fact, the regular Culling went off without a hitch, and while the beasts were distracted at Haarwatch's walls, the crew moved out into the Foglands. In the dead of night."

Magda fished out a leather folder, unwinding a cord that bound it closed. "The operation had close to three hundred souls assigned. Most were scholars and such for the Hierocracy, brainy types, but more than a third were skilled fighters. My...Our former teammate, Calesca Boscal, was hired on as an Extractor for the operation. It was a high-risk, high-reward outing, something that was right in Callie's wheelhouse."

A thief. Felix translated, taking his eyes off Magda a moment to look at Evie, who had put a hand up to her mouth. Her face radiated worry and concern, a stark difference from her previously mounting annoyance with her sister.

Magda continued. "The Guild lost contact with the operation two months ago. A month later, the Elders were ready to cut their losses. No rescue attempts, not even a lone scout." She ripped open the leather folder, using more force than needed. She passed the opened folder around, starting with Atar. "It was suspicious. Everything about this was kept quiet. Harn and I didn't know about it until recently, and even then it was like pulling teeth."

"Almost exactly like that, in one case," Harn smiled, his scars making it look more like a smirk.

The paperwork made its way from Atar to Vessilia, who poured over it. Felix glanced over her shoulder, curious. He was met with a wall of handwritten text that was as impenetrable as the wall from earlier. *It isn't just bad handwriting*, Felix realized, slightly shocked. *Apparently, I can't read.*

His thoughts went to the Henaari's journal, still in his pack, filled with scribbles and notes that were basically gibberish to him. Felix had figured it was written in a foreign language, one belonging to a strange new people, and of course he wouldn't be able to read that. This was different, or at least it felt different. *Are the Henaari's notes in the same language as this? It's hard to tell through the fancy script here.*

Magda paced on the other side of the fire, clearly agitated. "When we figured out the full lay of the land, I knew we had to do something. That document right there says it all; they sent men and women out to die for a land-grab."

"What?" Evie asked, confused. Felix echoed her confusion. He was missing something. To his surprise, it was Vessilia who spoke up.

"Heirocracy law states that if a force takes possession of a land, creates a bastion and defends it against all comers for six months, they gain a provisional hold on the land itself." She looked up from the paperwork, her eyes wide and mouth open. "They meant to take the Foglands as *territory*?"

"Got it in one." Harn smirked. "Took us a lot longer to figure that one out."

"But *why*?" Evie asked. "It's all just monsters and fog out here."

"Because of the resources," Atar said, joining the conversation for the first time.

Magda pointed at the mage. "The Foglands are an untouched treasure trove, Evie. The only reason it hasn't been plundered bare already is the endless fog. No one who enters can sense much, and all information gathering Skills fail to work in here."

"Then what's the point?" Felix asked. "Build an outpost or fortress or whatever, but if you can't find the resources, why bother?"

"But what if you could?" Magda asked. Felix suddenly felt extremely uncomfortable, like a spotlight had been shined on him. He almost felt the Tin Ranks' eyes, making his skin itch. "What if you had a way to counteract the fog?"

"Wait," Vessilia interrupted. "You're saying they found something to see through the fog?"

Magda shook her head. "No, they found a way to remove the fog entirely."

Everyone went silent.

"What?" Atar gasped. His eyes widened, and a grin stretched his face. "That'd be the find of the century!"

"Exactly, Sparky. That's why they came out here. The artifact, whatever it is, was found in the center of this city. They planned to come out here, retrieve it, and then build an outpost to defend against the nasties in the mist." Harn hawked a wad of phlegm into the fire, the spit sizzling in the ashes. "A good plan, really."

"Except they fucked up. Didn't know giants had come south. How could they?" Magda kept pacing, never quite going still. "So there we were. We had this information and couldn't do much with it. The only people we could go to were involved already. So, I came up with a plan." She stopped pacing as she took a breath and released it, as if steadying herself. "We would go into the Foglands ourselves."

"But we weren't allowed," Harn added. "Guild rules. Can't

access the Foglands without a vetted contract. Too dangerous, usually, and the Guild doesn't like to hand a chance at artifacts out to just anybody."

"But you're Onslaught and the Shieldwitch!" Evie protested. "You're famous. Why wouldn't they let you go alone?"

"We ain't nearly as big a deal as you seem to think, kid," Harn's gruff voice was laced with humor. "Sure, we got some good strength on our side, and we're tough, but we ain't shit compared to some of the folk on the Continent."

"So we had to come up with another plan," Magda pressed on, rushing her words. "Trainees."

"Damn. Of course," Evie muttered. Vessilia's mouth firmed into a line as she stared at the Shieldwitch. Atar scowled but seemed unsurprised.

"Maybe I'm missing something. What do you mean?" Felix asked.

"It means, *Felix*, that they had to get trainees into a contract so that a foray into the Foglands would be approved. It means, simpleton, that we were *used*." Atar practically spat the words, his face reddening beneath his flesh-colored trash stache. Magda cut in quickly before Felix could retort.

"Yes, we did. We used all of ya for this, and I'm sorry," she gripped the fingers of her left hand in her right, clasping them in agitation. "It was always our intention to honor the contract. Reveals and all. But all of this caught us off-guard."

"We figured it was another surge that took 'em out." Harn stretched in his seat, metal creaking. "A horde too big to stop, especially with only a hundred guards to protect two hundred noncombatants. We didn't expect a legion of giants out of the fuckin Hoarfrost, that's fer sure."

"Honestly, we wanted to round out our team with simple but talented folks. People we could help, but who could also stay low-profile. Get in, get out." Magda sighed, heavily. "But then *politics* got involved."

The Tin Ranks and Felix all shared a look. The Shieldwitch kept explaining.

"The Guild Elders got wind of our plans to bring trainees out into the Foglands to gain their Omens, and they all wanted a say," she shook her head.

"Too many cooks in the kitchen," added Harn. Magda scratched the back of her neck, nodding along with him.

"Let me guess, the Elders chose me as a favor to my master," Atar spoke up, his voice cutting.

"Yeah. Like I said, politics. Even more so for you, Vessilia."

The woman in question looked up from the paperwork in her hands, eyes weary. "Of course," she nodded. "I imagine my father made it happen?"

Magda shrugged. "We're newly-minted Silver Ranks with a stellar record. You're newly-minted Tin Rank with exceptional potential. As far as the Duke and the Elders were concerned, it was a no-brainer."

Vessilia nodded and sighed. She looked disappointed, though Felix couldn't quite work out why. More importantly, he eyed his new allies with fresh eyes. It didn't change who they had been during his time here, but being the daughter of a duke? He wasn't exactly boned up on his medieval nobility rankings, but that sounded extremely important.

"The last choice was taken from us too, but that wasn't politics. Just run of the mill nosiness." Magda smiled gently at her sister. Evie opened her mouth, but had been rendered speechless. Felix was impressed; he didn't think that could ever happen.

"When Evie found out about the contract, she insisted on coming along. Her damn stubborn pride and obvious skill made the decision for us, as well as our timeline," Magda's smile turned bitter. "It had been over five months since Callie and her team went missing. We were running out of time. So we finalized it, got approval, and here we are."

"Neck deep in it," remarked Harn, humor entirely absent in his voice. The entire room fell silent, save for the occasional crackle and pop of the fire. Pit looked from face to face, his wings drooping.

"Well, we're here, so we'd better get to helping, right?" Evie perked up after a minute. She stood and walked over to her sister. "That's what my big sister always taught me, anyhow."

Magda smiled and wrapped Evie in a bear hug. "Thank you, Evie."

"Yeah, well," Evie straightened her leathers after escaping the hug. "Callie means a lot to me, too. We'll find her."

"Oh excellent!" cried a shrill voice. "You're best friends and sisters, and everything is perfect now. Except we're still in the middle of enemy territory, surrounded by monsters, without our Omens, and at the mercy of a conniving pair of Guilders!" Atar was practically screaming by the end, veins in his neck and forehead popping alarmingly.

Holy shit, this dude's gonna have an aneurysm. Felix leaned away from the kid, frowning.

"Calm yourself, Sparky. You ain't—"

"Shut up, you oaf! This is unacceptable. We paid our fees and you-"

"Enough!"

The voice was loud and full of an authority Felix hadn't heard before. He turned in surprise to Vessilia, who glared down at Atar. "Do not be petty, Atar. You are better than this! They have fully explained themselves, yet you insist on clinging to your grievances! We were misled, yes, but it was in service of something greater. I for one would rather be here where I can be of use, helping others in peril." Atar shrank into his seat, face suddenly mortified. She turned toward Magda, the storm clouds in her expression easing up. "I am saddened that you did not choose me for my talents, and that my father has once again mixed into my affairs. But I offer you my complete support. I wish only to help."

Silence reigned again as Atar tried to become as small as possible, pulling away from the rest of them, and Magda and Harn both looked at Vessilia like she was some sort of mythical beast. Or so Felix assumed, since he was doing much the same.

He was still staring at Vessilia when she turned to him. "And you, Felix? Will you join us?"

Felix turned and saw that everyone was looking at him, and he felt his mouth go dry. "Ah," he started, before Magda interrupted him.

"Felix, I know we haven't spoken on the best of terms. I know that I've been suspicious and hard on you. So I understand if you don't wanna risk your life for strangers you met by chance." She took a deep breath and touched her locket, then met his eyes again. "But I'm gonna be honest, we need all the help we can get."

Felix scratched his arm, his skin prickling uncomfortably as the warmth of the fire and rising flush competed. "Ah, damn. Yeah. I'll help."

He laughed, the sound a little forced.

"After all, you're the only ones who know the way outta here, right?"

CHAPTER FORTY-FIVE

They spent some time discussing strategy and plans for their...infiltration was probably the best term, Felix decided. The Silver Ranks had done their scouting that morning but wouldn't be able to do anything that night, not with the giants on their guard. That assassin had stirred up the entire encampment, and now nearly a hundred giants and Hoarhounds were combing the city. What's more, the Silver Ranks still had not found any trace of her.

Felix's mood soured at the thought of Ilia.

"What about Callie? Can we afford to wait?" Evie asked.

Magda's face was drawn, but her voice was sure. "We don't have a choice. With the giants on the move and no idea of the comings and goings in that central building, we're blind. We can't move without more information, not if we plan to get out alive."

"Callie's strong. She'll make it through," Harn added, patting Evie on the shoulder.

That reminded Felix of what he hadn't yet told them, and he spoke up. "I saw her this morning. Your friend."

"Where?" Magda half rose from her seat, pinning him down with her stare.

"In the square before the bronze domed building, when that huge Risi leader was doing his evil monologue," Felix said. "She looked pissed."

A laugh bubbled up out of Magda's throat, surprising everyone, even herself.

"Yeah. That sounds like her." She scratched near her eye and blinked a couple times. "Thanks. Again."

Felix just inclined his head. What else could he have done? He cleared his throat. "Do you know what the giants meant by the Song? Or what this 'Mother' supposedly is?"

"Hoarfrost superstition. Some of the 'smarter' monsters find religion, somehow," Harn sucked at his teeth before fishing out a small side knife. "Dunno if I'd cahll thaht smaht, but..." he shrugged, knife picking at his teeth.

"The point is, the giants think there's something of value down in that hole. But it's probably just the artifact the Guild's been after," Magda added.

"Right, the one you mentioned," Felix shook his head. "Gotta be honest, a lot of what they said made zero sense."

"Yeah, same here. I heard a lot of that speech from my perch, I just couldn't see much of the square. Saw that huge blue bastard, though. Big chunks of floating ice and all." Evie took a long pull from a metal flask before passing it back to Harn. "If we have to fight him and all the others...I don't know how we can."

"We will think of a way," Vessilia chimed in, hands carefully cleaning her spear. "We have to." Evie nodded, picking idly at her food.

Ultimately, they decided to hunker down for the night before Harn would venture out again in the early morning to scout. In the meantime, all of them began to train under the direction of their team leaders. Each of the Tin Ranks immediately moved out and began a set of exercises that differed pretty wildly, but all seemed tailor-made for their physiques.

Felix watched them a bit before turning to Harn and Magda himself. He wanted to train his Skills and body, but he had something to do first.

"Magda, Harn," Felix started, and the two of them turned toward him. They were still wearing their impressive armor, though their weapons were set aside or sheathed. Felix swallowed and began again. "I need to talk with you both."

Harn looked at Magda with a frown, his scar pulling at his mouth and turning it into a grimace. For her part, Magda simply waved her hand. "Let me have my say first, kid."

Felix blinked, surprised. "Uh, sure."

"It was a big thing, helping us without knowing anything about us. Frankly, when I saw you putting dents in iron armor with your fists, I thought you musta been a plant. Someone from the Guild sent to spy on us." She let out a small bitter laugh, clearly at herself. "I'm not—it's been a tough few months."

Felix waved his hands. "Nothing to be sorry for. After hearing your story, I get it."

Harn grunted. "Point is, after seeing you in action and how you've helped us out, it's time for us to start trustin' ya."

Magda smirked and nodded. "What he said. He's a big galoot, but he can spin a phrase when he wants." Harn shoved her with his elbow, but it wasn't even hard enough to rock her. "I've said it a few times now, but thank you. You don't have a pony in this race, so stickin' around isn't something you have to do." She stuck out her hand.

Felix felt himself flush again, cursing his stupid sense of embarrassment even as he grasped her hand and shook it. "I'm just doing what anyone would do. There are people in trouble. We can get them out. Least I could do is help."

Magda gave him a look, like she wasn't sure what she was seeing. "Not really a common impulse, not around here. But it's appreciated." She cleared her throat and took her hand back. "Now, what did you have to tell me?"

"Oh, ah," Felix extemporized. He had come over here with a half-formed plan about his origins. To spill the beans, as it were. But now he had a perfect excuse to keep those details to himself, which was a relief. *What they don't know can't hurt me.* "I need teachers. My own education has been...self-administered."

Harn and Magda shared a look before they both nodded.

"How can we help?"

The first thing Felix wanted to do was get some answers. While Magda went about instructing her trainees, Harn sat down and started grilling Felix.

It was the opposite of what Felix intended, but Harn explained that if he was going to help train him, the grizzled warrior would have to know what Felix's baseline status was at this point.

"Do you have your Omen Revealed?" Harn asked, leaning back against the carved wall.

"Yeah," Felix said, standing awkwardly in front of him. It felt weird to be looming over the warrior, who seemed more interested in his flask than the questions.

"Care to tell me what it is?" Harn tried, though his voice sounded doubtful.

"Um, sure. It's the Magician."

Harn's eyebrows went up, and he pulled his flask away from his mouth. "Magician? Ya sure?"

"Yeah? Why?" Felix asked.

"Nothing, really. Just ain't a common one, is all."

"Oh...that doesn't make sense. Isn't Atar a mage?" Felix wondered, looking up at the slender teen, who was busy doing push-ups of all things, and not well.

"Sparky?" Harn shrugged. "Yeah, he's a magic focused kid. It's how he was raised down in Te'thys. He hasn't Revealed his Omen yet, but I doubt it'll end up the Magician."

It still didn't make sense. Magic was the Magician's whole deal right? That's why Felix's Willpower and Intelligence got bumped. Right?

"Why?" Felix asked.

Harn shrugged again, taking another pull of his flask. "Magic ain't a Human specialty, never has been. Elves though, yeah they got magic in spades. Probably find the Magician Omen all over 'em."

Felix chewed at his lip, mentally going over his list of questions. "Then what *is* an Omen? I thought it had something to do with your class..."

"Class? What's that?" Harn asked, eyebrows furrowed.

"Like your specialty? Warriors are good at physical combat, mages are good at magic, clerics are good at healing? And so on?" Felix explained, miming a few punches and magical looking flourishes for good measure.

Harn laughed.

"That's the dumbest thing I've heard. It's Skills and Titles that determine your specialty, and even then, that's only a guideline." Harn's face soured slightly. "And don't talk about priests. You don't want anything to do with them."

Felix wanted to ask more, but could tell Harn wasn't going to answer anything along those lines. *I'll just ask the others at some point.*

"You ready to answer my other questions, or do you just got like, a list of these?" Harn spat something thick off to the side. Felix could hear it splat nearby.

Gross. "Yeah, sorry. I just got a couple more questions. This wasn't really, uh, it... yeah, just a few more." Felix recovered his train of thought before he let too much slip about his origins. He had at least thirty different questions he wanted to follow up on, but he figured he'd have to narrow this down. He wanted to get training soon. "Do you know what all the Omens are?"

Harn rolled his eyes. "Some. Quill-pushers back at the Guild probably got a whole list, but ya learn a few from time to time. Let's see, mine is Strength, Magda's got the Star, and I've heard tell of the Wheel, Chariot, Justice, and even one called the Lovers, if you can believe it."

Harn chuckled, but Felix's eyes grew wide. "What?"

"I know. Odd. But hey, they give solid boosts per level, so any Omen is good."

Felix barely heard him, focused instead on his own revelation. *The Omens are named after...tarot cards? How? Or do I have that backwards? Are our tarot cards named after the Omens here?* The correlation raised more questions about this world and his own, and just how interconnected they were.

Harn stood up and started walking to the far side of the room. "Alright, that's enough questions. Wait," Harn paused and turned back to Felix. "What's your Born Trait?"

"Uh, Keen Mind."

Harn looked nonplussed. "What's that?"

Felix straightened up and said, "Perfect memory."

Harn quirked an eyebrow and walked away. "...Alright."

Felix followed, more than a little deflated.

Harn's method of training felt a lot like gym class at first.

Felix was made to do fifty push-ups, fifty sit ups, and then run around the room five times. At the end of it, Felix was a little out of breath but mostly felt fine. His Strength and Endurance scores had grown far beyond such a simple exercise.

"What's your Stamina down?" Harn asked as he came to a stop.

"About five percent," Felix said after checking his display. Harn made a noncommittal noise and sucked at his teeth again.

"Gimme a list of yer highest-leveled Skills," he said after a moment.

"All of them?" Felix clarified.

"Nah. Anything over, say, level 20. That'd do it."

Felix looked at his Status, briefly considering how much he wanted to reveal to the powerful warrior. *Should I keep some of this secret?* He waffled for a dozen seconds before deciding to keep all of his Epic rarity Skills a secret. *No need for him to know everything, right?* After compiling his list, he looked around for paper. "Do you want this written down, or should I read it off?"

"What?" Harn asked, frowning. "No, just show me the Skill list."

Felix's head rocked back in surprise, but he quickly reorganized his Skill list and, on a guess, *willed* it over to Harn. It was strange, but Felix could immediately see a blue window pop into existence before the Silver Rank.

So you can share your windows with anyone? That's handy.

Skills:
Acid Resistance (C) 20
Acrobatics (U) 21
Analyze (C) 21
Acid Stream (R) 22
Exploration (U) 21
Influence of the Wisp (R) 22
Stealth (C) 23
Dodge (C) 24
Unarmed Mastery (C) 24
Stone Shaping (R) 24
Poison Resistance (U) 25
Pain Resistance (U) 28
Fire Within (R) 29
Meditation (U) 30
Manasight (U) 31

"Blind gods, why do you have so many Skills?" Harn looked alarmed as he scrolled through the window Felix sent.

"Kinda just happened, really," Felix explained with a shrug. "I've been through some weird stuff recently."

"I'll say. Ya got three different Resistances here, a bunch of spells, some evasion Skills, one combat Skill, and the rest are all mental buffs a'one kind or another. Lotta Rare and Uncommon Skills too..." Harn gave Felix a surprised but respectful look. "This is almost as impressive as it is completely ridiculous. How're ya expecting to keep up with all these Skills?"

Felix didn't know how to answer that, so he just shrugged. "I'd try my best, I guess. I mean, I got them this far, right?"

Harn smirked, but Felix wasn't sure how to read the man. Was that amusement? Criticism? Nervous tic? The man kept talking, though.

"Normally, I'd put together a regimen based on yer highest Skills, the ones ya use the most. But seeing as yer some sorta high achiever, I figure we can focus on the basics a fightin' before we worry about Tempering." Harn walked over to his huge rucksack and began shoving items around inside. Felix felt a sudden rush of excitement as he registered what the warrior was telling him.

"You mean my Formation?"

"Hm? Yeah, I can sense you haven't completed any Tempering yet. You got, what? One Body Essence?" Harn asked over his shoulder.

"Yeah. I got it when I made Apprentice Tier in Poison Resistance," Felix confirmed. "How can you tell?"

Harn laughed without turning around. "Do this long enough, and ya get the knack. Sides, my Brawler's Physique does more'n make me fight good." Harn turned back around, this time holding a hard leather-looking case. He walked back toward Felix and set it on the ground before speaking up again. "Ya used a poison of some sort, right? Pretty strong one, if strange. It feels slow, like Narvum Oil," he paused. "It ain't Narvum Oil, is it?"

Felix felt like Harn's eyes were seeing right through him, somehow. Whatever his Brawler's Physique was doing, it was an unpleasant sensation that squirmed against his Perception. "Uh, maybe? It was a strong poison, some sort of paralytic that slowly made all my everything stop. I don't know what it was called," Felix rubbed his side, where the dagger had stabbed him. "And I didn't dose myself, if that's what you're saying. That assassin got me."

"Nah, that ain't Narvum Oil. Venom of the Narvum don't paralyze, and woulda given ya the runs fer a week." Harn's eyes narrowed, inspecting something about Felix's body, like he was reading a book Felix couldn't see. Abruptly he whistled, low and long. "Hoo, didn't know ya got the Sworn ta poison ya during yer Formation though! Hah! I'd kill ta have seen the look on her face when you stood back up."

Felix found himself chuckling. "It was pretty good, yeah."

"What Essence ya take?"

"The Essence of Inevitability. Though I'm not sure what that does, or even means," Felix admitted. "I don't fully understand why my Apprentice-Tier Skill even took parts of the poison into itself."

"That makes sense. Most keep the details on Tempering from the younger ones fer their own protection. Too many promising students thought themselves too special ta wait; Tempering before yer ready is deadly." Harn took another swig from his flask. "Special potions or rare treasures are used to Temper your Body, Mind, and Spirit. Yer system extracts a number of Essences from the brew, and ya pick during your Tier Formation.

"I got a few basic Iron types here, meant for the Tin Ranks ta bring them up to snuff." Harn unsnapped the locks on the leather case he brought over, throwing open the lid and displaying a series of small vials, each containing a silvery liquid. Like mercury, almost. "But even these common-type Essences can go twisty quick. They can as easily kill ya as strengthen ya. Much like yer poisoning."

Felix Analyzed them, and they all came back with similar descriptions: Essence Draught of Iron Mind, Essence Draught of Iron Body, and Essence Draught of Iron Spirit.

Name: Essence Draught of Iron Mind
Type: Essence Draught
Lore: Essence Draughts are used to Temper the Body, Mind, and Spirit. Used upon achievement of a Tier, they help to expel impurities and refine the vessel. This Essence Draught is infused with the Mind Essences of Iron.
Rarity: Common

Abruptly, the spark of memory flared in Felix's head. He had a liquid just like that. He'd had it ever since he found the Henaari's corpse.

"Other things can be used, but it's easier and cheaper ta get an alchemist to make up a basic Iron Essence Draught for Apprentice Tier." Harn gestured to the manifold rack of silver vials. "Less effective than a natural treasure or the like, but helluva lot easier ta take. Still hurts like a bitch, though."

"What if you reach Apprentice Tier in more than three Skills? Or have already reached apprentice tier and didn't Temper yourself?" Felix buckled down and asked the questions that were burning in his mind, the ones he'd worried about from the moment he learned about Tempering.

"Tempering more than three Skills is a waste. Resources and time. It won't have any added benefit, not at Apprentice Tier." Harn gestured to the vials again. "If ya failed to Temper yourself the first time, ya got two choices. Both ain't great. One is to raise another Skill to Apprentice Tier, which ain't easy and'll take time. Option two is a lot more painful and highly dangerous." Harn frowned, his eyes drifting down to the Skill list Felix sent to him.

"I've got Pain Resistance, I can handle it," Felix quietly asserted, feeling confident in that at least.

Harn's expression wasn't lazy confidence or smirking amusement. It was stone solid and just as cold. "No ya can't, kid. To Temper yourself for a Skill that passed beyond yer Tier Formation, you have to break the Skill itself."

"What?" Felix wasn't quite sure he heard that correctly.

"Break the Skill. Ya sunder yer understanding, sacrificing the Skill to alter yerself. It's not something done by anyone except the desperate, but I've heard stories. It's not pleasant and can have...side effects."

Shit. So I did *screw it up.* Felix bit his lip. *No way I'm gonna go breaking my Skills just for this.*

"So what should I do? I figure Tempering is my next step, right?" Felix asked.

"I'd suggest you put Tempering out of your mind for now. If one a yer Skills goes into Tier Formation, then ya can snag one a my Essence Draughts. Just do it quick, mind." Harn picked up the vials and set them off to the side.

At Harn's insistence, Felix changed his Skill display, reorganized into new broad categories of Body, Mind, Spirit, then broken down from there.

Skills:
BODY
Resistances: Acid Resistance (C), Level 20; Cold Resistance (C), Level 6; Fire Resistance (C) Level 14; Heat Resistance (U), Level 14; Pain Resistance (U), Level 28; Poison Resistance (U), Level 25; Bastion of Will (E), Level 28;

Combat Skills: Blunt Weapon Mastery (C), Level 3; Dodge (C), Level 24; Long Blade Mastery (C), Level 9; Parry (C), Level 2; Small Blade Mastery (C), Level 8; Staff Mastery (C), Level 1; Thrown Weapons Mastery (C), Level 10; Unarmed Mastery (C), Level 24; Blind Fighting (R), Level 18; Corrosive Strike (R), Level 18

Physical Enhancements: Running (C), Level 18; Stealth (C), Level 23; Swimming (C), Level 3; Acrobatics (U), Level 21; Breath Control (U), Level 17; Free Climbing (U), Level 15; Armored Skin (R), Level 16; Physical Conditioning (R), Level 19

MIND
Mental Enhancements: Acting (C), Level 6; Improvisation (C), Level 4; Intimidation (C), Level 2; Make An Entrance (U), Level 3; Meditation (U), Level 30; Lessons of the Past (R), Level 13; Deep Mind (E), Level 24

Information Skills: Analyze (C), Level 21; Tracking (C), Level 13; Exploration (U), Level 21; Herbalism (U), Level 17

SPIRIT
Spiritual Enhancements: Companion Pact (U), Level 14; Dual Casting (U), Level 13; Mana Manipulation (U), Level 4; Manasight (U), Level 31

Spells: Cloudstep (R), Level 1; Acid Stream (R), Level 22;

Fire Within (R) Level 29; Influence of the Wisp (R), Level 22; Invocation (R), Level 1; Mantle of the Long Night (R), Level 1; Shadow Whip (R), Level 13; Stone Shaping (R), Level 24; Reign of Vellus (R), Level 26; Sigils of the Primordial Dawn (E), Level 3

Admittedly, some of the Skills didn't quite fit in the categories he envisioned, but other than have a "Random" grouping, it was the best he could manage so far.

As he did that, he opened his satchel and fetched his hard potions case. Inside were a number of empty vials, he had six now, plus the filled one. That one was filled with a measure of liquid silver, heavy and thick. For the first time in days, he tried to Analyze it.

Analyze is level 22!

Name: Essence of Wandering Spirit
Type: Essence Draught
Lore: Essence Draughts are used to Temper the Body, Mind, and Spirit. Used upon achievement of a Tier, they help to expel impurities and refine the vessel. This Essence Draught is infused with the Essence of Wander.
Rarity: Uncommon

So it's a Spirit Essence. Wander...does it have something to do with the Henaari's religion? The Endless Raven?

"Alright," Harn clapped his hands, the sound startling Felix from his menus. "Now that's outta the way, first thing we gotta do is teach you how to fight. From what I've seen, you've got a lot of bad habits, kid."

Felix laughed. "You're not wrong. Fighting isn't exactly my thing."

Harn grunted. "Good thing you met me, because it's what I know best. C'mon," he smacked his chest, the metal on metal sound clanging.

"Attack."

CHAPTER FORTY-SIX

As the evening turned to true night and the Humans sparred within their bubble, Vvim watched.

Watched and waited.

The Old Ways were not forgotten, not by the Geist. The Tower was Vvim, and Vvim was the Tower. They stretched, their thoughts moving through the old structure like blood within a limb, focusing on the connection as they hadn't in Ages. Eyes of stone and metal, ears of wind and flame, Vvim could feel the Humans like ants upon their skin.

And the boy. The Nym Who Was Not.

Something about the boy irked his senses. What Vvim first recognized as the song of sorcery was but an echo in the child's movement. A...shadow that trailed behind. Vvim felt the rush of excitement fade away, resolving into the dim beat of realism.

He was no Sorcerer; he was barely Nym at all.

But how did he navigate the Tower? None should be in the Lower Annals. The Towers were attuned to the Geist. Lesser creatures were kept to the lower levels, like the Irontooth Apes or the Ofrenok. Yet somehow this strange child had moved through the Tower at will, acting on thoughts that he could not possess.

He knows so little, yet stares at things with such...hunger in his eyes. The hunger of the unlearned, perhaps, eager to be altered by the hum of knowledge. Vvim could feel him Analyzing everything he saw, sometimes repeatedly. What he found so interesting in stone walls and burning sticks, the Geist was unsure, but it intrigued them.

Indeed, Vvim could feel the flicker of discordance earlier as the boy listened to the Large One speak of betrayals and lies, an echo of the terrible promise the Geist felt before. To their delight, the boy responded with compassion when offered a choice between safety and sacrifice. As was only proper for even his diluted blood.

Perhaps he was more Nym than they thought.

They spoke on, and Vvim grew concerned over the artifact they chased, for the Geist knew what it was. To meddle with such things was beyond arrogance; Vvim should know.

The Geist had lost so many already.

So, the ancient creature sank deeper within the Tower, their self poured into this task, their first in far too long. And so the night stretched onward.

And Vvim watched.

"Uoufff!"

Felix smashed into the wall with a muffled *thump*, already used to the way the jellied air seemed to cushion both his body and the sound of impact. Groaning and sore, Felix rolled to his feet, pushing tiredly off a knee before dropping into what he referred to as his "battle stance."

"Pff," Harn laughed. "Stop doing that. It's not...just stop."

Felix dropped his fists and stood from his crouch, feeling a little embarrassed. They had been fighting for an hour, and it felt like an eternity. Harn had him use his fists, a sword, a dagger, even going so far as getting a heavy wooden stick from the fire pile to swing like a staff or club. What's more, the man wouldn't let Felix use any spells. His body was battered and bruised from the day, and the grizzled warrior wasn't gentle.

He's a monster.

Harn walked over to a set of waterskins that had been filled to bursting nearby. One of the side chambers had a functioning water basin, which was extremely strange to Felix, but everyone else just took it as a lucky break. A lever on the back let out ice cold water, just like a sink back home. Felix couldn't figure out what made it work, and any inquiries came back with a raised eyebrow and a single word. "Magic."

Of course. What else? His only comfort was that he was half-certain none of them actually knew the right answer.

"What," Felix panted after a long drink. "What next? More fighting?"

Harn took a measured sip of his water and eyed Felix, noting his bare and bruised torso. "Ya up for more?" Felix straightened himself, hiding the grimace that tried to steal across his face, and nodded. Harn smiled.

"Good. A glutten' fer punishment. That'll serve ya well, kid." Harn slapped him on the back, hard enough to send him stumbling forward several steps.

Armored Skin is level 18!

Harn followed right behind him, drawing one of his axes again. "Alright. So ya got a good foundation, and some solid stats seems like, especially fer yer level." Harn swung his axe in a set of looping slashes. "That's yer problem. Yer strong, but ya don't know what ta do with it."

"That seems right," Felix readily agreed. "I've been mostly flailing around during fights. It's worked out so far, but..."

"But ya can't rely on luck and stats forever. You got a balance Skill?" Harn asked.

"You saw that I've got Acrobatics. Does that count?"

Harn waggled his free hand. "It'll help. Focus on yer center, don't overextend. An' also," he pulled a second axe, this one a dull gun-metal color and tossed it to Felix. "Use this."

Felix, in a panic that was a left-over from his previous life, immediately felt like was going to fumble the catch. When his hands smoothly caught the haft of the axe, he was almost surprised. Then he registered what Harn was saying.

"Use the axe? I don't have Axe Mastery. I thought I was supposed to be learning about the Skills I already have?" Felix protested. Harn just raised his silvery axe up while dropping his own body lower.

Felix hurriedly raised his axe. He knew what was coming next.

In an instant, the warrior was on top of him, swinging down with his wicked blade. Felix jerked his own axe wide, trying to knock the silver strike away, but only succeeded in opening himself up. Panicking, he flexed his legs and hopped back a solid three feet. The axe still came down only inches from his chest, whistling in the air as Harn maneuvered it effortlessly.

A second swing came. Felix hopped back again, this time the attack missing him by a foot, before he charged in with an overhand chop of his own. The first few times they fought, Felix had been worried he would hurt the man, but by this point, Felix was more concerned his axe would break on the man's armor.

Which was stupid, since he missed by approximately a mile.

Felix tucked into a roll, intending to tumble past the warrior, a favored tactic against many beasts he'd fought. He managed the roll, but felt a blade burn a line down his back. As he came back to his feet, Felix gritted his teeth as the sharp pain faded to a dull burn thanks to his Pain Resistance. Harn stood casually, his axe held loosely in his grip and dripping a line of red.

Felix charged back in.

Blow after blow, chop, slice, swing, Felix tried everything he could to penetrate Harn's impossible defense. But the man was impervious to his attacks, moving his axe in a dizzying net of blocks and parries using the blade and haft. As a last ditch effort, Felix threw his weapon straight at the man's smirking face. Harn simply raised a hand and deflected the axe with his vambrace. It clattered to the ground the same time Felix did.

"Holy..shit..." Felix panted, his breath in big gulps. "An axe...is a...bullshit weapon."

Harn laughed. "Ya just don't know how ta use it. Yet."

"Whaddya...mean...'yet'?" Felix asked, but renewed blinking of his minimized notifications drew his attention. He toggled it and scrolled to the most recent addition.

New Skill Learned!
Axe Mastery (Common), Level 1!
You've taken a step down the path of axes! Like a lumberjack! Damage and speed increases with Skill Level.

Axe Mastery is level 2!

"All that...for a new Skill?" Felix laid back, letting his Stamina regenerate for a moment. Eyes closed, he asked, "Why?"

"Like I said, ya got the stats, ya just don't got the finesse." There was a tap of metal against stone as Harn walked closer. "I aim ta change that."

"By giving me MORE Skills?" Felix leveraged himself up into a sitting position and stared up at him. "Don't get me wrong, thanks and all, but were you just telling me not to get more Skills?"

"I said what ya got is weird, not wrong. Skills are our lifeblood, and a high-level Skill will win over higher levels any day a'the week." Harn smirked. "Yer problem is a lack a focus. Spells an' stealth an' fist fightin' an' Yyero-touched meditation? Ain't that just thinkin' hard fer too long?" This time he laughed, though not unkindly. "Yer all over the place. You practice these combat Skills with me, and I'll get you fightin' fit."

Felix huffed a breath, but smiled. *Finally, someone who's got this shit figured out.*

"Alright, I'll trust your judgement. At least until I can beat you in a fight," Felix half-muttered the last part to himself. Harn just smirked. Again.

He's infuriating.

The man wandered off, letting Felix recover and go over his notifications. *Dude's not lying. He knows what he's doing.*

Long Blade Mastery is level 10!
...
Long Blade Mastery is level 12!

Small Blade Mastery is level 9!
Small Blade Mastery is level 10!

Blunt Weapon Mastery is level 4!
...
Blunt Weapon Mastery is level 7!

Staff Mastery is level 2!
...
Staff Mastery is level 5!

Parry is level 3!

Parry is level 4!

Thrown Weapon Mastery is level 11!

Physical Conditioning is level 20!
Physical Conditioning is level 21!

The list of Skill increases made Felix feel capable, in an abstract sort of way. He knew he still had a long way to go.

I wonder if Harn would let me have some of his blood..I'm sure he's got some good Skills. Felix felt a vague ache in his gut, but shook off the uncomfortable pressure. *No chance that's acceptable behavior around here, though.*

And yet...

His Gourmand Title and Lessons of the Past Skill were such an advantage that he'd be a fool not to make the most of them. *Gotta find some more monsters, stat. Speaking of...*

Felix pulled up the description of one of his newest Skills: Mantle of the Long Night.

Mantle of the Long Night (Rare), level 1!
The cold of the Long Night cannot be stopped, only delayed. Extends an aura of cold centered on yourself. Range and strength increases with Skill Level.

Haven't even tried this out yet. Got too excited about Cloudstep. Felix smiled to himself. *Should I train it now?*

No one was around him, and while his Stamina was very low, his Mana was completely topped off. Felix shrugged into a comfortable sitting position, and double checked where everyone was located. Magda was nowhere to be seen, but Vessilia was fighting Evie, while Atar sparred against Harn, of all people.

Good luck with that. Felix chuckled, but stopped when his ribs ached. Pain Resistance was exactly what it said on the tin; it seemed to numb or make pain more tolerable, but it didn't make it go away. *If only*, he sighed.

He sensed Pit was near the actual stairs. Not, of course, where Felix had descended. He still couldn't find that stairwell, and the lack annoyed him. The whole tower was a weird little mystery wrapped in the larger mystery of what the hell happened to this huge city. Harn didn't know, neither did the others, only saying it happened long ago. *Evie referenced the Third Age, which sounds like a long time ago, but are Ages a hundred years? A thousand? What Age is it now?*

Felix's thoughts ran in circles, and he resolved to ask more pointed questions of the others, mentally adding the concept of time to his list of questions. *List is getting pretty long.*

Felix shook himself. He was losing focus. *Might be more tired than I thought. Whatever. I'll sleep when I'm dead.*

Mantle of the Long Night

A swirling gust of wind surrounded Felix, pushing outward a few feet before it terminated. The wind was chill, but not uncomfortable, and it never settled down, constantly rotating at low speed around him like a tiny, invisible hurricane.

This is cool. He rolled his eyes. *Neat. It's like a personal air conditioner.* No doubt it'd get stronger as it leveled, but it also didn't take up much Mana, only three or four points per second. At his current rate of regen, as long as Meditation was active, he could keep it up for a little over seven minutes. He left it on and turned toward his other spells.

Reign of Vellus got the most use of his spells, and it had already reached Apprentice Tier. As such, he'd noticed it was harder to level than before, taking either more usage or more unique insights to move it along. Felix decided to focus on his lesser-used spells, maybe amp up his firepower. Not to mention he might even complete that Apprentice Quest he had lingering.

Okay, so Acid Stream, Influence of the Wisp, and Stone Shaping are the closest to Tier, but my Sigils, Invocation, and Shadow Whip all need serious work. Cloudstep uses a lot of Mana and at least some *Stamina, so I'll set that aside for now. Hmm.*

Tottering to his feet, Felix made his way to the fire pile, retrieving a bundle of sticks from the remarkably large stack. He idly wondered if Harn had snuck out and chopped down a tree and the thought made him laugh. After a bit and some twine from their pack, he had produced three bundles of sticks that were his best attempt at targets.

Improvisation is level 5!
Mantle of the Long Night is level 2!

Huh, didn't expect that. Then, as he watched, the nearest bundle started to ever-so-slightly silver along the edges. When he touched a stick, it was frigid. *Awesome.*

Retracting his Mantle, Felix took several paces back from the impromptu targets and focused. He activated Shadow Whip and it shot forward from his left hand, smashing one of the targets down. He let the spell fade and frowned. *I didn't mean to knock it over. How did I make it spread out?* He cast again, this time acting on instinct and splaying his fingers out wide.

The Whip launched again, but the end of it fanned outward instead of staying a single solid whip-shape. The fanned out pieces of it easily engulfed and secured around the target. With a quick yank, the entire bundle flew back toward Felix, who caught it in delight.

Shadow Whip is level 14!

He returned the target.

Ok so I can control the shape of it. But how much? Felix cast again, this time trying to split the whip into two pieces after it had cast. There was a slight pressure behind his eyes, but then the spell did it; two wriggling tendrils of shadow writhed in time with each other, extending from the same hand. He tried to use both tendrils to simultaneously attack two targets at once...and failed spectacularly.

A sharp spike of pain lanced up his forehead. "*Ah*, shit!" He held his hand to his head before pulling it back, expecting blood. There was nothing. The pain had been inside his head. *Oh that's probably not good. Maybe leave the dual targeting for higher levels.*

Instead, Felix dual cast the spell, throwing two Shadow Whips at two separate targets. This time, it went as expected. Both targets were ensnared as he splayed his fingers, and both were yanked back toward him with a casual tug.

Dual Casting is level 14!

And on it went. He gained two more levels in Shadow Whip, and Felix discovered two things about it in that time. One, he could split the whip into four tendrils for each casting, but no more; he also couldn't move them independently, and all four tendrils would strike the same target. The only benefit he saw there was that each tendril was a different angle of attack, so maybe it would be harder to defend against?

And two, it was definitely tacky to the touch, which must help bind it to the target. What Felix didn't understand was why *this* shadow spell was tacky while the passive shadow cloak skill Illia had possessed had remained stubbornly slick. It was something he kept returning to: *If they're both made of shadow Mana, why are they different? What's the cause?*

As he sat, recovering his Mana and pondering the nature of his spellwork, he let his mind wander to the Rockstrike from whom he'd taken the Skill. The thing was a shadow/earth elemental and used its own tendrils as partial locomotion and offense. It had *definitely* used its tendrils independently, as had all the others he'd fought in that cave. None had used the tendrils to bind him, though, instead focusing on whipping and blunt force trauma. *Then why does mine? Did I get a variant?*

Felix closed his eyes, focusing on the spell itself. Like all the rest, Shadow Whip was a lingering feeling in his core, a phantom limb that he knew would activate if he prodded it in just the right way. It was strange, really, but that was how all of his Skills worked. Felix could feel a faint network of pulsing lines throughout his flesh, his pathways, and echoed out among them were the elaborate designs he recognized as Stone Shaping and Manasight. But they all started in his center, he felt. His core, where a blue-white fire roiled and azure sparks crackled.

He homed in on Shadow Whip, teasing out the feel of its pattern. It undulated, like a wave, but it was compressed, turned in on itself in a recursive manner that was dizzying to follow. Felix lost the path quickly, despite his recall; it was less about memory and more about...something else. Something vague that he didn't have the words for. Not yet.

Opening his eyes felt like he was resurfacing from a deep sea dive, and there was a brief moment of disorientation where the world felt too loud, too bright. He could almost hear a ringing in his ears, like a feedback loop from a hot mic, which was ridiculous—

Felix stopped. He focused on the sound, a not-quite ringing that definitely did *not* shake the inner portions of his ear. No, the ringing was coming from inside the house. His core, specifically.

Fire Within is level 30!

What is...Felix traced it back to the undulating pattern for Shadow Whip. He knew sound had some place in the development of Skills, just as the imprint within his core channeled and defined them. Meditation worked by feeding back into itself, *harmonizing* with his stats to produce more of the same. So what was Shadow Whip doing?

Felix pushed again along the undulating trail of his spell, feeling that ringing become more of a buzz as he neared those ineffable lines. The patterns were drawn in Mana itself, and as he focused closer, he could see pulses of blue-white light flaring along the lines of the Skill, followed closely by waves of grey-black shimmers. The buzz modulated, speeding up and slowing down as each blue-white pulse flared by, almost like a wave.

A grasping tide that surged and ebbed, each time grasping and pulling. Pushing away yet simultaneously never letting go.

Shadow Whip is level 17!
...
Shadow Whip is level 20!

Fire Within is level 31!
Fire Within is level 32!

Felix's eyes snapped open wide.

And he smiled.

CHAPTER FORTY-SEVEN

He didn't manage to level any more spells before Harn returned, fresh from beating Atar into the ground. Felix would've almost felt bad, if the kid wasn't a huge dork. Still, he felt some grudging respect as the mage kept getting back up. Harn got right back into it with Felix, starting up the same sort of weapons training as before, pushing him into spar after spar until time blurred.

It was late, though no one seemed to be settling down. Too much work to be done, too much to prepare.

Not that Felix had the time to think about it.

Harn came at him again, his two swords moving in opposite directions. Felix twisted sideways and used his bronze blade to catch one sword even as the second sliced open his hip.

"Fuaaa!" Felix kicked out, catching Harn's bicep. Harn shifted backward, not so much shoved as flowing with the momentum, spinning into a new set of strikes. Felix flailed, golden sparks rising from his Crescian blade as the steel swords caught and flung it from his grasp. He stared after it a moment before springing into a backwards roll.

Acrobatics had become increasingly easier, his body more flexible due to his Dexterity and Agility, but his fights with Harn were pushing him to a new limit.

"No retreating!" Harn came after him, swords striking deep furrows into the solid stone floor. Felix tumbled three times, each revolution ending with those blades closer and closer to his face. On the last, he pushed up onto his hands and twisted his body into an awkward round off.

Acrobatics is level 22!

It was weird and looked bad, but it was effective. Harn's blades once again barely scraped against Felix's skin, though still managing to draw two gouts of blood into the air. Gritting his teeth, Felix reached down and grabbed the axe resting against the wall. As Harn came in again, Felix swung the axe in a low arc, intending to catch the bastard on the knees. And he did.

The axe clanked dully against the armor, not even scratching it.

Faster than he could blink, the two swords crossed and came to rest against his neck. Felix swallowed audibly.

"Ya lose," Harn smirked. "Again."

Felix stood up as the warrior retracted his swords, sheathing them in a single fluid motion. "Again," Felix said.

"Yeah, again," Harn smirked as he turned to walk away. "That was the sixth time ya lost. I'm startin' ta think yer throwin' this on purpose."

"No," Felix said, his voice firmer. "*Again.*"

Harn half turned and eyed him up and down. Then he grinned.

"Oh, you got it, kid."

Twenty minutes later, Felix was exhausted. He laid out on the ground, the stone cooling his sweaty body. Harn sat down heavily next to him, his armor clanking dully on the floor.

"Siva's eyes, where'd that last bit come from?" Harn asked.

Eyes closed, Felix smiled. He'd managed to catch Harn off guard in the last bout, using Shadow Whip to grasp and pull the man's weapon just slightly off target, letting Felix get close enough to land a single punch. For the first time all night, Felix heard Harn gasp, though he doubted it was from pain.

Still, it was music to his ears.

"That was some clever Skill use. Didn't expect the spell. What was it?"

Felix cracked open an eye, looking at Harn from where he laid on the floor. Felix was covered in sweat, blood, and no small amount of bruises, while the burly human was still in his near-pristine armor. Small scratches covered Harn's armor, but it wasn't from him. "Shadow Whip."

Harn grunted. "Interestin'. Next time though, no spells. Can't learn weapons proper if ya have a crutch."

Felix frowned. He'd been proud of using his new understanding of Shadow Whip to get one over on the walking suit of armor. "It's a good spell, though."

Harn held up his hands. "I'm not sayin' it ain't. Can see a lotta utility in somethin' like that. My point is, weapon mastery'll get you more over the long run. Spells are...well, they're gimmicks. Level to level, Skill to Skill, ain't no mage is gonna hold up against a true warrior."

Felix chewed on his lip, considering the words.

Harn shook his head and smiled as he stood up. "Yer a weird one, Felix. Take a rest for the night. I gotta focus on the other kids." He walked off.

Frowning at being included with the term "kids," Felix took a breath and cleared his mind. His hip still hurt from where Harn had sliced him earlier, though it was nearly healed over by this point. After thirty seconds, he checked his notifications.

Acrobatics is level 23!
Parry is level 8!
Physical Conditioning is level 22!
Armored Skin is level 21!
Axe Mastery is level 5!
Blunt Weapon Mastery is level 8!
Long Blade Mastery is level 14!
Small Blade Mastery is level 13!
Staff Mastery is level 9!
Thrown Weapons Mastery is level 13!
Blind Fighting is level 19!
Mantle of the Long Night is level 3!

Even Blind Fighting jumped up? Felix was impressed, though his body wasn't. Aches and pains littered his flesh, and though the worst of it was dulled, it certainly wasn't a picnic. He'd sure as hell worked for those gains.

*I could rest now. Take a nap by the fire...*Felix eyed one of the side rooms and huffed a small breath. He stood up.

Too much to do. He had come up with some training ideas, and now was as good a time as any to try them out.

Pit, he sent to his nearly asleep Companion. *Can you watch over this doorway, bud? Squawk if anyone comes near.*

Felix could feel the tenku's grudging assent over their connection, though the lazy bird didn't rush. Felix could sense him take a long luxurious stretch, flexing his wings out in a show of not being hurried. He grinned before ducking under one of the cloth-covered archways. This was where the "magic basin" was, and the room was filled with several bench-like objects. Like the basins themselves, the benches were somehow carved from the stone itself, as if the entire room was chiseled from one piece of rock. *Or someone had a Stone Shaping spell.*

Felix walked over to one of the unused basins, a waist-high pedestal carved with pale figures along the four corners. It was deep enough to submerge half his body were he to jump in, and was one of many that had a non-functioning lever and still caked with dust. No windows dotted these rooms, unlike others, though there was a drain in the floor and odd holes bored into the ceiling. What they were for he wasn't certain, though the entire setup looked like some sort of communal shower.

Regardless, anthropology wasn't why he had come in here, no matter how fascinating all of this stuff happened to be. Felix held out his arms, raising them above the basin.

Acid Stream.

Two orbs of green acid bulged in his palms, suspended by some strange aspect of magic, before jetting a concentrated stream directly into the basin itself. He paused, letting the acid bubble and burn for a while. He didn't know if it would eat through the stone or not. When the bottom of the basin didn't fall out, he cast again. Felix had to stop and regenerate his Mana twice before filling the entire thing. By the end of it, he felt a little light-headed due to Mana loss and the pungent odor of the acid, which was an acrid tang in the air. It was gross and reminded him viscerally of the copse grubs and their pale, wriggly bodies.

His stomach gurgled, his body reminding him that he'd been training for hours now and wanted more food. *Wonder if there's any more of that Hoarhound left? Feels like I could eat a horse.*

Felix shook himself, exercising his Willpower to reorient. Food was later. Now was the experiment.

The basin was full of thick green acid, merrily bubbling away. Taking a deep breath, Felix lifted his left hand and pushed it wrist-deep into the liquid.

Ahhssshhh—that burns! Felix held back from screaming, but the pain was excruciating as the acid ate away at his skin beneath the surface. Moments later, his Pain Resistance must have kicked in, because it dulled down to a mild roar. Once that happened, he gritted his teeth and pushed the rest of his forearm into the basin.

His arm shook, muscles spasming as nerves misfired. The smell of acid wafted into his face, mingling with the scent of dissolving flesh. This close he could see bits of his skin peel off the top of his forearm and slowly disintegrate, each second the pain mounting higher and higher. In the corner of his vision, he saw his Health begin to dip, dropping 25% in as many seconds.

Acid Resistance is level 21!

It worked!

His Health loss started to slow, and Felix could almost feel his body fighting back. The acid was mostly opaque and the roiling bubbles occluded the rest, but the top of his forearm didn't get much worse, though he couldn't stop the shaking. Tick after tick, his Health dropped, until he reached 50% and the shaking was almost uncontrollable. The pain felt like it had dug sizzling needles into his muscles, a fizzing torment that was getting increasingly difficult to ignore.

And then, finally, relief.

Pain Resistance is level 29!

Acid Resistance is level 22!

The acid, once merrily bubbling away at his arm, stilled. Felix pulled his arm out of the acidic goop and stepped away from the basin, taking big lungfuls of clean air as he did. His arm was angry and red, covered in welts and burns from the acid. Felix held it up awkwardly, the pain of it only intensifying as his scoured flesh met the air, and held his elbow as if that would somehow stem the worst of it. Only after a minute passed, and his Health began to slowly creep back upward, did he let himself relax.

Can't believe that worked. Felix had suspected that his own acid would hurt him, but wasn't positive. He had Acid Resistance, right? And it was his own spell, so why would it hurt him? *I was right. My Acid Stream was higher level than my Acid Resistance, so it hurt me. The moment they evened out, the acid was less able to affect me. So if I can get Acid Stream higher than Acid Resistance again, I can power level it, probably right alongside Pain Resistance.*

Felix held out his arm, still pink and tender, but much better than only minutes before. Patches of new skin slowly spread across his flesh, his Perception picking out the morbid details easily. He leaned against another basin and stared into the middle distance as he pondered resistances. What did Tempering your body do to affect this sort of training? *If I were stronger, would this not work?*

Better get all the training he could before that happened.

Ever since Harn explained Tempering, Felix was careful not to push any Skill into Apprentice Tier, even going so far as to refuse to dodge some of the man's strikes. It helped that it seemed to take a lot to make that jump from level 24 to 25, but he had a couple Skills that were on the cusp, and even more that were within five levels of it. As much as he ached to finish his Apprentice Spell quest, Felix felt a deep sense of unease when he thought of Tempering himself. He wasn't sure what it was, but the more he pondered it—the closer he got—the more he shied away.

If Tempering myself is like burning away that poison, I'm not in a big rush to try that again. His thoughts flashed back to the silver vials Harn had shown him. *Besides, weren't those basic Essence Draughts? If I wait, am I missing out on better Essences? It's stupid, but I'd be kinda pissed if I missed out on something better for something right now.*

Felix tilted his head back and considered the ceiling. *Then again, if I don't live through the next few days, what's the point? Ugh. This is a pointless debate to have with myself.* Instead, he folded his legs and sat down on the ground, letting his mind wander toward his core. He wanted to see the results of his resistance training.

Previously, his Resistances were all hard to perceive within his core. The imprint of their ethereal patterns were vague and strangely inert. Felix assumed that was because they were passive rather than active abilities, only engaging when circumstances required. Sensing his Acid Resistance now, he thought he could perceive something, but it was either extremely faint or not there at all. He couldn't focus on it like he had with Shadow Whip, sadly, and would likely have to train it in a normal way.

His Mantle of the Long Night was similar, only appearing as a simple impression in his core. It was an active Skill for sure, but maybe because it was so low level it did not generate enough activity within his core to really show him anything. The pattern it displayed was a simple spiral and contained no extraneous or convoluted details, nothing that gave him a hint as to its nature. *Why is that? Shadow Whip is a maze of shapes and Stone Shaping is a corkscrewing roller coaster, comparatively.*

Every Skill he owned had a uniqueness to its pattern, though many were at least passingly similar. Resistances, for instance, were all inert and faded. His spells were all wild variations, though. It was like learning a language based on pictures of someone else's notes, written in *another* foreign language. The further he investigated his core, pathways, and intricate Skill imprints, the more he realized he needed to level his Fire Within Skill. Which was another Skill that was faded and inert, though likely for different reasons, and investigating it led nowhere.

No ringing. No humming or buzzing. Just the crackle and flare of his own core, burning just out of sight.

Makes sense that I can't level up my Fire Within Skill so easily. Not gonna lie though, that's disappointing.

Grooooouuuuugglle

Felix's concentration broke as his stomach let out a powerful gurgle. He patted his bare stomach, enjoying the sensation of having a flat midsection. "Better go eat, though. Who knows when I'll get more meat."

Felix stood and walked back into the main chamber, still not liking the feeling of the thickened air against his skin. Pit slept quietly near the archway, his little beak open as he snored. Felix smiled and kept going.

The room was still abuzz with activity, despite the late hour. In fact, Felix was a little surprised at how alert he was feeling despite the training he just did. *Must be an effect of higher Endurance?* He could still feel the urge to sleep, but it was easily put off, like riding a caffeine high without the jangly nerves. His body even ached less since his Pain Resistance went up again, and his regeneration was taking care of the bruises and cuts left by Harn.

The Tin Ranks were sparring again, this time Evie versus Vessilia. As Felix climbed down into the tiered fire pit, he watched the two young women fight with their respective weapons. Vessilia utilized the reach of her spear to keep her distance from her much more agile opponent, but Evie was hard to pin down. She flipped and twisted, moving up and over the spearwoman's attacks in a dizzying dance. Vessilia tried to keep up, but it looked like she was trying to grab dandelion fluff from the air. Each attempt only made it float further away.

Wonder what her Acrobatics Skill is? He ate as he watched, grabbing whatever was left over of the meat from a nearby tin platter. The thing was piled high with scraps carved from the carcass. *Definitely higher than mine, which means at least Apprentice Tier. And Vessilia has that way she jumps. Evie called her a Dragoon. But Harn said classes weren't a thing. So what's she referring to?*

Felix licked his fingers, the meat juices cold but still good. *Maybe it's an organization? So there's the Guild and now Dragoons. What else is out there?* Felix felt a flutter of excitement race through him at the idea of exploring this world. Maybe he was trapped here and he'd never see home again, but it was a taste of freedom he'd never had. *If only things stopped trying to kill me.*

Felix reached down for another piece of meat and found the simple tin plate empty. "Huh?" He looked around, but there was nothing left.

"How'd that happen?" There had to have been five or six pounds of meat in that pile. He even had a pile of bones left next to him, evidence of his massacre. *Is my metabolism that high now?* He didn't even feel full. *If I could, I would probably eat more.*

Felix held his hands out, feeling the sticky residue of pounds of monster meat and grimaced. Full or not, he was done, and he couldn't go back to training like this. He stood, luxuriating in a long stretch before finding his waterskin and a rag, using them to carefully wash his hands and chest. He was remarkably dirty, covered in dust and dirt, a bit of blood and acid, and now greasy smears of meat. What's more, it had been literal days since he last showered, and oh man did that feel gross.

He was basking in the warm memory of hot, daily showers

while scrubbing himself with a cold rag when someone threw something in his face. Felix turned and caught it, but the item ended up being cloth and bigger than his hands and just flopped onto his head. Pulling it down, he recognized it as a faded green shirt. He looked back up.

"Time to stop being naked, weirdo," Evie said, sipping on a dull yellow potion.

Felix laughed, more happy he had a shirt than embarrassed. He'd been on and off bare-chested for weeks now. "Yeah, I have a problem with shirts, I guess."

"Psh," she scoffed. "I don't see a problem." Evie looked him up and down while sipping on her potion. "But you're distracting people."

Felix, caught between a blush and a snarky reply, turned to see Vessilia and Atar looking his way. The noblewoman quickly found herself busy and turned back toward whatever she was doing...some sort of slow fighting stance routine. *A kata, is that what those are called?*

Atar, as he half expected, wasn't even looking at him. He was looking at Vessilia. When they did meet eyes, Felix could practically feel the anger radiating from the teen wizard.

Felix rolled his eyes.

He put on the shirt.

CHAPTER FORTY-EIGHT

"Hey what is that?" Shirt comfortably on, Felix nodded at the vial she held.

"This? Haven't seen a stamina potion before?"

Felix felt a rush of excitement. If he could replenish his Stamina even faster, then he could train far longer. "You have any more?"

"Some, but we burned through a lot during that big battle, back when we met. They get less effective over time anyway." Evie shrugged and tipped back the last of the potion before letting out a tiny burp. "Just taking one now to replenish before I gotta fight Harn. Bastard's tough as hell."

"I noticed," Felix rubbed his ribs, a phantom ache from one of many bruises the warrior had put on him. It was all healed by now though. "Hey, I've been meaning to ask. How much do you know about other races?"

"Hm?" Evie looked up as she rooted around the fire pit. "Which ones? I know lots." She peered around again and grumbled to herself. "Where'd that meat go?"

Felix looked down at the tin platter and moved surreptitiously away from it, scooting down the circular bench. "How, uh, how many races do you know?"

"Like met? Damn near all of em, if I had to guess. At least the common ones." She gave up her fruitless search for the remaining monster meat and plopped down on the bench alongside him. Her armor was beaten and scratched but sturdy, and the blue tabard thing she wore hung limp in the firelight. Felix couldn't spot her chain, which was usually wrapped around her arm or shoulder. "Elves, Dwarves, Alfein, Nixies and Naiads, though they're the same thing really. Just don't let ‘em know that. Learned that one the hard way."

Evie reached into the huge rucksack and somehow found a stack of hard biscuits and jerky. She started munching while she talked. "Goblinoids, of course. I even saw an elemental spirit once, but they were pretty standoffish. Don't see them much in the cities. Birdfolk I heard of, but never met one, same with the lizardmen down Te'thys way. Atar'd probably know more about them." She chewed loudly, food spraying slightly as she spoke. "Why?"

Felix was slightly overwhelmed at the list of races she just...spat out. He added them to a list of details for the future, when he had more time. He tried to steady his thudding heart, evening out his breath with his control Skill. He had to be careful here. "I was looking around upstairs. Saw a sculpture of a bunch of chimera and of another race, this one called a 'Nym' or something. You ever hear of them?"

Acting is level 7!

Keep that face nice and neutral!

Evie tapped her lips, chewing slowly. "Nym Nym Nym. Why does that sound familiar?" She snapped her fingers. "That's right! The Night Market in Amphora! They had this weird floaty pyramid with that name on it. Nym. No one knew what it did, on account of it bein' too weird. What'd that guy say about it..."

Evie drifted off, eyes up and staring at the middle distance. She screwed up her face, as if trying to eke out the last drop of a memory. "Said something about old ruins? Real old, like Third Age old. I *do* remember that no one could even Analyze it. Kinda like the fog here..." She stopped scrunching her face and turned to Felix, her green eyes bright. "Hey, speaking of which; how can you see through the fog?"

Felix frowned. "You still don't believe me?"

Evie waved her hands. "No, no. After today, I'm a believer, but it's weird. You came outta nowhere, you can see through the fog, you got a chimera friend who, no offence, is creepy as Yyero's backside..." Pit quietly growled from his slumber across the room, interrupting them. Felix frowned. Maybe the mishmash of bird and fox/dog was ungainly, but Pit was far from creepy. What did she see when she looked at Pit?

He asked her.

“Uh same thing you do? Got eyes, don’t I? Blurry and dark, like smoke made monster. Four eyes. Great huge claw wing things in its back. Like I said. Creepy." Her neck and shoulders twitched involuntarily, and she gave Felix an apologetic look.

Felix’s head rocked back, though he realized he shouldn’t have been surprised. *So the illusion was affecting how they saw Pit? Does it extend to all monsters?*

“How about the giants? What do they look like?”

“You’ve seen em. Blue skin, ugly, big beards. Why all the questions?”

“I don’t think we’re seeing the same things. The giants sound the same, so that’s weird, but Pit doesn’t look like that. He’s a chimera, sure, but he just looks like a cross between a black bird and a big fox. Normal feather wings and all," Felix said, scratching his jaw. His beard was slowly coming in—barely more than bristles at the moment—and it finally was starting to irritate him.

“Huh. No shit?” Evie shoved another hunk of bread in her mouth and chewed as she considered Pit from afar. She swallowed and said, “Wish I could see it. However you do it, it’s not somethin’ I got.”

Felix shrugged. "Maybe it's my Manasight? I'm pretty sure the fog you're seeing isn't real either."

"Manasight? What's that?" She paused. "Wait, what? Of course it's real. Just cuz you got special peepers doesn't mean—"

"It's an illusion. A really good one, probably, since it affects such a large area. I don't really know how magic works," Felix added. "But it's not really there. It clearly affects how you all see the monsters around here too, like Pit."

"That’s nuts." Evie took a big bite of jerky and chewed it for a moment. "Never heard of a spell that big or one that could last so long. Not even at the capitol. Can’t be possible, right?"

"It makes sense," chimed in Magda, who had been sidling up into the conversation for the last twenty seconds. Felix had eyed her out of his periphery, but didn't want to mention it. *Why not just come sit down? What's that about?*

"The fog being a spell fits with the idea that an artifact can dispel it. If it were natural, I figured it'd be easier to get rid of, yeah?" Magda sat down, her leather creaking as the metal bit jangled. "But how can a spell affect even information gathering Skills? Analyze doesn't work out here; neither does Herbalism or Tracking."

Felix shrugged, absolutely out of his depth. "Not a clue. Is there such a thing as large-scale magic? Like a big, I dunno, ritual or something that would activate over a large area?"

Magda tilted her head. "Maybe. But the amount of Mana you're talking about is...it's bigger than what everyone in Haarwatch could pool together, and then some."

Evie let out a low whistle. "That's a lotta juice."

"Yeah, a lot," Magda agreed, still looking thoughtful. She turned to Felix casually. "You said you found some carvings of Nym? Where?"

Knew you were listening in. Do you still not trust me? Despite his thoughts, he half-smiled and gestured to the wall where he had descended. "You're welcome to check it, if you can make it up there. Not even sure how I did; the staircase disappeared after I came down."

Magda half rose to her feet before making a series of gestures to someone out of Felix's line of sight. He could hear metal scraping softly against metal as presumably Harn walked toward where Felix had indicated. She turned back to Felix. "Are you sure?"

"Well, yeah. I walked through the archway and then it was gone when I—"

"No," Magda interrupted him. "About the Nym?"

"Uh, yeah," Felix felt his pulse suddenly spike. "Why? What's...is something wrong?"

Magda had pulled a dagger from a sheath at her back. Felix looked at Evie, who met his eyes and shrugged. When Felix looked back, the big woman had stepped out of the fire pit and toward one of the carved walls. She searched them a moment before she pointed with the dagger at a particular scene. "Was *this* there?"

Felix stared at her a moment longer before following the direction of her dagger. Among the natural scenes depicted along the carved walls, here the nature motif changed into curling vines that formed an elaborate circular frame. A figure stood among the smaller white stone figures, the ones that looked like children. The taller one was made of slightly different stone, darker and smoother than the off white of the walls. The figure held a crooked scepter in their hand, and was wearing long flowing robes with armor belted on over it.

And above their head, a tiny but definite four pointed star.

"Well, that looks familiar," Felix muttered. He could practically hear Magda's eyes affix onto him, and he turned toward her. "Yeah, it looked just like that."

"*That's* a Nym? They look boring." Evie grumbled through a mouthful of food. "No horns or nothin'?"

"You're sure? *Just* like this?" Magda repeated.

"Yes, damn it. Why?" Felix was getting annoyed with the shield warrior's constant confirmations.

"Harn and I spotted this earlier, though I didn't see any others. I had hoped it didn't mean anythin', maybe just a decoration. But if you saw what you saw, then we're in trouble." Magda stared at Felix with worried eyes. At some point, Vessilia and Atar had wandered over toward them all, and Felix could see them look on questioningly. Magda started talking again, her voice softer.

"We've been to a lot of ruins over the years, and out of all of them, the only one that nearly killed us was littered with pictures of *them*." She pointed again at the robed Nym with her dagger. "After that job went sideways, we found others that had seen these figures before. All of them were in ruins, ones that were hidden or sunk beneath the earth. All of them, without exception, were deadly."

Harn spoke up, and Felix turned to regard the warrior. "Those carvings can be found across the Continent. Always the worst places, but also the ones with the greatest treasure, too. This tower and the others like it might be somethin' these creatures built, somewhere they hid their deadly treasures."

"But who *were* they?" Atar asked, his eyes bright in the firelight. He seemed eager for this knowledge, and Felix wondered why. But he turned his attention toward Harn and Magda, hoping they could shed more light on his own newborn heritage. Magda shook her head and shrugged.

"Don't rightly know," Harn said. "We know the name, we know

they were around up until the Third Age, and we know they're Lost." Gasps rose among the Tin Ranks, and Felix perked up. He'd heard the term too many times to miss out now.

"Lost?" Felix asked, working to project an earnest ignorance. For a moment no one answered, but then Atar hopped in, no doubt happy to prove his knowledge.

Acting is level 8!

"The Ruin." Scattered nods and solemn looks crossed their faces. Felix just stared, eyes bouncing between them all.

"More importantly, it means this city is much more important than we realized," Magda continued, looking between them all. "Entire nations would bankrupt themselves to find intact Nymean artifacts."

"That also means we're in for a shitload'a trouble." Harn walked over to join her. "Like Magda said: Nymean ruins are dangerous, deadly so. Yer lucky ya didn't die on those stairs, Felix. The same goes for the rest of ya; no wanderin' around."

"How dangerous?" Vessilia's voice was soft, but her tone demanded answers. *Nobility, huh?*

"Let me put it this way, Lady Dayne," Magda said, capturing their attention again. "The old timers at the Guild have a rule for Nymean ruins. Count the stars."

"Count the stars?" Vessilia asked, eyebrow raised. "As in, how many figures?"

Magda's face was grim. "No. The star points. The more there are, the worse the danger ahead."

"And how many points did the stars have in that ruin of yours, Lady Aren?" Vessilia asked.

Magda swallowed and sheathed her dagger.

"Two."

An hour later, Felix laid uncomfortably on his borrowed bedroll, with Pit snoring lightly next to him. The big lump had been sleeping for the entire time, and he envied Pit's relaxation. Ever since Magda had revealed what she knew of the Nym, he hadn't relaxed once.

I'm a Lost Race, that's what the system notification said, way back when it altered my Apprentice Quest. That has something to do with the Ruin, which, okay, sure. Seems obvious enough on the surface. Big cataclysm comes along, wipes a people out. People later call it something ominous.

Felix bit his lip as he stared up at the ceiling. They had banked the fire and it had all but gone out, filling the space with only a dim red glow off to his right. Still, orange Mana flared and danced across the ceiling tiles, each one perfectly etched into the monolithic stone of the tower itself. Felix found it so easy to get lost in his own Manasight, gazing from one iridescent marvel to another. He didn't know if everyone could see Mana like he could, but he couldn't imagine going back to how it was before.

It's beautiful, this place. Despite everything I've gone through; brushes with death more often than I care to count, the terrifying joy of growing stronger, the constant low buzz of fear. It's all so beautiful, just the same.

Felix thought back to Magda's words, his Born Trait perfectly replicating her voice: *count the stars*. He had seen stars like that before; not upstairs of course, though he'd have to maintain that lie later. No, he had seen an entire array of those stars in the Waterfall Temple. Each alcove contained a Nym holding a star, increasing in complexity until he came to the massive green metal door. That portal had been carved with an elaborate and highly detailed mural showing Nym standing amid some sort of tree branches. And surmounting it all was an *eighteen*-point star.

If the star points dictate danger, then just what *is behind that door?* Nothing good, of that he was certain. Thinking back on it, Felix was almost glad he had left that Temple, otherwise there was a non-zero chance that he would have already attempted to open that damn door.

Balfur saved me from myself. He sighed. Pity for the hurt and displaced Irontooth Ape still ate at him; a product, perhaps, of his Memory. *Perhaps his family survived. He was chased by what I assume was the giants, away from these towers and into hiding. Could they still be around?*

Felix squeezed his eyes closed, cutting off that thought. What would be the point? *What could I even do for them? Except force us into a fight that they probably would lose.*

Balfur was their champion, he could clearly recall. The strongest of them, and Felix had ended him three levels ago.

He held up a hand, regarding it in his special sight as near-invisible wind Mana buffeted against it and dim orange fire Mana splashed against its edges. His hand was muted flesh, but spinning through him like blood was the blue electric fire of his Mana, sparked with a faint golden brilliance.

Whatever I am, whatever I've become, seeing these things has changed me. Maybe the Nym were evil masterminds who littered the world with death traps, or maybe there's more to them. Either way, my changed Race doesn't change who I am. Not even my Omen can do that, another choice taken from me somehow.

What was it Atar said? "You don't choose your destiny..." He was so certain about that, in a way that only a teen can be. *Last time I was that certain, I had convinced myself that smoking cigarettes was definitely cool. Teens don't know shit.*

Destiny is whatever the fuck I make of it.

Only fifty feet away and separated from the group by a thick blanket, Magda leaned against a nondescript block of stone.

Perhaps it's a counter, like a kitchen? She looked around herself, unable to identify any of the functions of the various blocks and holes scattered about the room. *Fuck if I know. This whole tower gives me the creeps.* There was no telling what unpleasant surprises the Nym might have left here.

The blanket suddenly lifted, revealing the silvery form of Harn as he ducked nimbly into the chamber. Magda grumbled to herself, pushing down a familiar jealousy of the warrior's Agility. *I had to carefully slide into this room or else pull that entire blanket down around my head.*

Harn stepped up to her. Nearly six inches shorter but nearly as wide, he was a badger of a man. Loyal, tenacious, and fierce in a fight. There were few she'd rather have at her side, and none were as good with an axe. Magda trusted her partner's eye, especially in regards to combat. Which is why they were meeting.

Wall of Force!

With a slight mental exertion, Magda gathered up and let spread her Mana, pushing out a solid dome of yellow light. It was bright and obvious, but with the others asleep and the archway covered, it should stay unnoticed. Besides the redirection of force, the wall also muffled sound, which was the reason she used it.

"So, what do you think?" She asked.

Harn sucked his teeth. "He's...somethin' else."

Magda narrowed her eyes. "Explain."

Harn sighed. "The kid is determined, I'll give em that. Didn't stop once, not even when I cut into his hip with a sword. He just kept movin' forward. It was impressive."

"Nothing strange about him? Nothing on where he's really from?" Magda was concerned about that part the most. She had her suspicions, but that's all they were. *For now.*

"No, he didn't really give nothin' up," Harn said.

"Not even his stats?" Magda pressed. Harn let out a short bark of a laugh.

"What, you want me to go out and just ask him? He's tighter than a barquist with lockjaw. Shoulda' seen him clam up when I asked for a list of his Skills. Had to back it up to anything above level twenty."

"You must have some idea? He used a spell on you, right?"

"Oh yeah, he damn near yanked the sword outta my hand. *Me*," he added, making sure Magda noticed his emphasis. "He's prolly at least above 90 Intelligence, 100 maybe if he's nearly whoopin' my Strength."

"What? How? His Strength must be 70 alone, and his Endurance...you saw him running today."

Harn nodded. "Coulda been potions, though."

Magda scoffed. "You know it wasn't. I heard him ask Evie what she was drinking. It's like he hadn't even seen one before."

"That's another thing. He's...the gaps in his knowledge're huge."

"He's a noble, I bet my shield on it," Magda nodded. "Sheltered and raised on high-level mobs and dangerous stat farming. Why he's out here is impossible to guess, but I put my bets on him knowing someone in that Guilder op. The way he stumbled outta the mist? Fighting off giants to save someone he didn't know? No one does that without a grudge to settle."

"Maybe," Harn scratched his jaw and sighed. "But still, he seems like a good enough kid."

Magda nodded, less reluctantly than she might have that morning. "He's...well he's earned at least some trust. Not too much, though. I'm not letting anyone compromise the mission."

Harn nodded and patted the big woman on the back. "We're close. We'll get her out."

"We better. Cassie would do the same for either of us. Not to mention all of the others. Those Guilders don't deserve to die at the hands of those blue bastards." Magda clenched her hands, hard enough that she could hear her tendons creak like old wood. "Speaking of, you ready to go soon?"

Harn nodded. "Just gonna catch me a wink or two, then I'm gone," Harn paused a moment while he looked at his partner. "What'll you be doing in the morning?"

"Sparring. I think it's time to see what our new recuit can do," Magda said through a wide grin, already focusing on the morning.

She didn't see Harn shudder.

CHAPTER FORTY-NINE

The morning came too early.

Felix woke to Pit huffing in his sleep, kicking his big feet and pushing the Nym nearly off his bedroll.

"Gah, buddy," Felix groaned, shifting out of reach of the tenku's paws. He looked up, at first only seeing a hazy darkness before activating his Manasight. The air was warm with trapped heat, the light outside blocked by the heavy blankets on the archways...but with Manasight, Felix could catch the ambient glow all around him as he picked out the others who were likewise slowly getting moving. He sat up and felt a sudden gnawing at his core, a gurgling ache that he couldn't ignore. It was accompanied by a familiar pressure on his bladder.

Fantasy world with magic and monsters, and I still gotta pee. He grumbled as he got up and half stumbled his way to the basin room. It had a big drain in the center. What else good was it for?

Four minutes later, Felix ducked back through the blanketed archway to find the fire rekindled and a savory scent in the air. He breathed deep, enjoying whatever it was even as he moved closer to the fire. The ache in his gut grew painful, like a hard cramp in his side.

Oof. Feels like my body's eating itself, heh. Felix hobbled down the tiered steps and picked up one of the tin plates sitting below. Evie was already there, cutting slices off the strangely-orange hunk of meat that was the size of Felix's torso. At first he thought it was some sort of seasoning, but as Evie's dagger cut deeper into the meat, he noticed zero variation in the ochre coloration. He Analyzed it.

Name: Roasted Ofrenok Meat
Type: Protein
Lore: Meat from the Ofrenok. Spicy.
Effect: None

Haha, what? Had he ever tried Analyzing cooked food before? He had been too preoccupied to bother with the Hoarhound meat, and that was the first bit of cooked food he'd had in weeks. Everything else was foraged. *Food can have effects? That's interesting.*

The others had joined them while he stared blankly at the meat, Vessilia and Atar still in simple woolen-like clothes. Felix Analyzed the material, but it only came back as "organic weave" which was almost annoyingly vague. *Analyze can really be hit or miss, huh?* He pondered whether that was due to the level of the Skill or something else, like his own understanding. The four of them all took turns quietly cutting off hunks of meat, piling their plates.

As Felix considered the modest pile in front of him, he recalled the Hoarhound meat the day before. *Hm...I didn't learn anything from the cooked Hoarhound meat, despite ingesting it. Why? Because it was cooked? Not enough blood? But the Wisp didn't have blood, they were just...just like a big blob of magic.* His Title and Skill both called for digesting the Mana of his targets, not specifically blood. Maybe the creatures were too dead to impart anything?

Felix watched the others eat the meat, seeing Atar gag slightly at the taste of it. Still, the kid muscled up and chewed mechanically. Vessilia also pulled a face, eating but mostly picking at it with a set of utensils she retrieved from her belt pouch. Evie, of course, ate without a word of complaint. Felix took a bite, and his eyebrows rose.

Tasty, if oily. He was braced for something, anything to happen. Usually there was a burning sensation and some vertigo with his Title; but he felt nothing. *I guess there's no Mana left in it to digest. Does the fire kill it, or does Mana flee with its life?* He observed the meat with his Manasight, and it was still awash in fire Mana, though he couldn't tell how much of that was a remnant of the fire that cooked it.

He tried to chew slowly, finding the meat aromatic but gamey. However, it wasn't the worst thing he had eaten. And damn, he was *hungry*. He went through two plates before the rest of them finished their first.

Wonder where she got this? The thought rattled around his head as he took another thick cut from the nearly-depleted haunch. *Did Magda go hunting before we woke? Why risk leaving the tower now?*

Almost as if the thought had summoned her, the large warrior stepped forward from a side chamber, fully armed and armored.

"Mornin', boys and girls. Hope you are rested and fed, because now it's time to work," She pointed to a cleared off side of the room, where Felix and Harn had sparred the night before. "Each of you are gonna spar one on one, then three on one. Then do it again. It's fifth glass now, so you can rest at noon. Let's go."

Felix felt more than heard the other three grumble their reply. Magda simply strode past them toward the sparring area, and the rest of them followed like moths to a flame. Felix made sure to scarf down as much food as he could before going after them.

It was still ten or so minutes before everyone (except Felix) was armed and armored. The closest thing Felix had to armor were his well-made leather boots, and those were starting to show their wear. He slung his pack down next to him, keeping the hooked blade close.

The first to fight was Evie and Vessilia. Felix, who had caught a bit of their sparring the other day, hadn't had a real chance to study them. Evie was just as fast and as acrobatic as he remembered, while Vessilia was preternaturally talented at being where a strike would just barely graze her. They traded blows for two minutes, neither one gaining the upper hand as Evie flipped and dodged around Vessilia's spear, and Vessilia sidestepped and blocked Evie's spiked chain.

"By the ancients, she is remarkable," Atar breathed, a little louder than he realized, Felix thought.

"They both are," Felix agreed, almost entranced by their smooth movements. Atar gave him a look that was a cross between embarrassment and outrage.

"You dare to compare a Duke's scion to a feral urchin? Are you mad as well as stupid?" Atar said.

Felix sighed, but felt his temper start to spike. "Are you always like this, or am I just lucky? Look, I get it. You like her. Whatever, man. You're all pretty impressive at this sort of thing, right?"

Atar turned his nose up and folded his arms. "Of course I am. My training began when I was a babe in arms. I assume your training started last night."

Felix almost laughed at that one. *Pretty close there, Atar.* "Hey, I know my knowledge has some holes in it, but gimme a break with all this superiority bull. Live and let live, yeah?"

Atar simply ignored him.

Gonna count that as a win.

The fight went on for another ten minutes, each of them running ragged by the end of it. Even pushing at the edge of her Stamina, the way Vess moved was... it was like a dancer through water; graceful, slow-seeming, but she was repeatedly just out of reach of each attack. Most of the time using the bare minimum of energy to reset and strike.

Evie, on the other hand, was a frenetic dynamo, a ballistic ricochet that never settled in one place, always moving always changing angles of attack. Her chain whipped and swept through the area, extending and retracting like it had a will of its own. Felix recalled that her Born Trait was about altering the weight of herself and the chain, and the girl seemed to have spent a lot of time mastering it.

In the end, Vessilia was able to win by exhaustion, pushing Evie to the end of her Stamina and causing her to collapse. Both of them were covered in cuts and scratches, the sole reminders of their fight.

They are really, really good. He wasn't sure he'd be able to face off against either of them, not without substantially more injuries.

Magda helped the two of them off to the side, where they drank water and rested.

"You and me next," Felix said, hoping to get something that wasn't vitriol from the teen mage. All he got was a glare. *Of course,* he sighed. The two of them took their places in the impromptu sparring area, one at either end with approximately thirty feet separating them.

"When I call it, you can begin," Magda said, standing off to the side with one hand raised. "Ready? Begin!"

An apple-sized orb of fire abruptly splashed against Felix's chest, and the heat and flame licked against his body painfully. Atar laughed.

"Ah, shit," Felix slapped at his chest before looking up. "Jumped the gun a little—"

Five more orbs were already flying toward him.

Felix leaped forward, tucking into a roll and pushing up onto his feet, already running. He dodged the first two and rolled beneath the third, but the fourth and fifth he took on the chest and forearm. He didn't flinch though, instead barreling forward toward the mage, fists raised.

Atar seemed to only see him as he drew within ten feet, the young man wheeling backward in startled fear. Felix didn't let him escape, instead pushing his advantage and closing the distance. One step, two, and Felix was inside Atar's guard, already winding up for a straight right.

"Spirit Immolation!"

The mage lit up in flames, as if his body transmuted to fire itself. Felix reeled backward, his momentum interrupted, as he was assaulted by fire and heat.

Fire Resistance is level 15!
Heat Resistance is level 15!

Atar stood taller, confidently sneering at the larger man. "Where's your muscle now, fool?"

Gritting his teeth, Felix reminded himself that this was just a friendly spar, and he *definitely* shouldn't kill the kid. Probably. Instead, he chose to do the only thing that came to mind: he stepped closer, letting the fire lick against his body and start burning his hair.

Fire Resistance is level 16!
Heat Resistance is level 16!

"What're you—!" Atar tried to pull back, to evade, but he was too slow.

Felix punched the little shit right in the jaw. Just a regular, everyday punch.

Atar fell like his bones had turned to jelly. The fire winked out. The fight had lasted less than twenty seconds.

"Ah, whoops." Felix turned to see Evie and Vessilia watching with a frown and frustrated surprise, while Magda only shook her head.

"Just pull him out of there. Ladies, you're up again." Magda clapped her large hands. "Let's move!"

They fought for hours, just as Magda promised.

The Silver Rank brought them to the edge of exhaustion again and again, letting them recover only the bare minimum of Stamina. Atar slept off his knockout with little ill effect as far as Felix could tell, which was a relief. Not that he'd thought he'd killed him, but getting knocked unconscious back on Earth was never a trivial thing. It could seriously mess with your brain.

No, ultimately Atar was only nursing his bruised pride after a half hour's rest. Felix didn't have time to worry about that though, because he was thrown up against both Evie and Vessilia together. The pair of them outclassed him fairly solidly, their ranged abilities preventing him from getting up close while their evasive maneuvers kept his Shadow Whip and Acid Stream from being as effective as they might have normally. Felix could tell he might be able to wear them down, but not before they'd riddled him with wounds.

They rotated again and again, Magda forcing Felix to fight all of them over and over as his Stamina seemed to regenerate the fastest. He wasn't sure how she could tell he wasn't as tired as the others, but Magda knew, somehow. His Meditation kept his Stamina regen at a little over 1 point per second, so as long as he kept his movements from getting too wild, he never dipped below 30%. Even when Atar returned to the fights and began pelting them all with his Sparkbolts.

His biggest problem? He was hungry again. Two hours in and it felt like he hadn't eaten anything in days, like his stomach was trying to escape through his back. It was distracting, but nothing he couldn't ignore, at least in the short term. *Just have to make it to lunch,* he kept repeating to himself while he muscled down the ache.

It was a slog, a marathon of Endurance and Willpower. Luckily, he had plenty of both stats, but it proved something to him again; stats were less important than Skill, overall. Maybe he could take down Evie with a Corrosive Strike, but only if he actually could hit her. He was plenty fast, but she was more Skilled at evasion.

When they finally sat back down at the fire pit around midday, Felix was nursing several new wounds on his arms and thighs. His pants were beginning to fall apart too, now, though his new tunic was only faintly singed. The others all had bloody gashes or gnarly bruises in varying states of healing. Rapid regeneration or not, getting hurt was unpleasant, and it seemed the others didn't heal quite as fast as he did, for whatever reason.

As he eagerly watched a new spit of Ofrenok meat begin roasting, Felix toggled his notifications for his training.

Fire Resistance is level 18!
Heat Resistance is level 18!
Acrobatics is level 23!
Physical Conditioning is level 22!
Long Blade Mastery is level 13!
Axe Mastery is level 5!
Staff Mastery is level 7!
Blunt Weapon Mastery is level 8!
Armored Skin is level 22!
Meditation is level 31!
Bastion of Will is level 30!
Dual Casting is level 15!
Acid Stream is level 23!
Shadow Whip is level 21!

Holy hell, the hits keep comin'. His Skill was improving significantly thanks to these training sessions. He had incorporated Harn's advice on switching out weapons, giving himself a chance to get better at all of them. Most of these were simple one or two point jumps, but he felt suddenly...better; more knowledgeable, though he couldn't for the life of him pinpoint where this knowledge originated. Felix had long since experienced a vague instinctual knowledge when it came to Skills, so perhaps this was the same effect, only amplified due to the larger amount of gains?

Either way, despite his aches and bruises, it was a morning well spent.

Now to eat some fucking grub.

Felix barely waited for the meat to cool, cutting off huge chunks and putting them away at a rapid pace. He was dimly aware of the others staring at him, but honestly he didn't care. He had to feed this strange, superhuman body he had created. By the time the meat was all gone, Felix had eaten around half his own weight in protein.

And I could still go for a bit more. He shook his head. *This new metabolism is wild.* He side-eyed Evie's plate as he idly played with his empty platter.

She rolled her eyes and scraped the rest of her food onto his plate. "You're a monster."

Felix only grinned and said, "But it's so good."

Vessilia sniffed, still picking at her food. "It is...a challenging meal, I'd say."

"You don't like it?" Felix mumbled through a mouthful. "It's just the right amount of spicy, I think."

"It is not that," Vessilia frowned, before setting her silverware down on her plate. She looked up at Felix. "Why aren't you exhausted?"

"Hm?" Felix paused, mid-bite as juices ran down his chin. He swallowed. "Oh, my Stamina isn't too bad off, especially now that we're resting."

"Feh, speak for yourself," Evie said, leaning back against the step behind her. "I'm barely past 20% now. Ain't gonna be fit to do real fighting for an hour, at least."

"That is my point. Felix, you fought all of us, repeatedly. Often with little breaks. How?" Felix could feel the others lean in toward him, each of them eager in their own way to hear the answer.

"I've got, uh, some pretty good Endurance. Plus, I've got a few helpful Titles," Felix started to explain, before every one of them simply nodded quickly and looked away.

What the hell?

"Did I say something wrong?" Felix looked between them all, eyebrow raised. "Do you not talk about Titles?"

Atar pursed his lips before responding. "One does not speak of their Titles with just anyone. Not a civilized person, at least."

"It's like revealing your strengths and weaknesses and exposin' a trump card,"Evie explained. "And having stuff close to the chest can keep you alive."

"Well, can you tell me how people get a Title? In a general sort of way?" Felix prodded, unsatisfied with their evasions.

"You have some, correct?" Vess asked.

"Mhm, some." It was hard but he kept his face straight for that one.

"How did you get them? Generally speaking, of course. Was there a lot of emotion and stress involved?" Vessilia picked delicately at her food, eating one small piece after another with her little fork.

"Oh, yeah. Almost all of them were like that." He blinked. "So Titles are like Skills? They are only garnered when you, what, meet a prerequisite and are stressed out?"

"Heightened emotional state, as it was called by my tutors. Titles and Skills, as you pointed out, are two sides of the same coin; the System is pushing them onto you due to circumstance, need, and strain. The more you encounter of any of those, and you'll have a high likelihood of gaining one." Vessilia gestured with her hands, ticking off each prerequisite.

"So what's an easy, common Title then?" Felix asked.

"Ehhh, hard to say," Evie supplied, her mouth still full. *Does she do that on purpose? Shit. Do I look like that when I eat?* His hand, which held a piece of orange meat, paused midway to his mouth.

Vessilia kept talking. "It tends to vary from person to person, though most professions usually employ similar Titles. Those are passed down by master to apprentice during training, I understand."

"Passed down? As in, the circumstances are repeatable?" Felix asked.

"Of course, bumpkin. In fact, my Master passed down unto me several of his Titles and Skills," Atar said, puffing up in pride. "Sparkbolt and Spirit Immolation are my prized possessions."

Felix opened his mouth, impressed despite himself. "Does that mean you started off at a high Skill level? Or just that it ensured you learned the same thing? Is there a worry about learning a slightly different version of the same Skill?"

"Calm down, man!" Evie laughed, slapping him on the back. It felt like a piece of paper hitting his shoulder. "How many questions you got in that head'a yours?"

Felix laughed, a little self-consciously. *It's a hard line to walk, asking enough to learn but not enough to raise suspicions even further.* "Too many, I think." He laughed it off, hoping to throw them off the scent of his strange ignorance.

Vessilia cleared her throat, and looked a bit uncomfortable for some reason. "Your tutors...were they not concerned with this aspect of your training?"

"My what?" Felix laughed. "No, no tutors for this guy. Self-taught, if you can believe it," Felix added sardonically. She sighed and leaned back, her armor creaking slightly.

"Oh we can believe it," Atar muttered. Evie gave him a look, but he just smiled innocently.

"You're kind of an ass, huh? That punch didn't knock any common decency loose, did it?" Felix asked. Atar screwed up his face, ready to retort with vitriol, but was interrupted by Evie's braying laugh.

"Haah haaahaha!" The young woman spit up a wad of meat into the fire, nearly choking. "Haha, shit. That's good."

"Alright enough fun, I think," came Magda's voice. The four straightened and turned, looking toward the arched stairwell where Magda was standing, arms akimbo.

"Time for a real challenge."

CHAPTER FIFTY

They geared up and, surprisingly, filed down the stairwell. Felix took the rear, eyes on the walls to make sure they didn't change again, while Pit walked alongside him.

Why are we going down? Don't we want to avoid the streets?

Down they went, however, level after level. They passed their original entry point, their footprints still discernible in the dust, and kept going. Felix worked his mental image of the structure, mapping out the floors as they went. He was reasonably sure they were camped out on the fifth level, so as they turned the last arc of the stairwell, he realized they were at the ground floor...and the archway leading out was entirely closed off.

The group piled onto the landing before the sealed archway, and Evie ran her hands across it.

"How do we open it?" She spoke softly, not really a whisper so much as a lower voice. Magda held up a finger, forestalling any further questions before walking to the *other* side of the landing, where the stairwell would have continued down had it not been ground level. She reached out toward a section of stone carved vines and *puff*, a faint wisp of Mana vapor poured onto the surface.

She has Mana Manipulation? Felix realized with some shock. He had taken Magda for a more physical-type fighter, but considering her penchant for magical shields, he supposed it made sense. *Maybe she can give me some pointers.* He didn't think that was too likely, though. Despite her professed thanks, Felix didn't entirely get the vibe that she trusted him much more than before.

It's more like I'm useful at the moment. Another body for the raid.

He shook himself from his thoughts, refocusing in time to see the wall before them...melt open.

That was the best way he could describe it. First, it was a wall of carved stone, and then it faded like a time-lapse video of a melting candle. A breeze released from the now open space like a pent up breath, stinking of stale air, damp stone, and something fetid. The air in Felix's Manasight looked...the only word that came to him was *foul.* Like something that had been left rotting beneath a shed.

"Follow me. And stay quiet," Magda warned. She turned and continued down the darkened tunnel, her eyes glowing green just as the rest of them.

The Tin Ranks and Felix all shared a look. Then, one-by-one, they followed.

The steps were slick, the slightest of moisture that felt awfully precarious to Felix in his leather boots. His soles didn't even have score marks, just flat slabs of leather. Felix made sure his Manasight was activated as high as he could manage, taking each step cautiously as they descended. The trip wasn't a long one; less than a minute later, Felix spotted the warm glow of a fire ahead. As they followed the circular path, two torches were revealed, lit and stuck into the ground in front of an open archway.

The fire flickered but burned steadily, even as another gust of uncomfortably moist air blew from the darkened opening.

"Wha—" Evie started to speak, but Magda raised a silencing finger. She followed that with a series of hand slashes and finger waggles in handspeak toward Atar. The mage cast his silence spell, letting the wispy yellow energy expand and envelop them all.

"Why can't we speak? And what's with the torches?" Evie asked, nodding at Atar in thanks. The fire mage just clenched his jaw in concentration. Felix could tell the spell took a lot out of him.

"Speaking is dangerous here. And the torches? They're to keep *that* out," she gestured into the dark archway, where a soft moan echoed from the shadows.

"What is that?" Vessilia asked, her voice slightly higher than normal.

In response, Magda only scooped up one of the torches and

hurled it into the adjoining room. The light spiraled crazily around the area, highlighting a packed earth floor and large blocks of worked stone formed into semi-circular walls. The torch clattered to a stop roughly in the center of the room...and it illuminated a nightmare made real.

It was bipedal but hunched until it nearly touched the floor with its spindly arms, its body cadaver-thin and covered in what looked like lumpy growths at the neck, armpits, and inner thighs. As the creature oriented on the torch, Felix saw its face, or what passed for one: it was all mouth, from the chin up to the forehead, gaping open and filled with three rows of crooked triangular teeth set into an ovular head. It pounced toward the light in a weirdly graceful way, its longer arms propelling it forward as a second, smaller pair of arms reached out toward the light. But the moment the creature got too close to the torch, it *skreeled* in pain and retreated. The torch flickered wetly off its dark flesh as it hissed toward the source of its pain.

It looks like it has scales. Its skin was slick like a slug, covered in some sort of viscous slime.

Analyze...

Name: Umber Ofrenok
Type: Chimeric Aberration
Level: 21
HP: 615/615
SP: 845/900
MP: 180/189
Lore: Standard Ofrenok are sightless predators, roaming the darkened places of the Continent. They are a stalking predator, able to move quickly and silently over long distances.
Strength: Endurance and Agility.
Weakness: Intelligence and Willpower. They fear fire's heat.

Lot more information on these things than the giants. Why? In games, it's usually a level difference thing, but this chimera is two levels above *me. What other factor is involved here? Wait—* Felix blanched. *Did we just* eat *that? Oh god. Oh god, it was so good, too...*

"It's an Ofrenok. Seen em a time or two, even outside the

Foglands. They're hunters, work in the dark, and have a bite worse than any snake," Magda grunted, gesturing at the creature. "They track by sound, so keep it quiet. The fire is to keep it at bay; it fears the heat, even if it can't see the light."

"Avet's own, that's terrifying," Vessilia whispered. Felix agreed, only belatedly realizing that his focus on Analyze was to distract himself. *That thing is nasty-looking. I cannot believe we ate it.* He shuddered, but didn't feel sick. Hell, he was *still* hungry. "But, I believe we could take it."

"Glad you think so. You're up first," Magda said. "Alone."

Vessilia turned to the Silver Rank, a small trace of fear in her features before she firmed them up and nodded. Magda gestured to Atar and the mage dropped his silence spell, his forehead dripping with sweat.

I gotta ask him about that. Maybe I can make that work better. It seems...inefficient. Felix patted Atar on the back in thanks, but he had his hands on his knees and didn't respond. When Felix looked up, Vessilia was already striding out toward the creature.

This will be interesting. How effective will her strange footwork be against an Ofrenok's Agility? Felix took a measured, careful breath. And he watched.

The creature stood still in the room, but had straightened slightly from its pained huddle. It lifted its head, bobbing it as if...sniffing? Vessilia approached it at an angle, holding her spear between the two of them. The torchlight glinted off of her spear's polished surface, but the creature didn't react, only tilting toward the far wall as the spearwoman carefully padded up.

As Vessilia drew near, she reared back with her spear and thrust forward.

The Ofrenok twisted unnaturally, body stretching into an arc around the spear. It used its smaller left hand to push at the steel polearm, rotating its body to get inside Vessilia's reach. Felix was certain that was it for her, but the noblewoman somehow got under the creature's strike, somersaulting forward and coming up to her feet with her spear and guard reestablished.

There's something...The creature reminded him of something, but he couldn't place it. Which, in itself, didn't make sense; he had perfect recall. It nagged at him, however, like a smell from his childhood, or a sound from an album he hadn't heard in years. As the monster lunged and snapped at Vessilia, Felix kept coming back to its mouth. *Something about it...something terrible...*

A sudden spike of dread washed over him, a weightlessness in his gut, as if he'd just dropped several floors in an elevator. Vertigo assaulted his senses and a dim clash sounded in his ears, a clash that resolved itself in the Ofrenok's claws against Vessilia's silver spear. With an effort of will, he shook it off. It was probably nothing.

Probably.

During the entire battle, the distance between them stayed the length of a spear. Vessilia used her graceful footwork to evade the Ofrenok's teeth and talons. The creature's body took wound after wound, even suffering a sudden flurry of high speed thrusts that punched five holes in its torso. The Ofrenok stumbled at that, suddenly retching a dark blood from its oversized maw. With a sudden spin and flourish, the spearwoman severed the creature's head from its body.

Snicker-snack. Hot damn. It had been so smooth, from start to finish, as if she wasn't wasting any extra movement on useless things. He stole a glance at the Silver Rank, but she didn't seem terribly impressed. *Maybe Magda's seen better, but it was flawless compared to my scrapes.*

Vessilia returned to them, breathing heavily and sweating, but victorious. A round of silent congratulations went out from the other three, Felix giving a smile and a thumbs up, which apparently confused her. He figured he'd explain later. They all looked to Magda, who strode back out into the dark room.

Exchanging looks, they watched as the shield warrior walked over to one of the curving walls, feet squelching in the mud that appeared as the walls loomed closer. Close to the far left wall, she made a strange strangled cry, startling all of them.

"What the hell was that?" Felix asked.

Magda looked at him, her eyes glowing green in the dark, and angrily put her finger to her lips as she walked back toward them.

Then they waited.

Felix had started to contemplate revisiting his stolen Memories again when they all heard a grotesque sloshing sound. It was faint, but Felix's eye caught movement in the shadows. A dark shape emerged from the mud at the base of the far left wall, exactly where Magda had made her call. It slid through the muck, a fish in water, until it regained its feet and made its cautious, head-bobbing advance into the chamber.

Magda glanced at them and pointed to Atar, who paled slightly. He rallied as he became aware of their gazes, and strode forward purposefully. His feet struck the earth solidly, with confidence.

The Ofrenok was on him in seconds.

"Sparkbolt!" Atar cried, an orb of fire materializing in his hands only to zip into the charging monstrosity's face. The Ofrenok reeled back, screaming in pain.

These things really don't like fire. Felix observed. *Is that noise gonna call more of them, though?*

The Ofrenok rounded on the mage quickly, reoriented with a snap of its gruesome jaws.

"Crown of Ignis!" Atar threw his hand into the air, where a crown made of red-orange fire flickered into existence. One, two...five Sparkbolts appeared and began to hover around the crown. The Ofrenok hurtled forward, jaws snapping and long limbs lunging toward the mage's scrawny neck. One after the other, the Sparkbolts whizzed unerringly toward the creature, pelting it in the head and shoulders and causing it to retreat in pain.

*Holy shit, is that what he did to me? I didn't see the crown before...*Felix watched the fight, enthralled at the strange magic Atar utilized. It was fascinating to him.

As the Sparkbolts regenerated around the Crown, Atar threw his arms out wide. "Spirit Immolation!" His entire body burst into a familiar flame, from his boots to his curly blond locks. The Ofrenok retreated back a pace, the heat from the fire too intense for it.

It never recovered.

Sparkbolts rained down on the monster five at a time, sizzling into its flesh until its hide was withered and cracked like the bottom of a dry riverbed. Thirty seconds later, it wobbled on its feet as the Crown finally disappeared in a flare of light, nearly finished. But as the light of Atar's magic faded, the fire seeming to soak into the mage's body. The Ofrenok grew bold; it hurled itself at the robed teen.

Atar caught its large claw in one hand. He wrenched its arm

down and to the side, causing it to shriek in anger. Then, he delivered a straight punch at the monstrosity's chest.

His fist went entirely through it.

WHAT! Felix was blown away. He looked incredulously at the others, who looked similarly impressed. *Where did that come from?*

Atar slumped forward onto the corpse, a sudden glow disappearing from his body. Felix hadn't noticed it at first, but he had been flooded with a strange combination of orange fire Mana and green-gold life Mana. Magda and Evie went out to help him. It took some doing to get Atar's fist out of the Ofrenok's chest cavity, as apparently whatever he had done left him fairly weak for a bit afterward. Ultimately, Magda had to cleave the thing apart. While she was busy luring another of the nasty creatures from the depths of the dark, Felix gave Atar an impressed nod.

"Why didn't you do that against me?" Felix whispered.

Atar looked at him, irritated. "Are you mocking me?"

"What? No, why? That was seriously impressive," Felix mimed a punch. "Just wondering why I didn't get that treatment before?"

Atar's dour expression eased toward a guarded one. "You're too fast." He turned away from him, walking to the other side of Evie.

Felix smiled.

Evie's turn went fairly quickly. She dispatched the Ofrenok with her spiked chain at a distance, similar to Vessilia's tactic. The core difference was that she used her high mobility to disorient the gnarly brute, and whatever that Born Trait of hers did, it was more than enough to deal with the Ofrenok. Once she wrapped one of its limbs in her chain, it was over. She ripped the limb from its body with only a grunt of effort.

She took its head with equal ease.

Evie was back among them at the stairwell in only fifteen seconds, and Magda sought out one more.

Felix felt himself getting a little jittery. *Do I have stagefright?* He shook his head ruefully. *Just another day in the Foglands, Felix.*

He shook his hands and legs in turn, getting them loose. Doffing his satchel and sword, Felix set them carefully next to Pit, who laid his head down on it. *Poor guy is probably bored as hell down here.* Felix could in fact feel the tenku's disdain for the

Ofrenok...as if it weren't worthy of even worrying about. He smiled and scratched his Companion's head, cheered by his confidence.

Magda had returned, and soon so had another chimeric creature. This one looked the same as all the rest, dark, scaly, and covered in viscous slime. Felix took a breath and walked forward.

He tried to do so stealthily, perhaps raise that Skill a little bit, but the ground was too loose and gritty. Felix's boots scraped against the earth loudly, and the Ofrenok's face swiveled directly toward him.

So much for that. Plan number two, the—

The creature was somehow already halfway to him, its face-mouth open and drooling. *Fast!*

Felix dove to the side, coming up in a roll to find that the hunched abomination was turning quickly to follow. Felix thrust his right hand forward, straining himself as he cast.

Reign of Vellus!

A cascade of blue lightning speared through the air as kinetic force slammed into and lifted the Ofrenok straight into the wall behind them. It hit with an audible thud, a wet meat sound against stone. The creature screamed, its mouth wide and jagged teeth bared to the sky. It struggled against his control, applying pressure against his Skill in a way he hadn't experienced since the giants, and for a second, it felt like something was pressing down on his...his everything.

The mouth. The teeth.

The Maw...

Vertigo assaulted Felix abruptly, as images cascaded through his mind, thoughts and sensations that were both familiar and hideously other. And somewhere, buried deep in his mind, held captive for weeks, a Memory surged to the front...

Of eyes in the acidic deep...of writhing appendages coursing through dark, brackish water...of a secret in stone and golden light....

Skreee—!

The Ofrenok stopped screaming as Felix came back to himself, a fraction of a second later. Blinking away the Memory, he focused on the now with considerable effort, and looked up.

The creature...was "watching" him, even as lightning and a pulsing blue light held it up and against the wall. It tilted its head as if curious, mouth closed but teeth still exposed, considering Felix in turn.

Felix felt that familiar surge of unnamed dread, a horror that crawled from the deepest parts of himself. He shoved it away, glaring hate at the creature that dared invade his mind.

"Acid Stream," he growled. A powerful jet of potent acid sprayed from his left hand, caught up in the waves of kinetic force and deluged the Ofrenok. It started screaming again, but that didn't last long. The acid ate away at its chest and throat, rushing through its massive mouth and burning it from the inside out.

In less than a minute, mush was all that remained held in his mental grip, and he dropped it carelessly to the ground. He was breathing heavy, and there was some ringing in his ears, but he turned away from the mush-pile once Magda laid a hand on his shoulder. She tilted her head back toward the group and patted him on the back, her face...kind, actually.

It was surprise enough that it brought him back, and the full realization hit him that the others had watched him pin a creature to a wall, then melt it into constituent goo with acid. He followed the shield warrior back to the others and braced for their reactions. Instead, all he received were approving nods and a pat on the back. Even Atar nodded and smirked in a not-entirely dickish way.

Huh.

Magda let them rest a moment as she did something out in the dark, but when she came back, she spoke to them for the first time in what felt like an hour.

"You've all impressed me today. I was aware of your skill before bringin' you on, and I've seen most of you in action in the field over the course of weeks, but I'm impressed with your growth. Come," she said as she led them back into the dark chamber. They walked until they were more or less centered in the room. "This was an assessment. Very soon, we will make our assault on the giant's camp, and it will be the most difficult thing you have attempted in your young lives. To that end, you all deserve to be as prepared as we can make you. So, this is it. Your Reveal."

The Tin Ranks looked at each other excitedly, but Felix only frowned. His Omen was already Revealed; he had told them that.

"I can tell you're wondering why you're here, Felix, since your Omen is already Revealed." The Tin Ranks turned to look at him in various ways, though he really only caught Evie's exaggerated eyeroll. That almost made him smile. "You're here to help. This is going to be difficult, and only three would not be enough."

"Help? Help with what, exactly?" Felix asked.

Vessilia tapped him on the shoulder. He turned, following her pointing finger. By the wall, a stretch of mud was bubbling.

No.

He turned, looking at all of the walls encircling them. All of the mud was bubbling, and a sloshing sound inundated the chamber.

"Good luck."

CHAPTER FIFTY-ONE

They came, like a midnight wave, surging from the vile muck.

Evie spun toward them. "Get into a circle! Atar, make with the fire! They fear the heat, so keep them from surrounding us!"

"Got it!" Atar immediately began conjuring Sparkbolts.

"Vess! Guard the mage! Anything that gets too close gets stabbed, yeah?" Vess nodded grimly, leveling her spear and stepping in front of Atar. Evie turned toward him then, grinning wildly. "You'n I are on long range. Wreck em before they step too close!"

Felix felt his face grin back, almost against his will as a surge of energy flooded his veins. Blinking, he noticed a small icon flashing: a head and torso, arms akimbo and chest pushed out.

Affected by Skill: Rally The Troops
Effect: +2% Combat Regen, +0.5% Endurance

Felix laughed, the joy bubbling forth despite knowing the monsters were only seconds from crashing into them. *This is extremely cool. She's better at this than I thought.*

Six of the abominations lunged out of the dark, ebon claws grasping toward their shouting, and the four of them burst into action. A crown of fire manifested above Atar's head, and from this close Felix could feel the searing heat of it. How the mage was able to withstand it only inches above his hair, he had no clue. Five more Sparkbolts whirled into existence, joining the previous five and spinning out thirty feet with a gesture from Atar. They began to rotate quickly around them, forming a loose barrier.

"It'd be better if we had flammable materials I could set on fire!" Atar grunted. "This won't be a perfect defense!"

"Doesn't have to be perfect. Just has to give us room to breathe," Evie insisted, nodding at the mage. "Vess, hold the fort. Felix, c'mon!" With that she ran forward, her chain already unspooling from her shoulder. Glancing quickly at Vessilia and Atar, he followed. At the same time, the first of the Ofrenok reached the whirling barrier.

SKREEEEEEAAAA!

The creature took a fiery orb to the shoulder, skidding to the side as it screamed in pain. Evie got to it first, her chain whipping forth to smash the Ofrenok directly in the face. Its head snapped backward and it stumbled, giving the woman enough time to sling the chain back and lash it forward again with preternatural speed. The Ofrenok got an arm up in time, somehow sensing the bladed chain, but it only entangled itself. It suddenly found the chain difficult to hold up at all, falling into the dirt arm first.

Felix focused away from Evie as he spotted two more of the monsters heading his way. He cleared his mind and shaped his Mana, tracing pathways that felt more than a little familiar by this point.

Reign of Vellus!

The lightning surged from the ground as the chimeras were immediately smashed forward into the earth. Felix hadn't even felt them resist it, likely due to their forward momentum. He didn't stop to ponder, though, instead pouring dual cast Acid Streams all over their prone forms. The powerful corrosive ate into their bodies rapidly, dissolving large portions of their hide and revealing orange muscle and blood beneath.

Sick. He stomped on their prone bodies, shattering the skull of one and feeling something crack in the chest of the other.

You Have Killed An Umber Ofrenok (x2)!
You Have Gained XP!

That was easier than the first time. He looked up, seeing Evie flip around three different opponents as she used her chain to bash and bind by turns. The bladed links would slash open their bodies even as they caught and redirected blows meant for her, and her strange Born Trait made it all the more unstoppable. His fight had brought him closer to her, and for a brief moment, he felt the concussive wave of clashing metal, like cymbals the size of city crashing together. Felix blinked, alarmed, but the sound faded just as quickly. It was replaced by Evie's face, lit up in a manic smile, her joyful spirit unimpressed by the increasing odds.

And they were increasing. Felix's quick scan noted at least a dozen of the creatures either arrayed against them or emerging from their mud tunnels. It was strange. None of the Umber Ofrenok carried with them the same dread as he experienced previously. Their features were still terrifying, but that familiarity had faded.

The Dread is only a Memory. You escaped it. He shook it off, clenching his fists.

Four more chimeric aberrations rushed toward him, and Felix went to meet them. This time, he brandished his hooked sword and flared one of his lesser used spells.

Influence of the Wisp!

Blue fire burst across his body before echoing across the distance and ensnaring one of the creatures. Body limned by flickering, heatless fire, its weak Will crumbled before him.

An Umber Ofrenok is Enthralled for 2 Seconds!

He ran forward, using his sword to decapitate the monster before it could recover. Before the body even fell, he moved onward, engaging two more of the beasts, one with a parry and the other with a point-blank Reign of Vellus that swept its feet out from under it. A swift knee smashed the Ofrenok's face into his leg, shattering teeth even as it tore his pants further. It went down, and he dismissed the kill notifications as he focused on the remaining two.

Felix was grinning now, his blood singing and muscles warm. He dove and ducked beneath the monsters' blows, though a few times their smaller arms caught him on his shoulders and forearms, slicing neat lines into his toughening hide. Yet, still the combat called to him, like when he had fought his first giant, and he felt an inexplicable need to laugh.

Strange. He blinked, wiping away sweat from his brow. *I think I'm having fun now.*

Vessilia was not having fun.

She ranged about, circling Atar as he conjured bolt after bolt of arcane fire, making sure to keep well away from his crown of intense heat. His circling ward did some good against the mounting odds, but as more of the disgusting creatures poured from their fetid lair, the ward gradually weakened. She jabbed her spear into the throat of another creature that had made it through, spinning into a slashing sweep to trip up two more. She dispatched them, too, an efficient motion that penetrated the heart of the Ofrenok with brutal speed. She moved on, unable to pause, to catch her breath. Five minutes had passed, an eternity in battle, and Vessilia found herself flagging as she moved through the forms drilled into her since childhood.

Step, half-step, turn, evade, thrust...

The movements weren't so rigid as a dance, but the Seven Steps of the Dragoon were infinitely versatile, able to be combined endlessly. She chained her movements, if for nothing else than for the conservation of her own Stamina. Without her movement technique and spear mastery, she'd have fallen to the ground minutes ago.

Which is why she was especially jealous of her friend Evie, who despite her weaker Endurance, had enough Skill in Acrobatics that she had Stamina to spare. Even after evading the multiplying attacks of the Ofrenok, her friend was like a ghost, unable to be touched. For all that Vessilia was touted as a genius, Evie outshone her in battle ten times over.

Felix, on the other hand, was simply impossible.

He was barreling through the monsters, taking them out with spells and sword and more of his insane fist fighting. He had been at it the entire time, his Stamina apparently endless as he moved quickly but gracelessly between enemies. Once she even saw him barrel bodily through one of the monsters, knocking the both of them to the ground, where he simply pummeled it to death.

His Skills are unpolished and wildly inefficient, but he has such raw power. She frowned. *He must have come across quite the collection of Titles to amass such stats at level 19. It is the only answer.*

Then it went quiet.

Evie landed next to her with a soft thud, bending her knees to absorb the impact. "Is that it?"

Vessilia looked around, her eyes (normally so sharp) were of limited use in the Foglands. Even here, inside this stone structure the thick mist was ever-present. "I am not sure. I somehow doubt it."

"Yeah," Evie grunted in agreement. "Can't see this being Magda's real test anyway. Too easy."

"Maybe...for you," panted Atar, who still wore his Crown of Ignis. Despite the lack of enemies, he was playing it smart and still had Sparkbolts circling them. "I can't...keep this up...forever. Those *bastards* took out...nearly half of my...Mana pool already!"

"Incoming!" Felix's voice shouted out from the fog. He sounded close, but that was never a sure thing in the murk. Then she heard it. Not the wet squelch the creatures had been making as they left their muddy burrows, but a distinct bubbling noise.

The mud all around them was *boiling* with movement.

"Night! Redouble that barrier, Atar! Vess, take the left side. I'll take the right! Felix!" Evie shouted into the fog.

"Yeah?"

"Get the back side of the chamber! How many are out there?"

"At least...twenty!" He replied.

"Shit," Evie cursed, looking to Atar and Vessilia. "This is gonna be hard. Whatever Magda did stirred up a whole nest of these bastards, and they're hungry. The fight before was just a snack. Time for the main course, now!"

Vessilia could feel Evie flare her leadership Skill, Rally. She let it wash over her, as did Atar, feeling the small bump to her Endurance and regeneration. It was not much, but it could make a difference today, and would only grow stronger in the future. Spinning her spear and resetting her grip, Vessilia nodded at her friend before taking her position.

I cannot fail. Not here.

Felix could feel them.

Insane as that was, Felix could feel the abominations rushing at him. He could see them, sure. They shone with some sort of twisted life Mana, a pus green twisted around a dark red core. But now, for some reason, their very presence was beating against Felix's senses. Like a sore tooth, an infection.

What is this?

He didn't have long to consider it. They converged on him, five of them heading directly for him, their senses stronger than the fog.

He fought. With a rising, ruthless joy, he fought.

It was madness. The ground shook and sounds echoed all around him as his companions used their Skills and special abilities, doing undoubtedly remarkable things he did not have the attention to see. Instead, he was overwhelmed by dark, scaly flesh and multiple sets of claws that raked and slashed at his vitals. He blocked and parried with his sword, using it with one hand while making Corrosive Strikes with the other. But these creatures were smarter or perhaps just faster than the previous ones; one of them grabbed Felix's arm, wrenching him around, and threw him down into the mud. The ground had gone soft with spilled blood and acid, their steps churning it all into a gnarly muck. Felix splatted down and was quickly pounced on by two of the Ofrenok.

Maws of stained yellow teeth set in blackened gums filled his vision, and he lashed out with successive Corrosive Strikes. He smashed them away, but more came, swarming his apparently vulnerable form. Their presence felt like a broken guitar string, twanging and out of place. So close, their Mana tasted like sickness, a corruption different and yet similar to the bloody Mana from the Orit and Archon.

It soured against his vision, befouling his senses.

No, get away!

Influence of the Wisp!

The three on him briefly froze as blue fire engulfed them.

"Get off!"

Reign of Vellus!

The creatures exploded away from him, launched up and into the air in twenty foot arcs even as Felix pressed deeper into the mud by the counter-force. Without a way to leverage his Strength, he could only endure the sudden mass of four full-grown Ofrenok as they sailed away.

Groaning in discomfort, Felix pulled himself to his feet in time for two of the four monsters to reconverge on him once more. Then screams emitted behind him.

Rather than look, he only frowned and yanked one of the Ofrenok toward him. At the same time, he used his right fist to conjure a Corrosive Strike. The combined force blasted his fist and forearm straight through the abomination's skull, shattering teeth and skull fragments in a shower of putrid green-black ichor. Throwing the body off his arm, he did the same to the next one, ramming his fist up and into their chest before driving their newly-made corpse into the ground. The last one reached him too late, and Felix spun to his feet and backhanded it. He had aimed for its head, but its sudden evasion took the bone-breaking blow against its shoulder, then tumbled away.

"Shit," Felix said, watching the chimeric aberration struggle to stand again. "I'll deal with you later."

He ran off. Back toward the others.

He had gotten caught up. His job hadn't been to kill as many as he could. He was there to help protect the others.

He arrived to a madhouse.

"Ahaha! Come! Challenge my might, foul beasts!"

The Tin Ranks were surrounded by black-scaled monstrosities. There had to be at least three dozen of them, each snapping and clawing at the pile. The only thing keeping them at bay seemed to be Atar's frantically-conjured Sparkbolts, which whirled around him even as he laughed maniacally. The crown atop his head was brighter than ever, and the waves of heat pushed back at the Ofrenok; those closest even had their hide rapidly blister, scorching from heat alone. There was a manic gleam in Atar's eyes, and his curled hair was sticking up in all directions as he laughed again.

"I am the greatest fire mage in all of Te'Thys! None shall survive!"

What the hell? Felix spotted Vessilia fighting a section of the Ofrenok, spear whirling near constantly as she sliced and stabbed and parried the long talons of the abominations. She was coated in green-black ichor, and arterial spray spouted into the air as she decapitated another monster. Of Evie, he could only make out a swinging chain on the far side of the group. They were fighting for their lives, and Felix wasn't sure how much longer they could keep it up.

Then the earth thudded beneath him.

Once.

Twice.

A different version of the Ofrenok emerged, elongated and somehow more upsetting. It had six legs, heavy scale plates on its limbs, face, and back, and was entirely black and slick with viscous slime. Its mouth still took up its entire head, but that head was now the size of Felix's entire torso. If the Ofrenok were infantry, then this was the tank.

Analyze...

Name: Umber Ofrehulk
Type: Chimeric Aberration
Level: 25
HP: 844/844
SP: 984/1100
MP: 150/150
Lore: Sightless behemoths, Ofrehulks are known to grow to gargantuan sizes if left unchecked. They are not as fast as their smaller brethren, but they are far stronger.
Strength: Endurance and Strength.
Weakness: Intelligence and Willpower.

SKKKKREEEEEOOOOOONK!

The beast's cry reverberated through Felix's chest like the biggest subwoofer he'd ever experienced. It dwarfed his own heart-beat, and for a second, Felix forgot how to breathe.

Then it charged.

"Finally! A worthy challenger!"

Atar spotted the behemoth heading his way, plowing through the skeletal Ofrenok that weren't worthy to fight him face to face. None of them could stand up to the Greatest Fire Mage in Te'thys, Apprentice to Sig'nyh Kel'lyv, Grandmaster of the Desert's Fire!

The six-legged beast trumpeted out a cry, crushing more of its fellows as it sought Atar, who only laughed louder.

In a dim portion of his mind, panic stirred, but it was overridden by an ecstatic anger and terrible joy. The Crown atop his head was the sovereign of true destruction, and he its avatar! Fear had no place in his mind, not so long as his magic sang in his veins. With a word and gesture, the young man's flesh went up in flames as Spiritual Immolation surged across his limbs.

A relentless, overpowering heat poured from Atar. The Crown amplified the effects of Immolation as he became subsumed in light. The beast slowed its charge, finally feeling the effects of Atar's powerful Spirit, or perhaps the resistance of the Ofrenok surrounding it. *True fear must be surging in its primitive brain,* he crowed internally. *Only natural, for true destruction invokes terror in all.*

"Face me, beast!" Atar sent a flurry of Sparkbolts out toward the monstrosity, each one a sizzling speck against its immense hide. But they did their job, driving the mindless beast into continuing its charge.

Rising up within him, a strident horn sounded, a call to arms and a rush of thunderous beats upon a drum the size of a mountain. It filled his body with a terrifying vigor even as that dim portion of himself cried out in despair.

Something was coming. Something he had never before experienced, a tearing within his soul that his compartmentalized self found agonizing. But confidence and rage poured from his Crown, and Atar laughed away the limb-rattling anticipation even as his Mana use surged.

The beast was within twenty feet now; it wasn't stopping, heat or no.

Atar snarled, his face a rictus of pain and ecstasy. He would tear this beast limb from limb, rendering its body into Avum chow with nothing more than his bare hands. Only two seconds, then he'd soak his Spiritual Immolation deep into his flesh, burning it for a boost in physical stats: Strength Ignition, his greatest trump Skill.

The beast bore down, only a dozen feet away now, and Atar shifted his Skill and *pushed.* The fire invaded his flesh, filling him to bursting as his physical stats skyrocketed beyond his limits. He felt invincible, untouchable. He rushed forward, tearing down two of the lesser creatures on his path toward the behemoth. He went through them like tissue paper. He came up short and braced himself, confident in stopping its rampage.

Then his Mana guttered out.

"No," eyes wide, the mage stared at his darkened hands. "No!" Weakness invaded Atar's flesh like a rot, withering his muscles and dropping him to the ground. The hulking monster didn't stop, it only bellowed out rage and an all-consuming hunger from its faceless maw.

Then, from nowhere the muscle-bound bumpkin hurtled into the behemoth, diverting its forward momentum just before it hit the mage. The earth shook as the hulk took several booming steps to catch itself, even as Felix crawled over and jumped aside.

A sudden glimmer of steel caught Atar's fading vision, the last flickers of firelight gleaming from her chain as it lassoed the beast about the neck. Blades dug into scaled flesh with a heavy *shunk* as the chain massively increased in weight, and Evie hauled on the line. Mere moments later, the crackle of azure lightning assaulted the monstrosity as well; Felix's strange magic grabbed hold of it, tipping the scales and sending it toppling to the ground.

No! That's my kill! Rage beyond words tumbled through his mind, and something in his chest finally tore completely. Like a cheesecloth put to torch, whatever covered him was consumed in a flash of pain and power.

Atar's body suddenly surged with unspent potency as a chord within him reverberated uncontrollably. The mage's skin burst with scorching hot fire Mana until it flowed out from him like an insufferable cloak. The Ofrenok all around him evaporated into ash as this concentrated power splashed against them, until the area within three yards of him was completely clear of life. All he could hear was a resounding beat that shook his body, all he could feel was the crashing melody of a triumphant horn that shook his very bones.

But he could still see. The shirtless fool rushed toward him, intent on stopping Atar's glorious ascent.

No! The ever-dimming portion of himself cried out. *You're burning yourself up! Wake up!*

Wake up!

But he only dimmed further, until the world faded to black.

Felix rushed to Atar, lifted his body up and checked his pulse. He was surprisingly light.

"He's alive," Felix breathed. This close, the residual heat of the Crown the mage once wore remained, and the ground itself was baked dry in a range of four yards. Moreover, the remnant of the orchestral music from before faded, a denouement that settled into silence.

Felix looked up, but there was only silence from his party. He turned, finding Evie on her knees, eyes half closed as she was wracked by a similar distress. He called out to her, but she didn't respond. Then, a wave of deep blue Mana poured from her body, crashing against the few remaining Ofrenok arrayed against her. Distantly, a frenetic drumming pounded, a cymbal crash against a stormy sea made of a series of rising chords, pushing at the sky itself. It peaked, then fell.

The music...it's their Reveal? I'm hearing *their Reveal?*

The Ofrenok had all fallen, scorched into nothing or bashed against the rocky ground by relentless waves. Seeing both Evie and Atar down but breathing, Felix searched for the third. Some distance away, surrounded by the minced corpses of her enemies, Vessilia half-knelt against the earth. Spear planted and body heaving, he caught the last moments of her own Reveal. Near-invisible gusts spun around her, shearing through any corpse too close. The ground around her was a soaked field of offal and gore, her body covered in more of the green ichor.

Setting Atar down again, Felix moved closer to her in the hopes that she was likewise alright. Once within a few yards, he could make out a fading sound. However, before it vanished, he perceived a cool clarity, a balm of trilling uptempo woodwinds. This song was an allegro spring breeze, balanced between winter's cold edge and summer's promised warmth.

She didn't move except to breathe, eyes closed but somehow locked in place.

"The Reveals are complete."

Felix turned toward Magda, who had reappeared on the field after leaving them to fight.

He was bone weary, and only mustered a frown. "They're hurt. We need to leave before more monsters arrive." Felix's own Stamina was dangerously low, though he'd be fine given a few minutes' rest.

Magda nodded, face serious but a certain pride showing through her eyes as she regarded the Tin Ranks. "They did well, all things considered." She turned to Felix. "As did you, Felix. I'm impressed you're still able to stand after your display."

Felix straightened, his body creaking and popping in protest. "I did what I could."

"And it was enough." Magda nodded and turned toward her sister and Atar. "Thank you."

Felix chewed his lip, considering the shield warrior as she walked away. Then he turned toward Vessilia and got his arm under her.

It was going to be a long walk back up those stairs.

CHAPTER FIFTY-TWO

Felix was right. The stairs were a haul.

Carrying a fully-armed and armored Vessilia was a challenge. She wasn't hard to lift, however, and was surprisingly easy considering she and all her gear was likely clocking in at 190 pounds. Mostly, it was her limp form and having to drag around a goddamn eight-foot spear.

It got caught on everything.

The struggle eased into monotony after a short while though, and Felix's mind began to unpack. They had fought and killed a large number of creatures in a short period of time. His kill notifications indicated he had dispatched twenty-one, both alone and in concert with the Tin Ranks. Now, he didn't find himself choked with guilt or anything. Those beasts wanted to eat him, and he was just fine destroying them instead. It had been a wild and hectic battle, yet he had felt a profound rightness to it all that, in retrospect, felt odd. When had he reveled in combat?

Perhaps it was inevitable. So much of his time on the Continent had been spent in fear, in confusion, or a combination of the two. Now that he was finding himself more potent than ever, why wouldn't he marvel at his own strength? He punched a monster straight through its chest! It hadn't hurt him at all! It had, in fact, felt like breaking through drywall. Feats like this were impossible back on Earth.

This entire world feels impossible. Terrifying and awful at times, but astounding just the same. His mind drifted to the magical Skills he was accruing, a childhood dream he had long since abandoned, now coming true. *They* have *to have wizard schools here, right? Felix the Wizard sounds too good not to happen.*

He even had potentially more Skills to acquire after today's fight. He patted his satchel, within which were the two vials of blood he'd managed to fill from the Ofrenok and Ofrehulk's corpses. Those were for later.

Around halfway up the third floor, Felix finally gave into his curiosity. He toggled his notifications, solidifying his new growth.

Heat Resistance is level 19!
Long Blade Mastery is level 15!
Blind Fighting is level 19!
Corrosive Strike is level 20!
Armored Skin is level 23!
Intimidation is level 4!
Bastion of Will is level 30!
Analyze is level 23!
Dual Casting is level 17!
Acid Stream is level 24!
Influence of the Wisp is level 23!

+1 AGL
+1 DEX

Hell. Yes. He had bumped up so many things, all of which were among his lower Skills. *Ah, damn. I completely forgot to use Shadow Whip and Mantle of the Long Night. Ugh. Wasted opportunity.*

Felix had decided he was in desperate need of a way to incorporate as many of his Skills as possible into a solidified fighting style. It'd maximize his leveling gains and keep that nagging voice quiet, the one that insisted that any Skill below level 20 was dragging him down and should be leveled *immediately*. It wasn't wrong, per se, but it was an echo of his childhood when he'd not be done with a game until he'd reached max level, max stats, all the important items and weapons. Felix had long ago accepted that this was not a game, and that his new life had deadly consequences. But, even still...

Gaining Skill levels and stats was immensely satisfying.

Felix frowned at his notifications, realizing he didn't make his next level. While no XP bar existed (to his knowledge), he could still *feel* how close he was to another level, and Felix felt only a hairsbreadth away from level 20.

Pit, however, did level up.

Your Companion Pit Has Gained 2 Levels!
+4 VIT! +4 PER! +8 AGL! +8 DEX! +6 WIL! +2 END! +4 INT!

"Scavenger," Felix eyed his Companion who trotted up the stairs beside him. "You snaked my experience!"

Pit warbled enthusiastically. He'd been extra affectionate since he rejoined Felix; the distinct feeling of being left out and worried had dominated the tenku. Felix had found out that Magda had sealed the archway with one of her force walls, allowing Pit to look into the room but be unable to help. This all came to him in a rush from Pit, who pushed his strange sense-emotions onto Felix with all the grace of a dump truck.

He had hugged his friend for a long while, sending his regret and assurance that he was fine.

Still, he grumbled to himself. *Having a Race with an experience penalty is bad enough, but I'm also sharing with Pit. Hard not to feel a little cheated.*

The stairs finally ended. They had felt interminable, long enough that Vessilia was beginning to come around in his arms.

"Who—?" She mumbled. Her face was in the crook of his neck as Felix had her in a classic princess carry, and she blinked up at him with half-closed eyes. "Where are we?"

"Back at the top of the tower, Duchess," Felix grunted as he took the last step into their floor.

Vessilia shook her head. "I'm not-" Her eyes shot open wide as she got a better look at Felix. "P-put me down!"

"Oh, sure," Felix set her on her feet, and the woman quickly backed up. "Sorry if I—sorry. Here." Felix held out her silver spear, and Vessilia snatched it from his hand. She was blushing furiously.

Shit, did I do something inappropriate? He had held her, but that wasn't weird, right? He was just bringing her back up the tower, just like Magda was doing...

Felix turned to see Magda walk into the room, holding her sister and Atar by the back of their armor. Their bodies dragged limply against the floor, and both were starting to come around. Felix grimaced; their shins were gonna be bruised all to hell.

"Took ya all long enough," groused a familiar voice. Felix spotted Harn in the tiered fire pit, which was still unlit. He looked tired from this distance, and he slapped at the large corpse next to him. It was another Hoarhound. "C'mon and help me cook this damn thing before it dissolves on us."

Magda and Felix got to work. The Tin Ranks were left to recuperate at the edge of the fire, though Harn managed to coax Atar into lighting some kindling, though from the look on his face, the mage regretted it immediately. Magda had Felix move the monster over to the side, where she started dressing the kill.

"Why did they pass out?" Felix asked, looking back at his ragged allies.

"You didn't?" Magda asked without looking up or stopping her knife. "The old-timers think a Reveal is all about a build up of energy that eventually wears away at the nugget of destiny that each of us holds within. But once Revealed, all that energy's gotta go somewhere, so it spills out." Magda punctuated her words by scooping a mess of blue-grey sacks from the Hoarhound's chest cavity. She slopped them over to the side, unceremoniously. "The energy takes from your body, too, draining Stamina, Mana, and a little Health, too. Leaves most people damn near unconscious, if not completely out." She made a few more cuts along the creature's underside that Felix couldn't see.

"How are you doing that?" Felix marveled as the Hoarhounds fur almost jumped off its body, Magda's Skill at Skinning or Butchering or whatever proving to be much higher than even his best Skill. "All the monsters I've fought turn to greasy smoke not long after."

Magda nodded at her hand, where she held her knife against the meat of the beast. "Enchanted knife. Preserves the kill and stops it from decaying. Once butchered, the meat won't smoke up anymore, just rot like normal flesh does."

"Handy."

Magda grunted in affirmation and got back to work.

Thirty minutes later, the fire was crackling and a heaping slab of meat was cooking on the makeshift spit. Pit was off in the corner, chowing down on the guts from the Hoarhound. The Tin Ranks were more alert and less shaky, though Evie was uncharacteristically silent and Atar resolutely stared anywhere but at the fire. Felix, meanwhile, chewed the inside of his cheek and watched them all, silently hoping the food would get done faster. He was, of course, starving again.

Most surprisingly, up close, Harn looked even more tired looking than the Tin Ranks. He had bags under his eyes, several bruises on his face, and his armor was covered in new scratches.

"So," Magda said, breaking the silence. "What happened?"

He let out a slow breath before answering.

Using Felix's directions, Harn had easily found the shit pit where the prisoners were kept. Getting close to it, however, was a damn sight harder.

His Brawler's Physique and specialized Body enhanced his senses much more than Magda's Tempering. He could navigate the blasted fog better than most, but distances still frustrated him. Harn had to evade several large patrols between the tower and the Risi encampment. Each was made up of four Hoarhounds and three or more Risi Warriors, and though most only had a half-stage Body at best, he still had to take the long way around. It wasn't that they were tough; far from it, Harn could have taken their lives easy as breathing. It was that he was scouting, not fighting.

Scoutin' not fightin', He repeated to himself. Even *if* his axes were getting real thirsty.

Once inside their encampment, the giant's security was much more lax. Groups of warriors congregated around their strange cold fires, while food and drink was passed around heartily. Harn slipped among them like a fish into water, his Stealth more than a match for careless eyes. The structure where the prisoners were being kept was off a little ways from the plaza square, tucked behind a large ice-covered colonnade. Within the enclosure, which had only the barest suggestion of walls, ice coated everything, a permanent decoration courtesy of the giants' bitter magic. Rags and paltry blankets were strewn about, as well as the charred remains of a fire. Bones of some sort were piled in a corner, and in another, someone had carved a large hole into the ice for a latrine.

Harn frowned. There were no people.

The prisoner's area was completely empty. He hadn't been expecting it to be full, but no sick? No injured? The icy conditions and lack of shelter alone would lead to sickness among the weaker-constituted folk, not to mention the wounded from down below. Harn worried that the weak were either left in the sinkhole, or they were disposed of up here. He could find no evidence either way, mostly due to the disarray of the encampment. *Someone* had at least made the latrine and had *most* of the garbage piled in one corner. He was betting that was Cassie's influence.

There was little to examine there, and Harn went about on the second part of his mission. He headed to the bronze dome.

Situated in the center of the camp, the squat building dominated the area. Not only was it the tallest structure standing for nearly a mile, but it was covered in an almost delicate layer of ice. The ice itself shimmered dully in the darkness, giving off a distinct purple-white glow.

The whole building's warded. Didn't know ice magic could do that...

Yesterday, when he was scouting this camp, he had noted the building but not the wards. In the dim sunlight and heavy fog that sheen was nearly invisible. Harn found a spot across the square, hidden and high, where he could wait and watch. He had a good angle and could even see directly into the building, to an extent. The mist confused his senses a time or two, but Harn had spent a long time honing his abilities, and he knew how to be patient. Regardless, nothing happened for a painfully long hour. When it did, it all happened at once.

The sky was just barely lightening up with the approaching sun when the purple-white Mana flickered and disappeared. The massive bronze doors in the front of the building creaked open on ancient hinges, making an almighty racket, and out strode the biggest giant Harn had ever seen. When he had first caught sight of them, he had been impressed by the Risi's imposing aura. Today was no different. Easily twenty-five feet tall, he was a slab of muscle and fur, striding purposely out of the bronze dome. Trailing behind him were three other giants, and for the first time Harn saw a Risi that wasn't bearded. Built very similar to their male counterparts, the female Risi were dressed in robes and furs as they all but glided along after their leader.

Harn wasn't sure where the big Risi was going, and he put it out of his mind when four guards marched wearily out of the building in their leader's wake. Another set of guards shuffled forward, taking their place.

Shift change. Harn nodded to himself. It was similar to what he'd seen the day before. *But how long before the leader comes back?*

Turned out, about an hour. Whatever the leader was doing, it seemed to tax him in some way, as the massive Risi seemed visibly fatigued when he returned. Only two women returned with him, their third mysteriously missing, though they did not seem tired at all. Again, same as the day before, when Harn had watched the leader disappear further into the city with his helpers. During that hour, Harn had watched the new guard scarf down food, drink mugs of ale, and ignore the captives that were dredged up from the sinkhole. From his vantage point, Harn could occasionally see a Human or Dwarven face that looked haggard and gaunt. Food wasn't given to the prisoners, neither did the giants use any healing potions or poultices.

It was extremely clear that the prisoners' best quality was that they were disposable.

Within a few minutes of the leader's return, the prisoners were led out, back to their enclosure, where a dozen Risi watched them like hawks. The rest of the morning proceeded as normal, and Harn ducked out before he was caught.

"The return trip was nasty, though," Harn added. "Had to fight my way through another patrol, then lead the survivors on a chase across town."

"At least you got some meat out of 'em!" Felix munched appreciatively. He was halfway through his second serving, while Magda cut pieces for the others. "After this morning, this is very good."

Harn eyeballed the three Tin Ranks. "Ya'll went through yer Reveals? All a ya?" Harn chuckled and bit a hunk of meat from a skewer. "Damn, wish I coulda seen that."

"They did good," Magda said, half-smiling at the others.

"They're about as ready as we can make 'em, considering our timeline."

Harn nodded and encompassed everyone in it. "Alright. Time to plan." He grabbed a charred stick and cleared some space at the bottom of the fire pit. He began to sketch a rough outline of the giant's encampment, as far as Felix could tell. "This is where we need to go. In the center of the camp is the bronze building, easily found, very recognizable. We need to sneak in during the shift change, when the wards on the building are dropped."

"Where does the massive leader go?" Evie asked, staring over the fire at his charcoal drawing.

"No clue. All I know is that he's done it twice in a row, and hopefully he keeps that schedule. If he doesn't, this whole thing's gonna go tits up fast." Harn drew a couple slashes near the circular representation of the dome. "Here is where the replacement guards come from, and here is where the old guards go. Both places are teeming with giants, so we avoid those at all costs. No stirring up the hornet's nest."

Magda folded her arms. "Points of entry?"

"There's three. One is the main big doors. Second is a side access door that was built for folk much smaller than giants, though you might have a time gettin' in. And the third ain't worth the risk." Harn grunted.

"What's that?" Felix asked.

"Third way is to somehow scale the sinkhole and use the stairwell itself. Bypass the whole building. Problem with that is we don't know exactly how long the wards will be down, or what dangers the sinkhole poses. And hell, the sheer drop alone makes it nearly impossible." Harn slashed his hand through the air, cutting off the idea. "We'll have to come through the small side door the moment the wards drop, which means we'll have to hide somewhere close."

"Here, perhaps?" Vessilia pointed at a squarish block to the side of the dome. "Is this a completed building or more ruins?"

"Ah, hm. I'm not—" Harn began.

"Ruins," Felix answered, his mind already recreating the scene. "We could hide there. It's got space enough for all of us while also being too small for use by the Risi." He glanced up, startled to find everyone staring at him. "What?"

"How do you remember that?" Atar asked. "You saw the place once."

"Oh, it's my Born Trait. Perfect recall."

Atar's mouth quirked up in a grin, and he shook his head. "Of course."

"Glad that's settled!" Harn clapped his hands before pointing at the dome again. "We get inside before the new guards show up. We ain't fightin' ‘em, might as well send out invitations then. No, we knock ‘em out, take'm down quietly. They've got a communal pot of food and they do *not* like sharing. A little poison'll do wonders."

"Good idea. It'd only weaken them, I assume?" Magda asked.

"Yeah, I ain't got poison strong enough for a giant's Endurance. It'll do, and I'll concern myself with killin' em while they're weakened." Harn took a breath and looked at them all, charcoal dangling from his fingers. "It all goes smoothly, we'll grab the prisoners and make it back here by noon."

Magda stood up, drawing their gaze. "I've heard better plans, but I've also been part of much worse. Time is not on our side. The prisoners are dying, a handful each night, as far as we can figure. We do this right, we can save a lot of lives. We do this wrong..." Magda trailed off.

She didn't go on. But then, she really didn't need to.

CHAPTER FIFTY-THREE

"What about that assassin?" Felix asked, interrupting the heavy silence. He looked around. "What happens if she shows up?"

"The Sworn aren't assassins, exactly...they're contractors. That means she has a specific job, and it don't have to be about killin'." Harn scratched his jaw with a gauntleted hand. *Why doesn't he take that off? Seems like it'd get uncomfortable after a while.*

"It seemed like that job involved siccing a dozen giants on you all," Felix rubbed his side, memory of the pain fresh for the next month. "What are the Sworn, anyway?"

"Ain't important. They're bad news, is all. They take a job and don't quit. Did she say anything to you?" Harn asked.

"No, though I asked. She just kept trying to kill me." Felix shrugged, eating another mouthful of monster meat. *Man, this is good. What is* in *these monsters?*

"I doubt that; the Sworn aren't known for pulling their punches. She has plans, we just don't see 'em yet," Harn sighed and looked at everyone. "If she shows up, leave her to me or Maggie, yeah? The only way to deal with the Sworn is to run away or put 'em down. Hard."

Magda nodded and added. "Felix, how did you encounter her in the first place? She attacked you?"

Felix quickly swallowed another mouthful before replying, grease spilling down his chin. "Oh, ugh. Sorry." He wiped his chin with his wrist. "I spotted her across the street, running under some sorta shadow magic. Like a cloak to help her hide, I think."

"Hmm," Magda tapped one of her shields, one of the smaller kite-style shields usually strapped to her arms. "That settles it. Felix, you're lookout during the rescue mission. If you're seeing an activated stealth Skill from a street away while also in this fog, you've got better eyes than all of us combined. You up for it?"

"Yeah," Felix replied, a spark of pride worming its way into his chest. Acknowledgement felt nice, if suspicious, especially when it was from the shield warrior. "I can do that."

"Good!" Harn laughed. "Let's finish off this beast and get some rest in. We gotta be fresh for tomorrow."

———

Over the next twenty minutes, Felix and the others polished off the rest of the meat, temporarily filling the endless void in his belly. Near the end of their meal, Felix received a startling notification.

Congratulations!
Your Title Gourmand Has Garnered Your Companion Insight!
They Have Fully Digested Their Opponent's Mana!

Your Companion, Pit Has Learned A Skill From A Hoarhound!
Cold Resistance (Common), Level 1!
Pit has felt the powerful effects of frost and has grown stronger for it. Damage reduction increases with Skill Level.

He nearly dropped his plate in surprise. Felix turned toward his Companion and found him stretching his wings over in the corner, the blue-grey offal of the Hoarhound utterly cleaned from the floor.

Must have been an elemental core in there. He looked at Magda and smiled to himself. *She did us a favor, huh boy?*

Elation and sleepiness floated over their connection, and Felix smiled wider. *Get some rest, buddy. Big day tomorrow.*

"What is so funny?"

Felix glanced up at Vessilia, who sat on the tier above him. "Nothing, just talking with Pit."

"Talking?" She looked around. "Is that a Skill?" Felix nodded, and her eyes lit up. "That is fascinating! You said you made a pact with the—with Pit?"

He noticed her slip but shrugged it off. "Oh yeah, when he was still real little...that makes it sound like it was years ago. It was last week," Felix peered over at his friend, who was sprawled on Felix's bedroll, belly up. He rolled his eyes with a smile. "They grow up so fast."

Vessilia laughed, throaty yet oddly self-conscious. She was strange for a noble. Felix's idea of the aristocracy was one hundred percent informed by TV and popular media rather than any personal experience, but she was surprisingly down to earth, even if she held some lofty ideals. Felix easily remembered her words about saving people, about doing good in the world.

Not bad goals. Not at all. Oh! That reminds me. He cleared his throat. "I was meaning to ask, what did your Omen turn out to be? If it's not too personal!"

"No no, it's exciting, really!" Vess gushed. She beamed as she announced, "My Omen is the High Priestess. Bonuses to Perception, Endurance, and Willpower."

"Pfft, typical. Rich, pretty, noble, now ya got a Royal Omen?" Evie playfully jostled her friend and smiled. "That's amazin', really. I Revealed the Devil. Bonuses to Agility, Dexterity, and Endurance."

"Of course you Revealed that one." Vessilia smiled back at Evie.

Not to be outdone, Atar raised his chin and said, "I Revealed the Chariot."

Harn whistled. "That ain't half bad at all. Bonuses to Willpower, yeah?"

Atar smiled and nodded. "Yes, as well as Endurance and Agility."

Evie laughed. "Siva's Touch! That's a good way to round you out, Atar," she exclaimed. "Get that Stamina up and you moving faster, all while workin' with a bigger Mana pool." Atar puffed up even more, adjusting his fancy robes.

"Wait," Felix put out his hands. "What are Royal Omens? I

thought everyone had access to the same ones?" This time, it was Atar who jumped in.

"More of an informal designation. Omens tend to run along family lines, same as nobility. The Royal Omens are the ones that everyone considers part of the upper crust: the Emperor, the Empress, the Heirophant, and of course, the High Priestess."

"Interesting," Felix hummed to himself, adding the tidbit to his mental notes. He was so busy going over his thoughts that it took him a whole minute to realize the Tin Ranks were all watching him expectantly.

"Well?" Evie asked, gesturing to the rest of them. "We've shared. What about you? Maggie said you'd already Revealed your Omen."

"Oh, yeah. Sure, of course. My Omen is the Magician. Bonuses to Willpower, Intelligence, and Perception," Felix said.

"What?" Atar went wide-eyed. "You have the Magician?"

"Yeah, surprised me, too. But it's worked out. My Willpower is my highest stat now." Felix surreptitiously watched his allies as he said that, receiving two reactions of note. The first was Harn, *no surprise*, who seemed faintly nonplussed at the admission; it was hard to tell with his stony features. The other was Atar, who simply sat staring at the fire for a long moment, then stood up and walked away from the fire pit.

Felix watched him go before turning back to the others with a raised eyebrow. "What was that about?"

Evie waved her hand dismissively before shoveling the last of her food in her mouth. Vessilia actually answered.

"He was probably surprised at your Omen. It is uncommon for Humans to have it."

"Right, yeah. Harn was saying that. But still, that was a weird reaction," Felix said.

Evie swallowed and laughed lightly. "He's probably just jealous. Those bonus stats are perfect for a mage. He got Chariot, which ain't bad at all, though. Noctis knows he needs more physical stats."

"Hm, just when he was warming up to me," Felix muttered. Vessilia smiled.

"I would not worry overmuch. I have only known the man for a month, and he is competitive to a fault. Perhaps he only wishes to improve upon his spellcasting." She shrugged, her long brown hair tumbling down her shoulder as the braid that usually bound it finally came loose.

Felix considered Atar, who had retreated to his corner and was seated cross-legged upon his bedroll. *Maybe I can convince him to help me. He certainly understands magic better than I do.* When his attention returned to the group, he found Evie in the middle of speaking to Harn.

"-some Essence Draughts. Just in case."

"Sure," Harn replied, pulling over his pack and getting a few silver vials out. He handed two of them to Evie, though Vessilia waved the offer away. "That's what they're here for, right? What about you, Felix?"

"What?" Felix said.

Evie turned to him. "We're close to hitting our next Apprentice Tiers, so Harn's handing out some Essence Draughts."

"Ah," Felix nodded. "Yeah I could use some."

"Some? How many? One, two? Mind, Body, or Spirit?" Harn asked, reaching back into his bag.

Felix checked his Skill list and then his Formation table.

Skills:
BODY
Resistances: Acid Resistance (C), Level 22; Cold Resistance (C), Level 6; Fire Resistance (C) Level 18; Heat Resistance (U), Level 19; Pain Resistance (U), Level 29; Poison Resistance (U), Level 25

Combat Skills: Axe Mastery (C), Level 5; Blunt Weapon Mastery (C), Level 8; Dodge (C), Level 24; Long Blade Mastery (C), Level 15; Parry (C), Level 4; Small Blade Mastery (C), Level 10; Staff Mastery (C), Level 7; Thrown Weapons Mastery (C), Level 11; Unarmed Mastery (C), Level 24; Blind Fighting (R), Level 19; Corrosive Strike (R), Level 20

Physical Enhancements: Running (C), Level 18; Stealth (C), Level 23; Swimming (C), Level 3; Acrobatics (U), Level 23; Breath Control (U), Level 17; Free Climbing (U), Level 15; Armored Skin (R), Level 23; Physical Conditioning (R), Level 22

MIND
Mental Enhancements: Acting (C), Level 8; Improvisation (C), Level 5; Intimidation (C), Level 4; Make An Entrance (U), Level 3; Meditation (U), Level 31; Lessons of the Past (R), Level 13; Bastion of Will (E), Level 30; Deep Mind (E), Level 24

Information Skills: Analyze (C), Level 23; Tracking (C), Level 13; Exploration (U), Level 21; Herbalism (U), Level 17

SPIRIT
Spiritual Enhancements: Companion Pact (U), Level 14; Dual Casting (U), Level 17; Mana Manipulation (U), Level 4; Manasight (U), Level 31

Spells: Cloudstep (R), Level 1; Acid Stream (R), Level 24; Fire Within (R) Level 32; Influence of the Wisp (R), Level 23; Invocation (R), Level 1; Mantle of the Long Night (R), Level 2; Shadow Whip (R), Level 21; Stone Shaping (R), Level 24; Reign of Vellus (R), Level 26; Sigils of the Primordial Dawn (E), Level 3

Formation, Apprentice Stage, Essence(s)
Body, 1 of 3, Inevitability
Mind, 0 of 3, N/A
Spirit, 0 of 3, N/A

"I've got two Body Skills at level 24, two Mind Skills, and three Spirit Skills nearly at Apprentice Rank," Felix scratched his head as he looked over his Skills. "I figure most of them might rank up soon."

"Huh." When he looked back to Harn, the man was sucking on his teeth and holding out his potions case. The silver vials were segmented into Body, Mind, and Spirit slots in the case, and Felix saw that there were not many left. If he took what he needed...

"It's alright if I take seven of them? I wouldn't want to take so many if others needed them," Felix asked.

"Avet's own, Felix. Seven?" Evie said, laughing a little. "How do you have so many Skills that high? I've got one Body and one

Mind already, but only two more are even close to Apprentice Tier. My Spirit and Mind Skills are too low." She waggled the silver vials in her hand. "These two draughts will be enough for me."

Vessilia cleared her throat and nodded as well. "I am fine. My," she sighed, almost apologetically. "My father gave me a selection of Essence Draughts that were hand-picked for me. I will not need any from the Guild's store."

"Oo, fancy. Let me see em!" Evie teased.

"They are nothing too interesting, just very...focused. Hey, stop going—that is my-!" Vessilia was suddenly fighting off an extremely curious Evie, who had plucked a hard-cased satchel from her friend's side. She snatched it right back. "You rabid harnoq," she laughed. "Hands to yourself."

"C'mon, I just wanna see how the Upper Crust lives," Evie pled, eyeing the satchel. "All I'm ever gonna get is the Iron Essence trifecta, and hey, it ain't nothing. But you know, it's also not as exciting as a *Dragoon's* hand-picked Essences!"

Vessilia rolled her eyes, but Felix watched with interest. "I'd be very interested to see what you have, as well. If you wanted to share. But you don't have to!" He added the last when Vessilia started looking worriedly down at her satchel. "Uh, you do you, uh, yeah."

Fucking hell, what was that? Might as well staple that foot into my mouth, it's not going anywhere soon.

"*Fine*, if it will calm you down, Evie." Vessilia unsnapped the bright metal buckles on the satchel, opening another, much fancier version of Harn's potion case. The moment it opened, the ambient Mana around them started swirling and flaring, like a time lapse video of storm clouds. Felix sat up straighter, the phenomenon obviously having something to do with what was inside the case. The top opened up on hinges, and inside were two trays that folded up and out, revealing an entire bevy of crystalline vials. Six in total, they shimmered with various jeweled hues, and each held a tightly-contained aura of magic. It was not quite the physical presence of stone or even fire, but was quite thicker than Mana vapor alone.

Felix Analyzed all of them as quickly as he could, but got back only their names.

Name: Essence Draught of Dragon's Fire

Name: Essence Draught of Dragon's Wing
Name: Essence Draught of Orichalcum
Name: Essence Draught of Sky's Light
Name: Essence Draught of Wind's Grace
Name: Essence Draught of Clarity

"What are *those*?" Evie's eyes were wide as she held a hand out, fingers splayed like they were in a breeze. "They feel powerful."

"They should. Those're Rare Essences, the lot of em, unless I miss my guess," Harn grunted, obviously impressed. "Put 'em away. That much Mana surging is noticeable. Don't want it slipping past the wards." Vessilia nodded, embarrassed, before pushing the trays back in and closing the case with a snap.

The storm of Mana that had been building stopped growing, and over the next few seconds dissipated completely.

Rare Essences, huh? Now *those* were good Essences. As before, Felix felt an unpleasant disquiet when he regarded the silver vials in Harn's case. Harn caught his eyes and laughed.

"Yeah, these ain't so fancy, but they're a solid base. You make a solid foundation, and you can go far." Harn shrugged. "Or don't. Build yer tower on sand, and watch it fall."

Harn had his number, that was for sure. Despite knowing what Harn was doing, Felix still felt his need for the Iron Essences surge in him. *Stupid reverse psychology.*

"Ok yeah. Gimme the seven, then."

Harn handed them over, and Felix carefully put them away in his own potion case, which was too full. Several empty vials, two filled with blood, and his own Draught of Wandering Spirit. He handed one back to Harn. "Sorry, just six. Forgot I had one."

"Oh?" Harn said, taking the Iron Spirit Essence back. "What one?"

"Essence Draught of the Wandering Spirit," Felix said, holding up the vial. "Uncommon rarity."

Harn sucked at his teeth and nodded. "That's a good one. Don't find those outside Henaar too much, though. How'd you get one?"

Felix tucked the vial back into his case before answering. "Found it in the forest. Someone lost it, I guess." He wasn't sure why he omitted the Henaari corpse, it just felt...inappropriate to bring up. He looked at Harn. "Do you know what Essences it offers?"

"Essence of Wander, for sure, but I ain't positive on the others. Usually offers two related Essences, but that one is tied deep to their goddess. The Endless Raven is known for knowledge and exploration," he said, packing away the case and starting to get up. "Chances are the other two're about one or both."

The women were talking about Vessilia's Essences, but Felix stepped away from them, cutting off Harn before he left. "One more question, Harn."

"Always one more with you. What?" Harn groused, and Felix got the impression he was genuinely tired.

"I'll make it quick, if I can. How long can you put off Tempering? As in, how long after reaching Apprentice Tier before you lose the chance to take an Essence Draught?" If it worked like he hoped, then he thought he'd be ok. If.

"If you ignore yer Apprentice notification, it won't activate. Just like any system prompt. Ya only got so long with that tactic though; at most a day, dawn ta dawn." Harn sighed and glanced at his bedroll. "After that, formation starts as normal, and if you don't have an Essence in ya, then yer outta luck."

Harn started to turn away before he stopped and looked back. "Oh, and ya won't be able to rank up the Skill either, until you finish formation, so that's a waste a time, too. Take my advice: it's better to settle for common Essences in the hand than rare ones ya can't find." With a final, piercing look, Harn stumped toward his bed.

Later that night, Felix spent some more time in the basin room.

He had some ideas about Skill training that he wanted to test.

After filling up the same basin with Acid Stream, he once more dunked his arm into the foul solution. Again, his flesh started to melt and sizzle, making the green liquid bubble furiously. His Acid Resistance was only 22, but his Acid Stream had jumped up to 24 after fighting the Ofrenoks. Now it was all about patience.

And pain.

Felix pushed at the pain, letting it drift around him like steam, feeling his Pain Resistance do its job as his Willpower buoyed the entire effort. As he held off the agony, Felix purposely let his mind float into Meditation. Pain Resistance flared, Acid Resistance building, Felix let himself fall deeper into Meditation than ever.

Everything went dark.

No pain. No weight. No scents or sounds or anything at all. It was a perfect void.

Just that ocean-loud roar of silence that was everything and nothing.

When he resurfaced, Felix was unsure if he'd been down for a few minutes or an hour, but his notifications indicated the latter.

Acid Resistance is level 24!
Pain Resistance is level 30!
Meditation is level 32!

"Haha! It worked!" Not only did he rank up three of his Skills, but he didn't have to endure the acrid stink of his own acid. Felix pulled his arm out of the once-sizzling goop and looked at it: it was hale and whole, without a single mark of pink or healing patch of skin. His resistance must have ranked up a while ago, and his Health regen did the rest.

After taking a moment to stretch his back, Felix sat on one of the stone benches and pulled out his two blood vials.

Ofrenok and Ofrehulk. Which to do first? He weighed them in his hands. *Both are gonna be gross, I can almost guarantee that.* He sighed. *Why blood? The Title and Skill both talk about digesting Mana, not blood specifically. I ate the shadow tendril of the Rockstrike previously, and the Wisp didn't have blood at all, just sparky magic...stuff. Could I just eat an enemy's spell instead?*

Felix snorted at the mental image of catching a fireball with his mouth. *Maybe, but am I getting hit with Mana when a fireball hits me? Or is it Mana that turns into fire?* A question worth asking. *Maybe Atar will tell me when he stops training.*

The mage had been pushing himself and his fire spells hard since dinner, resting only to recover some of his Mana before pushing forward again. He was dedicated, that was for sure. His Mana regen must have been pretty decent as well, since he was risking a low tank when they all got up in a few hours.

Felix's stomach growled, loudly, reminding him of his ever-present friend. *This is getting really annoying. I'm eating like a cartoon character, just piles of food, and still I have this...It's even making this blood look tastier.* He shuddered, but popped the cork on the Ofrenok vial. Better now than later. "Bottoms up."

"What are you doing, child?"

Felix scrambled to his feet, an orb of acid in his hand before he even turned.

"What?" He asked, blinking and tilting his head. "What are *you*?"

CHAPTER FIFTY-FOUR

Before him appeared to be a child-sized...anthropomorphic ermine. Perhaps only four feet tall, their body was long in proportion but stood upon two solid legs and held small, withered hands folded before them. A series of wrappings surrounded their body, like layered and elaborate robes once elegant, now moth-eaten. They were also old, their wedge-shaped face wrinkled and sagging as their almost emaciated neck strained to hold it up. Their ears were large triangles that flopped down from the top of their head, and eyes the unstained blue of summer sky regarded him with a cool sort of amusement.

They reminded Felix immediately of the Orit. He kept his hand raised, the spell still primed and spinning. He tossed an Analyze at them.

Name: ???
Race: ???
Level: ???
HP: ???/???
SP: ???/???
MP: ?????/????
Lore: Unknown
Strength: Unknown
Weakness: Unknown

So they're either way too strong or have the ability to hide from my Skill. Felix mentally groused. *I need to level this up faster.*

"Who are you?" Felix asked again, amending his question; this was clearly a person, despite his first confused impression. The ermine face stretched into a sharp-toothed smile, the large blue eyes crinkling heavily at the edges. Felix stifled the urge to call for the Silver Ranks; he'd see where this went first.

"This one is Vvim." Their voice was strong and high, but rusty, creaking with disuse.

"...Good evening, Vvim. Why are you here?" Felix didn't see the need to beat around the bush, the creature had obviously been watching him for at least some time. Probably longer, since Felix had not been able to sense him previously. Curious, Felix flexed his Manasight in an attempt to see Vvim's aura. Nothing appeared. The creature laughed, a dusty cough that seemed kind.

"This one is very old. These eyes have seen many things in many lands, but this one was convinced there was so little left. Then you stepped into Shelim."

"Shelim? Is that the name of the city? You're..." Felix assessed the creature's size and proportions. "The carvings and statues. You're one of the original inhabitants of this city?" Felix was somewhat amazed; he'd expected any people from this ancient ruin to have long been dust.

"Ah. So soon our name is forgotten. Yes, that was unavoidable. We flirt with the edge of Ruin here." The creature shifted slightly, but Felix saw their face twitch in discomfort. *They're in pain and their movement is slow. If this goes sideways, I should be able to get out the door before they can kill me...maybe.*

"Ruin? You're Lost?" Felix pulled himself back in, recalling the term bandied about the Nym.

"Not quite," Vvim's tone softened slightly. "But soon, perhaps."

Felix didn't know what to say to that.

"My...condolences, if that means anything," Felix frowned, feeling a reluctant pity kindle in his chest for this odd creature. Still, he kept Acid Stream in his raised hand, ready to use. "You still didn't answer my question, though. Why are you here?"

"This one is an Eye of the People. Long have we watched the city. A vigil measured not in days or years, but in centuries. The Eyes were told to wait for one thing, above all others, one sign that the end we sought might soon come," Vvim fixed Felix with a gaze at once both mild and unyielding. "We wait for the return of the Nym."

Felix's breath caught in his chest, and his heart hammered wildly. *What? Is he saying...?* "You wait for the return of a—a Lost Race? I'm told they're all gone."

"Not all," Vvim said softly, eyes turning to the southwest before flicking back to Felix. "Not all."

Felix's mind worked furiously, trying to find a way through this conversation. *Vvim is waiting for the Nym. Do they know* I'm *Nymean? They can't, right? The fog should still be interfering.*

"Vvim's eyes are old, but not blind," the creature continued, shifting their weight from foot to foot. "The fog does not blind this one as it does those poor mortals who wander into our land. The Geist are strong, they are wise, and they see much, Nym Who Is Not."

Surprise after surprise, this Vvim was delivering them like knockout punches. Felix reeled slightly, his secret exposed...but after a moment of thought, a number of ideas rushed to the fore. "You see through the fog? Like me?"

"Oh yes. The fog is an old friend, an ally to the People when we needed one the most." Vvim didn't appear to move, but Felix was startled to realize that they had somehow gotten within five feet of him. He took a hesitant step backward.

"So you see my Race, yeah? You can see that I'm Nymean, obviously," Felix half-laughed, but Vvim made a short slashing motion with one small hand.

"No. You smell of something else, of some*where* else." Vvim's nose wriggled. "The Grand Harmony names you Nym, but you are not."

"Then what am I?" Felix asked, irritated yet genuinely curious. For the first time, it felt like someone had answers to his core questions.

"This one...thinks you are a promise kept."

"That's vague." Felix frowned. "But I wasn't sent here by anyone. I'm here by accident."

"Are you? How do you know, child?" Vvim tilted their head, blue eyes earnest as they sought Felix's own. "Do you truly know why you are here?"

"...Do you?" Felix asked.

Vvim shrugged. "This one can only guess. And hope."

The...Geist, was it? The Geist spread its arms wide, as if in admission of some failing. "You appear as the Nym once did, and the Grand Harmony sings that truth into being. Perhaps you were something else once, perhaps not. But this one has watched you, Nym Who Is Not, and this one finds themself...curious."

"Watched me? For how long?" Vvim didn't answer. "What makes you so curious? And what gives you the right to spy on me?"

"*You* are the one who entered *this one's* Tower, no?" Vvim answered with some mirth. "And this one is curious about your relationship with the Large One and her metal attack dog."

"Magda and Harn?" Felix raised an eyebrow. "I've only known them for a couple days."

"And what do you think of their plan? Their rescue attempt?"

Felix was immediately on guard. If this creature heard everything, they could easily tell the giants. *If they haven't already.* "I think it's the right thing to do."

"Are you not afraid? Or are you so stone-hearted that the threat of four hundred giants does not touch you?" Vvim steepled their hands, tapping short black claws at the tips.

Felix didn't answer, and instead stared stonily at the Geist. He waited for their point.

"What is your goal, child? Not the Large One's goal, the safety of a paltry few from the hands of one of countless threats in this world. That is nothing. A few lives means little in the end." Vvim stared at him, his wide blue eyes searching Felix for...something.

What is this? Felix felt a hot, skin-prickling anger heat him from the inside out. The back of his neck itched and his jaw clenched. "What-?" Felix started to ask, but the Geist kept speaking in that same high, creaky voice.

"Why do you not run? Why save prey that has fallen into the hands of predators? Unless you mean to take them yourself." Vvim paused, nose wrinkling. "Is *that* your plan, Nym Who Is Not? Do you seek more meat for your fire? More blood for your belly?"

Felix's back went cold, his freehand that held the vials suddenly feeling clumsy and obvious.

"No! Of course not!" Felix protested, but he felt as if his guilt flashed across his face; he easily recalled considering the consumption of his allies' blood to learn their Skills. "I would never."

"Then why? You are mighty. This one saw what you did to the corrupted Ofrenok. Why not flee this place? Why risk your life for prey? Why defend those you have never known, for whom you have no reason to care?" Vvim's voice rose, not in volume, but in depth until it shook the air all around him. Felix couldn't think. Couldn't process even as icons flashed in his vision.

"*Why?*"

"Because I'm terrified!"

Felix's voice felt gunshot-loud in the basin room, echoing slightly against the stone. Silence had fallen, the Geist's voice gone. Once more, they were only a small creature, more than a dozen feet away.

"Because ever since I arrived here, I have fought against *everything.*" He dropped his spell and considered his right hand, calloused and coarsened by his experiences. "I have survived on luck, on Skills I barely understand, and on a hope that it's all been leading somewhere. That I can find a way *out.*"

Felix looked up at Vvim. "But I can't leave someone else here. To be killed and eaten and-and-and *used up?* For what? More power? More Skill levels?" He shook his head. "I couldn't live with myself if I did that. I wouldn't want to."

Vvim was silent, their raspy breathing the only sound in the basin room. Felix swallowed several times to soothe the lump in his throat, his emotions still a frenetic ball in his head that he couldn't quite parse.

Vvim nodded at the vials in Felix's free hand. "What do you intend to do with those, Nym Who Is Not?"

Felix narrowed his eyes, anger rising to the top. "Why do you care?"

"Mana lies within blood; life-force itself. Within that Mana is an ancient cry, far older than this one or even the People themselves," Vvim continued, not quite explaining. "The music, the lilting sounds of the Mother, the Song that ties the universe together. It calls to us through Mana."

"The Mother?" Felix repeated. "That's what the Risi called it. I don't."

"But you hear it, yes? A soft sigh beneath every movement, every action? A trumpet blast beyond victory, a lilting note with each sad ending."

Felix felt those emotions, one after the other, as Vvim described them. He was dizzied, his mind boiling with excess feelings. He answered honestly, too disoriented to do otherwise. "...Yes."

"Good. Then you are not beyond hope." Vvim shifted their weight, leaning back and...smiling at Felix. Their teeth were sharp and very white. "Hold tight to that feeling in your chest, the one you felt for the weak. It will serve you well."

Vvim snapped a clawed finger, the sound startling Felix into blinking, and when he opened his eyes again, they were gone.

"And beware the hunger, Nym Who Is Not," their voice creaked across the room, though Felix could no longer sense them at all.

"It is not to be trusted."

The silence after Vvim's departure was loud. It stood prominent in Felix's senses as he strained himself to perceive the tiniest of evidence that the Geist was still there. He found nothing.

All the while, Felix's heart hammered in his chest, his blood still roaring and adrenaline pumping into his veins. That messy ball of emotion still tangled his thoughts, and only after a few more deep breaths did he feel a wobbly sort of balance form. *Meditation levels are paying off, I guess.*

That icon was still flashing in his vision, temporarily forgotten in the heat of the moment. Felix toggled it and bit back a curse.

Affected by Skill: Touch of Catharsis
Effect: 50% Reduction in Alacrity, Emotional Instability Increased

That weasel made me upset on purpose! Felix huffed an aggrieved breath, but drew it out with an effort of Will. He took two more deep breaths, centering himself.

That tangle of emotions still affected his mind, and it felt like a sort of poison. He activated Fire Within.

Delving within his channels, Felix visualized the emotions as a cloud of pale pink energy. Pieces of it wafted through his channels, but the vast majority was within his head, a storm cloud of rose vapor that shimmered with an internal light. But he'd encountered foreign elements in his system before, so Felix knew what to do.

He fed it to the Fire.

Wisp after wisp was pulled down into his core, where his Fire

Within devoured it, burning it for fuel and sustenance. He only stopped when the main concentration of the pink Mana was dissipated, though Felix could still sense wisps floating free within him. Even so, the notification cleared. He opened his eyes and sighed in relief.

Fire Within is level 33!

The emotions were cleared away, leaving Felix feeling steady. His mind felt raw, like an exfoliated stretch of skin, but clean.

Then Felix felt rage. This one was fresh and entirely his own. *How dare they do that! Why? What was the point?* Felix detected no benefit to the spell, other than upsetting him. *Wait, what is Alacrity?*

Felix sat down, careful not to break the vials he still held in his hands. He checked through his status page but could find nothing on the term. It wasn't even in his Harmonic Stats listing, which he hadn't checked in a while. Then he felt his core, which had been steadily consuming those few wisps of pink Mana found in his channels, burn up the last of it.

He heard a sound like a far-off trilling, sharply rising.

You Have Unlocked A Harmonic Stat!
Alacrity - Affects feats of the mind. Confluence of Intelligence and Agility.
Current Value: ALA - 26.530*

Huh. Felix toggled open his Harmonic Stats and yup, there it was. *Alacrity. Did I get that* because *of Vvim's Skill?*

Harmonic Stats
RES: 43
REI: 21
ALA: 26

How many more of these are there? Despite himself, Felix felt a surge of excitement as he sat there, looking at his new stat. *What exactly is a "feat of the mind?" It doesn't seem like it affects mental resistance, necessarily. Perhaps mental abilities in general? Harmonic Stats are strange.*

He was getting distracted, he knew. Felix had been affected by an emotional manipulation spell. It had blasted right past his

Willpower and his Bastion of Will Skill, the stat and Skill he was pretty sure protected his mental state the most. That meant Vvim was powerful. But what did they do with Felix when he was compromised? They asked questions.

Why? What was so important to the Geist that it had to talk to *him*?

They said they were waiting for the Nym. For me. "A promise kept," they said. Felix shook his head. *It seemed more like the Geist was seeing if* I *knew why I was here, like it was...judging me.*

A chill ran down his back.

For what?

Vvim left the boy to ponder their words. It was all they could do.

The strange child was Nymean, that was certain. The Song spoke of his Race, and the Song did not lie. It could be blinded; it could be made false, but not to Vvim.

The Touch of Catharsis made it very clear. The boy seeks out the prisoners not for vanity or power, but out of sympathy. Vvim shook his head in amazement, fragile hands splayed against their heavily dust-coated desk.

The Nym had made it a policy to stamp out those predators that sought dominion over the weak, a policy that long made them the hated enemy of many powerful monsters. Now this strange child appeared in Shelim, Nym of Body and Mind, to save the weak from the corrupt.

It would be storybook perfect, were it not for the hunger Vvim sensed within him.

A mark was upon the boy. Within Vvim's Sight, there was a marring of his flesh, of his Spirit. In the Geist's powerful senses, they could sense Felix's body as a wash of electric blue and radiant gold; a strange Spirit to be sure, but not entirely remarkable. It was the bottom corner of his Spirit that raised concerns; it was marred by a sickly, insidious red, one that would have been hidden from most, but not Vvim. They would recognize that discordant touch anywhere.

Upon the boy's Spirit, there was the faint imprint of teeth, and between them, circular suction cups.

"We are at a crossroads, my dear Family. The world stands on the precipice of a great reckoning, and this one cannot tell if it will be triumph or despair." Vvim's creaking voice sounded flat in the small chamber, the undisturbed dust muffling all sound. It was a sad noise, like an old door shutting behind a loved one headed on a long journey; one they might not survive.

Still. Not every infected fell. The mark was not death, nor was it the end. And despite the Geist's mounting concern, Vvim felt their chest quicken and blood rush through ancient veins. The boy was fierce, and a compassion drove his heart, one that marked him as strange far more than his scent.

Alongside the rising excitement, a bubble of odd nerves rose up from Vvim's belly. A puff of ancient breath quivered the thick skein of dust upon the desk, dislodging a fair amount into the air. Only after the third such puff did Vvim realize what was happening.

They laughed.

They *hoped.*

CHAPTER FIFTY-FIVE

Felix poked his head out of the covered archway, checking on the group.

Everyone had settled into sleep or something like it, and the fire had been banked low. His Manasight easily picked out their forms, and a quick flex proved that green-gold life Mana still flowed through their blurry auras. It was hard for him to see auras properly—if that's what they were called—but it was enough. Pit, meanwhile, was snoring contentedly right next to the door, oblivious to everything that had just happened. Felix smiled wryly. "Some watchdog you are."

He gently petted the tenku on the head, causing him to snort and roll over.

Felix retreated back into the basin room, still considering the Geist's words. *If Vvim was trying to tell me something, why not just come out and say it? Why the run around and literal emotional manipulation?* It felt needlessly convoluted to Felix, but maybe that's how life was when you were an ancient ermine-person. *And was there a connection to the Orit?* They both looked like weasel-ish creatures, though the Orit had resembled some sort of mutated hybrid. Vvim was far smaller, too, and much more eloquent than the Orit's guttural mumblings. They were similar...but was it in any meaningful way? Or was it like humans and gorillas; common ancestors and divergent evolutionary lines?

He felt his stomach gurgle, almost as if it was reminding him of his purpose that night.

Right. The blood. He held out the two vials, regarding them again. *Vvim warned against the hunger, but did that mean my normal sped-up hunger? Or something else? Is there a difference?*

Felix considered his strange appetite with a new perspective; he had assumed it was an increase in his metabolism due to enhanced stats, and maybe it was. It was also true that Felix had started craving the power these vials could grant him, but that felt like an easy answer. Who wouldn't crave power if they could easily obtain it? In the end, Felix was trying to survive, and as far as he was concerned, that outweighed some nebulous, potentially moral danger to himself. Felix knew who he was; some stolen monster Skills weren't going to change that.

Steeling himself, Felix tipped the first vial up and downed it in one.

The hunger pains in his stomach flared violently for a moment, and Felix doubled over in sudden pain. The world stretched, rippling like usual, the world vanished into the void.

Oh right, he panted. *This again.*

The void was quickly populated by an infinite variety of Ofrenok, their snarling, slobbering visages dominating the horizon in all directions. They undulated, time playing out in physical space, extending outward from Felix's position like ten thousand snakes. It was, in a phrase, the worst.

I thought thirty of them was bad enough. This is a nightmare.

Unwilling to wait for the void to splinter and shear again, Felix reached out and selected one of the many bodies. A sensation of falling consumed him, and an instant later, he became something else.

Hunger.

Always hunger.

His slick body wriggled through a river of muddy slop, seeking out noises in the utter dark. He couldn't see, for he had no eyes. But sound shivered and shook all around him, pulsing like waves in the ocean. The small, muddy world beneath the surface was narrow and cramped until it reached the deeper parts, where the wet ran free and pools collected in the tight confines of sloppy stone.

Crawl-fish darted, here and there, too many legs, too fast; but he was smarter, quieter. Patient.

Snap! Snap!

Crawl-fish in his belly. Hunger happy, for now. But still, the hunt continued, because the hunger always came back.

Many crawl-fish later, he was in the underneath, where he fought against currents and sluicing muck. There he sensed a big crawl-fish. A huge one, made of something...hard, and shiny. He could not tell how he heard the shine, just that it pushed against his senses, a hundred crawl-fish legs waving in the wet.

Shiny and big and...and old. So old.

Too old. Too big. Too strong. The crawl-fish grabbed his brothers and sisters who swam among the muck, breaking them, snapping them.

Stealing them.

He swam. Swam fast and far. Into the upper dark, out of the wet beneath. Up. Up. Into the sky rock.

Where he will be safe from the Lost.

Felix snapped back to himself, more gently than usual, but with the same disconcerting sense of dislocation. It took him several long moments to reorient to his own senses, especially the confusing jumble of light and Mana that was his sight.

Ooofa. Wish that would improve faster. Felix shook his head, which only resulted in more spinning. Instead he closed his eyes and took deep breaths for thirty seconds. Slowly, everything settled.

Lessons of the Past is level 14!

That was about what I could expect from the Ofrenok. Slimy bastards. Felix felt a ripple of disgust spread from his neck, still able to perfectly envision the scaly, slimy body he had inhabited during the Memory. *And what did I learn? Ofrenok eat crawl-fish, which are nightmarish fish/crab hybrids, and something was eating them. No, wait.* Stealing *them. Ugh. Why?*

Felix sighed. *Another mention of the Lost. First the Orit, then Vvim, now some nameless Ofrenok.* A Memory rose to his attention, a stray thought tugged upon by the word "Lost." It was dim for a moment, before Felix's Born Trait drew sudden clarity.

The Copse Grub, that's right! It experienced something it called the Lost too. Broken. Unmade. Felix pondered. *I know it's not talking about me.*

He shrugged. Who knew how many "Lost" races there were? It wasn't important at the moment, but he made sure to file it away at the top of his questions. What was more immediately concerning was that Felix had not garnered a single Skill from the Memory. Not even a hint of one.

Is mud swimming a Skill? He chuckled to himself. *Would I want it if it was?*

So that was a bust. His first time garnering a Memory without any Skill use within it. His Gourmand Title didn't activate, so digesting the Mana was also fruitless.

Oh well. Move on. Don't dwell. He tipped the next vial up, gagging as the Ofrehulk blood poured past his tongue. It was thick and sour and black as pitch. He gulped audibly, and screwed up his face in disgust.

Then, again, the world stretched...then rippled, flinging him into the void.

Two hours later, Felix laid on his bedroll contemplating the ceiling.

Well, to be clear, he was laying *above* his bedroll. Then, with a puff and thump, Felix fell six inches down onto his back.

"Oof!"

His breath rushed out of him as he hit the hard ground, but he tried to turn it into a quiet wheeze. It was late, and his allies were well and truly asleep. The room was extremely dark, the fire having given up the ghost, though of course that didn't matter to him. The glow of ambient Mana all around was enough, not including the dissipating Mana of his Cloudstep Skill.

Cloudstep is level 5!

Felix had been doing this for about fifteen minutes, each time pushing himself a little higher than before. Turned out, Cloudstep created a platform of Mana that could cushion him, and he could also make it large enough to hold his whole body. The Mana cost was prohibitive, but it was good to know that, were he to have truly outrageous Mana or regen, he could sleep in a comfortable magic hammock.

It's the little things. He sat up and rubbed his face, feeling the long day weigh on him. His Stamina was still ok, and his Mana would regenerate quickly, but Felix had been through a *lot* in the past twenty four hours. He was mentally exhausted, and like he admitted to Vvim, he was terrified.

Turning his thoughts away, he considered the Skill he had stolen from the Ofrehulk.

Relentless Charge (Uncommon), Level 1!
Lay waste to your enemies by engaging in the ancient art of running real fast into them! Temporarily increases speed and weight when charging in a straight line. Speed and weight increased moderately by Skill level, Stamina use decreases slightly by Skill level, Mana use decreases slightly by Skill level.

He hadn't gained any Memories from the behemoth, for which Felix was grateful. He imagined the experiences of the Ofrehulk to be limited at best. He was still flung into the void, but the whole of it collapsed before he even saw any time-displaced strings of monsters. When he became aware of his own body again, his core had already finished digesting the creature's Mana.

The Skill was fueled by both Stamina *and* Mana, so he wouldn't be able to utilize it as much as his spells, but it was an interesting ability to have in the tank. Felix could imagine escaping an ambush by bashing through an enemy horde, or using it to get up close quickly. He hadn't tried it yet as the space in the tower was extremely limited, so he'd have to test it once they left in the morning.

Admittedly, this would be a lot easier if I had some sort of armor. Though it might be useful to train up Armored Skin and Pain Resistance even more. Felix winced at the thought. As normalized as the pain of combat was becoming, he didn't enjoy it. *If only they had some spare armor or something, I could at least protect my chest. Maybe a helmet?*

Felix let out a heavy sigh and closed his Skills again. He returned to contemplating the ceiling; the fall had interrupted his thoughts. It was vaulted, which he hadn't bothered to notice before. Delicately designed stone braces arced across like the ribs of some creature, and between them were small hexagonal tiles, almost like scales.

The tiles on the ground are five-sided, and the ones on the roof are six. Does that mean anything? The Nymean Temple had six-sided tiles on the ground, he recalled. *Here, there are five. Does that indicate some sort of...subservient status? The way Vvim had spoken of the Nym was almost reverent.*

Or am I drawing connections that aren't there?

Perhaps the architecture here was just meant to baffle everyone, he grumbled to himself. It was baffling to him, at the very least. He still hadn't been able to find the hidden door, and a trip up the original staircase only let him to an open area where wind and rain had damaged much of the architecture. No stairs went further up.

How did I get up there? Was it Vvim? The little creature said the Tower belonged to them, the Geist. Felix went over the conversation in his head again, reliving it, picking out bits the Geist said...and didn't say. *They said they were old. Centuries old? They looked ancient, for sure. Their fur was white and thin, their face super wrinkly. But they were also powerful, crazy fast, and perceptive.* How it watched them at all still eluded Felix, though he suspected the creature had some sort of spying or observation Skill.

Maybe Vvim can melt into the walls or something. He glanced at a nearby wall, solid and impervious in his Manasight, and scooted a few inches away. He knew so little about Vvim, the Geist, or even his companions currently. As the night went on and the dark pressed in closer, Felix felt adrift, just a little.

So many things could go wrong tomorrow. The Guilders are skilled and powerful, and I feel like I can hold my own for at least a little while. But the 'what ifs' concern me. The giants could return, the assassin could attack at the wrong moment, the prisoners could be too hurt to move. Felix felt inundated by the immensity of it all, and almost heard those whispering voices in the acid sea. They scraped against the ship of his mind, tipping it, scratching it, looking to drag him down again.

Felix's breath quickened. He knew he wasn't in that place anymore, but it still hit him like a punch in the dark. His blood felt thick and heavy, yet his pulse raced a thousand miles per hour, and he squeezed his fists so hard his tendons creaked. Haltingly, he re-imagined that castle, the fortress of high walls and impervious gates. His bastion.

The water crashed against those walls but couldn't get in, the creatures lashed the stone but found no purchase. Slowly, he firmed his resolve, flaring his Willpower to push his terror away. Felix's mind steadied, solid ground rising beneath his feet, his bastion surrounding him. The scraping of beasts in the dark water receded, the voice of failure pushed down and away.

I can do this.

Then again, maybe I could train a little more...

Felix gave up on the idea before he so much as sat up. He was beat. He might need a few more Skill levels, but he needed sleep, too. They had a scant few hours before the assault. Enough time to rest, prepare, and then go. No more training. No more time.

Was he strong enough?

He considered his stats, his Skills. Many were close to Apprentice Tier, which would likely grant him a big stat boost; but he still felt that reluctance in his gut toward using the Iron Essences. It didn't make sense, but it was there, gnawing at him. Grunting and mentally shaking himself, Felix resolved to use them, as it was pure stupidity otherwise. The way Harn and the others spoke of Tempering sounded like it was an all new echelon of strength; it should help him more than simply raising a few Skills to Apprentice Tier. His spells were closest to ranking up, he could almost feel it, so he planned to use his Wandering Spirit Essence Draught the moment he crossed the threshold.

Tomorrow, they assaulted the giants. Tomorrow, they would save the prisoners. Tomorrow... they would win.

He closed his eyes, finally letting himself drift off.

In the cold, weeping fog, Illia prowled.

She had taken to following the various Risi patrols as they looped through the city ruins, each one moving stiffly yet untiringly across the large metropolitan area. As far as Illia could suss out, this ancient city was easily larger than Setoria, and undoubtedly filled with precious artifacts. It was enough that she was almost tempted to abandon her contract. Almost. But then, the fog occluded all, and even if she had the Skills of a treasure hunter, she'd need to be damn close to use it in all this murk.

So she shadowed them, the giants unable to see beyond the fog and her Cowl. Not that they even tried. Someone in camp was puppeting the warriors, moving them with magic strings. They could only stare ahead and report until their patrol ended.

Blood magic. Illia frowned. *The Risi are dabbling in dark things indeed.*

It did not change her mission, however.

She had howled in rage when the Guilders had slipped once more from her grasp. Somehow, she had lost them during their latest escape. Illia had known they were in the eastern portion of the city, but those damn wardstones hampered her senses. With the addition of the night-cursed fog, it was only blind luck and her Brightsense Body that let her see Harn slipping through the streets.

The man was fast enough for someone his size, but no match for Illia. She duplicated his pace, stride for stride, watching him scout the giant's encampment. Moreover, she observed him return east, back toward the tall towers that dominated the higher elevated portions of the city.

She had guessed at their plans, but now she knew for certain. They intended to mount a rescue.

Foolish. Even for two Silver Ranks, facing even two dozen of these giants would spell their end. She didn't know their timetable, but with the rate the prisoners were dying, she assumed they would do it soon. She was betting on today.

The sky was still dark as she paced along the crumbling rooftop, and she felt herself flagging. The sun was a little over an hour from rising, and the Guilders could show up at any moment. Illia slugged back another cloudy potion and perked right up, feeling the effects immediately. The expensive things improved alertness and bumped up her Perception by 2% for four hours. They had the drawback of being addictive, but that was why she had brought a whole stack of them. They were indispensable on long watches.

Off in the distance, just at the edge of her new Perception, steel armor gave off a dull flash and a faint, far-off *crunch.*

The Shieldwitch and her charges were coming to her.

This time, she'd be ready.

CHAPTER FIFTY-SIX

They woke him well before dawn.

Bleary-eyed, Felix lurched to his feet and proceeded with a number of stretches. He still felt tight from yesterday's activities, though not nearly as bad as he should have. *Endurance probably helps with fatigue and strained muscles. Probably Agility and Dexterity too.*

As Felix stretched, the rest of the camp had broken out into a quiet flurry of activity. Armor was put back on, weapons were cleaned and inspected, and bags were repacked. Without armor to buckle or weapons to clean, and only his small satchel to carry, Felix used the time to train a little.

Since his Mana would regenerate well before they made the giant's camp, he decided to push his Shadow Whip closer to Apprentice Tier. Stone Shaping wouldn't work in the tower—he'd already tried—so it was the next best thing to train. Summoning his spell to hand, he aimed at the stick bundles he had created the other day, looking to grab and move them. It was easy enough to hit and yank them back into his reach, but Felix wanted flexibility from his Skills. *Gotta do better than that to push those gains. Can I...hmm, what if I move them around?*

Felix tried grabbing and moving the bundles from one point to another. It felt like using a twenty foot long wet noodle to do it; the strength of the Skill seemed tied to grabbing and snatching, or bludgeoning directly. But he kept trying. Each move was difficult, but after ten minutes or so, he was moving the bundle relatively close to where he wanted it. Give or take five feet.

This is just a three-pound bundle of sticks. Imagine doing this accurately to a person? Felix clucked to himself. *Impossible. For now.*

Focused on his task, it took Felix a long time to realize that Atar was standing nearby, watching. Grinning sheepishly, he turned to the mage, who was fully robed for battle. Atar even had his thin metal staff in hand.

"That's an interesting spell you have. I've seen you use it a few times before. What is it?" Atar asked.

"Oh, Shadow Whip," Felix replied, surprised at the amount of...agreeableness in Atar's voice. "It uses shadow Mana to create a tacky tendril that can extend about twenty or twenty-five feet. Haven't tested the max range, though." Felix pursed his lips in thought. "Hm, I could probably extend it with more Mana. Right?"

"Oh, for certain. Pumping additional Mana into a spell usually overcharges it in some capacity," Atar agreed. "Distance and power are usually the two main factors, though there's a cap. Always is."

"Capped by the Skill level?" Felix asked, receiving a nod in return. "Makes sense."

"Your available Mana limits it as well. Most people around level twenty have 210-230 Mana, so they can't afford to overcharge every spell." Atar glanced at Felix. "You have more than that, don't you?"

Shadow Whip is level 22!

Felix paused, Shadow Whip still extended. Then he yanked it back, hurtling the bundle of sticks into his arms. "Ah yeah, a little. Enough that I can push myself, at least."

"Ah, of course. With the Magician Omen that...that makes sense." Atar fiddled his fingers together, staring off into the middle distance. Felix glanced over at him when it became a little too silent for a little too long.

"Um, how's it feel, Atar? Having an Omen yourself?" Felix attempted to keep the conversation going. Who knew when the irritable mage would want to talk again?

"It feels surprisingly good. Like I'm finally moving forward."

Atar took a breath and shook himself out of his reverie. He shot a sideways look back over his shoulder, toward the firepit.

"Still sore at Magda?" Felix asked in a low voice, unsure if she could hear. She was busy talking to Harn and Evie across the chamber, so he assumed they were in the clear.

Atar glanced at him, smirk on his lips. "More than a little. She finally fulfilled the terms of the contract, insofar as getting us our Omens. That doesn't change the fact that she lied to us."

"I can't really argue with you there," Felix nodded, using another Shadow Whip to place the bundle back out ahead of him. It flung too far too fast and hit the wall with a clatter of snapping twigs. Felix grimaced. "But it does seem like she had good intentions. I mean, saving people from monsters? That's kinda the whole deal of the Protectors' Guild, right?"

Atar nodded, reluctantly. "True enough." He sighed and picked at the mud stain on the front of his robes. "This is above our rank, though."

"Can't argue that either. Four hundred plus frost giants is...a lot." Felix dismissed his spell with a sigh. "I've faced tough odds out here, too, many times. But the giants, the hounds, the...everything out here in the city. It's intense. Can't blame you for worrying or getting mad. But," Felix half gestured toward the walls. "If we don't save these people, who will?"

Atar went quiet, his face serious and drawn. Felix could see how young he was, barely out of his teens, and felt for him. As scared as Felix was, Atar knew this world better and probably appreciated the dangers even more.

"We'll keep an eye out for each other, right?" Felix smiled.

Atar looked up abruptly, meeting Felix's gaze. He smiled, a small, nervous thing. "Yeah."

"Felix. A moment, please."

Felix turned away from Pit, having just fed the little monster a handful of jerky. The tenku had snapped it all up in a single, gluttonous bite. He found Magda headed his way, while the rest of them had begun to gather near the stairwell.

"Sure. What's going on?" Felix stretched his shoulders, feeling some tightness from his Shadow Whip training. Magda slowed to a stop a few feet from him and she clenched her jaw for a few moments.

"You're an enigma, Felix. I don't understand why you're out here or how you've survived *alone* for weeks at your level. But after the past day, I know you're capable, and right now that is what we need." The words tumbled out in a rush, and Felix just stared, flabbergasted.

"That's...extremely honest of you," he managed, his anger rising. "And thanks, I guess. Glad I've proven my worth. Is that all?"

The last bit came out more than a little waspish, but frankly, Felix was *done* with Magda's suspicion. *It doesn't help that she's not entirely wrong for mistrusting my story.* He frowned, shaking off the thought.

Magda put her arms on her waist, metal clanking against metal; she wore that intricate mix of leather and steel armor that looked terribly complicated to put on. She regarded Felix with an exasperated sort of glare. "I'm just—I wanted to say I appreciate your help. You did well protecting the Tin Ranks during their Reveal, and I think you'll help us succeed at this mission. You don't *have* to help us, and that's why I wanted to give you this."

Magda reached into a pouch on her belt, fishing out a folded-up piece of vellum. Felix took it and unfolded the thick material, seeing a number of scrawled markings and symbols.

"A map?" He asked, eyebrows raised.

"Yes. It has the path from here to Haarwatch mapped out," Magda pointed at several triangular-shaped symbols scattered on the crudely-drawn map. "Here're waypoints that the Guild made a long time ago to help guide folk into the Foglands; it's how we found our way out here in the first place. They're hidden, but they're all marked with this symbol. With your eyes, you should be able to pick them out easily."

Magda pulled back as Felix looked up at her. "This is...this is a thank you. You don't have to come with us, but we—I would appreciate it. If not, use this map, find your way back to Haarwatch with my blessing."

Felix didn't quite have the words. He hadn't expected this, since as far as they knew, the way out had been the only leverage Magda had. "I'm here to help. I can't see those prisoners and do nothing. But, yeah. This is cool. Thanks."

Magda smiled and nodded before turning around.

"Then let's get going."

They were out of the tower minutes later. For all that trudging up the stairs with an unconscious teammate took forever, they fairly flew down the steps. Slowly, carefully, they emerged out into the chill pre-dawn dark.

The roads were clear of ice here, the giant's touch not having spread this far. Felix was fairly certain it was their Mantle of the Long Night generating so much ice, and either so many auras all together created a multiplicative effect....or some of them just had it at a ridiculously high Skill level. Felix activated his own version, keeping his distance from the others, but could see approximately zero ice accumulation.

Maybe because I'm moving? It's still only level 2, after all. Shrugging, he decided to turn it off. It was a drain on his Mana that his regen couldn't quite keep up with yet, and it would take quite a bit of leveling before it was a threat to anyone. *Not to mention ice-resistant frost giants.*

Pit's Cold Resistance is level 2!

Huh! Felix looked back, seeing Pit had jogged up into his aura before it cut out. *I can use it to level his resistance! Just like my Acid Stream. Hell. Yes.*

Back on it went. Pit quickly gathered what they were doing and got closer. Felix kept it up until his Mana hit 50% before cutting it off and letting himself regenerate. By the time they hit the spots where ice had begun to form again, they'd gone through six rounds of resistance training.

Pit's Cold Resistance is level 9!
Mantle of the Long Night is level 10!

The way was easy enough, even as the roads iced over. They had traveled perhaps ten miles in their original flight, and heading back toward the giant's camp was generally downhill. Still, they spread out, with Evie, Harn, and Felix taking the lead since they had stealth Skills. The others hung back, moving slowly but steadily toward their goal.

Harn and Evie relayed information back toward the others with their elaborate handspeak, something which Felix mentally chastised himself over; he had never learned the basics from Vessilia. *Next time, I hope.* Felix could arguably see the best out of all of them, though he was a little hazy on what exactly Harn could do with his specialized Body. He'd overheard them call it a Brawler's Physique, and wasn't sure if that was a Skill or Body Tempering or both. Regardless, Felix and Pit took the lead, able to see the patrols well before they ever saw him.

And boy, were there ever patrols; they encountered no less than eight groups of Risi and Hoarhounds as they moved toward the encampment. The warriors were stiff and ill-equipped to sense through the fog, but the hounds had exceptional senses of smell. This led to a couple close calls, but they remained unseen.

"Blood magic," Atar whispered after they passed the third wooden and dead-eyed patrol. "That's forbidden."

"No one told the giants, I guess," Evie muttered.

"They're being manipulated," Magda agreed in a low voice. "Don't make eye contact and don't draw close. We don't know what their controllers are sensing."

Still, the fog must have deadened their controllers' senses, as they were able to progress with relatively little issue. His Stealth and Breath Control Skills even leveled up to 24 and 20, respectively. It was only when they drew up to the actual encampment that they saw their first challenge.

Ruins had been knocked down and laid out in a circle around the camp, providing a makeshift barricade of fallen stone, pillars, and carved facades. Risi Warriors lingered in groups of two or three on the other side of the wall, sometimes tall enough to see over it, usually not. It ranged between seven and eight feet tall, and, depending on how industrious the builders were feeling, was either completely impassable or riddled with small openings.

They slipped through one such opening, Felix going first. Immediately through the wall, the Risi were nowhere in sight, and he cautiously waved everyone through. He opened up his Manasight and regretted it: the entire area was blanketed in a shimmering field of purple-white ice Mana. It laid thickly on the conjured ice at their feet and draped off the wall and buildings.

One of those bonfires his Memory called an "icefire" burned nearby, giving off a stark white light that practically *seethed* with ice Mana. All together, it was a jumble to his magic senses, and Felix had to deactivate his most useful ability. He worried he'd go blind otherwise.

Harn led the way at this point, and all of them made it into the hollowed-out building adjacent to the bronze domed capitol building. *That's what it looks like*, Felix decided. *Like a state capital building or somewhere a legislature meets. Strange how many architectural analogues there are between here and Earth. This entire place looks like a cross between ancient Rome and perhaps ancient India. Why?* They settled in to wait as Felix thought it over. *What connection is there between the Continent and Earth? Tarot cards are Omens here. Passingly similar architecture. And am I speaking English? Are they?*

Felix was partly distracting himself, he knew. He looked over his companions, who ranged the gamut of emotions from nervous to intensely stoic. It was a surreal feeling, crouching in a crumbling building while monsters prowled outside, just feet from almost-certain death. Felix felt his insides lurch from time to time, but he was getting a hang of this whole life or death thing. He pressed lightly with his Willpower, and the lurching faded, settling into a steely resolve.

They sat there, minute after minute, the cold slowly seeping into their clothes and armor. Felix could almost feel his Cold Resistance ticking up, the ice pushing a chill into his body to which his Fire Within flared in response. *Huh, almost forgot about that aspect of it. Strange*, he pondered as his limbs grew warm. *Is this an actual fire, or just my Mana heating me up?* He started to delve within himself, but a high-pitched whine that Felix hadn't quite registered before suddenly cut out. The grind of massive objects scraped against shattering ice.

The doors. It's happening.

Everyone stood up, watching Harn as he made several gestures. Felix turned to Pit, who was on his feet and ready to go. He focused and sent a series of images to his friend, telling Pit to stay out here, to be on lookout. Felix felt a flush of confusion and anger from the tenku, but followed up with a sense of care, of caution. And of frightened people just inside that building that Pit might accidentally terrify. Reluctantly, Pit sent back agreement before sitting back down. Felix bent over and hugged the chimera, squeezing him tight while Pit nuzzled his beak against his shoulder.

He stood up, turning from his friend, and saw that the adventurers were all filing out of the building. Felix scrambled after them, squeezing under a falling wall to the backside of their abandoned building. Just in time, he glimpsed Atar and Magda waiting for him. The others were nowhere to be seen.

"Cross when I say," Magda muttered. "Okay, now."

The three of them crossed the alleyway, only twenty or so feet, and into the open side door, though Magda had to stoop to enter. No shouts, no alarms.

They were in.

"Perfect. They're in." Illia sat atop the abandoned building the Guilders had just vacated, cross-legged and eating a handful of berries. "Mm, these aren't bad."

Finishing them off, the Sworn stood and stretched. She felt like a new woman, or she was about to. She only had a few more tasks before the Shieldwitch's plans all came crashing down, and Illia could make off with a hefty payday.

"Now where did that huge general of theirs get to?" she mused, spinning a dagger in her hand as she hopped off the wall.

Sixteen hours, Cas thought, spitting blood from her mouth. The copper taste of it seemed a constant companion. *Sixteen hours and seven souls lost. Ten lost yesterday. Twenty the day before. Thirteen before that. More, and more besides.* She spat again, thick globs slapping against the wooden stairs she climbed. *I will make you pay for every hour, every life, you blue pieces of shit. I keep a tally, and I will not break.*

Mechanically, Callie climbed the steps, one after the other. Her people, fellow Guilders all, trudged behind her. *Always behind. Leaders lead from the front. That's...that's what she'd say. I say kill em all, cuz I keep my tally. I will not break.*

With a grunt, she ran into the icy doors of the *temple*, as they called it. Callie raised her eyes, taking in the elaborately-carved bronze doors, larger than her by three feet. They were still too narrow to fit most of the giants. Too tired, she slapped her open fist against the metal, feeling the cold bite into her skin.

Cold Resistance is level 27!

That made her laugh, but it was laced with more than a little madness. She stifled it, pushing the wild laughter down as the doors opened. A hulking Risi guard, a new one perhaps, leered down at her while it fondled the haft of its club, its dumb blue face and bushy white beard split by a gap-toothed smile. She sobered up quickly.

"Lok tani?" It asked, as usual.

"Nothing. We found nothing." She tried to push her way forward, but the giant held out a thick fingered hand.

"Lok tani," it repeated, more forceful.

"I said, 'nothing.'" Callie said, looking up at the giant. "Are you stupid? There is *nothing* down there. Just death and more death."

"Lok tani!" The guard yelled, its face beginning to flush bluer than normal and a flop sweat appearing on its brow. "Rikta lok folar, esta tani!"

Callie growled, her hands almost reaching for the daggers these monsters allowed her. "I don't know what you're saying, you dumb, chimera-sucking, ice-licking asshole. I. Have. Nothing!"

"Hrggk!"

A sudden spurt of blue blood washed over Callie and the few Guilders immediately behind her, and a line appeared across the giant's throat. Slowly, like in a dream, the giant's head and its body separated in opposite directions. Gore pumped out, a morbid rain as Callie's eyes fixed on her adversary, finally dead.

"Well, you still have me," a voice said, maddeningly familiar.

And then the room exploded into chaos.

CHAPTER FIFTY-SEVEN

It was extremely dark within the capital building. Squinting in anticipation, Felix was forced to reactivate his Manasight, but instead of a wash of purple-white energy, only the now-routine glow of earth and shadow Mana remained. It was a balm to his senses, and Felix reveled in his restored capacity. He had felt almost crippled without the additional sense, one he easily considered his most useful Skill.

The hallway they were now in was short and straight, only ten or fifteen feet long, and lined with the usual assortment of bas-relief murals and nature motifs. The exits consisted of the door they had entered and another metal portal leading out, presumably into the central chambers they sought. Turning toward the others, Felix saw that almost everyone was grouped together in the dark, each of them with their eyes glowing a bright green.

"Wh-" He began to ask, but a hand clamped onto his shoulder and squeezed. Not very tightly, certainly not hard enough to hurt him, but it made Felix look; he could tell it was Vessilia somehow, though her body was only a vague outline in the dark filled with hints of green-gold life Mana and bare flashes of other colors. She raised a finger to her lips.

Right. The plan. Harn had already disappeared, no doubt poisoning the giant's food as they waited.

Two minutes passed before Harn returned, his armor moving

near soundlessly, and two more minutes before the first groans could be heard. Felix's breath quickened and his palms dampened. Usually flying by the seat of his pants, this careful patience reminded him uncomfortably of hiding from the Razorwing Skinks in the bushes near the coast. Or worse yet, of the Dread which lurked just beyond the shore, waiting and watching for Felix to dare return to the Bitter Sea.

Worst part of Keen Mind, hands down. Felix shook himself, trying to dislodge the perfect memory of orange eyes in brackish water and endless tentacles fitted with hooks and barbs. The memory was fixed though, at least for a few more weeks. Even then, his chance of perfect recall was still higher than he appreciated. Felix wasn't sure why the thought of the Dread bothered him so, why it had been creeping back into his consciousness, and could only reassure himself that it was simple nerves.

The rustle of Guilder bodies pulled him from his dark reverie, the impression of barbed appendages fading into the vault of his mind once again. Felix's allies rushed down the short hall before bursting through the metal door, now a rectangle of brilliant light. The groans and roars of the giants went from murmurs to a crashing wave of sound as Felix entered, the flurry of activity almost overwhelming even as his hands hissed with the unreleased might of his Skills.

Four giants were on the ground, clutching their stomachs and voiding their poisoned meals, while two others were more or less standing. Harn and Magda darted out, axes and shields swinging as they engaged the standing warriors. Felix loosed his Acid Stream directly into the eyes and mouth of the closest crippled Risi, causing the giant to rear back in agony even as it wretched. Foul bile and blue blood poured from its face, disorienting it and leaving it open for a single Corrosive Strike to its melting nose.

You Have Killed An Unknown Risi Warrior!
You Have Gained XP!
Corrosive Strike is level 21!
Make An Entrance is level 4!

The giant's face pulped against Felix's hand, its skull bursting like a rotted melon. It surprised Felix, not expecting such an easy kill; but he moved on, not willing to tempt fate by investigating quite yet. The next Risi Warrior was already dead, their body pierced through by a silver spear even as it burned with vivid orange flames. Nodding at Vessilia and Atar, Felix kept moving. Harn was trading blows with a Risi guard that apparently had barely partaken of the tainted food, his twin axes smashing against the crude might of the giant's club. That left two more. Felix spotted the next sickened guard and the giant cauldron, bubbling atop a bonfire made of icy white flames.

Relentless Charge!

Felix's body *clenched* as a powerful sensation of magic surrounded and enveloped him, even as he ran forward at a greater clip than he anticipated. His Agility stat made him fast, but with Relentless Charge, Felix reached the giant before either of them were prepared, hurtling bodily into the Risi Warrior and smashing them into the white bonfire. The giant attempted to roar in pain, but only choked on the rising bile that spilled out of its mouth even as flames ate at its Ice Demon fur and beard. Felix grimaced in disgust.

Relentless Charge is level 2!

Dual Casting!

Acid Stream!

Pushing extra Mana into the spell, Felix sought to make a quick end. Twin jets of acid shot from Felix's hands like fire hoses, quickly and easily coating the giant in his empowered acid magic. The fire went out. The guard's pained cry became a messy, sobbing gurgle before he saw another kill notification.

You Have Killed An Unknown Risi Warrior!
You Have Gained XP!

Grunting with the effort, Felix cut off his streams, shaking out his hands as if that could alleviate the sharp pain he felt in his channels. *Was that too much magic at once? Did I not shape it correctly?* The excess Mana in his attack felt like sandpaper on his insides for a moment at the end, which wasn't something he'd experienced often. *Why—?*

"Felix! Behind you!" Vessilia cried.

As he threw himself forward into a roll, something clipped

Felix's back as he tumbled to his feet. The nearest giant had disengaged with Evie and had whipped a long dagger in his direction. Felix snapped his head along the blade's path, seeing it shear into the ice on the far side of the room, sending an explosive cascade of crystalline shards raining down upon Vessilia and Atar. Perception screaming at him, Felix turned and flared his second most useful Skill.

Reign of Vellus!

Lightning exploded around Felix as the Risi Warrior's lunge was halted moments before connecting with its massive club. Pushing with all his magical might, Felix hurled the giant backwards, sending it careening into the warrior Harn was battling. With a series of rapid slashes, Harn finished both giants.

You Have Killed An Unknown Risi Warrior!
You Have Gained XP!

You Have Gained A Level!
You are now Level 20!
+3 to WIL! +2 to INT! +4 to DEX! +1 to END! +2 to PER! +2 to VIT! +4 to AGL!
You Have 5 Unused Stat Points!

Finally!

The rush of earned stats and experience flooded Felix's senses for a moment, as if his body and mind were buoyed up on a thrilling raft of light and orchestral music blared a heavenly crescendo. When he came back down, the fight was over. Panting, flesh tingling pleasantly, Felix turned toward the others, who had slowly gathered closer.

"Hah, hey," Felix nodded at Vessilia and Atar. "You both ok?"

Atar nodded, flexing his hands and rubbing them together. "The falling ice wasn't too bad, didn't have enough to bury us or cut into us, but this cold is getting awful."

"You are right about that," Vessilia agreed, tucking her spear under her arm as she brushed some frost and ice chips from her armored side. "But had that blade been an inch closer...It almost clove into me as it was."

Evie hopped over, chain whipping around her shoulder to store itself. "Vess! You ok? Can't believe that bastard got a cheap shot like that in! I—"

"Evie! I am fine! The blade barely nicked my belt!" Vessilia held out her hands in a supplicating gesture toward Evie, staving off her guilt. Felix's quick glance took in that some of the thin steel plates of her armor had been dented and a nice notch had been gouged from her thick leather belt.

She's right. Any closer and that would have gutted her. Felix swallowed and glanced around the chamber. *We got all of em, right? Wait, who...?*

The grate of metal on metal still crashed around the chamber. Across the room, eight-foot-tall metal doors had been thrown open, and a gaggle of beleaguered and injured people had stumbled inside. Magda had thrown up one of her yellow force bubbles and was trading blows with one of the survivors.

"The prisoners," Vessilia whispered. "Why is Magda fighting them?"

The giant had barely hit the ground when Callie's eyes met with the tall, gore-covered warrior just beyond it. She didn't move, just stood there and stared.

"Ma'am? W-who is that?" Bodie asked her, his Adam's apple bobbing nervously. "What's going on?"

"That's the Shieldwitch!" Someone cried behind Callie, Vivianne probably. Still, their leader stood stock still, unwilling to move.

This isn't real. It can't *be.* She was still in the Labyrinth. They had never gotten out. An agonized moan of mounting horror crept from her lips, even as her face creased into a snarl. *Not this. I will not fall for this trick again, Geist!*

So caught up was Callie in her internal struggle that she couldn't react in time to the cage of steel that clamped around her body, pinning her to the monster before them.

"Gerroff!" Callie twisted her body, attempting to slip the fearsome grapple, but the creature's powerful limbs only clamped harder. "I know your tricks, you rat! ACK!"

"Shh, calm down Callie. It's ok. I'm here." The familiar voice battered against her senses, pushing her mind to accepting what was clearly another illusion. Callie reared back before slamming the thickest part of her skull directly into the creature's fake face, causing the monster to snap its head up in reaction.

Fluid Shift!

The arms, loosened incrementally, slipped from around Callie as if she were made of water, and the treasure hunter dropped into a wide split before kicking into a backwards roll. Flipping back to her feet, she took a run at the automaton wearing her ex's face, long daggers summoned to her hand with a brief pulse of her Mana.

"Callie! Stop!"

Her deadly strikes only found air, sparks flying as they clashed against a yellow haze of power. "Copy her voice, her face, her abilities all you want Geist! I'll still best you!" She dove to the side, flickering out of phase with the physical for a single brief second before coming up on the other side of the force wall. "Who do you think she trained this power with? Hm?"

The treasure hunter was on the monster in moments, her long daggers slashing and stabbing in a flurry of attacks that flowed seamlessly into one another. But still, she found no purchase, no flesh to rend on her opponent. And Callie was tired. They had been in the Labyrinth for sixteen hours...her reserves were already dangerously low, and if this fight was to be one of attrition, she would not make it. Desperate, she called out to her allies, those few Guilders who still survived.

"Bodie! Vivianne! Karp! Flanking maneuvers!" She spun on her heel, delivering a solid roundhouse kick that was stopped by an immovable kite shield on the creature's arm. Long moments passed, mere fractions of a second, but Callie felt zero movement from her team. "What are you—?"

She spared a glance backward, but all of them, all of her fellow prisoners, were stock still and staring; some had hands over their mouths and shook their heads in disbelief, and others had smiles on their faces and tears in their eyes. Vivianne met her gaze and shouted something. It took a moment to work its way into the shield, muffled as they were, but Callie heard it clear as day.

"Stop fighting, Cal!"

They're mad. They've all succumbed! Callie's heart quailed for a desperate instant before resolving harder than ever. *But I won't. I keep my tally, Geist and Giant!* I will not break!

She returned her attention to her enemy, diverted for only a second, but a second is all you need to turn a battle.

She taught me that.

Then a wall of steel crashed into her, and Callie was swept into darkness.

Felix watched in awe as Callie fought like a demon against Magda's impenetrable defense. She flowed like mercury, weighted but unable to be pinned or stopped. Until she was. The final shield bash seemed to be a mercy, as far as Felix could tell. Her estranged friend seemed more interested in gutting Magda than greeting her.

That's a rough reunion. The other prisoners watched apprehensively after Callie went down, clearly unsure what was going to happen next. Luckily, Vessilia hopped forward and began speaking, as it seemed she had a knack for it.

"Ladies and gentlemen, we apologize for any confusion! We are from the Guild, and we are here to rescue you! Please, please come into the chamber so we can begin." She radiated such warmth and honesty that many of the former prisoners shook loose of their ennui and stumbled forward, moving closer to the group of adventurers that had clearly just killed their guards.

Felix stared at them all as they came forward, a slow-moving flood of people that he quickly counted. *There's only thirty here...so many have been lost in two days?* He felt a brief pulse of regret for their delay, necessary as it may have been. He shook it off, though; regret was useless and guilt, in this case, just selfish.

There was work to be done.

With a nod from Harn, Felix found a set of stairs and climbed up to a balcony, one with a window facing the rest of the Risi encampment. He peered through the window, keeping his body to the side and keeping his Stealth active. Outside the building the dark was just barely lightening with false dawn, but the moons were bright and the stars a shimmering sea in the sky, providing more than enough light for him to see. Clumps of various Risi moved about, but only a few. Most appeared to be sleeping, if the multiple gatherings of large, shadowy lumps were anything to guess by. He saw no evidence of any giants coming their way, and no sign of their leader or his witches.

The warm bundle of emotions in his chest flared with a query, a simple question. Felix smiled and replied back, pushing his emotions and thoughts along their connection. *I'm fine, Pit. Keep an eye out. Let me know if you see danger coming.* He received back a blooming warmth, affirmation and confirmation both.

Best dog I've ever had, Felix grinned to himself, before his current situation wore the expression away. He squinted as he flared his Manasight, scouring the square outside for any evidence of strange magics. *Who knows what those witches can do. The Circle sounds ominous, and the fact that their leader is both a giant twenty-five foot tall warrior* and *a spellcaster? Makes me nervous. But there's nothing here. Just those banked wards and all that ice Mana around the rest of the camp.*

The purple-white wards were subdued, waiting for something before they sprang back up and over the capitol building. Just what that was, Felix wasn't sure. He *was* certain that no giant watched them, no witch waited to recast the wardings. They were simply on standby. *Waiting for a trigger?*

Then he saw something, glinting near the peak of the ceiling, along the arc of the dome. It shone with a bright purple-white shimmer, but felt curiously inert.

What's that?

Dressed in rags or the damaged detritus of once useful armor, the Humans, Dwarves, and Elves all looked haggard at best. A few, like Callie apparently, had to be coaxed along; they seemed sure that the team was no more than an illusion. Magda, who had carried the unconscious form of Callie over to the central area, had quashed that notion before it went wild.

"This is real. We're here to help and bring you back out of the Foglands." She fished her silver plate from around her neck, flashing it for everyone to see it. "I promise you. Everything is gonna be fine."

That did a world of good, far as Evie could tell. Everyone started moving more freely, a few securing temporary weapons from the corpses of the giants. A few of them stared at the mushy remnants of one of the creatures, clearly disgusted, yet appearing triumphant. She couldn't agree more; Felix had done a number on that one. *Melted their damn faces off, euugh. Ain't like they deserved better, though.*

Evie watched as Vess spoke to the former prisoners, using her fancy diplomatic training, no doubt. The people were quickly organized into six groups of five, one for each of them to lead so that they could move quickly out of the encampment. Vess smiled an easy, caring smile at a female Dwarf then shook her hand firmly, probably bonding easily with her charges.

"Um, kid? How're we doin' this?"

Evie snapped her head toward the man speaking, a Human with a scraggly red beard, bald head, and stooping posture. "We're gathering everyone together uh..."

"Karp," the man offered.

"Karp. Karp? Ok. We're splitting up into groups, Karp. Keeps us speedy, ya know?" Evie pointed at herself and then the rest of the team around the area. "One of us is gonna lead you out of here, starting with Vess over there, then Atar," she nodded at the blonde mage, speaking to his own group of prisoners. "Then me. Once we're outside the walls, we'll split up and reconvene at our hidey-hole. Got it?"

Karp nodded, his smile wide and even beneath his wild beard. "Honestly, I'm just thrilled someone is here. That the Guild finally sent aid," his eyes seemed brighter as unshed tears gathered. "It's been so long."

Noctis' tits, what do I do? Evie wasn't as good with soothing people as Vess was, the woman now offering *hugs* for Siva's sake, all smiles and easy grace. She reached out and thumped the man on his back, earning a surprised look and relieved smile.

"It'll be alright," she managed, smiling widely. "'Sides, if more giants come, we'll thrash em, yeah?"

Karp bobbed his head, his teeth white against his red hair. Then he paused, looking up.

"Who is that?"

"Hm?" Evie glanced up, noticing for the first time that Felix was...climbing up the dome of the building, for some reason. "Oh...that's Felix. He's the lookout. Focus on me, though. When I say to—"

"What's he doin?" asked another of her group, this one a woman with dark brown hair and amber eyes, dark smooth skin only broken by two scars across the bridge of her nose. "Why's he climbin up there?"

"I don't know. Lookout stuff. C'mon, our turn is next." Evie motioned them to follow her, and slowly they did, gathering toward the exit. "Harn left first to scout the way; his senses're better than most. Then our mage Atar left. We'll follow them up, crossing between this building and another nearby; it's empty so we can gather from there. Understand?" They nodded, focusing back on her.

Hey, not too hard. I can do this people thing.

"C'mon then. Time to move."

"Hey, Cal. Time to wake up now."

A deluge of near-frozen water made the treasure hunter lurch up, gasping for breath and reaching for weapons that were no longer at her waist.

"Where-?" She tried to get to her feet, but her head felt fuzzy and floaty, her concentration disrupted.

"Take it easy. I had to go harder than I wanted," a familiar voice said, and Callie had to close her eyes to ease the disorientation as well as the string of painful memories that danced across her mind.

"You're not real," she whispered. She couldn't be. Not if this was a fair world. *Don't let her have been captured too.*

"Oh I'm very real, and if you ever come at me like that again, I'll beat your ass with my barn door here." The voice cracked near the end, but Callie could tell without looking that she was smiling. She cautiously cracked her eyelid, taking in the powerful woman crouching next to her wearing a set of worn and battered armor. Kite shields were strapped to her arms, smaller than Callie remembered but well made, certainly in better condition than the rest of her armor. Maggie's face was the same as ever, her sandy hair cut shoulder length and tied back, her strong nose and dark eyes. Her mouth, usually wide with a smile, was fixed in a grim line.

"Barn door is the only way you could've hit me, Mags," Callie breathed, her heart thudding in her chest as she considered the mad possibility. "Your aim sucks."

"Well, if I can't hit the broad side of a barn, just hit a broad with the barn, eh?" Magda said, a familiar rhythm to her speech, this joke shared a thousand thousand times.

"Oh gods wept, Maggie. You're real." She set her hand on Maggie's, tattered leather glove tightening on her metal gauntlet before she was pulled into a tight hug.

"Yeah. I'm here," Magda choked out before pulling Callie even closer. "I'm here."

CHAPTER FIFTY-EIGHT

Vessilia nodded at Evie as the latter left, ducking out the side exit and leading her small group on their journey. Atar and Harn had already left, presumably were even beyond the encampment even now, well on their way to the tower. The plan was working, though she feared almost too well.

Stop those thoughts. May the grace of Siva guide us. Vessilia had often turned toward her father's religion for comfort, usually finding it a warm blanket to soothe her thoughts. It was less than comforting today, however. Swallowing, she turned toward the room, doing a final count.

Other than Magda's friend (who was even now getting to her feet), there were nine prisoners still there. One group each for Felix and Magda to lead out of this place. She considered her own group, five of the survivors with impressive physiques but all the hallmarks of exhaustion. All were weakened, tired, and bloody, near the end of their Stamina and Mana after hours in the Labyrinth below.

Vessilia had learned much in talking to Vivianne, the Dwarven woman who had rushed to Callie's side after Magda had originally knocked her down. Apparently, she was a journeyman in Field Medicine, though unfortunately without talent for Mana Skills, so lacked any true Healing in her repertoire. Impressive, nonetheless;

the woman had a good head on her shoulders and helped to keep everyone else calm.

Smiling at her group, she led them to the exit. They were running low on time, having projected only a fifteen-minute window to get in and out. Vessilia feared...*No*, she insisted. *It will be fine.*

"*Ah*!"

One of the survivors, an Elvish man by the name of Pell, collapsed to the ground. Moving quickly, Vessilia rushed to his side, Vivianne right behind her. Ice was scattered all around the area, remnants from the weapon that nearly chopped her in half, and it was clearly on these chunks that the Elf had tripped. She glanced down at his leg, and his tattered pants revealed an ankle swollen and red, streaked with something dark just beneath the skin.

"Tsk, Pell, why didn't you say something? Did it bite you?" Vivianne asked, her eyes intense. Pell only grimaced and nodded, looking away. Vessilia watched the Dwarven woman's face soften slightly before she pulled a few rags out of a pocket. "What'll I do with you, Pell? Foolish Elf." Quickly, she wrapped up his ankle, and the two of them helped the Elf to his feet.

"Can you not heal it here?" Vessilia asked, looking at the Dwarf who shook her head, braids swinging. The noblewoman reached for her hardened potions case, a side pouch where she kept her two emergency Health Potions. Vivianne's squarish hand stopped her.

"No, those won't do any good. The wound needs cleansing, and we can't do that here. All we can manage is a brace, for now." The Dwarf furrowed her brow, frustrated. Vessilia put her hand on her shoulder and smiled gently, both at her and all the others.

"We will take care of him, of all of you, once we're free." She looked about, noticing that Magda had started to gather her people around her. "We must go. There is not much time."

The spearwoman got Pell's arm over her shoulder and neck, supporting his lanky weight. He stumbled, a slight tearing sound as he leaned against her and hissed in pain. Vessilia slipped, feeling something drop from her waist, likely Pell's patchwork armor. She fetched up against the icy wall for the briefest of moments. "I've got you, Pell. Everything is going to be fine."

Oration is level 16!

The Elf nodded, his face smoothing slightly, and the noblewoman kicked ice chunks out of her way while extolling her charges to follow her path.

"Come, my friends! We must be quick."

Magda released Callie, loath to let her go, but knew that they were short on time. The nine remaining survivors gathered around them, all of them watching with some measure of nervousness.

"You good, Cal?" One of them asked, a dark skinned man, heavy with muscle beneath his tattered leather armor. Clearly, he'd developed his Body well beyond his first Temper, likely past his second as well.

Callie wiped her face and smirked. "I'm fine, Bodie. Thanks." She stood straighter and noticed the empty room. "Where is everyone?"

"Evacuated," Magda answered, gesturing toward the side exit. "My people led three groups out already. Just two more to go and we're done in this cursed city." Only silence met that declaration, and Magda looked askance at Callie. "I know that silence. What?"

Callie hesitated, looking back toward the bronze doors they had just entered. "We...we can't leave, Mags."

"What?"

"There's something...whatever got buried here? It's bad. It's real bad. We can't let it be." Callie put her hands on her hips, scowling at the ice all around them. "Can't leave it to these frosted bastards."

"Explain," Magda frowned.

Cal grunted and started pacing. "The Labyrinth they had us run every day? It's a maze of traps and illusions, filled to the brim with chimera and elementals and who knows what else. It's a nightmare of torment, worse than any Nymean ruin I've ever seen."

"So why stay?" Magda asked, exasperated. "My plan was to leave all that behind. Get us back to civilization. Safety."

"Pfha!" Callie snorted, nose wrinkling in that familiar way it did. "Safety? Back in Haarwatch? Do you know why we're out here?"

"Territory grab," Magda shrugged. "Guild overreach."

"Right. And if that don't stink like Yyero's backside, I'm a mage." The treasure hunter shook her head and opened her mouth a couple times, as if working out what she wanted to say.

Magda scrubbed her face with her gauntleted hands, not caring that the metal scratched at her skin. She had two Tempers of her own. "Fair enough. That doesn't answer my question though, Callie."

The blond shook her head, like she was worrying at a bone. "It's a hunch, alright? Most of these giants, they don't speak like people do, just that monster tongue of theirs so I can't figure out what they're sayin. But...they're after what's in the center of this place. And that has to be awful. Why else put all these monsters here? Why build a Labyrinth? These Geist did it for a reason, and I know it's meant to hold in something much worse."

"Geist?" Magda hadn't heard the word before. "Is that who built it?"

"Yeah, some damn mad illusionists far as I can tell. They mess with your mind down there, turn everything...everyone. They're nasty pieces of work." Callie scratched her jaw and wouldn't meet Magda's gaze. "We're almost to the center. Another day, maybe two, and we'll be there. The giants have been throwin us at it, grinding down the Labyrinths' defenses, pushing us harder and harder. And now it's there, almost in reach." This time she did meet Magda's eyes, her stare bright and intense. "We *can't* let them get it. Whatever it is."

Magda sucked in a breath, unfamiliar with this intensity, this drive in her oldest friend. She crossed her arms and frowned. "We have minutes, at most, before the Risi and their leader return here. I'll gladly come back to this ruined city with an entire legion of mages and bombard the place to dust, but we have to *go*. Or else none of us are leaving."

Callie stood tall and rigid, anger in her eyes as bright as Magda's own. She opened her mouth, clearly intent on arguing, when a chunk of ice rapped off her skull.

"Ow! Hey! What the hell?"

They all looked up, and Magda groaned.

The *boy* was climbing the ceiling.

———

As Vess left, Felix signaled Pit that she was coming out and to watch out for her group. Pit, positioned atop the ruined building they had hid within, had excellent vantage of the square outside as well as the nearby gathering of giants that even now rolled fitfully in the tail end of their nightly rest. He would send Felix frequent pulses of contentment or even hazy images and smells of Atar, Harn, and Evie leaving the area safely with several prisoners in tow. Now, with Vessilia on the move, they were down to the last of the prisoners, still being gathered by Magda below. Everything was apparently going as planned.

Well, almost everything.

Felix' grip had been sure as he navigated the first portion of the wall, ascending vertically with little issue. His levels in Free Climbing did him wonders. It was the horizontal approach that terrified him, and his first attempt had almost led to a very long fall and near certain death. So, he got clever. Once he reached the highest he could climb and before the dome started to curve, Felix fished out his brightweave coil and imbued it with Mana.

The rope came alive in his grip, vibrating just slightly as the end quested about like a creature tasting the air. With a gentle pulse of Will, Felix sent the rope snaking along the ceiling, the imbued fibers easily clinging to the craggy ice that covered everything, easily reaching the central point of the dome before tying itself off with another pulse of intent. Still holding onto the rope, Felix ordered it to knot itself every five feet and held on tight.

"Whoa!"

The coil shortened considerably, dragging him off his perch and swinging him into the center of the room. Mastering the stomach-flipping disorientation, Felix began climbing up the rope, dislodging a growing pile of ice and snow to fall below him.

He distinctly heard swearing, but couldn't really do anything about it at this point. *Sorry!* He kept climbing, hand over hand, his Strength and the knotted rope making the ascent child's play. At the top, he came face to face with a glowing shard of ice embedded into the dome's interior. A small balcony ringed this part of the building, undoubtedly for maintenance, which meant that there was probably a *much* easier way to get up there. *Then again, probably not,* he thought as he swung over the railing and saw the eight inches of enchanted ice that coated the walls.

Exploration is level 22!

He turned and inspected the ice shard, which was easily the size of his entire torso.

Analyze...

Name: Elemental Shard
Type: Elemental Core
Lore: While an elemental core is a central node to an elemental being, an elemental shard is an order of magnitude greater. Can be used for many crafts up to and including Epic ranked artifacts.
Rarity: Epic

Wow. Imagine if Pit ate this one? If he could even get his mouth around it, that is. Felix gazed at the shard embedded in the ceiling with wide eyes, walking around the circular balcony to see it from all angles. His eyes snagged on something on its surface, a faint sheen that seemed too orderly to be mere light reflections. He stared hard, tilting his head this way and that, trying to catch the light from below on its angled planes. Then he had it. It appeared to be a series of shallow engravings on the upper third of the shard, and the more he looked, the more he saw.

Sigils of the Primordial Dawn is level 4!

They're sigils! Felix perused them a moment longer, noting only a few squiggles he recognized from the markings in the Temple. Working off a hunch, he tried Analyzing it again.

Name: Elemental Shard
Type: Elemental Core
Lore: While an elemental core is a central node to an elemental being, an elemental shard is an order of magnitude greater. Can be used for many crafts up to and including Epic ranked artifacts. This shard is being used as a focal point for a large area of effect spell, evidenced by the sigils gracing its surface.
Rarity: Epic

Analyze is level 24!

Oh shit, finally! Analyze was his first Skill he'd ever earned, and he definitely planned on Tempering his Mind once it hit Apprentice Tier. He looked again at the new Lore entry for the Elemental Shard and grinned. *Aha! This is the focal point of the wards around the building! I knew it!*

Felix started to inspect the ceiling, certain that if he could somehow get this shard out of the roof he could break it up, feed it to Pit piece by piece. He was strong, he could probably carry the thing easily, right? He circled the icy balcony several times, but each time he couldn't quite figure out a way to leverage it out. Then he smacked his forehead, feeling like an idiot.

Magic. Use your damn magic, man.

Reign of Vellus!

He reached his hands forward and lightning began to arc around the ceiling and shard. With a tug of his Will, the ice shuddered and groaned...before sliding loose.

Hell yeah!

Felix floated the Elemental Shard toward himself, tilting it slightly so that it wouldn't bang into the iced-over railing. The moment he put his hands on it, a notification popped up.

Do You Wish To Claim This Shard?

"Um, yes," Felix said with no little trepidation.

Shard Already Claimed. Contest Claimant?

Already claimed? Realization hit him. *The giant. Or the Circle witches maybe. Whoever had cast the ward.*

Directing his thoughts toward the prompt, he reluctantly said, "No."

Then the shard became *absurdly* heavy, almost ripping through his hands and into the floor beneath. "Holy shit!" He wheezed, veins standing out on his forehead. Felix could feel the ice-laden floor creak beneath his combined weight, and he did the only sensible thing he could think of: *Reign of Vellus.*

Lightning rapidly arced around the shard, but the weight lessened greatly as his Willpower took on the load. The shard bobbed in the air, lifted with much more grace than Tides of Vellus ever managed. "This Skill is so cool. If only I could stop all the lightning. Reduces the utility a lot."

Suddenly the building shook, ice shivering off and falling the hundred or so feet down to the ground floor.

What was that?

Then the doors, those massive bronze doors that fronted the building, exploded inward.

CHAPTER FIFTY-NINE

Felix felt a sharp, acrid emotion across his pact, swiftly followed by the scent of ice moving toward them. Pit's warning was too late, however.

The giants had arrived.

Shit, shit, shit, shit! He cursed himself before glancing guiltily at the Elemental Shard. *I had one job to do!*

A sense of panic suddenly swelled in his chest, though it was clearly from Pit. It had been getting easier and easier to differentiate that. Felix tried to calm his heart, taking slow, deep breaths while simultaneously sending a warning to his Companion: *No! Stop! Stay out there buddy. It's too dangerous here.*

A pregnant pause, then Pit sent back an anxious and surly concession. Felix breathed a sigh of relief. *One less worry.*

Felix crouched low, angling himself so he could see beyond the lip of his domed alcove. Barely, just barely, he could make out the massive bronze doors and the figures that strode through it. Wrapped in dark cloaks that nearly blended with the night outside, three female Risi glided upon gaits so smooth it was like they were floating. They were easily eight feet tall, and differed from their male counterparts only in that they actually had hair on their heads: long flowing manes of white hair whipped wildly about as they came in like a thunderstorm. Purple-white and deepest blue Mana flared along their bodies, visible even to normal eyes as it gathered along their shoulders in an arc of ethereal power. The ambient Mana in the room swirled, drawn toward the powerful Risi.

The Circle. Felix bit his lip. *Then that means...*

A mountainous figure followed after them, several shards of ice orbiting a body covered in dark iron armor. A massive sword, easily ten feet long, was sheathed at his hip, tilted slightly so it didn't drag on the floor. Felix was reminded again of how tall this bastard was, as he nearly skimmed the top of the archway, which was easily twenty five feet high. His beard was white and braided, different than many of the other Risi, though his massive head was just as bald.

*Grimmar. That's right. He had those same shards floating around him the other day too. Then this one...*He looked over at the shard still floating next to him in a light crackle of blue electricity. *This must be his, too.*

Both the witches and Grimmar stopped below the dome so that Felix was looking directly down on them from his hidden vantage. *Perfect spot to play sniper...if I had anywhere to escape to. I'm a sitting duck up here, and the only way out is down.*

"A little bird spoke to me of intruders in my temple," Grimmar's voice was deep, seeming to vibrate the air itself, the cacophonous sound of a rockslide. "I dared not believe prey would ever be so bold. What wild confidence bolsters your spirit? What foul misconception believes that you could *take* from *me?*"

Magda and the former prisoners spread out warily. The shield warrior held out her hands. "We seek only our people's freedom, giant. Let us leave, and there will be no more death here."

"Is that a threat, little Human?" One of the female Risi spoke up, her voice melodious and light.

"It's a damn promise, witch!" Callie snarled, daggers in hand.

The giant laughed, a cruel sound in his too-large throat. "What fire! Sigrun, show these *Humans* what we think of fire, hmm?"

Before Felix could blink, a veritable *storm* of ice Mana swirled around one of the witches, and with a flick of her wrist, she sent it howling toward Magda.

That was when all hell broke loose.

Clouds of *near-physical* ice Mana screamed toward the Guilders, tearing up the floor in a series of staccato explosions that hurt Felix's ears even a hundred feet up. Enveloped in moments, Felix's mouth went dry as he considered the power needed to cast such a spell, even as he felt a bone deep hunger for such a Skill.

Gotta get some of her *blood*, came the thought, heavy with an ache in his stomach. Felix shook the thought away. Now wasn't the time. Now was for survival.

Below, as the Mana cloud swirled, tearing stone and ice into the air, two figures burst outward: Magda and Callie. They ran in opposite directions, circling around Grimmar, both glowing ominously. Behind them, the Mana cloud dispersed, revealing a large Force Wall dome of yellow light. It flickered and faded, and the nine Guilders within surged forth.

Grimmar unsheathed his blade, brandishing it before him as the two Silver Ranks converged on their target. He roared. "Come, then! Try and claim what is the Kin's by right!"

Leading with her equipped kite shields, Magda struck first."Shield Bash!"

A wave of energy slammed into the giant, forcing him to block with his ten-foot-long blade, and capturing his focus. With a sudden burst of motion, Callie appeared behind Grimmar with her daggers poised above his achilles heel. But the leader of the Risi was no slouch, surprising Felix and Callie both with his speed and ferocity. Grimmar kicked backward, catching the treasure hunter square in the chest and launching her twenty feet; and he was more than ready for Magda's subsequent flurry of blows, warding them off with almost casual grace.

"Are you even trying, little fawns?" He laughed. "Why bother playing at predator with fangs such as these? Blunted claws were not meant to hunt!"

Felix pivoted, looking at the other Guilders, who even now rushed at the witches. The big man in front led the charge, and an impressive array of Skills suddenly filled the room. For all that they were on their last legs, these prisoners weren't holding back. Felix was impressed. The witch, assaulted on all sides, formed a barrier of ice, but found it battered down in moments. The furious, desperate strength of the prisoners overcame the spell in a spectacular flash. The purple-white light of her spells soon washed to blue as the first witch breathed her last.

A ragged cheer rose from the prisoners, though the large man with the hammer was trying to redirect their forces to the next target. Felix saw it coming, much as their leader did.

Influence of the Wisp!

Failed. Target Not In Range.

He couldn't stop Sigrun, the powerful witch from hurling a column of deep blue Mana at them. A roar of displaced air and when it cleared, three of the nine were down, their bodies pierced by prehensile tendrils of living water.

No! He couldn't do *anything* up here!

"Prey does not take from the predators! You are our hunt, our meal, our revel!" Grimmar's laugh boomed outward as he back-handed Magda's Force Wall, causing it to shimmer and quake. "You will fall because that is your destiny! You—*argh!*"

Magda smashed into Grimmar's knee, knocking it inward with an audible crunch, even as her left gauntlet screeched out as it crumpled.

I need to do something, he thought frantically. *I can't stay up here and do nothing!*

You could hide, a soft voice in the back of his mind suggested. It batted blue-green eyes at him, tempting him into the easier path. *Run away, and no one would blame you.*

Felix gave that line of reasoning more consideration than he should have before pulling away. *No. Enough hiding. No one else is dying so I can go free.* He paused and looked down at the chaos below him. *I just wish I had a plan that didn't end with* me *dying.* He couldn't attack directly for fear of counterattack without a way to dodge, and he couldn't use his utility Skills because he was too far away. Felix's mind raced, considering his options.

Then Grimmar roared as one of Callie's daggers struck true, drawing great dollops of blue blood. Suddenly, the ice shards that floated around him pulsed with purple-white light, sigils glowing and projecting outwards into a complex series of circular designs. To Felix's Manasight, it was as if a massive glacier had erected itself around the giant, encasing him in its protective embrace. Then, the spell circles reoriented on his attackers, and Grimmar laughed again, wild and vicious. Honestly, it was becoming annoying.

"Die where you belong! Mewling in the dirt!"

Twelve-foot-long ice spears formed within the spinning spell circles and began launching rapid-fire, like a magical machine gun.

Callie bobbed and weaved her way across the room, dodging most of them, but she was peaking; Felix could tell by her slouching shoulders and slowing gait. She wasn't as fast as she was at the start of the fight. And when she stumbled, Magda was there with a shield raised, letting the ice spears shatter on her power. Still, Magda fell back against the onslaught.

Worse yet, Felix's captured shard began to glow in response to the display. Sigils lit up the majority of the shard, and it attempted to fly down and join its siblings. Only Felix's Willpower kept it at bay, Reign of Vellus restraining it with azure lightning. However, slowly but surely, it was slipping away.

Felix looked below at Grimmar's marked rise in power, saw how he was dominating the field with his three Elemental Shards. The two witches were working together, casting spell after spell at the remaining seven prisoners, quickly wearing them down.

I can't let him have another, he gulped. Then, before he could overthink it, he slapped his hand onto the Elemental Shard.

Do You Wish To Claim This Shard?

YES!

Shard Already Claimed. Contest Claimant?

YES, MOTHERFUCKER!

Vessilia had made it.

The run to the outer wall was flawless, the cover of night enough to keep her group unseen and unheard. They slipped through the gaps in the makeshift wall and sped off into the city proper, angling in the direction of the tower. The group didn't speak, more concerned with conserving their limited Stamina, and Vessilia herself was preoccupied with both leading them and carrying Pell, who was only getting worse. Still, she traded a few handsigns with Vivianne, who proved to be an able scout, helping to keep the six of them within the deeper shadows and alleyways.

A few minutes beyond the wall, Vessilia brought them all up short before sending them back to hide within a half-collapsed ruin nearby. From within those deep shadows, they saw dozens of giants rushing past, moving at a far faster clip than any patrol she had seen previously. Handing Pell off to Enod, a strapping old man who was as wide as a Dwarf, Vessilia crept forward. The giants kept coming, group after group, as if all the patrols were converging on one spot, rumbling down the street toward...the encampment.

Oh no. Felix. Magda. They're in danger!

Still in a crouch, Vessilia spun back toward her new allies, intending to announce a change of plans. To say she was heading back to the Risi camp. But the words died in her throat.

The entire group was lying still on the ground.

W-what is this?

"Tsk tsk, heiress," whispered a voice. "You really should pick better company. Look at 'em. Asleep on the job."

Vessilia sensed a presence behind her and spun around, reaching for the knife she kept on her belt. But it was gone. Her whole belt was gone. Belatedly, she remembered the sound of ripping back in the encampment.

My belt! My...my pot..potions...

She wobbled on her feet, acrid fumes flooding in her nose, before falling unceremoniously onto her face.

Illia, masked and armored, manifested from the shadows wearing a wide grin.

"Time to go!"

Magda covered her eyes, barely able to see. A flare of visible purple-white light had burst from the three shards floating above Grimmar, well above the ambient light given off by whatever gods-cursed Skill the beast was utilizing. As her eyes cleared, Magda caught the flare of the same-colored magic above them, in the alcove at the top of the dome.

Felix...what is he doing?

The ice spears were still firing, but their power seemed diminished, as if the massive giant's full attention was no longer on them at all. As the spots disappeared from Magda's vision, she saw that the massive giant's eyes were unfocused and staring off into the middle distance.

"Something is happening...It's not...What is the blue bastard doing?" Callie growled, getting up from the ground after chugging a yellow Stamina potion; specifically one stolen from Magda's own belt.

"I have a feeling my...associate is involved with this," Magda admitted, glancing up again.

"The climbing kid?" Callie looked up, keen eyes making out a handsome young man with pale skin, dark, shaggy hair and piercing blue eyes that glowed brightly. One of those weird ice crystals floated next to him. "He's a mage?"

"Something like that," Magda grunted, using her shields to bat away more ice spears. "Come! We'll attack while it's distracted!"

They rushed forward.

Felix was in a dark void.

Again.

Well this is familiar.

He was once more lit by a sourceless light, except this time he wasn't alone. Grimmar was there, too.

Where am I? What is this? The Risi leader suddenly noticed Felix as the only other thing in the nothingness around them. *Prey! What is the meaning of this?*

Felix didn't answer, partly because he wasn't entirely sure, and partly because he was terrified of the giant.

You dare to ignore me, whelp? You are nothing!

Then a purple-white shard of ice appeared, materializing from the void in the exact middle of the space.

What? That is my.... Felix had to admit, Grimmar was quick on the uptake. He raised his arm and the shard began to fly toward the giant, gathering speed as it did.

No! Felix raised his own hand and strained his muscles, dragging on some invisible line to make the shard stop. It quivered and came to rest, shaking ever so slightly. *This one is mine, Grimmar!*

The giant snarled at him, but that snarl faded as the shard slowly but surely began to creep back toward Felix. Redoubling his efforts, the giant's arm muscles bulged and his hand turned to claws as the shard began reversing toward the Risi leader.

I will end you, Human. I'll strip the flesh from your bones, boil your hide, feed my hounds your cursed entrails, all while my witches keep you on the cusp of life and death, until you howl for me to stop. But I will not. The shard lurched alarmingly closer to Grimmar, and his huge smile became sharper. *I'll tear your friends apart as well, feeding them piece by piece to the monstrosities in the Labyrinth. But not you. You'll know horror and torment for all of time.*

Felix swallowed, sweat pouring down his face as he applied everything he could, straining his arms to pull the shard back toward him. But it was no use. The giant was strong, impossibly strong.

Hahaha! You stand no chance, boy! Grimmar's laughter echoed through the void, buffeting Felix like a burst of wind. *You are but a fawn, pretending to be the wolf! You have not the claws to tear nor the teeth to bite!*

The shard zipped another ten feet closer to the giant.

You were made to be ruled, to be put in your place. This world only has one constant: strength dominates, and the weak must serve...or perish.

The words struck Felix like physical blows, his arms shaking and his head growing dizzy. *What...what is this?* Felix felt like his Strength had become nothing in this place, as if his stats were meaningless in this contest of strength. The giant's words reminded Felix of all the times he came close to death, of the creatures large and small that had nearly killed him, that *would* have killed him were it not for luck. Grimmar's voice oozed across his mind, a foul presence that stank of blood and fear, and it finally struck him: He was going to lose.

Yessss! You see it now, I can tell! I know that look of defeat, of anguish! Grimmar's words were gleeful, even as they boomed out. *You have begun to realize, haven't you? Your proper place in this world.*

Grimmar dragged his arm back, the shard flying toward his open hand at speed.

Beneath my boot.

No!

The void rippled all around them, like a stone dropped in a puddle, and Grimmar seemed to lose his concentration. The shard slowed to a stop, mere feet from the giant's grasp.

What was that? Grimmar demanded, eyes swiveling toward Felix. *What did you say?*

I said no, you piece of shit! Felix straightened his legs, pushing up against the force that weakened him. Except he didn't push with his Strength or his Endurance; he didn't push back with his physical body at all. They weren't here physically anyway, so how would that make a difference? Here, in the void, it was a world of the *mind. You might be strong, Grimmar. You might be powerful. Maybe you even have some magic and cunning enough to use it.*

Felix straightened fully, his arm extended once again.

But I bet you don't have 169 points in Willpower, asshole!

Felix suddenly blazed with potency, his Willpower actively engaged in the contest for the first time. The shard shook, wobbling at first as Grimmar strained against it, but then it sped up toward the Nymean.

Grimmar howled. *That is mine! Taken by right of combat at the Kingsrock! You cannot claim it! You are prey!*

Shut the fuck up, Felix gasped, his concentration pushing the edge of his capability. The shard zipped across the intervening distance, faster and faster, and nothing the giant did made it sway at all. Then, with a final pop, the shard flew into Felix's arms.

The void dissolved, and the last thing Felix heard was the rage-fueled scream of the giant.

CHAPTER SIXTY

Felix reeled backward, his left hand slamming onto the balcony behind him and sending a loud *crack* through the ice. Once he blinked after images of purple-white light from his eyes, he saw that an icon was flashing in the corner of his vision. His notifications; he ignored it for now.

Instead, Felix focused on the Elemental Shard in his right hand. It was light as a feather somehow, still covered in sigils, still emitting a powerful aura of ice and frost, and it was...shrinking? It grew smaller and smaller as he watched, until it was barely the size of an apple. It slipped from his fingers and flew up to his head, where it started to hover, just out of sight on his left side.

Elemental Shard Claimed!
Mana Storage Gained
+20% Effectiveness To All Ice Magic
+20% Resistance to Cold

You Are Victorious In A Duel Of Wills!
You Have Earned XP!

New Title Gained!
Iron Will (Rare)!
You have proven yourself gifted in the arena of the

Mind. Must defeat an opponent of a higher stage in a Duel of Wills. +6 WIL, +6 REI, +10 ALA

Holy shit. Holy shit!

The hot thrum of power arced through Felix's veins, neatly distracting him from the danger he was in, but then Felix heard a scream of rage and pain from down below, so loud that ice literally fell from the ceiling.

———

The giant woke after only six strikes from Magda's Shield Bash and a single Stone Break. Callie had gotten off several dagger Skills, but had likewise encountered the brute's massive reserve of Health. Wounds covered the behemoth, but he had not collapsed.

"Damn! Fall back, Cal!" Magda leaped backwards over fifteen feet, bubbling up the moment she landed. Even before the yellow wall of energy rose, Callie was there, her preternatural quickness and flexibility allowing her to move in unexpected ways.

"What changed?" Callie asked, blades held to the side as she assessed their situation. The giant was shaking his head and screaming out in rage, as if all of the damage they had inflicted hit him at once, while the shards floating around him flickered and faltered in their constant discharge of those ice spears.

"Not sure. But I think the kid did something to him," Magda glanced up, where she could see Felix leaning over the railing with his eyes wide and a shard of his own hovering at his shoulder.

"Blind gods! The kid took one of the bastard's shards!" Callie crowed, more jubilant than Magda expected. "Take that, you greasy harnoq fucker!"

The giant stumbled, clutching his head in both hands, blood pouring from the wounds they had inflicted. Magda could almost read his thoughts, so clear was the expression of disbelief and anger.

"What have you *done?!*" the giant roared, body pivoting upwards toward the ceiling. He pointed a blue muscular arm directly toward Felix. "You pathetic child! I can sense your pitiful, stolen power!" The three shards began to glow once more as the Risi grunted in pain. Sigils lit up along their lengths, and those blasted magic circles appeared again.

"He's doing it again! Callie! Under Over!" Magda rushed forward, not waiting for a reply. She angled her left shield up, her Born Trait extending phantom edges of her arm-strapped kite shields to five times their original size. A sudden weight depressed her arm as Callie leaped on top of it, and Magda threw her left arm straight up. Callie burst upward, her impressive Agility given explosive power by Magda's Strength, and she landed onto the giant's angular chest armor.

"Remember me, asshole?" Callie screamed, her twin daggers glowing black and brown respectively. She struck with Fatal Flurry, one of her best dagger Skills, but Magda didn't see if it connected. She slid below the giant, coasting along on the ice beneath until she passed through the massive Risi's legs. The giant roared again, more wordless rage, and Callie's body blurred as she was thrown from his chest.

Clarion Call!

A high-pitched wail erupted from Magda's throat, a taunt that the giant shouldn't be able to deny. The Risi leader spun in place, swinging its massive ten-foot sword down directly at Magda.

Force Wall!

A bubble of yellow power formed seconds before impact, but it flickered wildly as the blade hit, shattering the ice and stones all around her. The giant snarled at her, blood pouring down its face from Callie's blades.

"You'll not distract me from my purpose, Humans!" Spittle flew as he pressed with considerable Strength against her Skill. "Your meager tricks are nothing! *Nothing*!"

With a roaring cry, he released one of his hands and pointed it straight up, directly at the center of the dome.

Directly at the boy.

All three shards oriented on his will, and a massive magical circle appeared in the air before them. Purple-white Mana shimmered in her vision, compacting into a spellform brighter than the sun.

"*Die! Die as the wretch you are!*" The Risi howled.

"No!" Magda cried out. "Force Wall!"

A yellow orb of power formed around the spell circle, but then the shards discharged: the coruscating brilliance of the purple-white beam swelled, tipped out of true, then shattered her Skill like it was nothing. The power exploded upward and through the roof itself.

THOOM!

Harn pulled up short, his armor clanking against the fog-slick cobbles below. He stood atop a hill, a little more than halfway back toward the tower, and the fog absolutely dominated his vision. He couldn't see or otherwise sense farther away than a hundred feet; yet he felt it clearly when a beam of purple-white magic exploded in the distance.

From the giant's encampment.

"What was that?" One of the more skittish survivors squealed.

"It came from the camp!"

"Quiet!" Harn snapped. *Maggie, ya better be outta there...*

Harn extended his senses, taking stock. He immediately knew that Magda and Felix hadn't passed him, but Harn had previously felt Evie move ahead of him. She was likely at the tower already, accounting for the leadership enhancements she could dole out. The girl might've chafed at Maggie's insistence that she learn those Skills, but they were solid tools. Atar was...yes, he was nearby, on the other side of the buildings north of Harn's position. Vessilia she...wait.

He couldn't sense her at all.

"Shit," Harn cursed, glancing at the ex-prisoners with him. He pointed to the most hale among them, a Human woman with red hair and a vast number of freckles across her face. "You, lead 'em to that tower. You can see it there, even through the fog. Get inside, climb to the fifth floor, and follow the lead of Evie Aren. Do nothin' else."

Harn started briskly walking away from them, back toward the giants.

"What? Where are you going?" One of them cried, their voice thick with fear. Harn growled, and he felt them shrink back from him.

"Are you going back to the giants? Is something—-"

"No," Harn said, already moving away. "This is somethin' else."

He disappeared into the fog only a few steps later, his armor barely making any noise. They were all adults, weakened as they were, they would be able to finish the last leg of the trip. And if they didn't, then Harn figured he'd have their blood on his hands, too.

Harn shook the thought of them off; they were a distraction at this point. His mind turned instead toward his goal, zeroing in on the most likely reason why the girl would vanish.

Hope ya can pull through, Maggie, cuz if it's the Sworn, then I'm gonna need some time ta bury all the pieces.

Felix woke up cold and confused.

"Wha—?" Felix blinked up at a dark grey sky, overcast but lightening to the east. "The sky?"

Armored Skin is—

Felix had the presence of mind to cut off the notification before he could see what level it had reached. but he knew. *Shit, not now.* His head felt full of cotton and a sharp pain stabbed him behind his eyes. *Where am I?* He quickly became aware that his entire back felt numb, and his hands came back slick with water. Twisting slightly, he realized he was on an ice-covered surface. Twisting just a bit more, and Felix could make out the jagged hole above and behind him where huge chunks of dark ice and bronze metal bloomed outward like a gnarly flower. Chunks of the balcony surrounded him, most of them half-frozen. Understanding came swiftly, even as his body began to slip on the ice.

"Whoa!" Felix threw his arms out, attempting to catch anything he could to slow his descent. His boot hit against a small lip of ice, and he stopped moving. *I'm on the fucking roof! How—?*

His head felt stuffed full of cotton, and the sky squirmed unpleasantly as he jostled to a stop. The last thing he remembered was a beam of ice Mana blasting through the ceiling and tearing the balcony he was on off the walls. *It must have—what?—exploded through the roof? How the hell did I live through that?* The shard floated into his field of view at that point and he remembered. *It boosted my Cold Resistance...*

He checked his Health and saw it was down to a little under 40%.

Goddamn. It's...it's really hard to think...

Felix saw an upsettingly familiar icon flashing next to his notifications. It featured a nondescript human head with a jagged line through it.

Status Condition: Concussion (Major)

Ugh, of course. Feels like I got hit by a truck. Once again, Felix was happy to have Pain Resistance to take the edge off his aching joints and muscles, which only felt mildly terrible. *Gotta get off this roof...somehow.*

Felix tried to twist again, to see how far he'd slid down, but he couldn't make his legs move the way he wanted. Something between his brain and muscles misfired, and he slipped.

"AH!" Felix sped down the arc of the dome, moving faster and faster. He reached out, attempting to grasp onto something, anything, but there was nothing in reach. The dome was covered in a faceted coating of magical ice, which thanks to their interference, was starting to thaw. It was the world's worst and coldest slip and slide, and Felix soon saw where the ride would stop: the capitol building sat right at the edge of the sinkhole, and the dark abyss yawned before him.

Shit shit shit shit shit shit shit!

Desperate but still woozy, Felix threw one, two, three attempts at Shadow Whip. The first two ricocheted pointlessly off the icy dome, but the third found purchase on some half-melted crag. Skidding to a stop at the very lip of the dome, Felix's body tilted dangerously forward, and it took all his concentration to keep his balance while gripping the Shadow Whip. With a desperate gasp, he leveraged himself back onto the ledge, back smacking against the slowly melting ice.

A sudden flood of anxiety and concern flowed into his chest, and despite his muddled thoughts, the source of it was clear. Felix sent back terse images of him standing comfortably on a wide ledge, totally fine; and definitely not on the edge of an icy roof above a mile-deep sinkhole.

Concern and rage bloomed in his chest, and Felix realized he had fucked that up. Vaguely, he got the impression that Pit was running off somewhere, but Felix couldn't quite piece it together.

I'm sure that's fine. He blinked rapidly and tried to slow his racing heart as he stared out into the sinkhole before him.

How the fuck do I get down from here?

Bodie sucked in a shaking breath, feeling his Stamina close to bottoming out. But it didn't matter; they had done it.

The final witch was down.

He only wished he could take the full credit for the kill, instead of having half of a roof fall on her.

Bodie felt a hand clap onto his shaking deltoid, and he turned to see Trendle give him a grim smile and nod. A burst of energy suddenly flowed into Bodie, and the large warrior's Stamina bar shot up by 15%. He straightened up, feeling his wind coming back to him, just in time to catch Trendle before he fell onto the ground. The man was big, but Bodie was stronger than most. He caught him easily.

My friend, why did you do that? He was only unconscious, thank the gods, because he had used up the last of his Mana. In fact, as Bodie looked around at his surviving allies, he realized it wasn't just him who had been gifted. The four remaining prisoners—*ex-prisoners*, he reminded himself—were all standing with a measure of ease. Fighting the witches had killed nearly all of them and brought the rest to the edge. *But now we have a chance. Sleep well, Trendle.* Bodie hefted the big mage over his shoulder, ready to run.

"*Ruooooaaaargggh*!"

Bodie pivoted toward the other end of the chamber, where Cal and a huge warrior he only belatedly recognized as the Shieldwitch fought Grimmar. They were all beat up, though the giant looked the least damaged. That figured; that bastard was likely the highest leveled out of any of the Risi Warriors or Circle Witches, and damn if he didn't move like it. Each move and strike with that huge, ten-foot sword was precise and powerful, and the bastard was probably a Journeyman Sword Master. As they watched, the Shieldwitch was slammed into the air by a powerful blow, her body arcing above them to fetch against the far wall in an impressive explosion of ice.

Bodie feared that Cal and her friend weren't going to be able to win this fight.

We could run, a dark voice said to him. *The door is right there, beyond the Shieldwitch. Freedom is so close.* For a brief, brilliant moment, hope surged in his chest like a wildfire. Hope for his old life.

He cursed himself for even considering it.

Bodie looked to the others, meeting each of their gazes and getting a fierce nod in return. Callie had nearly burned herself out holding their group of survivors together; they'd be less than worthless if they abandoned her now.

The large warrior set his friend gently onto the ground before picking up his battered mace again.

"Let's end this," he said, voice hoarse.

He received a wordless cry in response, and the four of them charged forward.

Felix was blind up there on the icy ledge, and had decided that had to change.

It took him several false starts to lean forward without catapulting himself off the edge, but eventually Felix was able to see down the side of the building. A wooden platform stuck out of the back of the structure, thirty or so feet to his right and perhaps a hundred feet below him.

He had an idea, and like most of his ideas it wasn't great. Perhaps if he wasn't concussed he could figure out something better, but a traitorous part of his mind doubted it. All of his plans were like this. Resigning himself to it, Felix readied another Shadow Whip in his left hand before letting go of his current tendril with his right hand. He tottered precariously, but despite a fierce dizzy spell, he maintained balance. Then he swallowed and took a single, steadying breath.

Reign of Vellus!

Felix's body exploded outward as he thrust his kinetic power against the surface of the dome behind him. His body arced out into the night, completely untethered for a wild, utterly insane moment; a powerful exaltation rose in Felix's veins, even as his stomach did somersaults. He spun his body, using the angled blast to twist himself so that he was facing the capital building once again. With a desperate thrust, Felix cast Shadow Whip outward with his left hand.

The tendril raced outward, quick as he could blink, and latched onto a window casement.

YES!

Felix still dropped, only this time when he hit the lowest point, he swung back up in an arc. With a graceless thump, the Nymean landed belly-first upon the wooden platform.

"Ow," he grunted, refusing to move for several blissful seconds.

His notifications started blinking faster, as if telling him more had been added.

"Hah...haha," he laughed between heavy breaths. "Stupid world."

Slowly Felix stood up, his legs still a little shaky with adrenaline. His back was to the building, and before him lay the massive sink-hole he'd seen previously. It was utterly dark in the predawn light, the overcast sky doing nothing to illuminate its depths. He took a single step closer, peering over the edge of the wooden platform. There were no railings, which wasn't ideal, but an awful curiosity arrested Felix's mind. It was like those times he'd gone to Chicago and New York, staring down off the top of the Empire State Building and Willis Tower. It both terrified and thrilled him, and Felix felt the same rush this time. Except...more, somehow.

There was a tickling sensation at the back of his mind, as if a half-remembered thought was trying to emerge. It was a sound, a...music, perhaps. A crooning in the air that crawled under his skin, made him want to move his limbs, to leap, to flail...to jump.

For a dizzying moment, Felix felt the distinct impression of hot breath against the nape of his neck. The sensation of being watched...of blue-green eyes in the dark.

He shuddered, his entire body quivering as he pushed the thought away. *That debuff must be fucking with my head more than I thought...*

Then the icon disappeared.

Mind suddenly steady, he took several steps back from the edge and turned toward the massive bronze doors behind him. They were carved with more nature motifs including the crawling vines and leaves, but the center of each door was dominated by a single large spike and a round object filled with triangles. It was a strange addition, he thought, as the artwork in these ruins was normally very good. These looked crude, the messy ovals given barely any thought. The doors had apparently drifted shut at some point earlier, but even still he could hear screams and shouts, as well as the occasional explosion from the other side.

That sounds...not fun. Why do I want to go back in there, again?

Taking a deep breath, Felix straightened his body, still feeling slightly lightheaded. Miraculously, he still had his satchel, though it had seen better days. He reached for his potions case, intent on fishing out...something. But halfway there the thought petered out, and Felix was left gazing at his satchel with blank eyes. That crooning increased. Shaking his head, Felix rested his hand on the pommel of his hooked sword, still kept strapped to his pack. Its presence felt reassuring, for some reason, though he still was much better at fighting with his fists than any weapon.

Felix checked his Health, Mana, and Stamina again. The last two were in the green, though his Health was still only a little less than half full. He held up his hands, staring at the calluses he had grown since coming here, and clenched them into fists.

It was time to get back in there.

CHAPTER SIXTY-ONE

"Ugh," Magda groaned. "That hurt."

Ice spilled off of her back, sharply clattering to the hard ground. She leveraged herself up, the weight of a large slab of ice still resting against her lower back and legs.

Force Wall!

A brief flare of her favorite Skill threw the slab up and back against the wall, where it cracked into three smaller chunks and slid to the ground. The yellow bubble dissipated, and Magda got to her feet, her blood burning and heart eager to rejoin the fight. Her rage boiled in her veins.

That blue bastard threw *me!* She hadn't been hit that hard since the Warlord of Neven, and she'd been a full stage behind at the time. She spat out a mouthful of blood. *Blighted giant must be at its second Temper at least...Guild records didn't say they were that strong naturally. Hope they weren't wrong. Because if that beast isn't at second Temper yet, then Haarwatch is going to have some mighty foes knocking on its doors.*

Her Health was too low, hovering near 50%, so she knocked back one of the basic healing potions they'd prepped. They didn't have many, but each of them got some, even the new kid. The red liquid fizzled slightly as it went down her throat, and she watched as her bar filled back up to 90%. *Did he even get a chance to use it? Or was it...maybe it was too quick.*

Magda stretched and cracked her neck, making sure she hadn't pulled anything. Doing so, she noticed something half-buried in the icy debris: a severed belt with an ornate and entirely too familiar buckle. Sucking in a breath, she reached down and pulled it free. On it was an empty sheath made for a dagger, and a battered-but-still-whole potions case.

That fool of a girl, Magda cursed. She hurriedly strapped the case to her own belt, cinching the buckles tight. *Just like a noble to misplace three thousand crowns worth of draughts.* She felt nervous even having the precious items on her; they were worth enough to feed and outfit an entire company of Tin Rank Guilders for a solid year, training included. Entirely too precious to be left behind.

Magda straightened and assessed the situation.

The four remaining survivors had finished off the witches and had joined Callie in fighting the leader. Five against one would normally be excellent odds, but the brute was monstrous. Staggeringly high Health, bottomless Stamina, and apparently enough Mana to bombard them with those ice spears for nearly three minutes. If this was to be a battle of attrition, Magda wasn't sure they'd survive.

We should run while we can.

Callie was a whirling dervish of sharpened edges, her knives flashing out at dizzying speeds to carve up whatever patch of flesh she could reach. However, she was encountering the same wall as the others: the giant was a mighty foe. His Strength was off the charts, and his Endurance and Vitality were likely also bolstered. And those spells he wielded...

Magda's gaze lifted to the roof, which had a large hole torn through it. Not melted, but pure force had smashed up through the dome. Right into the kid.

Blind gods. I...this...I'm sorry, Felix. Truly. She had asked, begged the boy to come with them. *Were it not for me, you'd still—*

Thud thud thud.
Thud thud.
Thud thud thud thud.

*Noctis' tits....*Some small part of her had been hoping the Risi were stupid or still sleeping, somehow able to ignore the sounds of their conflict. But that roof exploding would have been like a beacon to the entire encampment. She started running toward the doors, skirting the fight that was growing more and more intense. She flashed <Retreat> in handsign at Callie, but couldn't tell if the damned woman was gonna listen. Gritting her teeth, Magda glanced out the front doors.

A quick count into the fog marked easily two dozen Risi Warriors headed their way, with more close behind she was sure. Snarling in frustration, Magda grappled with one of the doors, a huge thirty-foot bronze monstrosity that had been left wide open after the leader's arrival. Her muscles strained, screaming with exertion as one of the doors ever so slowly began to close. It took about ten seconds, but she got half of the double doors to close with a resounding *slam.*

"*Rautka*! Falla lokti!" One of the giants cried, throwing its club overhand. Magda flared her Born Trait, extending the size of her kite shields, and slapped the crude projectile out of the air with a crash. Magda wanted to grab the second half of the door, but the Risi were too close.

She had to stem the tide here.

"C'mon then, blue bastards!" Magda reached her left arm up before slamming it into the ground right outside the doors, shattering the thick ice and exposing the rock beneath. Two more strikes and chunks of rock began flinging upward with each blow, and the giants were nearly upon her.

"*Ruaaahhhh!*"

Force Wall!

Magda flared her spell, expanding a wide bubble of yellow energy all around the door and catching six of the approaching giants right in their chests. The force of their collective weight strained and broke the spell, to Magda's annoyance, but it did its job. They rebounded, not particularly painfully, but their charge was broken, causing those behind them to trip and stumble. Risi Warriors fell into a mad jumble of limbs, each new warrior adding further confusion to what was once a straightforward run up.

Waiting no longer, Magda hefted two stones the size of her head, then lobbed them directly into the pile up.

Stone Break!

The rocks burst as they hit, sending a powerful explosion of shrapnel deep into confused Risi flesh. Magda didn't let up, instead reaching down and grabbing stone after stone, throwing with impressive accuracy and bursting them all. Within thirty seconds, all of the charging giants were on the ground, groaning in horrible pain, but not quite dead.

Tsk. I'll have to kill them up close, most likely. Damn, I—The fog ahead of her swirled, vomiting forth another line of eight-foot warriors, each as fresh as the last.

"Noctis grant me patience," she muttered, striking the ground again and leveraging another round of projectiles. "Again, then."

Callie ducked and twisted, nimbly avoiding the massive edge of Grimmar's blade. For all its awesome size, the giant was able to maneuver the sword with preternatural grace. His movements were unreal, well beyond what she'd come to expect from the giants who were hulking brutes and fought like them. She had been kept prisoner by the threat of their numbers (and the threat against the lives of her team) more than their actual ability. She was unhappy to find out that their leader was head and shoulders above them all.

Despite the difficulties she was having, and even though Mags was sent careening into the wall, Callie held onto a fiercely-burning hope. For the first time in *months*. The fire flared all the brighter when she saw Bodie and his team rush to her aid, pride welling up inside her. He, along with Vivianne and Karp, were her closest confidants since the giants had taken them. Ever since...

Screams in the dark. Human flesh bent from within. Something in the blood. Teeth in the night, a great and awful maw...

An errant blow from Grimmar clipped her leg, and Callie cried out as her entire lower body was flipped into the air. Only her second-stage Body kept her alive and functional, her Journeyman Acrobatics serving to reorient herself onto the wall. She pushed off the vertical surface, flipping forward again to fetch up inside the giant's guard. Her daggers smoked black and sepia in her eyes as she activated Fatal Flurry again. Seven slashes happened in the span of a second, each blow laid precisely atop the last.

She was rewarded with a gout of dark blue blood fountaining into the air, narrowly missing her body as she rolled to the side. Even still, the mad giant was unstoppable, especially with those damned shards floating about his head. Callie counted herself lucky that they seemed to have gone passive ever since they blasted the fucking roof off. She sheathed her daggers.

"Bodie! Flanking positions! We're wearing him down!" Callie

called out while her hands moved in a series of short, choppy gestures.

Bodie nodded. "You heard her! Move seven, triple, and four!" The Guilders spread out, clearly intending to encircle the massive Risi.

The giant only laughed, a sneer on his face. "You are all of you fools! My kind once ruled this Continent, masters of all and able to take a master's due!" Grimmar settled into a low stance, his huge meat cleaver held before his legs. The three shards rotated above his head, gleaming with unspent Mana. A distant roar of many voices came from behind them, beyond the front doors. Grimmar grinned a too-white smile that spread his forked beard and revealed his dark blue tongue. "Haha! You cannot win! You are cattle, meant to be herded. Too stupid to know what is right and good. So, if you lay down your weapons now, I promise to not be too hard on you. We'll only eat some of you."

Callie watched as Magda ran behind the giant, heading for the front doors. She flashed her the handsign for <Retreat> and she frowned before setting her mouth in a grim line. Mags would handle the oncoming giants; they just had to take care of this one. She signaled to Bodie.

"Eat this, ya blue fuck!"

Yan rushed forward, short-tempered and eager for giant blood. He was a shortsword specialist, one of the more popular weapons on the Continent, having devoted himself to Strength and Agility; so it was little surprise that the Risi's first blow missed the short man. At only five feet tall, he used his smaller stature to duck beneath the blade, sliding on the ice toward the giant's feet. At almost the same time Kelgan rushed forward, coming in from the opposite side, his salvaged halberd held high. He spun the pole above his head, building momentum for a power chop aimed at the giant's heel.

"Children. Pathetic!"

Grimmar spun in a low circle, his massive blade striking nearly simultaneously at each of the four defenders, making them all waste Stamina evading the deadly edge. At the same time, a creaking boom sounded from the front doors. One of the doors had been shut. Callie grinned.

They could do this.

<Now!> Callie signaled.

Just beyond Grimmar's range, Portia brought forth hands that had been shaping a complex spellform. It shone brilliantly in the cold chamber, the light of it refracting off the faceted ice all around them.

"Chains of Light!"

Spectral chains of golden Mana emerged from the air itself, snaking around the giant and snapping onto one another. In less than a second, a huge net of six thick chains laid over the giant, their ends fading into the ether, yet rigid with power.

Grimmar shrieked in rage, straining against the spell, but it held.

For now. Callie glanced a question at Portia; the woman wasn't in top shape after a day in the Labyrinth, none of them were, but she gave a shaky nod.

<One minute, max.>

Callie relayed that to everyone else. They took up their weapons again, their faces grim, and they rushed in to finish the job.

They were met by a torrential downpour of ice spears.

"You think me defenseless, worms? I am the Chieftain of the Kin! Champion of the Mother, Chosen of Battle at the Kingsrock! You are nothing!" Spell circles shaped and formed repeatedly, more ice spears launching at them as he spoke. Her men were driven back, unable to dodge all of the spears, and more than a few ended up dyed red with their own blood.

Then she heard a splintering sound, and Magda was knocked backward, a flickering yellow shield dissipating as she flew. The shield warrior easily landed on her feet, sliding backwards for a moment before stopping her momentum with one of her shields. Said shield was smoking, the remains of two ice spears embedded in the powerful metal. She looked at Callie with angry eyes. "We have company!"

The thunderous sound of heavy footsteps shook the air, and fifteen Risi Warriors streamed into the chamber. The first half dozen looked beaten and bruised, their armor and skin pitted and pierced by Magda's unique fighting style. The rest, unfortunately, were fresh and hale.

"Fall back to the side passage!" Magda cried, angling her shield to deflect a thrown axe. "Retreat!"

Callie's team, all that was left, ran pell-mell toward the exit.

She gritted her teeth and followed, loath to abandon the fight when the bastard Grimmar was so close.

I'll be back, monster.

Grimmar just laughed, letting them flee as his minions filled the room. More than thirty had poured in from the front entrance. "Yes! Run, my prey! Flee before the wolves." He grasped one of his three floating shards and threw it straight up, sinking it into an undamaged portion of the dome above. Immediately, a wash of purple-white light flooded over the ceiling and walls, extending in a flash to the ground. Just as Callie and the rest reached the side passage, it froze as icy Mana snapped into a wall of thick ice.

"Run as you like, little fawns. You'll never escape us." The bastard didn't move, but the Risi Warriors spread out, surrounding their location with slow, sure steps.

Shit! He reactivated the wards! Callie glanced around, seeing the drawn and grim looks on her friends' faces. A hand landed on her shoulder, heavy and clanking. She looked up at Mags, taller than everyone except Bodie.

"Can any of you break this down?" She nodded at the wall. Callie shook her head, though Bodie answered.

"Kelgan, perhaps you..?" The large warrior asked the bearded halberd user. Kelgan was panting, all of them were, their Stamina having been used up again and again in this fight. He held up a hand and straightened, though still leaning on his polearm.

"I can try," he offered before looking at his weapon. "I only hope this salvaged thing will last."

Callie clasped his wrist, helping him stand fully. "You're too stubborn a bastard to fail, Kelgan. I know you'll make it happen." She turned to look at the rest of them, fire in her eyes. "We've been here before. The edge of the cliff. Enemies all around us. All..." she broke a moment, her throat catching slightly. "All of us won't make it. All of us already haven't. But blind gods, some *have*! So pick up your weapons and lift your chins. We've already succeeded, no matter what happens here."

Mags grinned and let out a rowdy "Huah!" that was quickly echoed by the rest. The Shieldwitch stepped forward. "I'll take the vanguard and create some space. We do this right, and we can take a bunch with us."

"I like the sound of that," growled Yan, his shortswords out and eager. Bodie gripped his mace and Portia clasped her quarterstaff with her elbow, fingers already shaping some sort of spell.

"I'll augment your shields, Lady Aren," Portia offered, before pushing her working toward the tall woman. A wave of golden light flowed toward her, splashing onto her armor and sinking in. A notification must have popped up in front of her, as Mags simply smiled and waved it away.

"Thanks. That'll help."

Then the asshole spoke again.

"Do you truly wish to die cowering in the corner? You thought of yourself as a wolf, but you've no teeth at all, do you?" A deep belly laugh echoed through the chamber, muffled only by the sound of his advancing warriors. "I admit you have hurt this flesh, though it is only a passing injury, as are all who follow the Song of the Mother. I had hoped that you would have learned something from the Labyrinth, angry one, that perhaps the Mother's voice would reach you. You were so very close, after all."

Callie felt a flash of fear at the mention of the twisting maze down below, but she squashed it. *Later. Deal with it later.* Grimmar was still talking.

"—beautiful music. Perhaps if we consume you, the Mother will let you hear it before you die? A comforting thought, no?" A wave of laughter rolled through the giants, white teeth and white beards shaking in dark mirth. "I—"

He was interrupted by the sound of banging.

"What is that?" Grimmar asked, motioning his men to check.

The sound was faint at first, but steady, like a ticking clock. Bang. Bang. Bang.

Four Risi converged on the spot, the rear doors that led out into the sinkhole, the nightmarish portal that fanned the flames of Callie's fear. The ice was shaking, small pieces chipping off with each successive impact.

Something is trying to get in. Callie's fear screamed in her mind. *It's free. It's free. Noctis wept, it's free!*

Crash!

The ice shattered into huge pieces as the twin doors slammed open, framing an eight-foot portal into the night and a single, heaving young man with dark hair and gleaming blue eyes.

"Felix?" Magda shouted.

The kid? What? Callie's mind spun, her fear still running rampant. *He lived?*

"*What? Impossible!*" Grimmar shouted, and, for some reason, slightly...afraid? He gestured to his warriors. "Kill him! *Now!*"

For his part, the kid looked damn surprised to find so many giants fixated on him, but then he did something that would stay with Callie for the rest of her days. He charged in.

And he was *fast.*

Felix's body flickered, suddenly appearing twenty feet closer than he was, a spray of ice pluming behind him. He encountered the first warrior, ducking beneath their slow but powerful swing before jumping upward with a devastating uppercut. Green liquid sprayed out from his hand as he struck, and the giant fell backward with a strangled cry. He moved on, leaping toward the next Risi Warrior in line and laid into them. The warrior was enveloped in a bright blue flame for a moment and seemed to lose his nerve, because the kid rode the giant's body down to the ground as he let loose a flurry of blows.

One of those deadly metal clubs swung horizontally at Felix, but he somersaulted over it, tucking into a roll and coming up within melee range of the Risi Warrior. That close, the giant had little it could do other than attempt a grapple, which it did. Callie sucked in a nervous breath, but felt it push free in a huff of surprise; the giant that grabbed him found himself blasted away by some sort of blue lightning spell.

Who the hell is *this kid?* She turned to Maggie. "If we survive, you gotta tell me that one's story."

Mags grunted, smiling in a relieved sort of way. "Without a doubt. Assault Plan A?"

Callie tilted her head in agreement before turning to the others. "Kelgan! Break that ice down! If a kid can do it, so can you! Bodie, Yan, Portia, let's thin the herd!"

"Huah!"

CHAPTER SIXTY-TWO

Why are there so many giants here?

When Felix broke open the door, he expected Grimmar and his witches, but not an entire...*platoon* of warriors to flood the place. He'd reacted, bringing the fight to them before he could get swarmed. Miraculously, it was working so far.

Felix's notifications blinked rapidly at him again.

Gah! That's gonna drive me nuts! He ducked under another clumsy blow from one of the Risi Warriors. He couldn't afford to Tier up at that moment; he didn't have the time! *I could have outside though*, he realized as he kicked the left knee of the giant before him. *Why didn't I...?*

Screams arrested his attention. More warriors were swarming his position as Grimmar spat out some rage-fueled diatribe that Felix couldn't hear over the roar of combat. He could probably focus on it, but that seemed pointless. Instead, he dropped a final Corrosive Strike onto the prone giant before him, before he diverted all of his attention on the four new charging warriors.

Relentless Charge!

Felix zipped forward again, his Stamina and Mana taking a hit, but he closed the distance with two of the giants in a fraction of a second. The closest barely had time to react when Felix buried a Corrosive Strike into his solar plexus, crumpling its iron armor and knocking the bastard onto his ass. Senses flaring in warning. He dropped into a crouch as a metal club swung at his head before bouncing back up to cast Shadow Whip.

The black tendril shot outward, attaching to the giant's hand and wrist. With a mighty yank, Felix overbalanced the warrior and sent him stumbling to his left.

Stone Shaping!

The ground exploded upward, a craggy column bursting forward to bash into the giant's falling face. The Risi hit so hard the stone itself broke in two. Felix winced, involuntarily, though his sympathy for the brutes had run out long ago. Instead, he only felt a sudden swelling of...hunger. His appetite surged, apparently not satisfied with the dried meat he'd downed only a few hours ago.

However, Felix was starting to worry that this was something else entirely.

The last two giants screamed a challenge as they raced toward him, and Felix pushed back his hunger with an effort of will. He focused entirely on the approaching enemy, but for some reason they were moving...not slow, exactly. But predictably? Felix couldn't figure out why. He hadn't improved his Perception *that* much, only a hair over two points. How would that affect anything?

He thought back to his tabletop gaming days with a sudden, vivid Born Trait-induced clarity. Terms and phrases tumbled through his mind within a fraction of a heartbeat. *Is that it? Opposed rolls?* That particular concept sprang to the fore. *My Perception is going up against their, what? Agility? Since they aren't faster than I can perceive, they appear slower than normal. Add in the fact that my Agility is nearly 90, then huh.* Felix grinned.

Influence of the Wisp!

The Skill affected two Risi this time, freezing them in place for two whole seconds. More than enough time for Felix to blast them with dual casted Acid Streams. The powerful spell ate away at their exposed flesh with alacrity, turning their blue skin to green paste within seconds. They fell to the ground, clutching their throats and gurgling fluid from their melted tracheae. After a moment, even that went still.

For half a beat, Felix waited for the kill notification, but remembered he was suppressing them. Which meant he wasn't getting ANY experience or rank ups just yet. He groaned in annoyance, mostly at himself. Why *didn't I check my notifications on the scaffolding? I could have taken whatever draught I needed!* Felix looked up from the presumably dead bodies (they didn't seem to be breathing) as a crowd of Risi poured steadily into the capitol building. Ahead, a thick knot of them were congregating around a flashing yellow dome of energy, and Felix grinned in relief.

They're still here. Gotta get to them and get outta this hellhole!

Felix started running, pushing his Agility and Dexterity to the limit, dodging around giants and ducking between legs. He didn't have any sort of advanced movement technique like Vessilia and Evie, but his Acrobatics pulled its weight. Each tumble and spin, cartwheel and flip had Felix reveling in the power at his fingertips. Even here, in the midst of a battle he might not survive, he felt that same heady rush.

Something is definitely wrong with me, he thought, though his face was fixed in a wild grin.

He was close to the dome. If he could clear up a few more of them, then Magda and the prisoners could get out. They all could.

Skidding to a stop, Felix raised both of his hands as azure lightning gathered along his arms.

Reign of Vel—!

A wave of unformed, malicious ice Mana sheared across the chamber, forming a wall of jagged, razor sharp ice inches before him. It was thick and over ten feet tall, cutting Felix off from the others. The wall was bone-chillingly cold and felt like it was sucking the warmth out of him. Felix stepped back, turning toward the source.

"Grimmar," Felix swallowed, fear flashing down his spine. The giant stood twenty feet away, only a couple strides for the huge Risi.

The giant chieftain looked at the shard floating above Felix's shoulder and snarled his displeasure. "Of course. Your stolen shard. No wonder you barely took damage." He thrust his meaty hand forward. "I'll have that back now, vermin!"

"Sorry pal," Felix said, facing the giant fully and raising his fists. "Won this fair and square."

Grimmar snarled toward someone Felix Analyzed as another Risi Commander. "Kill the others. This one is *mine.*" The Commander nodded and saluted before rushing toward the yellow bubble.

Felix gulped, the fear tingling across his body like sour lightning. *Grimmar is level 50 at least. How the hell am I gonna live through this?*

Felix cast his eyes around the room, hoping for an answer, for someone to jump forward and offer to fight the massive chieftain in his place. No such luck.

Clenching his jaw and quelling his thunderous heartbeat, Felix took a slow, calming breath; he let Meditation wash over him, hoping that, if nothing else, it'd help with healing up. The briefest of moments passed as he did so, but in that time, the Risi chieftain surged forward and struck down with his insanely huge greatsword.

Smash!

Felix threw himself out of the way, his Strength shattering the ice below him milliseconds before the sword did a far better job of it. *One hit from that, and I'm dead, Armored Skin or not.* He slid to a stop, one hand on the ground to balance on increasingly slick ice. *Step one: don't get hit.*

Relentless Charge!

Felix got inside Grimmar's guard instantly, a thin spray of melted water behind him the only evidence of his passage. Grimmar pulled back, startled for an instant.

Step two: hit him back.

Influence of the Wisp!

Both Felix and Grimmar lit up with blue-white fire, and the Nym immediately channeled acid into his clenched fists.

Corrosive Strike!

Corrosive Strike!

Corrosive Strike!

Corrosive Strike!

Four hits were all he could manage before the giant back-handed Felix across the right shoulder. He was sent skidding across the ice at speed until he fetched painfully against the jagged ice wall Grimmar had conjured.

"Ahh!" The cold was beyond freezing, and it burned his neck and arm where it touched him. With another scream of pain, Felix tore himself from the conjured wall, leaving red, fleshy patches on its surface.

"Mmm, the blood of cattle about to be culled," Grimmar practically purred, his nostrils wide. "It is a strange vintage. Different than other Humans. Why is that?" Grimmar was already stomping toward him, wide, predatory grin plastered on his face.

"It is red, just as any other prey," Grimmar kicked out with a massive boot, crushing a section of the ice wall when he missed Felix. For his part, the boy scrambled forward on all fours, just barely avoiding the concussive force of the giant's stomps as they followed him. "Who trained you? Who taught you to fight back against your betters?"

Felix used Relentless Charge to hurl himself forward, only going half the usual distance, but getting well and truly clear of Grimmar's boot. He stood, back of his arm and neck bleeding, though his Health didn't take a noticeable dive. "No one trained me, idiot. All natural talent!" He smiled, aiming for annoying.

The shot landed; Grimmar roared again, clearly unwilling to manage his temper. "*Tell me!* You dared to walk the Void, Human! That is not something that is just *done*! Who taught you this?" The giant leaped toward him, sword leading the way.

"I'm more of a hands-on learner," Felix managed, ducking beneath the giant's massive blade. It sped by him like a semi-truck, buffeting him with the wind of its passage. "Same as you, probably!"

"*Not* the same, I assure you!" The chieftain's eyes were manic, not that Felix could spare much attention. All of his considerable Agility and Dexterity was poured into not getting skewered. "I was Chosen! I have been blessed by the Mother's eternal voice! You are a weak, disgusting Human!"

"The Mother again? That wouldn't—" He threw a stream of acid at the giant, making Grimmar tilt his blade to deflect it. "—wouldn't be the same as the Grand Harmony, would it?"

Grimmar snarled. "You dare dishonor Her! That is a lie, pushed by the weak! The Mother is not *Harmony*. She is *Dominance*!"

"Potato tomato." Felix shrugged.

Grimmar only screamed louder. He expended another blast of malignant ice Mana at him, and followed up with a savage kick.

Felix got caught as he dove out of the Mana wave, his body careening back onto the smoking corpses of three giants. An icon of a ribcage with a jagged line through it flashed in his vision.

Status Condition: Broken Ribs (x2)

Oh holy fuck, he groaned. It was the hardest hit he'd ever taken, hands down. Even if the icon hadn't confirmed it, Felix was sure something was broken, and an unpleasant sensation in his guts felt like something was leaking. His head was spinning, but even still he could see his Health drop precipitously. It halted somewhere around 15%. *God damn it.* He reached out, blindly grasping until he found his satchel. It had gotten lifted and tangled with his left arm, but he was able to fumble out the one Health Potion he'd been given.

A blur of ice smashed it out of his hand, shattering the vial against the rocks beyond.

Stunned, Felix turned toward Grimmar, who only sneered from behind his forked beard. One of his two remaining shards still glowed with a purple-white sigil circle that leaked Mana vapor into the air above.

"God, you're an asshole," Felix breathed.

"And you are a liar, and a thief," Grimmar sheathed his sword and placed his huge hands on his waist. "You stole your knowledge, somehow. But it doesn't matter if your lips are silent." Grimmar smiled, and it was goddamn creepy.

"I'll take the Memory from your blood myself."

Wait. What?

That was when a dagger exploded into the giant chieftain's throat.

It shimmered black and brown by turns in his Manasight, some strange combination of shadow and earth Mana he'd not seen before. Startled, Felix followed the trajectory to Callie grinning atop a pile of dead Risi Warriors. Her arm was outflung, and her expression was utterly triumphant.

Grimmar staggered, drawing Felix's morbid attention. Blue blood poured thickly from his neck, like syrup, and only gushed further when the Risi pulled the blade out. It left a jagged hole so deep Felix swore he could see the giant's spine. Grimmar dropped to a knee.

Felix almost stepped forward, the sight of the blood nearly too enticing. It was his busted body that stopped him, sending javelins of pain up through his chest. *Don't be an idiot.*

"C'mon kid! Time to go!" Magda's voice grabbed him as she jogged over, her armor scuffed and scored but unbroken. "Can you walk?" She reached down and helped him to his feet.

"Maybe, but why risk it?" Felix tried to laugh, but it sent a jagged pain through his abdomen.

"Keep it up, and I'll just leave ya here," Magda said, some warmth in her voice. Felix was rather shocked. "That was some impressive fighting you did."

"Uh, thanks," Felix replied, feeling short of breath. They took several steps further before the sound of hacking and spitting drew their attention. They didn't stop, but when it became a sort of rhythmic grunting Felix paused to look back. It reminded him of something, tickling his brain. What he saw behind them was a large inverted cone made of unattributed Mana swirling above Grimmar who had collapsed onto all fours. As he watched, the smell of rot and taste of corruption nearly overpowered his senses, and Felix knew the stench. It was tainted blood Mana. And it wasn't coming from Grimmar.

It was coming from the corpses all around them.

"We need to run," Felix insisted, moving faster and trying to keep his breathing even. It hurt enough that it was blazing past his Pain Resistance almost completely. At least whatever else that had torn inside him was patching up; he didn't feel leaky anymore.

"What's happening? What's he doing?" Magda asked as they quickly approached Callie. The blonde woman answered instead, brow furrowed and jaw clenched.

"Blood magic. Fuck."

Suddenly, blood rose from the corpses of the dozens of Risi Warriors that surrounded the wounded chieftain. It drifted up into the sky and was sucked into a tornado of blood, spinning around until it funneled directly into Grimmar's open mouth.

"Shiiit," said Magda. They moved faster.

Felix's chest was in agony, but he didn't slow down. The similarities between Grimmar and the Seven-Legged Orit were suddenly clear, his strange mind drawing immediate parallels between their words and actions. But it wasn't fear of the giant's blood magic that propelled Felix forward, it was the fact that the smell of it, the awful rotten sickness scent of it, was making him hungry.

Once they got passed Grimmar's ice wall, Felix could see the survivors up ahead. They were battling four Risi Warriors, all of them engaged by the powerful giants' attacks. Whispering a sudden curse, Callie zipped forward with outrageous speed, appearing as if by magic behind the Risi Warriors. Her single dagger flared with power as she stabbed, once, twice, three times. The giants fell like puppets with their strings cut, and Callie dropped to the ground some distance away, clearly exhausted.

Magda rushed forward, Felix close behind. She aimed a shield bash at the last giant, knocking them back and providing an opportunity for the short guy with two swords to run him through.

"Why'd you do that?" she asked, looking at Callie on the ground.

"Gotta...gotta be quick," Callie huffed, clearly spent. She looked up at Magda. "Got any extra?"

"Just one. How many've you had already?"

"Two."

"That'll barely put a dent in it," Magda started, but Callie held up her hand.

"It'll let me run, and won't slow you down," Callie panted. Magda reached into one of the two potions cases on her belt and pulled out a small vial of yellow liquid. She handed it to Callie, who immediately knocked it back.

"You folks ready? We gotta go now," Felix insisted, turning toward the other survivors who appeared close to breaking through the ice. "Hey you need help or—"

Felix's senses went haywire as a presence gathered behind him.

He threw himself forward, landing on his chest with a pained grunt, but avoiding the ten foot length of sword that hurled where his head once was.

A short scream cut off, but the pain made Felix's eyes go watery. All he saw was red blood pooling ahead of him. With extreme effort, he rolled onto his side, but before he could get up, he saw a nightmare looming above him. Grimmar stood there, but it wasn't Grimmar, not any more. Still huge, but red corruption poured from his body like smoke, and his eyes were completely black. Sharp teeth jutted out of his face, sticking out at strange angles and varying length; it was the jaw of some sort of deep sea monstrosity. Its face was torn all around the mouth and cheeks, as if it split apart when the extra teeth grew in.

Felix's mind seized as the creature stared down at him. The presence of its Mana alone was pressing him into the ice, and that was only compacted when Grimmar grabbed him by the shirt and *pushed*.

"*Aggh!*"

"Such sweet mewling cries," the thing that was Grimmar said, it's voice guttural and strange. It spoke like it had three voices, each a slightly different pitch. "Almost a song, you might say."

"Fuck off!" Above Felix, the massive greatsword Grimmar had thrown was used against him. Magda swung it horizontally, but Grimmar simply held out a hand and deflected the blow. Then he grabbed her by the arm and threw her behind him. Then with a wave of his hand, Grimmar summoned another wave of Mana that crashed against the others.

Magda disappeared from Felix's field of vision, but his ears picked up a distant crash around forty feet away. Of the other survivors, he heard nothing.

Holy shit, he's strong. Felix's thoughts raced through his pain, trying to come up with anything.

"I should thank you, boy. You have given me cause to use this form, a blessing from the Mother." The toothy maw of the giant loomed forward, his hot breath reeking of corruption and rot. "A piece of the Song, handed down Champion to Champion, waiting for the day it could be reunited in our flesh." A dark, snaking tongue slithered from Grimmar's now cavernous mouth.

"You look...like shit," Felix painfully laughed.

"Disrespectful til the end, aren't you?" Grimmar spat in his face, tongue lolling. Then, he gripped his chest in a single fist and lifted Felix up into the air. Felix screamed in pain, his vision almost whiting out from the intensity of it. Dimly, Felix could hear shouts and the clatter of metal, but for a moment, none of it mattered. Only the pain.

He came to not far from where they started, the giant simply striding farther toward the back end of the building. Felix's breath came in short, excruciating gasps.

Status Condition: Broken Ribs (x3)

Oh...great...

The giant was speaking, and had been for a while, Felix assumed.

"—bask forevermore in Her glory. I—" Grimmar stopped speaking abruptly, and Felix swiveled his head to see the giant's ruined face. His expression was...rapturous. Disgustingly so. "Yes!

Your Will be done, Song of Songs!" Grimmar adjusted his grip on him, easing pressure off Felix's damaged ribs. He looked into the young man's eyes, his black orbs eerie in the pale light of his elemental shards. "You've been chosen, boy. A great honor, whispered to me by the Mother Herself."

The giant scoffed, but his teeth made the sound wet and sloppy. "I do not dare oppose her will, as much as I'd like to crush your pathetic skull. Still," he mused, placing a meaty hand on either of Felix's arms. "She did not require you to be whole."

Felix was given no time to respond before Grimmar began to pull. White hot pain splintered up his arms, muscles tearing and bones creaking audibly. He screamed.

REIGN OF VELLUS!

Blue lightning arced out of him, dancing across Felix's body and Grimmar's too, but the giant didn't flinch, barely moved at all. The azure lightning, the kinetic force itself, was drawn like a magnet directly into the giant's fanged mouth. Felix's eyes widened. Grimmar laughed, even as he pulled excruciatingly slowly on Felix's limbs.

"So stupid, little fawn. The Mother has made me perfect. A true predator, I do not simply eat. I devour!"

A red and black blur flashed across Felix's vision, and Grimmar screamed. Felix fell to the ground, just barely able to land on his feet though his arms felt torn and useless. He looked up, just in time to see a dog-sized tenku clawing at the giant's face.

"*Pit!*"

The little chimera furiously slashed at Grimmar's head, and the giant sported a large gash across his left eye where dark sclera ran like pus down his face. Still screaming, Grimmar caught Pit by the tail and threw him to the ground. The ice beneath the tenku shattered, cracking in a wide radius.

"No!" Felix rushed over, utilizing Relentless Charge to appear next to his Companion. Felix tried to grab his friend, but couldn't get his hands to close properly around him. The chimera seemed dazed, and though he lifted his head, Pit seemed unable to move his legs for some reason. Felix toggled Pit's status and saw his friend's Health had dropped to barely above 10%.

The ground shook. Felix looked up at Grimmar, who approached slowly. His left eye was a ruin, and his right eye stared with terrible intent.

"Vile chimeras. Worth less than Humans," the elemental shards above Grimmar's head shimmered with purple-white light as an nebulous sphere of ice Mana appeared in the giant's right hand. "You want to save the boy? Fine! Then you both die!"

A wave of familiar, malicious energy burst from the giant, massive spears exploding in a line toward them.

"*Force Wall!*"

A bubble of yellow energy appeared around them, and Felix had only a bare moment to see that Magda, bleeding and half frozen, had placed herself in the path of the giant's spell.

Then the wave hit.

The three of them were sent flying, bursting through the open doors at the back of the chamber and shattering a portion of the wooden scaffolding before shooting straight out into the air.

Then they dropped into the abyss.

CHAPTER SIXTY-THREE

He was still.

Small and still and hidden. But it wasn't enough.

Something moved, an undulation through thick waters. Too many appendages flicking, twitching. They circled him.

They were close.

He was seen.

Felix woke to darkness.

It wasn't complete, some dim glowing lights he couldn't place proliferated from a low angle, but all he saw was blue-grey mist on black.

Mist? Felix blinked, but the fog didn't dissipate or fade into static. The space above him was absolutely thick with it. He tried to activate his Manasight but...it was already on.

What's going—uunf.

When he tried to lift his head, an awful spasm of pain rippled through his body, and Felix was suddenly reminded how he had gotten here. He had fallen.

Into the sinkhole.

Oh damn. Oh shit am I...? He tried moving his arms and legs, which was like unblocking a dam as a flood of awful sensations rushed into him at once. Shoulder muscles torn, joints yanked and strained, his forearms were bruised and cut, and his ribs...they were sharp daggers in his side. Worse than the gritty grinding of the bones in his chest, worse even than the lightning and flame of his abused muscles and lacerated flesh: the hunger had returned.

It came roaring back to life, an empty gnawing that felt like a creature was eating him from the inside out. Felix felt the beast in his gut actively steal his strength as he attempted to sit up; instead he only managed a weak flop which upset his delicate balance on whatever rock was beneath him. He slid sideways from it, landing onto moss-covered stone.

Felix could see more of the area at this angle, and he looked to be on a stone pathway, covered in moss and punctuated by odd standing stones. Nearby, to either side of him and close enough that they didn't fade entirely into the fog, there loomed sheer walls. They faded into misty darkness only fifty or so feet up. Faint swirling marks etched into the rocks he could see, twisty and convoluted enough that he found looking at them hurt after too long. He blinked and turned his head away, still stifling the growing pains in his body, and his eyes fell on the raised platform he had fallen off: it was Magda.

She was face-up, her arms and legs splayed to the side, and her armor was battered all to hell. Her eyes were closed, but after a panicked moment Felix realized she was breathing...barely. Despite feeling like he was going to shatter at any moment, Felix nudged himself just a bit closer, reaching a shaking hand out to nudge her. All he managed was a light touch, barely pushing against her arm.

Wait, I was on top of her? He realized. *Then she..?* She had saved him. Cushioned his fall with her own body and powers, just like before. *She jumped in front of that Mana wave. If she hadn't, I would've died. Guaranteed. And Pit...*Pit! Shock surged through him as he remembered his friend, even as shame wormed across his mind for forgetting. Unable to move well, even to properly lift his head and look around, Felix instead sent a questing sensation through their bond.

It was faint, but tiny reverberations echoed between them, resounding in his mind more than his ears. Flexing his Willpower and Pain Resistance, Felix dragged himself toward the echo, his body rioting. There. Just beyond the nearest standing stone, he saw a black paw. The paw twitched, and a wet nose quivered forward.

He's alive! Felix breathed, even though his ribs stabbed at him with every inhalation. *Is he hurt?* Unable to fully see him, Felix instead focused on their connection, searching for anything wrong with his Companion. It wasn't something he'd done before, but the fearsome need he felt drove his instincts, and after a brief resistance, he was met with a series of distinct...concepts, he guessed. Self-contained images that also held limited sensations like touch, taste, scent, and of course pain. A lot of pain.

Oh buddy. Pit's hip was sprained, if not broken, as were his two front legs and right wing. He was in an excruciating amount of pain. Felix wasn't sure what had happened, but either Magda hadn't been able to shield him completely, or he'd tried to slow his fall with his wings. Felix's own memories blanked out somewhere during that fall, despite his perfect recall; that must mean they hit *something* and got knocked out.

Felix looked up again, trying and failing to pierce through the gloom. For all he could tell, they were beneath a starless night sky. But if that were true, then the sun should be up, right? *How long have we been out?* A sudden thrill of fear raced up his agonized spine. *Are the giants coming?*

Heart hammering, Felix couldn't make out a single sound, other than a soft breeze brushing against rock and moss. He swallowed, the act as painful as everything else, and marshaled his thoughts. He only had one path forward, and that was to advance his formation. It had saved his ass in the past. He took a deep breath, and toggled open his neglected notifications.

Dodge is level 25!
Acrobatics is level 25!
Sigils of the Primordial Dawn is level 5!
Exploration is level 22!
Analyze is level 24!
Deep Mind is level 25!
Bastion of Will is level 32!
Armored Skin is level 25!
Shadow Whip is level 24!
Relentless charge is level 5!
Make An Entrance is level 10!
Intimidation is level 8!
Running is level 20!

Cold Resistance is level 17!
Dual Casting is level 19!
Acting is level 10!
Influence of the Wisp is level 25!
Corrosive Strike is level 24!
Unarmed Mastery is level 25!
Pain Resistance is level 31!
Blind Fighting is level 20!
Manasight is level 32!
Companion Pact is level 17!
Reign of Vellus is level 27!

"H-holy hell," Felix breathed. The rush of subtle knowledge, usual with each rank up in a Skill, was a torrent. His neck and back muscles screamed in pain as Felix convulsed, his mind near to bursting with unrestrained knowledge, concepts, and the strange system-given muscle memory. They faded, drifting even from his prodigious mind, leaving his head spinning with the vague residue of a series of notes, chords, string strummed like a sun setting beyond the horizon.

Then his core spasmed. A horrific pain many times the magnitude of his previous agony, dwarfing the ache of his shredded shoulders and broken ribs. The music *distorted*, the chords going minor like a mournful howl, and a deep gnawing ache that was so strong and alien that for a moment he couldn't identify it. It was the hunger, primal and utterly contemptuous of his Pain Resistance.

—Apprentice Tier in Dodge!
You Gain The Following:
+3 to AGL...

No! He fumbled at his waist, hands clumsy and numb, that faint pain still skittering down his arms. Then he noticed it.

His satchel was gone.

FUCK!

...
+3 to DEX
+3 to END

Felix felt a surge of power, that same rising concerto that marked all of his stat gains. Energy poured into him from the System, burning through his pathways as even this minor boost remade him in subtle ways.

Clarity came shortly after.

Damn it! With no Essence Draught in him, he had wasted the gains from Dodge. *Where did it go?*

It was nowhere to be found, the ground around him only studded with stones, mist, and moss. He must have lost it in the fall. He grimaced, the flare of pain through his core spearing upward like hell's heartburn. *What the hell* is *this?!* This couldn't be normal. This wasn't...he wasn't....

Magda shifted slightly, still unconscious, and Felix's eyes were drawn inexplicably to a rent in her armor. It exposed her neck, and his Perception keyed into the flush there, the thready beat of erratic heartsblood, pumping along her sturdy flesh.

—Tier in Acrobatics!
You Gain the—

The Mana she uses to generate those shields is strong. Her Skills must be...powerful. It would be worth it...right?

She wouldn't feel a thing.

+5 DEX
+5 AGL
+3 PER

"AHH!" Another pulse of power, injected straight into his soul, and the sudden burst weakened the hold of whatever had just grabbed him. "What the fuck was that?" Felix felt Bastion of Will fortify his mind, pushing at the hunger that even now reached for him with greedy tendrils. "What the *fuck* was that?" He found himself only inches away from Magda's bare throat, and Felix threw himself violently away.

Injured, he only managed to push himself as far as Magda's waist, where he scrabbled against her armor, kicking his legs to put as much distance between him and that potentially fatal mistake. As he did, his eyes landed on Magda's belt and the *two* potions cases she had strapped there. And though it was scuffed and battered, he instantly recognized the bright metal buckles and expensively inscribed leather. *Vessilia's potion case! Then that means—!*

With zero hesitation, Felix grabbed it and yanked it off the warrior's belt, the clasp breaking and sending bits of metal pinging off into the darkness. He unclasped the top and threw it open. Immediately, the ambient Mana in the area began to gather and roil, drawn toward the jewel bright vials of a ducal heir's personal Essence Draught stash.

Congratulations! You Have Reached Apprentice Tier in Deep Mind!
You Gain The Following:

With nothing more than a perfunctory Analyze, Felix grabbed the first Mind draught and slugged it back.

+10 ALA
+10 RES
+...
Rare Essence Draught Detected During Formation!
[Draught Essence of Clarity]

Choose a Feature:
Precision
Purity
Incarnation

What do these even mean? As with the poison, Felix found himself at a loss on what to choose. *Precision is important for survival. I have a few ranged abilities. Purity...not so much. Incarnation? What would that even be good for?* Felix fumbled with indecision, though something told him he only had finite time here. He hovered over Precision for a moment, feeling 98% sure in the decision...but swerved at the last second and made his choice.

Congratulations!
You have absorbed the Essence of Incarnation!

A spear of pain thrust through his mind and body, but after everything, it felt like being stabbed after a car crash. It still hurt, but his body couldn't even focus on it. Electricity rolled across his ribs and hips and shoulders, crackling along his broken bones like salt in a wound, until finally it buried itself in his skull. Felix dropped forward onto his hands, his body still mostly prone.

Holy shit, he panted. *I've gotta do that...three more times?!*

Grunting with effort but finding his body moving somewhat better than before, Felix reached into Vessilia's case and pulled out three more Essence Draughts. Two Body and a Spirit.

Felix felt the rising rush of his next Apprentice Tier Skill, and he gritted his teeth as he tossed back another draught. This one was thick and earthy, with a tang to it like copper.

Congratulations! You Have Reached Apprentice Tier in Armored Skin!
You Gain The Following:
+5 VIT
+5 END
+...
Rare Essence Draught Detected During Formation!
[Draught Essence of Orichalcum]

Choose a Feature:
Mountain
Red-Gold
Unforged

Again with unhelpful choices. Felix frowned. *Orichalcum is a metal right? Mythical. Mountain sounds strong. Red-Gold sounds weirdly specific. Unforged seems bad...unforged metal is just scrap, isn't it? This is my Body, I don't want an Unforged Body.*

Felix chose, once again following his gut.

Congratulations!
You have absorbed the Essence of Mountain!

More pain, more strange and minute changes to his body. Something was happening but he couldn't track what. By the end of it, he felt sturdier somehow, stronger maybe. And, mother of mercy, his ribs didn't hurt anymore.

Only a thousand other pains left. He tipped the next draught into his mouth, grimacing at the scorching heat of it.

Congratulations! You Have Reached Apprentice Tier in Influence of the Wisp!
You Gain The Following:
+5 WIL
+5 INT
+...
Rare Essence Draught Detected During Formation!
[Draught Essence of Dragon's Fire]

Choose a Feature:
Immolation
Fervor
Rage

Now these *are some options!* Felix found it in himself to rejoice before paling. *Immolation is...isn't that when people set themselves on fire? Fervor is intense passion and Rage...do I want either of those as a basis for my Spirit? Whatever that even means?*

Felix mashed his selection. *I hope this is the right one!*

Congratulations!
You have absorbed the Essence of Immolation!

A wave of heat burned through him, but it wasn't painful this time, just intensely uncomfortable. The burning spun and coiled up into his chest, just above his core.

One...more!

Felix was dripping sweat, his body visibly steaming in the chill mist, his arms and legs shaking uncontrollably. He wasn't sure if taking this many Essences at once was a good idea. Did Harn mention that? Did he ask? Felix shook his head, banishing distractions as he mustered his strength and raised the last vial to his lips. He glanced over at Magda.

And met her eyes, wide open and staring at him.

Oh shit.

Congratulations! You Have Reached Apprentice Tier in Unarmed Mastery!
You—

"Do it," she whispered, just at the edge of his hearing. Her voice was rough, somehow burred and pinched at the same time. "Do it, you fool."

Felix didn't need any more encouragement. He quaffed it.

+5 STR
+...
Rare Essence Draught Detected During Formation!
[Draught Essence of Wind's Grace]

Choose a Feature:
Liberation
Intangibility
Breath

The energy was building up in him even before he could select an Essence, a billowing power that made it hard to focus. His core flared, while that constant hunger ripped at his guts like a cat in a bag, desperate to be released. Felix pushed it down, harder and harder, until it all gave way. *Focus.* Focus!

Choose!

Felix slammed his choice, and his world spun away into oblivion.

Chitinous legs clacked in the dark, while hooked limbs swam the brackish waters.

"You're almost there, Felix."

Pale eyes watched him.

"Don't give up yet."

A slap to his face woke him up.

. . .

"Uagh!" He shouted, half sitting up and throwing his hands over his head. When more hits didn't follow, he risked a glance.

Magda half stood, half leaned against one of the standing stones next to him, smiling wearily with a grim sort of humor. "No more sleeping, princess."

"I wasn't sleeping, I was...my Formation!" Felix quickly brought up his notifications. He'd missed the last bit when he passed out.

Congratulations!
You have absorbed the Essence of Liberation!
3 of 3 Body Essences Formed!
Tempering Has Begun!

"Tempering has begun? What's that mean, exactly?" Felix asked, risking a look up at Magda.

"Your Body?"

"Yeah," Felix said.

She swallowed, then hobbled a few steps back.

"Brace yourself, kid."

Felix heard a rising chord, a deep basso strum that rolled over him like a wave. His skin crackled and tightened, while his muscles and very bones began to quiver inside of him. He bent over and hurled up his breakfast, his sick coming in waves of bile, while his joints swelled and popped, snapping into strange angles. His teeth ached, some hidden pitch shaking his nerves in his body, destroying them and remaking them all at once. He thought he screamed, but wasn't sure. Then a foul muck poured from his gullet, and he didn't care. His only thought was ridding himself of the stinking corruption that poured all over the mossy stone beneath him.

Five minutes and an eternity later, he collapsed.

"Siva's breath, that's a lot of impurities, Felix," Magda sounded impressed, if tired. "Ugh, now I have to fish you out."

Felix barely listened, his body still humming at a pitch his ears could barely recognize. Notifications streamed before him.

Congratulations!
You Have Tempered Your Body!

You Have Formed: the Moving Mountain Body
+10 STR
+10 END
+5 AGL
+5 DEX
+15 VIT

"C'mon, up you get. You can finish resolving your Temper on the way." Felix felt Magda grab him and haul him up, grunting with effort. "Seven Hells, you got heavy. What kinda Body did you Form?"

Felix didn't answer, at first distracted by the chiming that slowly faded from his ears, and then by the soft whimper of a dear friend.

"Pit!" Felix ran to where the tenku was laying, still hurt. Pit's gold eyes looked up at him, wide and wet, and his bird beak opened in a soft caw. "Oh buddy, how do I—? The potion case!"

Felix stumbled over to the case, which had been closed and latched again, probably by Magda. He flung it open and rooted out a single red Health Potion. Seconds later, he was back at Pit's side, carefully pouring the liquid down his Companion's throat.

"There you go. It'll be ok," Felix pet the side of Pit's head, skritching his feathers in that way he liked. Felix watched Pit's Health jump up nearly a hundred points, putting him at over 50%. Some gross twisting and cracking sounded out in the dark corridor as bones and muscles realigned in the chimera's legs. His wing, however, was still bent unnaturally.

"We have to go, Felix. That light show you put on will have attracted visitors, and I don't know how close the giants are, either." Magda's face was drawn as she looked up into the darkness. "This place is...it's bad. It's very bad."

So Felix scooped up his friend and turned to the Silver Rank.

"Alright. Where to?"

CHAPTER SIXTY-FOUR

The wind blew hard across the desolate city, though it barely moved the heavy fog that clung to its streets. The sun had risen an hour ago, filling the sky with jeweled tones and providing much needed light for his warriors. Grimmar stared once more into the sinkhole, the entrance to the Holy Depths less than a mile below.

So close, but...

"Lord Champion," a youthful voice said from behind him. Grimmar turned and beheld a youngling, kin barely grown into his beard but wearing the armor of a Warrior proudly. The youngling flinched when he noticed Grimmar's regard.

"Does something trouble you, warrior?" Grimmar said through his teeth. He knew exactly why the youngling flinched, why most of his warriors no longer would meet their chieftain's eyes. *They are in awe of the gift She has given. In awe of* me.

"No, Lord Champion. I have come to tell you that we have found traces of the escaped prisoners." He all but quivered with relief as he finished. Grimmar burst into a delighted laugh, which only grew stronger when he noticed the youngling cower.

"Excellent! And the Angry One?"

"Her body was not found. All signs point to her being with them."

Grimmar clapped his hands, a rush of powerful wind expelled by the motion. "Then we begin. Send half our warriors and all of the Circle to find the prisoners. If they cannot be returned, kill them all. The rest shall come with me."

"W-with you, my lord?" The youngling's voice cracked, and Grimmar decided to give him an encouraging smile.

"Into the Labyrinth. We seek the center. No matter the cost."

Grimmar turned away, already contemplating the descent. He did not see the youngling's face pale at his smile, but he could smell the fear in his blood.

It smelled delicious.

As they ran, Felix kept toggling his notifications.

Your Companion Pit Has Gained A Level!
+2 VIT! +2 PER! +4 AGL! +4 DEX! +3 WIL! +1 END! +2 INT!
Pit's Bite is level 18!
Pit's Rake is level 20!
Pit's Skulk is level 25!

Pit's Skulk Has Reached Apprentice Tier!
Your Companion Gains:
+5 PER
+5 AGL
+5 DEX

Energy swelled within his Companion's form as power from the System poured into him. This close, Felix felt the vibrations of a song blare out before fading to silence, like triumphant horns. Fascinated, Felix focused on the sensation, both with his eyes and the unique pact sense buried in his chest. Pit relaxed in his arms as the energy soothed away his remaining hurts, the stat bumps fuel to the fires of his regeneration. Felix had always healed a touch faster after leveling, so it was the same with his friend.

Companion Pact is level 18!

That wing is gonna be a problem, though. It hadn't healed much, though it didn't appear to be bleeding anymore. Felix imagined they should set it or something, but he didn't have the foggiest idea on how to do field medicine. He decided to keep an eye out for herbs or something that might help, though he felt that was a long shot.

Focusing on Pit was a good distraction for Felix, because Magda pushed them at a punishing pace, intending to put as much distance between them and the giants as possible. It had been at least an hour so far, and he kept up easily enough, but that wasn't the issue. A storm of energy still raged in his belly, flaring around his core and traveling in uncomfortable flashes to each of his limbs at random. When he stumbled for the third time, she explained.

"You're feelin' the after-effects of Tempering your Body," she said as they navigated a path densely coated with half-burned inscriptions. They were traps, his Analyze said, and those he could see were all discharged. Magda continued, "You get decent gains dependin' on the type of Body you Form, but it's almost *always* an upgrade. So what your feelin' is your new Body beginning to work for the first time. You're like a...really strong baby."

Felix huffed a laugh, easily done through the low-level pain. He'd experienced worse only a half hour ago. "Big, strong baby body, that's an image."

Magda flashed him a grin. "Honestly, I'm kinda jealous at what sorta boost you got from those Rare Essence Draughts."

"They're better than Iron, yeah?" Felix asked.

"Definitely better. But not in the way you might think. It's more about particulars. The Essences offered by the higher-rarity draughts are obscure, arcane, and specific. Iron Draughts woulda gotten you something like Hard or Unforged, both of which are common enough to metal Essences, if broad and general."

"Hey," Felix said, hoisting Pit farther up his shoulder. He was getting *big*. "Unforged was one of my options for the Orichalcum draught."

"Sure. It's a metal. They all got things in common. But the difference between iron and somethin' like orichalcum is great, so you'd still have gotten a better boost." She paused, her torn armor creaking as she shifted her weight and hopped off a small stone ledge. It was a five foot drop, and the path continued onward. Another trap, already set off. "If you don't mind me askin', did you pick that one?"

"Nah. Picked Mountain." Felix half shrugged, careful not to

disturb his sleeping Companion as he also hopped down. "Unforged sounded bad."

Magda coughed and held up a hand for a break. They stopped, leaning against a wall covered in withered plant-life. Ten seconds later she looked back up and nodded. They started up again. "Unforged isn't bad. It's about potential. Iron can be made into passable weapons and armor, perhaps great if a powerful Smith was involved. Orichalcum is used to build city walls and magical weapons. They're not in the same league."

Felix considered that as they kept moving. It made sense, as a higher rarity generally meant an increase in value, at least in the games on Earth. *Interesting that there could be the same Essences for different draughts. The quality of materials affected the result apparently, orichalcum over iron for instance. How did alchemy get involved?* He itched to find out more about that particular skill set, the idea of mixing potions and powers a strong draw, but he shook off the impulse. That was for another time. If they survived.

"Felix," Magda said as she slowed her pace to a fast walk. She turned to look at him, as he walked slightly behind and to her left. "Don't push yourself too hard. You're gonna feel some...backlash from using those Rare Essences."

"Backlash?" Felix asked, sending his senses inward. Other than the intermittent pulses of pain from his core, what she had termed the resolution of his Body Formation, he felt nothing was amiss. Interestingly enough, his hunger had faded as well, having become nothing more than a faint ache in his gut ever since he'd completed his Temper. *Why is that? What exactly is this hunger?*

"Rare Essences take more of a toll on a body than Common or Uncommon Essences. Somethin' about higher concentrations of Mana." Magda shrugged but sent a concerned glance his way. "You might feel more than twinges soon."

Felix frowned at that, but kept moving. "I'll deal with it."

They ran onward.

After a half hour of traveling, he couldn't really determine if they were any closer to getting out. Since they couldn't go back up the scaffolding, the two of them were forced deeper into the Labyrinth. However, Felix had expected more danger and resistance than what they had experienced. The Labyrinth was desolate, picked clean as far as he could tell. The dark was nearly complete, his Manasight not nearly as useful as it was on the surface, and the only light was from glowing lichen and an odd glow from the fog itself. They hadn't heard the sound of pursuit, but even now the giants could be barreling toward them and Felix wouldn't know until they were on top of them.

If this is what everyone had to deal with all the time on the surface, no wonder they were so jumpy. His nerves felt frayed with anxiety, but the quivers and pangs of his newly-Formed Body weren't helping. Admittedly, Felix was thrilled with his new Body, the name alone had the ring of something extraordinary. *Moving Mountain Body*, he mused as he climbed atop a series of standing stones, following Magda's lead. *Vessilia wasn't messing around with those Rare Essence Draughts. I feel so much stronger than before...sturdier, too.* His body hadn't seemed to have changed physically; Felix still felt he looked the same, it was just the power within his muscles had increased dramatically. *Those stat boosts from Forming this new Body were wild. What will happen when my Mind and Spirit Form?*

Despite the danger they were in, he was excited to find out.

Running is level 21!

After another two hours, they came to a circular room, as Felix came to think of these places. There were long passages and discrete rooms in this maze, and it honestly matched his idea of what a maze would be: high stone walls, twisty turns, even a few dead ends. This circular room was an interruption in the path, with one entrance and three exits in various directions. Magda chose to lean against the far wall, near the exit opposite where they entered, and slowly slid to the ground. The fog flowed through the room, filling it with a slight glow that made it both easier and harder to see.

"Rest up. Ten minutes," she half muttered, her eyes closing almost immediately.

Felix was surprised. The shield warrior was usually more tireless than this, though she had been pushing them hard. The pain of his Tempering had faded to almost nothing, just the occasional twinge in his calf or forearm, and Felix felt bursting with energy. His Stamina regeneration had jumped up, and with the Running Skill hitting level 21, his Stamina usage had declined dramatically when all they were doing was running.

Attempting to make use of the break, he did a round of

stretches that Harn had taught him, bending his legs, arms, and hips. His new Body might be strong, but he had no idea what to expect until they actually got into a fight, and a pulled muscle could spell doom for him and Pit. Magda too, probably.

She seems hurt. Weakened, somehow. Felix looked up, back toward the way they came. *What happened to her up there?*

Pit was feeling better, so Felix asked him to keep watch on the path back, which the tenku did with a huff of annoyance. *Remember, Pit. If you see someone, send me a message this way, then run to me as fast as you can. Got it?* Felix received a warm assent that felt like a beak nudging against his leg, for all that Pit was over forty feet away by then. *Companion Pact is such a cool Skill.* It was getting closer to Apprentice Tier, and Felix hoped they gained another benefit, as they had at level 10.

He took the time and contemplated the Skill within his core, trying to reach some sort of new understanding. Magda roused before he was able to do much, however. Felix got to his feet, calling Pit over with a brief pulse of intent through their pact, and the tenku obediently trotted their way.

"He's different," Magda said from behind Felix. He turned and raised an eyebrow at her.

"He's grown an inch or so," Felix agreed. Magda waved her hand.

"No, he looks different. I didn't notice when you had him in your arms. He's not as...blurry. He had four eyes before, and now I only see two. And his wings..." Magda scratched her head and blinked a couple times, as if she wasn't believing what she was seeing.

Holy shit, Felix had a hunch. "What does he look like now?"

Magda frowned. "Like a bird and a fox had a weird baby. His wings look like normal bird wings now."

"Up on the surface, I'm pretty sure he was being affected by whatever illusion made the fog. It made him seem scarier, from what I could tell, which made others attack him," Felix explained. "This is what he normally looks like. What he's always looked like to me."

Magda tapped her chin. "Then the spell that makes the Foglands the Foglands isn't in effect here. Why?" Her eyes lit up, suddenly transforming her entire tired face. "The artifact. We were right. It's down here, negating the power of the illusion."

Felix's eyes widened. He'd forgotten about the artifact. It wasn't important anyway, not to him. *He* could see just fine in the Foglands.

"Tch, damn. Still no Analyze, though." Magda grunted, and Felix's eyes widened. He hadn't thought of that.

That's lucky for me. No illusion, but still interference. Why?

Magda seemed charged with a new energy, moving quickly to the nearest passage off the circular room. "Since we can't go back, and we can't climb out, our only option is to move forward. Deeper."

Felix nodded. They had learned that early when Magda attempted to scale one of the impossibly high walls. She had done just fine up until the fog completely obscured her, then she described the wall as becoming slick and impossible to hold onto. They assumed it was a spell of some sort, though Felix's Manasight wasn't able to pick up anything from them.

"And what will we find when we go deeper?" Felix asked, worried he already knew the answer. "I don't imagine it'll be puppies and rainbows. Not if the giants were after it."

Magda frowned. "All I know is that Callie said it was something bad. Something that spooked even her, and she's one of the toughest people I know. She figured it had to do with the artifact, though. Could be if we find the artifact and destroy it, then this entire place stops functioning. Then we can escape."

"That reminds me, how is this spell still working? Haven't the Foglands been like this forever?"

"Not forever, but for the past two Ages, yes, as far as we can tell. Haarwatch has only existed for a few hundred years, barely a blip compared to some places on the Continent." Magda ran full out through the empty corridors, Felix pushing himself to keep pace despite his Agility almost reaching 100. *Her Running Skill must be sky high!*

"Right, so this spell might have been around since the...Second Age?" Felix asked, innocently as he could.

"What?" Magda panted and gave him a brief look. "No, the Third Age."

So that means it's the Fifth Age now. "But that means this spell has been running for...?"

"Two thousand years, give or take a few centuries," Magda shrugged, her damaged armor squealing slightly. "That's why I think this artifact must be powering it. It's probably a Mana Battery of some kind. Some Nymean ruins had things like that, fist-sized objects that drew in ambient Mana to power simple workings."

"But this spell is the size of the entire Foglands. How big is that? How much Mana would that require for two thousand years?" Felix's mind boggled at the numbers he was hearing, even as he grew excited at the knowledge.

"Big. No one's been able to map the Foglands before. So this artifact is gonna be huge, maybe the size of a building or a ship." Magda shook her head and grit her teeth. "At least it won't be hard to find," she grunted.

Felix hoped not.

Another thirty minutes passed this way, with Magda taking the left tunnel at each intersection.

As obviously dangerous as this place was, Felix was continually surprised at the amount of death and destruction he encountered. The walls were scorched, pierced, and liquefied in spots where deadly traps had triggered, and they found bits and pieces of humanoid bodies scattered all around. It was clear that the imprisoned Guilders had died over and over to push this far into the Labyrinth. The only upside, as far as Felix was concerned, was that they hadn't encountered a single armed trap themselves.

Pit was feeling better, at least able enough to run on his own. They made better time that way, and unburdened Felix was able to truly feel his new Body in motion. The ease of movement was exhilarating, each step smoother than before, an explosive power in his muscles that had not been there previously. With Magda in the lead and Pit taking up the rear, Felix let himself revel in the sensation.

That, of course, was when he stepped into the trap.

They had entered a "T" shaped room, two twenty-foot-wide corridors set perpendicular to each other, the walls carved with the same flowing, intersecting lines as always. The floor was dressed fieldstone, big, rough blocks of blue-grey stone placed into the ground in whatever combination fit, and half of it was coated in a thick moss. As Felix stepped on an innocuous stone, he heard a terrifying clicking noise, likely the last thing many prisoners had heard in this life.

Then the wall beside him exploded in green fire. He was hurled sideways.

"Aah-!" Felix howled, cut short by a sudden impact into the far wall. The wall gave slightly as a deep crack formed in the stone, and Felix fell heavily to the ground.

Fire Resistance is level 19!

"Felix! Get up!" Magda shouted from what seemed a very far distance away, but Felix's vision was blurry and his ears were ringing. A sense of alarm and fury radiated into his chest. Then the clash of steel and low-pitched snarls pushed past the buzzing in his ears. With a snap, his vision and hearing refocused, and Felix came to his feet.

Nearby, Magda was fighting two huge serpents, each the size of a school bus and made of a solidified green fire. She blocked and smashed at them with her shields, but they were strong, and between the two of them, they were wearing down her shields quickly. Pit was launching Frost Spears at them from a distance, but the ice was melting before it hit their fiery hides, doing only minimal damage. Since she was tanking both of them, Magda kept getting in Felix's line of sight, so he gathered himself and rushed into battle.

Relentless Charge!
Mantle of the Long Night!

Felix blasted forward, ripping up the moss between him and the monsters in a wave of concussive force. He moved faster than ever, appearing before one of the two serpents almost as if he had teleported. Without hesitation, Felix let loose his aura skill, hoping his ice might have more benefit than Pit's. A wave of freezing wind radiated outward from Felix, spinning in a ten foot radius and instantly coating the moss beneath his feet with a layer of frost. He heard Magda curse slightly, but didn't have time to apologize for catching her in the radius. The serpent struck.

Corrosive Strike!

Meeting its darting head with his own fist, Felix watched almost in slow motion as the emerald flames dimmed within his aura, leaving it vulnerable as his acid-coated fists clobbered the serpent right in the snout. Its face crumpled, burning blood squirting in all directions as he broke the skin and cartilage that made up this nightmare beast. He threw Analyze at it.

Name: Greenfyre Serpent
Type: Elemental
Level: 30
HP: 735/981
SP: 555/562
MP: 156/234
Lore: Composed of poisonous flame, the Greenfyre Serpent is dangerous to engage in melee. Attack from a distance.
Strength: AGL, DEX
Weakness: INT, WIL

Already committed to his actions, Felix shrugged off the warning and waded in with another three strikes.

Corrosive Strike!
Corrosive Strike!
Corrosive Strike!

The serpent's head snapped back each time, more and more of its burning blood launching up into the air and sizzled against its own flames. His Mantle was hurting it more than his unarmed attacks, so Felix took a chance and dropped his fists. The serpent immediately struck, flinging its wide open mouth in the Nymean's direction.

Moments before its maw snapped closed, Felix put a hand on the upper and lower jaw, stopping the beast in its tracks. With a burst of Willpower, he flared his Mantle, shaping its effect directly into the serpent's open mouth. Not all of the aura moved how he wanted it, but his 182 Willpower was not to be denied, and most of it shaped into a wide blast of icy wind. A flare of purple-white light went off above Felix's left shoulder, and the Serpent's green flames flickered and died in seconds.

Mantle of the Long Night is level 11!
Mantle of the Long Night is level 12!

Its body fell limply to the ground, now a dark, burnished brown. Felix panted lightly, surprised at how easily it died. He turned and saw Magda still using her shield to bash her opponent senseless, its body-fire guttering. As he watched, the Greenfyre Serpent reared back and struck, lightning quick, clamping onto Magda's left arm with its huge fangs.

Before Felix could react, a barrage of yard-long icicles speared the creature's head. He grinned at a panting Pit, whose mouth still glowed from the icy discharge. The serpent fell with a resounding *thud*, its mouth opening and releasing Magda. Unwilling to take a chance, Felix ran forward and blasted it with Acid Stream. Devoid of lifeforce, its body began melting almost immediately, so he cut it off.

"You ok?" Felix asked, putting a hand on the shield warrior's large shoulder. She had fallen to a knee, cradling her left arm close. A few seconds later, Magda leaned back and looked up at him.

"Yeah," she breathed, her eyes red and jaw clenching. "I'll be fine."

Her arm was pierced straight through, a large yellowed fang still embedded in the flesh. It glowed an awful, sickly green.

She was poisoned.

CHAPTER SIXTY-FIVE

It was nearly noon by the time Harn returned to the tower.

Slogging up the five floors, the heavily-armored man tried to control his breathing...and his anger. His fists creaked on the handle of his axes, metal faintly groaning under the influence of his immense Strength. Even so, Harn's finely-tuned Brawler's Body sensed the enemies with spears from an entire floor below.

Happy to give vent to his bile, Harn rushed up the stairs. Unfortunately, he had to stop short when the spears were held by two of the ex-prisoners. They jumped a full second later when they actually noticed him, one of them even giving a pathetic yelp.

"W-who goes there!" The pathetic one stuttered.

The other one, a woman with freckles and dark brown hair, merely lowered her spear and sighed. "It's the Onslaught, Frederick." To Harn she apologized. "Sorry for that, sir. We're all still a bit shaken. Go on in."

Inclining his helmeted head, he brushed past them without a word. Inwardly, he seethed. Harn would have loved a fight at this point. His blood was burning for it.

"Harn! Thank Siva you're back!" As soon as the warrior had pushed past the hung blanket, he was rushed at by Evie. She looked around and behind him expectantly before her face started to fall. "Did you...Where is she?"

"Vess still lives, near as I can figure," Harn held out his hands placatingly before pulling off his helm. He was a sweaty mess, and his grizzled face was less grizzled and more bearded with every passing day. "I lost the trail near the edge of the city. That...*woman* is good, unfortunately."

Evie nodded, not meeting his eye, instead turning to the crowd. The room was filled with the survivors of their rescue mission, most in small knots talking in soft voices. "Well, almost everyone is here. What do you want to do?"

Harn raised an eyebrow. "Almost everyone? Who's missin'?"

Evie didn't answer for a moment, but didn't have to as a familiar voice cut across the crowd. "Maggie's not here."

Harn turned, orienting on the voice he knew so well. "Callie. What's goin' on? Explain."

Callie stood from her seat by the tiered fire pit, not so much sauntering as stalking in his direction. She was bandaged up and her armor was beat to hell, but Harn felt an aura of danger around the treasure hunter that he hadn't felt in a long time.

"Mags saved that kid from the Risi Chieftain. Shielded him, the idiot," she spat to the side, the sputum coming out too red. She held her side a moment. "They both got knocked into the sinkhole."

"What?" Harn's eyebrows rose and his heart thundered again, readying his Body. "Then what're we waitin' fer? We can get 'em back by sundown."

Callie frowned and lowered her voice. "You expect these rundown dregs to make it back though the giant's encampment, down into the Labyrinth, and back out again? You'd be sending em to die, Kastos."

Harn gritted his teeth, his worry boiling in his guts. But she was right. Even if they left the prisoners here to fend for themselves, they'd likely get found and die. The Risi had increased their patrols a hundred fold, and even Harn had a tough time evading their notice on the way back.

"Someone has to lead these folk outta here," Callie went on, poking her long slender finger at Harn's chestplate. "You and Evie and the Te'thys boy have the best chance at that. Evie told me about the Sworn too, and I bet a dozen crowns that she's already halfway back to Haarwatch. You might even catch her, if she's stupid."

Harn deflated, knowing a good idea when he heard it, even if he didn't like it. He looked around, noticing for the first time that each of the Guilders were ready to go and eyeballing their group. "Fine. You're right. If nothing else, Maggie would want us to get them to safety first." He looked back at the treasure hunter. "What'll you be doin'?"

Callie spread her arms, daggers suddenly appearing in her hands with a blink of purple-blue Mana. "What I do best. Infiltrate and extract. Maggie's down that hole, and I aim to get her out."

Harn nodded, and Evie placed a reassuring hand on his bicep. She turned to Callie. "Make sure you save Felix, too. He didn't have to go on this mission. He...Promise us you'll do what you can."

Callie nodded, her eyes serious and her mouth grim. "If he's alive, he's coming, too, even if we have to drag 'im."

"You're hurt," Felix insisted, pointing at the obvious giant fang. "Let me help you."

"No, don't touch it!" Magda hissed, pulling her impaled arm away from him. "The poison is too strong. It'd kill you."

Oh shit. Felix took a step back, the woman's tone more than enough to convince him she knew what she was talking about. Magda grimaced and lifted herself onto her uninjured arm, propping herself up against the stone wall. "Get back while I deal with this. It ain't gonna be pretty."

Felix took another three steps back, unable to tear his eyes away as Magda braced herself and lifted her pierced arm. Felix's Manasight flickered, its normal perception still subdued down here, but even so he could identify a thick, powerful vein of power coursing through the fang, unloading a vile mixture straight into her body. With a strangled cry, Magda struck her left forearm against the Labyrinth wall and the stone itself shattered in a spiral of cracks. With a grunt and cry, she did it again. And again. Until finally, with a meaty *schlorch,* the fang dropped from her arm and onto the ground, where it began to dissolve the moss around it.

Magda pushed herself away, letting her body roll to the right. Her arm pumped out thick red blood with abandon, drenching the stone. "Don't approach it," she panted at him while still lying prone and fetching a bandage from her hip pouch. She pressed on it with her right hand, hard. "That's Rotvein poison. Nasty shit that I haven't seen in years. Not since," she grunted, attempting to sit up to no avail. Felix leaned over and helped her. "Not since that Nymean ruin we found. Bastards."

Felix, his face hidden from her eyes, bit his lip and furrowed his brow as he watched her blood darken the bandage. He felt a sluggish ache in his gut, a sleepy predator sniffing a fresh kill. He reoriented. "Are you...is the poison gonna kill you?"

Magda sighed and pressed harder against her wound. "I'll live. But I ain't gonna be shit for a while. Rotvein does what it says, meant to eat your body from the inside out. I've got an Ironblood Body, second Temper, which is fairly resistant to poisons and wounds; but Rotvein is *strong*." She coughed, a wracking fit that went on for a full minute. Breathing heavily, she looked up at Felix. "I'm...weakened. This poison is just the final hair on Yyero's darkened backside. Whatever that *bastard* did to me, it hurt me."

"Grimmar? What'd he do?" Felix asked.

Magda coughed, this time spitting out a mouthful of blood. "The damn giant bit me during the fight. It sounds impossible but he tore a hole in my leg and...ripped out one of my Skills."

Felix felt the ground give way beneath him, his head and gut doing upsetting things with his balance. He stumbled back, suddenly dizzy as pieces started to fall into place. "He...ripped out one of your *Skills*?" Felix was incredulous. "How? Is that even possible?"

"No clue," she grunted, wrapping her arm with strips of dark paper. Felix didn't recognize what they were. "It's still there, it's just...in pieces. Damn near killed me, though."

Felix recalled Harn mentioning breaking one's Skills to undo a Tempering...is that what happened? He kept his speculation to himself, but his mind raced. The giant had claimed its transformation was a gift from the "Mother," but what did that mean? Why was it so similar to his Gourmand Title? Hell, the blue chieftain had even said it'd steal Felix's memories. That was explicitly the same as his Lessons of the Past.

What the fuck is going on? Harn said the Mother was some made up religious nonsense, right? This is...it's a weird coincidence; too weird. What's the connection? It came to him, faster than he expected. *The Song. The Grand Harmony. The music of the System, whatever it is. Grimmar said that the Mother was down here, and that the...Holy Deeps contained the Song more strongly.* Felix paced as he wracked his memories. *Then maybe...*

Felix listened with that special sense he seemed to have, the one that let him perceive the...musicality of the system around him. Felix didn't have a Skill for it, no stat or icon, but he could do it all the same. He tilted his head, hearing the silent roar of mist, the distant clack of stones shifting, pushing his Perception to the limit. But...nothing. Just silence and stone, fog and darkness.

So he relaxed, kept his mind loose, freeing it from conception and direction. Felix sought to hear the music beyond everything, the burgeoning concerto that seemed to weave in and out of reality here on the Continent. And almost instantly, the song began.

There was a swelling of stringed chords before it diminished, then rose again. Like...like something breathing.

Something immense.

"Ayyshhh!" Magda cried, her forearm suddenly bathed in steam as the paper she had placed upon it glowed with a series of bright orange characters. Felix flinched and took a half step forward before he realized she was fine.

"What the hell was that?" he asked.

"Script seal," Magda panted, flexing her left hand. "Seals the wound, but it hurts like Avet's hook. Gimme a second to rest and regenerate. My Health is too low to keep moving."

Felix nodded and stepped away, eager to get some distance and think things through. He approached Pit, who had been watching the entire ordeal with a tilted head. Felix felt gentle curiosity and confusion through their pact, as if the chimera were wondering how the big one got injured. Gathering his thoughts, Felix sent back his impressions: fang, bitten, poisonous injury, hurt and weak. Pit's golden eyes met Felix's blue and nodded before he started to root around the two serpent corpses.

Sighing to himself, Felix toggled his notifications he'd minimized during the aftermath of the battle.

You Have Gained A Level!
You are now Level 21!
+3 to WIL! +2 to INT! +4 to DEX! +1 to END! +2 to PER! +2 to VIT! +4 to AGL!

You Have 5 Unused Stat Points!

The usual stream of energy poured into Felix, but after his Tempering it felt...mild. It was still equal parts pleasurable and painful, a confusing mix that he didn't like to dwell on, but it just seemed reduced in some way. Perhaps if he gained multiple levels at a time it'd feel different. *And that has to be the plan now*, he decided. *Whatever is making that music is down here with us. I'm gonna need all the levels I can get.*

A flutter of excitement burst against Felix's chest like a wave, and the Nym turned to see his Companion digging frantically at the body of a Greenfyre Serpent. The first of the two was slowly evaporating into that greasy black smoke, its stink already filling the hall. Their bronze-like scales had been resistant to damage, though it seemed the lack of living energy within it weakened its endurance, and Pit was already paw-deep in the elemental's entrails.

Elemental, Felix realized dully. *Of course he's excited.*

Felix reached down and tore the corpse asunder with his bare hands, congealing blood spilling like thick slurry onto the floor. Soon after, the Nym felt more than heard Pit crunch into an elemental core. A thrill of power vibrated through their pact, and Pit gained +2 Agility. Felix frowned. No Skill this time.

They moved onto the second serpent. A few strikes and this one split open too, Pit diving forward again. The tenku emerged covered in blood and offal, but his one uninjured wing pushed the entrails away from Pit's face, revealing a flickering green and orange crystalline core. Greedy pig that he was, Pit chomped down without waiting a second. A ringing chime undercut by the basso percussion of a gong announced a different result than before:

Your Companion Pit Has Learned A New Skill!
Poisonfire (R), Level 1!
A defensive Skill, it burns Mana and Stamina to provide an offensive barrier. Increases physical damage and inflicts damage on anyone attempting to harm the caster. Damage increases moderately with Skill level.

Briefly, Pit activated the new Skill, engulfing his body with a flickering green flame. It was an exact replica of the serpents' own ability. Felix grinned, happy that his Companion had a defensive Skill, even though it'd need a lot of levels before it became very useful. *At least now Pit has a better Mana pool and can make use of this sort of thing much better.*

Felix's thoughts trailed away as he watched the serpent's blood drain out onto the floor, quickly turning into that putrid smoke. He silently bemoaned that his vials were missing and a brief, wild thought flashed through his mind: of himself on all fours, lapping up the blood from the ground. Like an animal.

He shook that image off and stepped away from the serpent's corpse. He paused and thought. *It doesn't have to be blood, I know this. It's just Mana, which happens to reside most heavily in blood. What if I use the fang?*

The off-white ivory of the fang still sat in the corner, surrounded now by a foot-wide radius of charred moss. The idea of touching such an object with his bare hands...unwise, to say the least. So Felix got clever. Asking for Magda's skinning knife, he peeled off a few of the brown-bronze scales on the nearest serpent, building a collection of twenty of the palm-sized scales. Then, using Reign of Vellus, he lifted the fang up into the air to hover gently before him.

Azure lightning crackled and discharged around the fang, and Felix could feel Magda's questioning gaze on him, but he ignored it. Using his impressive Strength, he took the scales and bent several of them around the base of the fang, forming a handle of sorts. But they kept slipping off, the metallic scales not sticking to the fang in any meaningful way. Inspired by a sudden and perhaps mistaken thought, Felix realized that his Reign of Vellus could produce lightning; perhaps it could also produce an arc? Flaring Reign of Vellus through his hands, Felix grimaced as his arms were deluged with a flood of crackling pain. The scales bent and deformed under his Strength, and slowly Felix could feel them...mushing together.

Pain Resistance is level 32!

He kept adding scales, building up the casing around the deadly fang, and applying his improvised arc welder again and again. A flurry of blue and gold lights gathered at the edges of his vision as his arms shook, and electricity tried to eat through the flesh of his hands. Then finally, blissfully, it was done.

New Skill!
Lightning Resistance (Rare), Level 1!
You touched lightning with your bare hands! That's insane! Keep it up! Damage reduction increases with Skill level.

Heat Resistance is level 20!
Pain Resistance is level 33!

Felix winced as he peeled his hands off the burning hot metal and set the entire thing down. The fang was covered in a metallic sheath that left only the last four inches bare. Feeling proud of his creation, he quickly Analyzed it.

Name: Crude Poisonous Fang Dagger
Type: Piercing
Lore: Made from bits of a Greenfyre Serpent, it still retains a powerful amount of poisonous fire Mana. Contains 4 charges of Rotvein Poison.

Improvisation is level 6!
...
Improvisation is level 11!

Immediately ideas swirled in Felix's head on how to make his little danger dagger better, but he set them aside. He had what he wanted.

"What was that all about?"

Felix turned to see Magda standing tall on the path, looking far better than just a few minutes ago. If it weren't for the damaged armor and large script bandage on her arm, Felix would have assumed she was perfectly healthy.

Ironblood Body sure must be something.

"I wanted to take the fang with us. See if I can improve my Poison Resistance with it. So I made a...a handle, I'd guess you call it." Felix explained with a shrug. Magda nodded, seemingly impressed.

"That's smart thinking. The scales will restrict the effect a bit, and...of course, you already Tempered with Poison Resistance right?" Felix nodded and she started walking. "That'll help level your Skill, if you're careful. But do it on the way. We've still got a lot of walking to do before we get to the center."

Feeling slightly nonplussed, Felix started walking, Pit close to his heels.

CHAPTER SIXTY-SIX

Now that it was proven that not *all* traps were disarmed, the trio proceeded far more cautiously. The last thing Felix wanted was to be catapulted into a wall again, or have his legs incinerated, or his head pulped. And those were just three of the traps they managed to avoid. The sheer variety was remarkable to the Nym. What's more, his Manasight had trouble picking things out down here, otherwise he wouldn't be as tense as he was. For some reason he didn't understand, using his Manasight was like lifting a barbell with his pinkies. Potentially possible, but extremely taxing. Felix kept at it, though; the Skill was one of his most useful, and he was all but blind without it.

Maybe this is like weight training for my eyeballs, he mused as he once again flexed his Skill. There was a definite ache behind his eyes, not quite a headache. He mentally shrugged. *Just another bit of pain. Add it to the pile.*

Cautious as they were, they were still moving fast, or as fast as Magda could manage. She claimed to be fine, but was white as a sheet after only twenty minutes of running, which led to more breaks. It grated on Felix's nerves, which were unable to escape the feeling that the giants were out there, closing in. Maybe they had stayed up above, but he doubted it. The bastard wanted whatever was down here. He could only groan in frustration each time they had to slow or backtrack from a dead end.

The Labyrinth was well named, as it was filled with twisting paths and strange formations. Those line-carved standing stones were everywhere, sticking up from the ground or from the walls themselves. Often, they and the ground were covered in thick, faintly bioluminescent moss. Like the heavy fog, it was meant to distract and conceal. As Felix found out the hard way, nothing down here was safe.

They traversed two more rooms, areas of the Labyrinth where the corridor walls bulged outward in various shapes, and which were (usually) the most dangerous places. The traps were half-disarmed in both sections, Felix's Manasight flaring enough to note the thick cloud of Mana vapor clinging close to a number of the floor tiles. Following his guidance, the three of them made it through without incident.

The stretch after that, however, was a gauntlet.

Not only were the traps more unpredictable and varied (fire blast, conjured crushing pillars, even a type of sonic wail), but monsters emerged. At first, Felix mistook them for chimeras, but both Magda and his Analyze dissuaded him from that. They were basic elementals.

Name: Charwing
Type: Elemental
Level: 29
HP: 222/222
SP: 255/255
MP: 430/430
Lore: Elemental creatures of fire, they have a pack mentality and work most effectively as a group. Their limited senses are easy to fool.
Strength: AGL, STR
Weakness: VIT, PER

Six of them swarmed from the dark ceiling, dark shapes that burst into fire only moments before they struck. Felix and Magda dodged and tanked the hits, respectively, the woman's powerful shielding ability knocking them aside. The flock circled up and around for another attack.

Fire elementals? Felix felt that hunger again, though he was hard-pressed to determine if it was that gnawing emptiness or his own avarice.

Magda let out a piercing wail, like a high pitched siren almost, and the Charwings immediately oriented on her alone. Recognizing a taunt Skill when he heard it, Felix reached out with Reign of Vellus and attempted to grapple them.

Lightning sparked in midair, leaping from creature to creature as azure light flared and held fully half of them in place. The other three sped onward to Magda, buffeted by the invisible edge of her right arm shield.

Felix held the first three in place and, with a burst of mental effort and fully a quarter of his Mana, crushed them. They burst like charcoal, fire spouting outwards before extinguishing. All that was left were three small cores that clattered to the ground as he released the spell.

Reign of Vellus is level 28!

Felix sensed Magda and Pit dispatching the remaining Charwings, but his attention was truly captured by two larger foes that emerged from his immediate right. Both were shaggy beasts with rake-like claws, multiple curved tusks, and bone spurs that raced along their tapered backs. Quadrupedal, they stumped out of the mossy earth as if swimming from the depths.

Analyze...

Name: Mogru
Type: Elemental
Level: 39
HP: 849/849
SP: 522/535
MP: 325/325
Lore: Elemental creatures of earth, Mogru are very strong and sturdy. Their mossy fur and flabby body provides excellent protection from bludgeoning damage.
Strength: END, STR
Weakness: AGL, DEX

"Mogru, hmm," Felix considered them a moment longer

before deciding to experiment. They felt...dangerous, like a mudslide about to happen, so he knew he had to stop them quickly if he could. Reaching out a hand toward the two earth elementals, Felix cast.

Influence of the Wisp!

Mogru (x2) have been Enthralled for 5 Seconds!

The blue-white fire limned both Felix and his targets, and this time both of the elementals were enveloped in the effect. And what an effect: Enthralled for an entire 5 seconds, an eternity in a battle. But Felix felt there was something else happening, and when he looked closer at the elementals, he noticed that, instead of the illusion of fire, the Mogru were literally burning up. Startled, Felix simply watched as the beasts' shaggy fur curled and blackened, their small, beady eyes revealed beneath skin folds that began to crack and char. They couldn't even scream...until the effect ended. Then they bellowed with a pitiful vigor, and both charged at Felix in a rage.

Influence of the Wisp is level 26!

The Mogru were slow, their ponderous bodies not made for quick turns or pivots, but their huge foreclaws were deadly weapons. Twice they struck against Felix, once against his left arm held up in a block, and another tearing into his back. The claws dug deep furrows into his skin and muscle, bleeding him and shredding his shirt.

Ugh. He grunted as he ripped off the rest of his shirt. The loss of his top hurt more than the pain itself. *I really need armor.*

Armored Skin is level 26!

He tried repeatedly to counterattack, but each Corrosive Strike and unarmed blow against them only did minimal damage. Their massive, flabby bodies, easily the size of a riding mower, were heavily resistant to his bludgeoning attacks. If only he had still had his Crescian blade, then he'd have a better way. However, when one of his Corrosive Strikes hit an eye, one Mogru squealed in rage and disappeared into the ground. The other quickly followed.

Felix stood still, senses straining. He could hear Magda and Pit killing the last of a second batch of Charwings, and could almost feel their deadly heat waft against his neck. Felix pulsed his Manasight, pushing to see more. It was like shoving a boulder up a hill, but in a quick flash he caught a rapidly-rising hunk of dusty brown and green-gold life Mana. He grinned.

Felix jumped backward, landing nearly ten feet away, precariously close to the unspent traps that dotted this section of the corridor. Shaping a quick spell in his core, Felix shoved it into the earth before him, just as the Mogru burst from the earth in a powerful charge. Heads down and tusks out, the elementals had built a deadly inertia after swimming the earth. Felix almost felt bad, but not enough to let them kill him. So, in the instant before they came within five feet of him, there was a discharge of dusty brown Mana beneath the ground, and two three-foot thick spikes erupted mere inches before the charging Mogru. Too late to change their momentum, the elementals just lowered their heads and barreled through. The stone held for only a moment before it began to crumble and crack, but Felix was already airborne, leaping over them in a wide if ungainly arc.

Then the Mogru ran right into the traps.

The explosion was deafening as a variety of lethal measures erupted. Heat and cold washed in turns through the relatively small area, and it wasn't until well after the Mogru had perished that the traps stopped discharging.

Acting is level 11!

Felix breathed a sigh of relief, wincing as the tender bits of his arm and back pulled. They were clotting nicely, even scabbing over rapidly in some places, but his Health regeneration would take some time to catch up. Another pop of discharging Mana grabbed his attention, and he closed his eyes in annoyance. *Shit, their bodies were destroyed.* No more blood for him, not even a bone to gnaw on.

Whoops.

Magda and Pit were sitting together on a standing stone, the large woman's hand gently petting his back. Felix raised an eyebrow when he saw it but made no comment. Pit chirruped happily and hopped down, while Magda seemed amused.

"Dead enough for you, kid?" She nodded at the charred stretch of landscape. "Everything in this maze would have heard that."

Felix grimaced. "I didn't really think that through. Thought they'd trigger a trap or two, then I could finish them off." He shrugged, then winced again. "We should get moving then, yeah?"

"Agreed."

———

Running. More and more running.

Felix tried to set the pace, feeling a rise in that unnerving sense of urgency. Still, Magda's injuries restricted them all. Every time they rested, Felix paced or practiced a Skill, unable to place the rising unease that prickled at his skin. The fog felt...inhabited, sentient. Like the breath of a beast the size of a mountain, the dimming exhalation of a song that even now lingered at the edge of his hearing.

Beckoning.

Felix.

He bolted upright and spun in place, searching for the source. He saw only fog and the diffuse glow of moss.

"Pit, did you hear that?" He turned to see the tenku on his feet, hackles raised and beak wide. Pit growled in that strange way of his. Felix could feel surprise and fear through the pact, directed outward into the dark. *He heard it, too,* he thought with relief. *I'm not crazy.*

"Hear what?" Magda asked, getting back to her feet.

"I uh..I heard someone call my name," Felix explained.

"Callie said this place was full of illusions. It's probably that. Don't pay it any mind, focus on movin' forward." She started walking. "Let's go."

Felix frowned, still turning to regard the darkness around them. *Something is out there.* He gulped. *And it knows my name.*

———

Dual Casting is level 21!
Manasight is level 33!
Meditation is level 33!
Cloudstep is level 8!

Physical Conditioning is level 23!
Relentless Charge is level 9!

More monsters loomed in the murk, each stranger than the last. They faced elementals of all stripes, fire, earth, even a couple water types. They also contended against increasingly-convoluted traps and obstacles. Giant stone presses, exploding walls, air that literally *became* fire, nothing seemed beyond the craft of whatever built the Labyrinth.

When Magda mentioned the Geist were the builders, some pieces started falling into place for him. The towers and the Labyrinth, the whole city itself, built by the Geist. And the Geist had some sort of relationship with the Nym. So what did the Geist, and likely the Nym, want to lock away down here? Was it some incredible monster? Was it the Mother?

And why did he keep hearing her song? It was growing increasingly hard to put it out of his mind, the mournful tune intruding at the oddest moments. Only if he flexed Bastion of Will was Felix able to completely silence it.

The further they traversed, the stranger everything became. There were rooms that appeared to be underwater, yet the water was contained in an upright cube, something they had to swim through while evading dark orbs that swarmed in the liquid. More than a few impacted against him, though Magda's shields helped stave off the worst of the damage.

Swimming is level 6!
Armored Skin is level 27!

Occasionally, they would encounter a grouping of metallic creatures. Appearing humanoid, they were built from a dark metal and furnished with plates of quartz-like armor across the chest, shoulders, and appendages. Even Magda worried about them, and Felix's Analyze pulled back only their name, type, and levels.

Name: Etheric Automaton
Type: Golem
Level: 44

Thus far, they had been lucky enough to elude them. Stealth

had been a big part of that, and as a result, it finally hit Apprentice Tier.

Congratulations! You Have Reached Apprentice Tier in Stealth!
You Gain:
+3 PER
+3 AGL
+3 VIT

The stats rushed into him, but again, it felt somewhat lackluster compared to Tempering himself. Though, admittedly, he was avoiding Tiering up in his remaining Mind and Spirit Skills; Felix wasn't entirely sure Magda would be able to protect him if he locked up due to Formation. She wasn't her usual self by any means.

At their next rest stop, Felix decided to feed the collected Charwing cores to Pit. He had been only able to retrieve eight in total, as some of the enemies consumed or depleted their cores somehow. The cores were small, maybe the size of a marble, and Pit ate them nearly all at once.

"Slow down, little pig," Felix admonished, ruffling the tenku's head.

"Are you feeding him elemental cores?" Magda asked, her voice slightly strained. She had started walking with more of a limp after the last mile, claiming to be low on Stamina. They were moving down a broken pathway, the ground falling away in jagged chasms that crisscrossed the area.

Felix and Pit traversed the wide crevasses with ease, Felix using his new Body to effortlessly clear the five to six foot gaps while carrying the still injured Pit. Magda, however, took pains to make it across each one and had to rest every couple of jumps. They were resting now, about halfway through the chamber.

"Yeah, he likes 'em. Makes him stronger." Felix gestured to Pit, who had started to glow slightly as a small amount of orange vapor escaped between his feathers.

"Huh," Magda grunted. She shook her head. "Expensive taste."

"Hm? What do you mean?" Felix asked.

"Elemental cores. Used by nearly every profession. You just put about six hundred silver worth of cores in that chimera," Magda said, taking a swig of water from their dwindling supply.

What? Felix looked at Pit, who tilted his head curiously. *That sounds like a lot of money...maybe I should start saving some of these.* Pit nudged his thigh, hard enough to make Felix sway, and he laughed as he batted the tenku away from him. *Ok, ok! You get all the cores.*

"You're not what I expected, Felix," she said, interrupting his thoughts.

He looked at her askance. Felix had been enjoying Magda's change of attitude since getting stuck with him, so he was hesitant as he replied. "And what did you expect?"

"A spy," she said. *There it was. Suspicious Magda.*

Felix's laugh had an edge to it. "A spy? For who?"

Magda grunted and shook her head. "I don't know. The Guild, maybe. We stepped on a lot of toes to get out here, and plenty of Elders didn't want us out here. For official reasons, of course. No one would admit to the lost operation and squandered Guilders, so they couldn't block us outright." She frowned and growled. "I thought you were a plant. Someone who came out here to either stop us or report on us."

"What? Why? I didn't even know what the Guild was when I met you," Felix said.

"Yeah, and that's part of it. You're an enigma, kid. You've got too many Skills, stats that are through the roof for your level, a fog-touched *chimera* as a pet that you feed precious cores to like they're biscuits." She scoffed. "You don't know half the stuff all of us were taught in childhood."

"But I'm not a spy. I'm just...lost, I guess," Felix countered, still nervous to admit anything to the warrior. "You folks have taught me a lot, and I appreciate it. What I don't appreciate is the constant suspicion that you bombard me with; it's exhausting."

Magda held up her hands, her script seal starting to flake. "I know, I know. And I'm sorry, for what it's worth. The last few months, I haven't...I've been in a bad place."

Felix was silent a moment, chewing over his thoughts. There was more to say, but he didn't know how to approach it. So he just settled for: "Well, apology accepted, I guess."

The silence after was uncomfortable to say the least. Moreover, it was interspersed with the undulating song in his head, an intermittent urge to keep going and leave everyone else behind.

Shoving that drive away, Felix turned to Magda, who seemed to be contemplating the darkness above them.

"So...you and Callie, huh? She seems...intense." *Oh my god, what are you doing?* Felix's internal social critic railed at him even before he finished the sentence, causing him to stumble on the dismount. Magda was quiet for several minutes after that, which led to even more self-condemnation. *Ahh, why did you say anything? Just sit in silence. Or go find a monster. Yes, that's better. Let's go fight.* Felix almost stood up when the Shieldwitch spoke.

"Once we were something. I don't know if that means anything now." She sighed, a big one she dredged from her core.

"What happened, if you don't mind me asking?"

Magda looked at him and smirked. "No. It's fine. I've interrogated you enough." She adjusted her seat, leaning once again on her uninjured arm. "We worked together for years, even before Harn joined up. Before that, we were friends, back at the Academy."

Academy? Felix wanted to ask, but now that she started, he was loath to interrupt.

"We did a few harrowing trips into the interior of the Continent, gained some levels and renown, and during all that we grew closer. It was nothing we ever said, not out loud, but before we knew it, we were together. It was...it was nice." Magda's smile turned wistful. "Those were the good days, shortly after we were promoted to Bronze Rank and formed our own team. Harn joined up, and off we went. Hotspot to hotspot. There wasn't a contract we didn't take if it was within our rank. We were a perfect team."

Felix smiled. "That sounds nice. So what happened?"

Another sigh, deeper and more meaningful this time. "We got famous, in our own way. We were on track to be promoted to Silver Rank after some harrowing contracts, and things...fell apart. It's my fault, in the end." She closed her eyes and knocked her head against the stone wall. "Callie proposed. And I...I got scared. Silver Rank is a big deal, something fewer than one in a thousand might reach it. She wanted to get away from it. Do our own thing, away from the Guild. I...I couldn't. So she left."

The silence that followed was worse than what came before. Felix felt terrible for bringing it up. He opened his mouth to say something, anything, but each time had nothing more than empty platitudes. "I'm sorry, Magda. That's rough."

Magda nodded and with some effort stood up. She looked less pale, though the skin around her eyes was a little red now. "Don't let your mistakes linger, Felix," she said, looking into the foggy distance. "You'll try to bury 'em, but they come back. Regrets never really leave."

She gestured ahead. "Let's get moving."

CHAPTER SIXTY-SEVEN

Time was difficult to gauge down in the Labyrinth. The light never changed; there was no sun nor moon nor even stars, just the stones and the fog. If it weren't for his impeccable memory, Felix would have been as lost as Magda seemed to be, but he could at least estimate the amount of time they'd been down there. Technically, as it was within the past thirty days, Felix could count out the seconds and minutes, but that was both exhausting and worthless. It was enough that he could approximate the time: it had been around four hours since they had fallen into the sinkhole.

For much of that time, they were simply running, though battles occurred with increasing frequency. The Labyrinth lived up to its name, folding and moving through space in unpredictable ways. Multiple times, Felix was positive they were rushing down a corridor that seemed to turn and take up the same dimensional space as another. His eyes told him it was just a turn, but his memory said it was *exactly* the same. More than his Manasight (which was still restricted, somehow), his memory proved to be their greatest boon. He kept leading them back, unerringly remembering the path they had traversed.

The enemies they found ranged the gamut of elemental types, and he found a chance to sample most of their Mana.

Lessons of the Past is level 20!

His Skill increased multiple times, but not *once* did Felix learn a new Skill or gain a Memory from the elementals' blood and Mana. Ever since his Body Formation his hunger had quieted, only rising up once in a while, as if it was slumbering. Without the engagement of that growling in his core, it seemed his Title and Skill had a far lower chance of activating. It was frustrating, to say the least. To focus that frustration, Felix threw himself into clearing the enemies before them with greater gusto. They had to get out of here, and to do that, Felix needed to be far stronger than he was now...

To that end, Felix had dumped all of his Mana into the Elemental Shard that hung over his left shoulder. He didn't know at first how much Mana Storage was available in the shard, and decided to feed it slowly whenever they weren't fighting. Within the first ten minutes, it was at capacity, holding exactly five hundred Mana and not a drop more. It was a significant bump in his pool, and meant he could be even more cavalier about his spell usage. That thought just led him back around to his annoyance at the lack of new monster spells, though he supposed he had a pretty damn wide repertoire already. *No need to be greedy*, he admonished himself. *I still need to level up what I have.*

The song still continued, of course. It was an endless refrain, a track on repeat with only minute changes in pitch and tone as the hours blurred by. It was maddening to listen to, and Felix kept his Bastion of Will engaged nearly all the time, despite the toll it took on his mental fortitude.

Bastion of Will is level 35!

During breaks and those stretches of corridor without enemies, however, Felix attempted to level his Poison Resistance with the sheathed fang. Since the scales held in the poisonous aura, it was safe to hold along the bottom eight inches. The top was tricky, however. He held the crude dagger in one hand while slowly edging that poisonous miasma closer to his left forearm. The skin sizzled and eroded before his eyes, but the pain was no worse than an acid bath; better, perhaps, since his Body Formation. When the tip of the dagger got within six inches of his arm, his skin finally broke and blood poured out. Hissing in pain, he yanked the fang away, letting his natural regeneration repair it.

It was painful, but effective.

Poison Resistance is level 28!

He was healing faster now, his poison resistance neutralizing a portion of the Rotvein's potency. Still, he'd yet to even *touch* himself with the fang.

How'd Magda withstand getting this through her fucking arm? Felix shuddered before capping the fang with an improvised scale plug. He had no way to carry it except in his belt or in his hand all the time, and the last thing Felix wanted was to touch the fang before he was ready. They had encountered a few more of the Greenfyre Serpents, and he had fashioned a casing for the remaining four inches, knocking his Improvisation Skill to level 12.

He was growing by leaps and bounds down here in the dark. Despite the pain and the fear that dogged his every step, Felix felt an exhilaration that was both heady and freeing. Each encounter ended with at least a few Skill gains, and all the while his highest Skills edged closer to Apprentice Tier. The stats he gained during each Tier bump were significant increases to his power, and now he was extremely close to having all of his base stats above the one hundred mark.

STR: 102 PER: 111
VIT: 144 END: 120
INT: 111 WIL: 185
AGL: 105 DEX: 98

Pit was developing rapidly as well. The elementals they faced dropped a core at least twenty percent of the time, and each core was enough for 1-2 points in their favored stat. This led to an odd and scattered allotment of stats, but the results were more than satisfying.

STR: 49 PER: 52
VIT: 60 END: 53
INT: 37 WIL: 51
AGL: 93 DEX: 66

With the greater power, Pit was better able to take on the monsters with Felix, and their teamwork increased by the battle. He had always been fast, but he was lightning-quick now. Wingblades and Frost Spears were the tenku's weapons of choice, allowing Felix to get within melee range and providing support. The support was Pit's idea, strangely enough. Their communication was evolving in a way that Felix found remarkable; it wasn't speech but the bundles of image, senses, and emotions becoming stronger and more concise. Pulses of sensation through their pact were enough for near-instant understanding, and their Skill levels reflected that.

Pit's Wingblade is level 14!
Pit's Frost Spear is level 12!
Pit's Cry is level 24!
Pit's Rake is level 21!
Pit's Bite is level 20!

Companion Pact is level 23!

Frustratingly, Felix wasn't able to get Acid Stream, Shadow Whip, or Stone Shaping to level 25, despite how often he used them. Simple repetition wasn't cutting it anymore, the final jump taking far more effort than others. Felix didn't really understand why, and Magda's advice was to "think about how the Skill works and how it affects you." Which was...not exactly unhelpful, but Felix didn't make headway, not with those spells.

Exploration, on the other hand, had jumped to level 24 fairly quickly. This place was a treasure trove in important, unexplored crannies. That Skill seemed to apply toward places of significance, and Felix couldn't claim that this two-thousand-year-old death maze wasn't significant. They had encountered a wide variety of fascinating structures within the Labyrinth, ranging from the omnipresent carved standing stones to delicately-detailed frescoes painted on the walls and mostly hidden beneath thick moss. They depicted white-furred, robe-wearing creatures standing among a gaggle of elementals. Most were simply ordering the elementals around or using them to build something. A few, however, swarmed around strangely amorphous...blobs. They had no clear size or shape, only a dark discoloration that seemed to seep into whatever pigments were used on the paintings. The white-furred folk (Geist, clearly) were fighting against the blobs with spears and spells, but seemed to be in a stalemate.

Magda thought it curious, but likely irrelevant. "I've seen thousands of these sorts a' things. All of ‘em have their heroes fighting off monsters or demons, or whatever nonsense you wanna imagine. It's usually just braggin'."

"Then why aren't they winning?" Felix asked. Magda shrugged and kept moving.

Another twenty minutes later, they found the statue chamber. At least, that's what Felix called it.

It was massive, easily the largest space they had found within the Labyrinth. The dense fog and smothering darkness blocked their senses beyond fifty feet in any direction, but brief flashes of his Manasight convinced Felix the room was easily a mile in all dimensions.

Manasight is level 35!

The tiled and mossy floor extended about thirty feet from the entry before it tilted down into a lake. That was the only way to describe it, as it filled most of the space, dark water that slowly surged and receded with tiny waves yet was absolutely silent. Still, in the corridor just outside the chamber, Felix and Magda shared a look before stepping in. Now beyond the threshold, the sound of the water roared up from nothing, a constant susurration that filled the immense chamber.

"Some sorta seal or something on the door," Magda muttered, briefly looking back at the entryway. "Why bother, though?"

Felix shrugged and knelt down, pushing aside the omnipresent moss. A strip of carved rock was at the base of the archway, the markings in it etched in a familiar script. Felix went over his memories of the script he'd seen up to that point, a relatively short list. The script consisted of four characters, repeated over and over until they formed a dense banner of sigils. Felix considered them each in turn, and while his understanding of sigils was shaky at best, he was able to tease something from them. Uncertain as to why, Felix felt that the largest of the four characters meant "quietude" and that the rest modified that declaration for an unknown purpose.

Sigils of the Primordial Dawn is level 6!

"No clue why, but yeah, some sort of silence sigil is inscribed here." Felix stood up and brushed off his hands. "At least that means any monsters behind us won't hear us?"

Magda snorted before sitting down on a large rock. "That's something. I'm taking thirty seconds. Then we move. We're close, I know it."

Felix nodded, silently agreeing. They *were* close. The song was louder, more strident, more...insistent...though he still blocked it out with Bastion of Will. His Skill formed a metaphysical castle wall around his mind, dark stone repelling the sinuous notes like ransacking invaders. If he focused on it, Felix could easily picture those soaring walls of stone, each block the size of two men and growing larger and more ornate as the Skill leveled. Was it real?

As real as anything else in this bonkers place, he decided.

Felix walked to the water's edge, careful of his movements and scanning everything around him with a combination of Analyze and an intermittent Manasight. With no obvious traps underfoot, he gazed out into the water and his eyes widened. Closer now, the fog had parted to reveal massive statues partially submerged in the dark water, each of them depicting a wild beast that combined a handful of opposing features.

Chimeras.

There were dozens of them, perhaps hundreds placed in the water in a regular pattern. The water sloshed against them, the sunken statuary varying in height from enormous fifty-foot-tall constructions to barely peeking above the surface. They appeared to be all made in the same fashion, a fluted pillar supporting a chimeric beast in some sort of action pose. From his position, Felix could make out Wyverns, Harnoqs, Wendigos, and yes, even a few Tenku. But there were more, beyond the range of his Analyze, things he hadn't encountered before and were startlingly graceful meshes of monstrous creatures.

"What *is* all this?"

A chill wind blew across the water, the fog swirling in its passage, raising goosebumps on Felix's skin even as he ignored the temperature. His Cold Resistance made it inconsequential. What wasn't to be dismissed was that, when the fog parted, his peripherals caught the shape of something fluttering near the water line.

"Is that..?" Felix's attention pivoted and his mouth widened into a grin. "My stuff!"

There, sitting on the mossy stone was a slew of pages and the splayed open form of his ragged notebook. Felix rushed over, keeping his eyes open for any more traps, and scooped them up. The notebook was more or less intact, though a number of pages in the back were coming loose from the binding. It even still had the few pages he stole from the Archon. Felix only briefly glanced at their fell designs before snapping them shut again. Of the actual satchel there was no sign, nor of his grease pen or the locked box Pit had stolen. It appeared as if the bag had fallen from a great height and scattered, which unfortunately made sense.

We must be closer to our landing point then, right? How would the bag have fallen here if it was really four hours away from where we *landed?* Felix frowned. *We did double back on many of the pathways...this Labyrinth is too strange though. How big is it, exactly?*

Ten feet away, further from the water, he spied a dented and crumpled potions case. Cursing, Felix strode over and picked it up with gentle hands. It was his alright, and the case had been half-crushed by the fall, leaving several of the vials leaking a thick silver liquid. Remnants of liquid, at least, most of the essence draughts having leached into the ground. *Damn it, I need some of these.* Vessilia's draughts only contained enough for two Mind, two Body, and two Spirits. The ducal heiress already had partially tempered her Body, Mind, and Spirit, and only needed enough to finish the job. As Felix went through the case's remains, he found only a single Iron Body Essence Draught and the Wandering Spirit Essence Draught. The Body draught was useless to him, since he couldn't Temper his Body again at Apprentice Tier, but the Wandering Spirit Essence was lucky. It was his only uncommon ranked draught, and it meant he could fully Temper his Spirit with the Essences on hand.

Now I just have to worry about my Mind Skills. Both Exploration and Analyze are close to Tier.

The soft sound of something rubbing against stone caught his attention. Felix's Perception zeroed in on it without hesitation. It sounded high-pitched in a way he couldn't place, but it definitely was something dragging against stone. Almost at the water line, Felix spied a glittering bronze shape, crooked and sharp.

My sword!

As he watched a wave crashed over the blade, and it began to slip into the dark water. This time he didn't even check for traps, pushing himself quickly to the edge in an attempt to snatch the Crescian blade away from a watery grave. The moment his hand wrapped around the hilt, however, was when they struck.

The water thrashed, and suddenly a line of blood appeared on Felix's forearm, followed by a sharp, burning pain. He fell backward on his ass, looking for whatever attacked him. At first, he saw nothing. Then his high Perception picked out a slight distortion in the air before him, a distortion that was now lunging at him. With an undignified squawk, Felix rolled to the side as three somethings sparked against the stone ground, their path so fast and form so transparent that he couldn't follow the attack.

Pushing up with his free hand, Felix shoved himself into the air, cracking the stone beneath his hand with a sharp retort. Even before he landed back on his feet, the invisible creature struck again. The blow hit him square in the chest, sending the Nym sliding backward a few feet, stopping once he fetched up against a standing stone.

Invisible monsters? No...fair, he managed groggily before flaring Bastion of Will. His mind snapped back together. Felix leaned forward, surprised to find his hooked sword still in his hand. Then he tucked it into his belt and raised both of his hands.

Acid Stream!

Twin jets of acid exploded outward, extra Mana increasing their flow and speed. Felix sprayed down the area before him, panning to the side to ensure he got the invisible bastard. The viscous green liquid spat and sizzled against the stone, eating through the moss and rock at a steady rate, and a good portion of it coated a collection of spindly limbs that began to charge towards him. Felix couldn't quite make out what it was, or how many of them there were, but he did notice that the acid only sloughed off their form, doing no damage.

Shit.

Then the water exploded.

What seemed like a hundred dark blurs launched out of the water all along the coastline, shooting up before buzzing forward toward them. They were fast, fast enough that he couldn't make out details, but they weren't faster than thought.

Reign of Vellus!

Felix released the spell in an arc, and azure lightning exploded up from the earth as a wall of force shimmered and slammed everything backward. The near-invisible creature toppled back as the flying monsters bashed into midair as if hitting a massive window, their momentum stopped dead cold, though not reversed. They were like giant aquatic insects, sectioned carapaces, faceted eyes and all covered in glistening scales. Within moments, a few had recovered and buzzed their awful wings toward him again.

"Clarion Call!"

That high-pitched siren song belted out into the area, and nearly all of the fly-fish swerved toward her. Felix spared a glance toward her and saw Pit at her side, launching Wingblades and Frost Spears at the approaching monsters.

Good job, Pit. Watch out, they seem fast. Pit chirruped at him mentally, acquiescence that became a warning screech. Barely registering the warning, Felix turned in time to catch a blurring limb to the face.

Crash!

The stones shattered beneath him as his body was driven to the ground, but when the second limb hit his gut, Felix grappled with it. Refusing to let go, Felix dragged the invisible bastard down with him, using his leverage to yank on their glass-like limb until a loud *thud* echoed from beside him. Felix rolled on top of it, swinging out with Corrosive Strike. Something grabbed at his fist, but not hard enough to stop his blow.

Crack!

Splintering cracks formed on the surface of nothing, revealing the shape of several thrashing limbs beneath his fist.

Blind Fighting is level 21!

Strike after strike, Felix didn't let up. Not even as the glass monster beneath him lashed at him with razor-sharp claws and fangs, slashing into his legs, thighs and back. Felix pushed through the pain, focusing on pushing each Corrosive Strike harder and further through this beast's remarkable defense. The cracks spread, making it more and more visible as its form clouded with fractures, and Felix could make out a snarling wolf-like head atop an emaciated body with far too many limbs.

Analyze...

Name: Glassbone Stalker
Type: Aberration
Level: 35
HP: 90/433
SP: 418/683
MP: 94/94
Lore: Near invisible on land and water, they are aquatic beings that have been corrupted by a blood curse.
Strength: WIL, END, AGL
Weakness: INT, Bludgeoning Attacks

With a roar, he brought both hands down onto the Stalker's face, shattering the stone beneath it as it was reduced to glass powder.

"Huff, huff." Felix sat atop the beast a moment longer, catching his breath. One of the disgusting fly/fish hybrids buzzed his way, but he crushed it out of the air with a burst of Reign of Vellus.

Corrosive Strike is level 25!

Congratulations! You Have Reached Apprentice Tier In Corrosive Strike!
You Gain:
+10 STR
+10 PER
+10 END

Energy poured into him again, the stats vibrating his flesh and bones in ways too minor to keep track of while something like adrenaline pumped into his veins. It was enough of a boost for Felix to suddenly sense the presence of three other creatures, all of them slowly moving forward...toward him.

Felix flared his Manasight, and for the briefest of instants, he could see their forms: a latticework of green-gold Life Mana filled with dark violet light.

Manasight is level 36!

Felix pulsed outward with Reign of Vellus, sending a staggering jolt into the near-invisible Glassbone Stalkers and following up with a blast of his Mantle of the Long Night. The air around him began to steam as the temperature instantly dropped by thirty degrees and kept on dropping.

Mantle of the Long Night is level 13!

Ice formed on the ground as the air around them swirled in a frigid breeze, and the frost crawled over the Stalkers' forms as well, highlighting them against the darkness as they recoiled in pain. Alien, warbling yowls filled the air.

"Don't like the cold, ya jerks?" Felix scowled before pumping more Mana into the aura spell. The ice started to accumulate a little faster while his Mana began to drain like a sieve. The Stalkers yowled louder and lost their patience: with a blurring of frosted limbs, they charged.

Reign of Vellus!

Influence of the Wisp!

Another blast of kinetic force burst from him, this time barely stopping their braced forms. He followed up with his Influence spell, and while the blue-white fire seared them, the Enthrall failed to take hold. Their strong Willpower defended them. Growling with frustration, Felix gathered his Mana for a Stone Shaping, pushing his Fire Within to sound out the familiar patterns. Yet, as he did so, his ability to focus on Bastion of Will faltered, and an echo of something else shuddered through his pathways, something strange yet solidly familiar...

The Mother's song...

The pattern deviated, branching outward wildly as his Mana dumped into the spellform like a flood. Felix tried to stem the flow, but could only watch as power gushed from his core and channels, spilling out into the greedy earth in flashes of dusty brown and glistening silver. Groaning in pain and muscles straining with effort, he cast the spell.

Stone Shaping!

The Stalkers didn't pause a moment as creaking groans sounded from all around them, their numerous clawed limbs mere milliseconds from eviscerating Felix. Then, the outstretched claw of a massive statue slammed down upon the glass beasts, shattering two of them instantly and throwing the third into the path of a standing stone. Its impact was lost in the immense sound of the fallen statue, which had rung the earth like a gong and thrown everyone from their feet.

One of the nearest statues, one depicting a half feline/half reptilian Harnoq had been bent and knocked over somehow, though Felix suspected he knew why. His flickering Manasight could still trace wispy vapors of dusty brown Mana from the far end. It was just...so far away.

How did I do that?

Stone Shaping is level 25!

"Ah shit!" Felix gave the issue no more thought as he frantically cast around for his half-destroyed potions case. At the same time, the dark waters surged as another two dozen insect-fish creatures emerged, all of them darting in his direction. He threw himself down to dodge the first few, and though they missed him, a strident pain flashed across his spine and brain, like red-hot fireworks. Then, more buzzing creatures converged on him.

"Felix!" A yellow dome formed around him as he fell to his knees. "Hold it together!"

Congratulations! You Have Reached Apprentice Tier In Stone Shaping!
You Gain:
+5 STR

Felix could only grit his teeth and bear it as energy surged through him, pinging off an invisible wound. Close to twenty fly-fish hurled themselves at the shield around him, each of them chittering for his flesh. Another sharp cry, and close to half were diverted, streaming around him to attack the shield warrior who waded into the thick of it.

There! The case!

The pain surged again, just out of sight. He couldn't place it, he only felt the extreme agony of its presence, like an infected tooth. Felix snatched the Wandering Spirit draught from the ground, uncorked it with shaking limbs and quaffed it.

+5 WIL
+...

Uncommon Essence Draught Detected During Formation!
[Draught Essence of the Wandering Spirit]

Choose a Feature:
Wander
Dauntless
Chiaroscuro

What? A dull grinding resonated through his legs and it felt like his bones were splintering. *Wander, that's...ah..that's ok. Moving aimlessly? Dauntless sounds..agh!...sounds good. Bold and fearless. But...chiaroscuro? Isn't that a painting thing? Something about light and dark? Why is that...eyaah...even here? Why is* Italian *here in the System at all?*

The pain was coming increasingly fast. This was nothing like how his Body Tempered...or even the one Spirit Essence he tried. *What is happening?* The pain was transcending from bodily to something else, something that tugged at his heart and core as if someone was trying to tear away his skin. It was limb-weakening agony, and Felix fell to all fours. Felix blinked away sweat from his eyes and focused. The choice was before him, and he didn't have much time.

He chose Dauntless.

Or he tried to. His mental choice didn't register. And then the box did something he had never seen before. It..glitched. The blue system message flickered and twisted, suddenly flaring an angry red as the three options all scattered around him like loose leaf paper in a breeze. Pain tore through him, more savage than ever, and his left leg and forearm were at the center of it. Felix reached out, but each time the options flitted away.

GAH! Just choose, damnit!

He screamed as he closed his eyes and jabbed his arm forward, somehow trying to flare his Blind Fighting passive Skill.

Congratulations!
You have absorbed the Essence of Chiaroscuro!

Suddenly his body stopped hurting. The phantom injuries along his left side faded in an instant, and his skin felt normal and whole. That lasted for all of a second before the space around his core seemed to ignite, his internal fire eating away at his own flesh as soundless lightning crackled beyond his body, beyond anything tangible, and struck at the heart of who he was...it was pure agony. Pure ecstasy. Then, utter nothingness consumed his entire world.

CHAPTER SIXTY-EIGHT

"My lord Champion!"

Grimmar paused his inspection of the Song, which crooned so lovely into the air, and turned to his subordinate. "What is it?"

The kin before him was older and seasoned, a battle veteran Grimmar had taken out on many attacks against their enemies. However, the elder kin's name slipped from Grimmar's mind almost instantly, leaving only a curious blank in his memories. The old kin cleared his throat and pointed to a few smudges on the floor. "They were here, my lord. They fled that way."

Grimmar straightened to his full twenty-five-foot height and grinned, pushing his massive teeth outward in a display that all of his men found extremely upsetting.

"Good. They're close. I know it." Grimmar turned to his men, who were taking a short breather. "Full speed ahead! The enemy has revealed themselves! They must not be allowed to enter the Mother's presence!"

This would all end, soon.

Felix woke up and felt like twelve pieces of shit held together with scotch tape and dryer lint.

Everything hurt. Even his hair.

"Uglhgbl," he groaned. His lips and tongue felt a little numb, as if the nerves had been blasted to smithereens. He opened his eyes to black feathers and huge golden orbs that stared wetly at him from an inch away.

"*Squawk*!" A rush of warmth flooded his chest, and Pit nuzzled his glossy head against Felix's face for an entire minute, scratching at him with his sharp beak. Luckily, Felix had grown more than strong enough to withstand a few pokes, otherwise the tenku's razor-sharp beak would have ripped him open.

"Okay," Felix croaked as he waved the affable chimera away and sat up. Or tried to; his core muscles were like jelly, lasting no longer than a simple flex before going wobbly and dropping Felix back to the ground. "Unf!"

"Alright alright. Take it easy," Magda stepped over from his left and helped the Nym to a sitting position. "That was a nasty Temper. Maybe those Rare Essences hit you harder than you thought."

Felix's mouth felt dry as if stuffed with sand. "What do you mean?"

"I said Rare Essences would strain ya, right? Too much Mana in your channels can stretch and tear 'em, burn 'em out if you're not careful. And, unless I miss my guess, you just Tempered your Spirit," Felix nodded, and she continued. "Temperin' in the middle of a fight...you got some balls. That's usually a sure way to get dead."

Felix grimaced and looked around himself, noting the dark greasy smoke still wafting into the air all around them. It was a dark counterpoint to the pale fog, thicker and more potent. He sighed. "Thank you for keeping me alive. If you hadn't shielded me..."

"You woulda pulled something outta your hat, I'm sure. Frankly, kid, you're ridiculous. I've never met someone who advanced so quickly or accumulated so much strength as fast as you." Magda shook her head and sat on a tilted stone. "But still...there's something wrong with you. Your Spirit, I mean. But...huh, it's more than Mana strain, since your channels don't seem the worse for wear. My senses ain't the best, my Ironblood Body and Stonesteel Mind were formed for durability, not sensitivity. Story of my life," she added in a mutter, still peering at him. Felix felt exposed under that gaze, piercing even without the green glow of her Nighteye spell.

"Did somethin' happen to you? Was it that giant fuck? Did he break one of your Skills, too?"

Felix swallowed painfully, throat still dry. "No. Grimmar didn't do anything to me, thankfully."

"Well somethin' nasty got you at one point. Maybe scarred your Spirit. It has to be why your Temper went so bad."

Unbidden, the image of the Dread swam up from the dark depths of his mind, a mass of tentacles and eyes that extended into infinity, orange and inhuman. Of hooks and barbs and deadly danger mere moments after his arrival.

"Yes," he said in a quiet voice as events started to replay behind his eyes. "Something did."

Magda watched him closely, Felix's tone drawing her brows down contemplatively. She waited, letting him gather his thoughts, but a few minutes passed before he spoke. Felix, caught up in memories, vividly remembered the Dread's dire form in the brackish waters of the Bitter Sea. Moreover, he recalled the horror and pain he felt when the thing had wrapped its hooked tentacles into his flesh, piercing his left forearm and left ankle as it pulled him slowly deeper into the water.

Felix shuddered within the power of his perfect memory, almost surprised that he was not choking on the Dread's acidic ichor but breathing cold, humid air instead. The pain of those wounds and of the sharp, burning blood as it coursed down his throat echoed into the present. Felix felt his core flare with a terrible, aching hunger. The dark smoke swirled around them, and for a second all he could envision was tearing into one of those insectoid fish hybrids. With his teeth.

Sweat poured down his face despite the cool air, and Felix realized that his hands were shaking. He clenched them together, the spasm flitting through his forearms and biceps like an electric shock. He felt a laugh bubble up from his chest, one that shook his weakened abs unpleasantly. A soft warmth butted against his back, nudging him before putting a raven-like head over his shoulder and cooing softly. Impressions flitted through his chest, his pact, compact messages of warmth, of a nest, of...safety.

Companion Pact is level 24!

"Love you too, little bird," Felix scritched the tenku's head, moving to the side of his neck as Pit's uninjured wing briefly wrapped around him. Leaning back against that comfort, Felix felt a weight drop off his chest, one he almost hadn't realized he'd been carrying. He started talking, not filtering his words or gauging responses, the words pouring out of him in a deluge that had been a long time coming.

"I arrived here less than a month ago. I...woke up on a tiny spit of sand in the middle of a green ocean. I was alone, and I had no idea where I was or how I got there," Felix said.

Magda tilted her head but didn't interrupt.

"I uh, I fell in the water," he continued, the remembered splash and bite of the Bitter Sea washing over him. "Something grabbed me. A monster. It latched onto me and tried to...to pull me into the deep. I remember thinking that I was gonna die. I turned and saw its glowing orange eyes and tentacles, and I knew that this *thing*, this bastard was gonna eat me. So, I did it first."

He laughed, a small sound in the echoing chamber. "Ate it, really. Its blood was nasty and burned, but it was worth it. The thing let go. I got out of the water and ran my ass off."

Magda's snort interrupted his narrative, and Felix was confused as she began to laugh. "You got grabbed by a sea monster? And you lived because you...you bit it? Haha!" She screamed in laughter, the echo of her voice carrying far in this strange lake room. "That's the most ridiculous thing I've ever heard!"

Felix blushed even as he frowned at the Shieldwitch. "That's what happened. I don't know why it let me go. Maybe I just surprised it, I don't know! It nearly killed me as I ran down the sand spit, though. It didn't let me off easy, and those wounds nearly killed me."

"From a sea creature? I would expect so. Never seen one myself, but anything that *lives* in the Bitter Sea is deadly. They should be able to kill either of us with a single swipe of their claw, paw, tentacle, whatever. What level were you when you got away?"

Felix swallowed again, forgetting that his throat was still dry. Magda caught his expression and tossed him a full waterskin; filled from the lake, no doubt. He took a swig. *Here goes nothing.* "I uh, I didn't have a level."

"What?"

"I didn't have a level at the time. Or a status screen. Or Skills or anything," Felix felt his heart pound in his chest as he admitted these things, watching the shield warrior's face and hands, half ready to run away. He knew he was faster than her, now. "Where I'm from, we don't *have* levels."

Magda stood up, wincing slightly as something twinged in her side. "What do you mean? *Where* are you from?"

Felix scratched his neck, uncomfortable under her stare. "I'm from a place called Florida. On Earth. And, in my home, there are no adventurers, Titles...no magic."

"Noctis wept," Magda's hand drifted closer to her mouth. "You're Unbound."

"What?" Felix straightened. Magda took a step backward as he did so, which didn't escape his attention. "I've heard that term before. What does it mean?"

"Unbound. Unmoored. Untethered to this world, but brought in just the same. How?" Magda watched him with wide eyes, refusing to blink. Felix saw her body language shift subtly, her arms in front of her torso. Shields out.

"I don't know how," he answered slowly. Last thing he wanted to do was spook her. "That's what I'm saying. I woke up on the beach, got attacked by a nightmare, and when I woke up, everything started going weird."

"Weird how?"

"Well I...I went through character creation," Felix shrugged. At Magda's blank look he grunted. "Ugh. I got to choose my Race, my Omen, and my Born Trait."

"What!" Magda's voice boomed out, and this time her arms swept out in astonishment.

"Except I didn't. Not really," the words were coming fast now that he was saying them, the truth spilling out like a leaking balloon. "For some reason, all I got was some error messages from the System, and then it told me that my Race and Omen were already picked. The only thing I really got to pick was my Born Trait."

Magda started pacing, the stone beneath her shifting and clattering with her every step. "Your Race...what...the stories talk about the Unbound, call them demons, monsters. Calamity personified. But you're so...."

"Human-looking?" Felix asked. Magda only stared. "Are you asking what Race got picked for me?"

She nodded, and Felix grimaced.

"Nym."

Magda went remarkably still, but the tension in the air was suddenly thicker than the fog. Felix felt sweat pour down his back, and he had the very serious urge to run as far away as he could. "I'm not Nym, though! Not really. I was human before I came here. The System just...changed it on me. Like I said, I didn't get to choose. Didn't even get to see many other options."

There was a long minute of silence, a time that stretched on for several eternities to Felix. Then, unexpectedly, the tension eased by the barest fraction, something loosening in the air. Magda took a shaky breath. "A Lost Race...No wonder you're so damn strong."

"What?" Felix asked. "What does that have to do with anything?"

"Your ignorance makes *so* much more sense now," Magda half-muttered. "A Lost Race is one that fell to Ruin, and Ruin only comes to those who...reach too far. Burn too bright. Humans have been around for Ages, longer than history is recorded. That's because we're weak, all things considered. We only get three free stats each level, after all."

"Really? No bonuses?" Felix asked.

"Nothing else. We're shafted compared to almost any other Race; we just make up for it by sheer numbers. Talent, too, that counts for a lot. But we're safe from the Ruin." She laughed, a trace of wildness in her tone. "We thought you were a noble who lost his retinue. Hah! You're just a kid in over his head, Lost race or no."

Weirdly, Magda seemed almost happy about it all. Felix felt his chest loosen. "Is being Unbound a bad thing?"

Magda shrugged. "Old folk, specially the religious kind, they say the Unbound were demons sent by the gods to ravage the world."

"I'm not planning on any ravaging any time soon," Felix offered with a tentative smile.

"No didn't—didn't think you were," she coughed, hacking something wet and phlegmy onto the ground. "*Achem.* You're probably the least terrifying demon I've ever met. And the first."

Felix, finally feeling stronger, leveraged himself to his feet. "Glad of that. I certainly wouldn't want you for an enemy."

"Damn straight."

"Is this better or worse than a spy for your Guild?" Felix asked.

"About an even split. One the one hand, you're a cursed Unbound monster sent by the Blind Gods. On the other, you're *not* a boot-licking toady for the Elders." Magda fixed him with a grin. "Tall tales or no, the latter is heavily in your favor."

Felix laughed, a bit awkwardly, but the last of the tension drained away. Pit cautiously nosed his way between the two of them, cooing as both of them started petting him.

"Still doesn't change the fact that your Spirit is fucked up," Magda added. "You shouldn't Temper the last bit just yet. No telling how bad it might go. Even for a Nym."

Felix bit his lip and eyeballed his two, no three Spirit Skills that were close to Tier. Acid Stream, Shadow Whip, and Companion Pact. With a deep sigh, he dismissed his Skills and rubbed his temples. "So, what next?" Felix asked after a moment, looking out over the waters.

"Next, we figure out a way across the waters. Got any ideas?"

Felix did, in fact, have an idea.

Using Stone Shaping, he formed a wide boat to hold the three of them. It took exactly twenty-three tries before he figured out the air to stone ratio, feeling out the shape until the thing was thin enough to float but strong enough to hold their weight. Felix got absolutely soaked and wasted a bunch of Mana, but the thrill of creation was almost a reward in and of itself. The end result was a wide rowboat with a deep draft, and he even added a few bits of carvings to the edges, little geometric shapes that had no real rhyme or reason. He also made two oars out of the same stone, which was the easiest part.

However, his Stone Shaping had greatly improved since it Tempered. Whatever the hell Chiaroscuro did for his Spirit Formation, it somehow increased his dexterity with the spell by an order of magnitude. Shaping stone felt as natural as breathing, and Felix had to devote less mental energy to sounding out the spellform with Fire Within. So far, all of his Tempered Skills had improved greatly in some way, which Magda explained as one of the main effects of Tempering aside from forging yourself anew.

Forty minutes later, the three of them moved confidently onto the calm waters of the Statue Sea, as Felix dubbed it. While at first the traversal seemed oddly easy, they soon found that each statue would shift alarmingly each time they drew close. Unsure whether they were designed to collapse onto them or something even more sinister, they made it a point to avoid them at all costs. The waves grew in strength as they drew deeper into the waters, and by the first mile, their stone boat was riding up and down eight-foot waves while swarms of monsters burst from below to attack them. While a few were Glassbone Stalkers, they were mostly those fly-fish amalgams that thoroughly grossed him out. They were called Felkies, apparently, and nothing about them was good except that they were easy to kill. They attacked in swarms, even. Felix's best tactic was simply blasting them with Reign of Vellus, often having to keep the kinetic spell up for several minutes while it discharged blue lightning all around them. Pit helped with well-placed Frost Spears as often as he could, though the constant motion threw off his aim.

By the time they dragged their boat ashore on the other side, it had been two hours. Their strength was enough to propel them at great speed, despite the rough waters. They had also killed hundreds of Felkies, enough that Felix felt he was at the cusp of another level. Pit, meanwhile, had already leveled up twice, to 13.

Smug bastard, Felix thought, feeling the tenku's exhilaration as he strutted around on shore. He cracked a smile though, happy that at least his Companion was getting stronger. In fact, the double level ups had boosted the tenku's regeneration enough that his wing had healed completely, though not before Magda had insisted on rebreaking the malformed joint. It was painful, for Felix and Pit both, but necessary. Pit agreed to it, and despite the flare of pain he felt during it, the tenku was grateful toward the large shield warrior. Especially once the extra energy from the System helped heal it properly this time.

At the edge of the room was a set of stairs, twenty feet wide and going up at a steep angle until they disappeared into the fog. A smaller set of stairs was carved into the center, built for shorter legs and smaller feet.

Geist steps, Felix mused.

They climbed. For nearly an hour, they climbed. It was exhausting, even to Felix's quick Stamina regeneration. He didn't have a "stair climbing" Skill, so his usage soon outdrew his regen by a healthy measure. They had to take several breaks, mostly for Magda. She seemed...not great. Felix didn't mention it to her because he had no solutions, and surely she already knew what was going on. Whatever Grimmar had done to her, plus the Rotvein Poison, was taking its toll.

As they crested the staircase, Felix realized they were on top of a large platform, overlooking a substantial section of the Labyrinth. The fog blocked most sights, but looming nearby they could see a dark, ruined building. It was huge, big enough to be seen somewhat through layers of the damn mist, but close enough that it wasn't completely obscured. Trading nervous looks with Magda, they kept going.

The way forward was twisty and full of dead ends, as much of the rest had been, but it was remarkably lacking in traps of any sort. Or monsters. It was utterly quiet, save for their footsteps and Pit's clacking claws.

It was damn eerie.

When they finally came to the foot of the building, they found it to be a dark, dingy fortress made of dark stone and bronze metal. It was monolithic, with not a single visible join or seam, rising far above them and disappearing into the fog. The plaza they entered was wide open with no standing stones or structures and it measured somewhere along the lines of three hundred foot square. Across the plaza, directly opposing Felix and Magda, was a massive circular door, easily fifty feet in diameter, and banded with strips of that same bronze metal. Metal that seemed very similar to Felix's hooked sword.

More Nymean structures? He'd noticed that they enjoyed building with that particular metal, for whatever reason.

Felix looked at Magda, who was busy inspecting the plaza before them.

"This feels like a trap," he said.

"Oh yeah. Big trap."

Felix flexed his Manasight, which had been coming a bit easier recently. He could see the faint impression of...something...that had rubbed against the ground nearby. Traces of thick crimson energy were splattered here and there, and Felix's eyes went wide when he recognized the scent of it.

"Magda, there is—"

The screeching sound of metal on stone interrupted them, and they both whirled toward the source. A massive black and brown creature dropped from the wall, as long as a school bus and half as tall, its massive metallic claws ringing unpleasantly on the ground. Eyes of black with red-irises stared at them with undisguised hunger, though any sound it tried to make was turned into a wheeze by its strange collar.

Wait. Felix looked again and noticed that it wasn't a collar at all. Someone had hammered three bronze-gold spikes through the creature's neck.

Analyze...

Name: Bloodtainted Guardian
Type: Blood Beast
Level: 49
HP: ???/???
SP: ???/???
MP: ???/???
Lore: Corrupted by blood rituals, this creature was punished by its own people.
Strength: ???
Weakness: ???

Then the screeching sound came again, and a second Guardian joined the first.

CHAPTER SIXTY-NINE

The two Bloodtainted Guardians let out rasping hisses, and Felix felt animosity burn through the air. His Manasight perceived clouds of corrupted Mana steam from the creatures' undulating forms. A croaking yowl sounded from the first Guardian, bronze spikes vibrating unpleasantly. The second answered that call, its glottal thrum a buzzing dissonance that set Felix's teeth on edge.

Then they charged.

Their metallic claws struck sparks from the ground as they loped toward them, and Felix launched himself to the right while Pit ran to the left. In less than a second, the first creature had crossed the intervening distance and slammed its entire body against a hastily-erected Force Wall.

Felix tumbled, rolling himself forward onto his feet as the second Guardian peeled off toward him. His leap had taken him quite the distance, so Felix had a moment to inspect the creature before him. The creature was giant, a cross between a serpent and a weasel, yet worse than both. They were both, aside from their sheer size and fur patterns, near replicas of the Seven-Legged Orit. Sleek muscles rippled beneath their matted, brown and off-white hides, while their faces were gaunt and skeletal, dark pits for eyes and sharp, yellowed teeth, longer than his forearm, that dripped thick drool. The thinning fog revealed a plethora of shattered weapons, swords, and blades of all kinds that still remained in its thick hide; all this without even considering the strange bronze spikes through their necks.

But Felix's brief respite was over as the Guardian rushed him.

Reign of Vellus!

Blue light washed forward, lightning crackling up from the ground, but it did little more than flatten the fur on the Guardian's face.

Shit.

Felix shot out a Shadow Whip, securing it against the cobbled flooring before yanking hard. The Guardian leaped into empty space, barely missing his form, while Felix landed in an ungainly roll. His Dexterity and Agility were both high, but he still wasn't as graceful as Evie. The Guardian let out a choking roar, those throat spikes buzzing again.

Felix breathed hard, not tired but more than a little terrified of these creatures. They were nearly thirty levels above him! Felix had dealt with more than a few higher-leveled foes, but the last time he'd tangled with someone this high was Grimmar...and that hadn't ended well.

The Guardian twisted, its long body folding unnaturally as it followed Felix with its dead eyes. Those eyes burned with a crimson illumination, and Felix's Manasight spotted streams of dark vapor gathering between the creature's cadaverous jaws.

Manasight is level 37!

The dark vapor condensed in seconds into a liquid-like ball of crackling energy, dark as night. Felix's instincts screamed at him to get away, and he wasn't stupid enough to ignore them. Jerking a hand upward, Felix raised a stone wall from the floor between them and utilized Reign of Vellus to push himself up and away at an angle. Just in time, as the crackling ball burst into a beam of dark lightning, shearing through the stone wall like a hot knife through butter. It splashed against the massive structure behind him, rebounding off a glittering shield of green-gold light. Felix took note of that.

It has a shield? How do we get in? He ran, pushing his new Body to evade another dark lightning blast. *Focus. Kill them first, then the door.*

Frost Spears flew past Felix, close enough to feel their bitter energy, as the second Guardian battled against Magda and Pit.

Feelings of frustration and increasing aggression poured across the pact, causing Felix to glance over in concern. Magda was getting pummeled on by the beast, the original Force Wall gone, though it hadn't yet gotten through her kite shields. Pit, meanwhile, circled it and fired off Wingblades and Frost Spears, which it either dodged somehow or were deflected by its hide.

"*Oof!*"

He paid for his momentary distraction as his opponent surged forward and swiped him with a massive tire-sized paw. Felix sailed through the air before landing in a painful roll on the ground. A flash of bright white light suffused his vision for a moment, the pain blinding before numbing down to tolerable levels.

Pain Resistance is level 34!
Armored Skin is level 28!

"Ugh," Felix pushed himself to his feet, rushing despite several ugly twinges in his legs and lower back. Felix summoned twin streams of acid into his hands and blasted them back at the Guardian.

"Kkrrraaaaahhhh!" It roared in full defiance of his onslaught, bronze spikes rattling with the sound. The acid pattered against the creature, even burned it in many places, but Felix could see those same burns healing over only seconds later.

It's regenerating! What must its stats be to regenerate damage that fast? Or was that a blood beast thing? He considered his own Health, down now by 15% from that hit alone. *I didn't even get the claws, either.*

However, his magical assault had one good side effect; it made the Guardian wary of him. Despite the healed damage, Felix had still wounded the beast. It prowled in a slow circle around the Nym, and Felix took the breather to assess their situation.

Magda is holding her beast off, though for how long...? He looked around the room, never quite taking his eyes off the Guardian. *This room is huge, but there's nothing really to use here. Stone Shaping could make obstacles, but it's so strong, and that bullshit dark lightning spell shattered my wall.* He felt a growl in his core, and smiled despite himself. *That'd be a good spell to have...*

The Guardian paused, tipping its head like a dog with a scent, before dropping low and snarling at Felix. Those bronze spikes, so painful to look at, buzzed again.

What is the deal with those? Felix peered at the bronze spikes, trying to get a bead on them, but Analyze was slippery and only gave back the Guardians' stats. *They're part of it, somehow. A weak point? Or something else?*

Then his sharp eyes recognized that the plethora of broken blades in the creature's back held something else. A torn and tattered bag, half-pierced by a jagged sword. The Guardian dipped its head, undulating as it moved, and the bag twisted to reveal a lumpy square shape within.

My satchel!

It was beaten up, nearly beyond recognition, torn and strained by the fall and whatever these monsters had done to it. However, Felix could still see the boxy outline of the lockbox Pit had stolen from the Archon. With a flash of recollection, he checked his Active Quest List.

A Light In The Dark! 0 of 4 Remnants Found

The lockbox had one of the blood remnants, and Felix had tucked the other remnant into one of the satchel's pockets. He frowned as he confirmed that, since losing his bag, he was back to 0% on the Light in the Dark quest.

More sounds of frustration from Magda and the other Guardian, and Felix got an idea. Well, two ideas.

"Magda! Use these!" With a burst of Mana, Felix conjured a series of stone spears around Magda, much as he had against the Risi Commander. He saw her fierce grin as she snapped one of the spears from the ground before hurling it forward.

"Stone Break!"

The spear exploded into razor sharp shards, throwing her Guardian to the side and piercing its thick hide.

Felix spun back to his opponent who, as expected, was nearly on top of him.

Influence of the Wisp!

Shadow Whip!

Stone Shape!

A tendril of shadow snapped outward, tangling with the Guardian's legs. Felix flexed his Willpower and split the whip into four tendrils, each of which tangled with the long creature's powerful legs. The Shadow Whip barely tripped them up, the Guardian tearing through them in moments, but it paused the beast's charge long enough to become subsumed in blue-white fire.

Enthrall Failed. Target Is Immune.

The Enthrall didn't stick, but the new effect of his spell did: the Guardian made croaking screams as the fire ate away at its flesh and fur. Still the beast didn't stop, barrelling forward as its body went up like a torch.

The last spell was for him.

A platform of stone rocketed Felix upward, mere moments before the monster hit him. Felix leaped from this rising pillar, his Strength and Agility more than enough to send him flying over the head of the Guardian and directly onto its back. The pillar shattered into pieces as the monster charged through it, but Felix had already landed on its back and raced forward among the jagged hilts of doomed weapons.

Ah, shit! That's hot! In retrospect, using his new fire spell *then* jumping on a creature was not a great idea. But beggars couldn't be choosers.

Fire Resistance is level 19!
Heat Resistance is level 21!

Luckily, his aim hadn't been too far off. He was within a few yards of his satchel.

Felix got a hand around one of the tattered straps when something hit him like a freight train. Something pierced through him, a white hot bar of torment, and then he went flying. He flew so fast that he barely had time to tumble, smashing into the wall forty feet away. The wall cracked and shattered, sheets of rock shearing from the surface as his body was driven a foot into the stone.

"Hruuh!"

Pain Resistance is level 35!
Armored Skin is level 29!
Armored Skin is level 30!
Armored Skin is level 31!

Felix could only stare, eyes bulging, as his body failed to respond. He couldn't even breathe, his lungs unable to move for several long seconds. He saw Magda getting smashed to the ground, her Force Walls shattered. He saw Pit limping, blood trailing on the ground behind him but still managing to fire off a Frost Spear. And directly in front of him, Felix watched as the Bloodtainted Guardian untwisted itself, its impossible surrealist body contorting and stretching. The blue-white fire of his spell faded, and the damage done began to heal at a visible rate. A sharp, wet coughing sound drifted to Felix's ears, accompanied by a dissonant buzzing. It took him a second to realize that the monster was laughing.

In a whoosh, his breath returned, and Felix panted as he eyeballed his Health. That hit had dropped him to 30% Health. His mind raced as his body pulsed with pain. He couldn't survive another full-on strike. His new Body, augmented by Armored Skin and an Endurance stat at 131 were likely the only reason his spine wasn't shattered right then.

With a pained grunt, Felix pulled himself out of the wall and landed heavily onto the ground below. The Guardian still advanced, though it had slowed to a cautious walk. The thing was cunning, that was certain. It started to gather dark vapor in its mouth again.

He didn't have much time.

My spells aren't strong enough to penetrate its defenses for long, and I can't get close enough to pummel it without getting swiped again. Felix wiped sweat and blood from his eyes. Something had cut open his scalp. He needed a stat boost, something to juice up his damage enough to put the hurt on this monstrosity. Aside from somehow earning another Title or gaining a level for no reason, he only had one option. Well, two really.

Apprentice Tier.

He started running forward.

Shadow Whip!

Shadow Whip!

Two castings, this time both of them tacky tendrils of conjured shadow Mana. With a cry, he flung them forward and up, their length stretching as they did so to bash into the Guardian's triangular snout. With a Strength of 120 behind it, the whips snapped their head back, the dark lightning spell discharging into the air.

Spinning around, Felix used his own momentum to increase his attack, bringing the whips across the Guardian's exposed throat.

Croaking in surprised pain, it stumbled backward. And Felix grinned.

I can do this.

Applying his will, both whips split into two, then four, then with a burning stab in his mind, he split them again into eight. Something hot and wet rolled down his face, but he ignored it. Felix cast them forward, spreading their ends to tangle the Guardian's limbs. The creature leaped out of the way, but Felix didn't stop. Whip after whip, tendril upon tendril, he threw everything he had into it, burning his Mana at a prodigious rate. His head felt like it was cracking open, each split of the whips taxing his mind in ways he didn't understand, yet flared like white-hot fire. But he was used to pain; it was an old friend at this point.

Pain meant it was working.

Over and over, the whips lashed the Guardian, though they managed to counter and slice many of the tendrils before they hit. Still, wounds accumulated as fast as they healed, and Felix's arms burned with exertion. The Guardian yowled, another orb of liquid darkness forming in its jaws, and Felix wrapped a whip around its snout. The spell aborted with a resounding thunderclap, sending gobbets of cheek flesh flying as the monster's mouth blew from the inside.

Blunt Weapon Mastery is level 10!

Shadow Whip is level 25!
Congratulations! You Have Reached Apprentice Tier in Shadow Whip!
You Gain The Following:
+10 STR
+10 PER
+10 INT

Finally! Mindful of his Spirit damage, Felix let it pass without an essence draught. Still, a stabbing pain jolted from his left ankle, though it was soon lost amid the general flurry of energy the System poured directly into his veins.

The Guardian ripped through his tendrils, shredding their

conjured substance with its steel talons and freeing its mouth. Flesh re-knit across its cheeks, covering the gruesome teeth and tongue with ropes of withered skin. And it looked *pissed*.

Felix didn't pause, using hands shaky from stat gain to conjure dual orbs of Acid Stream. In a fit of inspiration, he pressed the two orbs together; a moment of tension and resistance, then an audible pop as the acid sloshed and mixed together. He now had a double-sized orb of acid rotating quickly between his two hands. It was stronger than his standard acid, but Felix felt it would have to be far stronger to do anything to this foe. He also did not miss that the Guardian was starting to move again.

My hands are busy; I can't cast Shadow Whip again.... He had little choice. *God, I hope this doesn't destroy my stuff.*

Influence of the Wisp!

Enthrall Failed. Target Is Immune.

Blue-white fire immolated the creature, and it began screaming in that choking way again. The Guardian was smart, however, and it didn't try to put out the flames. It cut to the chase and simply began running at Felix. Eyes wide, Felix frantically poured more Mana into his spellform, dumping nearly three hundred Mana into it as it ballooned outward, now the size of a beach ball and wobbling between his hands.

The ground shook with the Bloodtainted Guardian's loping advance. If he had the attention to spare, Felix would have thrown stone obstacles in its way, but it took everything he had to keep his spell from going haywire. *It's not ready!* He frantically poured Mana into the unsteady spellform, stretched beyond its intended function. *It's not-!*

It was too late. Guardian upon him, unable to dodge or else lose the spell entirely, Felix raised the globe of corrosive up into the air and gritted his teeth.

"*Force Wall!*"

With milliseconds to spare, a wall of yellow energy blinked into existence between Felix and the furious Guardian. It crashed into the magical barrier, the yellow Mana flaring red as the behemoth blood beast strained its limits. Blinking in surprise, Felix darted a glance at Magda. She stood nearly fifty feet away with her arm outflung in two directions. One toward him and one toward the *other* blood beast, likewise restrained by a Force Wall.

Felix nodded at her, blood and sweat dripping down his face.

"Cast! Quickly!" She shouted at him.

So he did. The acid globule had destabilized further during his lapsed attention, losing about a quarter of its Mana and cohesion before he firmed up its shape with his Willpower. A little less than three hundred Mana invested in the orb, it still wasn't enough, and he had plenty to spare. The Guardian strained against the barrier, flaring it orange and red in places as its claws and snout pushed and snapped at the magic. Felix focused, expending his Willpower further by shutting the enormous death beast out of his mind, putting every single iota of attention onto this spell.

It was a giant water balloon of acid, but that would do little to the blood beast. It had to be more. He had to DO more. Sounding out the shape of his Skill, he altered it, tweaked the pattern until the orb grew again, feeding on another two hundred Mana. Then he took a breath...and he tapped his shard, dumping all five hundred stored Mana into the spellform.

The acid orb grew huge until it was nearly six feet in diameter...but still, Felix wasn't done. Sunk deep into the pattern within his core, he knew this wasn't enough. So he lifted his hands, now spread as wide as they could go, and *pushed*, compressing the conjured magic. The acid steamed, the unsteady orb becoming a furious, boiling shape as Mana was pressed against Mana. Acrid vapor poured outward, falling like green mist as he compressed it, further and further, forcing it smaller with every pass. The Mana fought back, pushing at his hands with a bitter burn, eating away at his flesh until his hands were raw and dripping blood.

Felix gritted his teeth and bore the pain, letting it wash over him as he forced his spell to become something else. Something better.

"IT'S BREAKING THROUGH!"

The sound of thunder blasted across his senses, but Felix couldn't afford to look away from the dizzy lights within his own core; the rhythmic pound of huge feet and Magda's screams crashed against him, a terrible cold and anger blasting across his chest as Pit did something brave and foolish and...Felix tore himself away. There was only the spell. Or else...

Compress!

Mana leaked, boiling around him like a roaring waterfall, the sound like crashing cymbals and rolling timpanis. He pushed, his Strength and Endurance taking the load as much as his Willpower and Intelligence. Making a desperate gamble, Felix took the 10 free points he had saved and put all of them into Intelligence.

Compress!

A rising tremolo of notes came to a terrible crescendo and stuck there, sound stretched and strung between the beats of time. He opened his eyes. It was as if time had slowed down, his Intelligence and Perception working in tandem with something...else, to grant him an impossible snapshot. Green waves of acid and Mana were exploding all around him, expanding in a wave around his body as if he had splashed down in a puddle made of magic and death. Inches in front of him, battered by the corrosive waves, was one of the Bloodtainted Guardians, mouth wide in a snarl of pain while its legs still charged forward. Forward and to his right, only fifteen feet away, the second Guardian was frozen mid-lope, a dark power already gathering in its jaws.

He looked down.

In his hands Felix held an orb no bigger than his fist, matte and a green so dark it was nearly black. It spun, quickly even in his enhanced senses, and within that spinning there was a terrible, awful dissonance. As if in a dream, Felix cast it forward, hand thrusting out at the Guardian before him.

The wretched dissonance unraveled the frozen tremolo, time resuming with a furious lethality. The orb blasted forward like a shot and the Guardian...dodged it.

Still, it passed within inches of the blood beast's flesh, and it left a trail of dissolving meat and the monster *screamed*. Its body undulated away from the horrid spell's passage. But not fast enough. The orb zipped through several broken swords and impacted Felix's bag, tearing through leather and burst apart the locked box within.

Then it exploded.

A fireball as big as a house subsumed the Guardian instantly, so powerful it threw Felix back like a ragdoll, and even caught the second Guardian in its radius.

Felix landed hard on his ass, and he came back to his feet haltingly, more than a little woozy from discharging so much Mana at once. He peered into the fire, which twisted around itself and poured thick smoke into the dark sky above. There was no evidence of his opponent, its body entirely engulfed in that fireball, while the second Guardian stumbled painfully out of the flames before half falling to its side. Felix blinked and backed away, the monster entirely too close for comfort, and the wretched blood beast fixed him with a baleful eye.

"You...cannot...kill...us," it wheezed, the bronze spikes rattling and buzzing with every word. "We...cannot die. She...promised...."

Felix didn't know what to say, so naked was the hate and sorrow on its rat-like face. He'd almost feel pity if it hadn't just tried to kill them.

"We are...chosen!" The blood beast lunged forward, attempting to grab Felix; but he'd learned his lesson from the Orit, and used Relentless Charge to zip backward. It cost him in Mana and Stamina, but it was worth it. The monster fell flat on its face, his legs scrabbling against the hard ground, and it began to roar.

Beyond the Guardian, the fireball had died away, instead replaced with a crimson glow, one that began reversing the explosion. The fire and light and air all collapsed upon a single, brilliantly red point. Something bright and blood red ripped from the ground where the first dead Guardian had been, and the second, chattier one began to whine in terror.

"No! No!" It cried, pushing itself away. "We are...one...with the Maw..."

Then a blood red light tore from its chest to join the crimson singularity. It dropped to the ground, dead.

You have defeated a Bloodtainted Guardian (x2)!
You have earned XP!

Felix shook, like a leaf in the wind. His Health, Mana, and Stamina were all critically low, and his body was only barely coping. Luckily, his Stamina and Mana began to regenerate quickly...his Health would take far longer.

Acid Stream is level 25!
Congratulations! You Have Reached Apprentice Tier in Acid Stream!
You Gain The Following:
+10 INT

+10 ALA

Rarity of the Skill has upgraded!

Acid Stream (Rare) has become Wrack And Ruin (Epic)!

Wrack And Ruin (Epic), Level 25!
Nothing withstands your calamitous might! Not earth, not stone, not flesh. Potency, density, and speed increases moderately with Skill level.

The thrum of power echoed through him, and he smiled despite the fissure of pain that followed. The undeniable song that for a brief moment overwhelmed the constant concerto that was the Mother's symphonic breath. This was a chorus of life and power and possibility, pouring through him, into him, as he grew past his own limits once again.

The glowing red light slowly grew softer before floating gently to the ground, landing a few feet away with a soft *plink*. He glanced at it before a soft whine captured his attention. Magda lay on the ground fifty feet away, and Pit was nearby, nosing her entirely-too-still hand.

He stumbled toward them, but before he could get very far, two things happened in quick succession. The first, a notification:

Hidden Quest Complete!
Survive The Labyrinth!
You have bested the final guardians of the Labyrinth and are granted your just rewards!

And then, the massive door began to open.

CHAPTER SEVENTY

The massive door, more like a circular bank vault than anything else, pulled upward slowly with the sound of shrieking metal and grinding stone. Beyond was a soft darkness that almost seemed to...breathe. Felix flared his Manasight (a task that had become far easier), and he perceived a whirlwind: streams of multicolored vapor and light were being pulled into the doorway, all of the ambient Mana in the area gone in an instant.

Devoured.

Bastion of Will is level 35!

Felix gulped audibly, his pulse a rapid tattoo in his neck and chest. In the few moments before his Bastion of Will reestablished itself, he had heard that entrancing song, louder and more persuasive than ever. It sent through him a wave of dizziness that, coupled with his copious blood loss, was enough to stagger him. But then it was gone, and Felix was left staring at the void beyond the doorway.

Another notification hit him.

Quest Complete!
Advance Five Spells To Apprentice Level!
You have proven yourself an apprentice mage!

You Gain The Following:
Title: Apprentice Magus (Rare)
You have shown the bare minimum required of a Magus. You advance...for now. Gain +10 to Mental Stats, +10 to RES, +10 to ALA

ERROR!

...Rewards Increased Due to Advancing 6 Spells to Apprentice Tier
...Rewards Increased Due to Advancing 6 Spells of Rare or Higher Rarity
...Rewards Increased Due to Advancing 2 Spells of Epic or Higher Rarity
Unlocking Resonance and Alacrity...
Already Unlocked!
Accessing Options...

Unlocking Intent and Affinity...
+10 To All Harmonic Stats
+25% XP Gain Toward Next Level

You Have Unlocked A Harmonic Stat!
Intent - Affects influence upon the Harmonics. Confluence of Willpower and Strength.
Current Value: INE - 63

You Have Unlocked A Harmonic Stat!
Affinity - Affects empathy and connection. Confluence of Vitality and Perception.
Current Value: AFI - 57

The usual currents of effervescent energy boiled through him, expanding Felix in ways he could neither see nor understand. He simply felt...more. The music swelled higher and higher, the sound sweeping away the breathy call of the dark doorway, pure and crystalline. Vibrating through his entire being, as if he were the world's biggest tuning fork, struck upon the bones of the world.

When the rush faded, he was on his hands and knees, blinking at the cracked and riven ground. Before him was a crimson gemstone the size of a plum. It glittered in the glowlight of the Labyrinth's moss and fog, bright with a certain vitality that attracted him even as it repelled him. Instinctively, he Analyzed it.

Name: Bloodstone (Complete)
Type: Core
Lore: A complete bloodstone, made of a powerful creature's raw, immutable essence.

Felix picked it up, certain he knew what it was; another notification soon followed, confirming his suspicions.

Quest Complete!
A Light In The Dark!
You have collected 4/4 Blood Remnants! All four Remnants have fused into a single Bloodstone.
You Gain The Following:
x1 Essence Stone of Consumption (Mind Essence)

Name: Essence Stone of Consumption
Type: Essence Stone (Legendary)
Lore: A rarefied and crystallized Essence from a high tier source. It will grant the Essence of Consumption, a Mind Essence.

The Bloodstone dissolved in his hand, transmuting from a plum-sized gem to an oblong rock approximately an inch long and a half inch in diameter.

Essence...stone? Legendary? Felix shook his head and palmed it as he got to his feet. He'd worry about it later. For now he was more concerned about Pit...and Magda.

The two of them were fifty feet away, and Magda was still on the ground. She wasn't moving at all. Felix walked a bit, then when his body didn't fall apart, he started to jog over. Pit was nervously pacing around her downed form, and he gave a small chirp at Felix when he approached. Felix couldn't tell if she was breathing, her armor too bulky. There was a slow ooze of blood from a nasty gash in her forehead, but that was the least of her wounds. Her left shield was broken, just a hunk of twisted metal, and the arm underneath it was mangled, too. The armor was rent even further than before, the script seal nearly gone. Gashes extended all over her mail and leather kit, the edges melted or burnt by that dark lightning the Guardians used. It had been a powerful spell, capable of blasting apart her mundane and magical shields, its dark energy having left clear marks where it traveled up her left arm and discharging from her shoulder. Both were a charred mess, and Felix imagined her left side was basically shot at this point.

"Magda? Magda?" Felix knelt down, but his leg muscles were a little shaky so it was more of a sudden squat. "Are you-?"

"I'm...alive," she wheezed. "For now."

Felix breathed a sigh of relief, dearly wishing he could get a read on the woman with Analyze. "You got any more of those script seal things? You've got an awful lotta wounds." Felix felt a pang of worry from Pit. *When had the tenku gotten so close to Magda?*

"Side pouch...right hip," Magda offered. Her eyes were scrunched closed with what looked like concentration. "You know...how to use em, Unbound?"

Felix was already at her hip, pulling out a supply of cloth bundles, each marked with a different symbol in red. "Not a clue, Shieldwitch."

She grunted, annoyed and amused in equal measure. "Grab...the one labeled...with yarrow."

Felix's attention pinged at the word. Yarrow, his favorite herb. The only problem was that he still couldn't read their language. "What's that look like?"

"Blind gods...you can't read?" Magda groaned. "Circle...with seven hooks. Two lines....at the bottom...like legs."

Felix quickly found what she spoke of, a roll of thin cloth that was held closed by a red wax seal. "Got it."

"Good. Put...put it on me. Arm...and shoulder. Wrap it up."

To do that, Felix had to pull off her armor. It was *fairly* straightforward, but Felix had to bend and rip apart a couple straps he couldn't figure out. After five minutes, he had her left shoulder and arm completely bare, the clothing (*Gambeson?*) beneath having also been ruined by the Guardian's dark power. Magda's naked skin was all inflamed and bloody, the armor removal causing some more sluggish bleeding as it tore open some of her more minor wounds. With great care, Felix broke the wax seal and began to wrap Magda's arm and shoulder. The bundle didn't seem particularly large, but it had more than enough to secure her wounds. At the end, Felix was left with a small red character inscribed on the edge of the bandage.

"Now prick your finger...put your...your blood on the script," Magda wheezed through her teeth, which had been grinding the entire time he'd worked. Felix did just that, but nothing happened.

"It's not working. What do I do?" Felix felt a touch of panic settle onto his mind. As much as the woman had annoyed him, he didn't want her to die. "What does the blood do?"

"Wha...it charges the...script. Like a...fire."

A spark to ignite it. Then it's transferring Mana. What if I just pour Mana directly into it? Would that work, or would it ruin it? Felix ran his hand over his face in frustration. "How much blood does it take?"

"Just...a drop is...fine," Magda breathed.

Then say...a hundred Mana should be good, right? Felix didn't ask, he just held a hand over the inscription and willed out a portion of his unattributed Mana. It poured from his hand like a cloud of crackling blue, a tiny storm cloud in his palm. Felix pushed the Mana down and into the inscription itself.

The bandages suddenly clung to her shoulder and arm, tightening as if vacuum sealed. Magda hissed in pain before relaxing, while the script seal began to glow with a bright green gold writing all down its length. The light traced the script being written *(revealed?)* before fading into a dark black ink, and it terminated at the far end of the seal bandage.

Mana Manipulation is level 5!
Mana Manipulation is level 6!

After a moment, Felix helped Magda to her feet. She wobbled a bit, but quickly regained her composure.

"I'll be...ach, alright. I think. That damn poison is still screwin' with my Body. Can't heal properly with all this muck in my system," she grunted, still treating her left side gingerly.

Felix eyed his own Health. He'd only gained around 26 points back in the ten minutes since the battle, and his aches were slow to dissipate. Stamina moved a lot faster however, having regenerated all of his 721 points, and his Mana was simply insane at this point. In the last ten minutes, he'd regenerated not only enough to refill his Mana pool, but to also recharge his shard back to full.

Gotta do something about that Health Regen. Either that or find a way to boost the hell out of my Meditation Skill.

"C'mon. We should get moving." Felix nodded at the open door. "I'm willing to bet that's the center we've been after."

Magda followed his gaze and nodded, her expression warring between pained and trepidatious. Felix didn't blame her. He wasn't relishing the idea of entering that doorway either.

Suddenly, Pit's head perked up and swiveled to look behind them. Moments later, Felix heard it, too.

Something was shaking the ground. And it was getting closer.

"Yyero's ass, what now?" Magda muttered, readying her lone shield and turning toward the source, the same path they had traversed.

Less than two seconds later, a massive figure emerged from the fog, dark and near featureless despite the glowlight of the maze. Teeth that reminded Felix vividly of a shark and boar-tusks led the way, the giant's blue skin and dark iron armor the same as ever.

"Well, well, well," Grimmar chortled. "What's happened here?"

From behind him came twelve more giants, each visibly winded but grinning viciously at Felix and his friends. The Nym's sharp eyes picked out signs of battle damage, wear upon their armor and skin that indicated that they hadn't been as careful as Felix and Magda had in their advancement.

"Grimmar," Felix growled. "How great to see you. How's the eye?"

The chieftain snarled at him, his hand lifting halfway to his left eye before stopping. It was still a ruin, the four angry red claw marks swollen and inflamed.

"I'll gut you for that, worm. You and your tame chimera." The giant glared at a space above Felix's left shoulder before flicking back to his face. "For that and so much more."

Oh right, the shard.

"I won this, fair and square," Felix said, trying to keep his voice mild as he glanced at the dissipating flesh of the Guardian beasts. The bronze spikes that had been within their necks were the only thing left from the first one, and the second was soon to follow. "You should have put more points into Willpower, Grimmy."

"Ta'katha! Riktu na fala!" One of the giants beside the chieftain surged forward, held back only by the hands of his fellows. The way the giant spit at him as he raged made it clear he took offense to Felix's flippant words. He didn't know why the others held the giant back, but he was happy for it.

Good. Gimme just a little longer.

Felix doubted he'd get that wish.

Grimmar held up a hand and the snarling of his subordinates died away instantly. He fixed Felix with a smarmy, insincere grin...or something close to it. The amount of teeth in the giant's mouth made normal facial expressions a challenge. Felix didn't fully understand how the Risi even spoke coherently.

"This posturing bores me, and I have better places to be. Ossun," Grimmar signaled an older Risi that was nearly fifteen feet tall. A Commander. "Dispose of them."

All twelve giants rushed in.

Reign of Vellus!

Reign of Vellus!

Reign of Vellus!

The three bronze spikes, the only remnants of the first Blood-tainted Guardian zipped through the air, propelled by Felix's will toward the three giants leading the charge. Ossun dodged out of the way, but the next three took the spikes directly to the neck, chest, and gut respectively. The spikes were extremely sharp, preternaturally so, cutting through the armor like tissue paper. Which was what Felix was counting on...what he didn't expect was what happened after.

Eldritch Contaminant Found...
Isolation Wards Initiated

Bright yellow lightning discharged from the three spikes, the giants attached to them seizing as thousands of volts coursed through their massive bodies. Sigils illuminated along the sides of the spikes, words Felix could neither make out nor understand, and all three spikes were suddenly drawn together like magnets. This meant that the three electrified Risi Warriors were also slammed together, blue blood spraying in a fountain between them as the bronze spikes discharged another deadly charge of power. The crackle of buzzing dissonance was powerful and awful.

Holy shit.

The Risi didn't move for a beat, letting Felix and Magda seize the initiative. Magda grabbed a stone rod, leftover from their previous fight, and hurled it among the largest cluster of giants.

"Stone Break!"

As the giants were bombarded with rocky shrapnel, Felix entered range and hit them with Influence of the Wisp. Four giants were hit, all of them succumbing to the Enthrall status condition, even as a blue-white fire rapidly ate at their exposed flesh. Their screams shocked the others into motion, and the visceral presence of fire seemed to bring out an unbridled rage in all the giants. They ignored Magda and headed straight for Felix.

Guess they hate fire.

A Force Wall penned them in, but only resisted a few powerful blows from the Risi Warriors, amassed as they were; but by then, Magda was among them, using Shield Bash on anyone who came close.

Felix, meanwhile, was focused on Grimmar. The chieftain was attempting to bypass the fight completely, walking briskly toward the opened door and yawning darkness beyond. Felix cast out a Shadow Whip, intending to grab the massive Risi's leg and trip him up. Instead, something grabbed *Felix's* leg and hauled back. His aim was thrown, the spell falling short of the chieftain as his body was jerked backwards several steps. After those steps, Felix's new heavier Body helped him stop and brace, and he looked behind him. The prone form of Ossun had his outstretched hand clasped firmly around Felix's ankle. The older giant also had a surprised look on his face, as if he had expected that to go differently.

"Kill them all, Ossun," Grimmar said as he glanced backward without stopping. "Mother will forgive us."

He disappeared into the dark.

Shit!

"Rak len fala to'mak rati!" Ossun screamed at him, his rage reigniting from a momentary confusion. The giant's grip tightened on Felix's leg, then he was sent sprawling to the side.

Felix's body impacted the ground with an almighty crash, the stone giving way beneath his strengthened Body and Ossun's enormous strength. Felix gasped in surprise, the impact driving the breath from his lungs yet again. However, Ossun had released Felix's leg as the Risi Commander regained his feet and loomed over the prone Nym.

"You...are...worthless," Ossun said in a stilted voice. Then he raised his right foot up high and drove it downward for a powerful stomp.

Reign of Vellus!

Lightning blasted all around him as Felix stopped the giant's boot with a thought and about 150 Mana. Even still, Ossun's leg began to shake and strain, moving closer with each moment. Still lying on his back, Felix cast his newest spell.

Wrack and Ruin!

A green orb condensed in his right hand, so dark it was nearly black, before launching with a powerful thunderclap at Ossun's enormous face. The blue bastard didn't even have a moment to blink before the fist-sized sphere punched directly through his forehead and shot out with a spray of blue gore.

You have defeated Ossun, Risi Commander!
You have earned XP!

Wrack and Ruin is level 26!

Felix gasped, stepping back from Ossun's death-slackened grip, surprised and a little sickened at the devastation of the giant's head. Yet he wasn't a fool, at least not always. He summoned two more dark orbs and sent them rocketing outward.

The deadly spheres were able to rip through a single enemy before they dissipated and he had to recast. As long as he hit them in an unarmored section, they died instantly, their flesh too weak to fight against the spell's powerful acid. Each casting, however, cost Felix upwards of a hundred Mana. He could manage about eight more shots before he'd be on empty, or relying on his shard's reserves.

I'll have to make 'em count, then.

Four more castings in rapid succession blasted out from his grasp, each one finding a giant's chest, head, or shoulder. Headshots were instantly fatal, but where the ball of highly-condensed acid had to eat through armor, it lost much of its penetrating power. It dissolved the crude iron armor the giants wore, but only did moderate damage to whatever flesh was beneath. Pit, anticipating Felix's actions, used his Frost Spears and Wingblades to put the giants off balance. The tenku had embraced his Poisonfire as well, and was a green-lit torch on the dark battlefield, weaving between the relatively-slow Risi like an immolating ghost.

Magda kept up her Force Walls and Stone Break projectiles as often as she could, trying to give them breathing space from the giants' massive reach advantage, but she was slower than ever. She was still strong though, and each blast of Stone Break or angled Shield Bash knocked back enemies, keeping them too occupied to properly assault Felix or Pit.

You have defeated an unknown Risi Warrior (x6)!
You have earned XP!

Less than thirty seconds into their fight, the ground started rumbling again, much louder this time. Only four Risi Warriors remained, but that was about to change; Felix could see a wave of dark shapes moving forward in the fog....from two different entrances.

"We have to run!" Felix shouted. "They're coming from all sides!"

Magda deflected a club strike, using the momentum to power her own spinning Shield Bash. The Risi facing her fell backward, its knees smashed in at an awful angle.

"Into the doorway!" She started running in his direction immediately, and Felix made sure to whistle at Pit as well. They retreated.

"*Raukta!* Falla lokti! Falla!" a voice in the fog shouted, but Felix only ran harder. They were only twenty yards away from the door. *So close. We can make it.*

Then the air was filled with the sound of a whistling sort of hum, and Felix turned his head. Just in time to see dozens upon dozens of crude iron clubs spin out of the fog, hurled with enough force to launch them like helicopter blades in a deadly arc. The ground ripped up, the heavy metal tearing through stone as they impacted, the clubs becoming tumbling dervishes of demolition. Debris exploded in every direction as blades of ice followed the clubs' paths.

Pit nimbly evaded two of them, but was only at the edge.

Felix and Magda were in the epicenter.

A bubble of yellow energy appeared around Magda and was instantly bombarded, flaring a dangerous orange-red. Another flickered around Felix as well, much smaller and tighter than Magda's usual, but then he was engulfed. Dozens of metallic clubs lashed into him and sent him flying, ricocheting within the storm of metal and rock and icy magic. Felix felt his Health drain precipitously, his skin tearing and muscles ripping, and a bone snapped in his right arm. Felix's HUD indicator had dropped to a bare 5% above empty.

Above death.

Armored Skin is level 32!
Armored Skin is level 33!
Cold Resistance is level 18!

Pain Resistance is level 36!

Felix groaned as he came to a stop, half buried under rock and maybe forty different hunks of iron. He felt like a building had fallen on him. Dust and blood was in his eyes, but approaching footsteps thundered closer. Panicked, he shoved his way free, shifting enough of the clubs to squeeze out of his cage.

The area was devastated. Five-foot spikes of dark metal stuck up everywhere, piled together or lying at angles where they impacted the stone enough to stand erect. Ice swarmed over it all, frost clinging to the metal, and snaking trails of ice led back into the distance to either side of them. The fog swirled, thicker than ever with a haze of dust and the greasy smoke of dissolving monsters. Felix sent a quick pulse through his pact, and Pit emerged nearby, seemingly unharmed.

Thank god, Felix thought with relief. *But where's...?*

Then he spotted her. An armored hand sticking out from beneath a metric shit-ton of iron and ice. With a grunt, Felix leaped in her direction, his powerful legs easily carrying him the ten foot distance. With his left hand, Felix started yanking the metal away, careful not to cause any of it to collapse. The clang and clatter was deafening, but he didn't care. They had to move. Now.

Felix revealed enough of Magda that he was able to pull her out of the cocoon of crude iron, though it was a struggle with only a single arm. She was in rough shape, her armor further dented and torn, the leather portions almost completely chewed up. Her legs looked particularly bad, the metal having sheared in several places.

"Wake up, Magda!" Felix shook her gently before slapping her face with more urgency. The thundering was closer than ever.

Magda's eyes fluttered open, her blunt features creasing into a faint frown. "Don't need to yell."

Felix's breathing was harsh and loud, the pain of his arm and the thousands of lacerations on his body all screaming for attention. "The giants are coming. Stand up! We have to go!"

"I can't."

Magda pushed and pulled herself into a sitting position, but she didn't use her legs at all. Felix looked, really looked at the damage, and noticed a heavy smear of blood stretched between Magda and the iron pile he'd pulled her from.

"You can't walk?" He asked.

Magda shook her head. "Something...tore into my legs. Broke one, and my muscles gone all loose in the other," she didn't make eye contact with Felix, instead staring out into the fog as the tromp of booted feet grew louder. "I'm not going any farther."

"What?" Felix asked, flustered. "But it's right there! The doorway is so close, I can drag you."

And he started to do just that, despite Magda's half-hearted arguments. They had only gotten a few feet when a new sound joined the cacophony: the grinding and squealing of stone and metal.

The door was closing.

"Aaaargh!" Felix shouted, wordlessly hurling his rage. "C'mon!"

He reached down and lifted Magda, throwing her into a fireman's carry. He staggered under her weight, her six and a half foot frame far heavier than he had anticipated.

I've got 131 in Strength. I can do this.

Step by plodding step, Felix drew closer to the doorway. The ground was littered with debris, iron, chunks of stone, and slick patches of ice. Each step was more hazardous than the last, and when Felix stumbled for the third time, Magda pushed him away. He looked at the door, more than halfway closed.

"Stop this! We won't make it!"

"No, we can do it. I'm not leaving you behind."

Pit crooned sympathetically, echoing Felix's tone. Felix turned to the tenku. "Pit, run ahead! I'll be right there, ok?"

The chimera hesitated a moment before dipping his beak and darting off. Felix turned back to the shield warrior, who was tightening the straps on her last remaining shield.

"Go, Felix. Get out of here. I've got this."

"Why?" Felix asked, his eyes flicking between the closing doorway and the approaching Risi, who even now he could see through the mist. Magda swallowed twice before answering.

"Someone's gotta survive to deactivate the artifact," she ripped her pendant off and handed it to Felix, closing his fist over it. "Give that back to Callie when..."

"Yeah, I-"

Abruptly, an invisible force smashed into him, throwing Felix backward nearly thirty feet. He landed hard, rolling on the ground before fetching up against a hard object. Dizzy and a little nauseous from the pain in his broken arm, Felix turned back to see Magda staring back at him, her shield arm extended as if pushing something. Then the round vault door slowly closed between them.

No!

Shadow Whip!

Felix saw Magda smile gently at him an instant before the vault door closed, and his Shadow Whip flailed against impervious stone.

CHAPTER SEVENTY-ONE

He stared at the darkened door for a long time.

Why did she...? I could have saved her. We were right there.

He felt...what did he feel? Felix wasn't sure. There was an ache, a hollow just below the ribs and in the back of his throat. No tears though. Felix hadn't known Magda for long, and tears felt...It felt wrong. As if he was mourning someone, and that wasn't right.

Pit rubbed up against him, a soft warmth against his hands and legs. Worry and sadness and no little bit of fear wafted from the tenku with every pulse of his heart. Felix gripped his Companion with his left arm, hissing in pain as his body rocked the broken bone in his right.

She's not dead yet. She...can make it out.

He wasn't sure who the lie was for, Pit or himself.

Felix looked around. It was utterly dark within the chamber, a velvety black completely different from the gloom of the maze. This darkness had weight to it, and it pressed down upon him. Felix blinked and tried to activate Manasight. There was a moment of pressure, somewhere between his eyes and brain, and then it passed with a faint, inaudible *pop*.

Manasight is level 38!
Manasight is level 39!

He beheld a storm. A vibrant, resounding riot of colorful vapor streamed above him, roiling in the air, the earth...everything. It was like a thousand miles of ambient Mana had been compacted and stored in this place, held within like a stormhead that never broke. It was so intense that Felix had to turn off the ability after only a few seconds, plunging his world back into primordial darkness.

Ow. The sight of all that Mana had hurt his brain, stretching some part of his mind painfully. A full forty seconds after, Felix still saw flashes of blue and gold at the corner of his vision, a familiar and unpleasant sensation. Pit nudged him with his beak, and a sense of urgency flared along their pact.

He's right. Grimmar is here.

He stood up, using the stone object behind him for support and cradling his busted arm. Were it not for the pain that pulsed along his snapped humerus, he would have felt disembodied, a floating eye in a sea of inky black. He glanced at his Health, his HUD the only thing visible in there: it was only at 15%, barely rising above a hundred points.

I can't fight like this. Will my regeneration heal my broken bones? How long would that take? He panted into the darkness, the effort of standing up taking more out of him than he anticipated. *Do I have the time, anyway? Or is that giant just waiting around a corner, ready to rip my head off?*

He figured if it was gonna happen, it would have already. Grimmar didn't seem to be the patient type.

A blinking in his vision made itself known in that darkness. Truthfully, it had been blinking for a while before he'd been thrown into this chamber, but Felix had been...preoccupied. Flaring Pain Resistance and his Willpower to ignore his aching arm, he toggled his notifications.

Pit's Bite is level 24!
Pit's Rake is level 23!
Pit's Wingblade is level 19!
Pit's Frost Spear is level 17!
Pit's Cold Resistance is level 16!
Pit's Poisonfire is level 13!

Your Companion Pit Has Gained 2 Levels!

+4 VIT! +4 PER! +8 AGL! +8 DEX! +6 WIL! +2 END! +4 INT!

Pit fairly glowed with energy, a light that might have been faint in the daylight was nearly blinding here. Felix could tell the tenku fought to not make too much noise, but still let out small peeps as he fairly shook, his body washed by the System's energy.

Good. At least one of us—

You Have Gained A Level!
You are now Level 22!
+3 to WIL! +2 to INT! +4 to DEX! +1 to END! +2 to PER! +2 to VIT! +4 to AGL!
You Have 5 Unused Stat Points!

Oh hell yes. This is what I needed. I can dump these points into Vitality and boost my healing a little.

Felix took a shuddering breath as the System's energy ran through him, individual level gains not carrying quite the same oomph as before. Then, as he prepared to assign his free stat points, the stream turned into a raging torrent that physically shook Felix's body. He gritted his teeth, the vibrations making his arm clench and tighten; he could practically hear his bone grinding against itself. Blue and gold flashed across his vision, more powerfully than before as a rising chord vibrated within his soul. He fell to his knees, and something cracked beneath him.

What? His muscles rippled and twisted, agony to his bruised and battered limbs. *What is happening?*

Felix's heart beat a rapid-fire tattoo, less a beating and more thrumming along inside him, pushing his blood through his body that he felt change with every passing second. His skin hardened, his muscles tightened, his bones burnt as blood poured through them like magma. That magma felt all the worse along his right arm where the break was a discordant burr in the pulsing symphony that roared all around him. A twanging steel string, broken and buzzing among the punishing swell of harmony.

He screamed.

This felt like his Body was Tempering all over again, but that was impossible. He hadn't even used any Essences. Wisps of blue and sporadic gold streamed from his body and lit up the dark, a bonfire to Pit's candle flame. Wild shadows danced around a wide open antechamber as his senses pushed outward, expanding farther than they ever had before. His breathing became a stentorian labor, his every twitch and shift a groaning sigh in the stillness, and even the dark became less so, brightening to an impenetrable gray.

A jolt of power rushed up his spine, spinning with a fervent gusto as something within him was changed and...remade. It brought Felix to his feet, faster and smoother than he'd moved in a long while, the ground cracking once again beneath his feet. The storm of energy burst through his skin, his body unable to contain it all and it flared blue-gold around his flesh. A corona of fire and crackling azure lightning.

Then it was done.

Congratulations!
You Have Achieved The First Threshold!
All Primary Stats Exceed 100!

Title Earned!
The Broken Path (Rare)!
You walk a path toward terrible power. Pray you have the wisdom to use it, or else fall to Ruin. +10% Journeyman Tier Bonus (Body, Mind, Spirit)
Requires: All Primary Stats Exceed 100, Level Below 50, Lost Race (Nym)

"Haah, haah, heaah," Felix leaned against the wall, gulping for breath as his heart rate slowly returned to normal. "What...the shit was that? The Broken Path?" He shook his head, dismissing the notification. "That description is...ominous."

Felix wiped sweat from his face, flicking it away to his side before he realized he'd done it with his right hand. Surprised, Felix held up his right arm, feeling not a single pang or spasm of pain. Hesitantly, he poked his left hand fingers into his bicep, and beyond the skin and muscle he felt a slight ache to his bone. Whatever had happened to him hadn't healed him completely, it seemed, and he had a feeling that if he strained too hard, it might break again. Even still, it was a miracle.

How? He'd experienced bursts of healing before, namely when he'd Tempered his Body, but that had healed him thoroughly. This had...remade him, in some way. As if all the physical changes his body had been experiencing as he raised his stats was condensed and enhanced. His skin and the muscle beneath it felt rock hard yet pliant in a strange dichotomy of sensations that gave him a certain sense of power. He ran his hands over the rest of his body, marveling at the subtle yet definite changes. He took a single step forward, feeling his joints move just a touch quicker, as if oiled or something. Each step was followed with a faint cracking beneath him, and when Felix knelt down, he realized the tiled flooring was breaking beneath his weight.

Delicate flooring.

He stood back up and took a deep breath. Pit trotted toward him, moving unerringly in the dark. *Weakened arm or not, it's time to move forward.*

Though the darkness had lightened some, it was still an opaque curtain before him. With a little trepidation, Felix activated Manasight again. The riot of ambient Mana returned, but this time the piercing pain did not, and it only remained slightly uncomfortable to view the storm of power that filled the antechamber. With some effort, Felix focused his eyes beyond the swirling clouds of Mana, focusing instead on the details of the room itself.

Manasight is level 40!

He was in the entryway, and aside from the circular doorway out, there were a number of faint paintings on walls that curved into a semi-circle. The ceiling arced high above, a soaring design that reminded him of a cathedral, ribbed and vaulted. Behind him, on the other side of the pillar he'd fetched up against was an archway leading further into this...palace? Temple?

What is this place?

He knew it was the center of the Labyrinth, and so it must contain something powerful, important, or dangerous. But other than that, neither Felix nor Magda had a clue what they had been walking into; it was something they had discussed off and on, though without any real clue to the truth. Callie had said it was dangerous and deadly, and that had been enough for Magda. Felix frowned. It was enough for him, too.

Just assume this place is trying to kill me. After all, that's been the consensus so far.

In the spirit of survival, Felix checked his person. He had no shirt, of course, tattered pants, and boots that were on the edge of death. Tucked in his belt was Vessilia's potions case, his Crescian blade, and the crude fang...

Shit. I dropped it. He rubbed his temples, furious. *I must have lost it when the giants hit us. Fuck.*

Frustrated, Felix walked toward the paintings on the walls, stepping a bit closer to make out their details. He moved through the swirls of ambient Mana, their touch like a delicate caress along his senses that he fought to shut out. The murals were faded with age, far more than the murals out in the Labyrinth. For how long they must have been down here, Felix was surprised any sort of paintings existed at all. These depicted tall folk wearing robes and armor walking alongside a plethora of pale-furred people the size of human children. Other, more strange people populated the images, but each working seemed centered on those first two.

Nym and Geist.

Here in the antechamber, a Nym was wearing a crown of bronze and holding aloft a scepter of some sort of pale metal. The Geist beside them held an unfurled scroll, and had their mouth open as if they were reading aloud. Felix followed the mural along the wall, passing through the archway and into a long hallway. He moved as slowly and quietly as he could, though the racket he'd made previously would have woken the dead. The hallway was clear of any people thankfully, Risi or otherwise, so Felix returned to the walls.

A story was being told in these murals, and Felix was enraptured.

The Nym and Geist traveled all over the land, from rolling hills to deep forests, wide lakes and frigid mountains. Sometimes they were joined by others, more Nym and Geist or even a smattering of other races Felix couldn't identify. There was a stretch of silver forest, each leaf etched in shimmering metal. A deep, achingly beautiful lake, swarming with life hinted at beneath the languid ripples. A range of mountains that towered above the clouds, their peaks split. And through them all, Felix saw a familiar detail: a bronze spike, like two pyramids stacked atop each other, stabbed into the ground.

The same as the Guardians' enchanted collars, only several orders of magnitude larger.

The Nym and Geist were shown at each of these sites and many others, standing to thc side of the spikes as if investigating. Each time, the locations changed and the two figures seemed to grow wearier and wearier, subtly drooping at the shoulders and knees. The Nym did not raise the scepter quite as high, and the Geist unrolled less and less of its scroll until finally, the two stood in a verdant valley filled to the brim with flowering fruit trees. Here, a massive spike had been embedded, larger by far than any that had come before, and the two figures stood tall and proud. Jubilant.

Felix kept walking, the hall long and uninterrupted by nook or cranny. It was just the story.

The next mural showed a collection of buildings sprouting up, small and grey at first but quickly growing complicated as the mural extended down the hall, larger buildings with more ornate architecture populating the area around the spike. Flying creatures swarmed the air, colorful and wild, while a plethora of peoples filled the growing city. *Shelim*, he realized. *This is Shelim.* This *city.* Felix could pick out a familiar layout, done in multiple concentric circles that radiated outward and intersected. He recognized the groupings of towers, their heights far taller than the other buildings, save for the spike itself. He could even spot the bronze-domed capitol building, at the edge of the spike's grand grounds.

He found his eyes drawn upward as the mural changed again. Now the spike...shimmered, almost, despite the static nature of paint and dyes, appearing to pulse through the city entirely. A dark amorphous shape was painted above the bronze spike, its thundercloud shape radiating colorful lines into the city and land beyond. The lines were inlaid metals, sparkling as they described perfect parabolic arcs, each terminating in a swell of color that even the Ages hadn't much dimmed. It was, by nearly all accounts, a marvelous and powerful image.

But to Felix, who's eyes could barely leave that ominous thundercloud, he felt it radiate something else. A powerful sense of...need.

Deep in his belly, above his navel, Felix felt an ache. It howled softly with an echo of his empty hunger, the first wakening pangs of a slumbering beast. There was a connection, a kinship that he felt with that shapeless mass. A yearning that made moving his eyes away a feat of mental strength. When he did, he found the rest of the mural gone. The hallway stretched on for twenty more yards, but someone or something had shattered the walls, ripping the facade off with massive claws spaced feet apart. The ground was littered with chunks of broken rock.

There is something very bad in here, Felix swallowed as he looked at the jagged rents through solid stone.

He stepped forward, more cautious than ever among the fallen stone, moving toward the edge of the hall. He heard voices, faint but growing stronger with each step, and Felix was surprised to realize he recognized both of them.

"I am not worthy of your attention," rumbled Grimmar, his voice muffled for some reason. "It is an honor to breathe the air around your hallowed flesh."

"Indeed," said a far daintier voice, the simple word conveying a sense of resignation and weariness. "I see that you have claimed my gift, bestowed upon your ancestors so long ago."

"I have, Mother," Grimmar grated as Felix peeked around the corner, where the hall opened up into a huge open space. Polished granite stretched across the floor, smooth and unmarred. Shadowed alcoves dotted the far walls, which were circular much like the antechamber, surmounted by fluted pillars and covered in elaborate carvings of vines and leaves. The roof arched upward, unsupported by any beams or braces, and bright natural light filtered down into the chamber.

The sunlight filled the space with such radiance that, for a moment, Felix forgot to breathe, the bloom of illumination too bright to see beyond for the barest of instants. When it cleared, Felix could see Grimmar kneeling on the floor, head down and hands pointed forward as if he were praying or...or prostrating.

Beyond him, centered in the circular space, was a bronze spike that stretched forty feet up, maybe a quarter of the way to the ceiling, shimmering with a restrained power that nevertheless felt fearsome. The surface was crawling with sigils that flared and faded in rapid succession, never in the same sequence or position twice.

"I hope to be worthy of this smallest piece of your divinity, Mother."

Nearly hidden by the giant's bulk, a woman stood. She was dressed in a simple, flowing gown of pale, wispy cloth that seemed to float around her in a breeze that wasn't there. The woman laughed, a bright sound that sent a wave of serenity crashing through Felix. The walls of his Bastion of Will shook, the dark stone quaking beneath that gentle surge, but they held.

Bastion of Will is level 36!
Bastion of Will is level 37!
Bastion of Will is level 38!

Breath Control is level 21!
Breath Control is level 22!

Felix ducked back behind the wall while he strained to control his breathing, feeling as if he had just run a marathon. Sweat beaded along his forehead, mingling with the dried blood and grime from his recent battles, dripping down his bare chest and back. He flared Meditation, trying to calm his mind, but he was shaken.

That's...holy shit, that's not good. He swallowed, working spit from his dried tongue.

I think I'm in trouble.

CHAPTER SEVENTY-TWO

I need a plan, I need a plan, he thought frantically. *A good one, for once.*

Felix was still hidden, as far as he knew, held from Grimmar and that terrible presence by no more than a few dozen feet of stone wall and thin air. There was nowhere else to hide: the hallway ended here, and the chamber beyond was as wide open as a place could be, not to mention being lit up by what appeared to be a noontime sun.

If she's as powerful as I fear she is, I'm already exposed. My Stealth Skill is just barely in Apprentice Tier, and she...she's definitely not.

Felix's mind raced, looking at his Skills, at the terrain, at anything he could to survive this next deadly adventure. His mind felt somehow like an enormous greased wheel, spinning and spinning with greater speed and breadth than he'd experienced in his life. It felt similar to when he got his first significant Intelligence bump. His Primary Stats hitting one hundred plus had amplified his physical and mental stats beyond what he'd ever experienced. He reviewed what he'd just seen in his perfect mental eye.

Grimmar prostrated himself on the floor, the woman standing before him...above him, even. He called her Mother. *The* Mother, he assumed. Which, all things considered, was the worst case scenario. Facing off against a deified mother of monsters was not even remotely in his wheelhouse, despite the fatal danger he continually faced with every passing moment on the Continent....

Maybe he *should* have expected this.

He returned to the mental image, viewing it from all angles. Grimmar was sweating and dirty, his armor scuffed and torn. Evidence of a rough passage through the Labyrinth? Or something else? The giant was also bleeding slightly, from the ears, too, which Felix was pretty sure wasn't normal. He shied away from the woman, focusing instead on the massive pyramidal obelisk beyond her: the bronze spike. Curious just how far his perfect recall went, Felix attempted to use Analyze on the obelisk in his own mental image. Surprisingly, results came back.

Name: Essence Anchor
Type: Enchanted Structure
Lore: Used in Ages past to siphon, store, and transmit Mana across vast distances. Made of Crescian Bronze, the ancient Nym built them with the help of the Geist.

Exploration is level 25!

Congratulations! You have—

Felix cut the notification off and dismissed it. *Shit. This is* not *the time. Shit.*

There was a lurching sensation within him, like a jolt through the center of his belly. Concerned, he probed his core, visualizing by dint of his Fire Within Skill. Blue fire, shot with gold and crowned with crackling sparks, it remained largely the same. There was an...echo of that gnawing hunger, one that seemed to be growing louder. That wasn't the sensation Felix felt, so instead he looked beyond all that, to his Skills. Patterns etched in light, they spun a slow dance around his core. He knew that they lit up and shimmered as he used his Skills, but now several flickered with ephemeral light. The greatest of them flared wildly, burning bright with a sense of exuberance to it. Felix knew instantly that this was his Exploration Skill.

This is what it looks like when a Skill is about to Tier? He regarded the flashing, pulsing lights. *It's beautiful.*

A few others shone nearly as bright, among them Analyze and...Companion Pact. In addition to Exploration, they were his final two options to finally, fully Temper his Mind and Spirit.

But would even that be enough here?

Fire Within is level 33!

"Oh come now," said a bright and airy voice, half laughing. "Hiding is so childish."

Felix pulled from his core, his spine snapping straight as nerves and surprise got the best of him. Haltingly, he edged his head toward the corner and peeked an eye beyond. The woman was still standing in the same place, but now she stared right at him as she gently waved. Beckoning him closer.

"Come, Felix Nevarre." Her voice was soft and sweet. "I promise I won't bite."

Shit. I don't have a choice, do I? Pit, stay back...and be ready to run.

A surge of stubborn anger washed through the pact, surprising Felix enough to forget his nerves for a moment. Pit rammed his head into Felix's leg, clearly refusing to stay behind.

Ok, fine. We'll do this together.

Shuddering with adrenaline and fear, Felix and Pit took a hesitant step into the chamber. His booted foot clunked against the smooth flooring, which seemed to be made entirely of polished granite and inlaid with countless interconnected stars. *Count the stars*, he thought with a nervous laugh, pressing forward through air that felt thick with energies and a powerful swell of far-off music. His Manasight still ran, though not as strongly as before, and the entire chamber was awash in a storm of ambient power. The closer he drew toward the two figures, the more he realized that much of the power was emanating from the Essence Anchor, so much so that the other two were almost washed out by the noise of it all. Almost, but not quite. A faint buzz rattled in the background, a hum running counterpoint to the Anchor's powerful draw.

He walked until he came to the edge of an inlaid circle, one that surrounded the Essence Anchor, Grimmar, and the woman.

"You're here, and none too soon. I see you have grown stronger indeed since last we spoke." The woman's eyes twinkled at the last, and a spark of recognition flared within Felix. He knew that voice. Those eyes. Blue-green, summer leaves atop a pond. A yearning ran through him, sudden and complete, and the hunger in his belly fully woke. Its growl matched pitch with that hum in the air until the two resonated unpleasantly, his inner ear buzzing with a terrible and distracting dissonance. A far cry from the orchestral thrum of the Anchor only feet away.

"You," he gasped, fighting off what he knew to be an unnatural attraction. "I know you. You're..."

"The woman of your dreams? Naturally," she smiled, her face framed by a cascade of straight black hair, and it was like a second sun emerged from the clouds. Vertigo spun Felix's world for a moment, before his walls settled again.

Bastion of Will is level 39!
Deep Mind is level 26!

"How?" Felix's mind raced, connections appearing and disappearing. "My dreams. My...you've been speaking to me since the waterfall."

"Well before that, Felix," she said, her pale dress billowing in a breeze he could not feel. It was a diluted yellow. "You just couldn't hear me properly."

A low growl emanated from Felix's left. Grimmar, still bowed low to the ground so that his head touched the cool stone, turned and locked eyes with him. A thrill of fear raced across Felix's nerves, but he was quickly reaching a saturation point. Even the giant's toothy grimace was becoming old hat, gross as it was.

"Oh, come now, Grimmar," she chided, a pale hand bopping him atop his blue head. A sound like a gunshot echoed through the room, Grimmar's face smashing into the ground hard enough to shake it. "Don't be childish. You're *both* in line to be my Champion."

Felix licked his lips nervously. That love tap would have broken his bones. *What the fuck have I gotten into?*

Grimmar lifted his face, swollen and burst along his left cheek and jaw, and gasped. "Him, Mother? He is a disgusting *Human*...how could *he* be worthy of you?"

"Human?" She laughed, another bright, cheery thing that danced around the chamber. Blond locks fluttered on the same intangible breeze that shifted her dress. "No no, dear Grimmy. He is not Human at all. Are you, dear?

Felix's eyes darted between the two of them, one grimacing in anger and suspicion, another smiling beatifically. He could feel the flare of alarm in his chest, and he felt Pit press tighter against the back of his legs, his own head on a swivel.

"No, I'm not," he admitted.

"See? He's Nymean," she nodded.

Grimmar's eyes nearly bulged from their sockets, and a vein snaked down his forehead. His cheek and jaw were healing quickly, but the sudden strain sent blue blood pouring from the wound, and the giant began to visibly shake. A long moment passed where Felix was positive the Risi was going to attack him, but the giant mastered himself, though not without consequence. Blood dripped from his nose and ears.

"You stayed your bloodlust. That is good." The woman, whoever and whatever she was, patted the giant on the shoulder. "It would displease me were you to fight in my presence."

"Who are you?" Felix asked.

"She is the Mother, you fool," snarled Grimmar, the heat not yet banished from his tone. At a look from the woman, he leveraged himself up and onto his knees. "The beginning and the end of all life upon this wretched plane of mud and blood."

The woman made a *tutting* sound. "Grimmar is a bit...blinded by religious devotion. For which I give you full credit, dear," she directed at the giant, who blushed beneath the scowl he offered Felix. "I am Lhel. Or I once was, before...all this." She waved a delicate hand around her, indicating not just the vaulted chamber, but somehow all that lay beyond.

"Lhel," Felix repeated, hearing a soft musicality in the name. "Why are you here, in this...whatever this is? It looks like a palace, or a temple, but those don't usually have giant blood beasts guarding the doors."

"How...astute of you, Felix." Lhel sighed prettily, her dress flouncing. "Yes, I am a prisoner here. Trapped these long Ages by my vile enemies."

"Enemies?" Felix asked, eyeing the walls around him. They were at least a hundred feet in any direction.

"Why, the Geist, of course. You must have seen their statues and paintings they had erected all over Shelim. Vain little cretins," she muttered.

The Geist? Vvim didn't...wait, they said their People had been here a long time. Ages spent watching and waiting. Or were they guarding? Felix's mind raced, moving pieces around a mental chessboard. "Why would they imprison you?"

"Jealousy. And vengeance," she sniffed disdainfully. "The Geist are feral, deceitful creatures, you know. They rose up against us, throwing their rightful betters off our earned thrones and seized them."

"Their betters?" Felix asked, the word sour in his mouth. He was afraid he already knew the answer.

"Us, of course," Lhel said, blue-green eyes flashing in the sunlight. "The Nym."

Images flashed through Felix's mind, carvings and mosaics depicting the Nym all around the Foglands, even there, twenty yards behind him. "Is that you? In the paintings?"

"In the hallway? Yes, that is me, back before..." Her voice drifted and her eyes went distant for a moment, as if she were viewing a memory. Felix cleared his throat.

"So the Geist painted beside you...?"

"Ssev, my closest friend and bitterest enemy." Her eyes flashed again as Mana congealed there, sparking behind her retinas. "They who laid the path upon which the whole of our people walked. A broken path that ended in Ruin." Her voice had a sudden heaviness to it, a weight that pressed against Felix's shoulders. She looked behind her at the soaring Essence Anchor, its surface shifting with a glowing, flickering script. "A path that resulted in our empire shattering, our people Lost, and me imprisoned for two thousand years."

Felix shared a look with Pit, and he saw a flash of pity in the tenku's eye. Felix felt it too, though he was wary. *Is this my emotion...or hers?* He checked his HUD, but no status conditions were listed as when he'd been affected by Vvim's emotional manipulation Skill. *Best to be wary, though,* he sent to Pit.

Then he heard a chime. His eyes flicked toward the Essence Anchor, and upon its surface he saw three large sigils appear, fluid, organic shapes with which he'd been growing increasingly familiar. One of them was exceedingly similar to the first sigil he'd decoded: light. But it was covered in slashes and markings that seemed to...enhance and restrict it, changing the meaning from *light* to...*eternally retreating horizon.*

Sigils of the Primordial Dawn is level 7!

...

Sigils of the Primordial Dawn is level 10!

Meaning and composition flooded his mind, scattered and barely interrelated, but enough to drown a man. Having mental attributes above one hundred had its advantages, however: as quick as the knowledge filtered down, Felix sorted and settled it, pulling the disparate ideas and concepts of the sigil script into his steel trap of a mind. The large sigils faded with a second chime, but he'd gathered enough patchwork knowledge to know they said something like '*draw beast anchor eternally retreating horizon never void.*' It wasn't completely right, his conjugation sloppy and tenses confused; more like a gesture toward the truth, than the truth itself.

This is important, he suddenly knew. *I need to keep her talking.*

"Ugh, that noise. Hearing that twice a glass for two thousand years would drive anyone up the wall." She pinched the bridge of her nose, appearing truly tired. Shadows fell across her face, and something was...off there. It was gone by the time she brought her gaze back to Felix and Grimmar. "Where were we? Ah yes. Trapped by my best friend—"

"What is that?" Felix asked.

"Excuse me?"

"You do not interrupt her!" Grimmar hollered, toothy jaw flung wide, though he stilled at a glance from his goddess. Felix had felt his heart lurch in his chest when Grimmar had reared back, but he let himself breath again as he met Lhel's eyes.

"The bronze spike behind you. What is it?"

She stared at him a moment, a tiny smile on her full lips. Her red curls fell loose about her face, though she swept several locks behind her left ear. "Why play dumb, Felix? I know you have the Analyze Skill, so surely you could divine enough to call it by its true name: an Essence Anchor." Lhel's face twisted, the smile turning wistful. "It was our greatest achievement and starkest failure. You wonder why I label the Geist as monsters? Because of this."

She thrust her hands forward, and each one filled with a brilliant, bloody light. The Anchor too lit up, a protective barrier made of thousands of shifting, rotating sigils visible for an instant.

Felix saw that between them, the woman and the Anchor, there was a chain made of sunlight...and it was wrapped around her neck.

Tears glistened in her eyes. "It was an etheric device meant to draw and store energy from the world itself. We tested it everywhere, across the breadth of the Nymean kingdoms. Many places were powerful, many holding a store of power ready to be tapped...but only here was there an infinite source. A Mana Well of unbelievable potency and size, enough unattributed Mana to fuel our cities for an Age or more. Only, it wasn't meant to be." She clenched her hands at her sides. "Ssev and their family *changed* it, the script upon the Anchor. It was meant to draw from the earth, but instead it drew from the surface, capturing and draining those with the greatest pools of Mana: us."

She tugged on the chain of light, which held firm as if it were solid steel before fading from view. "It locked me here, the only one who could have stopped what came next. Ssev's changes woke a...hunger from the earth, drawn to our draining Mana. Something ancient and unstoppable. It...it devoured them all." She sagged, appearing all of her thousands of years of age as trauma and grief darkened her face. She clutched her hands around her elbows and looked away from the Anchor. "This is my prison. The Essence Anchor, a device I helped create, turned against me by those who were jealous of our rightful rule."

Pity once again tugged at his heart, yet something about her didn't sit right with Felix. Her dismissal of other peoples and casual use of violence against Grimmar were part of it, but it was something more. Something about how...connected he felt with her. It unnerved him that whenever she laughed or smiled or frowned, Felix felt it too, but somehow stronger. Like a feedback loop.

The Anchor still flashed rapidly, displaying different sigils in different locations each time. He had made zero headway, though some part of his mind was still working at it, trying to leverage his fledgling knowledge.

He shook his head, playing up the pity routine. Maybe he could tease more information from her...she seemed very chatty.

"I heard a...crooning, beckoning me here. That was you?" She nodded, her wavy brown hair hanging before her face like a curtain. "Why me?"

Grimmar grunted and spoke, and though his body was still kneeling, his giant frame and voice hinted at a precipice of violence. "A question I would like answered as well. If you would be so kind, honored Mother."

Pale hands parted her black hair, tucking half behind her left ear. She appeared...vulnerable to Felix, someone who had been hurt before and feared it happening again.

Felix blinked. Where had *that* thought come from?

Bastion of Will is level 40!
Deep Mind is level 27!

"You were called because you dared to survive," she half whispered, her blue-green eyes vivid. "You showed such potential in those first moments of your life here. I wanted you to succeed, for you are the last of us; Nym in truth if not by birth."

Felix's back went cold, the hairs on his neck lifting. "So then you know."

"Oh yes. Those who listen could hear your arrival, Unbound. Your kind are loud in a way that is particularly piercing in this sleepy corner of the Continent."

"Demon," Grimmar whispered, his bloody face alarmed. Despite how his jaw healed, Felix could still see blood seeping from his ears and nose, a slow but nonstop leak. "No wonder you bested me in the Black. Mother forfend, an Unbound."

"Tish tosh," scoffed Lhel, waving her hand at the giant. "They are simply stolen people. Pulled against their will to a world unlike any they've ever seen. You're not the first Unbound I've met, though you are the first I've seen survive a gauntlet of challenges as you have."

Felix watched both of them: Grimmar, who now looked with a measure of fear in his anger, and Lhel, who seemed inordinately...proud of him.

"You told me I needed to be stronger," he said, palms sweating. "Why?"

"Survival. Yours and mine. I would not see the Nym perish. To return to being well and truly Lost."

"How are they Lost if you still live?" Felix asked.

"I don't live, not truly. Not here in this desolate oubliette.

Forgotten and trapped by the schemes of lesser beasts." She scoffed. "It is not a fit fate for the proud Nym, a race that once strode across the skies and brought terror and devastation upon all who opposed us."

Her voice rose with such earnest ire that Felix felt buffeted by it. There was an awful predatory gleam in her blue-green eyes, like a naked blade poised above flesh. He still maintained Bastion of Will, but even still, Lhel's vehemence echoed through his soul. Felix found himself angry and irritable, frustrated at something he couldn't grasp. He flared his Skill harder, pushing the limits of what he could get out of it, but the sensation faded slightly, proving to him that it wasn't real at all. That unraveled the rest of it.

Bastion of Will is level 41!
Deep Mind is level 28!

"So, as you have survived and reached my humble abode, I ask this of you: become my Champion."

There was a crash as Grimmar leaped to his feet, his armor clanking around him. He did not speak at first, but Felix felt the pressure of his gaze just the same. He was not happy.

"Mother, you cannot possibly think that this...this Nymean Unbound can serve you better than I! I, who have fought the very Hoarfrost for this honor, who reigned supreme at the King's Rock, who carry your very blood in my veins." Lhel turned away from Felix and toward the giant, and Grimmar went pale. Felix was surprised to find he completely agreed with the Risi Chieftain.

"Personally, I'm not in favor of the terror and devastation you're talking about," Felix said with a nervous laugh. Pit whimpered slightly behind him. "It doesn't really fit what I thought I knew about the Nym, honestly. In the depictions I've seen they are...compassionate. Protectors."

"*Weakness*," Lhel replied, her voice rasping as she spun toward Felix. "A legacy of it, spread across our kingdoms. And for what? In the end, they were unable to do what had to be done. What I said must be done. And so Ruin came for them." She spat on the ground, and the liquid sizzled against the perfect floor, marring it.

"You remind me of them, child," Lhel's mood flipped on a dime, her lilting voice abruptly soft and sad. "My brothers and sisters, lost to desolation and predation. Gone before their time. Betrayed." At the last, Lhel's voice and tone shook menacingly.

Panic wormed through Felix's guts. He was dealing with a powerful being so far beyond him that she could kill him with a look...and she was quite likely insane.

"That is why I need a Champion, Felix Nevarre. My Champion would carry the core of me, bridging the wards of this prison and letting me breathe free air once more." She took a big breath, and all the air in the room shook, the ambient Mana going wild as it surged toward her....into her. She simply...ate it. All of it.

"Freedom is what I desire most of all, Felix Nevarre. And freedom is what one of you can give to me. Please," she added, her soft eyes bright with unshed tears. The light of the hidden sun gleamed off her lashes and stray hairs as she reached out a hand toward Felix. Open. Inviting.

"Please aid me. Become my Champion, and we may right these atrocities wrought against us."

Harps and chords strummed through his mind as he beheld what was likely the most beautiful woman he'd ever seen begging him for his help. Help that he could easily give, he knew. He could envision taking Lhel's core and walking out of here with it, untouched by trap or monster, able to devote himself to pleasing this perfect Nymean woman who—

A burr in the chorus caught his ear.

Felix frowned, his joyous train of thought burdened by mundanity. But he couldn't tear his attention away from it: the burr became a rasp, which transformed into a buzzing dissonance that unraveled the song entirely. As if his soul had left his body, Felix felt as if he slammed back into himself, fully aware of what had been about to happen.

His hand was inches away from Lhel's own.

"No," Felix said softly, then much firmer. "No."

He stepped back, out of the circle and away from the Nymean woman.

"What?" She asked, her face the perfect image of confused fragility, as if tears and sorrow were only moments from breaking across her features. Felix felt something inside him give, but he shored up the walls of his Skill, and his Bastion held firm.

Bastion of Will is level 42!

Deep Mind is level 29!

Then her face twisted, fine eyebrows drawing down above blue-green orbs that flashed with a sudden and terrible malice. "Fine," she said, and her mouth began to grow far too many teeth. "Then we do this the hard way."

CHAPTER SEVENTY-THREE

Bloody, crimson Mana surged all around them as Lhel breathed it out like steam. Sickly and rotten, it made Felix gag even from a dozen feet away. It clouded his senses for just a moment, and when he could see her again, Lhel's face had...cracked, splitting along her cheeks as two extra rows of teeth populated in her mouth, with more coming in behind them. As he watched, her hands lengthened into spindly claws, their tips darkening to a rusty, blood red.

"I thought you were Nymean. You're...what are you?" Felix and Pit backed away, putting another twenty feet between them and the creature that was once Lhel.

"I am perfection! I am a terror beyond time, Primordial and everlasting." She laughed, and even with the teeth, it was as sweet a sound as he'd ever heard. His Bastion resisted however, shrugging it off a little easier than a few minutes ago. "Frankly, I am disappointed, Felix! That you would believe one as wondrous as I could possibly be a *weak, pathetic* Nymean."

Pit squawked in terror. Between one blink and the next, the creature was inches away from Felix, and he could see that the blue-green in her irises had expanded to fill the entirety of her eyeball.

"I am far more than *anything* this fallen world has seen in ten thousand years. The Nym were *nothing*, a delicious light snack at best followed by two thousand years of indigestion. I am all that is left of Lhel, for I have consumed her, Body, Mind, and Spirit." She reared back, mouth agape and howling into the sky. "I am the Unending Maw, Last of the Three, Survivor of Ruin!"

"Consumed...?" Felix felt his stomach clench, his aching gut burning all the more with her proximity. Despite her shifting appearance, a part of him still yearned for her, somehow.

"Oh yes, dear one. And she was so very delectable. As were her colleagues she had attempted to save by submitting to me," a burbling laugh danced from her ruinous throat, still so close that Felix could see the barbed thorns lining her glottis rattle. "Such a fool."

"You ate them?"

"Mhmm, all that I could find. Practically did the Ruin's work for them." Another throaty, rattling laugh, another piercing buzz in his guts. It felt like a ball of razor blades spinning within, ripping him up from the inside. Felix felt something wet drip down his ear, and he reached up to find it was blood.

She was killing him without lifting a finger.

Felix backed up again, pulling Pit along with him, but he knew there was nowhere to go; the only exit was the dark hallway ending in a locked vault door. He looked up, toward the sunlight.

The windows....

They were easily two hundred feet up, and last he checked, he couldn't fly.

"I smell your fear, your despairing calculations. They are the same as all my prey, wide-eyed fawns too terrified to pose much challenge. You smell....delightful, dearest Felix, all the more so since you became a Nym. But I do not want to kill you, my dear." She spread her arms wide, her limbs slightly too long, the claws of her fingers too dark and corroded. "I am a monster in truth, but I come in good faith."

Her mouth pouted, teeth hidden for the moment. "I did not lie to you, Felix. The Geist were at first my allies...for it was they who dug deep enough to uncover my tumultuous skein of flesh beneath the endless earth. I was trapped there, hibernating after the War, sleeping so long that I had all but forgotten myself. Lhel and Ssev woke my Mind, and I will always be grateful for that." Her pout turned hideous once more, teeth sprouting further along her jaw. "They also betrayed me, them and all the traitorous Races who fought needlessly against my awakening.

"They needed only to submit. That is all I asked. Submit and be devoured.

"For I was so very hungry."

While speaking, Lhel had become a horror, her pale skin cracked and scaled, colored like dark rust. Her limbs lengthened, stretching to twice their size as her torso sagged and pulled, contorting into a parody of a humanoid spine. Muscle piled upon muscle as her once slender frame thickened and filled in, until her body resembled the agile grace of a panther mixed with the heavy, plated chest of a rhino. It was her mouth, however, that had the most dire change: widened and elongated, her jaw hung open, ten feet wide and filled with six rows of sharp teeth. Those teeth grew bigger as the transformation continued, until several curved out and upward like great tusks, and others went down like vicious fangs.

A monster...

Analyze...

Analyze Failed.

The stone flooring creaked beneath its sudden immense weight, for the creature was now twenty feet tall at the shoulder and twice that in length. A long, serpentine tail whipped behind the creature, its length capped with more tooth-like spikes that descended from its back. A frill of ivory tusks sprouted from its head and neck, as if its mouth split all the way around its skull.

Felix stumbled further back—heart humming, it beat so fast—and his mind raced.

Grimmar smiled, standing tall and looking proud to the far left of Felix, his own gruesome teeth a faint echo of the Maw's own. He raised his voice. "Mother! How could any be so foolish as to fight you? Even the ancient, pathetic Nym and their calamitous traditions were not so blind as to ignore that."

"You question me!?" The Maw let out a screaming roar, the sound overlaid with a thousand voices of all timbres screaming in unison. Grimmar folded like a house of cards, his legs going limp as blood poured from his eyes, ears, and nose.

"For-forgiveness, hon-honored Mother," he gurgled.

Shaking its toothy mane, it continued to speak, its voice once more Lhel's. "The Nym were fools, through and through, but not without their wiles. Lhel, researcher that she was, claimed curiosity and submitted to my clear superiority. But it was a trick! A dirty, underhanded trick by a dirty, underhanded Race! She attempted to wrest control from me! Me! I am unending, untiring, eternal and everlasting. It was a game Lhel was sure to lose...and she knew it!"

The Maw whipped its tail to the side, narrowly avoiding Grimmar but crashing into one of the pillars somehow. The pillar shattered, parts of it pulverized instantly while the rest tumbled down noisily. Grimmar paled and gurgled again.

Felix gaped. The Maw was over a hundred feet away from where the pillar had stood. The aftershock of its lashing tail was enough to shatter stone.

Everything about this is bad. Felix looked down at Pit, who had his wings spread, feathers fluffed, and tail bushier than ever, as if he could fool a primordial hellbeast. The terror the tenku was experiencing was an echo of his own.

The hunger pains redoubled, pushing a wheezing gasp from Felix's lungs. *How do I stop this?*

The Maw kept speaking furiously, heedless of Felix's agony. "The crafty Nym stalled me long enough for the cavalry to arrive. The Herald, you see, had come to call."

The Herald? Felix hadn't heard that name before. In the corner of his eye, Felix could see even Grimmar tilt his bloody head questioningly at the title.

"You question the title, Grimmar? Good!" The Maw laughed as the giant flinched. "Lost and Ruined, a fitting fate for those who would challenge me!

"Bold as you please, she strode from her skyhold and into Shelim, her blasted armies following behind. But I defeated them all, oh yes, yes I did! Consumed them, blood and bone! Muscle and sinew and guts and fats! Such delicacies had been denied me too long as I slept in the dark earth, and I dined with relish! Oh the glory! Oh the *MANA!*"

Another screaming roar echoed out into the chamber, its sound too loud for even that huge space. It reverberated from the walls, bouncing back and forth like white noise, a terrible static that set Felix's teeth on edge and incited his hungry core once more. Felix screamed, but the sound was lost in the cacophony of the Maw's ecstatic rage.

"Glorious battle turned to glorious feasting, but I was opposed! The Night-cursed Herald withstood my attacks, her Skill besting my power in the short term, but I knew—I knew!—that it was only a matter of time. I am the Unending Maw, and I am relentless and inescapable. I am the hungry gullet at the end of all things!" The Maw paced, its lashing tail scoring the flooring with each swing. "Yet, while the Herald and I fought, vile trickery was afoot. Ssev, the repugnant beast, had devised a trap. When the Herald had me distracted, they caught me in it! Lashing me to this wretched Anchor and sealing me in this prison."

Like a physical embodiment of its rage, crimson Mana vapor poured off of the Maw's back, wafting up and to Felix's right. He could taste it, just as he had with the blood beasts, rotten and corrupted and coppery, blood gone bad. Then the vapor was pulled faster and faster, stretching thin and spinning around the room as if circling a drain. Within two seconds, it was swallowed by the Essence Anchor, and the golden scripts flared.

It's a power sink, Felix suddenly realized. *It eats the power of the Maw, somehow keeping it trapped here. How?*

"Ah, but we have gotten off-track," the Maw murmured in its soft, feminine voice. "You have not submitted, nor agreed of your own volition to be my Champion." A grotesque, simpering smile creased the Maw's face, and it turned to view a kneeling Grimmar. The giant was no longer bleeding, but his dark blue blood had pooled around him like spilled paint. "*Make* him submit, Grimmar."

The giant was on his feet instantly, all fear banished and a wild, savage glee overtook his face.

"Your will is my pleasure, honored Mother."

Felix started, looking from the Maw to Grimmar, who had started to advance on him, drawing his huge, ten-foot-long greatsword. "What happened to acting in good faith?"

The Maw laughed, and Felix winced. "*I* am not trying to kill you, Felix! In fact, I truly hope you survive!"

Grimmar started to run, his face growing darker and uglier at the Maw's words. His huge gait ate up the distance, the giant's body twisting as he brandished his immense greatsword. The blade swung out horizontally, but with the tip dipped at an angle, a strike clearly designed for smaller foes.

More instinct than plan, Felix blasted down with Reign of

Vellus, launching himself thirty feet straight up into the air. He wasn't close enough to the walls to do that trick again, so instead he tried to activate Relentless Charge. He'd never used it mid-air before, but the Skill engaged, and the world blurred so fast Felix barely had time to lift his hands up.

Corrosive Strike!

Felix aimed a left-handed punch at Grimmar's remaining eye, but the giant had a warrior's reactions and tucked his chin, causing Felix's fist to impact the crown of his skull. Acid burst in all directions as the blow landed, but the thickness of the giant's skull blunted much of the force. Even still, Grimmar's head rocked back, the Risi's balance disrupted by the sheer mass behind the attack. Felix's new weight was a surprise for both of them, and as the giant's head tipped backward, the Nym toppled up and over his skull. Two steps Grimmar stumbled back, time enough for a falling Felix to latch onto the back of the Risi's fur collar and summon one of his new favorite spells.

Wrack and Ruin!

Felix still hanging tight to his collar, Grimmar threw himself to the ground and rolled. The fist-sized orb blasted forth with a roar, ripping a dissolving trench in the giant's right pauldron, but otherwise missing. Felix released his grip and pushed off, barely avoiding getting steamrolled by the massive warrior.

"Haha! Delightful!" Laughter trilled through the air, and Felix had to fight through the agony in his guts again. He rolled to his feet, watching his Health tick down by a percentage point each time the Maw laughed.

What is going on with that?

"Your abilities and Skills have only grown, dear boy! So much stronger now than when you arrived, weak and mewling upon the gray sands of the Bitter Sea. I had bet your pathetic weaknesses would burn away in the crucible of combat, and I was right! What remarkable foresight to have placed my hopes on you."

"How?" Felix growled, backing carefully away from Grimmar who was climbing onto his enormous feet. "How could you know I was coming here? Did you...did you bring me here?"

"No. I merely capitalized on your arrival, genius that I am," the Maw grinned. "The Unbound have not been seen in Ages, far longer than I have been imprisoned here. To be aware of your arrival alone was a fortuitous boon, one that I could not deny."

The Maw ran its barbed and hooked tongue along its yellowing fangs.

"So I sent my child for you."

Felix looked at the Maw, brow down in confusion. Then his senses screamed, just in time to notice a wave of malignant Mana plowing toward him. Felix threw himself to the side, tucking his shoulder into a roll. Spikes of ice as hard as steel punched up through the ground, tearing through the left leg of his pants and scraping an inches-long furrow in his calf.

Grimmar rushed forward at the same time, greatsword leading the way. Felix was barely to his feet when the giant thrust his weapon at his chest. But a Windblade knocked into the sword, just missing the Nymean and shearing its length along the ice-coated floor. The sword clanged against the rock beneath, and stopped.

Grimmar yanked on it, but the sword didn't budge.

Felix grinned as Pit screeched a challenge at the blue Risi Chieftain.

Shadow Whip!

The tendril of shadow bludgeoned the giant's right forearm before latching on. With a mighty haul, Felix yanked back, twisting Grimmar's hand and causing him to release the weapon. Grimmar looked over at Felix, black eyes wide with disbelief as his arm quivered with the effort of resisting the Nym.

"How did you gain such strength?" Grimmar tensed his arm again but was held fast.

"Killing—Ungh," Felix grunted, pulling back. "Killing giants is great for power leveling."

Grimmar roared, and his featureless black eyes suddenly burned with bloody crimson Mana. The chieftain's mouth, a ruin of mismatched fangs, opened far wider than ever before, and he inhaled. The ambient Mana in the air swirled and was sucked directly into the giant's maw, and even the Shadow Whip dissolved in Felix's grip. A swirling maelstrom of crimson rot surged through the giant's already corrupted aura, pouring out toward his extremities like a cancerous growth.

Grimmar tore off his beaten iron armor, revealing a blue chest covered in heavy slabs of muscle and countless scars. Suddenly, ivory spikes erupted along Grimmar's arms and shoulders, his ribs and abs, and his legs and feet. Three-foot long claws emerged from his uncovered hands, yellow and almost infected-looking.

Felix blanched, the corrupted Mana and visceral sight almost too much for his senses. The giant had become even more monstrous than before, and he reveled in it.

"Thank you, Mother," he crooned, the sound like three overlapping voices, both similar and inferior to the Maw's own voice. Felix also realized that the spikes and claws weren't either of those things: they were teeth.

Oh, that's gross.

Grimmar positively dripped with bloody Mana, his muscles twitching with its power. Ready as he thought he was, Felix didn't even see the blow coming.

Caught in the chest and left shoulder, Felix was hurled into flight before crashing hard into a shadowed alcove. Everything was white with pain, searing across his nerves until his resistance kicked in, muting it to an agonizing roar. He tried to stand up twice, not managing it until the third attempt. Something felt...loose inside of him. His Health had dropped 30%.

"Tsk tsk. I said submit, Grimmar." There was no mistaking the warning in her tone, and Grimmar paled.

"Yes, honored Mother." He stomped toward Felix.

"Where was I? Oh yes. My child. I saw you questioning that, but it is easily answered: you are not the first to hear my call." She smiled as Grimmar appeared before Felix and grabbed him by the arm. He was spun and slammed into the wall, cracking a pillar that had likely been there for thousands of years. Felix gasped. Something definitely burst.

His Health dropped another 20%.

"You see, when the Geist began to guard my prison, they erected only cursory wardings to keep me isolated. They trusted their wretched family to honor the laws of my incarceration, as passed down by the Nym and their blasted Herald." The Maw contemptuously tossed its mane of toothy spikes, and they rattled like chattering bones.

"But my song, it finds the cracks. The gaps in the wards and minds of those Geist foolish enough to guard a living god. I claimed them, turning them against their wicked brethren and showing them how to achieve true power." The Maw exhaled, and a crimson mist coalesced into a shimmering, oblong stone the size of an apple.

"I gave them a piece of my core, my true power. Most died, my power too great for their flesh, even diluted, and the cores came back. But a few...ahh, yes. A few proved they were worthy." With a quick inhalation, the stone dissolved into mist and was sucked back into the Maw.

"Those worthy few were broken by my touch, their flesh mutating with the power of my blessing." The Maw shifted its blue-green orbs to Grimmar, who still held Felix in an iron grip. "Their change was obvious, and the Geist reacted exactly as I knew they would.

"Sentiment!" The Maw hollered, its thousand voices howling. "Sentiment is what dooms this world, compassion and mercy the blade above your necks. It ended the Nym, and it ended the Geist. They were too broken with grief to execute their family. Most were cast into the wilds to live or die, acting as monstrous buffers against the outside world. An extra layer to their devious fog. Two were even kept close, collared and leashed, set within the Labyrinth they built as further security against my might.

"Guardians, if you will."

Felix's eyes widened and he gasped for breath, Grimmar squeezing him ever tighter. Oxygen was getting hard to come by, but his neurons sparked rapid-fire.

The Bloodtainted Guardians. Giant blood beasts collared with small Essence Anchors. And they...they looked exactly like...like the Orit.

"Yes, you begin to see. I'm quite surprised to find that you encountered nearly every one of my failed progeny," the Maw cooed in bloodthirsty delight. "You tore them apart with blade and acid and fire. Quite vicious for such a little thing."

Screeeeaaw!

A dog-sized projectile slammed into Grimmar's leg, and Felix could just barely see the fire-covered form of Pit slashing and biting furiously against the giant's exposed heel.

"Yaaa!" Grimmar shouted, pulling up his leg. "You little monster!" With a savage glance at Felix, he punted the tenku into the distance. Felix's eyes widened in rage. Pit landed, and the Poisonfire winked out. Pit didn't get back up.

Felix's vision was starting to turn colors, flashing blue and gold at the corners, and veins in his neck strained as he pressed against Grimmar's new, colossal might. Memories flashed behind his eyes, of the Guardians attempting to speak, only to emit a rattling buzz, of the Orit choking out vile words, of Grimmar, soaked in the corrupted Mana he wielded even now.

All touched by the Maw.

All of them remade.

"But the Orit was not the first of my children you met. I told you, did I not, that I called my child when you arrived?" The Maw smiled wide, an impossible amount of teeth on display, and its thick, barbed tongue lolled. "My child answered from the deep, swimming from hideous depths to find you walking upon a spit of sand."

A vision of countless orange eyes in the green-black water, of barbed tentacles grabbing and tearing, pulling Felix into the water.

"Oho! He knows! He's figured it out!" Grimmar crowed before throwing Felix across the chamber. He flew nearly forty feet before he hit the icy ground like a ragdoll.

Felix's Health bar started flashing, dangerously close to empty.

The Dread...impossible. Felix pulled himself up haltingly, feeling gashes on his legs, arms, chest, and back along with contact burns from the ice itself. *Pit...Pit are you...?*

He could feel a faint warmth through his pact, so he knew the tenku still lived. He brought up his Companion's status.

Health: 23 / 311

"Do you submit, boy?" Rumbled the tri-voices of the transformed Grimmar, already stomping toward him. "Please say no."

"F-fuck off, mama's boy," Felix grunted, then let loose two concentrated orbs of acid. They barreled outward, smashing into Grimmar's shins and knocking the massive Risi onto his face. The ground shook so hard Felix was thrown to his feet. He immediately started running for Pit.

"*Stop!*"

Between one step and another, Felix felt nearly every muscle in his body seize. He was just feet from Pit's side.

In his peripheral vision, a rust-red shape slinked towards him. A sense of terror welled up from within, and all along his Bastion, he felt the scraping tendrils of those segmented monstrosities, swimming, crawling, clawing their way up his walls. He was there, reeling in fright from their advances.

"You have such *spirit* in you, Felix Nevarre," the voice whispered in his ear, so close he could smell the fetid stink of its breath. "You are the same as when we first met in the brackish Bitter Sea. Devoid of hope, devoid of the possibility of victory, yet still you fight until the last."

Images of grasping tentacles and toothy maws filled his mind, the creatures pressing tight against his mental fortifications. Vicious howls pierced the dark, a terrible resonance that shook the air. Shavings of stone fell from his Bastion's walls, chunks that *plunked* into the rising waves of an acidic ocean. Felix huddled himself farther away, pulling up from the horrors beyond the walls. The Maw's soft voice found him there, just the same.

"My Dread marked you, branded your Spirit for my purposes. And then you did us one better! You bit him back!" The voice crooned in pleasure, and Felix's walls shook as if an earthquake had hit. "Imbibing my child's ichor let me help you, mold you into what you needed to become."

Images flashed across the sky, and Felix looked up, seeing himself as if from a distance, while green waves sloshed in the foreground.

"You were marked before the System could claim you. Mine. And so I did some...editing, you might say." Scrapings outside the walls and the howling increased in volume and intensity. "I chose your Race. The Nym are near-perfect Vessels for me, and there you were, ripe for the picking!"

Felix's Bastion was rocked, the very foundation shuddering and dropping several inches. *The* Maw *chose my Race?*

"Mmmm yes, your precious, special Race. It was your destiny to find me, to serve me," the Maw's purr turned into a growl. "I would have altered your damnable Omen too, but the Omen...fought back. Magician. Fah! A minor setback, nothing more."

The rust-red monstrosity paced around Felix, always just out of view to his frozen eyes. Felix strained against whatever Skill the Maw had laid on him, to no avail; it was like breaking through a steel wall with his bare hands. At times it was as if the massive hell beast was there, at others, he felt the soft touch of a dainty hand along his back and shoulders.

"With the remnants of my power coursing through your veins, you were far more susceptible to a few minor alterations. I know you've enjoyed them as you've eaten your way across the Foglands.

Bite by delectable bite, your hunger grows bigger by the moment. Your body craving the blood and guts and meat of monsters, of your enemies, even your friends." A laugh, soft and throaty and buzzing his inner ear. "Titles and Skills aren't my usual forte, but for you, I made an exception."

As if to illustrate the Maw's point, two blue windows appeared before him: the Title and Skill windows for Gourmand and Lessons of the Past.

Rumbling shook the air, dust pluming from below as waves crashed over the battlements. The tower, only a story above the crenelated walls, shuddered and listed to the side.

It all made sense. Felix could envision the moment he had received both Title and Skill, how exciting and strange it was to gain a Title for simply biting a monster and living to tell the tale. The thrill of gaining new Skills and abilities from eating the blood and Mana of other creatures. The...the rush.

There was more howling, and for the first time, Felix realized that it wasn't from the abominations in the sea.

It was his hunger. And it was coming from inside the walls.

CHAPTER SEVENTY-FOUR

The air quaked, and the stone beneath his feet shook as Felix regarded his Bastion of Will. His visualization of it was breaking apart, piece by piece, while the howling in his guts reached a fever pitch.

Crimson wind caressed his skin, pulling Felix from his mental construct back to physical reality, the Maw's face only inches from his own. It purred at him.

"A fine hunger, sharp and fierce. You do me proud, child."

His hunger rioted as it touched him, the volume within his mental space and pain within his body reaching all-new heights. It felt like he was being torn apart from the inside.

"And your Body, what marvels you have wrought. You've put your Skills to such good use. This...Moving Mountain Body is stalwart and resilient." A sharp claw ran along his left shoulder, tearing a painful line across his upper back as it circled him. "And you've passed the First Threshold. Remarkable. Mouthwatering."

The Maw crossed back into Felix's peripheral vision, and he could see that it was an unholy mix of woman and beast, changing between each step as it kept a humanoid hand against his bloody skin. Its talons were like fire as they scratched out fluid lines in his flesh. "Your Mind is...simple. Barely Tempered at all, hmm? Wonderful. That will make this so much easier."

It stopped, clawed feet suddenly clicking against the icy floor.

Then a growl, low and buzzing and terrible, shook Felix to his core. "Your Spirit, however, is still too strong. My Mark is not enough." It spat out the last words, then its voice grew softer. "Strange. You should be in agony, right now. Barely able to stand, let alone resist." Then there was a gasp, and Felix could hear a smile in its voice. "Ah, perfect."

Hands grabbed Felix's belt, ripping free the hardened potions case he had resting against his hip and tearing his belt off in the process. A metallic clatter rang throughout the room as his hooked sword fell to the ground, and his thin leather belt was tossed somewhere in the distance. The Maw wandered back into Felix's vision, this time almost entirely in the guise of Lhel, for that is what it was: a fleshy mask the creature used to lure people in. The creature fiddled with Vessilia's potions case, and for an unreasonable moment, he dared hope she couldn't get it open. Felix knew it was beaten and battered, but it had proven to be extremely durable during his misadventures.

With a slight flex in her forearms, the case was torn in two.

Felix saw it almost in slow motion. Vials went flying, mostly empty, while two were filled with brilliant multicolored light. The Maw plucked one of the two out of the air, letting the rest fall to the ground. A succession of shattering noises filled the room, and the Maw held up a vial filled with a greenish-white liquid that sparkled in the sunlight.

No...

The vials had fallen out of his line of vision, and locked up as he was, Felix couldn't quite see if any had made it.

"A beautiful concoction," it said, holding up the Essence Draught of Sky's Light. "Such strange delights these Humans are capable of now. Distilling Essences was once a high art, you know."

Unable to respond, Felix also couldn't scream when the Maw appeared inches away from his face again. His breathing sped up, that was it. It gripped Felix's jaw with a sharp-fingered claw, tipping his head back as it ripped the cork from the vial with its teeth. Without preamble, the Maw forced the vial into Felix's mouth.

"Take your medicine, dear."

He felt the draught burn a trail of fire down his esophagus, and yet the concentrated Mana was like rain on parched earth. It soaked into his tissues before it ever reached his stomach, moving directly to his core and flaring with a bright white light.

"And now, to make use of it, hmm?"

It placed a dainty claw upon his chest, moving it slightly until it was right above his navel. Then, without warning, its talons dug into his gut like five thrusting daggers.

Streamers of red corruption pulsed through his viscera. Though Felix couldn't look down, a feverish sickness swept outward from the Maw's talons. With Fire Within, however, he could visualize exactly what it was doing. The veins of crimson effluvia spread into him, invading his core like a bloody flood. Felix flared his blue-white fire, but it still dimmed and spat, flaring brighter for only a few seconds before fading again. The vile power twisted and congealed, roaming his core as if...looking for something. Then it paused, and in a flash pressed itself neatly against one of his Skills; it was only one of two that were burning brilliantly in the darkness of his mind.

A great and compounding dissonance shook him, inside and out. It was as if the song he'd been hearing in the back of his mind was suddenly interrupted, sheared into by atonal beats, snapped strings, and the rattled buzzing of discord.

***&(@ERR0#%$R**
#*(XpiERR—anges to System! Be Aware! Rogue Alterations Are Proscribed.
All Actions Have Consequences.
((%$Companion Pact is level 25!

Felix gasped as the notification ripped through his consciousness, unable to be repressed as the Maw's strange power forced his body into Spirit Formation. Then the pain came.

His body was locked, but within his Bastion, Felix screamed into the heavens as his soul *burned*. Those flaring tears at his ankle and wrist were scalding brands upon his flesh, torments that spread across his body like a virulent rash, leaving char and ash in their wake. Distantly, Felix could hear something laughing, a cruel and callous sound, one that reveled in his agony. But it was subsumed by the inferno that raged across his Spirit.

@#!$Congratulations! You Have Reached Apprentice

Tier In Companion Pact!
You Gain:
+5 AGL
+5 DEX
+...

The anguish of his soul redoubled, and Felix felt as if he were splitting in two. A deep and ruinous fissure ripped through him, sundering his Spirit in a way that he feared could never be fixed. That manic, cruel laughter grew louder, thick tongue lashing in anticipation.

A piercing cry echoed across his mind, a sharp implement cutting through the noise. Both the buzzing discordance and the cruel laughter cut off. Everything stopped...and Felix felt the resurgence of his pact bond. A golden thread of light thrummed across his mindscape, flickering with streaks of deep black and vibrant red, leading off into a far distance that rumbled with thunder. Fury surged and sang across the breadth of imaginary space, and Felix could see the fan of massive red and black wings spreading just beyond the horizon.

A glissando swept across Felix's mind, a dazzling shift from low to high notes that soared into the deepest reaches of his soul.

Rarity of the Skill has upgraded!

Companion Pact (Rare) becomes Etheric Concordance (Legendary)!

Etheric Concordance (Legendary), Level 25!
You have deepened the connection between you and your Companion, forming a concordance that will have echoing consequences for you both. The grandest heights and crushing depths lie in store, though what shape the future holds is up to you both. All previous abilities of Companion Pact are retained.

Upon reaching level 25, you have gained the ability Convergence - Merge with your Companion for 1 minute x Skill level, gaining additive bonus to Harmonic Stats. Companion is released at end of effect.

Without warning the pain returned, crashing into Felix like a tidal wave. Green waters overwhelmed his Bastion's walls, flooding through the crenelations and sizzling against the courtyard. Acrid smoke and fumes began to fill the air while crimson fire roared in Felix's soul. He fell to his knees, dark stone shattering beneath him as the tower listed further to the side.

Rare Essence Draught Detected During Formation!
[Essence Draught of Sky's Light]

Choose a Feature:
Horizon
Vaulted
Beacon

Barely cognizant, Felix couldn't muster the energy to choose. He felt the world sliding away from him, tilting toward collapse. Mental construction or not, his Bastion of Will was failing him. He tried again, but his thoughts unraveled as fast as he could form them.

I can't...

Another shriek cut through his mindscape, and Felix turned away from his Bastion and core, refocusing on the real world. He still stood, locked in place. The Maw still laughed, though it had wandered away, toward the fallen giant...the one who was sitting up shakily. A soft scraping noise caught his attention and out of his lower peripherals Felix could see a dark shape was dragging itself closer, claw by claw.

It was Pit, and he was in bad shape. Feathers had been torn out in several spots and a few wounds oozed thin blood from the tenku's back and shoulders. A trail of smeared red extended behind him, and he was shaking. Whether from cold or blood loss or exertion, Felix didn't know.

He didn't know.

Felix groped for the assuring presence of the pact, but it was gone, as was Pit's warmth. With a soft, yet insistent chirrup, Pit lifted his head and fixed him with a golden stare. Felix read grit and fury and something boundlessly *other* in the tenku's gaze, something he had never seen before.

Then Pit's paw touched him.

Convergence.

There was a blinding light, turning Felix's vision entirely white as Pit disappeared.

A great swell of melody as a dozen notes resounded within Felix. Power thundered through him, similar to a System level up but so much greater. The dissonant pain was driven away, drowned beneath the frenzy of harmony, too much for the Maw's power to dilute and break apart.

Felix brought up his Harmonic Stats with a thought. Then he felt them shift and expand, becoming something more.

Harmonic Stats
RES: 125 (+28)
INE: 78 (+14)
AFI: 74 (+15)
REI: 71 (+15)
ALA: 119 (+27)

Felix and Pit cut out a moment, a sliver of space where thought and action could exist within the maelstrom of the Maw's awful power.

A birdlike voice cried at him, the hint of a growl in the sound. The meaning was instantly clear.

Choose!

Felix chose.

Congratulations!
You have absorbed the Essence of Beacon!
3 of 3 Spirit Essences Formed!
Tempering Has Begun!

Then the pain came back.

Grimmar choked back a cry as he sat up. He had to leverage himself entirely with his arms, as the giant's legs below the knees were a ruin. His miraculously-accelerated healing was repairing the damage, but whatever that Nym had used was slowing it down.

That bastard boy! I'll rip this throat out, no matter what the Mother says!

So caught up in his own rage, Grimmar didn't notice his goddess' presence until he felt claws dig into his wounds.

"AHH!" Grimmar let loose an animalistic, basso scream.

"You live, yet you lie here," came the Mother's sweet voice, a balm to Grimmar's ears. Then her voice turned sharp. "While *I* had to finish the job!"

Though she regained the Nymean shape of Lhel, claws the size and weight of greatswords stabbed further into Grimmar's legs, tearing into his flesh with ease. Grimmar screamed again, panic flushing his voice.

"You are a disappointment, Grimmar. All of your advantages, and still you're *failing*." She shook her head, and Grimmar felt his world begin to crumble. "But I will give you one last chance to become my true Champion, my Vessel."

The Mother produced a bloody red stone the size of her head and held it aloft in dainty hands. The giant took it gingerly from her, the stone barely bigger than his massive thumbnail.

"Prove yourself. Survive."

Without thought or question, Grimmar threw the red stone back, swallowing it down instantly.

There was a long moment where the Risi Chieftain thought his goddess had made a mistake. *Surely not. I must be...*

Then he felt a crawling sensation, deep in the flesh of his wounds. It tingled, a shifting wave against his leg meat that pressed blue ichor out of him like a spilled tankard, but behind it Grimmar's muscle and skin began to stitch back together. He was healing, rapidly, even in the acid-touched injuries inflicted by that damnable child. He watched his Health rise steadily, then faster and faster as the healing gained steam. Grimmar grinned widely, even as a powerful heat built up within his legs and chest.

With this power, I will conquer the entire Continent, let alone that pathetic Nymean. Grimmar went to stand but found his legs, now fully healed, strangely too weak. *What is this?*

The wounds that had so recently closed up began to bulge, his calf muscles and thighs ballooning rapidly. His skin began to pop and burst, tearing in great stretches along his legs as the heat became an inferno.

Grimmar howled, the pain nearly too much.

"Wh-what is—?" He could barely get the sentence out as his abdomen began to cave, his muscles and fat and guts squeezing and ripping away from themselves. The muscles beneath his legs twisted and shivered, growing ever larger and slamming to the ground with a quaking *thud*. He couldn't breathe, couldn't scream, but blazing flames engulfed his chest and crept toward his arms and head. His skin shriveled and tore, muscles beneath them wasting away as black, rotting flesh chased after healthy blue. The nutrients of his body were being siphoned away, pulled in by the monstrous growth on his legs.

Grimmar stared in paralyzed horror, his body abruptly too weak to lift his head, as hundreds of teeth emerged in razor-sharp rows upon the agonizing growth. Mouths appeared, flexing and screaming without sound or reason. The giant's blood boiled, turning to thick, torpid sludge in his veins and pooling in his withered chest.

He choked, unable to clear his throat.

"Unsuitable," she declared, staring him in the face with no more concern than a bug. She scoffed. "Too rigid. Too weak."

His last thought was a plaintive wail for his goddess to save him. And then her immense teeth flashed in the sunlight, and Grimmar knew no more.

Congratulations!
You Have Tempered Your Spirit!

You Have Formed: the Dawnwalker Spirit
+10 WIL
+10 INT
+10 RES
+15 INE
+5 ALA

A storm of energy poured through Felix's form, once again changing him on a fundamental level that he still did not comprehend. Felix felt Pit thrum with the power of it too, somehow gaining from his consolidated Spirit.

Dawnwalker? What does that mean? It wasn't as straightforward as "Moving Mountain" but then again, the concept of Spirit was beyond Felix's normal experiences. Suddenly, without any warning,

Felix's body completely relaxed. He fell to the ground with a muffled *thump.*

"Uuhh," he groaned. Everything was burning, every muscle, tendon, and joint screaming with the agony of released tension. *It released me?*

The crimson flood in his core had gone.

His Spirit, maybe even his soul, felt ripped apart and beaten bloody. Whatever the Maw had done, his Spirit felt raw, like an open wound. Dimly, Felix realized that it was only with the combined effect of their Harmonic Stats that his regeneration was able to keep up with the damage the Tempering did. Even then, Felix wasn't sure that everything went the way it should have. He felt...weighted down, as if his Spirit was incomplete or malformed.

Magda...was right. Shit. And it did...all this so I couldn't resist...what? What is...the creature...planning?

Whatever it was, Felix wanted none of it. He cast about, unable to really move. His body was numb and unresponsive, but his eyes weren't.

There...has to be...something. Even thinking was starting to hurt, echoes of the Maw's terrible dissonance like a thousand knives in his thoughts. *Something...*

A thought surfaced, from Pit no less, a focused beam of intent. Felix was able to turn his head, reveling in the sensation as he did so. Glass covered the ground before him, but beyond that laid a blood-red stone and a vial filled with liquid light.

The Essence Stone! The last draught!

With excruciating slowness, Felix pulled his numb, tingling body over the broken shards of glass. He felt a few of them bite into his shirtless chest and belly, but his skin was too tough for them, and he didn't stop. He was so close. Pit screeched in his mind, closer than he'd ever been before, and they pushed together. The vial was within reach, but his numb arms wouldn't cooperate with delicate movements. So, Felix scooped it and the Essence Stone toward him with a single flailing arm. Trapping the vial against his chest, along with a bunch of glass and ice, he fumbled it up to his mouth. It was still corked and sealed.

To hell with it, Felix groused. He bit right into the vial, shattering the seal and top and driving a shard directly into his tongue. He ignored it, the pain nothing before the Maw's power, and swallowed down the draught.

It burned fiercely, tasting like musk and wind, and far off grasses beneath a summer sky. It sunk into his core, boiling away around his reignited fire, ready to be used.

Felix spat out the glass shard and shuffled around, looking for the Essence Stone. Grimmar started screaming across the chamber, and Felix rushed as much as he could. He panted, short, panicked gasps as he searched. Feeling was returning to his hands now, and when he found it, he snatched it out of the pile. The stone gleamed red, nearly an inch long and a half inch in diameter: it was a damn horse pill.

This grants the Consumption Essence...no options like a draught. It came from a Bloodstone that came from blood beasts created *by the Maw. That can't be good, can it? Can it?*

Pit warbled within his mind, the Convergence still in effect. A series of thoughts raced through their collective mind; Felix couldn't get over how weird it all was.

Whatever doesn't kill me makes me stronger? That seemed to be the direct translation of what Pit was implying. Felix looked down at the glittering stone. An image of the poison fang he'd crafted drifted through his mind, of someone viewing him at a low angle as he pressed the fang closer and closer to his arm. All for a few levels in Poison Resistance.

Ok...got me there. But this, he held out the stone. *It's different.*

Grimmar's screaming increased in intensity before cutting off completely. Softly, but far too close for comfort, Felix heard a voice.

"Oh, you naughty boy."

Quick as a flash, Felix threw the Essence Stone in his mouth, but before he could swallow, he locked up again. It sat upon his tongue, only inches from its destination.

"I cannot believe I dropped the Bloodbinding. I'm getting careless in my imprisonment," Felix heard the tap, tap, tap of bare feet upon the hard ice. The Maw drew closer. "Grimmar has failed me, Felix. His flesh was weak, unable to withstand my majesty. But then, he was always a long shot. One of many I've tried over the millennia." Felix heard its sigh of disappointment break into a smile, the sharpness of it hiding in its voice. "You are different, Felix. Your Body is strong, your Mind supple, and your Spirit..."

She ran her clawed hands along his back and sides, pressing and testing his flesh.

"Ah yes. Your Spirit is primed. Merely waiting on the final act.

The grand finale." The Maw walked until it stood in front of Felix. He realized he was nearly back in the same position as he started, a little outside the central circle, facing the Essence Anchor. Sigils flared and sank upon its surface, far more rapidly now than before, but still not making much sense to him. He didn't know enough.

The Maw cleared its throat, recapturing his attention, and Felix saw that it had become Lhel once more. Her appearance was without flaw, seemingly Nymean in every way that Felix could spot. She smiled, but it wasn't gentle or kind or sweet; it was the bared teeth of a predator, ready for their meal.

"Let us begin, yes?"

She took a pale, dainty hand and thrust it into her mouth, all the way up to her elbow. Blood and spittle poured from her gaping jaw as her left hand rooted around for something. Had Felix been able to speak, he would have been struck dumb by the vision before him; it was gruesome and appalling, even more so because Felix had no clue what the creature was doing. But then the Maw grabbed hold, and with an almighty tug, pulled a smoking, shapeless mass of crimson gunk, and then kept pulling. And pulling. Like a nightmarish stage magician, the Maw removed the shapeless mass of blood-soaked corruption until it filled the air, and Felix's eyes felt like they were going to explode. The sight of this...power, was absolutely terrifying on a primal level. The blob hovered above her, the size of a 747 airplane, pulsing with dim flashes of internal lightning and oozing in all directions. Clouds of Mana vapor poured off of it like dry ice.

With a flick of a hand, the entire mass was thrown behind her.

Felix watched as the gargantuan *thing* spun backward, floating almost casually until it was caught within the swirling whirlpool of the Essence Anchor. The pull of the Anchor yanked it into a huge spiral, threads of the mass spinning off, stretching around the ancient obelisk like blood down a drain.

It's Mana, Felix realized. *Liquid Mana.*

He sensed such power from the Mana that it had utterly overwhelmed him. Now that it was thinning, Felix felt a pang of longing for it, and his mouth began to actually salivate. What horrible things could be done with such corrupt, delicious power? As the liquid Mana was consumed by the Essence Anchor, another thought flickered through his mind.

Why had she given it up?

The Maw sighed, still in the guise of Lhel, and she looked...old. Haggard and drawn, the creature's skin was pulled taut against her bones, as if every ounce of fat had been expended by her actions. Stumbling forward, she coughed several times into her pale hand.

"The chain around my neck tightens the harder I fight against it. The Anchor is attuned to me, to my *power*, so I can never leave under my own strength. But if I give that up...well, that's entirely different." She gave him a smirk that was more like a corpse's grin. "Oh, I know you're dying to ask more questions. Questions, questions! So curious, little Felix." She looked up at the sunlight which had started to angle across the chamber at some point. "But I'm running out of time. And so are you."

Without another word, the Maw melted into a crimson mist and surged toward Felix. Unable to budge an inch, he couldn't stop it as the Maw's vaporous form poured through Felix's gut wounds...and into his channels. Much like before, the creature flooded into his pathways like a virulent pus, oozing at speed toward his center. It left behind only raw and shredded passages and flesh, throbbing with corruption that was like acid on nerve endings. Her coming was presaged by a buzzing dissonance that shook everything and sent his unnatural hunger into overdrive.

Hm, how fascinating. Fire and lightning. An interesting mix and quite nice, too. I can do so much with this space.

But it is entirely too crowded. Time to clean house.

Felix watched with mounting horror as the Maw flashed toward the lights that composed his Skills and began to tear them apart.

#&#D4NGER! YOUR SKILL ACTING HAS BEEN D#5%$mAGeD!
20% O))#_$RATING CApACITY!

The world shattered.

Felix thought he'd known pain before; this entire experience had been a lesson in it. But he'd known nothing. *Nothing.*

After two strikes, his Acting Skill sundered completely.

@#(U HAVE L0ST THE SKILL ACTING, LEVEL 11!

Lightning arced across his core, sparking in roiling coils that hummed like a generator. His internal fire, more white than blue, spiked in sympathetic rage, coursing through his veins like a molten dirge. Felix couldn't think, couldn't see or speak, couldn't feel anything but the agony of a piece of his core shearing off into the abyss.

Mmm, that was wonderful. Only level 11, was it? I have forgotten how good you Nym taste! It paused, the shapeless mass of bloody Mana clacking a thousand teeth. *Don't worry. I won't eat you. Not* all *of you.*

(*$5GER! YOUR SKILL IMPROVISATION HAS BEEN DAMAG($D!
33% OPERATING CAp—
YOU HAVE LOST $38F SKILL IMPROVISATIOn, LEVEL 11!

I need to make it more comfortable for myself, but honestly, I just can't help taking a nibble. Mm!

But Felix couldn't hear. He was overwhelmed by the agony of his soul being scoured and devoured by this abomination. His vision, both physical and not, was surmounted by flashes of blue and gold, flares that burst and shuddered with each tearing bite the creature took from him. Each Skill that was devoured was lost knowledge, lost capability, lost pieces of himself. And he knew he'd never get them back.

The Maw cooed at his evolved Skills, at his Epic ranked ones, the deep craving in her voice readily apparent.

No.

Felix pulled away from his inner turmoil, focusing on his physical reality. Pit chirruped, helping him maintain even as his vision nearly blacked out. His mind steadied.

This isn't the end.

He still had the Essence Stone. If he could swallow it....Felix tried to flex, to push, to goddamn vibrate but he was stuck, locked away from his body by the Maw's blood magic. Even with Pit's help, with the advantages of Convergence, his stats were no match for a creature older than anything he'd ever known. A creature that had infected him from the start, that molded and shaped him into a perfect host for its insanity and hunger. A—

The hunger.

Felix focused on the Maw, who was still rampaging within his core, still giving off that scent and taste and feel of rot deep in his veins and channels. But more than that. It was the song, the Mother's Song, the one the giants raved about. A raucous chorus of saw bands and crashing notes, chords that rattled against one another like a tool chest falling down a set of stairs, opposed, at odds. Not a Grand Harmony, like Vvim called it. *This* Song wasn't about Harmony at all.

It was about Dominance.

And part of him *loved* it.

His hunger ate it up, shrieking and vibrating within him, ripping outward with teeth sharp enough to shred, to devour. But it always wanted more. More and more and more. So Felix took that Song and funneled it into his hunger, gave it all it wanted. Fed it until it choked and drooled.

Within his physical body, saliva kept gathering, an involuntary reaction. And the Essence Stone...slipped.

Swallowed whole.

Boring down on his core, Felix focused on his last Skill, the one that started it all. It was a banked blaze, still untouched by the rampaging Maw, and Felix thrust his will within it.

He *pushed.*

Analyze...

Name: The Unending Maw (Transcendant)
Type: Primordial
Level: ??????????
HP: ????????????/????????????
SP: ????????????/????????????
MP: ????????????/????????????
Lore: The Unending Maw is a cataclysm from a previous Age, a Primordial being of eternal Hunger.
Strength: ???
Weakness: ???

The Skill flared up in a fiery inferno, a lighthouse bonfire that lit up the bloody dark.

What are you doing!

Felix opened his notifications.

CHAPTER SEVENTY-FIVE

Exploration is level 25!

Congratulations! You have reached Apprentice Tier in Exploration!
You Gain:
+3 INT
+3 END
...
Rare Essence Draught Detected During Formation!
[Essence Draught of Dragon's Wing]

Choose a Feature:
Soar
Eclipse
Guide

He had no time and no context for these choices. He chose with his gut. It hadn't failed him yet.

Congratulations!
You have absorbed the Essence of Eclipse!

A rising thrill of coruscating power hit him like a wave, but it was almost lost in the chaos as Skill up notifications streamed past his mind.

Sigils of the Primordial Dawn is level 13!
Shadow Whip is level 26!
Pain Resistance is level 42!
Armored Skin is level 38!
Cold Resistance is level 20!
Etheric Concordance is level 26!
Deep Mind is level 30!

Analyze is level 25!

Congratulations! You have reached Apprentice Tier in Analyze!
You Gain:
+3 INT
+2 PER
...

Legendary Essence Stone Detected During Formation!
[Essence Stone of Consumption]
Choose a Feature:
Consumption
Consumption
Consumption

Through the scintillating shimmer of System power, blue and gold sparks exploding like fireworks in his vision and mind, he reached out.

He chose.

Congratulations!
You have absorbed the Essence of Consumption!
3 of 3 Mind Essences Formed!
Tempering Has Begun!

It was like a tsunami, a roar that was his entire being, a screaming symphonic terror. And strangest of all, the hunger inside of him, that vast emptiness: it moved. Like a living thing, it crawled up his spine and into his head, where it nestled at the base of his skull.

No! What are you doing?

The Maw railed at him, rushing across his core. It was a blood-drenched hole in his gut, lit by the guttering flickers of his inner fire, but the creature flew straight and true; all the while tearing at everything within reach.

D4NGER! YOUR SKILL ACROBATICS HAS BEEN D/////#$MGeD!
54% OPErATING CApACITY!

DANGER! YOUR SKILL AXE MASTERY HAS B23N D)(_MGeD!
81% OPERATING (((((ApACITY!

You'll not take this from me! Your flesh is mine*!*

The Maw barreled directly for the grouping that burned the most fiercely: the Skills Deep Mind, Exploration, and Analyze. Paralyzed by paroxysms of power and sound, Felix could only watch as the pustulent effluvia of the creature's form rocketed toward his Skills, radiating a sinister and deadly light. Corrosion spread in its path, the space itself shaking as the Maw opened wide.

The three Skills exploded in a supernova of light and fire, releasing their own wave of untamed might.

The Maw was thrown back, its form disrupted until its oozing body was a mass of jagged spikes. It reeled in pain and fury.

What have you done?

A wall of shimmering light encased Felix's Skills, all of them, as trilling notes and strummed chords reached a stunning crescendo.

Congratulations!
You Have Tempered Your Mind!

You Have Formed: the Godeater Mind
+10 INT
+10 WIL
+5 PER
+25 ALA

Felix felt his mind *expand*, blooming like a flower in sunlight. Everything felt *more*, and each thought held such a weight as to be practically physical. His hunger raged at the base of his skull, pain shooting across his brain stem and flickering down his spine. Instinctively, Felix sucked in a breath, and the crimson energy that suffused his flesh was sucked into it. Suddenly, the Bloodbind locking his body failed, and Felix stumbled forward.

Without a second to lose, Felix ran toward the Anchor.

You terrible child! You'll ruin everything!

Felix crossed the circle, passing beyond the icy coating on the floor. Only ten feet away, a powerful force ripped him backward. As if a hook had been implanted in his gut, he folded in half and flew through the air to land on his ass just outside the circle again.

Stay!

Crimson power welled up within his channels, forcing itself into his muscles and sinews. Felix took another sharp breath and they too were consumed, Mana vapor devoured by his insatiable hunger. He stood back up.

Yearrgh! My Bloodbind—! The Maw's voice echoed across his flesh, sending quakes and tremors flinching through his entire body. *Then I'll do it myself!*

The Maw flooded his channels, snaking through his pathways like a malignant eel, and pieces of its purulent form plunged into him. These pieces were like spikes that began branching outward, vaporous veins and capillary-like formations that anchored its power. Felix stumbled and stalled, his body only responding in jerks and spasms as the Maw's dominance was reestablished.

"Get out of me!!"

Chirrruuup!

The hunger responded, eating away at the spikes in his body. But he couldn't keep up. The Maw was too old, too crafty, and still too strong by half. It sped up, traveling in loops through his pathways, at every twist and turn planting more root-like spikes to stop him. He didn't stop, not for long. Each pause was punctuated by another step, another inch forward.

You're too weak, Felix! You're a confused little boy in a strange new world, and you're weak! The Maw laughed, the buzzing dissonance of it still there, still jarring to his senses. *I'll hollow you out and wear you like a coat. I meant to leave you somewhat whole, but you've gone too far. I'll break your Skills one by one until you've nothing left, until you're just an empty sack for me to puppet! I'll make do with a broken Vessel, and you'll beg to be released into death by the time I'm done!*

"Why—" he grunted, taking a single step forward. "Isn't. This. Working!"

Felix flexed and pushed with his internal control, flaring his inner fire and sending it coursing down his channels. It barely made a dent, but was able to tear up a few more of the Maw's roots. He sucked in a breath, and more gaseous pieces of the Maw were consumed. Pit shrieked, a fierce attacking cry, and Felix felt reassurance through their bond. *My hunger isn't doing it! Something changed!*

Felix remembered fighting for his life on a rooftop, struggling to survive a brutal poison. He had fed the poison to his inner fire, burning it away, same as when he took a Draught or ate the Essence Stone. But now his hunger had separated from his core, moving to his head for some reason, and it wasn't working. It wasn't enough.

He needed more than Mana vapor, this time. He needed the Maw's oozing form itself.

Repressing his revulsion, Felix spun his core harder, pouring his Will and Alacrity into stoking that inner fire and sparking his azure lightning. He *pulled*, hard as he could, yanking more of the vapor through his channels and the barest, tiniest piece of the Maw itself. The fire flared purple where the crimson ooze hit the blue, and electricity danced at the contact point.

A...memory flashed by him, brief and dizzying, of facing off against an endless legion of bronze-armored warriors. Each armed with spears and swords that glowed with elemental Mana, mounted atop shrieking tenku and harnoq and wendigos. It was gone in a moment, but Felix grinned.

It had *worked.*

How dare you!

A rotten, corrosive power surged through his channels, and Felix's grin disappeared as he was thrown bodily into the air. Straight up, Felix didn't stop until he hit a buttress that arced across the dome of the ceiling, crashing into it and breaking it apart.

You sniveling little thief*!*

Felix was blasted again, sideways this time, colliding with another support and shattering it. Something snapped in his chest and a wet gurgle emitted as his breath flew from him in a wheeze.

Status Condition: Broken Ribs (x3)
Status Condition: Perforated Lung

You steal from me? Use my gifts against...You're not stopping*?*

Gritting his teeth, Felix *pulled* again, and again, pushing through the pain. Tiny, infinitesimal pieces of the Maw's form were torn free and burned up. This time only bare flashes of memories struck him, images that went by too fast to recognize anything except the dominant impression of fire and blood. He started to fall.

The Maw growled, and Felix's body rattled with vibrations. An immense pressure slammed him up against the ceiling, cracking the heavy stone of the dome and sending chunks falling below. Felix grew dizzy, the floor so far below him and his entire body being pressed upon, as if he were being crushed by Grimmar all over again. But his hunger was stronger than ever, sharper by the moment, a cavernous *void* in his being that demanded sustenance.

He *pulled.*

More memories flashed through his consciousness, flickering things that buzzed and broke into static after only a few seconds. Fire and blood and broken towers. Armies in bronze armor, opponents made of living rock and crystal, creatures devoured by the thousands. A jumble of violent, desolate imagery rampaged through his brain.

The Maw screamed again and dug itself deeper in his channels, pushing itself further, back toward his core. Its power buffeted Felix, pressing against his chest, his limbs, his neck; it crushed him ever deeper into the ceiling, until he feared he'd burst like a grape. He did the only thing he could. He *pulled.*

Raraaaagh! Curse you, Felix! I take it away! All of your gifts!

TITLE: GOURMAND IS LOST!

SKILL: LESSONS OF THE PAST IS LOST!

Blinding pain tore through him, head to foot. Fissures appeared on his skin, cracks that widened into bloody wounds that snaked across his abdomen. Felix tried to move his right arm, to stem the bleeding, but the Maw's power hurled it aside, and a bone-deep crunch and crack sounded as his right arm snapped again. Felix would have screamed had he the breath for it, and Pit cried out in sympathy. He felt feathers brush against his consciousness as the tenku tried to stem the tide, focusing on their wounds so Felix could fight back. It was all he could do to keep moving forward. To keep pulling.

And even though he was wounded and his Health was dropping fast, Felix took heart.

The Maw was getting desperate. It was losing ground.

Felix growled. *This is* my *body! And in here,* I'm *the monster!*

A piece far larger than ever before was ripped from the Maw's contorted form. It fell, screaming into his Fire Within. Teeth of fire and lightning chomped down on it, and the glistening ooze of the Maw, that bloody, rotten corruption fulfilled some part of him that Felix could no longer restrain. His hunger raged forth, eating as much as he could.

Synergy Detected Between Mind Formation And Primordial Foe!

All Choices Have Consequences.
Continue With Skill Creation?

YES, GODDAMN IT!

Discord built within his core, a reverberation that sent jagged bolts of pain in all directions, tearing at the fissures in his flesh. A new symbol written in light and fire and blood was scored into the walls of his core, a monstrous, inhuman pattern that snarled.

New Skill!
Ravenous Tithe (Epic), Level 1!
Consume completely an object or creature which you have claimed and can physically touch. Uses Mana to power conversion. Chance of gaining Skills and/or Memories from target if applicable.

Ravenous Tithe!

Without waiting, Felix engaged his new Skill and felt more

pieces of the Maw rip apart and disappear in his core. The Fire Within raged, growing larger than ever before as it fought to burn up the concentrated essence that piled on. Lightning struck, charring and shattering segments, electric teeth masticating the disgusting meal.

A horrible, bottomless wail echoed from the Maw.

Energy flooded his limbs and the fissures in his skin dimpled and twisted, closing even as his blood boiled in his veins. Steam, literal steam poured from his mouth as the Maw's pressure relaxed, and his teeth sharpened and grew longer and longer, pushing through his jaw and gums. Felix's body twitched and spasmed, each contraction throwing him across the ceiling like a bug, his muscles stretching and ripping as the corrupted power tore through him.

That is mine! You are mine!

Stop!

Sharp claws burst from Felix's hands, tearing furrows in the stone above him before rotting and falling off. Toothy spikes twisted and burst from his back and shoulders, points of agony that left him slick with his own blood. A second surge of released power made them explode in size, piercing the ceiling and dropping a rain of stone and plaster to the ground below.

No!

Felix screamed.

Everything went dark.

"Bumble?"

Felix started and sat up. His face felt wet, and he wiped drool from his chin and cheek. He was in a...kitchen? The walls were painted canary yellow and a variety of dried herbs and garlic was strung from the unpainted oak cabinets. A half-full sink sat nearby, chipped on the edge where someone had banged into it, and a pink frosted cake was sitting on the counter. Someone had cut a piece out of it. Crumbs were everywhere.

"Bumble, when did you get here?" The voice was warm and welcoming, and very familiar. Felix turned around and realized he was on a barstool in his mother's kitchen. His mother stood a few feet away, in the doorway with a bag of groceries.

"Mom!" Felix hopped off the stool and rushed over, so fast his mother blinked and swayed backward. He wrapped her in a hug that must have been entirely too tight.

"Okay! I'm happy to see you, too!" Felix let go as his mother gasped for breath and laughed. "What's gotten into you?"

Felix quickly took the bag of groceries from his mother's hands and set it on the counter. There was something cold in it, though he didn't bother checking. "I'm just...it feels like a long time."

His mother gave him a strange look before pursing her lips and giving him a once over.

"You're not drunk, are you?"

"What? No! Of course not," he said.

"Good. Those friends of yours have been a bad influence, I think." She started bustling around the room, taking items out of her bag and putting them away.

Felix's thoughts flashed back to his friends he would hang out with back home, the ones who threw the parties on the beach and got wasted every night after their shifts. He shook his head, almost unable to believe the kind of dumb stuff he had gotten up to with them. His eyes landed on a poorly-wrapped package on the counter, a gift covered in newspaper and not even the comics or anything. It was the Business section. There were a couple other presents on a small table near the archway to the living room, and something clicked in his mind.

Gabby's birthday. This was Gabby's birthday party.

He was in a memory.

"Oh no, Bumble! Did you eat some of Gabriella's cake? Tch." Felix looked down at the crumb filled plate before him before grinning sheepishly. His mother rolled her eyes and pulled more groceries out.

A bittersweet feeling swept through him as he let go of something he hadn't realized he'd been holding. He wasn't home. He was just hallucinating, probably while the Maw choked the last bit of life out of him.

Thoughts of the Maw made the memory flash an unpleasant reddish hue, and Felix quickly banished the idea. He didn't know how long he had.

"Mom?"

"Mm?"

"You know I love you, right?"

"Of course I do," she looked at him strangely from over the top of the ice cream she was doling out. He could hear the screams and cheers of teens in the backyard. They were probably playing in the pool, though he wasn't sure. He didn't end up staying at the party in real life.

"What's going on, honey?" His mom leveled her warm brown eyes at him, her brows tilted up in concern. Felix had to clear his throat a few times before he could manage to speak.

"Nothing special. Just...just a rough few weeks." His throat ached for some reason. "I got a dog, though. A rescue."

"Really? Do you have the space for a dog?" His mother smiled when she saw his face, knowing the answer. She patted his cheek. "You and your bleeding heart, Bumble. Someone's gonna take advantage of you, one day."

"Yeah," Felix swallowed, the room tinting vaguely red.

"Oh but don't change, honey. I know it's tough out there, with jobs and everything, but you're a good boy," she smiled at him again before picking up a platter of ice cream and cake. "You gonna come wish your sister a happy birthday?"

"Yeah I—" The room turned a deeper red, and this time it didn't relent. Felix looked around, wild-eyed.

"What's wrong?"

"I—I gotta go, Mom," he walked up and gave his mother another tight hug. "I'll miss you."

"Oh honey," she sighed in his ear before holding him out at arm's length. "You can always come back."

Felix smiled, and his throat ached ever more. He swallowed a few times, the room starting to pulse with crimson. "Bye, Mom. I love you."

He fled from the house, unable to look at her again, or at the party out back. As he ran outside, he thought he heard her say something behind him, but he couldn't make it out.

The door slammed.

Felix woke up still screaming.

Slowly, he stopped, instead taking big lungfuls of air. His breath was hitched and painful, his lung still not working correctly.

Status Condition: Collapsed Lung (x1)
Status Condition: Broken Ribs (x2)
Status Condition: Broken Arm (x1)

He was enveloped in a cloud of steam and pulsing crimson Mana. It sparked and sizzled against the blue and gold in his aura, though he didn't see much of it at all. The steam was still pouring from his mouth, and as he stopped screaming, he realized that his jaw was packed full of oversized fangs. They bristled like a nightmare angler fish. When he tried to reach his hand up to touch them, he found his upper arm immobile. His body was stuck, too, and Felix couldn't quite parse why everything felt...upside...down.

Shit.

He was hanging from the ceiling, the spike-like teeth that had erupted from his back, shoulders, and upper arms fixed him securely in the stone. As the steam cleared even more, Felix could see his skin had become rust red and scaled in places, like a rash was spreading across his chest and shoulders. Pain still blazed across his entire body, but it felt...muted.

You're mine, now.

The voice startled him, not because he'd forgotten about the Maw, but because he couldn't fully sense it at all. Whereas before the Maw was a congealed ooze within his Mana channels, now it felt...omnipresent.

Eat me, strike me, slay me! You'll never defeat my power! I am Unending!

The Maw kept screaming at him, hating him but reveling in its victory. Felix had consumed the Maw's power and essence using his new Skill. It was the only thing he could do. He could feel the creature's power roiling inside him, burning away the parts of him that were Felix and replacing them with...with itself. He was changing, slowly maybe, but inevitably. Felix could sense the Maw's consciousness was held back, much weakened by its sacrifice, so much so that Felix's newly Tempered Mind was able to restrain it for a time.

Still, its potency overwhelmed him, powerful in a way that Felix couldn't comprehend. He couldn't restrain it for long, and he knew that when he lost his grip, it would devour him whole.

And the Maw would be free.

Felix had consumed enough of its memories to understand what would happen next. What the Maw truly desired.

It would burn across the world, devouring all life, animate or otherwise.

Everyone would die.

Everyone.

Unless he did something.

He looked down at the Essence Anchor. It was over a hundred feet below him, but he could make out its details as if he were standing next to the thing. The sigils on its surfaces flashed rapidly, the same ones he'd noticed before. He knew what it said now, mostly: *Anchor The Beast and Draw Its Power Into The Infinite Void.*

The Maw still screamed, but it faltered when Felix stared at the Anchor.

There's no way out for you, Felix Nevarre. You're mine for all eternity.

Felix ignored it, instead visualizing his Bastion. It was whole again, not unmarred by its experiences, but the waters had been driven back. Atop the tallest tower, he stood and found Pit waiting. He knelt down, and the tenku rushed to give him a hug, chirping loudly.

"Hey buddy," Felix had tears in his eyes when they separated. "I'm gonna do something stupid, now. So you gotta go."

Pit ruffled his feathers and let out a rebellious, trilling note. Normally it would have been followed by sense images and pantomime, but the two of them were still bound closer than flesh. Felix understood Pit completely when he chirped.

No. To the end.

Then he headbutted Felix in the chest, pushing the rest of his body into another hug. Felix hugged him back, throat aching again.

"Ok," he managed. "To the end, little man."

Something dripped from his real eyes, but it wasn't tears. It was blood, and it fell downward until it came within twenty yards of the Anchor. A great pyramidal obelisk, it rose to a sharp, tapered point, and Felix's enhanced Perception marked the blood as it swirled around the Anchor, spinning closer and closer until it was absorbed by the bronze metal.

Felix pushed back with his left forearm, leveraging his left shoulder from the stone. The tooth-spike came free with a grinding *thunk*. Now free, he rotated his arm and placed it against the ceiling, bracing it for a final push.

No! You fool!

Felix pushed, straining against the stone.

You'll perish!

He was strong now, much stronger than when he'd started. It was easy. A final tug and he dropped.

Falling through the air, Felix couldn't help tensing, but he refused to close his eyes. This was his choice, made of his own free will.

And then, resounding in his mind, a memory dredged from beyond a slamming door, finally perfectly recalled.

I love you too, Bumble.

EPILOGUE

The earth shook and trees toppled all around them, forcing Harn to pull a few of the slower Guilders out of the way of a massive rotten trunk. Screams echoed all around him, both from the Guilders and the creatures in the fog.

"What in Avet's name was that?" Harn turned, pulled off his helmet and squinted into the distance. They had climbed the foothills outside the ruined city, nearly into the narrow pass between the valley and the rest of the Foglands, and were this normal terrain, Harn would have been able to see for miles. As it was, he was barely able to see a massive plume of smoke rising from the city center...exactly where the Risi encampment had been.

"Harn! Something's happening!" Harn whipped toward the voice and saw Atar braced against the trunk of a rotting tree. He was staring all around him with wild eyes. He looked up at Harn, and the warrior could tell the kid was terrified. "There's something happening in the ambient Mana, something, I don't know. Being removed."

Suddenly, the omnipresent fog flickered rapidly before it just vanished. In an instant, the thick fog was gone and Harn's eyes were blinded by beams of sunlight. Blinking at the brightness, Harn realized the sky was blue and unclouded, that the temperature had risen twenty degrees at least, and the forest...the forest had changed utterly. Where before the trees were rotting, corrupted stumps filled with grotesque shapes and withered vines, now they were full and lush. Fruit hung from branches all around them, healthy and delicious-looking. Grass, weeds, wildflowers, all of it had sprouted beneath their feet as if it had been there the whole time. A carpet of greenery that extended in all directions, and even the seemingly-rotten trunk before him resolved into a healthy, if uprooted, growth.

"I-I can Analyze!" Someone shouted gleefully.

"Herbalism is working, too!" Another had picked a fruit from a tree and was staring at it in fascination.

"Atar? What's goin' on?" Harn looked at the mage, hoping for an answer. Atar stared around him with wide eyes, no doubt reading System prompts. "Atar!"

"The interference in the Foglands has disappeared, completely. All Skills work normally," the mage blinked and looked up at Harn. "He was right," he said in a quieter voice.

"Who was right?"

"Felix. He said it was all an illusion, remember?" Atar looked up and closed his eyes, enjoying the feeling of sun on his skin. "They must have deactivated the artifact!"

Harn frowned, then looked back at the city. He could see it now, the ruined landscape crystal clear in his vision and enhanced senses. The center of the city was a mass of dust and debris, and it looked as if most of it had collapsed even further; the sinkhole there had expanded by several miles. Harn couldn't make out much more, but he had a sinking feeling in his gut.

His gut was rarely wrong.

"What happened?" Harn turned to see Evie standing there, staring out into the distance. Her face was pale, her jaw muscle jumping as she nervously clenched and unclenched. "Is...is she—?"

"I don't know," Harn said, softly. "Hopefully, Callie finds her. But we have to keep going."

He gripped the kid's shoulder tight before letting go. Evie stood there a while longer before turning away from the ruined city. Harn pretended not to notice her red eyes and running nose, instead turning around and shouting at his impromptu crew.

"Move out, folks! Double time!"

"On the outside!"

"Switch!"

The clang of battle was loud, but much softer than only minutes before. Callie and her crew had taken the fight to the Risi army that had assembled in these narrow halls. While the giants could only field three abreast, her entire group could navigate with room to spare, all attacking simultaneously. The giants were strong and many, but more than anything, it simply cost them time.

Something had happened ten minutes ago, however, something literally and figuratively earth-shaking. As the once-terrifying Labyrinth's ceiling opened up to the blue sky and the fog dissipated, something broke inside the giants. Many of them fell to the ground, twitching and bleeding from their eyes, and more still had half their Health disappear in an instant. Her team had pushed the weakened giants back into a large central chamber, one that was absolutely littered with corpses and metal clubs.

As her team finished the last stragglers, Callie stepped away, moving slowly but steadily through the debris strewn battlefield. Pure sunlight streamed down into the maze, banishing the darkness that clung to the edges and illuminated a slaughter. Dozens of bodies were turning to greasy black smoke where they laid, and it seemed many more had already dissolved, leaving clunking iron armor among the obstacles in her path.

Eye for Gold.

Callie activated her Perception Skill, useful for finding treasure among dross. Luckily, Magda's shields were made of an expensive alloy, worth enough to trigger her ability's auto-tagging feature.

Found: Mithril Kite Shield x1

The tag hovered over the object in question as Callie clambered over the spindly mountain of iron scrap. She slid down the other side, using her mobility Skill to its utmost. Coming to a stop, Callie pulled Magda's kit shield out from under a slagged pile of iron ore, grunting with the effort.

The shield was broken in half.

A swirl of black, greasy smoke caught her eye and Callie half turned from the half-melted mound before her. Beyond the smoke, she could see a bulky form, slumped atop a low hill. Abandoning all pretense, Callie flew forward, running across the complicated terrain as fast as she could. She came into clear view of the figure who was atop a literal hill of bodies, each of them slowly dissolving into dark vapor. In a flash Callie took off, leaping from body to body, until she knelt before Magda.

Up close, the woman was bloody and mangled, her armor riven in several places including both of her shields. Her sandy brown hair was mussed by sweat and blood, and half her face was an angry red from frost burns. She was leaning against a massive circular door, having clearly placed her back against it during her fight. Callie's breath caught in her chest.

"Mags?" Callie whispered.

Magda was quiet and still.

With shaking hands, Callie reached out and placed it against Magda's heart.

All she felt was cold.

The shadows faded as the fog did, revealing a very surprised face behind a familiar black mask.

Ilia stood stock still while the world around her changed completely, and she placed a quick hand on the platform that floated next to her. The Dayne girl was bound hand and foot to the platform, unconscious since she had "rescued" her from her dire straits. Which was the only official story the Sworn was going to be offering. The platform itself was an elaborately-crafted slab of dark-stained wood, intricately inscribed with glowing sigils all around the outer edge. It hovered four feet above the ground and easily kept pace with the Sworn, but her hand gripped its edge possessively.

When the changes ceased, Ilia marveled at the land's transformation: hundreds of blossoms bloomed on nearby bushes and trees, and nearly a dozen unusual herbs filled the ground all around her. She quickly Analyzed twenty-four different growths, each a rare crafting material, and that was only the immediate area. Untouched treasures littered the forest path, many that crafters in Haarwatch and beyond would pay out the nose for; she only regretted she hadn't the Herbalism Skill needed to pick them.

I need to get back to Haarwatch, now.

Some of her contacts would pay top dollar for this information, but only if she was the first to deliver it.

With a happy skip in her step, Ilia increased her pace. She smirked at the unconscious girl and tossed back another stimulant potion; her old one was wearing off fast. With luck, she could make it back to Haarwatch in two days. She smiled, bright as the sun above.

This is a good day.

Vvim watched from above as the giants fell.

The few Risi that had not entered the Labyrinth writhed among the city streets, the ice they generated having faded at a rapid pace. Their bodies, every one of them, were broken in some fundamental way. Most bled from every orifice they had as they shook and trembled upon the stones. Their elemental hounds fell, too, connected somehow to the warriors. The Geist simply watched.

There was no mercy in those eyes.

But then, something strange happened.

As Vvim watched, part of the street collapsed. This was not in itself strange; many sinkholes had formed in Shelim, and many more would undoubtedly form in the future. No, what was truly odd was that this hole was formed by the burrowing of six large wurms.

Vvim perked up, his eyes of stone narrowing from his Tower.

The large wurms were perhaps ten feet long and as thick as a barrel, their four-piece jaws working the rock and dirt into a solid ramp. Only the nearest of the giants even paid attention, and they simply watched as a rusted creature made of overlapping steel plates creaked out of the tunnel. It was large, but not as large as even the smallest Risi Warrior, though its Spirit flared with a dark corruption that set Vvim's teeth on edge. It was not mechanical in nature, for Vvim's sharp senses could detect the distinct thrum of life Mana in its form, faint though it was.

The creature stopped at the top of the ramp, placing its hand at either side, and began speaking.

"You have been abandoned, giants," it began, though its voice did not originate from itself. Vvim squinted. "Your Mother is gone, never to return."

It's a sonic relay, Vvim determined in alarm. The rare etheric device was implanted in the creature's chest, the originating signal coming from far below.

"Even now, you suffer from her leaving, bereft of her gifts," the deep voice continued. "I can feel your pain. I *ache* along with you. But I come with glad tidings: join with me, and you shall have your vengeance upon the prey that defied you. Join with me and never be left behind again."

Slowly, and much to Vvim's surprise, one-by-one the giants struggled to their feet. They shuffled like the wakened dead, but the Geist could see the gleam of fury in their eyes. These creatures were not cowed or beaten, they were cornered wolves.

"No!" cried a voice among them, and the few standing warriors turned to regard a long-haired female Risi wearing bloodied robes. "You spin lies against the honored Mother, creature! It cannot be trusted! She will return! Grimmar will return from below to raise us above the prey, just as was promiiiiaiiaaaaa-!"

The witch was engulfed by flames, a massive twenty-foot-long wurm having emerged behind her. Its breath was instant death for their kind, and the giants all shuffled nervously away from its blind gaze.

"Grimmar has already perished," said the voice, its timbre steady and unchanged. "He was too weak for the Mother, and the Mother herself is vanquished."

"Who! Who did this?" The voice was one among the crowd, faceless, but it was taken up by almost every giant there.

"A creature that should not be, and that no longer is. Felix Nevarre perished along with the Mother." The voice rose in volume, quelling the whispers. "If you seek strength, then come. Come to my Domain and be set free."

The tunnel was lit with a crimson light from far below, and the metal creature gestured to it.

"Your new Father awaits."

Vvim watched as the giants, one by one, filed down into the darkness.

Within the black expanse of the Void, there was nothing.

And then there was something.

"Unf!"

Landing face-first upon featureless, non-extant, yet very real ground, Felix Nevarre broke his nose. Blood gushed for a moment, dripping down his face and spattering against the black.

Shit, that...hurt? Felix looked up, fighting off vertigo as he did so, the lack of *anything* proving more than his inner ear could handle. *I'm alive?*

With the rustle of wings and clack of hard talons, Pit landed next to him far more gracefully.

Pit! Felix threw an arm around his Companion's shoulders, pulling him in for a hug. Pit's wings batted excitedly against Felix's back and shoulders, while the tenku let out a series of trilling chirps. After the moment passed, Felix stood up with a grin and looked before them. For as far as they could see, the world was a featureless black. Only Pit and Felix himself were lit with a sourceless glow.

Where are we? It looked like the void where he had battled Grimmar for the shard, and where his Lessons of the Past Skill...He shook his head.

How did we get here, Pit? Weren't we—?

New Quest!

Escape the Void!
You have saved the Continent from the Maw, but all choices have consequences. As a result of becoming the Maw's Vessel, however briefly, you have been banished to the Void!
Find a way out, if you can!
Rewards: Freedom, Title, Varies
Good Luck!

Felix closed his eyes and sighed. *At least we have each other for company, buddy.*

A slap and clatter sounded behind him, and a voice let out a growling, high pitched whine.

What is this?! Where am I?!

Felix whipped around, heart beginning to pound as he found the Maw, gaunt and shaking in the guise of Lhel. It was barely standing up, yet it pinned Felix with furious blue-green eyes.

What have you wrought, Felix Nevarre?

ABOUT NICOLI GONNELLA

Nicoli Gonnella spent his formative years atop a mountain, breathing deep of the world energy and expelling impurities from his soul. Also he went to school and stuff. He always wrote but now he's abandoned everything to do it full time. Readers give him strength, spirit bomb style, and there's no telling how strong he will become. This isn't even his final form.

He lives with his wife, two kids, and a corgi named Cornelius.

Connect with Nicoli Gonnella:
Discord.gg/sqQvJQhY8F
Patreon.com/Necariin
RoyalRoad.com/fiction/30321/Unbound
Facebook.com/Nicoli-Gonnella-Author-347428719693359

ABOUT MOUNTAINDALE PRESS

Dakota and Danielle Krout, a husband and wife team, strive to create as well as publish excellent fantasy and science fiction novels. Self-publishing *The Divine Dungeon: Dungeon Born* in 2016 transformed their careers from Dakota's military and programming background and Danielle's Ph.D. in pharmacology to President and CEO, respectively, of a small press. Their goal is to share their success with other authors and provide captivating fiction to readers with the purpose of solidifying Mountaindale Press as the place 'Where Fantasy Transforms Reality.'

Connect with Mountaindale Press:
MountaindalePress.com
Facebook.com/MountaindalePress
Twitter.com/_Mountaindale
Instagram.com/MountaindalePress

MOUNTAINDALE PRESS TITLES

GameLit and LitRPG

The Completionist Chronicles,
The Divine Dungeon,
Full Murderhobo, and
Year of the Sword by Dakota Krout

Arcana Unlocked by Gregory Blackburn

A Touch of Power by Jay Boyce

Red Mage and
Farming Livia by Xander Boyce

Space Seasons by Dawn Chapman

Ether Collapse and
Ether Flows by Ryan DeBruyn

Dr. Druid by Maxwell Farmer

Bloodgames by Christian J. Gilliland

Unbound by Nicoli Gonnella

Threads of Fate by Michael Head

Lion's Lineage by Rohan Hublikar and Dakota Krout

Wolfman Warlock by James Hunter and Dakota Krout

Axe Druid,

Mephisto's Magic Online, and
High Table Hijinks by Christopher Johns

Skeleton in Space by Andries Louws

Dragon Core Chronicles by Lars Machmüller

Chronicles of Ethan by John L. Monk

Pixel Dust and
Necrotic Apocalypse by David Petrie

Viceroy's Pride by Cale Plamann

Henchman by Carl Stubblefield

Artorian's Archives by Dennis Vanderkerken and Dakota Krout

Made in the USA
Columbia, SC
10 August 2023

21476799R00464